The Yemassee

The Yemassee: A Romance of Carolina

Selected Fiction of William Gilmore Simms
Arkansas Edition

John Caldwell Guilds
Editor

The University of Arkansas Press
Fayetteville 1994

Copyright 1994 by John Caldwell Guilds

98   97   96   95   94   5   4   3   2   1

Designed by John Coghlan

The paper used in this publication meets the minimum requirements of the American National Standard for Permanence of Paper for Printed Library Materials Z39.48-1984. ⊚

Library of Congress Cataloging-in-Publication Data

Simms, William Gilmore, 1806–1870.
    The Yemassee : a romance of Carolina / John Caldwell Guilds, editor.
    p.   cm. — (Selected fiction of William Gilmore Simms-Arkansas edition)
    Includes bibliographical references.
    ISBN 1-55728-302-8 (cloth)
    1. South   Carolina—History—Colonial   period,   ca.   1600–1775—Fiction.
2. Frontier   and   pioneer   life—South   Carolina—Fiction.   3. Indians   of   North
America—South   Carolina—Fiction. I. Guilds, John   Caldwell, 1924–   . II. Title.
III. Series: Simms, William Gilmore, 1806–1870.   Selections.   1993.
PS2848.Y5   1994
813'.3—dc20   93-24124
                                                                              CIP

Acknowledgment

I am grateful for the assistance of Caroline Collins in preparing the explanatory notes and the historical and textual data in the appendices.

CONTENTS

Preface to the Arkansas Edition[*]

William Gilmore Simms needs to be read to be appreciated, and he can be neither read nor appreciated unless his works are made available. Thus I am pleased to edit for the University of Arkansas Press *Selected Fiction of William Gilmore Simms: Arkansas Edition,* beginning with *Guy Rivers: A Tale of Georgia. Selected Fiction* will include novels originally designated by Simms as Border Romances, selected novels from his Revolutionary War Series, his three novels dealing with pre-colonial and colonial warfare with Native Americans, and several volumes of his best shorter fiction, including *The Wigwam and the Cabin.* In these volumes, Simms depicts the American frontier from pre-colonial times in sixteenth-century Florida in its ever-westward movement across the Appalachian Mountains to the Mississippi River Valley in the early nineteenth century.

Though the Arkansas Edition of Simms will not be a critical edition in the strictest sense, the principles in establishing copy-text are those recommended by the Committee on Scholarly Editions of the Modern Language Association. For each volume copy-text has been selected under the following procedures: (1) if the author issued a revised edition, such edition becomes copy-text; (2) if there was no revised edition, the original publication is the copy-text; (3) if a critical text (established under CEAA or other comparable standards) exists, such text is the copy-text. In each volume of *Selected Fiction* there will be explanatory as well as textual notes, with a list of the more significant substantive revisions made by the author in preparing the text for a revised edition. Simms's nineteenth-century spelling

* The Preface to the Arkansas Edition and William Gilmore Simms Chronology were originally published in William Gilmore Simms, *Guy Rivers: A Tale of Georgia,* ed. John Caldwell Guilds, Fayetteville: University of Arkansas Press, 1993.

remains unmodernized; all emendations in the text of typographical errors, redundancies, or omissions are recorded.

Each volume will contain both an introduction and an afterword. I am indebted to the University of Arkansas Press for permission to incorporate relevant portions of my *Simms: A Literary Life* for the introductions; the afterwords analyze the works by Simms in more detail and depth than was possible in the limited scope of a biography.

JCG

WILLIAM GILMORE SIMMS CHRONOLOGY

1806   Born in Charleston, South Carolina, April 17, the son of William Gilmore Simms, an Irish immigrant, and Harriet Ann Augusta Singleton Simms

1808   Mother died; left in the custody of his maternal grandmother by his father, who, frustrated by personal tragedy and business failure, deserted Charleston for the Southwest

1812–16   Attended public schools in Charleston

1816   At age ten made momentous decision to remain in Charleston with grandmother rather than join now-wealthy father in Mississippi

1816–18   Concluded formal education at private school conducted in buildings of the College of Charleston

1818   Apprenticed to apothecary to explore medical career

1824–25   Visited father in Mississippi; witnessed rugged frontier life

1825   Began study of law in Charleston office of Charles Rivers Carroll; edited (and published extensively in) the *Album*, a Charleston literary weekly

1826   Married Anna Malcolm Giles, October 19

1827   Admitted to bar; appointed magistrate of Charleston; published two volumes of poetry; first child, Anna Augusta Singleton Simms, born November 11

1832   Anna Malcolm Giles Simms died, February 19; made first visit to New York, where he met James Lawson, who became his literary agent and lifelong friend

1833   Published first volume of fiction, *Martin Faber: The Story of a Criminal*

1834   Published first "regular novel," *Guy Rivers: A Tale of Georgia*

1835   Published *The Yemassee: A Tale of Carolina* and *The Partisan: A Tale of the Revolution*

1836   Married Chevillette Eliza Roach, November 15, and moved to Woodlands, the plantation owned by her father; published *Mellichampe: A Legend of the Santee*

1837   Birth of Virginia Singleton Simms, November 15; first of fourteen children born to Chevillette Roach Simms

1838   Published *Richard Hurdis: or, The Avenger of Blood. A Tale of Alabama*

1840   Published *Border Beagles: A Tale of Mississippi* and *The History of South Carolina*

1841   Published *The Kinsmen: or, The Black Riders of Congaree: A Tale* (later retitled *The Scout*) and *Confession: or, The Blind Heart. A Domestic Story*

1842   Published *Beauchampe, or, The Kentucky Tragedy. A Tale of Passion* (later retitled *Charlemont*)

1842–43   Editor, *Magnolia*, Charleston literary magazine

1844   Elected to South Carolina legislature for 1844–46 term; published *Castle Dismal: or, The Bachelor's Christmas. A Domestic Legend*

1845   Published *The Wigwam and the Cabin* and *Helen Halsey: or, The Swamp State of Conelachita. A Tale of the Borders;* editor, *Southern and Western* (known as "Simms" Magazine)

1846   Published *Views and Reviews in American Literature History and Fiction, First Series* (dated 1845)

1847   Published *Views and Reviews, Second Series* (dated 1845)

1849–55   Editor, *Southern Quarterly Review*

1850   Published *The Lily and the Totem, or, The Huguenots in Florida*

1851   Published *Katharine Walton: or, The Rebel of Dorchester. An Historical Romance of the Revolution in Carolina* and *Norman Maurice; or, The Man of the People, An American Drama*

1852   Published *The Sword and the Distaff; or, "Fair, Fat and Forty," A Story of the South, at the Close of the Revolution* (retitled *Woodcraft*); *The Golden Christmas: A Chronicle of St. John's, Berkeley; As Good as a Comedy; or, The Tennessean's Story*; and *Michael Bonham: or, The Fall of Bexar. A Tale of Texas*

1853   Published *Vasconselos. A Romance of the New World* and a collected edition of *Poems*

1855   Published *The Forayers or the Raid of the Dog-Days*

1856   Published *Eutaw. A Sequel to The Forayers . . . ; Charlemont or The Pride of the Village. A Tale of Kentucky;* and *Beauchampe, or the Kentucky Tragedy. A Sequel to Charlemont;* disastrous lecture tour of North, in which he voiced strong pro-South Carolina and pro-Southern views

1858   Death of two sons to yellow fever on the same day, September 22: the "crowning calamity" of his life

1859   Published *The Cassique of Kiawah. A Colonial Romance*

1860   Vigorously supported the secessionist movement

1862   Woodlands burned; rebuilt with subscription funds from friends and admirers; birth of last child, Charles Carroll Simms, October 20

1863   Chevillette Roach Simms died September 10: "bolt from a clear sky"

1864   Eldest son William Gilmore Simms, Jr., wounded in Civil War battle in Virginia, June 12; most intimate friend in South Carolina, James Henry Hammond, died November 13

1865   Woodlands burned by stragglers from Sherman's army; witnessed the burning of Columbia, described in *The Sack and Destruction of the City of Columbia, S.C.*

1866   Made arduous but largely unsuccessful efforts to reestablish relations with Northern publishers

1867   Published "Joscelyn; A Tale of the Revolution" serially in the magazine *Old Guard*

1869   Published "The Cub of the Panther; A Mountain Legend" serially in *Old Guard;* published "Voltmeier, or the Mountain Men" serially in *Illuminated Western World* magazine

1870   Delivered oration on "The Sense of the Beautiful" May 3; died, after a long bout with cancer, at the Society Street home of his daughter Augusta (Mrs. Edward Roach) in Charleston, June 11, survived by Augusta and five of the fourteen children from his second marriage

Introduction to *The Yemassee*

Flushed with the victory of *Guy Rivers* (1834) and more confident than ever of his ability to compete with all comers in the creation of stirring American themes, young William Gilmore Simms was quick to follow his popular triumph with another major effort in the same genre. The first indication of Simms's thinking about a new novel came in his letter of July 19, 1834, to his New York friend and agent, James Lawson, long before the prolific South Carolinian knew the full extent of *Guy Rivers*'s critical acclaim. "I am doing nothing, but thinking much," Simms wrote, "and digesting the plan of an Indian tale—a story of an early settlement and of an old tribe in Carolina" (*L*, I, 61).[1] This first reference to *The Yemassee* was followed by another some three or four months later verifying that the new project was swiftly taking form. "My Yemassee gets on rapidly," Simms wrote in November 1834; though admitting that "the earlier chapters" were "only sketched" and could not be completed until "I have in *pro. per.* gone over the ground of the story, and become acquainted with its localities . . . ," he still planned "to have it ready for the publishers" by January (*L*, I, 63). Yet, typical of Simms, even before completing the draft of *The Yemassee*, the ambitious young novelist was already visualizing "other plans" he was "anxious to get on with" (*L*, I, 63)—plans which doubtless included the first of his Revolutionary novels, *The Partisan*, since by late May 1835, he had completed and sent to the Harpers "some five chapters of a new work upon which I am going to be busy" (*L*, I, 68). Simms, in 1834–35, was literally consumed with literary fire, which blazed with remarkable intensity and even more remarkable volume.

With *The Yemassee*, Simms had once again managed to publish a ground-breaking new novel better than anything he had previously written; even while the accolades of his previous success were still echoing in his ears, *The Yemassee: A Romance of Carolina*, like *Martin Faber* and *Guy Rivers* before it, was published in New York by Harper—in late March or early April, 1835. It was immediately hailed in the April number of the *Knickerbocker* as being superior to *Guy Rivers* and worthy of "high rank among our native fictions" (V, 341–43). Favorable reviews proliferated: the *Mercantile Advertiser and New-York Advocate* of April 15 proclaimed "there is talent in every page of it, and it will not pass away and be forgotten"; the *New York Times* of the following day reviewed the book "with extreme delight," stating that Simms's reputation was now "permanently established" and that the large first printing had sold out in thirty hours; the *New York Commercial Advertiser,* the *New York Mirror,* and the *New Yorker* all highly favorably reviewed *The Yemassee* on April 18; five days later the *Baltimore American* stated that "*The Yemassee* establishes its author, Mr. Simms, among the first class of modern novelists"; all these critiques appeared in well-known Northern papers or magazines within an eight-day period. No wonder that the first edition of twenty-five hundred copies sold out quickly, requiring two other printings before the end of the year. Simms, by his twenty-ninth birthday on April 17, 1835, had established for himself a literary reputation surpassed by no other contemporary American novelist.

The Yemassee was indeed Simms's best effort to date. While he retained all the advantages of the "new field" he had discovered—the Southern frontier—he also explored another of the "untrodden paths" to which his imaginative mind was attracted—the theme of the American Indian. By centering upon colonial South Carolina as his setting, Simms was able to utilize even more effectively than in *Guy Rivers* his great skill at depicting landscape, particularly that of his native state, which he loved and with which he was thoroughly familiar. By concentrating upon the wars between the early white settlers and the Indian tribe indigenous to coastal Carolina, he was able, while using notably different locale, theme, and philosophy, to take advantage of the great interest aroused by Cooper's Leatherstocking novels. But Simms, as Vernon L. Parrington pointed out in his monumental *Main Currents of American Thought,* "did not follow Cooper's example and plunge into the wilderness," but instead focused upon the "frontier psychology" of "the squatter and settler," mimicking "their sordid prose."[2] Simms crowded "a wealth of romantic material" into *The Yemassee*—"enough to serve Cooper for half a dozen tales" as Parrington observed—and though in so doing the young Southerner may have lost some of Cooper's "dramatic swiftness of movement," he gained an "abundance of accompanying action—the sense of cross purposes and many-sided activities, which *The Yemassee* so richly suggests." Compared with Cooper's Mohicans, Simms's Yemassees are much more complex human beings, with faults and virtues, much less the noble savage. In fact, nineteenth-century American literature produced no more realistic treatment of the American aborigines[3] than did Simms in his novels *The Yemassee, Vasconselos,* and *The Cassique of Kiawah.* But as Parrington noted, it is idle to compare Simms with Cooper. Not only is Simms "incomparably the greater master of racy prose, as he is much the richer nature," but Simms was also "far too rich in his own right to live as a dependent on anyone, and certainly far too original to be an imitator."[4] While Simms consciously and sympathetically portrayed the Indians as credible human beings, capable of corruption and destined for tragic defeat, he also was consciously creating a mythology about the Yemassee. In the 1853 preface to the Redfield edition of *The Yemassee,* Simms, while contending that his "portraits . . . are true to the Indian," confessed that he took "liberties" with "his mythology": "That portion of the story, which the reverend critics, with one exception, recognized as sober history, must be admitted to be a pure invention—one, however, based upon such facts and analogies as . . . will not discredit the properties of the invention" (see below, xxviii).

Simms was perhaps the first American writer to draw the distinction between *novel* and *romance,* as commonly observed in European literature—a distinction made notable in the United States by Hawthorne's famous statement in the preface to *The House of Seven Gables* in 1851. Though Simms was to make some modifications in the prefatory letter to the revised 1853 edition, he stated in the preface to the first edition (1835) of *The Yemassee*: "I have entitled this story a romance, and not a novel—the reader will permit me to insist upon the distinction." Rather than being restricted like the novel to the realistic representation of ordinary life, the *romance* (to Simms, and later to Hawthorne) gave the artist license to deploy legendary, imaginative, and poetic material usually associated with the medieval epic. In Hawthorne's words, the "legendary mist" of *The House of Seven Gables* has "a great deal more to do with the clouds overhead than with any portion of the actual soil of the County of Essex." Simms, on the other hand, contended that "Modern romance is the substitute which the

people of today offer for the ancient epic. . . . The modern romance is a
poem in every sense of the word."[5] This epic concept of the romance,
perhaps drawn from Simms's boyhood reading of Homer and Virgil, fit
perfectly with the South Carolina author's discovery that the American
readers of the day were attracted to heroic, dramatic, purposeful por-
trayals of national themes in their fiction. *The Yemassee,* then, is
Simms's first attempt to write an American epic—the Great American
Novel, as it were—dealing with American history in its initial, most
savage form, the warfare between European settlers and Native
Americans over the very land itself, and depicting an era fraught with
irreconcilable competing purposes, cultures, and philosophies of strikingly different peoples. The scope, the breadth, and the vision of *The
Yemassee* are indeed epic, and the work has an energy and raw power
unusual for American writing at the time. Despite flaws in structure,
diction, and characterization, it effectively presents a view of America
found nowhere else in our literature.

C. Hugh Holman has convincingly demonstrated that Simms was
consciously influenced by Sir Walter Scott in creating this and other of
his historical romances.[6] There can be little doubt of Simms's admiration for Scott. In "Modern Prose Fiction," an essay written earlier and
finally published in the *Southern Quarterly Review* in 1849, Simms
called Scott "more perfect, more complete and admirable than any
writer of his age," partly because he combined "the peculiar powers of
the *raconteur* with those of the poet, painter, and the analyst of events
and character" better than any other writer.[7] The Scott formula of a
dramatic encounter in which "the ancient rough and wild manners of
a barbarous age are just becoming innovated upon" (*The Fortunes of
Nigel*) is well represented in Simms's novel by the Yemassee war, a conflict between settler and savage; and the central love story, or aristo-
cratic subplot, of Gabriel Harrison (Governor Craven) and Bess
Matthews, seems to follow Scott's plot structure and his use of historical personages. But Simms's creative effort in *The Yemassee* owes little
or nothing to Scott; it was inspired, perhaps most of all, by his three
visits to the Southwest. During the first two he rode with his father
throughout the Indian country, visited the Creek and Cherokee
nations, and listened to the elder Simms's vivid stories of his own
Indian experiences. During the third visit, undertaken to settle his
father's estate in 1831, he evinced an even livelier interest in Indian
affairs. Taking a seventeen-day journey on horseback through the

Choctaw lands in Mississippi, Simms recorded with perception the startling changes that had taken place since his earlier visit. The most dramatic scene anywhere in Simms's work—the tomahawking murder by Matiwan of her own son, Occonestoga, undertaken to save him from ritualistic disgrace and humiliation—was probably inspired by the young writer's observation of a similar degradation of an Indian youth during his 1831 visit to Mobile, Alabama.

Certainly Simms's greatest achievement in *The Yemassee* is the creation of memorable characters like Sanutee, the sage chief of the Yemassees, and Matiwan, his wife, perhaps the most striking Indian woman in the literature of that day. Also worthy of recognition is the painstaking portrayal of the degeneration, by white man's alcohol, of the talented but weak and vain Occonestoga. Simms handles these Indian characters with unusual deftness and restraint, using direct characterization to allow them to reveal their dignity and their folly, their pain and their joy, in speech, manners, and action. The epic tradition that the fall of a worthy enemy is an event of tragic proportions— not an occasion for rejoicing—is preserved in Simms's skillful handling and the mood and tone of solemnity he conveys. The inevitability of the defeat of the Yemassee and the ascendancy of the white settlers evokes a sense of national tragedy in keeping with the epic dimension of the romance.

As the most forward-looking and realistic American novelist in his portrayal of the Indian, Simms also raised the question about the Native American's capability to adapt to the kind of civilization to which the white race aspired. In a heated debate with the Reverend Mr. Matthews, the young, untutored, but good-hearted stalwart Hugh Grayson states unequivocally his judgment that the inferior Indian can never live peacefully with the white settlers. "[I]t is utterly impossible that whites and Indians should ever live together and agree," Grayson proclaims. "The nature of things is against it, and the very difference between the two, that of colour, perceptible to our most ready sentinel, the sight, must always constitute them an inferior caste in our minds" (293). The racial philosophy expressed by his characters— based on the presumed superiority of the white race to the colored races, red or black—while disturbing to the modern reader because of its innate racism, nevertheless represents effectively and truthfully the thinking of Simms's day.

Similarly, though in 1835 the abolitionist movement was only beginning to inflame sectional feelings, the traditional concept that slavery under an enlightened owner was beneficial to the appreciative slave pervades the dialogue between Gabriel Harrison and Hector, the slave whom Harrison wishes to free for saving his life. Even though Harrison offers money, a house in Charleston, and freedom, because "You have saved my life, old fellow—you have fought for me like a friend, and I am now your friend, and not any longer your master," Hector is adamant in his rejection of the offer:

> I d——n to h——l, maussa, if i guine to be free! . . . I can't loss you company. . . . 'Tis onpossible, maussa, and dere's no use for talk 'bout it. De ting ain't right: and enty I know wha' kind of ting freedom is wid black man? Ha! you make Hector free, he turn wuss more nor poor buckrah—he tief out of de shop—he git drunk and lie in de ditch—den, if sick come, he roll, he toss in de wet grass of de stable. . . . No, maussa—you and Dugdale berry good company for Hector. I tank God he so good—I no want any better. [397]

The passage is worth recording for two reasons: first, it reveals Simms's knowledge of, and ability to transcribe accurately, the Gullah dialect spoken by some low-country South Carolina blacks from colonial times to the present; second, it reflects Simms's philosophical assumption that the black race, more adaptable than the red, would benefit from its association with the white, to the advantage of both,[8] whereas—in Hugh Grayson's view at least—the inflexible red race could never live peacefully with the white.

In keeping with the historical record of the Yemassee War, Simms reveals that black slaves fought with the English settlers against both the Indians and the Spaniards. This fact is not surprising for two reasons: the supposition that the English practiced a "gentler form of treatment" that "won the affections of their serviles" (378)[9]; and the opposing reputation of the Spanish for cruelty to its plantation slaves in the Caribbean—hence the concern lest Hector be captured and sold into slavery in Cuba (118, 124). What at first seems shocking, however—even though there is little reason to question the historical authenticity—is the unmerciful brutality of the blacks against the Indians.[10] Yet the fear of being scalped—or, worse, of being captured alive and sold for bounty to the Spaniards—was motivation sufficient to arouse hate and vindictiveness in the loyalist slaves, who in addition could thus impress their masters with the ferocity of their zeal. No better evidence of the brutalizing effect of war can be given than Simms's revelation that red, black, and white[11] alike become inhumanly cruel when caught up in its passion.

NOTES

1. The *New York Mirror* of August 2, 1834, announced that the author of the highly successful *Guy Rivers* was at work on another American novel (12, 39).

2. *The Romantic Revolution in America, 1800–1860* (New York: Harcourt, Brace, 1927), 135.

3. See Albert Keiser, *The Indian in American Literature* (New York: Oxford University Press, 1933), 154 ff.

4. *Romantic Revolution,* 131, 135.

5. In the revised preface addressed "To Professor Samuel Henry Dickson, M.D., of South Carolina," *The Yemassee: A Romance of Carolina,* new and revised edition (New York: Redfield, 1853), Simms modified his original statement, "The modern romance is a poem in every sense of the word," to read: "The Romance is of loftier origin than the Novel. It approximates the poem" (below, xxx).

6. "The Influence of Scott and Cooper on Simms," *American Literature* 22 (May 1951): 203–18.

7. *Southern Quarterly Review* 15 (April 1849): 41–83.

8. In her interesting and stimulating study, *A Sacred Circle: The Dilemma of the Intellectual in the Old South, 1840–1860* (Baltimore: Johns Hopkins University Press, 1977), Drew Gilpin Faust explains why the Southern intellectual of whatever origin living in the South was likely to hold these views. The intellectuals she concentrates upon

in addition to Simms are Edmund Ruffin and Nathaniel Beverley Tucker, both from Virginia; George Frederick Holmes, an Englishman who lived in both South Carolina and Virginia; and James Henry Hammond of South Carolina.

9. In the opening paragraph of chapter 6, Hector's remarks to Harrison, which reveal genuine concern and a sense of personal responsibility unusual in the portrayal of a slave-master relationship, is accounted for as follows: "Hector, though a slave, was a favourite, and his offices were rather those of the humble companion than of the servant" (36).

10. For instance, even after there was "no longer the form of a battle array" among the Yemassee, "the negroes cleared the woods with their clubs, beating out the brains of those whom they overtook, almost without having any resistance offered them" (379).

11. Not only criminals like Chorley, but also responsible white citizens like Dick Grimstead, Moll Granger, and even Gabriel Harrison display brutality while under the effects of war. After hurling Chinnabee "like a stone to the ground," the "fully aroused" Harrison stood before the now defenseless Indian and proclaimed, "Coosaw—thou are the last chief of thy people. The cunning serpent will die by the Coosah-moray-te, like the rest." To emphasize the tragic ramifications of Chinnabee's "knife . . . in . . . heart" execution, Simms allows the last words of the Indian to convey both his resignation to his fate and his awareness of its far-reaching impact and turns his execution into an act of genocide; "Chinnabee is the last chief of the Coosaw—his people have gone—they wait for him with the cry of a bird. Let the pale-face strike. Ah ha!" (377).

THE

YEMASSEE

A

ROMANCE OF CAROLINA

By W. Gilmore Simms, Esq
AUTHOR OF "THE PARTISAN," "GUY RIVERS," "MARTIN FABER," "RICHARD
HURDIS," "BORDER BEAGLES," ETC.

New and Revised Edition

REDFIELD
110 AND 112 NASSAU STREET, NEW YORK
1854.

R. CRAIGHEAD, PRINTER AND STEREOTYPER,
53 Vesey Street, N.Y.

TO PROFESSOR
SAMUEL HENRY DICKSON, M.D.,
OF SOUTH CAROLINA

My Dear Dickson,—

It is now nearly twenty years since I first inscribed the Romance of "The Yemassee" with your name. The great good fortune which attended the publication in the favor of the public, the repeated editions which have been called for, and the favourable opinions of most of the critics, who, from time to time, have sat in judgment upon it, seem to justify me in endeavouring to retouch and perpetuate the old inscription in the new and improved edition of my various writings which it is meant to herald. You will see, if you do me the honour again to glance over the pages of this story, that I have done something towards making it more acceptable to the reader. I could not change the plan of the story in any wise. That is beyond my control. I could make no material alterations of any kind; since such a labor is always undertaken with pain, and implies a minuteness of examination which would be excessively tedious to a writer who has long since dismissed the book from his thoughts, in the more grateful occupation of fresh imaginings and new inventions. It is my great regret that I can now do so little towards rendering the story more worthy of the favor it has found. I am now fully conscious of its defects and crudities. No one can be more so than myself. In reading it over, for the small revision which I have made, I am absolutely angry with myself, as Scott is reported to have been with Hogg while reading one of the stories of the Shepherd, at having spoiled and botched so much excellent material. I see now a thousand passages, through which had I the leisure, and could I muster courage for the effort, I should draw the pen, with the hope to substitute better thoughts, and improved situations, in a more appropriate and graceful style. But I need not say to you how coldly and reluctantly would such a task be undertaken, by one who has survived his youth, and who must economize all his enthusiasm for the new creations of his fancy. I can only bestow a touch of the pruning knife here and there, cutting off the more obtrusive excrescences, and leaving minor ones to the indifference or the indulgence of the reader.

Something, perhaps, should be said of the story as a whole. When I wrote, there was little understood, by readers generally, in respect to the character of the red men; and, of the opinions entertained on the subject, many, according to my own experience, I knew to be incorrect. I had seen the red men of the south in their own homes, on frequent occasions, and had arrived at conclusions in respect to them, and their habits and moral nature, which seemed to me to remove much of that air of mystery which was supposed to disguise most of their ordinary actions. These corrections of the vulgar opinions will be found unobtrusively given in the body of the work, and need not be repeated here. It needs only that I should say that the rude portraits of the red man, as given by those who see him in degrading attitudes only, and in humiliating relation with the whites, must not be taken as a just delineation of the same being in his native woods, unsubdued, a fearless hunter, and without any degrading consciousness of inferiority, and still more degrading habits, to make him wretched and ashamed. My portraits, I contend, are true to the Indian as our ancestors knew him at early periods, and as our people, in certain situations, may know him still. What liberties I have taken with the subject, are wholly with his mythology. That portion of the story, which the reverend critics, with one exception, recognised as sober history, must be admitted to be a pure invention—one, however, based upon such facts and analogies as, I venture to think, will not discredit the proprieties of the invention.

What I shall add to these statements, must be taken from the old preface, which I shall somewhat modify.

You will note that I call "The Yemassee" a romance, and not a novel. You will permit me to insist upon the distinction. I am unwilling that the story shall be examined by any other than those standards which have governed me in its composition; and unless the critic is prepared to adopt with me those leading principles, in accordance with which the book has been written, the sooner we part company the better.

Supported by the authority of common sense and practice, to say nothing of Pope—

"In every work regard the writer's end,
Since none can compass more than they intend—"

I have surely a right to insist upon this particular. It is only when an author departs from his own standard (speaking of his labours as a work of art), that he offends against propriety and merits censure. Reviewing "Atalantis," a fairy tale, full of fanciful machinery, and without a purpose, save the embodiment to the mind's eye of some of those

> "Gay creatures of the element,
> That, in the colour of the rainbow live,
> And play i' the flighted clouds—"

one of my critics—then a very distinguished writer—gravely remarked, in a very popular periodical, "Magic is now beyond the credulity of eight years;" and yet the author *set out* to make a tale of magic, *knowing* it to be thus beyond the range of the probable—knowing that all readers were equally sagacious—and never, for a moment, contemplated the deception of any sober citizen.

The question briefly is—What are the standards of the modern Romance? What is the modern Romance itself? The reply is immediate. The modern Romance is the substitute which the people of the present day offer for the ancient epic. The form is changed; the matter is very much the same; at all events, it differs much more seriously from the English novel than it does from the epic and the drama, because the difference is one of material, even more than of fabrication. The reader who, reading Ivanhoe, keeps Richardson and Fielding beside him, will be at fault in every step of his progress. The domestic novel of those writers, confined to the felicitous narration of common and daily occurring events, and the grouping and delineation of characters in ordinary conditions of society, is altogether a different sort of composition; and if, in a strange doggedness, or simplicity of spirit, such a reader happens to pin his faith to such writers alone, circumscribing the boundless horizon of art to the domestic circle, the Romances of Maturin, Scott, Bulwer, and others of the present day, will be little better than rhapsodical and intolerable nonsense.

When I say that our Romance is the substitute of modern times for the epic or the drama, I do not mean to say that they are exactly the same things, and yet, examined thoroughly, the differences between them are very slight. These differences depend on the material employed, rather than upon the particular mode in which it is used. The Romance is of loftier origin than the Novel. It approximates the poem. It may be described as an amalgam of the two. It is only with those who are apt to insist upon poetry as verse, and to confound rhyme with poetry, that the resemblance is unapparent. The standards of the Romance—take such a story, for example, as the Ivanhoe of Scott, or the Salathiel of Croly,—are very much those of the epic. It invests individuals with an absorbing interest—it hurries them rapidly through crowding and exacting events, in a narrow space of time—it requires the same unities of plan, of purpose, and harmony of parts, and it seeks for its adventures among the wild and wonderful. It does not confine itself to what is known, or even what is probable. It grasps at the possible; and, placing a human agent in hitherto untried situations, it exercises its ingenuity in extricating him from them, while describing his feelings and his fortunes in his progress. The task has been well or ill done, in proportion to the degree of ingenuity and knowledge which the romancer exhibits in carrying out the details, according to such proprieties as are called for by the circumstances of the story. These proprieties are the standards set up at his starting, and to which he is required religiously to confine himself.

"The Yemassee" is proposed as an *American* romance. It is so styled as much of the material could have been furnished by no other country. Something too much of extravagance—so some may think,—even beyond the usual license of fiction—may enter into certain parts of the narrative. On this subject, it is enough for me to say, that the popular faith yields abundant authority for the wildest of its incidents. The natural romance of our country has been my object, and I have not dared beyond it. For the rest—for the general peculiarities of the Indians, in their undegraded condition—my authorities are numerous in all the writers who have written from their own experience. My chief difficulty, I may add, has risen rather from the discrimination necessary in picking and choosing, than from any deficiency of the material itself. It is needless to add that the historical events are strictly true, and that the outline is to be found in the several chronicles devoted to the region of the country in which the scene is laid. A slight anachronism occurs in one of the early chapters, but it has little bearing upon the story, and is altogether unimportant.

But I must not trespass upon your patience, if I do upon your attention. If you read "The Yemassee" *now,* with such changes of mood and judgment as I must acknowledge in my own case, I can hardly hope that it will please you as it did twenty years ago. And yet, my friend, could we both read it as we did then! Ah! how much more grateful our faith than our knowledge! How much do we lose by our gains—how much do our acquisitions cost us!

Yours faithfully,

W. GILMORE SIMMS

CHARLESTON, *June,* 1853.

The Yemassee

Chapter One

"A scatter'd race—a wild, unfetter'd tribe,
That in the forests dwell—that send no ships
For commerce on the waters—rear no walls
To shelter from the storm, or shield from strife;—
And leave behind, in memory of their name,
No monument, save in the dim, deep woods,
That daily perish as their lords have done
Beneath the keen stroke of the pioneer.
Let us look back upon their forest homes,
As in that earlier time, when first their foes,
The pale-faced, from the distant nations came,
They dotted the green banks of winding streams."

THE district of Beaufort, lying along the Atlantic coast in the State of South Carolina, is especially commended to the regards of the antiquarian as the region first distinguished in the history of the United States by an European settlement.* Here a colony of French Huguenots was established in 1562, under the auspices of the celebrated Gaspard de Coligni, admiral of France, who, in the reign of Charles IX., conceived the necessity of such a settlement, with the hope of securing a sanctuary for French protestants, when they should be compelled, as he foresaw they soon would, by the anti-religious persecutions of the time, to fly from their native into foreign regions.

---

* We are speaking now of authentic history only. We are not ignorant of the claim urged on behalf of the Northmen to discovery along the very same region, and to their assertion of the existence here of a white people, fully five hundred years before this period;—an assertion which brings us back to the tradition of Madoc and his Welshmen; the report of the Northmen adding further, that the language spoken was cognate with that of the Irish, with which they were familiar. For this curious history, see the recently published *Antiquitates Americanæ*, under the editorship of Professor Rafn, of Copenhagen.

This settlement, however, proved unsuccessful; and the events which history records of the subsequent efforts of the French to establish colonies in the same neighbourhood, while of unquestionable authority, have all the charm of the most delightful romance.

It was not till an hundred years after, that the same spot was temporarily settled by the English under Sayle, who became the first governor, as he was the first permanent founder of the settlement. The situation was exposed, however, to the incursions of the Spaniards, who, in the meanwhile, had possessed themselves of Florida, and for a long time after continued to harass and prevent colonization in this quarter. But perseverance at length triumphed over all these difficulties, and though Sayle, for further security, in the infancy of his settlement, had removed to the banks of the Ashley, other adventurers, by little and little, contrived to occupy the ground he had left, and in the year 1700, the birth of a white native child is recorded.

From the earliest period of our acquaintance with the country of which we speak, it was in the possession of a powerful and gallant race, and their tributary tribes, known by the general name of Yemassees. Not so numerous, perhaps, as many of the neighbouring nations, they nevertheless commanded the respectful consideration of all. In valour they made up for any deficiencies of number, and proved themselves not only sufficiently strong to hold out defiance to invasion, but were always ready to anticipate assault. Their promptness and valour in the field furnished their best securities against attack, while their forward courage, elastic temper, and excellent skill in the rude condition of their warfare, enabled them to subject to their dominion most of the tribes around them, many of which were equally numerous with their own. Like the Romans, in this way they strengthened their own powers by a wise incorporation of the conquered with the conquerors; and under the several names of Huspahs, Coosaws, Combahees, Stonoees, and Sewees, the greater strength of the Yemassees contrived to command so many dependants, prompted by their movements, and almost entirely under their dictation. Thus strengthened, the recognition of their power extended into the remote interior, and they formed one of the twenty-eight aboriginal nations among which, at its first settlement by the English, the province of Carolina was divided.

A feeble colony of adventurers from a distant world had taken up its abode alongside of them. The weaknesses of the intruder were, at first, his only but sufficient protection with the unsophisticated savage. The white man had his lands assigned him, and he trenched his furrows to receive the grain on the banks of Indian waters. The wild man looked on the humiliating labour, wondering as he did so, but without fear, and never dreaming for a moment of his own approaching subjection. Meanwhile, the adventurers grew daily more numerous, for their friends and relatives soon followed them across the ocean. They, too, had lands assigned them in turn, by the improvident savage; and increasing intimacies, with uninterrupted security, day by day, won the former still more deeply into the bosom of the forests, and more immediately in connexion with their wild possessors; until, at length, we behold the log-house of the white man, rising up amid the thinned clump of woodland foliage, within hailing distance of the squat, clay hovel of the savage. Sometimes their smokes even united; and now and then the two, the "European and his dusky guide," might be seen, pursuing, side by side and with the same dog, upon the cold track of the affrighted deer or the yet more timorous turkey.

Let us go back an hundred years, and more vividly recall this picture. In 1715, the Yemassees were in all their glory. They were politic and brave—a generous and gallant race. The whites had been welcomed at their first coming to their woods, and hospitably entertained; and gradually lost all their apprehensions, from the gentleness and forbearance of the red men. The confidence of the whites grew with the immunities they enjoyed, and in process of time they came to regard their hosts in the character of allies and to employ them as auxiliaries. In this character, never suspecting their danger from the uses to which they were put, and gladly obeying a passion to the exclusion of a policy, the Yemassees had taken up arms with the Carolinians against the Spaniards, who, from St. Augustine, perpetually harassed the settlements. Until this period the Yemassees had never been troubled by that worst tyranny of all, the consciousness of their inferiority to a power of which they, at length, grew jealous. Lord Craven, the governor and palatine of Carolina, had done much, in a little time, by the success of his arms over the neighbouring tribes, and the admirable policy which distinguished his government, to impress this feeling of suspicion upon the minds of the Yemassees. Their aid, finally, had ceased to be necessary to the Carolinians. They were no longer sought or solicited. The presents became fewer, the borderers grew bolder and more incursive, and new territory, daily acquired by the colonists in some way or other, drove them back for hunting-grounds upon the upper waters of the Edistoh and Isundiga.* Their chiefs began to show signs of discontent, if not of disaffection, and the great mass of their people assumed a sullenness of habit and demeanour, which had never marked their conduct before. They looked, with a feeling of aversion which they yet strove to conceal, upon the approach of the white man on every side. The thick groves disappeared, the clear skies grew turbid with the dense smokes rolling up in solid masses from the burning herbage. Hamlets grew into existence, as it were by magic, under their very eyes and in sight of their own towns, for the shelter of a different people; and at length, a common sentiment, not yet embodied perhaps by its open expression, even among themselves, prompted the Yemassees in a desire to arrest the progress of a race with which they could never hope to acquire any real or lasting affinity. Another and a stronger ground for jealous dislike arose necessarily in their minds with the gradual approach of that consciousness of their inferiority which, while the colony was dependent and weak, they had not so readily perceived. But, when they saw with what facility the new comers could convert even the elements, not less than themselves, into slaves and agents, under the guidance of the strong will and the overseeing judgment, the gloom of their habit swelled into ferocity, and their minds were busied with those subtle schemes and stratagems with which, in his nakedness, the savage usually seeks to neutralize the superiority of European armour.

The Carolinians were now in possession of the entire sea-coast, with a trifling exception, which forms the Atlantic boundary of Beaufort and Charleston districts. They had but few, and those small and scattered, interior settlements. A few miles from the seashore, and the Indian lands generally girdled them in, still in the possession as in the right of the aborigines. But few treaties had yet been effected for the purchase of territory fairly out of sight of the sea; those tracts only excepted which formed the borders of such rivers, as, emptying into the ocean and navigable to small vessels, afforded a ready chance of escape to the coast in the event of any sudden necessity. In this way, the whites had settled along the banks of the Keawa, the Etiwan, the Combahee, the Coosaw, the Pocota-ligo, and other contiguous rivers; dwelling generally in small communities of five, seven, or ten families; seldom of more, and these

---

* Such is the beautiful name by which the Yemassees knew the Savannah river.

taking care that the distance should be slight between them. Sometimes, indeed, an individual adventurer more fearless than the rest, drove his stakes, and took up his abode alone, or with a single family, in some boundless contiguity of shade, several miles from his own people, and over against his roving neighbour; pursuing, in many cases, the same errant life, adopting many of his savage habits, and this, too, without risking much, if any thing, in the general opinion. For a long season, so pacific had been the temper of the Yemassees towards the Carolinians, that the latter had finally become regardless of that necessary caution which bolts a door and keeps a watch-dog.

On the waters of the Pocota-ligo,* or Little Wood river, this was more particularly the habit of the settlement. This is a small stream, about twenty-five miles long, which empties itself into, and forms one of the tributaries of, that singular estuary called Broad river; and thus, in common with a dozen other streams of similar size, contributes to the formation of the beautiful harbour of Beaufort, which, with a happy propriety, the French denominated Port Royal. Leaving the yet small but improving village of the Carolinians at Beaufort, we ascend the Pocota-ligo, and still, at intervals, their dwellings present themselves to our eye occasionally on one side or the other. The banks, generally edged with swamp, and fringed with its dark peculiar growth, possess few attractions, and the occasional cottage serves greatly to relieve a picture, wanting certainly, not less in moral association than in the charm of landscape. At one spot we encounter the rude, clumsy edifice, usually styled the Block House, built for temporary defence, and here and there holding its garrison of five, seven, or ten men, seldom of more, maintained simply as posts, not so much with the view to war as of warning. In its neighbourhood we see a cluster of log dwellings, three or four in number, the clearings in progress, the piled timber smoking or in flame, and the stillness only broken by the dull, heavy echo of the axe, biting into the trunk of the tough and long-resisting pine. On the banks the woodman draws up his *"dug-out"* or canoe—a single cypress, hollowed out by fire and the stone hatchet;—around the fields the negro piles slowly the worming and ungraceful fence; while the white boy gathers fuel for the pot over which his

---

* The Indian pronunciation of their proper names is eminently musical; we usually spoil them. This name is preserved in Carolina, but it wants the euphony and force which the Indian tongue gave it. We pronounce it usually in common quantity. The reader will lay the emphasis upon the penultimate, giving to the *i* the sound of *e*.

mother is bending in the preparation of their frugal meal. A turn in the river unfolds to our sight a cottage, standing by itself, half finished, and probably deserted by its capricious owner. Opposite, on the other bank of the river, an Indian dries his bearskin in the sun, while his infant, wrapped in another, and lashed down upon a board,—for security, not for symmetry—hangs rocking from the tree, beneath which his mother gathers up the earth with a wooden shovel, about the young roots of tender corn. As we proceed, the traces of the Indians thicken. Now a cot, and now a hamlet, grows up before the sight, until, at the very head of the river, we come to the great place of council and most ancient town of the Yemassees—the town of Pocota-ligo.*

---

* It may be well to say that the Pocota-ligo river, as here described, would not readily be recognised in that stream at present. The swamps are now reclaimed, plantations and firm dwellings take the place of the ancient groves; and the bald and occasional tree only tells us where the forests have been. The bed of the river has been narrowed by numerous encroachments; and, though still navigable for sloop and schooner, its fair proportions have become greatly contracted in the silent but successful operation of the last hundred years upon it.

Chapter Two

"Not in their usual trim was he arrayed,
The painted savage with a shaven head,
And feature, tortured up by forest skill,
To represent each noxious form of ill—
And seem the tiger's tooth, the vulture's ravening bill."

THE "great town" of Pocota-ligo, as it was called by the Yemassees, was the largest in their occupation. Its pretensions were few, however, beyond its population, to rank under that title. It was a simple collection of scattered villages, united in process of time by the coalition with new tribes and the natural progress of increase among them. They had other large towns, however, not the least among which was that of Coosaw-hatchie, or the "Refuge of the Coosaws," a town established by the few of that people who had survived the overthrow of their nation in a previous war with the Carolinians. The "city of refuge" was a safe sanctuary, known among the greater number of our forest tribes, and not less respected with them than the same institutions among the Hebrews.* The refuge of the Coosaws, therefore, became recognised as such by all the Indians, and ranked, though of inferior size and population, in no respect below the town of Pocota-ligo. Within its limits—that is to say, within the cordon of pines which were blazed to mark its boundaries, the criminal, whatever his evil deed, found certain security. Here he was sacred. The spot was *tabooed*

---

* This peculiar institution among the red men, and which seems to have existed among all the tribes, however unlike in other respects, constitutes one of the arguments among those who insist upon the aborigines as sprung from the Israelites, and who seek to find among them the remnants of the Lost Tribes. Adair has devoted a large portion of his otherwise admirable collection of notes to this wild illusion, to sustain which, he shows himself perversely ingenious in his misuse of history and reason.

to the pursuer and the avenger. The furies had to remain without. The murderer was safe so long as he kept within the marked circuit. But he might never venture forth with hope to elude his enemy. The vengeance of the red man never sleeps, and is never satisfied while there is still a victim.

The gray soft tints of an April dawn had scarcely yet begun to lighten in the dim horizon, when the low door of an Indian lodge that lay almost entirely embowered in a forest thicket, less than a mile from Pocota-ligo, might be seen to open, and a tall warrior to emerge slowly and in silence from its shelter. He was followed by a dog, somewhat handsomer than those which usually claim the red man for a master. In his gaunt figure, the beast was something of a hound; but he differed from this animal in his ears, and in the possession of a head exceedingly short and compact. He was probably the cross of a cur upon the beagle. But he was none the less serviceable to his present owner. The warrior was armed after the Indian fashion. The long straight bow, with a bunch of arrows, probably a dozen in number, suspended by a thong of deerskin, hung loosely upon his shoulders. His hatchet or tomahawk, the light weapon, a substitute for the stone hatchet, introduced by the colonists, was slightly secured to his waist by a girdle of the same material. His dress, which fitted tightly to his person, indicated a frequent intercourse with the whites; since it had been adapted to the shape of the wearer, instead of being worn loosely as the bearskin of preceding ages. Such an alteration in the national costume was found to accord more readily with the pursuits of the savage than the flowing garments which he had worn before. Until this improvement, he had been compelled, in battle or the chase, to throw aside the cumbrous covering which neutralized his swiftness, and to exhibit himself in that state of perfect nudity, which was scarcely less offensive to the Indians than to more civilized communities. The warrior before us had been among the first to avail himself of the arts of the whites in the improvement of the costume; nay, he had taken other lessons, of even greater value, from the superior race. But of these hereafter. He wore a sort of pantaloons, the seams of which had been permanently secured with strings,—unsewed, but tied. They were made of tanned buckskin of the brightest yellow, and of as tight a fit as the most punctilious dandy in modern times would insist upon. An upper garment, also of buckskin, made with more regard to freedom of limb, and called by the whites a hunting-shirt, completed the dress. Sometimes, such was its make, the wearer threw it as a sort of robe loosely across his shoulders; secured thus with the broad belt, either of woollen cloth or of the same material, which usually accompanied the garment. In the instance of which we speak, it sat upon the wearer pretty much after the manner of a modern gentleman's frock. Buskins, or as named among them, *mocasins*, also of the skin of the deer, tanned, or in its natural state, according to caprice or emergency, enclosed his feet tightly; and without any other garment, and entirely free from the profusion of gaudy ornaments so common to the Indians in modern times, and of which they seem so extravagantly fond, the habit of our new acquaintance may be held complete. Ornament, indeed, of any description, would certainly have done little, if anything, towards the improvement, in appearance, of the individual before us. His symmetrical person— majestic port—keen, falcon eye—calm, stern, deliberate expression, and elevated head—would have been enfeebled, rather than improved by the addition of beads and gauds,—the tinsel and glitter so common to the savage now. His form was large and justly proportioned. Stirring event and trying exercise had given it a confident, free, and manly carriage, which the air of decision about his eye and mouth admirably tallied with and supported. He might have been about fifty years of age; certainly he could not have been less; though we arrive at this conclusion rather from the strong, acute, and sagacious expression of his features than from any mark of feebleness or age. Unlike the Yemassees generally, who seem to have been of an elastic and frank temper, the chief—for he is such—whom we describe, seemed one, like Cassius, who had learned to despise all the light employs of life, and now lived in the constant meditation of deep scheme and subtle adventure. He moved and looked as one with a mind filled to overflowing with restless thought, whose spirit, crowded with impetuous feelings, kept up constant warfare with the more deliberate and controlling reason.

Thus appearing, and followed closely by his dog, advancing from the shelter of his wigwam, he drew tightly the belt about his waist, and feeling carefully the string of his bow, as if to satisfy himself that it was unfrayed and could be depended upon, prepared to go forth into the forest. He had proceeded but a little distance, however, when, as if suddenly recollecting something he had forgotten, he returned hurriedly to the dwelling, and tapping lightly upon the door which had been closed upon his departure, spoke as follows to some one within:—

"The knife, Matiwan, the knife."

He was answered in a moment by a female voice; the speaker, an instant after, unclosing the door and handing him the instrument he required—the long knife, something like the modern case-knife, which, introduced by the whites, had been at once adopted by the Indians, as of all other things that were most necessary to the various wants of the hunter. Protected, usually, as in the present instance, by a leathern sheath, it seldom or never left the person of its owner. It was somewhat singular, indeed, that an Indian warrior and hunter should have forgotten so important an implement, but the fact will better illustrate the vexed and disquieted nature of the chief's mind, which was greatly troubled from peculiar causes, than any act or omission besides. The chief received the knife, and placed it along with the tomahawk in the belt around his waist. He was about to turn away, when the woman, but a glimpse of whose dusky but gentle features and dark eyes appeared through the half-closed door, addressed him in a sentence of inquiry, in her own language, only remarkable for the deep respectfulness of its tone.

"Sanutee,—the chief—will he not come back with the night?"

"He will come, Matiwan—he will come. But the lodge of the white man is in the old house of the deer, and the swift-foot steals off from the clear water where he once used to drink. The white man grinds his corn with the waters, and the deer is afraid of the noise. Sanutee will hunt for him in the far swamps—and the night will be dark before he comes back to Matiwan."

"Sanutee—chief," she again spoke in a faltering accent, as if to prepare the way for something else, of the success of which, in his ears, she seemed more doubtful; but she paused without finishing the sentence.

"Sanutee has ears, Matiwan—ears always for Matiwan," was the encouraging response, in a manner and tone well calculated to confirm the confidence which the language was intended to inspire. Half faltering still, however, she proceeded:—

"The boy, Sanutee—the boy, Occonestoga—"

He interrupted her, almost fiercely.

"Occonestoga is a dog, Matiwan; he hunts the slaves of the English in the swamps for strong drink. He is a slave himself—he has ears for their lies—he believes in their forked tongues, and he has two voices for his own people. Let him not look into the lodge of Sanutee. Is not Sanutee the chief of the Yemassee?"

"Sanutee is the great chief. But Occonestoga is the son of Sanutee—"

"Sanutee has no son—"

"But Matiwan, Sanutee—"

"Matiwan is the woman who has lain in the bosom of Sanutee; she has dressed the venison for Sanutee when the great chiefs of the Cherokee sat at his board. Sanutee hides it not under his tongue. The Yemassees speak for Matiwan—she is the wife of Sanutee."

"And mother of Occonestoga," exclaimed the woman hurriedly.

"No! Matiwan must not be the mother to a dog. Occonestoga goes with the English to bite the heels of the Yemassee."

"Is not Occonestoga a chief of Yemassee?" asked the woman.

"Ha! look, Matiwan—the great Manneyto has bad spirits that hate him. They go forth and they fear him, but they hate him. Is not Opitchi-Manneyto* a bad spirit?"

"Sanutee says."

"But Opitchi-Manneyto works for the good spirit. He works, but his heart is bad—he loves not the work, but he fears the thunder. Occonestoga is the bad servant of Yemassee: he shall hear the thunder, and the lightning shall flash in his path. Go, Matiwan, thou art not the mother of a dog. Go!—Sanutee will come back with the night."

The eye of the woman was suffused and full of appeal, as the chief turned away sternly, in a manner which seemed to forbid all other speech. She watched him silently as he withdrew, until he was hidden from sight by the interposing forest, then sank back sorrowfully into the lodge to grieve over the excesses of an only son, exiled by a justly incensed father from the abode of which he might have been the blessing and the pride.

Sanutee, in the meanwhile, pursued his way silently through a narrow by-path, leading to the town of Pocota-ligo, which he reached after a brief period. The town lay in as much quiet as the isolated dwelling he had left. The sun had not yet arisen, and the scattered dwellings, built low and without closeness or order, were partly obscured from sight by the untrimmed trees, almost in the original forest, which shut them in. A dog, not unlike his own, growled at him as he approached one of the more conspicuous dwellings, and this was the only sound disturbing the general silence. He struck quietly at the door, and inquired briefly—

"Ishiagaska—he will go with Sanutee?"

---

* The Yemassee Evil Principle.

A boy came at the sound, and in reply, pointing to the woods, gave him to understand—while one hand played with the handle of the chief's knife, which he continued to draw from and thrust back into its sheath, without interruption from the wearer—that his father had already gone forth. Without further pause or inquiry, Sanutee turned, and taking his way through the body of the town, soon gained the river. Singling forth a canoe, hollowed out from a cypress, and which lay with an hundred others drawn up upon the miry bank, he succeeded with little exertion in launching it forth into the water, and taking his place upon a seat fixed in the centre, followed by his dog, with a small scull or flap-oar, which he transferred with wonderful dexterity from one hand to the other as he desired to regulate his course, he paddled himself directly across the river, though then somewhat swollen and impetuous from a recent and heavy freshet. Carefully concealing his canoe in a clustering shelter of sedge and cane, which grew along the banks, he took his way, still closely followed by his faithful dog, into the bosom of a forest much more dense than that which he had left, and which promised a better prospect of the game which he desired.

Chapter Three

"The red-deer pauses not to crush
The broken branch and withered brush,
And scarcely may the dry leaves feel
His sharp and sudden hoof of steel;
For, startled in the scatter'd wood,
In fear he seeks the guardian flood,
Then in the forest's deepest haunt,
Finds shelter and a time to pant."

WHAT seemed the object of the chief Sanutee, the most wise and valiant among the Yemassees? Was it game—was it battle? To us seemingly objectless, his course had yet a motive. He continued to pursue it alone. It was yet early day, and, though here and there inhabited, no human being save himself seemed stirring in that dim region. His path wound about and sometimes followed the edge of a swamp or bayou, formed by a narrow and turbid creek, setting in from the river, and making one of the thousand indentations common to all streams coursing through the level flats of the southern country. He occupied an hour or more in rounding this bayou; and then, with something of directness in his progress, he took his way down the river bank and towards the settlement of the whites.

Yet their abodes or presence seemed not his object. Whenever, here and there, as he continued along the river, the larger log hovel of the pioneer met his sight, shooting up beyond the limits of civilization, and preparing the way for its approach, the Indian chief would turn aside from the prospect with ill-concealed disgust.

"————He would the plain
Lay in its tall old groves again."

Now and then, as—perched on some elevated bank, and plying the mysteries of his woodcraft, hewing his timber, clearing his land, or breaking the earth—the borderer rose before his glance, in the neighbourhood of his half-finished wigwam, singing out some cheery song of the old country, as much for the strengthening of his resolve as for the sake of the music, the warrior would dart aside into the forest, not only out of sight but out of hearing, nor return again to the road he was pursuing until fairly removed from the chance of a second contact. This desire to escape the sight of the intrusive race, was not, however, to be so readily indulged; for the progress of adventure and the long repose from strife in the neighbourhood had greatly encouraged the settlers; and it was not so easy for Sanutee to avoid the frequent evidences of that enterprise among the strangers, which was the chief cause of his present discontent. Though without anything which might assure us of the nature or the mood at work within him, it was yet evident enough that the habitations and presence of the whites brought him nothing but disquiet. He was one of those persons, fortunately for the species, to be found in every country, who are always in advance of the masses clustering around them. He was a philosopher not less than a patriot, and saw, while he deplored, the destiny which awaited his people. He well knew that the superior must necessarily be the ruin of the race which is inferior—that the one must either sink its existence in with that of the other, or it must perish. He was wise enough to see, that, in every case of a leading difference betwixt classes of men, either in colour or organization, such difference must only and necessarily eventuate in the formation of castes; and the one conscious of any inferiority, whether of capacity or of attraction, so long as they remain in propinquity with the other, will tacitly become subjects if not bondmen. Apart from this foreseeing reflection, Sanutee had already experienced many of those thousand forms of assumption and injury on the part of the whites, which had opened the eyes of many of his countrymen, and taught them, not less than himself, to know, that a people once conscious of their superiority, will never be found to hesitate long in its despotic exercise over their neighbours. An abstract standard of justice, independent of appetite or circumstance, has not often marked the progress of Christian (so called) civilization, in its proffer of its great good to the naked savage. The confident reformer, who takes sword in one hand and sacrament in the other, has always found it the surest way to rely chiefly on the former agent. Accordingly, it soon grew apparent to the Yemassees, that, while proposing treaties for the purchase of their lands, the whites were never so well satisfied, as when, by one subtlety or another, they contrived to overreach them. Nor was it always that even the show of justice and fair bargaining was preserved by the new comer to his dusky brother. The irresponsible adventurer, removed from the immediate *surveillance* of society, committed numberless petty injuries upon the property, and sometimes upon the person of his wandering neighbour, without being often subject to the penalties awarded by his own people for the punishment of such offences. From time to time, as the whites extended their settlements, and grew confident in their increasing strength, did their encroachments go on; until the Indians, originally gentle and generous enough, provoked by repeated aggression, were not unwilling to change their habit for one of strife and hostility, at the first convenient opportunity. At the head of those of the Yemassees entertaining such a feeling, Sanutee stood pre-eminent. A chief and warrior, having great influence with the nation, and once exercising it warmly in favour of the English, he had, however, come to see more certainly than the rest of his people, the degradation which was fast dogging their footsteps. Satisfied of the ultimate destinies of his nation, unless arrested in its descent to ruin, his mind was now wholly delivered up to meditations upon measures, designed for relief and redress. With a sagacity and intelligence, such as are seldom to be found among any uncivilized people, he discussed with himself every possible form of remedy for the evils and dangers of his race, which could be conceived by a resolute and thinking spirit, warmed by patriotism and desirous of justice. We shall see, in the sequel, how deeply he had matured the remedy, and how keenly he had felt the necessity calling for its application.

At length his wanderings brought him to a cottage more tastefully constructed than the rest, having a neat veranda in front, and half concealed by the green foliage of a thickly clustering set of vines. It was the abode of the Rev. John Matthews,[*] an old English Puritan, who had

---

[*] One of the express conditions upon which the original patent of Charles II. was granted to the lord proprietors of Carolina, was their promulgation of the gospel among the Indians. Upon this charitable object the mission of Mr. Matthews was undertaken, though it may be well to add, that one of the grounds of objection made subsequently to the proprietary charter was the neglect of the duty. An objection not so well founded when we consider the difficulties which the roving habits of the savages must at all times and of necessity throw in the way of such labours.

settled there with his wife and daughter, and officiated occasionally as a pastor, whenever a collection of his neighbours gave him an opportunity to exhort. He was a stern and strict, but a good old man. He stood in the veranda as Sanutee came in sight. The moment the chief beheld him, he turned away with a bitter countenance, and resolutely avoiding the house until he had gone around it, took no manner of heed of the friendly hail which the old pastor had uttered on seeing him approach.

This proceeding was unusual: Sanutee and the preacher had always before maintained the best understanding. The unctuous exhortations of the latter had frequently found a profound listener in the red chief, and more than once had the two broken bread together, in the cottage of the one or the wigwam of the other. The good pastor, however, did not suffer his surprise at Sanutee's conduct to linger in his memory long. He was not of the class who love to brood over the things that bewilder them. "It is strange, verily," quoth he, as he saw the chief turn aside abruptly, and in silence, "very strange; what has vexed him, I wonder!" and here his reflections ended in regard to a proceeding which an old politician of the woods might have meditated with profit to the future.

Meanwhile, pursuing a winding route, and as much as possible keeping the river banks, while avoiding the white settlements, the Indian warrior had spent several hours since his first departure. He could not well be said to look for game, though, possibly, as much from habit as desire, he watched at intervals the fixed gaze of his keenly scented dog, as it would be concentrated upon the woods on either side—now hearing and encouraging his cry, as he set upon the track of deer or turkey, and pursuing digressively the occasional route of the animal whenever it seemed that there was any prospect of his success. As yet, however, the chase, such as it was, had resulted in nothing. The dog would return from cover, forego the scent, and sluggishly, with drooping head and indolent spirit, silently trip along either before or behind his master.

It was about mid-day when the chief rested beside a brooklet, or, as it is called in the south, a branch, that trickled across the path; and taking from the leathern pouch which he carried at his side a strip of dried venison, and a small sack of parched Indian meal, he partook of the slight repast which his ramble had made grateful enough. Stooping over the branch, he slaked his thirst from the clear waters, and giving the residue of his food to the dog, who stood patiently waiting for the boon, he prepared to continue his forward progress.

It was not long before he reached the Block House of the settlers—the most remote garrison station of the English upon that river. It had no garrison at this time, however, and was very much out of repair. Such had been the friendship of the Yemassees heretofore with the Carolinians, that no necessity seemed to exist, in the minds of the latter, for maintaining it in better order. The Block House marked the rightful boundary of the whites upon the river. Beyond this spot, they had as yet acquired no claim of territory; and, hitherto, the Indians, influenced chiefly by Sanutee and others of their chiefs, had resolutely refused to make any further conveyance, or to enter into any new treaty for its disposal. But this had not deterred the settlers, many of whom had gone considerably beyond the limit, and suffered no interruption. All of these were trespassers, therefore, and in a trial of right would have been soon dispossessed; but in the event of such an effort, no treaty would have been necessary to yield sufficient sanction to the adventurers for a defence by arms of their possessions; and many of the borderers so obtruding were of a class to whom the contiguity of the Indians was quite as grateful, and probably as safe, as that of their own colour. In the neighbourhood of the Block House, however, the settlements had been much more numerous. The families, scattered about at a distance of two, three, or four miles from one another, could easily assemble in its shelter in the chance of any difficulty. The fabric itself was chiefly constructed for temporary use as a place of sudden refuge; and could with comparative ease be defended by a few stout hearts and hands, until relief could reach them from their brethren on the coast. Though not upon the river, yet the distance of this fortress from it was inconsiderable—a mile or more, perhaps, and with an unobstructed path to a convenient landing. Retreat was easy, therefore, by this route, and succours by the same way could reach them, though all the woods around were filled with enemies. It was built after the common plan of such buildings at the time. An oblong square of about an acre was taken in by a strong line of pickets, giving an area upon either end of the building, but so narrow that the pickets in front and rear actually made up part of the fabric, and were immediately connected with its foundation timbers. The house consisted of two stories, the upper being divided by a thick partition into two apartments, with a single clumsy window of about three feet square in

the sides of each. These windows, one or other, faced all the points of
the compass; and loopholes, besides, were provided for musket shooting. Beyond the doorway there was no other opening in the stout logs
of which the walls were made. The lower story was a sort of great hall,
having neither floor nor division. The only mode of reaching the
upper story, was a common ladder, which might be planted indifferently against the trap-openings of each of the chambers; each being
thus provided separately from the others, though a slight effort only
was necessary to throw these several apartments into one. A line of
loopholes below, at proper intervals, seemed to complete the arrangements for the defence of this rude, but sufficient structure, serving for
the exercise of sharpshooters against an approaching enemy. The
house was built of pine logs, put together as closely as the nature of
the material and the skill of the artificers would permit; and, save
through the apertures and windows described, was impervious to a
musket bullet. It was sufficiently spacious for the population of the
country, as it then stood, and the barrier made by the high pickets, on
either side, was itself no mean obstacle in a sudden fray. A single
entrance to the right area gave access to the building, through a door-
way, the only one which it possessed, opening in that quarter. The gate
was usually of oak, stoutly made, and well ribbed, but, in the present
instance, it was wanting entirely, having been probably torn off and
carried away by some of the borderers, who found more use for it than
for the fortress. The friendly terms of relationship, between the red
men and the whites, had led to the utter neglect, and almost total
abandonment of their fortress by the latter. Men too much love their
ease not to believe promptly in the signs that encourage confidence,
and our woodmen, a people bold and adventurous, are usually quite
as reckless and incautious as adventurous. True, a few hours might
restore the Block House, but in seasons of surprise a few hours is an
eternity. We might as well expect the one as hope the other.

From the Block House, which Sanutee examined both within and
without with no little attention and some show of discontent, he proceeded towards the river. A little duck-like thing—a sort of half
schooner, but of very different management and rigging, lay in the
stream, seemingly at anchor. There was no show of men on board, but
at a little distance from her a boat rowed by two sailors, and managed
by a third, was pulling vigorously up stream. The appearance of this
vessel, which he beheld now for the first time, seemed to attract much

of his attention; but as there was no mode of communication, and as she showed no flag, he was compelled to stifle his curiosity, from whatever cause it might have sprung. Leaving the spot, therefore, after a brief examination, he plunged once more into the forest, and as he took his way homeward, with more seeming earnestness than before, he urged his dog upon the scent, while unslinging his bow, and tightening the cord of sinews until the elastic yew twanged at the slight pressure which he gave it; then choosing carefully the arrows, three in number, which he released from the string which bound the rest, he seemed now for the first time to prepare himself in good earnest for the hunt. In thus wandering from cover to cover, he again passed the greater number of the white settlements in that precinct, and, in the course of a couple of hours, had found his way to a spacious swamp, formed by the overflow of the river immediately at hand, and familiarly known to the warrior as a great hiding-place for game. He perceived at this point that the senses of the intelligent dog became quickened and forward, and grasping him by the slack skin of the neck, he led him to a tussock running along at the edge of the swamp, and in a zigzag course passing through it, and giving him a harking cheer common to the hunters, he left him and made a rapid circuit to an opposite point, where a ridge of land, making out from the bosom of the swamp, and affording a freer outlet, was generally known as a choice stand for the affrighted and fugitive deer. He had not long reached the point and taken cover, before, stooping to the earth, he detected the distant baying of the dog, in anxious pursuit, keeping a direct course, and approaching, as was the usual habit, along the little ridge upon the border of which he stood. Sinking back suddenly from sight, he crouched beside a bush, and placing his shaft upon the string, and giving all ear to the sounds which now continued to approach, he stood in readiness for his victim. In another moment and the boughs gave way, the broken branches were whirled aside in confusion, and, breaking forth with headlong bound and the speed of an arrow, a fine buck of full head rushed down the narrow ridge and directly on the path occupied by the Indian. With his appearance, the left foot of the hunter was advanced, the arrow was drawn back until the barb chafed upon the elastic yew, then whizzing, with a sharp twang and most unerring direction, it penetrated in another instant the brown sides of the precipitate animal. A convulsive and upward leap testified the sudden and sharp pang which he felt; but he kept on, and, just at the moment when Sanutee, having fitted another arrow, was about to complete what he had so well begun, a gunshot rang from a little copse directly in front of him, to which the deer had been flying for shelter. This ended his progress. With a reeling stagger which completely arrested his unfinished leap, the victim sank sprawling forward upon the earth, in the last agonies of death.

Chapter Four

"This man is not of us—his ways are strange,
And his looks stranger. Wherefore does he come—
What are his labours here, his name, his purpose,
And who are they that know and speak for him?"

THE incident just narrated had scarcely taken place, when the dog of the Indian chief bounded from the cover, and made towards the spot where the deer lay prostrate. At the same instant, emerging from the copse whence the shot had proceeded, and which ran immediately alongside the victim, came forward the successful sportsman. He was a stout, strange looking person, rough and weather-beaten, had the air, and wore a dress fashioned something like that of the sailor. He was of middle stature, stout and muscular, and carried himself with the yawing, see-saw motion, which marks the movements generally upon land of that class of men. Still, there was something about him that forbade the idea of his being a common seaman. There was a daring insolence of look and gesture, which, taken in connexion with the red, full face, and the watery eye, spoke of indulgences and a habit of unrestraint somewhat inconsistent with one not accustomed to authority. His dress was that of a seaman, but implied no ordinary service. It was that of a person who had his fancies, as well as ample means. It was fashioned of the very finest stuffs of the time. He wore a blue jacket, studded thickly with buttons that hung each by a link, and formed so many pendent knobs of solid gold; and there was not a little ostentation in the thick and repeated folds of the Spanish chain, made of the same rich material, which encircled his neck. His pantaloons, free, like the Turkish, were also of a light blue cloth, and a band of gold lace ran down the outer seam of each leg, from the hip to the heel. A small dirk, slightly curved, like that worn by the young officers of our navy in modern times, was the only apparent weapon which he carried, beyond the short, heavy German rifle he had just used so successfully.

The deer had scarcely fallen when this personage advanced towards him from the wood. The shot had been discharged at a trifling distance from the deer, which was pushing for the direct spot where the stranger had been stationed. It had penetrated the breast, and was almost instantly fatal. A few moments served to bring him to his victim, while Sanutee from the other end of the copse also came forward. Before either of them could get sufficiently nigh to prevent him, the dog of the chief, having reached the deer, at once, with the instinct of his nature, struck his teeth into his throat, and began tearing it voraciously for the blood, which the Indian sportsman invariably encouraged him to drink. The stranger bellowed to him with the hope to arrest his appetite, and prevent him from injuring the meat; but, accustomed as the dog had been to obey but one master, and to acknowledge but a single language, he paid no attention to the loud cries and threats of the seaman, who now, hurrying forward with a show of more unequivocal authority, succeeded only in transferring the ferocity of the dog from his prey to himself. Lifting his gun, he threatened but to strike, and the animal sprang furiously upon him. Thus assailed, the stranger, in good earnest, with a formidable blow from the butt of his fusil, sent the enemy reeling; but recovering in an instant, without any seeming abatement of vigour, with a ferocity duly increased from his injury, he flew with more desperation than ever to the assault, and, being a dog of considerable strength, threatened to become a formidable opponent. But the man assailed was a cool, deliberate person, and familiar with enemies of every description. Adroitly avoiding the dash made at his throat by the animal, he contrived to grapple with him as he reached the earth, and with a single hand, with an exercise of some of the prodigious muscle which his appearance showed him to possess, he held him down, while with the other hand he deliberately released his dirk from its sheath. Sanutee, who was approaching, and who had made sundry efforts to call off the infuriated dog, now cried out to the seaman in broken English—

"Knife him not, white man—it is good dog, knife him not."

But he spoke too late; and in spite of all the struggles of the animal, with a fierce laugh of derision, the sailor passed the sharp edge of the weapon over his throat. The deed was done in an instant. Releasing his hold, which he had still maintained with a grasp of steel, and in spite of all the efforts of the animal, he left him to perish where he lay, and rising, prepared to meet the redman. The dog, with a single convulsion, lay lifeless at his feet.

It was fortunate for himself that he was rid of the one assailant so soon; for he had barely returned his knife to its sheath, and resumed his erect posture, when Sanutee, who had beheld the whole struggle—which, indeed, did not occupy but a few minutes—plunged forward as furiously as the animal had done, and the next instant was upon the stranger. The Indian had hurried forward to save his dog; and his feelings, roused into rage by what he had witnessed, took from him much of that cautious resolve and prudence which an Indian never more exhibits than when his purpose is revenge. The sudden passions of Sanutee, kindled so unexpectedly, and by such a loss as that which he had just sustained, deprived him of his usual coolness. With a howl of fury, as he beheld the sharp knife passing over the throat of his faithful follower, he bounded forward. Throwing aside his bow, which now only impeded his movements, he grappled the stranger with such an embrace from brawny arms as might have compelled even the native bear to cry for quarter. But our red chief had found no easy victim in his grasp. The sailor was a stout fellow, all muscle, bold and fearless, and was prepared for the assault. It was very soon evident that Sanutee, though muscular also, and admirably built, was not exactly a match for his present opponent. He was taller, and less compact, and labored of necessity under a disadvantage in the trial of strength which ensued, with one so much shorter and more closely set. The conditions of the combat seemed to be perfectly well understood by both parties; for, with the exception of an occasional exclamation from one or the other, in the first movements of the struggle, no words passed between them. Their arms were interlaced, and their bodies closely locked for a desperate issue, without parley or preparation. At first it would have been difficult to say which of the two could possibly prove the better man. The symmetry of the Indian, his manly height, and easy carriage, would necessarily incline the spectator in his favour; but there was a knotted firmness, a tough, sinewy bulk of body in the whole make of his opponent, which, in connection with his greater youth, would bring the odds in his favour. If the sailor was the stronger, however, the Indian had arts which for a time served to balance his superiority; but Sanutee was exasperated, and this was against him. His enemy had all the advantage of perfect coolness, and a watchful circumspection that seemed habitual. This still defeated, in great part, the subtleties of his assailant. The error of Sanutee was in suffering impulse to defeat reflection, which necessarily came too late, once engaged in the mortal struggle. The Indian, save in the ball-play, is no wrestler by habit. There he may and does wrestle, and death is sometimes the consequence of the furious emulation;* but such exercise is otherwise unpractised among the aborigines. To regret his precipitation, however, was now of little avail—to avoid its evils was the object.

One circumstance soon gave a turn to the affair, which promised a result decisive on one side or the other. So close had been the grasp, so earnest the struggle, that neither of them could attempt to free and employ his knife without giving a decided advantage to his enemy; but in one of those movements which distorted their bodies, until the ground was nearly touched by the knees of both, the knife of the Indian warrior fell from its sheath, and lay beside them upon the turf. To secure its possession was the object, upon which, simultaneously as it were, both their eyes were cast; but, duly with the desire, came the necessity of mutual circumspection, and so well aware were they both of this necessity, that, it is probable, but for an unlooked-for circumstance, the battle must have been protracted sufficiently long, by exhausting both parties, to have made it a drawn one. The affair might then have ended in a compromise; but, it so happened, that, in the perpetual change of ground and position by the combatants, the foot of Sanutee at length became entangled with the body of his dog. As he felt the wrinkling skin glide, and the ribs yield beneath him, an emotion of tenderness, a sort of instinct, operated at once upon him, and, as if fearing to hurt the object, whose utter insensibility he did not seem at that moment to recollect, he drew up his foot suddenly, and endeavoured to avoid the animal. By separating his legs with this object, he gave his adversary an advantage, of which he did not fail to avail himself. With the movement of Sanutee, he threw one of his knees completely between those of the warrior, and pressing his own huge body at the same time forward upon him, they both fell heavily, still interlocked, upon the now completely crushed carcase of the dog. The Indian chief was partially stunned by the fall, but being a-top, the sailor was unhurt. In a moment, recovering himself from the relaxed

---

* In a fair struggle, engaged in this manly exercise, to kill the antagonist is legitimate with the Indians generally; all other forms of murder call for revenge and punishment.

grasp of his opponent, he rose upon his knee, which he pressed down heavily upon Sanutee's bosom; the latter striving vainly to possess himself of the tomahawk sticking in his girdle. But his enemy had too greatly the advantage, and was quite too watchful to permit of his succeeding in this effort. The whole weight of one knee rested upon the instrument, which lay in the belt innocuous. With a fearful smile, which spoke a ferocious exultation of spirit, in the next moment the sailor drew the dirk knife from his own side, and flourishing it over the eyes of the defenceless Indian, thus addressed him:—

"And now, what do you say for yourself, you red-skinned devil? Blast your eyes, but you would have taken my scalp for little or nothing—only because of your confounded dog, and he at my throat too. What if I take yours?"

"The white man will strike," calmly responded the chief, while his eyes looked the most savage indifference, and the lines of his mouth formed a play of expression the most composed and natural.

"Ay, d——e, but I will. I'll give you a lesson to keep you out of mischief for ever after, or I've lost my reckoning and have no skill in seamanship. Hark ye now, you red devil—wherefore did you set upon me? Is a man's blood no better than a dog's?"

"The white man is a dog. I spit upon him," was the reply; accompanied, as the chief spoke, with a desperate struggle at release, made with so much earnestness and vigour as for a few moments seemed to promise to be successful. But failing to succeed, the attempt only served to confirm the savage determination of his conqueror, whose coolness at such a moment, more perhaps than anything beside, marked a person to whom the shedding of blood seemed a familiar exercise. He spoke to the victim he was about to strike fatally, with as much composure as if treating of the most indifferent matter.

"Ay, blast you, but you're all alike. There's but one way to make sure of a redskin, and that is, to slit his gills whenever there's a chance. I know you'd cut mine soon enough, and that's all I want to know to make me cut yours. Yet, who are you—are you one of these Yemassees? Tell me your name; I always like to know whose blood I let."

"Does the white man sleep?—strike; I do not shut my eyes to the knife."

"Well, d——n it, red-skin, I see you don't want to get off, and I'm not the man to baulk a fellow's spirit when it's his own pleasure to walk the plank. It's as natural to me to cut a red-skin's throat as it is to him to scalp a white; and you seem to be one of that sort of people whom it's a sort of pleasure to help through the world. And yet, if you are one of these Yemassee red-skins!—"

This was spoken inquiringly. Sanutee did not answer. Neither did he remain passive. Whether it was that the grasp of the sailor had been somewhat relaxed upon him, that he had somewhat recovered his own strength, or beheld in the white man's eye something of that incertitude which seemed to lurk in his language, in spite of its ferocity, it would be difficult to say. But, just at this time, his struggles were renewed, and with a determined effort. But the knife was flourished over his eyes the moment after.

"Ah! blast you, there's no saving you! It's your throat or mine, I see; so here's at you, with as sharp a tooth as ever bit the throat of white skin or a red!"

Sanutee threw up an arm to avert the weapon; but the stroke had been a feint. In another moment the sharp steel was driven towards the side of the victim. The red chief, ere the blow was felt, conjectured its direction. His eyes closed, and in his own language he began to mutter sounds which might have embodied his chant of many victories. He had begun his death song. But he still lived. The blow was arrested at the very moment when it was about to penetrate his heart. The sailor, seized from behind, was dragged backwards from the body of his victim by another and a powerful hand. The opportunity to regain his feet was not lost upon the Indian, who, standing now erect with his bared hatchet, again confronted his enemy, without any loss of courage, and on a more equal footing.

Chapter Five

"His eye hath that within it which affirms
The noble gentleman. Pray you, mark him well;
Without his office we may nothing do
Pleasing to this fair company."

THE sailor turned fiercely, dirk in hand, upon the person who had thus torn him from his victim; but he met an unflinching front, and a weapon far more potent than his own. The glance of the new comer, not less than his attitude, warned him of the most perfect readiness; while a lively expression of the eye, and the something of a smile which slightly parted his lips, gave a careless, cavalier assurance to his air, which left it doubtful whether, in reality, he looked upon a contest as even possible at that moment. The stranger was about thirty years old, with a rich European complexion, a light blue eye, and features moulded finely, so as to combine manliness with as much of beauty as might well comport with it. He was probably six feet in height, straight as an arrow, and remarkably well and closely set. He wore a dress common among the gentlemen of that period and place—a sort of compound garb, in which the fashion of the English cavalier of the second Charles had been made to coalesce in some leading particulars with that which, in the American forests, seemed to be imperatively called for by the novel circumstances and mode of life prevailing in the region. The sur-coat was of a dark blue stuff, usually worn open at the bosom, and displaying the rich folds of the vest below to the taste of the wearer, but which on the present occasion was of the purest white. The underclothes were of a light gray, fitting closely a person which they happily accommodated, yet served admirably to display. His buskins were like those worn by the Indians. A broad buckskin belt encircled his waist, and secured the doublet which came midway down his thigh. In his hand he carried a light fusil of peculiarly graceful make for that period, and richly orna-mented with drops of silver let in tastefully along the stock, so as to shape vaguely a variety of forms and figures. The long knife stuck in his belt was his only other weapon; and this, forming as it does one of the most essential implements of woodcraft, we may scarcely consider it under that designation. A white Spanish hat, looped broadly up at one of the sides, and secured with a small button of gold, rested slightly upon his head, from which, as was the fashion of the time, the brown hair in long clustering ringlets depended about the neck.

The sailor, as we have said, turned immediately upon the person who, so opportunely for Sanutee, had torn him from the body of the Indian; but he encountered the presented rifle, and the clicking of the cock assured him of the perfect readiness of him who carried it to encounter his enemy in any way that he might choose. There was that in the stranger's eye which showed him to be as cool and confident, as he was vigorous and young. The sailor saw that he was no child—that he was not less powerful of make than the red man, and if his muscles had not yet the same degree of hardihood, they were yet much more flexible for use. The single, sudden effort by which he had been drawn away from his victim, indicated the possession of a degree of strength which made the sailor pause and move cautiously in his advance upon the intruder.

"Well, my good master," said the seaman, having arrived at some prudent conclusion which tended in a slight degree to moderate his fury— "what is this matter to you, that you must meddle in other men's quarrels? Have you so many lives to spare that you must turn my knife from the throat of a wild savage to your own?"

"Put up your knife, good Pepperbox—put it up while you have permission," said the person so addressed, very complaisantly, "and thank your stars that I came in time to keep you from doing what none of us might soon undo. Know you not the chief—would you strike the great chief of the Yemassees—our old friend Sanutee—the best friend of the English?"

"And who the devil cares whether he be a friend to the English or not? I don't; and would just as lief cut his throat as yours, if I thought proper."

"Ha! indeed! you care not whose throat is cut! you care not for the friends of the English! very wise indifference that, standing here, as you do, in the midst of an English settlement. Pray, who are you, my good fellow, and whither do you come from?"

Such was the response of the Cavalier to the sailor, whom the language of the former seemed for a moment to arouse into his former fury. But this he found it politic to restrain; a necessity which made him not a whit more amiable than before. There was some secret motive or policy, or it might be a sense of moral inferiority, in breeding or in station, which seemed to have the effect of keeping down and quelling, in some sort, the exhibitions of a temper which otherwise would have prompted him again to blows. The pause which he made, before responding to the last direct enquiry, seemed given to reflection. His manner became suddenly more moderate, and his glance rested frequently, and with an enquiring expression, upon the countenance of the Indian. At length, giving a direct reply to the interrogatory of the Cavalier, which seemed a yielding of the strife, he replied,

"And suppose, fair master, I don't choose to say who I am, and from whence I come.—What then?"

"Why then let it alone, my patient Hercules. I care little whether you have a name or not. You certainly cannot have an honest one. For me you shall be Hercules or Nebuchadnezzar—you shall be Turk, or Ishmaelite, or the devil—it matters not whence a man comes when it is easily seen whither he will go."

The countenance of the sailor again grew dark with angry passions. The cool, contemptuous, jeering language and manner of the cavalier were almost insupportable to one who had probably felt himself to be as great as Xerxes when on the quarter of his sloop or schooner. He showed clearly in the sudden flashing of his eye, and the reddening darkness of his cheek, that his passion was of a sort to prompt him to instantaneous grapple with his questioner, but he remained stubbornly silent. It was with evident effort, however, that he commenced the process of thinking himself into composure and caution. He had his own reasons, and there were purposes in his mind, that compelled him to consideration and forbearance. But for too frequent draughts of Jamaica, this self-subjection had been more easy from the first. Proceeding in a leisurely manner to reload his fusil, he offered no interruption to the Englishman, who now addressed himself to the Indian.

"You have suffered a loss, Sanutee, and I'm sorry for it, chief. But you shall have another—a dog of mine—a fine pup which I have in

Charleston. When will you go down to see your English brother at Charleston?"

"Who is the brother of Sanutee?"

"The governor—you have never seen him, and he would like to see you. If you go not to see him, he will think you love him not, and that you lie on the same blanket with his enemies."

"Sanutee is the chief of the Yemassees—he will stay at Pocota-ligo with his people."

"Well, be it so. I shall send you the dog to Pocota-ligo."

"Sanutee asks no dog from the warrior of the English. The dog of the English hunts after the dark-skin of my people."

"No, no, old chief—not so! I don't mean to give you Dugdale. Dugdale never parts with his master, if I can help it; but you say wrong. The dog of the English has never hunted the Yemassee warrior. He has only hunted the Savannahs and the Westoes, who were the enemies of the English."

"The eyes of Sanutee are good—he has seen the dog of the English tear the throat of his brother."

"The charge is a strange one, Sanutee, and I do not understand it. But you are angered now, and perhaps with reason. I shall see you hereafter. I will myself bring to Pocota-ligo, the dog that I promise you. He will prove better than the one you have lost."

"Sanutee would not see the young brave of the English at Pocota-ligo. Pocota-ligo is for the Yemassees. Let the Coosaw-killer come not."

"Hah! What does all this mean, Sanutee? Are we not friends? Are not the Yemassee and the English two brothers, that take the same track, and have the same friends and enemies? Is it not so, Sanutee?"

"Speaks the young chief with a straight tongue—he says."

"I speak truth; and will come to see you in Pocota-ligo."

"No; the young brave will come not to Pocota-ligo. It is the season of the corn, and the Yemassee will gather to the festival."

"The green corn festival! I must be there, Sanutee, and you must not deny me. You were not wont to be so inhospitable, old chief; nor will I suffer it now. I would see the lodge of the great chief. I would partake of the venison—some of this fine buck which the hands of Matiwan will dress for the warrior's board this very evening."

"You touch none of that buck, either of you; so be not so free, young master. It's my game, and had the red-skin been civil, he should have had his share in it; but, as it is, neither you nor he lay hands on it; not a stiver of it goes into your hatch, d——n me."

The sailor had listened with a sort of sullen indifference to the dialogue which had been going on between Sanutee and the new comer; but his looks indicated impatience not less than sullenness; and he took the opportunity afforded him by the last words of the latter, to gratify, by the rude speech just given, the malignity of his excited temper.

"Why, how now, churl?" was the response of the Englishman, turning suddenly upon the seaman, with a haughty indignation as he spoke— "how now, churl? is this a part of the world where civility is so plentiful that you must fight and quarrel to avoid a surfeit. Hear you, sirrah; these woods have bad birds for the unruly, and you may find them hard enough to get through if you put not more good humour under your tongue. Take your meat, for a surly savage as you are, and be off as quickly as you can; and may the first mouthful choke you. Take my counsel, Bully-boy, and clear your joints, or you may chance to get more of your merits than your venison."

"Who the devil are you, to order me off? I'll go at my pleasure; and as for the Indian, and as for you—"

"Well, what, Hercules?"

"Well, look to square accounts with me when I'm ready for the reckoning. There's no sea-room, if I can't have it out of you, perhaps when you're least able to pay out rope."

"Pooh! pooh!" replied the cavalier, coolly. "You threaten, do you? Well, as you please and when you please! and now that you have discharged your thunder, will you be good-natured for once, and let your departure be taken for a promise of improvement in your manner."

"What, go!"

"Exactly! You improve in understanding clearly."

"I'll go when I please. I'll be d——d, if I turn my back at the bidding of any man."

"You'll be something more than d——d, old boy, if you stay. We are two, you see; and here's my Hector, who's a little old to be sure, but is more than your match now" —and as the Englishman spoke, he pointed to the figure of a sturdy black, approaching the group from the copse.

"And I care not if you were two dozen. You don't scare me with your numbers. I shan't go till it suits my pleasure, for either red-skin, or white-skin, or black-skin; no, not while my name is—"

"What?" was the inquiry of the Englishman, as the speaker paused at the unuttered name; but the person addressed grinned, with a sort of triumph at having extorted this show of curiosity on the part of the cavalier, and cried:

"Ah! you'd like to know, would you? Well, what'll you give for the information?"

"Pshaw!" replied the cavalier, turning from the fellow with contempt, and once more addressing the red chief.

"Sanutee, do you really mean that you would not see me at Pocota-ligo. Is your lodge shut against your friend. Is there no smoking venison which will be put before me when I come to the lodge of Matiwan. Why is this? I meant to go home with you this very night."

Sanutee replied sternly:

"The great chief of the Yemassees will go alone. He wants not that the Coosaw-killer should darken the lodge of Matiwan. Let Harrison" —and as he addressed the Englishman by his name, he placed his hand kindly upon his shoulder, and his tones were more conciliatory— "let Harrison go down to his ships—let him go with the pale-faces to the other lands. Has he not a mother that looks for him at evening?"

"Sanutee," said Harrison, fixing his eye upon him curiously,— "wherefore should the English go upon the waters?"

"The Yemassees would look upon the big woods, and call them their own. The Yemassees would be free."

"Old chief,"—exclaimed the Englishman, in a stern but low voice, while his quick, sharp eye seemed to explore the very recesses of the red chief's soul,— "Old chief; thou hast spoken with the Spaniard!"

The Indian paused for an instant, but showed no signs of emotion or consciousness at a charge, which, at that period, and under the then existing circumstances, almost involved the certainty of his hostility towards the Carolinians, with whom the Spaniards of Florida were perpetually at war. He replied, after an instant's hesitation, in a calm, fearless manner:

"Sanutee is a man—he is a father—he is a chief—the great chief of the Yemassee. Shall he come to the Coosaw-killer, and ask when he would loose his tongue? Sanutee, when the swift hurricane runs along the woods, goes into the top of the tall pine, and speaks boldly to the Manneyto—shall he not speak to the English—shall he not speak to the Spaniard? Does Harrison see Sanutee tremble, that his eye looks down into his bosom? Sanutee has no fear."

"I know it, chief—I know it—but I would have you without guile also. There is something wrong, chief, which you will not show me. I would speak to you of this and other matters, necessary to the safety and happiness of your people, no less than mine, therefore I would go with you to Pocota-ligo."

"Pocota-ligo is for the Manneyto—it is holy ground—the great feast of the green corn is there. The white man may not go when the Yemassee would be alone."

"But white men are in Pocota-ligo—is not Granger there, the fur trader?"

"He will go," replied the chief, evasively. With these words he turned away to depart; but suddenly, with an air of more interest, returning to the spot where Harrison stood, seemingly in meditation, he again touched his arm, and spoke:

"Harrison will go down to the sea with his people. Let him go to Keawah. Does the Coosaw-killer hear? Sanutee is the wise chief of Yemassee."

"I am afraid the wise chief of Yemassee is about to do a great folly. But, for the present, Sanutee, let there be no misunderstanding between us and our people. Is there any thing of which you complain?"

"Did Sanutee come on his knees to the English? He begs not bread—he asks for no blanket."

"True, Sanutee, I know all that—I know your pride, and that of your people; and because I know it, if you have had wrong from our young men, I would have justice done you."

"The Yemassee is not a child—he is strong, he has knife and hatchet—and his arrow goes straight to the heart. He begs not for the justice of the English."

"Yet, whether you beg for it or not, what wrong have they done you, that they have not been sorry?"

"Sorry—will sorry make the dog of Sanutee to live?"

"Is this the wrong of which you complain, Sanutee? Such wrongs are easily repaired. But you are unjust in the matter. The dog assaulted the stranger, and though he might have been more gentle, and less hasty, what he did seems to have been done in self-defence. The deer was his game."

"Ha, does Harrison see the arrow of Sanutee?" and he pointed to the broken shaft still sticking in the side of the animal.

"True, that is your mark, and would have been fatal after a time, without the aid of gunshot. The other was more immediate in effect."

"It is well. Sanutee speaks not for the meat, nor for the dog. He begs no justice from the English, and their braves may go to the far lands in their ships, or they may hold fast to the land which is the Yemassee's. The sun and the storm are brothers—Sanutee has said."

Harrison was about to reply, when his eye caught a glimpse of another person approaching the scene. He was led to observe him, by noticing the glance of the sailor anxiously fixed in the same direction. That personage had cooled off singularly in his savageness of mood, and had been a close and attentive listener to the dialogue just narrated. His earnestness had not passed unobserved by the Englishman, whose keenness of judgment, not less than of vision, had discovered something more in the manner of the sailor than was intended for the eye. Following closely his gaze, while still arguing with Sanutee, he discovered in the new comer the person of one of the most subtle chiefs of the Yemassee nation—a dark, brave, collected malignant, Ishiagaska, by name. A glance of recognition passed over the countenance of the sailor, but the features of the savage were immoveable. Harrison watched both of them, as the new comer approached, and he was satisfied from the expression of the sailor that the parties knew each other. Once assured of this, he determined in his own mind that his presence should offer no sort of interruption to their freedom; and, with a few words to Ishiagaska and Sanutee, in the shape of civil wishes and a passing inquiry, the Englishman, who, from his past conduct in the war of the Carolinians with the Coosaws, had acquired among the Yemassees, according to the Indian fashion, the imposing epithet, so frequently used in the foregoing scene by Sanutee, of *Coosah-moray-te* —or, as it has been Englished, the killer of the Coosaws—took his departure from the scene, followed by the black slave, Hector. As he left the group he approached the sailor, who stood a little apart from the Indians, and with a whisper, addressed him in a sentence which he intended should be a test.

"Hark ye, Ajax; take safe advice, and be out of the woods as soon as you can, or you will have a long arrow sticking in your ribs."

The blunt sense of the sailor did not see further than the ostensible object of the counsel thus conveyed, and his answer confirmed, to some extent, the previous impression of Harrison touching his acquaintance with Ishiagaska.

"Keep your advice for a better occasion, and be d——d to you, for a conceited whipper-snapper as you are. You are more likely to feel the arrow than I am, and so look to it."

Harrison noted well the speech, which in itself had little meaning; but it conveyed a consciousness of security on the part of the seaman, after his previous combat with Sanutee, greatly out of place, unless he possessed some secret resources upon which to rely. The instant sense of Harrison readily felt this; but, apart from this, there was something so sinister and so assured in the glance of the speaker, accompanying his words, that Harrison did not longer doubt the justice of his conjecture. He saw that there was business between the seaman and the last-mentioned Indian. He had other reasons for this belief, which the progress of events will show. Contenting himself with what had been said, he turned away with a lively remark to the group at parting, and, followed by Hector, was very soon hidden from sight in the neighbouring forest.

Chapter Six

"Go—scan his course, pursue him to the last,
Hear what he counsels, note thou well his glance,
For the untutored eye hath its own truth,
When the tongue speaks in falsehood."

HARRISON, followed closely by his slave, silently entered the forest, and was soon buried in subjects of deep meditation, which, hidden as yet from us, were in his estimation of the last importance. His elastic temper and perceptive sense failed at this moment to suggest to him any of those thousand objects of contemplation in which he usually took delight. The surrounding prospect was unseen—the hum of the woods, the cheering cry of bird and grasshopper, equally unheeded; and for some time after leaving the scene and actors of the preceding chapter, he continued in a state of mental abstraction, which was perfectly mysterious to his attendant. Hector, though a slave, was a favourite, and his offices were rather those of the humble companion than of the servant. He regarded the present habit of his master with no little wonderment. In truth, Harrison was not often in the mood to pass over and disregard the varieties of the surrounding scenery, in a world so new and beautiful, as at the present moment he appeared. On the contrary, he was one of those men, of wonderful common sense, who could readily, at all times, associate the mood of most extravagance and life with that of the most every-day concern. Cheerful, animated, playful, and soon excited, he was one of those singular combinations, which attract us greatly when we meet with them, in whom constitutional enthusiasm and animal life, in a development of extravagance sometimes little short of madness, are singularly enough mingled up with a capacity equal to the most trying requisitions of necessity, and the most sober habits of reflection. Unusually abstracted as he now appeared to the negro, the latter, though a favourite, knew better than to break in upon his mood, and simply kept close at hand, to meet any call that might be made upon his attention. By this time they had reached a small knoll of green overlooking the river, which, swollen by a late freshet, though at its full and falling, had overflowed its banks, and now ran along with some rapidity below them. Beyond, and down the stream, a few miles off, lay the little vessel to which we have already given a moment's attention. Her presence seemed to be as mysterious in the eye of Harrison, as, previously, it had appeared to that of Sanutee. Dimly outlined in the distance, a slender shadow darkening an otherwise clear and mirror-like surface, she lay sleeping, as it were, upon the water, not a sail in motion, and no gaudy ensign streaming from her tops.

"Hector," said his master, calling the slave, while he threw himself lazily along the knoll, and motioned the negro near him: "Hector."

"Yes, sah—Maussa."

"You marked that sailor fellow, did you, Hector?"

"I bin see um, Maussa."

"What is he; what do you think of him?"

"I tink notin bout 'em, sah.—Nebber see 'em afore—no like he look."

"Nor I, Hector—nor I. He comes for no good, and we must see to him."

"I tink so, Maussa."

"Now—look down the river. When did that strange vessel come up?"

"Nebber see 'em till dis morning, Maussa, but speck he come up yesserday. Mass Nichol, de doctor, wha' talk so big—da him fuss show 'em to me dis morning."

"What said Nichols?"

"He say 'tis English ship; den he say 'tis no English, 'tis Dutch— but soon he change he min', and say 'tis little Dutch and little Spaniard: after dat he make long speech to young Mass Hugh Grayson."

"What said Grayson?"

"He laugh at de doctor, make de doctor cross, and den he cuss for a d——m black rascal."

"That made you cross too, eh?"

"Certain, Maussa; 'cause Mass Nichol hab no respectability for nigger in 'em, and talk widout make proper osservation."

"Well, no matter. But did Grayson say anything about the vessel?"

"He look at 'em long time, sah, but he nebber say noting; but wid long stick he write letter in de sand. Dat young Grayson, Mass Charles—he strange gentleman—berry strange gentleman."

"How often must I tell you, Hector, not to call me by any name here but Gabriel Harrison? will you never remember, you scoundrel?"

"Ax pardon, Maussa—'member next time."

"Do so, old boy, or we quarrel:—and now, hark you, Hector, since you know nothing of this vessel, I'll make you wiser. Look down over to Moccasin Point—under the long grass at the edge, and half covered by the canes, and tell me what you see there."

"Da boat, Maussa.—I swear da boat. Something dark lie in de bottom."

"That is a boat from the vessel, and what you see lying dark in the bottom, are the two sailors that rowed it up. That sailor-fellow came in it, and he is the captain. Now, what does he come for, do you think?"

"Speck, sa, he come for buy skins from de Injins."

"No:—that craft is no trader. She carries guns, but conceals them with box and paint. She is built to run and fight, not to carry. I looked on her closely this morning. Her paint is Spanish, not English. Besides, if she were English, what would she be doing here? Why run up this river, without stopping at Charleston or Port Royal—why keep from the landing here, avoiding the whites; and why is her officer pushing up into the Indian country beyond our purchase?"

"He hab 'ting for sell de Injins, I speck, Maussa."

"Scarcely—they have nothing to buy with; it is only a few days since Granger came up from Port Royal, where he had carried all the skins of their last great hunt, and it will be two weeks at least before they go on another. No—no. They get from us what we are willing to sell them; and this vessel brings them those things which they cannot get from us—fire-arms and ammunition, Hector."

"You tink so, Maussa."

"You shall find out for both of us, Hector. Are your eyes open?"

"Yes, Maussa, I kin sing like mocking bird," . . . . and the fellow piped up cheerily, as he spoke in a familiar negro doggrel.

> "'Possum up a gum-tree,
> Racoon in de hollow,

In de grass de yellow snake,
In de clay de swallow.'"

"Evidence enough. Now, hear me. This sailor fellow comes from St. Augustine, and brings arms to the Yemassees. I know it, else why should he linger behind with Sanutee and Ishiagaska, after his quarrel with the old chief, unless he knew of something which must secure his protection? I saw his look of recognition to Ishiagaska, although the savage, more cunning than himself, kept his eye cold—and—yes, it must be so. You shall go," said his master, half musingly, half direct. "You shall go. When did Granger cross to Pocota-ligo?"

"Dis morning, Maussa."

"Did the commissioners go with him?"

"No, sah: only tree gentlemans gone wid him."

"Who were they?"

"Sa Edmund Bellinger, who lib close 'pon Asheepoh—Mass Steben Latham, and nodder one—I no hab he name."

"Very well—they will answer well enough for commissioners. Where have you left Dugdale?"

"I leff um wid de blacksmith,—him dat lib down pass de Chief Bluff."

"Good; and now, Hector, you must take the track after this sailor."

"Off hand, Maussa?"

"Yes, at once. Take the woods here, and make the sweep of the cypress, so as to get round them. Keep clear of the river, for that sailor will make no bones of carrying you off to St. Augustine, or to the West Indies, if he gets a chance. Watch if he goes with the Indians. See all that you can of their movements, and let them not see you. Should they find you out, be as stupid as a pine stump."

"And whay I for fin' you, Maussa, when I come back? At de parson's, I speck." —The slave smiled knowingly as he uttered the last member of the sentence, and looked significantly into the face of his master, with a sidelong glance, his mouth at the same time showing his full white array of big teeth, stretching away like those of a shark, from ear to ear.

"Perhaps so," said his master, quietly and without seeming to observe the peculiar expression of his servant's face— "perhaps so, if you come back soon. I shall be there for a while; but to-night you will probably find me at the Block House. Away now, and see that you sleep not; keep your eye open lest they trap you."

"Ha, Maussa. Dat eye must be bright like de moon for trap Hector."

"I hope so—keep watchful, for if that sailor-fellow puts hands upon you, he will cut your throat as freely as he did the dog's, and probably a thought sooner."

Promising strict watchfulness, the negro took his way back into the woods, closely following the directions of his master. Harrison, meanwhile, having dispatched this duty so far, rose buoyantly from the turf, and throwing aside the sluggishness which for the last half hour had invested him, darted forward in a fast walk in the direction of the white settlements; still, however, keeping as nearly as he might to the banks of the river, and still with an eye that closely scanned at intervals the appearance of the little vessel which, as we have seen, had occasioned so much doubt and inquiry. It was not often that a vessel of her make and size had been seen up that little insulated river; and as, from the knowledge of Harrison, there could be little or no motive of trade for such craft in that quarter—the small business intercourse of the whites with the Indians being soon transacted, and through mediums far less imposing—the suspicions of the Englishman were justified and not a little excited, particularly as he had known for some time the increasing discontent among the savages. The fact, too, that the vessel was a stranger, and that her crew and captain had kept studiously aloof from the whites, and had sent their boat to land at a point actually within the Indian boundary, was, of itself, enough to prompt the most exciting surmises. The ready intelligence of Harrison at once associated the facts with a political object; and being also aware, by previous information, that Spanish guarda-costas, as the cutters employed at St. Augustine for the protection of the coast were styled, had been seen to put into almost every river and creek in the English territory, from St. Mary's to Hatteras, and within a recent period, the connected circumstances were well calculated to excite the scrutiny of all well-intentioned citizens.

The settlement of the English in Carolina, though advancing with wonderful rapidity, was yet in its infancy; and the great jealousy which their progress had occasioned in the minds of their Indian neighbours, was not a little stimulated in its tenour and development by the artifices of the neighbouring Spaniards, as well of St. Augustine as of the Island of Cuba. The utmost degree of caution against enemies so powerful and so easily acted upon, was absolutely necessary; and we shall comprehend to its full, the extent of this conviction among the colonists, after repeated sufferings had taught them providence, when we learn from the historians that it was not long before this when the settlers upon the coast were compelled to gather oysters for their subsistence with one hand, while carrying fire-arms in the other for their protection. At this time, however, unhappily for the colony, such a degree of watchfulness was entirely unknown. Thoughtless as ever, the great mass is always slow to note the premonitions and evidences of change which are at all times going on around them. The counsellings of nature and of experience are seldom heeded by the inconsiderate multitude, until their omens are realized, and then when it is beyond the control which would have converted them into agents, with the almost certain prospect of advantageous results. It is fortunate, perhaps, for mankind, that there are some few minds always in advance, and for ever preparing the way for society, even sacrificing themselves nobly, that the species may have victory. Perhaps, indeed, patriotism itself would lack something of its stimulating character, if martyrdom did not follow its labours and its love for man.

Harrison, active in perceiving, decisive in providing against events, with a sort of intuition, had traced out a crowd of circumstances, of most imposing character and number, in the events of the time, of which few if any in the colony besides himself, had any idea. He annexed no small importance to the seeming trifle; and his mind was deeply interested in all the changes going on in the province. Perhaps, it was his particular charge to note these things—his station, pursuit—his duty, which, by imposing upon him some of the leading responsibilities of the infant society in which he lived, had made him more ready in such an exercise than was common among those around him. On this point we can now say nothing, being as yet quite as ignorant as those who go along with us. As we proceed we shall probably all grow wiser.

While Harrison thus rambled downwards along the river's banks, a friendly voice hallooed to him from its bosom, where a pettiauger, urged by a couple of sinewy rowers, was heaving to the shore.

"Halloo, captain," cried one of the men— "I'm so glad to see you."

"Ah, Grayson," he exclaimed to the one, "how do you fare?" —to the other, "Master Hugh, I give you good day."

The two men were brothers, and the difference made in Harrison's address between the two simply indicated the different degrees of intimacy between them and himself.

"We've been hunting, captain, and have had glorious sport," said the elder of the brothers, known as Walter Grayson— "two fine bucks and a doe. We put them up in a twinkling; had a smart drive, and bagged our birds at sight. Not a miss at any. And here they are. Shall we have you to sup with us to-night?"

"Hold me willing, Grayson, but not ready. I have labours for to-night that will keep me from you. But I shall tax your hospitality before the venison's out. Make my respects to the old lady, your mother; and if you can let me see you at the Block House to-morrow, early morning, do so, and hold me your debtor for good service."

"I will be there, captain, God willing, and shall do as you ask. I am sorry you can't come to-night."

"So am not I," said the younger Grayson, as, making his acknowledgments and farewell, Harrison pushed out of sight and re-entered the forest. The boat touched the shore, and the brothers leaped out, pursuing their talk, and taking out their game as they did so.

"So am not I," repeated the younger brother, gloomily:— "I would see as little of that man as possible."

"And why, Hugh? In what does he offend you?" was the inquiry of his companion.

"I know not—but he does offend me, and I hate him, thoroughly hate him."

"And wherefore, Hugh! what has he done—what said? You have seen but little of him to judge. Go with me to-morrow to the Block House—see him—talk with him. You will find him a noble gentleman."

And the two brothers continued the subject while moving homeward with the spoil.

"I would not see him, though I doubt not what you say. I would rather that my impressions of him should remain as they are."

"Hugh Grayson—your perversity comes from a cause you would blush that I should know—you dislike him, brother, because Bess Matthews does not."

The younger brother threw from his shoulder the carcase of the deer which he carried, and with a broken speech, but a fierce look and angry gesture, confronted the speaker.

"Walter Grayson—you are my brother—you are my brother;—but do not speak on this subject again. I am perverse—I am unreasonable, perhaps! Be it so—I cannot be other than I am; and, as you love me, bear with it while you may. But urge me no more in this matter. I cannot like that man for many reasons, and not the least of these is, that I cannot so readily as yourself acknowledge his superiority, while, perhaps, not less than yourself, I cannot help but feel it. My pride is to feel my independence—it is for you to desire control, were it only for the connexion and the sympathy which it brings to you. You are one of the million who make tyrants. Go—worship him yourself, but do not call upon me to do likewise."

"Take up the meat, brother, and be not wroth with me. We are what we are. We are unlike each other, though brothers, and perhaps cannot help it. But one thing—nay, above all things, try and remember, in order that your mood may be kept in subjection—try and remember our old mother."

A few more words of sullen dialogue between them, and the two brothers passed into a narrow pathway leading to a cottage, where, at no great distance, they resided.

Chapter Seven

"Ye may not with a word define
The love that lightens o'er her face,
That makes her glance a glance divine,
Fresh caught from heaven, its native place—
And in her heart as in her eye,
A spirit lovely as serene—
Makes of each charm some deity,
Well worshipp'd, though perhaps unseen."

THE soft sunset of April, of an April sky in Carolina, lay beautifully over the scene that afternoon. Embowered in trees, with a gentle esplanade running down to the river, stood the pretty yet modest cottage in which lived the pastor of the settlement, John Matthews, his wife, and daughter Elizabeth. The dwelling was prettily enclosed with sheltering groves—through which, at spots here and there, peered forth its well whitewashed verandah. The river, a few hundred yards in front, wound pleasantly along, making a circuitous sweep just at that point, which left the cottage upon something like an isthmus, and made it a prominent object to the eye in an approach from either end of the stream. The site had been felicitously chosen, and the pains taken with it had sufficiently improved the rude location to show how much may be effected by art, when employed in arranging the toilet, and in decorating the wild beauties of her country cousin. The house itself was rude enough—like those of the region generally—having been built of logs, put together as closely as the material would permit, and affording only a couple of rooms in front, to which the additional shed contributed two more, employed as sleeping apartments. Having shared, however, something of the whitewash which had been employed upon the verandah, the little fabric wore a cheerful appearance, which proved that the pains taken with it had not been entirely thrown away upon the coarse material of which it had been constructed. We should not forget to mention the porch or portico of four columns, formed of slender pines decapitated for the purpose, which, having its distinct roof, formed the entrance through the piazza to the humble cottage. We are not prepared to insist upon the good taste of this addition, which was very much an excrescence. The clustering vines, too, hanging fantastically over the entrance, almost forbidding ingress, furnished proof enough of the presence and agency of that sweet nature, which, lovely of itself, has yet an added attraction when coupled with the beauty and the purity of woman.

Gabriel Harrison, as our new acquaintance has been pleased to style himself, was seen towards sunset, emerging from the copse which grew alongside the river, and approaching the cottage. Without scruple, he lifted the wooden latch which secured the gate of the little paling fence running around it, and slowly moved up to the entrance. His approach, however, had not been entirely unobserved. A bright pair of eyes, and a laughing, young, even girlish face were peering through the green leaves which almost covered it in. As the glance met his own, the expression of sober gravity and thoughtfulness departed from his countenance; and he now seemed only the playful, wild, thoughtless, and gentle-natured being she had been heretofore accustomed to regard him.

"Ah, Bess; dear Bess—still the same, my beauty; still the laughing, the lovely, the star-eyed—"

"Hush, hush, you noisy and wicked—not so loud; mother is busily engaged in her evening nap, and that long tongue of yours will not make it sounder."

"A sweet warning, Bess—but what then, child? If we talk not, we are like to have a dull time of it."

"And if you do, and she wakes without having her nap out, we are like to have a cross time of it; and so, judge for yourself which you would best like."

"I'm dumb,—speechless, my beauty, as a jay on a visit! See now what you will lose by it."

"What shall I lose, Gabriel?"

"My fine speeches—your own praise—no more eloquence and sentiment? My tongue and your ears will entirely forget their old acquaintance; and there will be but a single mode of keeping any of our memories alive."

"How is that—what mode?"

"An old song tells us—

"'The lips of the dumb may speak of love,
Though the words may die in a kiss—
And—'"

"Will you never be quiet, Gabriel?"

"How can I, with so much that is disquieting near me? Quiet, indeed,—why, Bess, I never look upon you—ay, for that matter, I never think of you, but my heart beats, and my veins tingle, and my pulses bound, and all is confusion in my senses. You are my disquiet, far and near—and you know not, dear Bess, how much I have longed, during the last spell of absence, to be near, and again to see you."

"Oh, I heed not your flattery. Longed for me, indeed, and so long away. Why, where have you been all this while, and what is the craft, Gabriel, which keeps you away?—am I never to know the secret?"

"Not yet, not yet, sweetest; but a little while, my most impatient beauty; but a little while, and you shall know all and every thing."

"Shall I? but, ah! how long have you told me so—years, I'm sure—"

"Scarcely months, Bess—your heart is your book-keeper."

"Well, months—for months you have promised me—but a little while, and you shall know all; and here I've told you all my secrets, as if you had a right to know them."

"Have I not?—if my craft, Bess, were only my secret—if much that belongs to others did not depend upon it—if, indeed, success in its pursuit were not greatly risked by its exposure—you should have heard it with the same sentence which just told you how dear you were to me. But, only by secrecy can my objects be successfully accomplished. Besides, Bess, as it concerns others, the right to yield it, even to such sweet custody as your own, is not with me."

"But, Gabriel, I can surely keep it safely."

"How can you, Bess—since, as a dutiful child, you are bound to let your mother share in all your knowledge? She knows of our love? does she not?"

"Yes, yes, and she is glad to know—she approves of it. And so, Gabriel—forgive me: but I am very anxious—and so you can't tell me what is the craft you pursue?" and she looked very persuasive as she spoke.

"I fear me, Bess, if you once knew my craft, you would discover that our love was all a mistake. You would learn to unlove much faster than you ever learned to love."

"Nonsense, Gabriel—you know that is impossible."

"A thousand thanks, Bess, for the assurance; but are you sure—suppose now, that I were a pedler, doing the same business with Granger, probably his partner—only think."

"That cannot be—I know better than that—I'm certain it is not so."

"And why not, my Beautiful."

"Have done!—and, Gabriel, cease calling me nick-names, or I'll leave you. I won't suffer it. You make quite too free."

"Do I, Bess,—well, I'm very sorry—but I can't help it, half the time, I assure you. It's my nature—I was born so, and have been so from the cradle up. Freedom is my infirmity. It leads to sad irreverences, I know. The very first words I uttered, were so many nicknames, and in calling my own papa, would you believe it, I could never get further than the pap."

"Obstinate—incorrigible man!"

"Dear, delightful, mischievous woman—But, Bess, by what are you assured I am no trader?"

"By many things, Gabriel—by look, language, gesture, manner—your face, your speech.—All satisfy me that you are no trader, but a gentleman—like the brave cavaliers that stood by King Charles."

"A dangerous comparison, Bess, if your old Puritan sire could hear it. What! the daughter of the grave Pastor Matthews thinking well of the cavaliers of Charlie Stuart? Shocking!—why, Bess, let him but guess at such bad taste on your part, he'll be down upon you, thirty thousand strong, in scolds and sermons."

"Hush—don't speak of papa after that fashion. It's true, he talks hardly of the cavaliers—and I think well of those he talks ill of;—so much for your teaching, Gabriel. It is you that are to blame. But he loves me; and that's enough to make me respect his opinions, and to love him, in spite of them."

"You think he loves you, Bess—and doubtlessly he does, as who could otherwise—but, is it not strange that he does not love you enough to desire your happiness?"

"Why, so he does."

"How can that be, Bess, when he still refuses you to me?"

"And are you so sure, Gabriel, that his consent would have that effect? Would it, indeed, secure my happiness?"

The maiden made the inquiry, slowly, half pensively, half playfully, with a look nevertheless downcast, and a cheek that showed a blush after the prettiest manner. Harrison passed his arm about her person, and with a tone and countenance something graver than usual, but full of tenderness, replied:—

"You do not doubt it yourself, dearest. I'm sure you do not. Be satisfied of it, so far as a warm affection, and a thought studious to please your own, can give happiness to mortal. If you are not assured by this time, no word from me can make you more so. True, Bess—I am wild—perhaps rash and frivolous—foolish, and in some things headstrong and obstinate enough; but the love for you, Bess, which I have always felt, I have felt as a serious and absorbing concern, predominating over all other objects of my existence. Let me be at the wildest—the waywardest—as full of irregular impulse as I may be, and your name, and the thought of you, bring me back to myself, bind me down, and take all wilfulness from my spirit. It is true, Bess, true, by the blessed sunlight that gives us its smile and its promise while passing from our sight—but this you knew before, and only desired its reassertion, because—"

"Because what, Gabriel?"

"Because the assurance is so sweet to your ears, that you could not have it too often repeated."

"Oh, abominable—thus it is, you destroy all the grace of your pretty speeches. But you mistake the sex, if you suppose we care for your vows on this subject—knowing, as we do, that you are compelled to love us, we take the assurance for granted."

"I grant you; but the case is yours also. Love is a mutual necessity; and were it not that young hearts are still old hypocrites, the general truth would have long since been admitted; but—"

He was interrupted at this point of the dialogue—which, in spite of all the warnings of the maiden, had been carried on, in the warmth of its progress, somewhat more loudly than was absolutely necessary—and brought back to a perception of the error by a voice of inquiry from within, demanding of Bess with whom she spoke.

"With Gabriel—with Captain Harrison—mother."

"Well, why don't you bring him in? Have you forgotten your manners, Bess?"

"No, mother, but—come in, Gabriel, come in:" —and as she spoke she extended her hand, which he passionately carried to his lips, and resolutely maintained there, in spite of all her resistance, while passing into the entrance and before reaching the apartment. The good old dame, a tidy, well-preserved antique, received the visitor with regard and kindness, and, though evidently but half recovered from a sound nap, proceeded to chatter with him, and at him, with all the garrulous freedom of one who saw but little of the world, possessed more than her usual share of the curiosity of the sex, and exercised the natural garrulity of age. Harrison, with that playful frankness which formed so large a portion of his manner, and without any effort, had contrived long since to make himself a friend in the mother of his sweetheart; and knowing her foible, he now contented himself with provoking the conversation, prompting the choice of material, and leaving the tongue of the old lady at her own pleasure to pursue it: he, in the meanwhile, contriving that sort of chat, through the medium of looks and glances with the daughter, so grateful in all similar cases to young people, and which, at the same time, offered no manner of obstruction to the employment of the mother. It was not long before Mr. Matthews, the pastor himself, made his appearance, and the cour- tesies of his reception were duly extended by him to the guest of his wife and daughter; but there seemed a something of backwardness, a chilly repulsiveness in the manner of the old gentleman, quite repug- nant to the habits of the country, and not less so to the feelings of Harrison. For a brief period, indeed, the cold deportment of the Pastor had the effect of somewhat freezing the warm exuberant blood of the cavalier, arresting the freedom of his speech, and flinging a chilling spell over the circle. The old man was an ascetic—a stern Presbyterian—one of the ultra-nonconformists—and not a little annoyed at that period, and in the new country, by the course of gov- ernment, and plan of legislation pursued by the Proprietary Lords of the province, which, in the end, brought about a revolution in Carolina, resulting in the transfer of their colonial rights and the restoration of their charter to the crown. The leading proprietors were generally of the church of England, and, with all the bigotry of the zealot, forgetting, and in violation of their strict pledges, given at the settlement of the colony—and through which they made the acquisi- tion of a large body of their most valuable population—not to inter- fere in the popular religion—they proceeded, soon after the colony began to flourish, to the establishment of a regular church, and, from step to step, had at length gone so far as actually to exclude from all representation in the colonial assemblies, such portions of the country as were chiefly settled by other sects. The region in which we find our story, shared in this exclusion; and, with a man like Matthews, who was somewhat stern of habit and cold of temperament—a good man in his way, and as the world goes, but not an overwise one—a stickler for small things—wedded to old habits and prejudices, and perhaps like a very extensive class, one who, preserving forms, might with little difficulty be persuaded to throw aside principles—with such a man the native acerbity of his sect might be readily supposed to undergo vast increase and exercise, from the political disabilities thus warring with his religious professions. He was a bigot himself, and, with the power, would doubtless have tyrannised after a similar fashion. The world within him was what he could take in with his eye, or control within the sound of his voice. He could not be brought to understand that climates and conditions should be various, and that the popular good, in a strict reference to the mind of man, demanded that people should everywhere differ in manner and opinion. He wore clothes after a different fashion from those who ruled, and the difference was vital; but he perfectly agreed with those in power that there should be a prescribed standard by which the opinions of all persons should be regulated; and such a point as this forms the faith for which, forgetful all the while of propriety, not less than of truth, so many thousands are ready for the stake and the sacrifice. But though as great a bigot as any of his neighbours, Matthews yet felt how very uncomfortable it was to be in a minority; and the persecutions to which his sect had been exposed in Carolina, where they had been taught to look for every form of indulgence, had made him not less hostile towards the government than bitter in his feelings and conduct in society to those who were of the ruling party. To him, the bearing of Harrison,—his dashing, free, unrestrainable carriage, directly adverse to Puritan rule and usage, was particularly offensive; and, at this moment, some newly proposed exactions of the proprietors in England, having for their object something more of religious reform, had almost determined many of the Puritans to remove from the colony, and place themselves under the more gentle and inviting rule of Penn, then beginning to attract all eyes to the singularly pacific and wonderfully successful government of his establishment. Having this character, and perplexed with these thoughts, old Matthews was in no mood to look favourably upon the suit of Harrison. For a little while after his entrance the dialogue was constrained and very chilling, and Harrison himself grew dull under its influence, while Bess looked every now and then doubtfully, now to her father and now to her lover, not a little heedful of the increased sternness which lowered upon the features of the old man. Some family duties at length demanding the absence of the old lady, Bess took occasion to follow; and the circumstance seemed to afford the pastor a chance for the conversation which he desired.

"Master Harrison," said he, gravely, "I have just returned from a visit to Port Royal Island, and from thence to Charleston."

"Indeed, sir—I was told you had been absent, but knew not certainly where you had gone. How did you travel?"

"By canoe, sir, to Port Royal, and then by Miller's sloop to Charleston."

"Did you find all things well, sir, in that quarter, and was there any thing from England?"

"All things were well, sir; there had been a vessel with settlers from England."

"What news, sir—what news?"

"The death of her late majesty, Queen Anne, whom God receive—"

"Amen!—but the throne—" was the impatient inquiry. "The succession?"

"The throne, sir, is filled by the Elector of Hanover—"

"Now may I hear falsely, for I would not heed this tale? What—was there no struggle for the Stuart—no stroke?—now shame on the people so ready for the chain;—so little loyal to the true sovereign of the realm!" and as Harrison spoke, he rose with a brow deeply wrinkled with thought and indignation, and paced hurriedly over the floor.

"You are fast, too fast, Master Harrison; there had been strife, and a brief struggle, though, happily for the nation, a successless one, to lift once more into the high places of power that bloody and witless family—the slayers and the persecutors of the saints. But thanks be to the God that breathed upon the forces of the foe, and shrunk up their sinews. The strife is at rest there; but when, oh Lord, shall the persecutions of thy servants cease here, even in thy own untrodden places!"

The old man paused, while, without seeming to notice well what he had last said, Harrison continued to pace the floor in deep meditation. At length the pastor again addressed him, though in a different tone and upon a very different subject.

"Master Harrison," said he, "I have told thee that I have been to

Charleston—perhaps I should tell thee that it would have been my pleasure to meet with thee there."

"I have been from Charleston some weeks, sir," was the somewhat hurried reply. "I have had labours upon the Ashepoo, and even to the waters of the Savannah."

"I doubt not—I doubt not, Master Harrison," was the sober response; "thy craft carries thee far, and thy labours are manifold; but what is that craft, Master Harrison? and, while I have it upon my lips, let me say, that it was matter of strange surprise in my mind, when I asked after thee in Charleston, not to find any wholesome citizen who could point out thy lodgings, or to whom thy mere name was a thing familiar. Vainly did I ask after thee—none said for thee, Master Harrison is a good man and true, and his works are sound and sightworthy."

"Indeed—the savages" —spoke the person addressed, with a most provoking air of indifference— "and so, Mr. Matthews, your curiosity went without profit in either of those places?"

"Entirely, sir—and I would even have sought that worthy gentleman, Lord Craven, for his knowledge of thee, if he had aught to say, but that he was gone forth upon a journey," replied the old gentleman, with an air of much simplicity.

"That would have been going far for thy curiosity, sir—very far—and it would be lifting a poor gentleman like myself into undeserving notice, to have sought for him at the hands of the Governor Craven."

"Thou speakest lightly of my quest, Master Harrison, as, indeed, it is too much thy wont to speak of all other things," was the grave response of Matthews; "but the subject of my enquiry was too important to the wellbeing of my family, to be indifferent to me, and this provides me the excuse for meddling with concerns of thine!"

Harrison paused for a moment, and looked steadfastly, and with something like affectionate interest in the face of the old man; and for a moment seemed about to address him in language of explanation; but he turned away hurriedly, and walking across the floor, muttered audibly— "Not yet! not yet! not yet! It will not do yet."

"What will not do, Master Harrison. If thou wouldst speak thy mind freely, it were wise."

The young man suddenly resumed his jesting manner.

"And so, sir, there were no Harrisons in Charleston—none in Port Royal?"

"Harrisons there were—"

"True, true, sir—" said Harrison, breaking in— "true, true—

Harrisons there were, but none of them the true. There was no Gabriel among the saints of those places."

"Speak not so irreverently, sir, —if I may crave so much from one who seems usually so indifferent to my desires, however regardful he may be at all times of his own."

"Not so seriously, Mr. Matthews," replied the other, now changing his tone to a business-like and straightforward character. "Not so seriously, sir, if you please; you are quite too grave in this matter, by half, and allow nothing for the ways of one who, perhaps, is not a jot more extravagant in his, than you are in yours. Permit me to say, sir, that a little more plain confidence in Gabriel Harrison would have saved thee the unnecessary and unprofitable trouble thou hast given thyself in Charleston. I know well enough, and should willingly have assured thee that thy search after Gabriel Harrison in Charleston would be as wild as that of the old Spaniard among the barrens of Florida for the waters of an eternal youth. He has neither chick nor child, nor friend nor servant, either in Charleston or in Port Royal, and men there may not well answer for one whom they do not often see unless as a stranger. Gabriel Harrison lives not in those places, Master Matthews."

"It is not where he lives not that I seek to know—to this thou hast spoken only, Master Harrison—wilt thou now condescend to say where he *does* live, where his name and person may be known, where his dwelling and his connexions may be found—what is his craft, what his condition?"

"A different inquiry that, Mr. Matthews, and one rather more difficult to answer—*now* at least. I must say to you, sir, as I did before, when first speaking with you on the subject of your daughter, that I am of good family and connexions, drive no servile or dishonourable craft—am one thou shalt not be ashamed of—neither thou nor thy daughter; and, though now engaged in a pursuit which makes it necessary that much of my own concerns be kept for a time in close secrecy, yet the day will come, and I look for it to come ere long, when all shall be known, and thou shalt have no reason to regret thy confidence in the stranger. For the present, I can tell thee no more."

"This will not do for me, Master Harrison—it will not serve a father. On an assurance so imperfect, I cannot risk the good name and the happiness of my child; and, let me add to thee, Master Harrison, that there are other objections which gather in my mind, hostile to thy claim, even were these entirely removed."

"Ha! what other objections, sir?—speak."

"Many, sir; nor the least of these, thy great levity of speech and manner, on all occasions; a levity which is unbecoming in one having an immortal soul, and discreditable to one of thy age."

"My age, indeed, sir—my youth, you will surely phrase it upon suggestion, for I do not mark more than thirty, and would have neither Bess nor yourself count upon me for a greater experience of yours."

"It is unbecoming, sir, in any age, and in you shows itself quite too frequently. Then, sir, your tone and language, contemptuous of many things which the lover of religion is taught to venerate, too greatly savour of that ribald court and reign which made merry at the work of the Creator, and the persecution of his creatures, and drank from a rich cup where the wine of drunkenness and the blood of the saints were mixed together in most lavish profusion. You sing, sir, mirthful songs, and sometimes, though, perhaps, not so often, employ a profane oath, in order that your speech—a vain notion, but too common among thoughtless and frivolous persons—may, in the silly esteem of the idle and the ignorant, acquire a strong and sounding force, and an emphasis which might not be found in the meaning and sense which it would convey. Thy common speech, Master Harrison, has but too much the ambition of wit about it—which is a mere crackling of thorns beneath the pot——"

"Enough, enough, good father of mine that is to be; you have said quite enough against me, and more, rest you thankful, than I shall ever undertake to answer. One reply, however, I am free to make you."

"I shall be pleased to hear you, sir."

"That is gracious, surely, on the part of the accuser:—and now, sir, let me say, I admit the sometime levity, the playfulness and the thoughtlessness, perhaps. I shall undertake to reform these, when you shall satisfy me that to laugh and sing, and seek and afford amusement, are inconsistent with my duties either to the Creator or the creature. On this head, permit me to say that you are the criminal, not me. It is you, sir, and your sect, that are the true criminals. Denying, as you do, to the young, all those natural forms of enjoyment and amusement which the Deity, speaking through their own nature, designed for their wholesome nurture, you cast a shadow over all things around you. In this way, sir, you force them upon the necessity of seeking for less obvious and more artificial enjoyments, which are not often innocent, and which are frequently ruinous and destructive. As for the irreverence to religion, and sacred things, with which you charge me, you will suffer me respectfully to deny. This is but your fancy, reverend sir; the fruit of your false views of things. If I were thus irreverent or irreligious it were certainly a grievous fault, and I should be grievously sorry for it. But I am not conscious of such faults. I have no reproaches on this subject. Your church is not mine; and that is probably a fault in your eyes; but I offer no scorn or disrespect to yours. In regard to manners and morals, there is no doubt something to be amended, in my case, as in that of most persons. I do not pretend to deny that I am a man of many errors, and perhaps some vices. You will suffer me to try and cure these, as worldly people are apt to do, gradually, and with as much ease to myself as possible. I am not more fond of them, I honestly think, than the rest of my neighbours; and hope, some day, to be a better and a wiser man than I am. That I shall never be a Puritan, however, you may be assured, if it be only to avoid giving to my face the expression of a pine bur. That I shall never love Cromwell the better for having been a hypocrite as well as a murderer, you may equally take for granted; and, that my dress, unlike your own, sir, shall be fashioned always with a due reference to my personal becomingness, you and I, both, may this day safely swear for. These are matters, Mr. Matthews, upon which you insist with too much solemnity. I look upon them, sir, as so many trifles, not worthy the close consideration of thinking men. I will convince you, before many days, perhaps, that my levity does not unfit me for business—never interferes with my duties. I wear it as I do my doublet; when it suits me to do so, I throw it aside, and proceed, soul and body, to the necessity which calls for it. Such, sir, is Gabriel Harrison—the person for whom you can find no kindred—no sponsor; an objection, perfectly idle, sir, when one thing is considered."

Here he paused somewhat abruptly. The pastor had been taken all aback by the cool and confident speech of his youthful companion, whom he thought to have silenced entirely by the history of his discoveries in Charleston—or his failure to discover. He knew not well what to answer, and for a brief and awkward moment was silent himself. But, with an effort at composure and solemnity, seizing on the last word of Harrison's speech, he said—

"And pray, sir, what may that one thing be?"

"Why, simply, sir, that your daughter is to marry Gabriel Harrison himself, and not his kindred."

"Let Gabriel Harrison rest assured that my daughter does no such thing."

"*Cha-no-selonee*, as the Yemassees say. We shall see. I don't believe that. Trust not your vow, Master Matthews. Gabriel Harrison will marry your daughter, and make her an excellent husband, sir, in spite of you. More than that, sir, I will, for once, be a prophet among the rest, and predict that you too shall clasp hands on the bargain."

"Indeed!"

"Ay, indeed, sir. Look not so sourly, reverend sir, upon the matter. I am bent on it. You shall not destroy your daughter's chance of happiness in denying mine. Pardon me if my phrase is something audacious. I have been a rover, and my words come with my feelings—I seldom stop to pick them. I love Bess, and I'm sure I can make her happy. Believing this, and believing too that you shall be satisfied, after a time, with me, however you dislike my name, I shall not suffer myself to be much troubled on the score of your refusal. When the time comes—when I can see my way through some few difficulties now before me, and when I have safely performed other duties, I shall come to possess myself of my bride—and, as I shall then give you up my secret, I shall look to have her at your hands."

"We shall see, sir," was all the response which the bewildered pastor uttered to the wild visitor who had thus addressed him. The character of the dialogue, however, did not seem so greatly to surprise him, as one might have expected. He appeared to be rather familiar with some of the peculiarities of his companion, and however much he might object to his seeming recklessness, he himself was not altogether insensible to the manly frankness which marked Harrison's conduct throughout. The conversation had now fairly terminated, and Harrison seemed in no humour to continue it or to prolong his visit. He took his leave accordingly. The pastor followed him to the door with the stiff formality of one who appears anxious to close it on such visitor for ever. Harrison laughed out as he beheld his visage, and his words of leave-taking were as light and lively as those of the other were lugubrious and solemn. The door closed upon the guest. The pastor strode back to his easy chair and silent meditations. But he was aroused by Harrison's return. His expression of face, no longer laughing, was now singularly changed to a reflective gravity.

"Mr. Matthews," said he— "of one thing let me not forget to counsel you. There is some mischief afoot among the Yemassees. I have reason to believe that it has been for some time in progress. We shall not be long, I fear, without an explosion, and must be prepared. The lower Block House would be your safest retreat in case of time being allowed you for flight; but I pray you reject no warning, and take the first Block House if the warning be short. I shall probably be nigh, however, in the event of danger, and though you like not the name of Gabriel Harrison, its owner has some ability, and wants none of the will to do you service."

The old man was struck, not less with the earnest manner of the speaker, so unusual with him, than with his language; and, with something more of deference in his own expression, begged to know the occasion of his apprehensions.

"I cannot well tell you now," said the other, "but there are reasons enough to render caution advisable. Your eye has probably before this beheld the vessel in the river. She is a stranger, and I think an enemy. But as we have not the means of contending with her now, we must watch her well, and do what we can by stratagem. What we think, too, must be thought secretly; but to you I may say, that I suspect an agent of the Spaniard in that vessel, and will do my utmost to find him out. I know that sundry of the Yemassees have been for the first time to St. Augustine, and they have come home burdened with gauds and gifts. These are not given for nothing. But, enough—be on your watch; to give you more of my confidence, at this moment, than is called for, is no part of my vocation."

"In heaven's name, who are you, sir?" was the earnest exclamation of the old pastor.

Harrison laughed again with all the merry mood of boyhood. In the next moment he replied, with the most profound gravity of expression, "Gabriel Harrison, with your leave, sir, and the future husband of Bess Matthews."

In another moment, not waiting any answer, he was gone, and looking back as he darted down the steps and into the avenue, he caught a glance of the maiden's eye peering through a neighbouring window, and kissed his hand to her twice and thrice; then, with a hasty nod to the wondering father, who now began to regard him as a madman, he dashed forward through the gate, and was soon upon the banks of the river.

Chapter Eight

"The nations meet in league—a solemn league,
This is their voice—this their united pledge,
For all adventure."

SANUTEE turned away from the spot whence Harrison had departed, and was about to retire, when, not finding himself followed by Ishiagaska, and perceiving the approach of the sailor, his late opponent, and not knowing what to expect, whether peace or war, he again turned, facing the two, and lifting his bow, and setting his arrow, he prepared himself for a renewal of the strife. But the voice of the sailor and of Ishiagaska, at the same moment, reached his ears in language of conciliation; and, resting himself slightly against a tree, foregoing none of his precautions, however, with a cold indifference he awaited their approach. The seaman addressed him with all his usual bluntness, but with a manner now very considerably changed from what it was at their first encounter. He apologized for his violence, and for having slain the dog. Had he known to whom it belonged, so he assured the chief, he had not been so hasty in despatching it; and, as some small amends, he begged the Indian to do with the venison as he thought proper, for it was now his own. During the utterance of this uncouth apology, mixed up as it was with numberless oaths, Sanutee looked on and listened with contemptuous indifference. When it was done, he simply replied—

"It is well—but the white man will keep the meat: —it is not for Sanutee."

"Come, come, don't be ill-favoured now, old warrior. What's done can't be undone, and more ado is too much to do. I'm sure I'm sorry enough I killed the dog, but how was I to know he belonged to you?"

The sailor might have gone on for some time after this fashion, had not Ishiagaska, seeing that the reference to his dog only the more provoked the ire of the chief, interposed by an address to the sailor, which more readily commanded Sanutee's consideration.

"The master of the big canoe—is he not the chief that comes from St. Augustine? Ishiagaska has looked upon the white chief in the great lodge of his Spanish brother."

"Ay, that you have, Indian, I'll be sworn; and I thought I knew you from the first. I am the friend of the Spanish governor, and I come here now upon his business."

"It is good," responded Ishiagaska—and he turned to Sanutee, with whom, for a few moments, he carried on a conversation in their own language, entirely beyond the comprehension of the sailor, who nevertheless gave it all due attention.

"Brings the master of the big canoe nothing from our Spanish brother? Hides he no writing in his bosom?" was the inquiry of Ishiagaska, turning from Sanutee, who seemed to have prompted the inquiry.

"Writing indeed—no—writing to wild Indians." The last fragment of the sentence was uttered to himself. He continued aloud, "Now, I have brought you no writing, but here is something that you may probably understand quite as well. Here—this is what I have brought you. See if you can read it."

As he spoke, he drew from his bosom a bright red cloth—a strip, not over six inches in width, but of several yards in length, worked over, at little intervals, with symbols and figures of every kind and of the most fantastic description—among which were birds and beasts, reptiles, and insects, rudely wrought, either in shells or beads, which, however grotesque, had yet their signification. This was the Belt of Wampum which among all the Indian nations formed a common language, susceptible of every variety of use. By this instrument they were taught to declare hostility and friendship, war and peace. Thus were their treaties made; and, in the speeches of their orators, the Belt of Wampum, given at the conclusion of each division of the subject, was made to asseverate their sincerity. Each tribe, having its own hieroglyphic, supposed or assumed to be especially characteristic, affixed its *totem*, or sign manual, to such a belt as that brought by the stranger; and this mode of signature effectually bound it to the conditions which the other signs may have expressed.

The features of the chief, Sanutee, underwent a change from the repose of indifference to the lively play of the warmest interest, as he beheld the long folds of this document slowly unwind before his eyes; and, without a word, hastily snatching it from the hands of the seaman, he had nearly brought upon himself another assault from that redoubted worthy. But as he made a show of that sort, Ishiagaska interposed.

"How do I know that it is for him—that treaty is for the chiefs of the Yemassees; and blast my eyes if any but the chiefs shall grapple it in their yellow fingers."

"It is right—it is Sanutee, the great chief of the Yemassees; and is not Ishiagaska a chief?" replied the latter, impressively. The sailor was somewhat pacified, and said no more; while Sanutee, who seemed not at all to have heeded the latter's movement, went on examining each figure upon the folds of the Wampum, numbering them carefully upon his fingers as he did so, and conferring upon their characters with Ishiagaska, whose own curiosity was now actively at work along with him in the examination. In that language, which from their lips is so sweet and sonorous, they conversed together, to the great disquiet of the seaman, who had no less curiosity than themselves to know the purport of the instrument, and the opinions of the chiefs upon it. But he understood not a word they said.

"They are here, Ishiagaska, they have heard the speech of the true warrior, and they will stand together. Look, this green bird is for the Estatoe;* he will sing death in the sleeping ear of the pale warrior of the English."

"He is a great brave of the hills, and has long worn the blanket of the Spaniard. It is good," was the reply.

"And this for the Cussoboe—it is burnt timber. They took the totem from the Suwannee, when they smoked him out of his lodge. And this for the Alatamaha, a green leaf of the summer, for the great prophet of the Alatamaha never dies, and looks always in youth. This tree snake stands for the Serannah; for he watches in the thick top of the bush for the warrior that walks blind underneath."

"I have looked on this chief in battle—the hill chief of Apalachy. It was the fight of a long day, when we took scalps from their warriors, and slew them with their arms about our necks. They are brave—look, the mark of their knife is deep in the cheek of Ishiagaska."

"The hill is their *totem*. It stands, and they never lie. This is the

---

* A tribe of the Cherokees, living in what is now Pendleton district.

wolf tribe of the Cherokee—and this the bear's. Look, the Catawba, that laughs, is here. He speaks with the trick-tongue of the Coonee-lattee;* he laughs, but he can strike like a true brave, and sings his death-song with a free spirit."

"For whom speaks the viper-snake, hissing from under the bush?"

"For the Creek warrior with the sharp tooth, that tears. His tooth is like an arrow, and when he tears away the scalp of his enemy, he drinks a long drink of his blood, that makes him strong. This is their *totem*—I know them of old; they gave us sixty braves when we fought with the Chickasahs."

The sailor had heard this dialogue without any of the advantages possessed by us. It was in a dead language to him. Becoming impatient, and desiring to have some hand in the business, he took advantage of a pause made by Sanutee—who now seemed to examine with Ishiagaska more closely the list they had read out—to suggest a more rapid progress to the rest.

"Roll them out, chief; roll them out; there are many more yet to come. Snakes, and trees, and birds, and beasts enough to people the best *show-stall* of Europe."

"It is good," said Sanutee, who understood in part what had been said; and, as suggested, the Yemassee proceeded to unfold the wampum, at full length, though now he exhibited less curiosity than before. The residue of the hieroglyphics were those chiefly of tribes and nations of which he had been previously secure. He continued, however, as if rather for the stranger's satisfaction than his own.

"Here," said he, continuing the dialogue in his own language with Ishiagaska, "here is the Salutah** that falls like the water. He is a stream from the rock. This is the Isundiga*** that goes on his belly, and shoots from the hollow—this is the Santee, he runs in the long canoe, and his paddle is a cane, that catches the tree top, and thus he goes through the dark swamps of Serattaya.**** The Chickaree stands up in the pine, and the Winyah is here in the terrapin."

---

* The mocking-bird. The Catawbas were of a generous, elastic, and lively temperament, and, until the Yemassee outbreak, usually the friends of the Carolinians.

** Salutah, now written Saluda, and signifying Corn river.

*** Isundiga, or Savannah.

**** Near Nelson's ferry and Scott's lake on the Santee.

"I say, chief," said the sailor, pointing to the next symbol, which was an arrow of considerable length, and curved almost to a crescent, "I say, chief, tell us what this arrow means here—I know it stands for some nation, but what nation? and speak now in plain English, if you can, or in Spanish, or in French, which I can make out, but not in that d——d gibberish which is all up side down and in and out, and no ways at all, to my understanding."

The chief comprehended the object of the sailor, though less from his words than his looks; and with an elevation of head and gesture, and a fine kindling of the eye, he replied proudly:

"It is the arrow, the arrow that came with the storm—it came from the Manneyto to the brave, to the well-beloved, the old father-chief of the Yemassee."

"Ah, ha! so that's your mark—totem, you call it? Well, its a pretty long thing to burrow in one's ribs, and reminds me of the fellow to it, that you kindly intended for mine. But that's over now—so no more of it, old chief."

Neither of the Indians appeared to heed the speech of the sailor. They were too much interested by one of the signs which now met their eyes upon the belt, and which they did not seem to comprehend. Sanutee first called the attention of his brother chief to the symbol, and both were soon busy in eager inquiry. They uttered their doubts and opinions in their own language with no little fluency; for it is something of a popular error to suppose the Indian that taciturn character which he is sometimes represented. He is a great speech-maker, and when serious business claims him not, is exceedingly fond of a jest; which, by the way, is not often the purest in its nature. The want of our language is a very natural reason why he should be sparing of his words when he speaks with us, and a certain suspicious reserve is the consequence of a certain awkward sense of inferiority.

The bewilderment of the chiefs did not escape the notice of the sailor, who immediately guessed its occasion. The symbol before their eyes was that of Spain; the high turrets, and the wide towers of its castellated dominion, frowning in gold, and finely embroidered upon the belt, directly below the simpler ensign of the Yemassees. Explaining the mystery to their satisfaction, the contrast between its gorgeous embodiments and vaster associations of human agency and power, necessarily influenced the imagination of the European, while wanting every thing like force to the Indian, to whom a lodge so vast and cheerless in its aspect, seemed rather an absurdity than any thing else; and he could not help dilating upon the greatness and magnificence of a people dwelling in such houses.

"That's a nation for you now, chiefs—that is the nation after all."

"The Yemassee is the nation," said one of the chiefs proudly.

"Yes, perhaps so, in this part of the world, a great nation enough; but in Europe you wouldn't be a mouthful—a mere drop in the bucket—a wounded porpoise, flirting about in the mighty seas that must swallow it up. Ah! it's a great honour, chiefs, let me tell you, when so great a king as the King of Spain condescends to make a treaty with a wild people such as you are here."

Understanding but little of all this, Sanutee did not perceive its disparaging tendency, but simply pointing to the insignia, inquired—

"It is the Spanish totem?"

"Ay, it's their sign—their arms—if that's what you mean by totem. It was a long time before the Governor of Saint Augustine could get it done after your fashion, till an old squaw of the Cherokees fixed it up, and handsomely enough she has done it too. And now, chiefs, the sooner we go to work the better. The governor has put his hand to the treaty, he will find the arms, and you the warriors."

"The Yemassee will speak to the governor," said Sanutee.

"You will have to go to Saint Augustine, then, for he has sent me in his place. I have brought the treaty, and the arms are in my vessel ready for your warriors, whenever they are ready to sound the warwhoop."

"Does Sanutee speak to a chief?"

"Ay, that he does, or my name is not Richard Chorley. I am a sea chief, a chief of the great canoe, and captain of as pretty a crew as ever riddled a merchantman."

"I see not the totem of your tribe."

"My tribe?" said the sailor laughingly— "My crew, you mean. Yes, they have a totem, and as pretty a one as any on your roll. There, look," said he, and as he spoke, rolling up his sleeve, he displayed a huge anchor upon his arm, done in gunpowder. This was the sort of writing which they could understand. That it was worked on the body of the sailor, worked into his skin, was making the likeness more perfect, and the bearing of the red chiefs towards the sea captain became in consequence more decidedly favourable.

"And now," said Chorley, "it is well I have some of my marks about me, for I can easily put my signature to that treaty without scrawl of pen, or taking half the trouble that it must have given the worker of these beads. But, hear me, chiefs, I don't work for nothing; I must have my pay, and as it don't come out of your pockets, I look to have no refusal."

"The chief of the great canoe will speak."

"Yes, and first to show that I mean to act as well as speak, here is my *totem*—the *totem* of my crew or tribe as you call it. I put it on, and trust to have fair play out of you." As he spoke, he took from his pocket a small leaden anchor, such as are now-a-days numbered among the playthings of children, but which at that period made no unfrequent ornament to the seaman's jacket. A thorn from a neighbouring branch secured it to the wampum, and the engagement of the sea chief was duly ratified. Having done this, he proceeded to unfold his expectations. He claimed, among other things, in consideration of the service of himself and the fifteen men whom he should command in the insurrection, the possession of all slaves who should be taken by him from the Carolinians; and that, unless they offered resistance, they should not be slain in the war.

"I don't want better pay than that," said he, "but that I must and will have, or d———n the blow I strike in the matter."

The terms of the seaman had thus far undergone development, when Sanutee started suddenly, and his eyes, lightening seemingly with some new interest, were busied in scrutinizing the little circuit of wood on the edge of which their conversation had been carried on. Ishiagaska betrayed a similar consciousness of an intruder's presence, and the wampum belt was rolled up hurriedly by one of the chiefs, while the other maintained his watchfulness upon the brush from whence the interruption appeared to come. There was some reason for the alarm, though the unpractised sense of the white man had failed to perceive it. It was there that our old acquaintance, Hector, despatched as a spy upon the progress of those whom his master suspected to be engaged in mischief, had sought concealment while seeking his information. Unfortunately for the black, as he crept along on hands and knees, a fallen and somewhat decayed tree lay across his path, some of the branches of which protruded entirely out of the cover, and terminated within sight of the three conspirators, upon the open plain. In crawling, cautiously enough, over the body of the tree, the branches thus exposed were agitated, and, though but slightly, yet sufficiently for the keen sight of an Indian warrior. Hector, all the while ignorant of the protrusion within their gaze of the agitated members—in his anxiety to gain more of the latter words of the sailor, so interesting to his own color, and a portion of which had met his ear—incautiously pushed forward over the tree, crawling all the way like a snake, and seeking to shelter himself in a little clump that interposed itself between him and those he was approaching. As he raised his head above the earth, he beheld the glance of Sanutee fixed upon the very bush behind which he lay; the bow uplifted, and his eye ranging from stem to point of the long arrow. In a moment the negro sunk to the level of the ground; but, in doing so precipitately disturbed still more the branches clustering around him. The lapse of a few moments without any assault, persuaded Hector to believe that all danger was passed; and he was just about to lift his head for another survey, when he felt the entire weight of a heavy body upon his back. While the black had lain quiet, in those few moments, Sanutee had swept round a turn in the woods, and with a single bound, after noticing the person of the spy, had placed his foot upon him.

"Hello, now, wha' de debble dat? Git off, I tell you. Dis dah Hector! Wha' for you trouble Hector?"

Thus shouting confusedly, the negro, taken in the very act, with a tone of mixed fear and indignation, addressed his assailant, while struggling violently all the time at his extrication. His struggles only enabled him to see his captor, who, calling out to Ishiagaska, in a moment, with his assistance, dragged forth the spy from his unconcealing cover. To do Hector's courage all manner of justice, he battled violently; threatening his captors dreadfully with the vengeance of his master. But his efforts ceased as the hatchet of Ishiagaska gleamed over his eyes, and he was content—save in words, which he continued to pour forth with no little fluency—to forego his further opposition to the efforts which they now made to keep him down, while binding his arms behind him with a thong of hide which Ishiagaska readily produced. The cupidity of Chorley soon furnished them with a plan for getting rid of him. Under his suggestion, driving the prisoner before them, with the terrors of knife and hatchet, they soon reached the edge of the river, and, after a little search, they found the place, Rattlesnake Point, where the cruiser's boat had been stationed in waiting. With the assistance of the two sailors in it, the seats were taken up, and the captive, kicking, struggling, and threatening, and all in vain,

was tumbled in; the seats were replaced above him, the seamen squat-
ted upon them; and every chance of a long captivity, and that foreign
slavery against which his master had forewarned him, was the melancholy prospect in his thoughts. The further arrangements between the
chiefs and the sailor took place on shore, and out of Hector's hearing.
In a little while it ceased—the Yemassees took their way up the river to
Pocota-ligo, while Chorley, returning to his boat, bringing the deer
along—which he tumbled in upon the legs of the negro—took his seat
in the stern, and the men pulled steadily off for the vessel, keeping
nigh the opposite shore, and avoiding that side upon which the settlements of the Carolinians were chiefly to be found. As they pursued
their way, a voice hailed them from the banks, to which the sailor gave
no reply, but immediately changing the direction of the boat, put her
instantly into the centre of the stream. But the voice was known to
Hector as that of Granger, the Indian trader, and with a desperate
effort, raising his head from the uncomfortable place where it had
been laid on a dead level with his body, he yelled out to the trader,
with his utmost pitch of voice, vainly endeavouring, through the mists
of of evening, which now hung heavily around, to make out the person to whom he spoke. A salutary blow from the huge fist of the sailor,
driven into the uprising face of the black, admonished him strongly
against any future imprudence, while forcing him back, with all the
force of a sledge-hammer, to the shelter of his old position. There was
no reply, that the negro heard, to his salutation; and, in no long time
after, the vessel was reached. Hector was soon consigned to a safe
quarter in the hold, usually provided for such freight, and kept to
await the arrival of as many companions in captivity, as the present
enterprise of the pirate captain, for such is Master Richard Chorley,
promised to procure.

Chapter Nine

"Why goes he forth again—what is the quest,
That from his cottage home, and the warm hearth,
Blest that its warmth is his, carries him forth
By night, into the mazy solitude?"

THE boats, side by side, of Sanutee and Ishiagaska, crossed the river at a point just below Pocota-ligo. It was there that Sanutee landed—the other chief continued his progress to the town. But a few words, and those of stern resolve, passed between them at separation; but those words were volumes in Yemassee history. They were the words of revolution and strife, and announced the preparation of the people not less than of the two chiefs, for the commencement, with brief delay, of that struggle with their English neighbours, which was now the most prominent idea in their minds. The night was fixed among them for the outbreak, the several commands arranged, and the intelligence brought by the sailor informed them of a contemplated attack of the Spaniards by sea upon the Carolinian settlements, while, at the same time, another body was in progress, over land, to coalesce with them in their operations. This latter force could not be very far distant, and it was understood that when the scouts should return with accounts of its approach, the signal should be given for the general massacre.

"They shall die—they shall all perish, and their scalps shall shrivel around the long pole in the lodge of the warrior," exclaimed Ishiagaska, fiercely, to his brother chief, still speaking in their own language. The response of Sanutee was in a different temper, though recognising the same necessity.

"The Yemassee must be free," said the elder chief, solemnly, in his sonorous tones— "The Manneyto will bring him freedom—he will take the burden from his shoulders, and set him up against the tree by the wayside. He will put the bow into his hands—he will strengthen him for the chase; there shall be no pale-faces along the path to rob him of venison—to put blows upon his shoulders. The Yemassee shall be free."

"He shall drink blood for strength. He shall hunt the track of the English to the shores of the big waters; and the war-whoop shall ring death in the ear that sleeps," cried Ishiagaska, with a furious exultation.

"Let them go, Ishiagaska, let them go from the Yemassee—let the warrior have no stop in the chase, when he would strike the brown deer on the edge of the swamp. Let them leave the home of the Yemassee, and take the big canoe over the waters, and the tomahawk of Sanutee shall be buried—it should drink no blood from the English."

"They will not go," exclaimed the other fiercely— "there must be blood—the white man will not go. His teeth are in the trees, and he eats into the earth for his own."

"Thou hast said, Ishiagaska—there must be blood—they will not go. The knife of the Yemassee must be red. But—not yet—not yet! The moon must sleep first—the Yemassee is a little child till the moon sleeps, but then—"

"He is a strong man, with a long arrow, and a tomahawk like the Manneyto."

"It is good—the arrow shall fly to the heart, and the tomahawk shall sink deep into the head. The Yemassee shall have his lands, and his limbs shall be free in the hunt."

Thus, almost in a strain of lyric enthusiasm, for a little while they continued, until, having briefly arranged for a meeting with other chiefs of their party for the day ensuing, they separated, and the night had well set in before Sanutee reappeared in the cabin of his wife.

He returned gloomy and abstracted—his mind brooding over schemes of war and violence. He was about to plunge his nation into all the difficulties and dangers of a strife with the colony, still in its infancy, but even in its infancy, powerful to the Indians—with a people with whom they had, hitherto, always been at peace and on terms of the most friendly intercourse. Sanutee felt the difficulties of this former relation doubly to increase those which necessarily belong to war. He had, however, well deliberated the matter, and arrived at a determination, so fraught with peril not only to himself but to his people, only after a perfect conviction of its absolute necessity. Yet, such a decision was a severe trial to a spirit framed as his—a spirit, which, as in the case of Logan, desired peace rather than war. The misfortune with him, however, consisted in this, that he was a patriot rather than a sage, and, though lacking nothing of that wisdom which may exist in the soul of the true and excited patriot; constituting, when it does so, the very perfection of statesmanship,—he yet could not coolly contemplate what he was about to do, without misgiving and great anxiety. The schemes in which he had involved himself, were big with the fate of his own and another people; and seeing what were the dangers of his attempt, his whole thought was necessarily given to the duty of lessening and averting them. But this was not the sole cause of anxiety. It was with a sentiment rather more Christian than Indian that he recalled the ties and associations which he himself, as well as his people, had formed with the whites generally, and especially with individuals among them, at the first coming of the European settlers. Ignorant of their power, their numbers, their arts, their ambition, he had been friendly, had cordially welcomed them, yielded the lands of his people graciously, and when the whites were assailed by other tribes, had himself gone forth in their battle even against the Spaniards of St. Augustine, with whom he now found it politic to enter into alliance. But his eyes were now fully opened to his error. It is in the nature of civilization to own an appetite for dominion and extended sway, which the world that is known will always fail to satisfy. It is for her, then, to seek and to create, and not with the Macedonian madman, to weep for the triumph of the unknown. Conquest and sway are the great leading principles of her existence, and the savage must join in her train, or she rides over him relentlessly in her onward progress. Though slow, perhaps, in her approaches, Sanutee was sage enough at length to perceive all this, as the inevitable result of her progressive march. The evidence rose daily before his eyes in the diminution of the game—in the frequent insults to his people, unredressed by their obtrusive neighbours—and in the daily approach of some new borderer among them, whose habits were foreign, and whose capacities were obviously superior to theirs. The desire for new lands, and the facility with which the whites, in many cases, taking advantage of the weaknesses of the Indian chiefs, had been enabled to procure them, impressed Sanutee strongly with the melancholy prospect in reserve for the Yemassee. He, probably, would not live to behold them landless, and his own children might, to the last, have range enough for the chase; but the nation itself was in the thought of the unselfish chieftain, upon whom its general voice had conferred the title of "the well-beloved of the Manneyto."

He threw himself upon the bearskin of his cabin, and Matiwan stood beside him. She was not young—she was not beautiful, but her face was softly brown, and her eye was dark, while her long black hair came down her back with a flow of girlish luxuriance. Her face was that of a girl, still round and smooth, and though sorrow had made free with it, the original expression must have been one of extreme liveliness. Even now, when she laughed, and the beautiful white teeth glittered through her almost purple lips, she wore all the expression of a child. The chief loved her as a child rather than as a wife, and she rather adored than loved the chief. At this moment, however, as she stood before him, robed loosely in her long white garment, and with an apron of the soft skin of the spotted fawn, he had neither words nor looks for Matiwan. She brought him a gourd filled with a simple beer common to their people, and extracted from the pleasanter roots of the forest, with the nature of which, all Indians, in their rude pharmacy, are familiar. Unconsciously he drank off the beverage, and, without speaking, returned the gourd to the woman. She addressed him inquiringly at last.

"The chief, Sanutee, has sent an arrow from his bow, yet brings he no venison from the woods?"

The red of his cheek grew darker, as the speech reminded him of his loss, not only of dog, but deer; and though the sailor had proffered him the meat, which his pride had compelled him to reject, he could not but feel that he had been defrauded of the spoils of the chase, which were in reality his own. Reminded at the same time of the loss of his favourite dog, the chief replied querulously:

"Has Matiwan been into the tree-top to-day, for the voice of the bird which is painted, that she must sing with a foolish noise in the ear of Sanutee?"

The woman was rebuked into silence for the moment, but with a knowledge of his mood, she sank back directly behind him, upon a corner of the bearskin, and, after a few prefatory notes, as if singing for her own exercise and amusement, she carolled forth in an exquisite ballad voice, one of those little fancies of the Indians, which may be found among nearly all the tribes from Carolina to Mexico. It recorded the achievements of that Puck of the American forests, the mocking-bird; and detailed the manner in which he procured his imitative powers. The strain, playfully simple in the sweet language of the original, must necessarily lose in the more frigid verse of the translator.

THE "COONEE-LATEE," or "TRICK-TONGUE."

I.

"As the Coonee-latee looked forth from his leaf,
He saw below him a Yemassee chief,
    In his war-paint, all so grim—
Sung boldly, then, the Coonee-latee,
I, too, will seek for mine enemy;
    And when the young moon grows dim,
I'll slip through the leaves, nor shake them,—
I'll come on my foes, nor wake them,—
    And I'll take off their scalps like him.

II.

"In the forest grove, where the young birds slept,
Slyly by night, through the leaves he crept,
    With a footstep free and bold—
From bush to bush, and from tree to tree,
They lay, wherever his eye could see,
    The bright, the dull, the young, and the old;
I'll cry my war-whoop, said he, at breaking
The sleep, that shall never know awaking,
    And their hearts shall soon grow cold.

III.

"But, as nigher and nigher the spot he crept,
And saw that with open mouth they slept,
    The thought grew strong in his brain—
And from bird to bird, with a cautious tread,
He unhook'd the tongue, out of every head,
    Then flew to his perch again;—
And thus it is, whenever he chooses,
The tongues of all of the birds he uses,
    And none of them dare complain."*

The silly little ballad may have had its effect in soothing the
humours of the chief, for which it was intended: but he made no

---

* The grove is generally silent when the mocking-bird sings.

remark. Though sad and vacant of look, he seemed soothed, however, and when a beautiful pet fawn bounded friskingly into the lodge, from the enclosure which adjoined it, and leaped playfully upon him, as, with an indulged habit, he encouraged its caresses. The timid Matiwan, herself, after a little while, encouraged by this show of good nature, proceeded to approach him also. She drew nigh to him in silence,—still behind him, and hesitatingly, her hand at length rested upon his shoulder. To the liberty thus taken with a great chief, there was no objection made: but at the same time, there was no acknowledgment or return, no recognition. Sanutee, silent and meditative, unconsciously, it would seem, suffered his own hand to glide over the soft skin and shrinking neck of the fawn. The animal grew more familiar and thrust its nose into his face and bosom, a liberty which Matiwan, the wife, was seldom emboldened to attempt. Suddenly, however, the warrior started, and thrust the now affrighted animal away from him with violence.

"Woman!" he cried, in a voice of thunder, "the white trader has been in the lodge of Sanutee."

"No! no! Sanutee,—the white trader,—no! not Granger. He has not been in the lodge of the chief!"

"The beads, Matiwan!—the beads! See!" with the words, he caught the fawn with one hand, while with the other he tore from its neck, a thick necklace, several strands of large particolored beads which had been wound about the neck of the animal. Dashing them to the ground, he trampled them fiercely under his feet.

"The boy,—Sanutee—the boy, Occonestoga—"

"The dog! came he to the lodge of Sanutee when Sanutee said no! Matiwan—woman! Thy ears have forgotten the words of the chief—of Sanutee—thine eyes have looked upon a dog."

"'Tis the child of Matiwan—Matiwan has no child but Occonestoga." And she threw herself at length, with her face to the ground, at the foot of her lord.

"Speak, Matiwan—darkens the dog still in the lodge of Sanutee?"

"Sanutee, no! Occonestoga has gone with the chiefs of the English, to talk in council with the Yemassee."

"Ha—thou speakest!—look, Matiwan—where stood the sun when the chiefs of the pale-faces came? Speak!"

"The sun stood high over the lodge of Matiwan, and saw not beneath the tree-top."

"They come for more lands—they would have all; but they know not that Sanutee lives—they say he sleeps—that he has no tongue,— that his people have forgotten his voice! They shall see." As he spoke, he pointed to the gaudy beads which lay strewed over the floor of the cabin, and, with a bitter sarcasm of glance and speech, thus addressed her:—

"What made thee a chief of Yemassee, Matiwan, to sell the lands of my people to the pale-faces for their painted glass? They would buy thee, and the chief, and the nation—all; and with what? With that which is not worth, save that it is like thine eye. And thou—didst thou pray to the Manneyto to send thee from thy people, that thou mightst carry water for the pale-faces from the spring? Go—thou hast done wrong, Matiwan."

"They put painted glass into the hands of Matiwan, but they asked not for lands; they gave it to Matiwan, for she was the wife of Sanutee, the chief."

"They lied with a forked tongue. It was to buy the lands of our people; it was to send us into the black swamps, where the sun sleeps for ever. But I will go—where is the dog—the slave of the pale-faces? Where went Occonestoga with the English?"

"To Pocota-ligo—they would see the chiefs of Yemassee."

"To buy them with the painted glass, and red cloth, and burning water. Manneyto be with my people, for the chiefs are slaves to the English; and they will give the big forests of my fathers to be cut down by the accursed axes of the pale-face. But they blind me not—they buy not Sanutee! The knife must have blood—the Yemassee must have his home with the old grave of his father. I will go to Pocota-ligo."

"Sanutee, chief—'tis Matiwan, the mother of Occonestoga, that speaks; thou wilt see the young chief—thou wilt look upon the boy at Pocota-ligo. Oh! well-beloved of the Yemassee—look not to strike." She sank at his feet as she uttered the entreaty, and her arms clung about his knees.

"I would not see Occonestoga, Matiwan—for he is thy son. Manneyto befriend thee, but thou hast been the mother to a dog."

"Thou wilt not see to strike—"

"I would not see him! but let him not stand in the path of Sanutee. Look, Matiwan—the knife is in my hand, and there is death for the dog, and a curse for the traitor, from the black swamps of Opitchi-Manneyto."

He said no more, and she, too, was speechless. She could only raise her hands and eyes, in imploring expression to his glance, as, seizing upon his tomahawk, which he had thrown beside him upon the skin, he rushed forth from the lodge, and took the path to Pocota-ligo.

Chapter Ten

THE house of council, in the town of Pocota-ligo, was filled that night with an imposing conclave. The gauds and the grandeur—the gilded mace, the guardian sword, the solemn stole, the rich pomps of civilization were wanting, it is true; but how would these have shown in that dark and primitive assembly! A single hall—huge and cumbrous—built of the unhewn trees of the forest, composed the entire building. A single door furnished the means of access and departure. The floor was the native turf, here and there concealed by the huge bearskin of some native chief, and they sat around, each in his place, silent, solemn; the sagacious mind at work; the big soul filled with deliberations involving great events, and vital interests of the future. No assembly of the white man compares, in seeming solemnity at least, with that of the red. Motionless like themselves, stood the torch-bearers, twelve in number, behind them—standing and observant, and only varying their position when it became necessary to renew with fresh materials the bright fires of the ignited pine which they bore. These were all the pomps of the savage council; it is but the narrow sense, alone, which would object to their deficiency. The scene is only for the stern painter of the dusky and sublime—it would suffer in other hands.

Huspah was at this time the superior chief—the reigning king, if we may apply that title legitimately to the highest dignitary of a people with a form of government like that of the Yemassees. He bore the title of Mico, which may be rendered king or prince, though it was in name

only that he might be considered in that character. He was not one of
those men of great will, who make royalty power, no less than a name.
In this sense there was no king in the nation, unless it were Sanutee.
Huspah was a shadowy head. The Yemassees were ruled by the joint
authority of several chiefs—each controlling a special section with
arbitrary authority, yet, when national measures were to be determined upon, it required a majority for action. These chiefs were elec-
tive, and from these the superior, or presiding chief, was duly chosen;
all of these, without exception, were accountable to the nation; though
such accountability was rather the result of popular impulse than of
any other more legitimate or customary regulation. It occurred sometimes, however, that a favourite ruler, presuming upon his strength
with the people, ventured beyond the prescribed boundary, and tran-
scended the conceded privileges of his station; but such occurrences
were not frequent, and, when the case did happen, the offender was
most commonly made to suffer the unmeasured penalties always consequent upon any outbreak of popular indignation. As in the practice
of more civilized communities, securing the mercenaries, a chief has
been known to enter into treaties, unsanctioned by his brother chiefs;
and, forming a party resolute to sustain him, has brought about a civil
war in the nation, and, perhaps, the secession, from the great body, of
many of its tribes. Of this sort was the case of the celebrated Creek
chief, Mackintosh—whose summary execution in Georgia, but a few
years ago, by the indignant portion of his nation, disapproving of the
treaty which he had made with the whites for the sale of lands,
resulted in the emigration of a large minority of that people to the
west.

Among the Yemassees, Huspah, the oldest chief, was tacitly placed
at the head of his caste, and these formed the nobility of the nation.
This elevation was nominal, simply complimentary in its character,
and without any advantages not shared in common with the other
chiefs. The honour was solely given to past achievements; for at this
time, Huspah, advanced in years and greatly enfeebled, was almost in
his second infancy. The true power of the nation rested in Sanutee—
his position was of all the others the most enviable, as upon him the
eyes of the populace generally turned in all matters of trying and
important character. However reluctant, his brother chiefs were usually compelled to yield to the popular will as it was supposed to be
expressed through the lips of one styled by general consent, the "well-

beloved" of the nation. A superiority so enviable with the people had the natural effect of making Sanutee an object of dislike among his equals. He was not ignorant of their envy and hostility. This had been shown in various ways; particularly in the fact that in council, it was only necessary that he should introduce a measure to find him in a minority. An appeal to the people would, it is true, make all right; but to the patriotic mind of Sanutee, particularly now, and with such important objects in view, the relation with his brother chiefs was a subject of great anxiety, as he plainly foresaw the evil consequences to the people of this hostility on the part of the chiefs to himself. The suggestions which he made in council were usually met with decided opposition by a regularly combined party, and it was only necessary to identify with his name the contemplated measure, to rally against it sufficient opposition for its defeat in council. The nation, it is true, did him justice in the end; but to his mind there was nothing grateful in this sort of conflict.

Under this state of things at home, it may be readily understood why the hostility of Sanutee to the approaching English, should meet little sympathy with the majority of those around him. Accordingly, we find, that as the favourite grew more and more jealous of and hostile to the intruders, they became, for this very reason, more and more favoured by the party among the chiefs, which was envious of his position. No one knew better than Sanutee the true nature of the difficulty. He was a far superior politician to those around him, and had long since foreseen the warfare he would be compelled to wage with his associates when aiming at the point, to which, at this moment, every feeling of his soul, and every energy of his mind, was devoted. It was this knowledge that chiefly determined him upon the conspiracy—the plan of which, perfectly unknown to the people, was only entrusted to the bosom of a few chiefs, having like feelings with himself. These difficulties of his situation grew more obvious to his mind, as, full of evil auguries from the visit of the English commissioners, he took the lonely path from his own lodge to the council-house of Pocota-ligo.

He arrived just in season. As he feared, the rival chiefs had taken advantage of his absence to give audience to the commissioners of treaty from the Carolinians, charged with the power to purchase from the Yemassees a large additional tract of land, which, if sold to the whites, would bring their settlements directly upon the borders of Pocota-ligo itself. The whites had proceeded, as was usual in such cases, to administer bribes of one sort or another, in the shape of pre-sents, to all such persons, chiefs, or people, as were most influential and seemed most able to serve them. In this manner had all in that assembly been appealed to. Huspah, an old and drowsy Indian, totter-ing with palsy from side to side of the skin upon which he sat, was half smothered in the wide folds of a huge scarlet cloak which the commis-sioners had flung over his shoulders. Dresses of various shapes, colours, and decorations, such as might be held most imposing to the Indian eye, had been given to each in the assembly, and put on as soon as received. In addition to these, other gifts, such as hatchets, knives, beads, &c., had been made to minister to the craving poverty of the people, so that, before the arrival of Sanutee, the minds of the greater number of the chiefs had been rendered very flexible, and prepared to give gracious answer to all claims and proffers which the policy of the white commissioners should prompt them to make.

Sanutee entered abruptly, followed by Ishiagaska, who, like him-self, had just had intelligence of the council. There was a visible start in the assembly as the old patriot came forward, full into the centre of the circle,—surveying, almost analyzing every feature, and sternly dwelling in his glance upon the three commissioners, who sat a little apart from the chiefs, upon a sort of mat to themselves. Another mat held the presents which remained unappropriated and had been reserved for such chiefs, Ishiagaska and Sanutee among them, as had not been present at the first distribution.

The survey of Sanutee, and the silence which followed his first appearance within the circle, lasted not long: abruptly, and with a voice of deep but restrained emotion, addressing no one in particular, but with a glance almost exclusively given to the commissioners, he at length exclaimed as follows, in his own strong language:—

"Who came to the lodge of Sanutee to say that the chiefs were in council? Is not Sanutee a chief?—the Yemassees call him so, or he dreams. Is he not the well-beloved chief of the Yemassees, or have his brothers taken from him the totem of his tribe? Look, chiefs, is the broad arrow of Yemassee gone from the shoulder of Sanutee?"

And as he spoke, throwing the loose hunting shirt open to the shoulder, he displayed to the gaze of all, the curved arrow upon his bosom, which is the badge of the Yemassees. A general silence in the assembly succeeded this speech—none of them caring to answer for an omission equally chargeable upon all. The eye of the chief lowered scornfully as it swept the circle, taking in each face with its glance; then, throwing upon the earth the thick bearskin which he carried upon his arm, he took his seat with the slow and sufficient dignity of a Roman senator, speaking as he descended:—

"It is well—Sanutee is here in council—he is a chief of the Yemassees. He has ears for the words of the English."

Granger, the trader and interpreter, who stood behind the commissioners, signified to them the purport of Sanutee's speech, and his demand to hear anew the propositions which the English came to make. Sir Edmund Bellinger—then newly created a landgrave, one of the titles of Carolinian nobility—the head of the deputation, arose accordingly, and addressing himself to the new-comer, rather than to the assembly, proceeded to renew those pledges and protestations which he had already uttered to the rest. His speech was immediately interpreted by Granger, who, residing in Pocota-ligo, was familiar with their language.

"Chiefs of the Yemassee," said Sir Edmund Bellinger— "we come from your English brothers, and we bring peace with this belt of wampum. They have told us to say to you that one house covers the English and the Yemassee. There is no strife between us—we are all the children of one father, and to prove their faith they have sent us with words of good-will and friendship, and to you, Sanutee, as the well-beloved chief of the Yemassee, they send this coat, which they have worn close to their hearts, and which they would have you wear in like manner, in proof of the love that is between us."

Thus saying, the chief of the deputation presented, through the medium of Granger, a rich but gaudy cloak, such as had already been given to Huspah;—but putting the interpreter aside and rejecting the gift, Sanutee sternly replied—

"Our English brother is good, but Sanutee asks not for the cloak. Does Sanutee complain of the cold?"

Granger rendered this, and Bellinger addressed him in reply—

"The chief Sanutee will not reject the gift of his English brother."

"Does the white chief come to the great council of the Yemassees as a fur trader? Would he have skins for his coat?" was the reply.

"No, Sanutee—the English chief is a great chief, and does not barter for skins."

"A great chief?—he came to the Yemassee a little child, and we took him into our lodges. We gave him meat and water."

"We know this, Sanutee." But the Yemassee went on without heeding the interruption.

"We helped him with a staff as he tottered through the thick wood."

"True, Sanutee."

"We showed him how to trap the beaver,* and to hunt the deer—we made him a lodge for his woman; and we sent our young men on the war-path against his enemy."

"We have not forgotten—we have denied none of the services, Sanutee, which yourself and people have done for us," said the deputy.

"And now he sends us a coat!" and as the chief uttered this unlooked-for anti-climax, his eye glared scornfully around upon the subservient portion of the assembly. Somewhat mortified with the tenour of the sentence which the interpreter in the meantime had repeated to him, Sir Edmund Bellinger would have answered the refractory chief—

"No, but, Sanutee—"

Without heeding or seeming to hear him, the old warrior went on—

"He sends good words to the Yemassee, he gives him painted glass, and makes him blind with a water which is poison—his shot rings in our forests—we hide from his long knife in the cold swamp, while the copper snake creeps over us as we sleep."

As soon as the deputy comprehended this speech, he replied—

"You do us wrong, Sanutee,—you have nothing to fear from the English."

Without waiting for the aid of the interpreter, the chief, who had acquired a considerable knowledge of the simpler portions of the language, and to whom this sentence was clear enough, immediately and indignantly exclaimed in his own—addressing the chiefs, rather than replying to the Englishman—

"Fear,—Sanutee has no fear of the English—he fears only the Manneyto. He only fears that his people may go blind with the English poison drink,—that the great chiefs of the Yemassee may sell him for a slave to the English, to plant his maize and to be beaten with a stick. But, let the ears of the chiefs hear the voice of Sanutee—the Yemassee shall *not* be the slave of the pale-face."

---

* The beaver, originally taken in Carolina, is now extinct.

"There is no reason for this fear, Sanutee—the English have always been the friends of your people," said the chief of the deputation.

"Would the English have more land from the Yemassee? Let him speak; Granger, put the words of Sanutee in his ear. Why does he not speak?"

Granger did as directed, and Sir Edmund replied:—

"The English do want to buy some of the land of your people—"

"Did not Sanutee say? And the coat is for the land," quickly exclaimed the old chief, speaking this time in the English language.

"No, Sanutee," was the reply— "the coat is a free gift from the English. They ask for nothing in return. But we would buy your land with other things—we would buy on the same terms that we bought from the Cassique of Combahee."

"The Cassique of Combahee is a dog—he sells the grave of his father. I will not sell the land of my people. The Yemassee loves the old trees and the shady waters where he was born, and where the bones of the old warriors lie buried. I speak to you, chiefs—it is the voice of Sanutee. Hear his tongue—it has no fork; look on his face—it does not show lies. These are scars of battle, when I stood up for my people. There is a name for these scars—they do not lie. Hear me, then."

"Our ears watch," was the general response, as he made his address to the council.

"It is good. —Chiefs of the Yemassee, now hear. Why comes the English to the lodge of our people? Why comes he with a red coat to the Chief—why brings he beads and paints for the eye of a little boy? Why brings he the strong water for the young man? Why makes he long speeches, full of smooth words—why does he call us brother? He wants our lands. But we have no lands to sell. The lands came from our fathers—they must go to our children. They do not belong to us to sell—they belong to our children to keep. We have sold too much land, and the old turkey, before the sun sinks behind the trees, can fly over all the land that is ours. Shall the turkey have more land in a day than the Yemassee has for his children? Speak for the Yemassee, chiefs of the broad-arrow—speak for the Yemassee—speak, Ishiagaska—speak, Choluculla—speak, thou friend of Manneyto, whose words are true as the sun, and whose wisdom comes swifter than the lightning—speak, prophet—speak, Enoree-Mattee—speak for the Yemassee."

To the high-priest, or rather the great prophet of the nation, the latter portion of the speech of Sanutee had been addressed. He was a cold, dark, stern looking man, gaudily arrayed in a flowing garment of red, a present from the whites at an early period, while a fillet around his head, of cloth stuck with the richest feathers, formed a distinguished feature of dress from any of the rest. His voice, next to that of Sanutee, was potential among the Indians; and the chief well knew, in appealing to him, Choluculla, and Ishiagaska, that he was secure of these, if of none other in the council.

"Enoree-Mattee is the great prophet of Manneyto—he will not sell the lands of Yemassee."

"'Tis well—speak, Ishiagaska—speak, Choluculla," —exclaimed Sanutee.

They replied in the same moment:—

"The English shall have no land from the Yemassee. It is the voice of Ishiagaska—it is the voice of Choluculla."

"It is the voice of Sanutee—it is voice of the prophet—it is the voice of the Manneyto himself!" cried Sanutee, with a tone of thunder, and with a solemn emphasis of manner that seemed to set at rest all further controversy on the subject. But the voices which had thus spoken were all that spoke on this side of the question. The English had not been inactive heretofore, and, what the influence gained from their numerous presents and promises to the other chiefs, and the no less influential dislike and jealousy which the latter entertained for the few more controlling spirits taking the stand just narrated, the minds of the greater number had been well prepared to make any treaty which might be required of them; trusting to their own influence somewhat, but more to the attractions of the gewgaws given in return for their lands, to make their peace with the great body of the people in the event of their dissatisfaction. Accordingly, Sanutee had scarcely taken his seat, when one of the most hostile among them, a brave but dishonest chief, now arose, and addressing himself chiefly to Sanutee, thus furnished much of the feeling and answer for the rest:—

"Does Sanutee speak for the Yemassee—and where are the other chiefs of the broad-arrow? Where are Metatchee and Huspah—where is Oonalatchie, where is Sarrataha?—are they not here? It is gone from me when they sung the death-song, and went afar to the blessed valley of Manneyto. They are not gone—they live—they have voices and can speak for the Yemassee. Sanutee may say, Ishiagaska may say, the prophet may say—but they say not for Manneywanto. There are brave chiefs of the Yemassee, yet we hear only Sanutee. Sanutee! cha! cha! I am here—I—Manneywanto. I speak for the trade with our English brother. The Yemassee will sell the land to their brothers." He was followed by another and another, all in the affirmative.

"Metatchee will trade with the English. The English is the brother to the Yemassee."

"Oonalatchie will sell the land to our English brothers."

And so on in succession, all but the four first speakers, the assembled chiefs proceeded to sanction the proposed treaty, the terms of which had been submitted to them before. To the declaration of each, equivalent as it was to the vote given in our assemblies, Sanutee had but a single speech.

"It is well! It is well!"

And he listened to the votes in succession, approving of the trade, until, rising from a corner of the apartment in which, lying prostrate, he had till then kept out of the sight of the assembly and entirely concealed from the eye of Sanutee, a tall young warrior, pushing aside the torch-bearers, staggered forth into the ring. He had evidently been much intoxicated, though now recovering from its effects; and, but for the swollen face and the watery eye, the uncertain and now undignified carriage, he might well have been considered a fine specimen of savage symmetry and manly beauty. When his voice, declaring also for the barter, struck upon the ear of the old chief, he started round as if an arrow had suddenly gone into his heart—then remained still, silently contemplating the speaker, who, in a stupid and incoherent manner, proceeded to eulogize the English as the true friends and dear brothers of the Yemassees. Granger, the trader and interpreter, beholding the fingers of Sanutee gripe the handle of his tomahawk, whispered in the ears of Sir Edmund Bellinger:—

"Now would I not be Occonestoga for the world. Sanutee will tomahawk him before the stupid youth can get out of the way."

Before the person addressed could reply to the interpreter, his prediction was, in part, and, but for the ready presence of the Englishman, would have been wholly accomplished. Scarcely had the young chief finished his maudlin speech, than, with a horrible yell, seemingly of laughter, Sanutee leaped forward, and, with uplifted arm and descending blow, would have driven the hatchet deep into the scull of the only half-conscious youth, when Sir Edmund seized the arm of the fierce old man in time to defeat the effort.

"Wouldst thou slay thy own son, Sanutee?"

"He is thy slave—he is not the son of Sanutee. Thou hast made him a dog with thy poison drink, till he would sell thee his own mother to carry water for thy women. Hold me not, Englishman—I will strike the slave—I will strike thee, too, that art his master;" and, with a fury and strength which, to check, required the restraining power of half a dozen warriors, he laboured to effect his object. They succeeded, however, in keeping him back, until the besotted youth had been safely hurried from the apartment; when, silenced and stilled by the strong reaction of his excitement, the old chief sank down again upon his bearskin seat in a stupor, until the parchment conveying the terms of the treaty, with pens and ink, provided by Granger for their signatures, was handed to Huspah, for his own and the marks of the chiefs. Sanutee looked on with some watchfulness, but moved not, until one of the attendants brought in the skin of a dog filled with earth and tightly secured with thongs, giving it the appearance of a sack. Taking this sack in his hands, Huspah, who had been half asleep during the proceedings, now arose, and repeating the words of general concurrence in the sale of the lands, proceeded to the completion of the treaty by conveying the sack which held some of the soil to the hands of the commissioners. But Sanutee again rushed forward; and seizing the sack from the proffering hand of Huspah, he hurled it to the ground, trampled it under foot, and poured forth, as he did so, an appeal to the patriotism of the chiefs, in a strain of eloquence in his own wild language which we should utterly despair to render into ours. He implored them, holding as they did the destinies of the nation in their hands, to forbear its sacrifice. He compared the wide forests of their fathers, in value, with the paltry gifts for which they were required to give them up. He dwelt upon the limited province, even now, which had been left them for the chase; spoke of the daily incursions and injuries of the whites; and, with those bold forms of phrase and figure known among all primitive people, with whom metaphor and personification supply the deficiency and make up for the poverty of language, he implored them not to yield up the bones of their fathers, nor admit the stranger to contact with the sacred town, given them by the Manneyto, and solemnly dedicated to his service. But he spoke in vain; he addressed ears more impenetrable than those of the adder. They had been bought and sold, and they had no scruple to sell their country. He was supported by the few who had spoken with him against the trade; but what availed patriotism against numbers? They were unheeded, and, beholding the contract effected which gave up an immense body of their best lands for a strange assortment of hatchets, knives, blankets, brads, beads, and other commodities of like character, Sanutee, followed by his three friends, rushed forth precipitately, and with a desperate purpose, from the traitorous assembly.

Chapter Eleven

"A vengeance for the traitors; vengeance deep
As is their treason—curses loud and long,
Surprising their own infamy and guilt."

SANUTEE, the "Well Beloved," was not disposed to yield up the territory of his forefathers without further struggle. The Yemassees were
something of a republic, and the appeal of the old patriot now lay with
the people. He was much better acquainted with the popular feeling
than those who had so far sacrificed it; and, though maddened with
indignation, he was yet sufficiently cool to determine the most effec-
tual course for the attainment of his object. Not suspecting his design,
the remaining chiefs continued in council, in deliberations of one sort
or another; probably in adjusting the mode of distributing their spoils;
while the English commissioners, having succeeded in their object,
retired for the night to the dwelling of Granger, the Indian trader—a
Scotch adventurer, who had been permitted to take up his abode in
the village, and from his quiet, unobtrusive, and conciliatory habits,
had contrived to secure much of the respect and good will of the
Yemassees. Sanutee, meanwhile, discussed his proposed undertaking
with his three companions, Enoree-Mattee, the prophet, Ishiagaska,
and Choluculla, all of whom were privy to the meditated insurrection.
He next sought out all the most influential and fearless of the
Yemassees. Nor did he confine himself to these. The rash, the thoughtless, the ignorant—all were aroused by his eloquence. To each of these
he detailed the recent proceedings of council, and, in his own vehe-
ment manner, explained the evil consequences to the people of such a
treaty; taking care to shape his information to the mind or mood of
each individual to whom he spoke. To one he painted the growing
insolence of the whites, increasing with their increasing strength,

almost too great, already, for any control or management. To another, he described the ancient glories of his nation, rapidly departing in the subservience with which their chiefs acknowledged the influence, and truckled to the desires of the English. To a third, he deplored the loss of the noble forests of his forefathers, hewn down by the axe, to make way for the bald fields of the settler; despoiled of game, and leaving the means of life utterly problematical to the hunter. In this way, with a speech accommodated to every feeling and understanding, he went over the town. To all, he dwelt with Indian emphasis upon the sacrilegious appropriation of the old burial-places of the Yemassee—one of which, a huge tumulus upon the edge of the river, lay almost in their sight, and traces of which survive to this day, in melancholy attestation of their past history. The effect of these representations—of these appeals—coming from one so well beloved, and so highly esteemed for wisdom and love of country, as Sanutee, was that of a moral earthquake; and his soul triumphed with hope as he beheld them rushing onwards in a momently gathering crowd, and shouting furiously, as they bared the knife and shook the tomahawk in air—

"Sangarrah, Sangarrah-me, Yemassee—Sangarrah, Sangarrah-me—Yemassee"—the bloody war-cry of the nation. To overthrow the power of the chiefs there was but one mode; and the aroused and violent passions of Sanutee and the chiefs who concurred with them, did not suffer them to scruple at the employment of any process, however extreme, for the defeat of the proceedings of the council. The excited chiefs, acting in concert, and using all their powers of eloquence, succeeded in driving the infuriated multitude whom they had roused in the direction of the council house, where the chiefs were still in session.

"It is Huspah, that has sold the Yemassee to be a woman," was the cry of one— "Sangarrah-me—he shall die."

"He hath cut off the legs of our children, so that they walk no longer—he hath given away our lands to the pale-faces—Sangarrah-me—he shall die!"

"They shall all die—have they not planted corn in the bosom of my mother?"—cried another, referring, figuratively, to the supposed use which the English would make of the lands they had bought; and, furiously aroused, they all struck their hatchets against the house of council, commanding the chiefs within to come forth, and deliver themselves up to their vengeance. But, warned of their danger, the beleaguered rulers had carefully secured the entrance; and, trusting that the popular ebullition would soon be quieted, they fondly hoped to maintain their position until such period. But the obstacle thus offered to the progress of the mob—for mobs are not confined to the civilized cities—only served the more greatly to inflame it; and a hundred hands were busy in procuring piles of fuel, with which to fire the building. The torches were soon brought, the blaze kindled at different points, and but little was now wanting to the conflagration which must have consumed all within or driven them forth upon the weapons of the besiegers; when, all of a sudden, Sanutee made his appearance, and with a single word arrested the movement.

"Manneyto, Manneyto—" exclaimed the old chief, with the utmost powers of his voice; and the solemn adjuration reached to the remotest incendiary and arrested the application of the torch. Every eye was turned upon him, curious to ascertain the occasion of an exclamation so much at variance with the purpose of their gathering, and so utterly unlooked-for from lips which had principally instigated it. But the glance of Sanutee indicated a mind unconscious of the effect which it had produced. His eye was fixed upon another object, which seemed to exercise a fascinating influence upon him. His hands were outstretched, his lips parted, as it were, in amazement and awe, and his whole attitude was that of devotion. The eyes of the assembly followed the direction of his, and every bosom thrilled with the wildest throes of natural superstition, as they beheld Enoree-Mattee, the prophet, writhing upon the ground at a little distance, in the most horrible convulsions. The glare of the torches around him showed the terrific distortion of every feature. His eyes were protruded, as if bursting from their sockets—his tongue hung from his widely distended jaws, covered with foam—while his hands and legs seemed doubled up, like a knotted band of snakes, huddling in uncouth sports in midsummer.

"Opitchi-Manneyto—Opitchi-Manneyto—here are arrows—we burn arrows to thee; we burn red feathers to thee, Opitchi-Manneyto,"—was the universal cry of deprecatory prayer and promise, which the assembled mass sent up to their evil deity, whose presence and power they supposed themselves to behold, in the agonized writhings of their prophet. A yell of savage terror then burst from the lips of the inspired priest, and, rising from the ground, as one relieved, but pregnant with a sacred fury, he waved his hand towards the council-house, and rushed headlong into the crowd, with a sort of anthem, which, as it was immediately chorussed by the mass, may have been usual to such occasions:

> "The arrows—
> The feathers—
> The dried scalps, and the teeth,
> The teeth from slaughtered enemies—
> Where are they—where are they?
> We burn them for thee,—black spirit—
> We burn them for thee, Opitchi-Manneyto—
> Leave us, leave us, black spirit."

The crowd sung forth this imploring deprecation of the demon's wrath; and then, as if something more relieved, Enoree-Mattee uttered of himself:

> "I hear thee, Opitchi-Manneyto—
> Thy words are in my ears,
> They are words for the Yemassee;
> And the prophet shall speak them aloud!—
> Leave us, leave us, black spirit."

"Leave us, leave us, black spirit. Go to thy red home, Opitchi-Manneyto—let us hear the words of the prophet—we give ear to Enoree-Mattee."

Thus called upon, the prophet advanced to the side of Sanutee, who had, all this while, preserved an attitude of the profoundest devotion. The prophet then stood erect, lifted, as it were, with inspiration, his eyes spiritually bright, his features sublimed by a sacred fury; his tongue was loosed, and with lifted hands and accents, he poured forth, in uncouth strains, a wild rhythmic strain, the highest effort of lyric poetry known to his people:

> "Let the Yemassee have ears,
> For Opitchi-Manneyto—
> 'Tis Opitchi-Manneyto,
> Not the prophet, now that speaks,
> Hear Opitchi-Manneyto.

> "In my agony, he came,
> And he hurl'd me to the ground;
> Dragged me through the twisted bush,
> Put his hand upon my throat,
> Breathed his fire into my mouth—
> That Opitchi-Manneyto.
>
> "And he said to me in wrath,—
> Listen, what he said to me;
> Hear the prophet, Yemassees—
> For he spoke to me in wrath;
> He was angry with my sons,
> For he saw them bent to slay,
> Bent to strike the council-chiefs,
> And he would not have them slain,
> That Opitchi-Manneyto."

As the prophet finished the line that seemed to deny them the revenge which they had promised themselves upon their chiefs, the assembled multitude murmured audibly, and Sanutee, than whom no better politician lived in the nation, knowing well that the show of concession is the best mode of execution among the million, came forward, and seemed to address the prophet, while his speech was evidently meant for them.

"Wherefore, Enoree-Mattee, should Opitchi-Manneyto save the false chiefs who have robbed their people? Shall we not have their blood—shall we not hang their scalps in the tree—shall we not bury their heads in the mud? Wherefore this strange word from Opitchi-Manneyto—wherefore would he save the traitors?"

"It is the well-beloved—it is the well-beloved of Manneyto—speak, prophet, to Sanutee," was the general cry; and the howl, which, at that moment, had been universal, was succeeded by the hush and awful stillness of the grave. The prophet was not slow to answer for the demon, in a wild strain like that already given them:

> "'Tis Opitchi-Manneyto,
> Not the prophet, now that speaks,
> Give him ear then, Yemassee,
> Hear Opitchi-Manneyto.

"Says Opitchi-Manneyto,
Wherefore are my slaves so few—
Not for me the gallant chief,
Slaughtered by the Yemassee—
Blest, the slaughtered chief must go,
To the happy home that lies
In the bosom of the hills,
Where the game is never less,
Though the hunter always slays—
Where the plum-groves always bloom,
And the hunter never sleeps.

"Says Opitchi-Manneyto—
Wherefore are my slaves so few?
Shall the Yemassee give death—
Says Opitchi-Manneyto—
To the traitor, to the slave,
Who would sell the Yemassees—
Who would sell his father's bones,
And behold the green corn grow
From his wife's and mother's breast?

"Death is for the gallant chief
Says Opitchi-Manneyto—
Life is for the traitor slave,
But a life that none may know—
With a shame that all may see.

"Thus Opitchi-Manneyto,
To his sons, the Yemassee—
Take the traitor chiefs, says he,
Make them slaves, to wait on me.
Bid Malatchie take the chiefs,
He, the executioner—
Take the chiefs and bind them down,
Cut the totem from each arm,
So that none may know the slaves,
Not their fathers, not their mothers—
Children, wives, that none may know—
Not the tribes that look upon,

Not the young men of their own,
Not the people, not the chiefs—
Nor the good Manneyto know.

"Thus Opitchi-Manneyto,
Make these traitors slaves for me;
Then the blessed valley lost,
And the friends and chiefs they knew,
None shall know them, all shall flee,
Make them slaves to wait on me—
Hear Opitchi-Manneyto,
Thus, his prophet speaks for him,
To the mighty Yemassee."

The will of the evil deity thus conveyed to the Indians by the prophet, carried with it a refinement in the art of punishment to which civilization has not often attained. According to the superstitions of the Yemassees, the depriving the criminal of life did not confer degradation or shame; for his burial ceremonies were precisely such as were allotted to those dying in the very sanctity and most grateful odour of favourable public opinion. But this was not the case when the totem or badge of his tribe had been removed from that portion of his person where it had been the custom of the people to have it wrought; for, without this totem, no other nation could recognise them, their own resolutely refused to do it, and, at their death, the great Manneyto would reject them from the plum-groves and the happy valley, when the fierce Opitchi-Manneyto, the evil demon, whom they invoked with as much, if not more earnestness than the good, was always secure of his prey.

Such, then, was the terrific decree delivered by the prophet. A solemn awe succeeded for a moment this awful annunciation among the crowd; duly exaggerated by the long and painful howl of agony with which the doomed traitors within the council-house, who had been listening, were made conscious of its complete purport. Then came a shout of triumphant revenge from those without, who now, with minds duly directed to the new design, were as resolute to preserve the lives of the chiefs as they had before been anxious to destroy them. Encircling the council-house closely in order to prevent their escape, they determined patiently to adopt such measures as should best secure them as prisoners. The policy of Sanutee, for it will scarcely need that we point to him as the true deviser of the present scheme, was an admirable one in considering the Indian character. To overthrow the chiefs properly, and at the same time to discourage communication with the English, it was better to degrade than to destroy them. The populace may sympathize with the victim whose blood they have shed, for death in all countries goes far to cancel the memory of offence; but they seldom restore to their estimation the individual they have themselves degraded. The mob, in this respect, seems to be duly conscious of the hangman filthiness of its own fingers.

Chapter Twelve

"This makes of thee a master, me a slave,
And I destroy it; we are equal now."

A NOT less exciting scene was now going on within the council-chamber. There, all was confusion and despair. The shock of such a doom as that which the chiefs had heard pronounced by the people, under the influence of the prophet, came upon them like a bolt of thunder. For a moment it paralyzed with its terrors the hearts of those who had no fear of death. The mere loss of life is always an event of triumph with the brave among the Indians, and, for the due ennobling of which, his song of past victories and achievements, carefully chronicled by a memory which has scarcely any other employment, is shouted forth in the most acute physical agony, with a spirit which nothing can bend or conquer. But to deprive him of this memory—to eradicate all the marks of his achievements—to take from him the only credential by which he operates among his fellows, and claims a place in the ranks of the illustrious dead—was a refinement upon the terrors of punishment, which, unfrequently practised, was held as a doom, intended to paralyze, as in the present instance, every spark of moral courage which the victim might possess. For a moment such was its effect in the assembly of the chiefs. The solitary howl of despair which their unanimous voices sent up, as the first intimation of the decree met their ears, was succeeded by the deepest silence, while they threw themselves upon their faces, and the torch-bearers, burying their torches in the clay floor of the building, with something of that hate and horror which seemed to distinguish the body of the Indians without, rushed forth from the apartment and joined with the assembled people. Their departure aroused the despairing inmates, and while one of them carefully again closed the entrance before the watchful mass without could avail themselves of the opening, the rest prepared themselves with renewed courage to deliberate upon their situation.

"There is death for Manneywanto," exclaimed that fierce warrior and chief— "he will not lose the arrow of his tribe. I will go forth to the hatchet. I will lift my arm, and strike so that they shall slay."

"Let them put the knife into the heart of Oonalatchie," cried another— "but not to the arrow upon his shoulder. He will go forth with Manneywanto."

The determination of the whole was soon made. Huspah the superior but superannuated chief, tottered in advance, singing mournfully the song of death with which the Indian always prepares for its approach. This song became general with the victims, and with drawn knives and ready hatchets, they threw wide the entrance, and rushing forth with a fury duly heightened by the utter hopelessness of escape, they struck desperately on all sides among the hundreds by whom they were beleaguered. But they had been waited and prepared for, and, forbearing to strike in return, and freely risking their own lives, the Indians were content to bear them down by the force of numbers. The more feeble among them fell under the pressure. Of these was Huspah, the king, whom the crowd immediately dragged from the press, and, in spite of the exertions of Sanutee, who desired the observance of some formalities which marked the ceremony, they fiercely cut away the flesh from that portion of the arm which bore the symbol of his people, while his shrieks of despair and defiance, reaching the ears of his comrades, still struggling with their assailants, heightened their desperation and made their arrest the more difficult. But the strife was in a little time over. The crowd triumphed, and the chiefs, still living and unhurt, saving only a few bruises which were unavoidable in the affray, were all secured save Manneywanto. That powerful and ferocious chief manfully battled with a skill and strength that knew no abatement from its exercise, and seemed only heightened by the opposition. A friendly hand, at length, whose stroke he blessed, encountered him in the crowd, and severed his skull with a hatchet. He was the only individual of the traitors by whom the vengeance of the Indians was defrauded. Not another of the clan proved fortunate in his desperation. The survivors were all securely taken, and, carefully bound with thongs, were borne away to the great tumulus upon which they were to suffer the judgment which they so much dreaded. There was no escape. They found no mercy. They did not plead for mercy, nor for life. Death was implored, but in vain. The prophet—the people, were relentless. The knife sheared the broad arrow from breast and arm, and in a single hour they were expatriated men, flying desperately to the forests, homeless, nationless, outcasts from God and man, yet destined to live. It is remarkable that, in all this time, suicide never entered the thoughts of the victims. It forms no part of the Indian's philosophy to die by his own hand, and the Roman might have won a lesson from the Yemassee, in this respect, which would have ennobled his Catos.*

Meanwhile, the deputation of the Carolinians lay at the house of Granger, full of apprehensions for their common safety. Nor was Granger himself less so. He felt assured of the danger, and only relied upon the interposition of Sanutee, which he knew to be all-powerful, and which, looking on the outbreak of the people as the result of their own impulse, he saw no reason to imagine would be denied on the present occasion. From their place of retreat, which lay on the skirts of the town and nigh the river, the embassy could hear the outcries and clamours of the Indians without being acquainted with particulars; and when at length they beheld the flames ascending from the house of council—which, when they had seized upon the chiefs, the rioters had fired—believing the chiefs consumed in the conflagration, they gave themselves up for lost. They did not doubt that the fury which had sacrificed so many and such influential persons would scarcely be satisfied to allow of their escape; and, firmly impressed with the conviction that their trial was at hand, Sir Edmund Bellinger drew his sword, and, followed by the rest of the deputation, prepared for a conflict in which they had but one hope, that of selling the life dearly, which seemed so certainly forfeited.

In this mood of mind they waited the coming of the storm; nor were they long kept in suspense. Having beheld the fearful doom carried into effect, and seen their ancient rulers scourged out of the town, the revolutionists rushed headlong, and with an appetite for blood duly heightened by the little they had seen, to the dwelling of the

---

* Ordinarily, such is the case; yet there are exceptions to the rule. The Cherokees have been frequently known to destroy themselves, after losing their beauty from the smallpox.

trader—vowing as they hurried along, to their infernal deity, Opitchi-Manneyto, an increase of slaves in the persons of the Englishmen, whom they proposed to sacrifice by fire. On their way, mistaking one of their own people who had dressed himself somewhat after the fashion of the English, in a dress which had been discarded by some white man, they dashed him to the earth, trampled and nearly tore him into pieces before discovering the mistake. In such a temper, they appeared before the dwelling of the trader, and with loud shouts demanded their prey.

Determined upon stout resistance to the last, the commissioners had barricaded the little dwelling as well as they could; and, doubtless, for a small space of time, would have made it tenable; but, fortunately for them, just as the furious savages were about to apply the fatal torch to the building, the appearance of Enoree-Mattee and Sanutee spared them an issue which could have only terminated in their murder. Sanutee had his game to play, and, though perfectly indifferent, perhaps, as to the fate of the commissioners, yet, as his hope in the forthcoming insurrection lay in taking the Carolinians by surprise, it was his policy to impress them with confidence rather than distrust. He aimed now to divest the embassy of all suspicion, and to confine the show of indignation on the part of the Yemassees, entirely to the chiefs who had so abused their power.

Addressing the mob, he controlled it in his own manner, and telling them that they wanted nothing from the English but the treaty which had so fraudulently been entered into by their chiefs, he engaged to them to effect its restoration, along with the skin of earth, which completing the bargain, was held equivalent in their estimation, to a completion of legal right as an actual possession. After some demur, Granger admitted the chief, who came alone to the presence of the deputation, the chairman of which thus sternly addressed him:—

"Are the English dogs," said Sir Edmund Bellinger, "that thy people hunt them with cries and fire? Wherefore is this, Sanutee?"

"The English have the lands of my people, and therefore my people hunt them. The bad chiefs who sold the land as chiefs of the Yemassee, are chiefs no longer."

"Thou hast slain them?" inquired Sir Edmund.

"No, but they are dead—dead to Sanutee—dead to the Yemassee—dead to Manneyto. They are dogs—the English have slaves in the woods."

"But their acts are good with us, and the English will protect them, Sanutee, and will punish their enemies. Beware, chief—I tell thee there is danger for thy people."

"It is good. Does the white chief hear my people? They cry for blood. They would drink it from thy heart, but Sanutee is the friend of the English. They shall touch thee not—they shall do thee no harm!"

"Thou has said well, Sanutee, and I expected no less from thee; but why do they not go? Why do they still surround our dwelling?"

"They wait for the wampum—they would tear the skin which carries the land of the Yemassee;" and the chief, as he spoke, pointed to the treaty and the sack of earth which lay by the side of Bellinger. He proceeded to tell them that they should be secure when these were redelivered to the Indians. But, with the commissioners it was a point of honour not to restore the treaty which they had obtained from the rulers *de facto* of the people—certainly, not to a lawless mob; and, regarding only the high trust of which he had charge, the speech of the chief commissioner was instantaneous:—

"Never, Sanutee, never—only with my blood. Go—you have my answer. We shall fight to the last, and our blood be upon the heads of your people. They will pay dearly for every drop of it they spill."

"It is well," said Sanutee. "It is well: Sanutee will go back to his people, and the knife of the Yemassee will dig for his land in the heart of the English." He left the house, accordingly; and, with gloomy resignation, Bellinger, with the other commissioners and Granger, prepared for the coming storm with all their philosophy. In a few moments the anticipated commotion began. The populace, but a little before silent and patient, now chafed and roared like a stormy ocean, and the fierce cry of "Sangarrah-me," the cry for blood, went up from a thousand voices. The torches were brought forward, and the deputies, firm and fearless enough, saw no hope even of a chance for the use of their weapons. The two subordinates, with Granger, looked imploringly to Bellinger, but the stern chief paced the apartment unbendingly, though seemingly well aware of all the dangers of their situation. At that moment the wife of Granger—a tall, fine looking woman, of much masculine beauty, appeared from an inner apartment, and before she had been observed by either of the commissioners, seizing upon the little skin of earth and the parchment at the same moment, without a word, she threw open the door, and cried out to Sanutee to receive them. This was all done in an instant, and before the stern commissioner could see or interfere, the deposits, placed in the grasp of the savages, were torn into a thousand pieces.

"Woman, how durst thou do this!"—was the first sentence of Bellinger, to the person who had thus yielded up his trust. But she fearlessly confronted him—

"My life is precious to me, Sir, though you may be regardless of yours. The treaty is nothing now to the Yemassees, who have destroyed their chiefs on account of it. To have kept it would have done no good, but must have been destructive to us all. Sanutee will keep his word, and our lives will be saved."

It was evident that she was right, and Bellinger was wise enough to see it. He said nothing farther, glad, perhaps, that the responsibility of the action had been thus taken from his shoulders. The assurances of the woman were soon verified. In a short time Sanutee re-appeared among the commissioners. The crowd without, meanwhile, had been made to hear his voice,—had shared in the destruction of the offensive treaty, and their rage was temporarily pacified. The storm gradually subsided.

"Sanutee is a friend of the English," was the soothing assurance of the wily chief. "The wise men of the English will soon go to their own people. The Yemassee will do them no hurt."

The commissioners waited perforce the signal of Sanutee to depart. The clamour having subsided, they prepared to go forth under the protection and presence of the old chief, which the proud Sir Edmund Bellinger had indignantly, but in vain, refused. Seeing that Granger and his wife remained, Sanutee turned suddenly upon him, and in a low tone, unheard by the commissioners, asked why he did not prepare to go also. He answered by avowing his willingness still to remain in Pocota-ligo, as before, for the purpose of trade.

"Go—Sanutee is good friend to Granger, and to his woman. Go all—there is fire and a knife in the hand of the Yemassees, and they will drink a deep draught from the heart of the pale-faces. If Granger will not go from the Yemassee, look, the hatchet of Sanutee is ready;" and he raised it as he spoke— "Sanutee will save Granger from the fire-death."

This is the last service which the Indian warrior may do his friend, and Granger understood the extent of the impending danger from this proffer, meant as a kindness on the part of the old chief. He needed no second exhortation to remove, and, though the hope of gain and a prosperous trade had encouraged him hitherto, to risk every thing in his present residence, the love of life proved stronger; for he well knew that Sanutee seldom spoke without good reason. Packing up, therefore, with the aid of his wife, the little remaining stock in trade which he possessed, and which a couple of good-sized bundles readily comprised, they took their way along with the commissioners, and, guided by Sanutee, soon reached the river. Choosing for them a double canoe, the old chief saw them safely embarked. Taking the paddles into their own hands, the midnight wayfarers descended the stream on their way towards the Block House, while, surrounded by a small group of his people, Sanutee watched their slow progress from the banks.

Chapter Thirteen

"And merrily, through the long summer day,
The southern boatman winds his pliant horn,
As sweeping with the long pole down his streams,
He cheers the lazy hours, and speeds them on."

THE fugitives reached the Block House in safety, and found the few hours of repose which they could snatch between the time of their midnight escape and daylight, highly grateful from the fatigues which they had undergone. The upper apartments were appropriately divided between the commissioners and Granger, who, with his wife, instead of seeking sleep on their arrival, proceeded with all the mechanical habits of the trader, to attend first to the proper safety and arrangement of his stock in trade; which, consisting of a few unsold goods, of a description adapted to the wants of that region, and some small bundles of furs, intrinsically of little value, were yet to the selfish tradesman of paramount importance.

It was early sunrise on the morning following the wild events narrated in our last chapter, when Gabriel Harrison, of whom we have seen little for some time past, appeared on the edge of the little brow of hill, known as the Chief's Bluff, which immediately overlooked the Pocota-ligo river. In the distance, some ten or twelve miles, unseen of course, lay the Indian village or town of the same name. Immediately before him, say one or two miles above, in the broadest part of the stream, rested motionless as the hill upon which he stood, the sharp clipper-built vessel, which has already called for some of our attention, and which, at this moment, seemed to attract no small portion of his. Sheltered by the branches of a single tree, which arose from the centre of the bluff, Harrison continued the scrutiny, with here and there a soliloquizing remark, until interrupted by the presence of the commissioners, who, with Granger, now came towards him from the Block House.

"Ha, Sir Edmund—gentlemen—how fares it, and when came you from Pocota-ligo?" was the salutation of Harrison to the deputation.

"At midnight, my lord—at midnight, and in a hurry; we had the whole tribe upon us. There has been a commotion, and by this time, I doubt not, the Yemassees have cut the throats of all the chiefs friendly to our proposed treaty."

"Indeed, but this is worse and worse. I feared something, and warned the council against this movement. But their cursed desire to possess the lands must precipitate all the dangers I have been looking for. I told them that the Yemassees were discontented, and that the utmost care must be taken not to goad them too far. I saw this in the sullenness of old Sanutee himself, and they have given wings to the mischief by their imprudence. But how was it, Sir Edmund? let us have particulars."

The circumstances, as already narrated, were soon told, and the countenance of Harrison bespoke the anxious thoughts in his bosom. Turning to Granger, at length, he addressed the trader inquiringly:

"Can you say nothing more than this—what have you learned touching Ishiagaska? Was it as I feared? Had he been to St. Augustine?"

"He had, my lord,—"

"Harrison—Harrison—Captain Harrison," impatiently exclaimed the person addressed— "forget while here, that I have any other title. Go on."

"Ishiagaska, sir, and old Choluculla, both of them have been to St. Augustine, and have but a week ago returned, loaded with presents."

"Ay, ay, the storm gathers, and we must look to it, gentlemen commissioners. This matter hurries it onward. They were making their preparations fast enough before, and they will now find reason enough, in their passions and our cupidity, for instant action. Yet you say that Sanutee saved you."

"He did, and seemed friendly enough."

"Said he aught of disapproval to their proceedings?—made he any professions of regard to the English?"

"He said little, but that was friendly, and his interposition for our safety—"

"Was his policy. He is a cunning savage, but I see through him. He does not wish to alarm us, for they can only conquer by disarming our caution; and this is my greatest fear. Our people are so venturous that they refuse to believe any evidence short of actual demonstration, and every day finds them thrusting their heads and shoulders farther and farther into the mouth of the enemy, and without the chance of support from their friends. They will grow wise at a fearful price, or I am greatly deceived."

"But what do you propose, my lord, if you look for an insurrection near at hand?" asked Sir Edmund Bellinger.

"I might answer you readily enough, Sir Edmund, by asking you wherefore I am here. But please style me Harrison, and if that be too abrupt in its expression, to your own ears—it will not be to mine—then make it Master or Captain Gabriel Harrison. It is something of my game to see for myself the difficulties and the dangers at hand, and for this reason I now play the spy. Here, I am perfectly unknown—save to one or two persons—except as the captain of a little troop, whose confidence I secured in the affair with your Coosaws and Ashepoos, and which I embodied on that occasion. Still, they only know me as Captain Harrison, and, somehow or other, they are well enough content with me in that character."

"And think you that there is an insurrection at hand?"

"That, Sir Edmund, is my fear. It is the question which we must examine. It is vitally important that we should know. Our borderers are not willing to come out, unless for serious cause, and to call them out prematurely would not only tax the colony beyond its resources, but would dismiss the present rulers of the people, with curses both loud and deep, to the unambitious retreats of home and fireside. They are turbulent enough now, and this matter of religion, which our lord proprietors in England, the bigoted old Granville in particular, seem so willing, with their usual stupidity, to meddle with, has completely maddened these same people, in whose watery country of Granville we now stand."

"And what do you propose to do?"

"Why, surely, to gain what information we can, before calling the people to arms. To render them cautious, is all that we can do at present. The evidence which I have of this approaching insurrection, though enough for suspicion, will scarcely be considered enough for action; and I must continue to spy myself, and engage others in the work, so as to keep pace with their movements. They must be watched closely,—ay, and in every quarter, Sir Edmund, for, let me tell you, that in your own barony of Ashepoo, they are quite as devilishly inclined as here. They are excited all around us."

"But I have seen nothing of all this," was the reply of the land-grave. "The Ashepoos, what are left of them, seem quiet enough in my neighbourhood."

"To be sure they are, while in the presence of Sir Edmund Bellinger, the immediate authority of the English in their country. But did you strip yourself of your authority, as I have done, for I am just from that very quarter; put on the dress, and some of the slashing and bilbo swagger of a drunken captain from the Low Countries, to whom a pot of sour ale is the supreme of felicity, they had shown you more of their true nature. Some of my evidence would amuse you. For example, I crossed the river last night to the house of Tamaita, an old squaw who tells fortunes in the very centre of Terrapin swamp, where she is sur-rounded by as damnable an assemblage of living alligators, as would have made happy all the necromancers of the past ages. She told me my fortune, which she had ready at my hand, and which, if true, will cer-tainly make me a convert to her philosophy. But, with her predictions, she gave me a great deal of advice, probably with the view to their being more perfectly verified. Among other things, she promised us a great deal of lightning soon; a promise which you would naturally enough suppose, meant nothing more than one of our summer afternoon thunder storms, which, by the way, are terrible enough."

"What else should she mean?"

"Her lightning signified the arrows of the Yemassees. In this way, they figure the rapidity and the danger attending the flight of their long shafts. The promise tallied well with the counsel of Sanutee, who advised me yesterday to be off in the big canoe."

"Which advice you decline—you propose still to continue here, my lord—Captain Harrison, I mean," replied Sir Edmund.

"Of God's surety, I will, Sir Edmund. Can I else now? I must watch this movement as well as I can, and make our people generally do so, or the tomahawk and fire will sweep them off in a single night. Apart from that, you know this sort of adventure is a pleasure to me, and there is a something of personal interest in some of my journeyings, which I delight to see ripen."

Bellinger smiled, and Harrison continued with an air of the most perfect business—

"But speed on your journey, gentlemen—the sooner the better. Make the best of your way to Charleston, but trust not to cross the land as you came. Keep from the woods; for the journey that way is a slow one, and if things turn out as I fear, they will swarm before long with enemies, even to the gates of Charleston. Do me grace to place these despatches safely with their proper trusts. The assembly will read them in secret. This to the lieutenant-governor, who will act upon it immediately. Despatch now, gentlemen—I have hired a boat, which Granger will procure for you from Grimstead."

The commissioners were soon prepared for travel, and took their departure at once for the city. Granger, after they had gone, returned to the conference with Harrison at the Chief's Bluff, where the latter continued to linger.

"Have you seen Hector?" asked the latter.

"I have not, sir."

"Indeed. Strange! He had a charge from me yesterday to take the track of a sea-faring fellow, whom I encountered, and of whom I had suspicions—after that, he was told to cross over, and give you intelligence of my being here."

"I have seen nothing of him."

"The blockhead has plunged into trap then, I doubt not. Confound him, for a dull beast. To be absent at this time, when I so much want him."

While Harrison thus vented his anger and disquiet, Granger, suddenly recollecting that he had been hailed the afternoon before, by some one in a boat, as he was proceeding rapidly to join the commissioners in Pocota-ligo—though without knowing the voice or hearing it repeated—now related the circumstance, and at once satisfied the person he addressed of the correctness of his apprehensions.

"Ha—he is then in that sailor's clutches. But he shall disgorge him. I'll not lose Hector, on any terms. He's the very prince of body servants, and loves me, I verily believe, as I do my mistress. He must not suffer. Look forth, Granger, you have sharp eyes—look forth, and say what you think of the craft, lying there at the Broad-bend."

"I have watched her, sir, for the last hour, but can't say for certain what to think. It is easier to say what she is not, than what she is."

"That will do—say what she is not, and I can readily satisfy myself as to what she is."

"She has no colours—her paint's fresh, put on since she has been in these waters. She is not a Spaniard, sir, nor is she English, that's certain."

"Well, what next, Sir Sagacity?"

The trader paused a few moments, as if to think, then, with an assured manner, and without seeming to annex any great importance to the communication which he made, he dryly replied—

"Why, sir, she's neither one thing nor another in look, but a mixture of all. Now, when that's the case in the look of a vessel, it's a sign that the crew is a mixture, and that there is no one person regulating. It's left to them to please their taste in most things, and so that paint seems put on as if Dutch and French, Spanish and Portuguese, and English, all had some hand in it. There's yellow and black, red and green, and all colours, I make out, where no one nation would employ more than one or two of them."

"Well, what do you infer from all that?"

"I think, sir, she's a pirate, or what's no better, a Spanish guarda-costa."

"The devil you do, and Hector is in her jaws! But what other reasons have you for this opinion?"

"What is she doing here—having no intercourse with the people—keeping off from the landing—showing no colours, and yet armed to the teeth? If there be nothing wrong, sir, why this concealment and distance?"

"You jump readily and with some reason to a conclusion, Granger, and you may be right. Now hear my thought. That vessel comes from St. Augustine, and brings arms to the Yemassees, and urges on this very insurrection of which you had a taste last night."

"Very likely, and she may be a pirate, too. They are thick about the coast."

"Ay, Granger, as the contents of some of your packages might tell if they had tongues," said Harrison, with a smile.

"God forbid, captain," exclaimed the trader, with a simple gravity which rose into honest dignity as he continued— "I can show bills for all my goods, from worthy citizens in Charleston and elsewhere."

"No matter; I charge you not. But you may be right. To be a pirate and a Spaniard are not such distinct matters, and now I think with you, the probability is, she is both. But what I mean to say, Granger, is this—that she comes here now with no mere piratical intent, but to serve other and perhaps worse purposes—else, what keeps her from plundering the shore?"

"The best reason in the world, sir; it's a long reach she must go through before she safely keels the sea. It's slow work to get from the bay of the Broad, and a wind takes its pleasure in coming to fill up a sail in this crooked water. Let them once do what they came for, and make the coast, then look out for the good merchantmen who find their way into the Gulf of Mexico."

"Well, whether Spaniard, or pirate, or Dutch Flyaway, we must get Hector out of her jaws, if it's only to keep him a gentleman, and—but stay, she drops a boat. Do you make out who comes in it?"

"Two men pull—"

"Certain. Who again, Mercury?"

"A bluff, stout fellow, sits astern, wears a blue jacket, and—"

"A gold chain?"

"He does, sir, with thick-hanging shining buttons."

"The same. That's Hercules."

"Who, sir?"

"Hercules or Ajax, I don't remember which. I gave him one or other, or both names yesterday, and shall probably find another for him to-day; for I must have Hector out of him! He shapes for the shore—does he?"

"Yes, sir; and from his present course, he will make the parson's landing."

"Ha! say you so, most worthy trader? Well, we shall be at the meeting." "Yes," muttered the speaker, rather to himself than to his companion— "we shall be at the meeting! He must not look upon my pretty Bess without seeing the good fortune which the fates yield her, in the person of her lover. We shall be there, Granger; and, not to be unprovided with the means for effecting the escape of Hector, let us call up some of our choice spirits—some of the Green Foresters— they know the signal of their captain, and, thanks to fortune, I left enough for the purpose at the smithy of Dick Grimstead. Come, man of wares and merchandises—be packing."

Leading the way from the hill, Harrison, followed by Granger, descended to the level forest about a mile off, in the immediate rear of the Block House, and, placing his hunting horn to his lips, he sounded it thrice with a deep clear note, which called up a dozen echoes from every dell in the surrounding woods. The sounds had scarcely ceased to reverberate before they were replied to, in a long and mellow roll, from one, seemingly a perfect master of the instrument, who, even after the response had been given, poured forth a generous blast, followed by a warbling succession of cadences, melting away at last into a silence which the ear, having carefully treasured up the preceding notes, almost refused to acknowledge. From another point in the woods, a corresponding strain thrice repeated, followed soon after the first, and announced an understanding among the parties, to which the instrument had been made ably subservient.

"These are my Green Jackets, Granger; you have made money out of that colour, my Plutus—my own green jacket boys, true as steel, and swift as an Indian arrow. Come, let us bury ourselves a little deeper in the thick woods, where, in half an hour, you may see a dozen of the same colour at the gathering."

Chapter Fourteen

"I know thee, though the world's strife on thy brow
Hath beaten strangely. Altered to the eye,
Methinks I look upon the self-same man,
With nature all unchanged."

THE boat from the unknown vessel reached the point jutting out into the river, in front of the dwelling of the old pastor; and the seaman, already more than once introduced to our notice, leaving the two men in charge of it, took his way to the habitation in question. The old man received the stranger with all the hospitalities of the region, and ushered him into the presence of his family with due courtesy, though as a stranger. The seaman seemed evidently to constrain himself while surveying the features of the inmates, which he did with some curiosity; and had Harrison been present, he might have remarked, with some dissatisfaction, the long, earnest, and admiring gaze which, in this survey, the beautiful features of Bess Matthews were made to undergo, to her own evident disquiet. After some little chat, with that bluff, free, hearty manner which is the happy characteristic of the seafaring man,—the frankness, in some degree, relieving the roughness of the man's speech and manner,—the stranger contrived to remove much of the unfavourable impression which his gross and impudent cast of face had otherwise made; and, in reply to a natural inquiry of the pastor, he gave a brief account of the nature of his pursuits in that quarter. A close and scrutinizing legal mind might have picked out no small number of flaws in the yarn which he spun, yet to the unsophisticated sense of the little family, the story was straightforward and clear enough. The trade in furs and skins, usually carried on with the Indians, was well known to be exceedingly valuable in many of the European markets; and, with this declared object the seaman accounted for his presence in a part of the world, not often honoured with the visit of a vessel of so much pretension as that which he commanded. From one thing to another, with a fluent, dashing sort of speech, he went on—now telling of his own, and now of the adventures of others, and, bating an occasional oath, which invariably puckered up the features of the old Puritan, he contrived to make himself sufficiently agreeable, and after a very passable fashion. Bessy did not, it is true, incline the ear after the manner of Desdemona to her Blackamoor; but in the anecdote, of adventure, which every now and then enriched the rambling speech of their guest, either in the tale of his own, or of the achievements of others, it must be acknowledged that the simple girl found much, in spite of herself, to enlist her curiosity and command her attention. Nor was he less influenced by her presence than she by his narrative. Though spoken generally, much of his conversation was seemingly addressed in especial to the maiden. With this object, he sprinkled his story with the wonders of the West Indies, with all of which he appeared familiar—spoke of its luscious fruits and balmy climate—its groves of lemon and of orange—its dark-eyed beauties, and numerous productions of animal and vegetable life. Then of its gold and jewels, the ease of their attainment, and all that sort of thing, which the vulgar mind would be apt to suppose exceedingly attractive and overcoming to the weak one. Having said enough, as he thought, fairly and fully to dazzle the imagination of the girl—and, secure now of a favourable estimate of himself, he drew from his bosom a little casket, containing a rich gold chain of Moorish filigree work, arabesque wrought, and probably a spoil of Grenada, and pressed it on her acceptance. Her quick and modest, but firm rejection of the proffered gift, compelled the open expression of his astonishment.

"And wherefore not—young lady? The chain is not unbecoming for the neck, though that be indeed the whitest. Now, the girls of Spain, with a skin nothing to be compared with yours, they wear such necklaces as thick as grape vines. Come, now—don't be shy and foolish. The chain is rich, and worth a deal of money. Let me lock it now about your neck. You will look like a queen in it—a queen of all the Indies could not look more so."

But the sailor blundered grossly. Bess Matthews was a thinking, feeling woman, and he addressed her as a child. She had now recovered from the interest which she had shown while he narrated adventures which excited her imagination, and set her fancy in glow;—conjuring up and putting into activity many of those wondrous dreams which the young romancer has so ready at all times in thought—and she soon convinced him that he had greatly mistaken her, when he was so willing to transfer to himself the attention which she had simply yielded to his stories. He began to discover that he had mistaken his person, when he beheld the alteration in her tone and manner; and sunk away, somewhat abashed, at the lofty air with which she rejected the gift, and resented the impertinent familiarity of his offer. But, his discouragement was only for a moment. He soon recovered his confidence. If he had surprised the daughter by his freedom, he was soon to astonish the father. Suddenly turning to the old man, he said abruptly:—

"Why, Matthews, you have made your daughter as great a saint as yourself. Ha! I see you stagger. Didn't know me, eh! Didn't remember your old parish acquaintance, Dick Chorley."

The pastor looked at him with some interest, but with more seeming commiseration.

"And are you the little Richard?"

"Little, indeed—that's a good one. I was once little, and little enough, when you knew me,—but I am big enough now, John Matthews, to have myself righted when wrong is done me. It is not now, that the parish beadle can flog little Dick Chorley. Not now, by thunder!—and it's been a sore sorrow with some of them, I think, that it ever was the case."

"Well Richard, I'm glad to find you so much better off in the world, and with a better disposition to work for yourself honestly, than in old times," said the pastor gravely.

"Hark ye, Matthews—no more of that. That's as it may be. Perhaps I'm better—perhaps I'm not. It's none of your business either one way or the other; and to look back too closely into old time doings, ain't a friend's part, I'm thinking. Blast me! old man, but you had nearly made me forget myself; and I wouldn't like to say rough things to you or any of yours, for I can't but remember you were always more kind to me than the rest, and if I had minded you I might have done better. But what's done can't be undone, and the least said is soonest mended."

"I meant not to speak harshly, Richard, when I spoke of the past," said the pastor, mildly, "but the exile finds it sweet to remember, even those things which were sorrows in his own land. I find it so with me;

and though, to speak plainly, Richard, I would rather not see you to know you as of old, yet the recognition of your person, for a moment, gave me a sentiment of pleasure."

"And why should it not—and why should it not? Blast me! old man, but you don't think I'm the same ragged urchin that the parish fed and flogged—that broke his master's head, and was the laughing-stock and the scapegoat of every gentleman rascal in the shire?—no, no. The case is changed now, and if I'm no better, I'm at least an abler man; and that stands for right and morality all the world over. I'm doing well in the world, Matthews—drive a good trade—own a half in as handsome a clipper as ever swum in the blue waters of the gulf; and, if the world will let me, I shall probably in little time be as good—that is to say as rich a man—as any of them. If they won't, they must look out for themselves, that's all."

"One thing pleases me, at least, Richard," said the pastor, gravely, "and that is to find your pursuits such that you need not be ashamed of them. This should give you an honest pride, as it certainly yields me great pleasure."

There was rather more of inquiry than of remark in this observation, and Chorley saw it.

"Ay, ay, if it pleases you, I'm satisfied. You are a good judge of what's right, and can say. For my part, I make it a rule to boast nothing of my virtue. It takes the polish off a good action to turn it over too often in one's mouth."

There was a satirical chuckle following the speech of the sailor which the pastor did not seem to relish. It seemed to sneer at the joint homilies which they had been uttering. The dialogue was changed by the pastor.

"And where is your mother now, Richard?"

"Ask the parish church-yard—it has one grave more, that I can swear for, than when you left it; and, though I'm bad at grammar, I could read the old woman's name upon the stick at the head. When she died I came off. I couldn't stand it then, though I stood it well enough before. They have not seen me since, nor I them—and there's no love lost between us. If I ever go back, it will be to see the old beadle and that grave-stick."

"I hope you harbour no malice, Richard, against the man for doing his duty?"

"His duty?"

"Yes, his duty. He was the officer of the law, and compelled to do what he did. Wherefore then would you go back to see him, simply—and why do you strangely couple him in your memory with your mother's grave?"

"Ha! that's it. He broke her heart by his treatment to me, and I would break his scull upon her grave as a satisfaction to both of us. I did wrong when a boy, that's like enough, for older people did wrong daily about me; but was my public disgrace to cure me of my wrong? They put me in the stocks, then expected me to be a good citizen. Wise enough. I tell you what, Matthews, I've seen something more of the world than you, though you've seen more years than I; and mark my word! whenever a man becomes a bad man—a thief, an outlaw, or a murderer—his neighbours have to thank themselves for three-fourths of the teachings that have made him so. But this is enough on this talk. Let us say something now of yourself—and first, how do you like this part of the world?"

"As well as can be expected. I am indifferent to any other, and I have quiet here, which I had not always in the turbulent changes of England. My family too are satisfied, and their contentment makes the greater part of mine."

"You'd find it better and pleasanter in Florida. I drive a good business there with the Spaniard. I'm rather one myself now, and carry his flag, though I trade chiefly on my own log."

The dialogue was here broken in upon by the entrance of Harrison, who, in spite of the cold courtesies of the pastor, and the downcast reserve in the eyes of Bess Matthews, yet joined the little group with the composure of one perfectly satisfied of the most cordial reception.

Chapter Fifteen

"Thou shalt disgorge thy prey, give up thy spoil,
And yield thee prisoner. The time is short,
Make thy speech fitting."

BEFORE resuming with these parties, let us retire to the green wood with Harrison and the trader. We have heard the merry horn of his comrades responding freely to that of the former. "You shall see them," said he to Granger— "brave fellows and true, and sufficient for my purpose. I can rely upon Grimstead, the smith, and his brother, certainly, for I left them but a couple of hours ago at the smithy. Theirs was the first answer we heard. I know not who comes the second, but I look for Wat Grayson from that quarter, and sure enough, he is here. Ha! Grayson, you are true and in time, as usual. I give you welcome, for I want your arm."

"And at your service, captain, to strike deer or enemy, for fight or labour. Ha! Granger—but you have forgotten my knife, which I've sorely wanted."

"It is here, at the Block House, ready for you."

"Good! Well, captain, what's the service now? I'm ready, you see, and glad that you feel able to count so free upon Wat Grayson."

"You shall soon see, Grayson. I wait for but a few more of the boys, to show you the work before us; and in order not to waste more time, wind your horn, and let the men come freely."

The horn was wound again, and but a few seconds had elapsed when a distant reply from two other quarters acknowledged the summons. In a few moments the sturdy blacksmith, Grimstead, followed by his younger brother, penetrated the little area, which was the usual place of assemblage. A moment after, a bustling little body, known as Dr. Nichols, the only medical man in that region, also entered the ring, mounted upon a little ambling pony, or tacky from the marsh—a sturdy little animal in much use, though of repute infinitely below its merits.

"Ha! doctor—our worthy Esculapius—how fares it? You come in time, for we look to have some bones for your setting before long," exclaimed Harrison, addressing him.

"Captain Harrison," responded the little professional, with a most imposing manner, "it gives me pleasure at any moment to do my country service. I am proud that my poor ability may be called into exercise, though I should rather have you invoke my personal than professional offices."

"We shall need both, doctor, most probably. We must first risk our bones before the surgeon may hope to handle them; and in doing so, have no scruple that he should risk his along with us."

"And wherefore, may I ask, Captain Harrison?"

"Simply, doctor, that he may be taught a due lesson of sympathy, by his own hurts, which shall make him tender of ours. But we are slow. Who have we here to count on for a brush?"

"Count on Dick Grimstead, captain, and you may put down Tom with him; but not as doctors.—I'm not for the doctoring, captain."

"Irreverend fellow!" muttered Nichols.

Harrison laughed, and proceeded to enumerate and arrange his men, who soon, including himself and Granger, amounted to seven. He himself carried pistols, and the short German rifle already described. The rest had generally either the clumsy muskets of the time, or the tomahawk, an instrument almost as formidable, and certainly quite as necessary in the forests. Some of them were dressed in the uniform of the "green-jackets," the corps which had been raised by Harrison in the Coosaw war, and which he commanded. Though ignorant entirely of his character and pursuits, yet his successful heading of them in that sudden insurrection, at a moment of great emergency, not less than the free, affable, and forward manner which characterized him, had endeared him to them generally; and, unlike the pastor, they were content with this amount of their knowledge of one whom they had learned not less to love than to obey.

Harrison looked round upon his boys, as he called them, not heeding sundry efforts which Nichols made to command his attention. Suddenly addressing Grayson, he asked—

"Where's Murray?"

"Sick, captain—on the flat of his back, or I had brought him with me. He lies sick at Joe Gibbons', up by Bates', where he's been running up a new house for Gibbons."

"He must come from that, Grayson. It is too far from the Block House for any of them, and for a sick man it will be hopeless, if there should be war. He is not safe there, Grayson, you must move him."

"That's impossible, captain. He can't move, he's down flat with the fever."

"Then you must bring him off on your shoulders, or get a cart, for he is not safe where he is. There is danger of insurrection here. The Yemassees are at mischief, and we shall, before very long, have the war-whoop ringing in our ears. We must clear the borders of our people, or the Yemassees will do it for us."

"And I'm ready, captain, as soon as they," exclaimed Grayson; "and that's the notion of more than Wat Grayson. The boys generally, long for something to do; and, as we go up the river, the Indians get too monstrous impudent to be borne with much longer."

"True, Grayson—but we must wait their pleasure. I only give you my suspicions, and they amount to nothing, so long as the Yemassees profess peace."

"Oh, hang their professions, captain, say I. I don't see why we should wait on them to begin the brush, seeing it must be begun. There's nothing like a dash forward, when you see you have to go. That's my notion; and, say but the word, we'll catch the weazel asleep when he thinks to catch us. All our boys are ready for it, and a ring of the horn round Alligator Swamp will bring a dozen; and by night we could have Dick Mason, and Spragg, and Baynton, who have gone up to the new clearing upon the fork of *Tuliffinee.*"

"It is well," said Harrison, "that you should be ready, but it is for the council to make war and peace,—not for us. We can only provide for our defence in case of assault, and against it I want to prepare you, for I greatly apprehend it. But, in the meantime, I have another job for execution."

Nichols, now finding a favourable moment, in his usual swelling manner, addressed Harrison and the company. Nichols, we may mention, is an incipient demagogue; one of an old school, the duties of which, under the hotbed fosterings of our benign institutions, have largely increased the number of its pupils since his day. His hearers knew him well. His vanities were no new things to his present companions.

"Captain Harrison, understand me. I protest my willingness to volunteer in any matter for the good of the people. It is the part of the true patriot to die for the people, and I'm willing when the time comes. Prepare the block, unsheath the sword, and provide the executioner,—and I, Constantine Maximilian Nichols, medical doctor, well assured that in my death I shall save my country, will freely yield up my poor life, even as the noble Decius of old, for the securing of so great a blessing for our people. But, captain, it must be clear to my mind that the necessity is such, the end to be attained is of so great moment, that the means to be employed are warranted by the laws, in letter and in spirit. Speak, therefore, captain, the design before us. Let me hear your purpose—let my mind examine into its bearings and its tendencies, and I will then declare myself."

Harrison, who knew the doctor quite as well as his neighbours, with singular composure preserved his gravity, while the foresters laughed aloud. He answered:

"Come with us, Constantine Maximilian—your own mind shall judge."

He led the party to the Chief's Bluff, and from the eminence he pointed out to them at a little distance below, where lay the boat of the schooner; one of the seamen was to be seen rambling upon the land at a little distance from it, while the other lay in its bottom.

"Now, Constantine," said he, "behold those men. I want them secured, bound hand and foot, and kept until farther orders."

"Show me, Captain Harrison, that the peace of the country, the lives of my fellow-countrymen, or the liberties of the people, depend upon the measure, and I am ready to yield up my life in the attainment of your object. Until you do this, captain, I decline; and must furthermore lift up my voice in adjuration to those about me, against acting as you counsel, doing this great wrong to the men whom you have singled out for bondage, depriving them of their liberties, and possibly their lives."

"You are scrupulous, doctor, and we shall have to do without you. We shall certainly secure those two men, though we meditate nothing against the liberties of the people."

"I shall warn them by my voice of your design upon them," was the dogged resolve of the doctor.

"Of God's surety, if you dare, Nichols, I shall tumble you headlong from the bluff," sternly responded Harrison; and the patriot—to

whom the declamation was of itself the only object aimed at, constituting the chief glory in his desire—acknowledged, while shrinking
back, that the threat offered quite a new view of the case. With the
others, Harrison found no difficulty. He proceeded—

"Those men must be secured—they are but two, and you are five.
They are without arms, so that all you may look for in the affair will be
a black eye or bloody nose. This will trouble neither of you much,
though less ready than Constantine Maximilian to die for the people.
Tumble the dogs into the sand and rope them—but do them no more
damage than is necessary for that."

"Who are they, captain?" asked Grayson.

"Nay, I know not; but they come from that vessel, and what she is
I know not. One thing is certain, however, and hence my proceeding:
in that vessel they have safely packed away my black fellow, Hector."

"The devil they have—the kidnappers!"

"Ay, have they; and unless I get him out they will have him in the
Cuba market, and heaven knows how many more besides him, in
twenty days, and we have no vessel to contend with them. There is but
one way to give them a taste of what they may expect. You secure these
lads, and when you have done so, bring them round to Parson
Matthews, sound your horn, and I shall then do my share of the duty."

Leaving them to the performance of this task, Harrison went forward to the cottage of the pastor; while, headed by Grayson, the whole
party, Nichols not excepted, went down the bluff, and came by a circuitous route upon the seamen. One of them slept in the boat and was
secured without any difficulty. On opening his eyes, he found himself
closely grappled by a couple of sturdy woodsmen, and he did not even
venture to cry aloud, warned as he had been against such a measure,
by the judicious elevation of a tomahawk above his head. The other
fellow took to his heels on seeing the capture of his companion, but
stood no manner of chance with the fleet-footed foresters. He was
soon caught, and Constantine Maximilian Nichols was the most
adroit of the party in bandaging up the arms of both, *secundum artem.*
Ah! if the good doctor could have been content with one profession
only! but like too many craving creatures—who enjoy the appetite
without knowing how to feed—he aimed at popular favour. His
speeches were framed solely with that end, and he accordingly prated
for ever, as is the familiar custom always among the little cunning,
about those rights of man for which he cared but little. He was not

judicious in his declamation, however; he professed quite too largely; and, in addition to this misfortune, it grew into a faith among his neighbours, that, while his forms of speech were full of bloodshed and sacrifice, the heart of the doctor was benevolently indifferent to all the circumstances and the joys of strife. But the prisoners were now secured, and, under close guard, were marched off, agreeably to arrangement, to the cottage of the pastor.

Chapter Sixteen

"'Tis the rash hand that rights on the wild sea,
Or in the desert—violence is law,
And reason, where the civil arm is weak."

THE entrance of Harrison, alone, into the cottage of the pastor, put a stop to the dialogue which had been going on between himself and the seaman. The reception which the host gave the new comer, was simply and coldly courteous—that of his lady was more grateful, but still constrained; as for poor little Bess, she feared to look up at all, lest all eyes should see how much kinder her reception would have been. Harrison saw all this, but the behaviour of the pastor seemed to have no effect upon him. He rattled on in his usual manner, though with something of loftiness still, which appeared to intimate a character of condescension in his approaches.

"Mr. Matthews, it gives me pleasure to find you well—better, I think, than when I had the pleasure to see you last. You see, I tax your courtesies, though you could find no relatives of mine in Charleston willing to extend you theirs. But the time will come, sir, and your next visit may be more fruitful. Ah! Mrs. Matthews, growing young again, surely. Do you know I hold this climate to be the most delightful in the world,—a perfect seat of health and youth, in which the old Spaniard John Ponce, of Leon, would certainly have come nigher the blessed fountain he sought, than he ever could have done in Florida. And you, Bess—Miss Matthews, I mean—still sweet, charming as ever. Ah! Mrs. Matthews, you are thrice fortunate—always blessed. Your years are all so many summers—for Providence leaves to your household, in all seasons, one flower that compensates for all the rest."

And thus, half playful, half serious, Harrison severally addressed all in the apartment, the sailor excepted. That worthy looked on, and listened with no little astonishment.

"D——d easy to be sure," he half muttered to himself. Harrison, without distinguishing the words, heard the sounds, and readily comprehending their tenour from the look which accompanied them, he turned as playfully to the speaker as he had done to all the rest.

"And you, my handsome Hercules—you here too?—I left you in other company, when last we met, and am really not sorry that you got off without being made to feel the long arrow of the Yemassee. Pray, how came you so fortunate? Few men here would have killed the dog of an Indian, without looking for the loss of his scalp, and a broken head in requital. Give us your secret, Hercules?"

"Look ye, young master—I'm not angry, and not going to be angry, but my name, as I told you before, is not Hercules—"

"Not Hercules,—indeed!—then it must be Ajax—Ajax or Agamemnon. Well, you have your choice, for you look any of these great men so well, that by one or other of their names, I must call you. I could not well understand you by any other."

It seemed the policy of Harrison, so he appeared to think, to provoke the person he addressed into something like precipitance, suspecting him, as he did, of a secret and unfriendly object; and finding him a choleric and rash person, he aimed so to arouse his passion, as to disarm his caution and defeat his judgment; but, though Chorley exhibited indignation enough, yet, having his own object, and wishing at that moment to appear as amiable as possible, in the presence of those who knew him as a different character in childhood, he moderated his manner, if not his speech, to his situation and his desires. Still, his reply was fierce enough, and much of it muttered in an undertone, was heard only by the pastor and the person he addressed.

"Hark ye, sir, I don't know what ye may be, and don't much care; but blast my liver, if you don't mind your eyes, I'll take your ears off, and slit your tongue, or I'm no man. I won't suffer any man to speak to me in this manner."

"You won't—and you'll take my ears off and slit my tongue. Why, Hercules, you're decidedly dangerous. But I shall not tax your services so far."

"Shall do it, though, by thunder, whether you like it or not. You are not two to one now, youngster, and shan't swing to-day at my cost, as you did yesterday."

"Pshaw—don't put on your clouds and thunder now, old Jupiter—you look, for all the world, at this moment, like a pirate of the gulf, and must certainly frighten the ladies should they happen to look on you."

All these speeches were made *sotto voce*, in an *aside* which the ladies could not hear; though it was evident, from the manner of both, that they were uneasy. The pastor fidgeted. He was very much disturbed. When the last sentence of Harrison fell upon Chorley's ears, he started visibly, and the fierceness of his look was mingled with one of decided disquiet, while the close, dark, penetrating eye of Harrison was fixed sternly upon his own. Before he could recover in time for a reply in the same manner, Harrison went on, resuming all his playfulness of speech and look.

"Don't mean to offend, Hercules, far from it. But really, when I spoke, your face did wear a most flibustier sort of expression, such as Black Beard himself might put on while sacking a merchantman, and sending her crew along the plank."

"My name, young man, as I told you before," began the sailor, with a look and tone of forbearance and meekness that greatly awakened the sympathies of the pastor, to whom the playful persecution of Harrison had been any thing but grateful— "my name is—"

But his tormentor interrupted him—

"Is Jupiter Ammon, I know—give yourself no manner of trouble, I beg you."

"Master Harrison," said the pastor, gravely, "this is my guest, and so are you, and as such, permit me to say that mutual respect is due to my house and presence, if not to one another. The name of this gentleman is Chorley, Master Richard Chorley, whose parents I knew in England as well as himself."

"Ha! Chorley—you knew him in England—Master Chorley, your servant,—Hercules no longer. You will be pleased to forgive my merriment, which is scarce worth your cloud and thunderstorm. Chorley, did you say—Chorley—a good name—the name of a trader upon the Spanish Islands. Said I right?" inquired the speaker, who appeared to muse somewhat abstractedly over his recent accession of intelligence, while addressing the seaman. The latter sulkily assented.

"Your craft lies in the river, and you come for trade. You have goods, Master Chorley—fine stuffs for a lady's wear, and jewels—have you not jewels such as would not do discredit to a neck, white and soft—a glimpse, such as we sometimes have through these blessed skies, of a pure, glorious heaven smiling and wooing beyond them? Have you no such befitting gauds—no highly wrought gem and ornament—in the shape of cross and chain, which a sharp master of trade may have picked up, lying at watch snugly among the little Islands of the gulf?"

"And if I have?" sullenly responded the seaman.

"I will buy, Hercules—Master Chorley I should say—I would buy such a jewel—a rich chain, or the cross which the Spaniard worships. Wouldst thou wear such a chain of my giving, dear Bess—Miss Matthews, I mean? Thy neck needs no such ornament, I know, no more than the altar needs the jewel; yet the worshipper finds a pleasure when he can place it there. Tell me, Miss Matthews, will you wear such gift of my giving?"

Harrison was a person of the strangest frankness of manner. The soliciting sweetness of his glance, as this was spoken, seemed to relieve it of some of its audacity. He looked tenderly to her eyes as he spoke, and the seaman, watching their mutual glance, with a curiosity which became malignant, soon discovered their secret, if so it may be called. Before his daughter could speak, the old pastor sternly answered for her in the negative. His feelings had grown more and more uncompromising and resentful at every word of the previous dialogue. In his eyes, the cool composure of Harrison was the superb of audacity, particularly as, in the previous interview, he thought he had said and done enough to discourage the pretensions of any suitor, and one so utterly unknown to him as the present. Not that there was not much in all that he knew, of the person in question, to confound and distract his judgment. In their intercourse, and in all known intercourse, he had always proved brave, sensible, and generous. He had taken the lead among the volunteers, a short time previous, in defeating a superior Spanish force and driving them in disgrace from a meditated attack on Port Royal Island and Edisto. For this service he had received from the men he had then commanded, an application for the permanent continuance of his authority—an application neither declined nor accepted. They knew him, however, only as Gabriel Harrison, a man singularly compounded of daring bravery, cool reflection, and good-humoured vivacity, and knowing this, they cared for little more information. The farther mystery—knowing so much—was criminal in the eyes of the pastor, who had better reasons than the volunteers for desiring a greater share of the stranger's confidence; and though really, when he could calmly reflect on the subject, uninfluenced by his prejudices of Puritanism, pleased with the individual, a sense of what he considered his duty compelled him to frown upon pretensions so perfectly vague yet so confidently urged as those of his visitor. The course of the dialogue just narrated contributed still more to disapprove Harrison in the old man's estimation.

"My daughter wears no such idle vanities, Master Harrison," said he, "and least of all should she be expected to receive them from hands of which we know nothing."

"Oh, ho!" exclaimed Chorley aloud, now in his turn enjoying himself at the expense of his adversary— "Oh, ho—sits the wind in that quarter of your sail, young master?"

"Well, Hercules, what do you laugh at? I will buy your chain, though the lady may or may not take it."

"You buy no chain of me, I think," replied the other— "unless you buy this, which I would have placed myself, as a free gift, upon the neck of the young lady, before you came."

"You place it upon Bessy's neck, indeed! Why, Bully-boy, what put that extravagant notion into your head?" exclaimed Harrison scornfully, aloud.

"And why not, master; why not, I pray you?" inquired the seaman, at the same time not seeking to suppress his pique.

"Why not—indeed! But it needs not to say it! will you sell your chain?"

"Ay, that will I, but at a price something beyond your mark. What will you give now?"

"Put like a trader—Granger himself could not have said it with more grace. I will give—" at that moment a distinct blast of the horn, reverberating through the hall, announced to Harrison the success and approach of his party. Fixing his eye upon the person he addressed, and turning full upon him, he replied—

"I have the price at hand—a fitting price, and one that you seem already to have counted on. What say you then to my black fellow, Hector? He is a fine servant, and as you have already stowed him away safely in your hold, I suppose you will not hesitate to ask for him three hundred pieces in the Cuba market—something more, I fancy, than the value of your chain."

The seaman was confounded—taken all aback—as well as the pastor and his family, at this unlooked for charge.

"Where, Master Harrison, did you say?" inquired Matthews. "Where? your fellow Hector?"

"Ay, Hector, you know him well enough! why stowed away in the hold of this worthy fur and amber trader's vessel—safe, locked up, and ready for the Spaniard."

"It's a d——d lie," exclaimed the ferocious seaman, recovering from his momentary stupor.

"Bah, Hercules—see you fool written in my face, that you suppose oaths go further with me than words? You are young, my Hercules, very young, to think so,"—then, as the accused person proceeded to swear and swagger, Harrison turned to the ladies, who had been silent and astonished auditors— "Mrs. Matthews, and you, Bess, take to your chambers, please you, for a while. This business may be unpleasant, and not suited to your presence."

"But, Captain Harrison, my son," said the old lady, affectionately.

"Gabriel, dear Gabriel," murmured the young one.

"No violence, gentlemen,—for heaven's sake, gentlemen," said the host.

Harrison kissed his hands playfully to the mother and daughter, as, leading them to an inner door, he begged them to have no apprehension.

"There is no cause of fear—be not alarmed. Hercules and myself would only determine the value of Hector, without unnecessary witnesses. Go now, and fear nothing."

Having dismissed the ladies, Harrison turned immediately to Chorley, and putting his hand with the utmost deliberation upon his shoulder, thus addressed him—

"Hark ye, Hercules, you can't have Hector for nothing. The fellow's in prime order—not old, and still active—besides he's the most trustworthy slave I own, and loves me like a brother. It goes against me to part with him, but if you are determined to have him, you must give me an equivalent."

The seaman, with many oaths, denied having him. We forbear the brutal language which he used in his asseveration. But Harrison was cool and positive.

"Spare your breath, my brave fellow," said he contemptuously as coolly, "I know you have him. Your swearing makes none of your lies true, and you waste them on me. Give up Hector, then—"

"And what if I say no?" fiercely replied the seaman.

"Then I keep Hercules!" was the response of Harrison.

"We shall see that," exclaimed the kidnapper—and drawing his cutlass, he approached the door of the cottage, in the way of which Harrison stood calmly. As he approached, the latter drew forth a pistol from his bosom, coolly cocked and presented it with one hand, while with the other, raising his horn to his lips, he replied to the previous signal. In another moment the door was thrown open, and Granger, with two of the foresters, promptly appeared, well armed, and, by their presence, destroying any thought of an equal struggle, which might originally have entered the mind of Chorley. The three new comers ranged themselves around the apartment, so as to encircle the seaman.

"Captain Harrison," interposed the pastor, "this violence in my house—"

"I deeply regret, Mr. Matthews," was the reply, "but it is here necessary."

"It is taking the laws into your own hands, sir."

"I know it, sir, and will answer to the laws for taking Hector from the unlawful hands of this kidnapper. Stand aside, sir, if you please, while we secure our prisoner. Well, Hercules, are you ready for terms now?"

Nothing daunted, Chorley roared out a defiance, and with a fierce oath, lifting his cutlass, he resolutely endeavoured to advance. But the extension of his arm for the employment of his weapon, with his enemies so near, was of itself a disadvantage. The sword had scarcely obtained a partial elevation, when the iron fingers of Dick Grimstead fixed the uplifted arm as firmly as if the vice of the worthy blacksmith had taken the grasp instead of his muscles. In another moment Chorley was tumbled upon his back, and, spite of every effort at release, the huge frame of Grimstead maintained him in that humiliating position.

"You see, Hercules, obstinacy won't serve you here. I must have Hector, or I shall see the colour of every drop of blood in your body. I swear it, of God's surety. Listen, then, here are materials for writing. You are a commander—you shall forward despatches to your men for the delivery of my snow-ball. Hector I must have."

"I will write nothing—my men are in the boat; they will soon be upon you, and, by all the devils, I will mark you for this."

"Give up your hope, Bully-boy, and be less obdurate. I have taken care to secure your men and boat, as fast and comfortably as yourself. You shall see that I speak truth." Winding his horn as he spoke, the rest of the foresters appeared under the conduct of Nichols, who, strange to say, was now the most active conspirator, seemingly, of the party; they brought with them the two seamen well secured by cords. Ushering his prisoners forward, the worthy Constantine, seeing Harrison about to speak, hastily interrupted him—

"The great object of action, captain—the great object of human action—Mr. Matthews, I am your servant—the great object, Captain Harrison, of human action, as I have said before, is, or should be, the pursuit of human happiness. The great aim of human study is properly to determine upon the true nature of human action. Human reason being the only mode, in the exercise of which we can possibly arrive at the various courses which human action is to take, it follows, in direct sequence, that the Supreme Arbiter, in matters of moral, or I should rather say human propriety, is the universal reason—"

"Quod erat demonstrandum," gravely interrupted Harrison.

"Your approval is grateful, Captain Harrison—very grateful, sir— but I beg that you will not interrupt me."

Harrison bowed, and the doctor proceeded:—

"Referring to just principles, and the true standard, which,— Master Matthews, this may be of moment to you, and I beg your particular attention—I hold to be human reason,—for the government, the well-being of human society, I have determined—being thereto induced simply by a consideration of the good of the people—to lead them forth, for the captivity of these evil-minded men, who, without the fear of God in their eyes, and instigated by the devil, have feloniously kidnapped and entrapped and are about to carry away one of the lawful subjects of our king, whom God preserve. —I say subject, for though it does not appear that the black has ever been employed as a colour distinguishing the subjects of our master, the King of Great Britain, yet, as subject to his will, and the control of his subjects, are more than all, as speaking in the proper form of the English language, a little interpolated here and there, it may be, with a foreign coating or accent—which it may be well to recognise as legitimately forming a feature of the said language, which by all writers is held to be of a compound substance, not unlike, morally speaking, the sort of rock, which the geologists designate as pudding-stone—pudding being a

preparation oddly and heavily compounded—and to speak profes-
sionally, indigestibly compounded—I say, then, and I call you, our
pastor, and you, Captain Harrison, and you, Richard Grimstead—
albeit you are not of a craft or profession which I may venture to style
liberal—you too may be a witness,—and you will all of you here
assembled take upon you to witness for me, that, in leading forth these
brave men to the assault upon and captivity of these nefarious kidnappers, rescue or no rescue, at this moment my prisoners, that, from the
first immutable principles which I have laid down, I could have been
governed only by a patriotic desire for the good of the people. For, as it
is plain that the man who kidnaps a subject has clearly none of those
moral restraints which should keep him from kidnapping subjects,
and as it is equally clear that subjects should not be liable to kidnapping, so does it follow, as a direct sequence, that the duty of the good
citizen is to prevent such nefarious practices. I fear not now the inves-
tigation of the people, for, having been governed in what I have done,
simply by a regard for their good and safety, I yield me to their judgment, satisfied of justice, yet not shrinking, in their cause, from the
martyrdom which they sometimes inflict."

The speaker paused, breathless, and looked round very compla-
cently upon the assembly—the persons of which his speech had vari-
ously affected. Some laughed, knowing the man; but one or two
looked profound, and of these, at a future day, he had secured the suf-
frages. Harrison suffered nothing of risibility to appear upon his features, composing the muscles of which, he turned to the patriot,—

"Gravely and conclusively argued, doctor, and with propriety, for
the responsibility was a weighty one, of this bold measure, which your
regard for popular freedom has persuaded you to adopt. I did not
myself think that so much could be said in favour of the proceeding;
the benefits of which we shall now proceed to reap. And now,
Hercules," he continued, addressing the still prostrate seaman, "you
see the case is hopeless, and there is but one way of effecting your liberty. Write—here are the materials; command that Hector be restored,
without stroke or stripe, for of God's surety, every touch of the whip
upon the back of my slave shall call for a corresponding dozen upon
your own. Your seamen shall bear the despatch, and they shall return
with the negro. I shall place a watch, and if more than these leave the
vessel, it will be a signal which shall sound your death-warrant, for

that moment, of God's surety, shall you hang. Let him rise, Grimstead, but keep his sword, and tomahawk him if he stir."

Chorley saw that he was in a strait, and in hands no ways scrupulous. Satisfied that the case was hopeless on other terms, he wrote as he was required. Sullenly affixing the signature, he handed it fiercely to Harrison, who coolly read over its contents.

"So your name is really not Hercules, after all," he spoke with his usual careless manner— "but Chorley?"

"Is it enough?" sullenly asked the seaman.

"Ay, Bully-boy, if your men obey it. I shall only take the liberty of putting a small addition to the paper, apprising them of the prospect in reserve for yourself, if they steer awkwardly. A little hint to them," speaking as he wrote, "of new arms for their captain—swinging bough, rope pendant, —and so forth."

In an hour and the men returned, bringing along with them the subject of contention, the now half frantic Hector. Chorley was instantly released, with his two companions. He hurried away with scarce a word to the pastor. Swearing vengeance as he went, for the indignity he had undergone, and the disappointment, he prepared to leave the dwelling in the humour to do mischief. But unarmed as he was, and awed by the superior numbers of Harrison, he was compelled, perforce, to keep his wrath in reserve; resolving upon a double reckoning for the delay, whenever the opportunity should offer for revenge. Harrison goaded him with words of new annoyance as he went—

"Keep cool, Hercules; this attempt to kidnap our slaves will tell hardly against you when going round Port Royal Island. The battery there may make your passage uncomfortable."

"You shall suffer for this, young one, or my name's not—"

"Hercules! well, well—see that you keep a close reckoning, for I am not so sure that Richard Chorley is not as great a sea-shark as Steed Bonnett himself."

The seaman started fiercely, as the speaker thus compared him with one of the most notorious pirates of the time and region, but a sense of caution restrained from any more decided expression of his anger. With a single word to the pastor, and a sullen repetition of a general threat to the rest, he was soon in his boat and upon the way to his vessel.

Chapter Seventeen

"Have a keen eye awake—sleep not, but hold
A perilous watch to-night. There is an hour
Shall come, will try the stoutest of ye all."

I SAY it again, Captain Harrison—fortunate is it for mankind, fortu-nate and thrice happy—Mr. Matthews, you will be pleased to respond to the sentiment—thrice fortunate, I say, is it for mankind—Richard Grimstead, this idea is one highly important to your class, and you will give it every attention—thrice fortunate for mankind that there are some spirits in the world, some noble spirits, whom no fear, no danger, not even the dread of death, can discourage or deter in their labours for the good of the people. Who nobly array themselves against injustice, who lift up the banners of truth, and, filled to over-flowing with the love of their kindred, who yield up nothing of man's right to exaction and tyranny, but, shouting their defiance to the last, fear not to embrace the stake of martyrdom in the perpetuation of an immortal principle. Yes, captain—"

The audience began to scatter.

"What,—will you not hear?—Mr. Matthews, venerable sir,—Master Grayson, Master Walter Grayson, I say—and you, Richard Grimstead—will nobody hear?—thus it is,—the blind and insensible mass!—they take the safety and the service, but forget the benefactor. It is enough to make the patriot renounce his nature, and leave them to their fate."

"You had better go now, doctor, and see poor Murray, instead of standing here making speeches about nothing. Talk of the good of the people, indeed, and leave the sick man without physic till this time of day."

"You are right in that, Master Grayson, though scarcely respectful. It concerns the popular welfare, certainly, that men should not fall victims to disease; but you must understand, Master Grayson, that even to this broad and general principle, there are some obvious exceptions. One may and must, now and then, be sacrificed for the good of many—though to confess a truth, this can scarcely be an admitted principle, if such a sacrifice may tend in any way to affect the paramount question of the soul's immortal happiness or pain. I have strong doubts whether a man should be hung at all. For, if it happen that he be a bad man, to hang him is to precipitate him into that awful abiding place, to which each successive generation may be supposed to have contributed in liberal proportion; and if he should have seen the error of his ways, and repented, he ceases to be a bad man, and should not be hung at all. But, poor Murray, as you remind me, ought to be physicked—these cursed fevers hang on a man, as that sooty-lipped fellow Grimstead says, in a speech, uncouth as himself, like 'death to a dead negro.' The only God to be worshipped in this region, take my word for it, Master Grayson, is that heathen God, Mercury. He is the true friend of the people, and as such I worship him. Captain Harrison—the man is deaf. Ah, Mr. Matthews—deaf, too! Farewell, Master Grayson, or do you ride towards Gibbons'? He turns a deaf ear also. Human nature—human nature! I do hate to ride by myself."

And with these words, in obvious dissatisfaction—for Doctor Constantine Maximilian Nichols was no longer listened to—he left the house and moved off to the wood where his little tacky stood in waiting. By this time the foresters generally had also left the old pastor's cottage. Giving them instructions to meet him at the Block House, Harrison alone lingered behind with the old Puritan, to whom the preceding events had somehow or other been productive of much sore disquietude. He had shown his disapprobation at various stages of their occurrence; and even now, when the restoration of Hector, more than ever, showed the propriety, or policy at least, of the course which had been pursued, the old man seemed still to maintain a decided hostility to the steps which Harrison had taken for the recovery of his property. Having once determined against the individual himself, the pastor was one of those dogged and self-satisfied persons who can never bring themselves to the dismissal of a prejudice; who never permit themselves to approve of any thing done by the obnoxious person, and who studiously seek, in regard to him, every possible occasion for discontent and censure. In such a mood he addressed Harrison when the rest had departed:

"This violence, Master Harrison," said he, "might do in a condition of war and civil commotion; but while there are laws for the protection of the people and for the punishment of the aggressor, the resort to measures like that which I have this day witnessed, I hold to be highly indecorous and criminal."

"Mr. Matthews, you talk of laws, as if that pirate fellow could be brought to justice by a sheriff."

"And why should he not, Master Harrison?"

"My good sir, for the very best reason in the world, if you will but open your eyes, and take off some few of the scales which you seem to prefer to wear. Because, in that vessel, carrying guns, and men enough to serve them, he could safely bid defiance to all the sheriffs you could muster. Let the wind but serve, and he could be off, carrying *you* along with him if he thought proper, and at this moment nothing we could do could stop him. There is no defending Port Royal, and that is its misfortune. You must always call the force from Charleston which could do so, and at this time there is not a single armed vessel in that port. No, sir— nothing but manœuvring now for that fellow, and we must manage still more adroitly before we get our own terms out of him."

"Why, sir—where's the battery at Port Royal?"

"Pshaw, Mr. Matthews—a mere fly in the face of the wind. The battery at Port Royal, indeed, which the Spaniards have twice already taken at noonday, and which they would have tumbled into ruins, but for Captain Godfrey and myself, as you should remember—for your own chance of escape, and that of your family, was narrow enough. A good wind, sir, would carry this Flibustier beyond the fort before three guns could be brought to bear upon her."

"Well, Master Harrison, even if this be the case, I should rather the guilty should escape than that self-constituted judges should take into their own hands the administration of justice and the law."

"Indeed, Reverend Sir, but you are too merciful by half; and Hector, if he heard you now, would have few thanks for a charity, which would pack him off to the Cuba plantations for the benefit of that scoundrelly pirate. No, no. I shall always hold and recover my property by the strong arm, when other means are wanting."

"And pray, sir, what security have the people, that you, unknown to them as you are, may not employ the same arm to do them injustice, while proposing justice for yourself?"

"That is what Nichols would call the *popular* argument, and for which he would give you thanks, while using it against you. But, in truth, this is the coil, and amounts to neither more nor less than this, that all power is subject to abuse. I do not contend for the regular practice of that which I only employ in a last necessity. But, of this enough. I am in no mood for hair splitting and arguing about trifling irregularities, when the chance is that there are far more serious difficulties before us. There is a subject, Mr. Matthews, much more important to yourself. You are here, residing on the borders of a savage nation, with an interest scarcely worth your consideration, and certainly no engrossing object. Your purpose is the good of those around you, and with that object you suffer privations here, to which your family are not much accustomed. I have an interest in your welfare, and—"

The lips of the pastor curled contemptuously into a smile. Harrison proceeded:

"I understand that expression, sir, upon your face; and, contenting myself with referring you for a commentary upon it to the sacred profession of your pursuit, I freely forgive it." The pastor's cheek grew red, while the other continued;—

"You are here, sir, as I have said, upon the Indian borders. There is little real affinity between you. The entire white population thus situated, and stretching for thirty miles towards the coast in this direction, does not exceed nine hundred, men, women, and children. You live remotely from each other—there is but little concert between you, and, bating an occasional musket, or sword, the hatchet and the knife are the only weapons which your houses generally furnish. The Indians are fretful and becoming insolent"—

"Let me interrupt you, Master Harrison. I have no fears! This danger of Indian war is always the cry among those who have *popular* objects. So far as my experience goes, the Yemassees were never more peaceable than at this moment."

"Pardon me, sir, if I say you know little of the Indians, and are quite too guileless yourself to comprehend the least portion of their deceitful character. Are you aware, sir, of the insurrection which took place in Pocota-ligo last night?"

"Insurrection at Pocota-ligo?—what insurrection?"

"The chiefs were deposed by the people, and by this time are probably destroyed, for selling their lands yesterday to the commissioners."

"Ah! I could have said the why and the wherefore, without your speech. This but proves, Captain Harrison, that we may, if we please, provoke them by our persecutions into insurrections. Why do we thus seek to rob them of their lands? When, O Father of mercies, when shall there be but one flock of all classes and colours, all tribes and nations, of thy people, and thy blessed Son, our Saviour, the good and guiding shepherd thereof?"

"The prayer is a just one, and the blessing desirable; but, while I concur with your sentiment, I am not willing to agree with you that our desire to procure their land is at all inconsistent with the prayer. Until they shall adopt our pursuits, or we theirs, we can never form the one community for which your prayer is sent up; and so long as the hunting lands are abundant, the seductions of that mode of life will always baffle the approach of civilization among the Indians. But this is not the matter between us now. Your smile of contempt, just now, when I spoke of my regard for your family, does not discourage me from repeating the profession. I esteem your family, and a yet stronger sentiment attaches me to one of its members. Feeling thus towards you and it, and convinced, as I am, that there is danger at hand from the Indians, I entreat that you will remove at once into a close neighbourhood with our people. Go to Port Royal, where the means of escape to Charleston are easy;—or, why not go to Charleston itself?"

"And see your family," coolly sneered the pastor.

"It will be yours before long, and you will probably then know all the members thereof. I trust they will be such as neither of us will be ashamed of," was the quiet reply. "But let not your displeasure at my pretensions, or my lack of family, make you indifferent to the safety of your own. I tell you, sir, there is a near and great danger to be apprehended from the Indians."

"I apprehend none, Captain Harrison. The Indians have always borne themselves peaceably towards me and towards all the settlers— towards all who have carried them the words of peace. To me they have always shown kindness and a respect amounting almost to reverence. They have listened patiently to my teachings, and the eyes of some of them, under the blessed influence of the Saviour, have been opened to the light."

"Be not deceived, Mr. Matthews. The Indian upon whom you would most rely, would be the very first to strip your scalp as a choice trimming for his mocasin. Be advised, sir—I know more of this people than yourself. I know what they are when excited and aroused; deception with them is the legitimate morality of a true warrior. Nor will they, when once at war, discriminate between the good neighbour, like yourself, and the wild borderer who encroaches upon their hunting grounds and carries off their spoil."

"I fear not, sir—I know all the chiefs, and feel just as secure here, guarded by the watchful Providence, as I possibly could do in the crowded city, fenced in by mightiest walls."

"This confidence is rashness, sir, since it rejects a precaution which can do no harm, and offers but little inconvenience. Where is the necessity for your remaining here, where there is so little to attract, and so few ties to bind? Leave the spot, sir, at least until the storm is over-blown which I now see impending."

"You are prophetic, Master Harrison, but as I see no storm impending, you will suffer me to remain. You seem also to forget that, in remaining in this region, which you say has few ties for me and mine, I am complying with a solemn duty, undertaken in cool deliberation, and which I would not, if I could, avoid. I am here, as you know, the agent of a noble Christian charity of England, as a missionary to the heathen."

"Be it so; but there is nothing inconsistent with your duty in leaving the spot for a season. Here, in the event of a war, you could pursue no such mission. Leave it, if for a season only."

"Master Harrison, once for all, permit me to choose for myself, not only where to live, but who shall be my adviser and companion. I owe you thanks for your professed interest in me and mine; but it seems to me there is but little delicacy in thus giving us your presence, when my thoughts on the subject of my daughter and your claim have been so clearly expressed. The violence of your course to-day, sir, let me add, is enough to strengthen my previous determination on that subject."

"Your determination, Mr. Matthews, seems fixed, indeed, to be wrong-headed and obstinate. You have dwelt greatly upon my violence to this sea-bear; and yet, or I greatly mistake my man, you will come to wish it had been greater. But, ask your own good sense whether that violence exceeded in degree the amount necessary to secure the restoration of my slave? I did only what I thought essential to that end, though something provoked to more. But this aside. If you will not hear counsel, and determine to remain in this place, at least let me implore you to observe every precaution, and be ready to resort to the Block House with the first alarm. Be ready in your defence, and keep a careful watch. Let your nightbolts be well shot. I too, sir, will be something watchful for you. I cannot think of letting you sacrifice, by your ill-judged obstinacy, one, dear enough to me, at least, to make me bear with the discourtesies which come with such an ill grace from her sire."

Thus speaking, Harrison left the cottage abruptly, leaving the old gentleman standing,—angry enough still, but still somewhat dissatisfied with his own conduct,—in the middle of the floor.

Chapter Eighteen

"Thou kill'st me with a word when thou dost say
She loves him. Better thou hadst slain me first;
Thou hadst not half so wrong'd me then as now."

Hector met his master at the door of the cottage with tidings from the daughter which somewhat compensated for the harsh treatment of the father. She had consented to their meeting that afternoon in the old grove of oaks, well-known even to this day in that neighbourhood, for its depth and beauty of shadow, and its sweet fitness for all the purposes of love. Somewhat more satisfied, therefore, he took his way to the Block House, where the foresters awaited him.

They met in consultation, and the duties before Harrison were manifold. He told the party around him all that it was necessary they should know, in order to ensure proper precautions; and, having persuaded them of the necessity of this labour, he found no difficulty in procuring their aid in putting the Block House in better trim for the reception of the enemy. To do this, they went over the fabric together. The pickets forming an area or yard on two of its sides, having been made of the resinous pine of the country, were generally in good preservation. The gate securing the entrance was gone, however, and called for immediate attention. The door of the Block House itself—for it had but one—had also been taken away, and the necessity was equally great of its restoration. The lower story of the fortress consisted of but a single apartment, in which no repairs were needed. The upper story was divided into rooms, and reached by a ladder—a single ladder serving the several divisions, and transferable to each place of access when the ascent was desirable. One of these apartments, built more securely than the other, and pierced with a single small window, had been meant as the retreat of the women and children, and was now in the possession of Granger, the trader, and his wife. His small stock in trade, his furs, blankets, knives, beads, hatchets, etc., were strewn confusedly over the clapboard floor. These were the articles most wanted by the Indians. Firearms it had been the policy of the English to keep from them as much as possible. Still, the intercourse between them had been such that this policy was not always adhered to. Many of their principal persons had contrived to procure them, either from the English tradesmen themselves, or from the Spaniards of St. Augustine, with whom of late the Yemassees had grown exceedingly intimate; and though, from their infrequent use, not perfect masters of the weapon, they were still sufficiently familiar with it to increase the odds already in their favour on the score of numbers. Apart from this, the musket is but little, if any thing, superior to the bow and arrow in the American forests. It inspires with more terror, and is therefore more useful; but it is not a whit more fatal. Once discharged, the musket is of little avail. The Indian then rushes forward, and the bayonet becomes innocuous, for the striking and sure distance for the tomahawk in his hands is beyond the reach of its thrust. The tomahawk, with little practice, in any hand, can inflict a severe if not a fatal wound at twelve paces, and beyond the ordinary pistol certainty of that period. As long as his quiver lasts—containing twelve to twenty arrows—the bow in the close woods is superior to the musket in the grasp of the Indian, requiring only the little time necessary after the discharge of one, in fixing another arrow upon the elastic sinew. The musket too, in the hands of the Englishman, and according to his practice, is a sightless weapon. He fires in line, and without aim. The Anglo-American, therefore, has generally adopted the rifle. The eye of the Indian regulates every shaft from his bow with a rapidity given him by repeated and hourly practice from his childhood, and he learns to take the same aim at his enemy which he would take at the smallest bird among his forests. But to return.

Harrison, with Grimstead, the smith, Grayson, Granger, and the rest, looked carefully to all the defences of the fortress. He employed them generally in the repairs considered necessary, nor withheld his own efforts in restoring the broken timber or the maimed shutter. The tools of the carpenter were as familiar as the weapon of warfare, to the hand of the American woodsman, and the aid of the smith soon put things in train for a stout defence of the fabric, in the event of any necessity. This having been done, the whole party assembled in Granger's apartment to partake of the frugal meal which the hands of the trader's wife had prepared for them. We have seen the bold step taken by this woman in delivering up to the Yemassees the treaty which conveyed their lands to the Carolinians, by which, though she had risked the displeasure of Sir Edmund Bellinger, whom the point of honour would have rendered obstinate, she had certainly saved the lives of the party. She was a tall, masculine, and well-made woman; of a sanguine complexion, with deeply sunken, dark eyes, hair black as a coal and cut short like that of a man. There was a stern something in her glance which repelled; and though gentle and even humble in her usual speech, there were moments when her tone was that of reckless defiance, and when her manner was any thing but conciliatory. Her look was always grave, even sombre, and no one saw her smile. She thus preserved her own and commanded the respect of others, in a sphere of life to which respect, or in very moderate degree, is not often conceded; and though now she did not sit at the board upon which the humble meal had been placed, her presence restrained the idle remark which the wild life of most of those assembled around it, would be well apt to instigate and occasion. At dinner, Hector was examined as to his detention on board of the schooner. He told the story of his capture as already given, and, though the poor fellow had in reality heard nothing, cr very little, of the conversation between the sailor and the Indians, yet the clear narrative which he gave, descriptive of the free intercourse between the parties, and the presence of the belt of wampum, were proofs strong as holy writ;—conclusive, certainly, to the mind of Harrison, of the suspicion he already entertained.

"And what of the schooner—what did you see there, Hector?"

"Gun, maussa! big gun, little gun—long sword, little sword, and hatchets plenty for Injins."

"What sort of men?"

"Ebery sort, maussa; English, Dutch, French, Spanish,—ugly little men wid big whisker, and long black hair, and face nebber see water."

This was information enough; and, after some further deliberations, the parties separated, each in the performance of some duty which, by previous arrangement, had been assigned him. An hour after the separation, and Walter Grayson arrived at the landing upon the river, a few hundred yards from the cottage where he lived, in time to see his brother, who was just about to put off with several bundles of skins in a small boat towards the vessel of the supposed Indian trader. The manner of the latter was cold, and his tone rather stern and ungracious.

"I have waited for you some hours, Walter Grayson," said he, standing upon the banks, and throwing a bundle into the bottom of the boat.

"I could come no sooner, Hugh; I have been busy in assisting the captain."

"The captain—will you never be a freeman, Walter—will you always be a water-carrier for a master? Why do you seek and serve this swaggerer, as if you had lost every jot of manly independence?"

"Not so sharp, Hugh,—and, my very good younger brother—not so fast. I have not served him, more than I have served you and all of us, by what I have done this morning."

He then went on to tell his brother of the occurrences of the day. The other seemed much astonished, and there was something of chagrin manifest in his astonishment—so much so indeed, that Walter could not help asking him if he regretted that Harrison should get his slave again.

"No—not so, brother,—but the truth is, I was about to take my skins to this same trader for sale and barter, and my purpose is something staggered by your intelligence."

"Well, I don't know but it should stagger you; and I certainly shouldn't advise you to proceed on such a business;—for the man who comes to smuggle and kidnap will scarcely heed smaller matters of trade."

"I must go, however, and try him. I want every thing, even powder and lead."

"Well, that's a good want with you, Hugh, for if you had none, you'd be better willing to work at home."

"I will not go into the field,"—said the other, haughtily and impatiently. "It will do for you, to take the mule's labour, who are so willing to be at the beck and call of every swaggering upstart; but I will not. No! Let me rather go with the Indians, and take up with them, and dress in their skins, and disfigure myself with their savage paint; but I will neither dig nor hew when I can do otherwise."

"Ay, when you can do otherwise, Hugh Grayson—I am willing. But do not deceive yourself, young brother of mine. I know, if you do not, why the labours of the field, which I must go through with, are *your* dislike. I know why you will rather drive the woods, day after day, in the Indian fashion, along with Chiparee or Occonestoga and with no better company, for, now and then, a poor buck or doe, in preference to more regular employment and a more certain subsistence."

"And why is it then, Walter?—let me have the benefit of your knowledge."

"Ay, I know, and so do you, Hugh; and shame, I say, on the false pride which regards the toil of you own father, and the labours of your own brother, as degrading. Ay, you blush, and well you may, Hugh Grayson. It is the truth—a truth I have never spoken in your ears before, and should not have spoken now, but for the freedom and frequency with which you, my younger brother, and for whom I have toiled when he could not toil for himself, presume to speak of my conduct as slavish. Now, examine your own, and know that as I am independent, I am *not* slavish; you can tell for yourself whether you owe as little to me, as I to you and to all other persons. When you have answered this question, Hugh, you can find a better application than you have yet made of that same word 'slave.'"

The cheek of the hearer grew pale and crimson, alternately, at the reproach of the speaker, whose eye watched him with not a little of that sternness of glance, which heretofore had filled his own. At one moment the collected fury of his look seemed to threaten violence, but, as if consideration came opportunely, he turned aside, and after a few moments' pause, replied in a thick, broken tone of voice:—

"You have said well, my elder brother and my better. Your reproach is just—I am a dependant—a beggar—one who should acknowledge, if he has not craved for, charity. I say it—and I feel it, and the sooner I requite the obligation the better. I will go to this trader, and sell my skins if I can, kidnapper or pirate though he be. I will go to him, and beg him to buy, which I might not have done but for your speech. You have said harshly, Walter Grayson, very harshly, but truly, and—I thank you, I thank you, believe me—I thank you for the lesson."

As he moved away, the elder brother turned quick upon him, and with an ebullition of feeling which did not impair his manliness, he grappled his hand—

"Hugh, boy, I was harsh and foolish, but you drove me to it, I love you, brother—love you as if you were my own son, and do not repent me of any thing I have done for you; which, were it to be done over again, I should rejoice to do. But when you speak in such harsh language of men whom you know I love, you provoke me, particularly when I see and know that you do them injustice. Now, Captain Harrison, let me tell you—"

"I would not hear, Walter—nothing, I pray you, of that man!"

"And why not?—Ah, Hughey, put down this bad spirit—this impatient spirit, which will not let you sleep; for even in your sleep it speaks out, and I have heard it."

"Ha!" and the other started, and laid his hand on the arm of his brother— "thou hast heard what?"

"What I will not say—not even to you!—but enough, Hugh, to satisfy me, that your dislike to Harrison springs from an unbecoming feeling."

"Name it."

"Jealousy!—I have already hinted as much, and now I tell you that your love for Bess Matthews, and her love for him, are the cause of your hate to Harrison."

"You think she loves him?" was the broken and huskily uttered inquiry.

"I do, Hugh—honestly I believe it."

And as the elder brother replied, the other dashed down his hand, which, on putting the question, he had taken, and rushed off, with a feeling of desperation, in the direction of the boat. In a moment, seated centrally within it, he had left the banks; and a little flap oar was plied from hand to hand with a rapidity and vigour more than half derived from the violent boiling of the feverish blood within his veins. With a gaze of sad sympathy and of genuine feeling, Walter Grayson surveyed his progress for a while, then turned away to the cottage and to other occupations.

In a little while, the younger brother, with his small cargo, approached the vessel, and was instantly hailed by a gruff voice from within.

"Throw me a rope," was the cry of Grayson.

"For what—what the devil should make us throw you a rope? who are you—what do you want?" was the reply. The speaker, who was no other than our old acquaintance, Chorley, showed himself at the same moment, and looked out upon the visitor.

"You buy furs and skins, captain—I have both, and here is a bag of amber, fresh gathered, and the drops are large.* I want powder for them, and shot—and some knives and hatchets."

"You get none from me, blast me."

"What, wherefore are you here, if not for trade?" was the involuntary question of Grayson. The seaman, still desirous of preserving appearances as much as possible, found it necessary to control his mood, which the circumstances of the morning were not altogether calculated to soften greatly. He replied therefore evasively.

"Ay, to be sure I come for trade, but can't you wait till I haul up to the landing? I am afraid there's not water enough for me to do so now, for the stream shoals here, as I can tell by my soundings, too greatly for the risk; but to-morrow—come to-morrow, and I'll trade with you for such things as you want."

"And whether you haul to the landing or not, why not trade on board to-day? Let me bring my skins up; throw me a rope, and we shall soon trade. I want but few things, and they will require no long search; you can easily say if you have them."

But this was pressing the point too far upon Chorley's good-nature. The seaman swore indignantly at the pertinacity of his visitor, and pouring forth a broadside of oaths, bade him tack ship and trouble him no longer.

"Be off now, freshwater, and wait my time for trading. If you bother me before I'm ready, I'll send you more lead than you're able to pay for, and put it where you'll never look for it. Put about, in a jiffy, or you'll never catch stays again. Off, I say, or I'll send a shot through your figure-head that shall spoil your beauty for ever."

Grayson was naturally surprised at this treatment, and his fierce spirit felt very much like a leap at the throat of the ruffian captain. But prudence taught him forbearance, in act at least. He was not sparing

---

* Amber, in Carolina, was supposed to exist in such quantities, at an early period in its history, that among the laws and constitution made by the celebrated John Locke for the Province, we find one, regulating its distribution among the eight lords proprietors. At present we have no evidence of its fruitfulness in that quarter, and the probability is, that in the sanguine spirit of the time, the notion was entertained from the few specimens occasionally found and worn by the Indians.

of his words, which were as haughty and insolent as he could make them. But Chorley could beat him easily at such weapons, and the young man was soon content to give up the contest. Sternly and sadly, and with the utmost deliberation, paddling himself round with a disappointed heart, he made once more for the cottage landing.

Chapter Nineteen

"The hunters are upon thee—keep thy pace,
Nor falter, lest the arrow strike thy back,
And the foe trample on thy prostrate form."

IT was about noon of the same day, when the son of Sanutee, the outcast and exiled Occonestoga, escaping from his father's assault and
flying from the place of council as already narrated, appeared on the
banks of the river nearly opposite in the denser settlement of the
whites, and several miles below Pocota-ligo. But the avenger had followed hard upon his footsteps, and the fugitive had suffered terribly in
his flight. His whole appearance was that of the extremest wretched-
ness. His dress was torn by the thorns of many a thicket in which he
had been compelled to crawl for shelter. His skin was lacerated, and
the brakes and creeks through which he had been compelled to plough
and plunge, had left the tribute of their mud and mire on every inch of
his person. Nor had the trials of his mind been less. Previous drunkenness, the want of food, and extreme fatigue (for, circuitously doubling
from his pursuers, he had run nearly the whole night, scarcely able to
rest for a moment), contributed duly to the miserable figure which he
made. His eyes were swollen, his cheeks sunken, and there was a wobe-
gone feebleness and utter desolateness about his whole appearance. He
had been completely sobered by the hunt made after him; and the
instinct of life, for he knew nothing of the peculiar nature of the doom
in reserve for him, had effectually called all his faculties into exercise.

When hurried from the council-house by Sir Edmund Bellinger,
to save him from the anger of his father, he had taken the way, under a
filial and natural influence, to the lodge of Matiwan. And she cheered
and would have cherished him, could that have been done consistently
with her duty to her lord. What she could do, however, she did; and,

though deeply sorrowing over his prostituted manhood, she could not, at the same time, forget that he was her son. But in her cabin he was not permitted to linger long. Watchful for the return of Sanutee, Matiwan was soon apprised of the approach of the pursuers. The people, collected to avenge themselves upon the chiefs, were not likely to suffer the escape of one, who, like Occonestoga, had done so much to subject them, as they thought, to the dominion of the English. A party of them, accordingly, hearing of his flight, and readily conceiving its direction, took the same route; and, but for the mother's watchfulness, he had then shared the doom of the other chiefs. But she heard their coming and sent him on his way; not so soon, however, as to make his start in advance of them a matter of very great importance to his flight. They were close upon his heels, and when he cowered silently in the brake, they took their way directly beside him. When he lay stretched along, under the cover of the fallen tree, they stepped over his body, and when, seeking a beaten path in his tortuous course, he dared to look around him, the waving pine torches which they carried flamed before his eyes.—

"I will burn feathers, thou shalt have arrows, Opitchi-Manneyto. Be not wrath with the young chief of Yemassee. Make the eyes blind that hunt after him for blood. Thou shalt have arrows and feathers, Opitchi-Manneyto—a bright fire of arrows and feathers!"

Thus, as he lay beneath the branches of a fallen tree, around which his pursuers were winding, the young warrior uttered the common form of deprecation and prayer to the evil deity of his people, in the language of the nation. But he did not despair, though he prayed. Though now frequently drunk and extremely dissolute, Occonestoga had been a gallant and very skilful partisan even in the estimation of the Indians. He had been one of the most promising of all their youth, when first made a chief, after a great battle with the Savannahs, against whom he distinguished himself. This exceeding promise at the outset of his career, rendered the mortification of his subsequent fall more exquisitely painful to Sanutee, who was a proud and ambitious man. Nor was Occonestoga himself utterly insensible to his degradation. When sober, his humiliation and shame were scarcely less poignant than that of his father; but, unhappily, the seduction of strong drink he had never been able to withstand. He was easily persuaded, and as easily overcome. He had thus gone on for some time; and, seeking the fiery poison only, he was almost in daily communication with the lower classes of the white settlers, from whom alone liquor could be obtained. For this vile reward he had condescended to the performance of various services for these people—offices which were held to be degrading by his own; and so much had he been discredited among the latter, that but for his father's great influence, which necessarily restrained the popular feeling on the subject of the son's conduct, he had long since been thrust from any consideration or authority among them. Originally he had been highly popular. His courage had been greatly admired, and admirably consorted with the strength and beauty of his person. Even now, bloated and blasted as he was, there was something highly prepossessing in his general appearance. He was tall and graceful, broad and full across the breast, and straight as an arrow. But the soul was debased within him; and there were moments when he felt all his wretched humiliations—moments when he felt how much better it would be to strike the knife to his own heart, and lose the deadly and degrading consciousness which made him ashamed to meet the gaze of his people. Even now, as he emerges from the morass, having thrown off his pursuers, the criminal purpose besets him. You see it in his face, his eye—you see it in the swift, hurried clutch of the knife, and the glance upward and around him. But such thoughts and purposes usually linger for a moment only. Baffled then, they depart as suddenly as they come. Occonestoga threw off his desperate purpose, as he had thrown off his pursuers. Once more he went, pressing rapidly forward, while the hunters were baffled in rounding a dense brake through which he had dared to go. He was beyond them, but they were between him and the river; and his course was bent for the settlements of the whites—the only course in which he hoped for safety. Day came, and he thought himself safe; but he was roused by the hunting cries of new pursuers. He almost despairs. His flight had taken him completely out of his contemplated route. To recover and regain it is now his object. Boldly striking across the path of his hunters, Occonestoga darted along the bed of a branch which ran parallel with the course he aimed to take. He lay still as the enemy approached—he heard their retreating footsteps, and again he set forward. But the ear and sense of the Indian are as keen as his own arrow, and the pursuers were not long misled. They retrieved their error, and turned with the fugitive; but the instinct of preservation was still active, and momentary success gave him a new stimulant to exertion. At length, when almost despairing and exhausted, his eyes beheld, and his feet gained, the bank of the river, still ahead of his enemy; and grateful, but exhausted, he lay for a few moments stretched upon the sands, and gazing upon the quiet waters before him.

He was not long suffered to remain in peace. A shout arrested his attention, and he started to his feet to behold two of his pursuers emerging at a little distance from the forest. This spectacle completed his misery. Exhaustion had utterly subdued his soul. He felt, once more, that death would be far preferable to the degraded and outcast life which he led—doomed and pursued for ever by his own people— and rising to his feet, in the moment of his despair, he threw open the folds of his hunting shirt, and placing his hand upon his breast, cried out to them to shoot. But the bow was unlifted, the arrow undrawn, and to his surprise the men who had pursued him as he thought for his blood, now refused what they had desired. They increased their efforts to take, but not to destroy him. The circumstance surprised him; and with a renewal of his thought came a renewed disposition to escape. Without further word, and with the instantaneous action of his reason, he plunged forward into the river, and diving down like an otter, reserved his breath until, arising, he lay in the very centre of the stream. But he arose enfeebled and overcome—the feeling of despair grew with his weakness, and turning a look of defiance upon the two Indians who still stood in doubt, watching his progress from the banks which they had now gained, he raised himself breast high from the water, and once more challenged their arrows to his breast, by smiting it with a fierce violence, the action of equal defiance and despair. As they saw the action, one of them, as if in compliance with the demand, lifted his bow; but the other the next instant struck it down. Half amazed and wondering at what he saw, and now almost overcome by his effort, the sinking Occonestoga gave a single shout of derision, and ceased all further effort. The waters bore him down. Once, and once only, his hand was struck out as if in the act of swimming, while his head was buried; and then the river closed over him. The brave but desponding warrior sunk hopelessly, just as the little skiff of Hugh Grayson, returning from his interview with Chorley, which we have already narrated, darted over the small circle in the stream which still bubbled and broke where the young Indian had gone down. The whole scene had been witnessed by him, and he had urged every sinew in the effort to reach the youth in season. His voice, as he called aloud to Occonestoga, whom he well knew, had been unheard by the drowning and despairing man. But still he came in time, for, as his little boat darted over the spot where the red-man had been seen to sink, the long black hair suddenly grew visible again above the water, and in the next moment was firmly clutched in the grasp of the Carolinian. With difficulty he sustained the head above the surface, still holding on by the hair. The banks were not distant, and the little paddle which he employed was susceptible of use by one hand. Though thus encumbered, he was soon enabled to get within his depth. This done, he jumped from the boat, and by very great effort bore the unconscious victim to the land. A shout from the Indians on the opposite bank, attested their own interest in the result; but they did not wait for the result, disappearing in the forest just at the moment when returning consciousness, on the part of Occonestoga, had rewarded Grayson for the efforts he had made and still continued making for his recovery.

"Thou art safe now, Occonestoga," said the young man; "but thou hast swallowed more water of the river than well befits an empty stomach. How dost thou feel?"

"Feathers and arrows for thee, Opitchi-Manneyto," muttered the savage, in his own language, his mind recurring to the previous pursuit. The youth continued his services without pressing him for answers, and his exhaustion had been so great that he could do little if any thing for himself. Unlashing his bow and quiver, which had been tied securely to his back, and unloosing the belt about his body, Grayson still further contributed to his relief. At length he grew conscious, and sufficiently restored to converse freely with his preserver; and though still gloomy and depressed, returned him thanks, in his own way, for the timely succour which had saved him.

"Thou wilt go with me to my cabin, Occonestoga?"

"No! Occonestoga is a dog. The black woods for Occonestoga. He must seek arrows and feathers for Opitchi-Manneyto who came to him in the swamp."

The youth pressed him urgently and kindly; but finding him obdurate, and knowing well the inflexible character of the Indian, he gave up the hope of persuading him to his habitation. They separated at length after the delay of an hour,—Grayson again in his canoe, and Occonestoga plunging into the woods in the direction of the Block House.

Chapter Twenty

"Thus nature, with an attribute most strange,
Clothes even the reptile, working in our thoughts,
Until they weave themselves into a spell,
That wins us to it."

THE afternoon of that day was one of those clear, sweet, balmy after-
noons, such as make of the spring season in the south, a holiday
term of nature. All was animated life and freshness. The month of
April, in that region, is, indeed,

> ——————"the time,
> When the merry birds do chime
> Airy wood-notes wild and free,
> in secluded bower and tree,
> Season of fantastic change,
> Sweet, familiar, wild, and strange—
> Time of promise, when the leaf
> Has a tear of pleasant grief,—
> When the winds, by nature coy,
> Do both cold and heat alloy,
> Nor to either will dispense
> Their delighting preference."

The day had been gratefully warm; and, promising an early summer, there was a prolific show of foliage throughout the forest. The
twittering of a thousand various birds, and the occasional warble of
that Puck of the American forests, the mocker—the Coonelatee, or
Trick-tongue of the Yemassees—together with the gleesome murmur of
zephyr and brook, gave to the scene an aspect of wooing and seductive
repose, that could not fail to win the sense into a most happy uncon-

sciousness. The old oaken grove which Bess Matthews, in compliance
with the prayer of her lover, now approached, was delightfully conceived for such an occasion. All things within it seemed to breathe of
love. The murmur of the brooklet, the song of the bird, the hum of the
zephyr in the tree-top, had each a corresponding burden. The
Providence surely has its purpose in associating only with the woods
those gentle and beautiful influences which are without use or object to
the obtuse sense, and can only be felt and valued by a spirit of corresponding gentleness and beauty. The scene itself, to the eye, was of
character to correspond harmoniously with the song of birds and the
playful sport of zephyrs. The rich green of the leaves—the deep crimson of the wild flower—the gemmed and floral-knotted long grass that
carpeted the path—the deep, solemn shadows of evening, and the trees
through which the now declining sun was enabled only here and there
to sprinkle a few drops from his golden censer—all gave power to that
spell of quiet, which, by divesting the mind of its associations of every-
day and busy life, throws it back upon its early and unsophisticated
nature—restoring that time, in the elder and better condition of
humanity, when, unchanged by conventional influences, the whole
business of life seems to have been the worship of high spirits, and the
exercise of living, holy, and generous affections.

The scene and time had a strong influence over the maiden, as she
slowly took her way to the place where she was to meet her lover. Bess
Matthews, indeed, was singularly susceptible of such influences. She
was a girl of heart, but a wild heart,—a thing of the forest,—gentle as
its innocentest flowers, quite as lovely, and if, unlike them, the creature
of a less fleeting life, one, at least, whose youth and freshness might
almost persuade us to regard her as never having been in existence for
a longer season. She was also a girl of thought and intellect—something, too, of a dreamer:—one to whom a song brought a sentiment—
the sentiment an emotion, and that in turn sought for an altar on
which to lay all the worship of her spirit. She had in her own heart a
far sweeter song than that which she occasionally murmured from her
lips. She felt all the poetry, all the truth of the scene—its passion, its
inspiration; and, with a holy sympathy for all of nature's beautiful, the
associated feeling of admiration for all that was noble, also, awakened
in her mind a sentiment, and in her heart an emotion, that led her, not
less to the most careful forbearance to tread upon the humblest flower,
than to a feeling little short of reverence in the contemplation of the

gigantic tree. It was her faith, with one of the greatest of modern poets, that the daisy enjoyed its existence; and that, too, in a degree of exquisite perception, duly according with its loveliness of look and delicacy of structure. This innate principle of regard for the beautiful forest idiots, as we may call its leaves and flowers, was duly heightened, we may add, by the soft passion of love then prevailing in her bosom for Gabriel Harrison. She loved him, as she found in him the strength of the tree well combined with the softness of the flower. Her heart and fancy at once united in the recognition of his claims upon her affections; and, however unknown in other respects, she loved him deeply and devotedly for what she knew. Beyond what she saw— beyond the knowledge gathered from his uttered sentiments, and the free grace of his manner—his manliness, and playful frankness—he was scarcely less a mystery to her than to her father, to whom mystery had far less of recommendation. But the secret—and he freely admitted that there was a secret—he promised her should soon be revealed; and it was pleasant to her to confide in the assurance. She certainly longed for the time to come; and we shall be doing no discredit to her sense of maidenly delicacy when we say, that she wished for the development not so much because she desired the satisfaction of her curiosity, as because the objections of her sire, so Harrison had assured her, would then certainly be removed, and their union would immediately follow.

"He is not come," she murmured, half disappointed, as the old grove of oaks with all its religious solemnity of shadow lay before her. She took her seat at the foot of a tree, the growth of a century, whose thick and knotted roots, started from their sheltering earth, shot even above the long grass around them, and ran in irregular sweeps for a considerable distance upon the surface. Here she sat not long, for her mind grew impatient and confused with the various thoughts crowding upon it—sweet thoughts it may be, for she thought of him whom she loved,—of him almost only; and of the long hours of happy enjoyment which the future had in store. Then came the fears, following fast upon the hopes, as the shadows follow the sunlight. The doubts of existence—the brevity and the fluctuations of life; these are the contemplations even of happy love, and these beset and saddened her; till, starting up in that dreamy confusion which the scene not less than the subject of her musings had inspired, she glided among the old trees, scarce conscious of her movement.

"He does not come—he does not come," she murmured, as she stood contemplating the thick copse spreading before her, and forming the barrier which terminated the beautiful range of oaks which constituted the grove. How beautiful was the green and garniture of that little copse of wood. The leaves were thick, and the grass around lay folded over and over in bunches, with here and there a wild flower, gleaming from its green, and making of it a beautiful carpet of the richest and most various texture. A small tree rose from the centre of a clump around which a wild grape gadded luxuriantly; and, with an incoherent sense of what she saw, she lingered before the little cluster, seeming to survey that which, though it seemed to fix her eye, yet failed to fill her thought. Her mind wandered—her soul was far away; and the objects in her vision were far other than those which occupied her imagination. Things grew indistinct beneath her eye. The eye rather slept than saw. The musing spirit had given holiday to the ordinary senses, and took no heed of the forms that rose, and floated, or glided away, before them. In this way, the leaf detached made no impression upon the sight that was yet bent upon it; she saw not the bird, though it whirled, untroubled by a fear, in wanton circles around her head—and the black-snake, with the rapidity of an arrow, darted over her path without arousing a single terror in the form that otherwise would have shivered at its mere appearance. And yet, though thus indistinct were all things around her to the musing mind of the maiden, her eye was yet singularly fixed—fastened, as it were, to a single spot— gathered and controlled by a single object, and glazed, apparently, beneath a curious fascination. Before the maiden rose a little clump of bushes,—bright tangled leaves flaunting wide in glossiest green, with vines trailing over them, thickly decked with blue and crimson flowers. Her eye communed vacantly with these; fastened by a star-like shining glance—a subtle ray, that shot out from the circle of green leaves—seeming to be their very eye—and sending out a fluid lustre that seemed to stream across the space between, and find its way into her own eyes. Very piercing and beautiful was that subtle brightness, of the sweetest, strangest power. And now the leaves quivered and seemed to float away, only to return, and the vines waved and swung around in fantastic mazes, unfolding ever-changing varieties of form and colour to her gaze; but the star-like eye was ever steadfast, bright and gorgeous gleaming in their midst, and still fastened, with strange fondness, upon her own. How beautiful, with wondrous intensity, did

it gleam, and dilate, growing large and more lustrous with every ray
which it sent forth. And her own glance became intense, fixed also;
but with a dreaming sense that conjured up the wildest fancies, terribly beautiful, that took her soul away from her, and wrapt it about as
with a spell. She would have fled, she would have flown; but she had
not the power to move. The will was wanting to her flight. She felt that
she could have bent forward to pluck the gem-like thing from the
bosom of the leaf in which it seemed to grow, and which it irradiated
with its bright white gleam; but ever as she aimed to stretch forth her
hand, and bend forward, she heard a rush of wings, and a shrill
scream from the tree above her—such a scream as the mock-bird
makes, when, angrily, it raises its dusky crest, and flaps its wings furiously against its slender sides. Such a scream seemed like a warning,
and though yet unawakened to full consciousness, it startled her and
forbade her effort. More than once, in her survey of this strange
object, had she heard that shrill note, and still had it carried to her ear
the same note of warning, and to her mind the same vague consciousness of an evil presence. But the star-like eye was yet upon her own—a
small, bright eye, quick like that of a bird, now steady in its place and
observant seemingly only of hers, now darting forward with all the
clustering leaves about it, and shooting up towards her, as if wooing
her to seize. At another moment, riveted to the vine which lay around
it, it would whirl round and round, dazzlingly bright and beautiful,
even as a torch, waving hurriedly by night in the hands of some playful boy;—but, in all this time, the glance was never taken from her
own—there it grew, fixed—a very principle of light,—and such a
light—a subtle, burning, piercing, fascinating gleam, such as gathers
in vapour above the old grave, and binds us as we look—shooting,
darting directly into her eye, dazzling her gaze, defeating its sense of
discrimination, and confusing strangely that of perception. She felt
dizzy, for, as she looked, a cloud of colours, bright, gay, various
colours, floated and hung like so much drapery around the single
object that had so secured her attention and spell-bound her feet. Her
limbs felt momently more and more insecure—her blood grew cold,
and she seemed to feel the gradual freeze of vein by vein, throughout
her person. At that moment a rustling was heard in the branches of
the tree beside her, and the bird, which had repeatedly uttered a single
cry above her, as it were of warning, flew away from his station with a
scream more piercing than ever. This movement had the effect, for

which it really seemed intended, of bringing back to her a portion of
the consciousness she seemed so totally to have been deprived of
before. She strove to move from before the beautiful but terrible presence, but for a while she strove in vain. The rich, star-like glance still
riveted her own, and the subtle fascination kept her bound. The mental
energies, however, with the moment of their greatest trial, now gathered suddenly to her aid; and, with a desperate effort, but with a feeling
still of most annoying uncertainty and dread, she succeeded partially in
the attempt, and threw her arms backwards, her hands grasping the
neighbouring tree, feeble, tottering, and depending upon it for that
support which her own limbs almost entirely denied her. With her
movement, however, came the full development of the powerful spell
and dreadful mystery before her. As her feet receded, though but a single
pace, to the tree against which she now rested, the audibly articulated
ring, like that of a watch when wound up with the verge broken,
announced the nature of that splendid yet dangerous presence, in the
form of the monstrous rattlesnake, now but a few feet before her, lying
coiled at the bottom of a beautiful shrub, with which, to her dreaming
eye, many of its own glorious hues had become associated. She was, at
length, conscious enough to perceive and to feel all her danger; but terror had denied her the strength necessary to fly from her dreadful
enemy. There still the eye glared beautifully bright and piercing upon
her own; and, seemingly in a spirit of sport, the insidious reptile slowly
unwound himself from his coil, but only to gather himself up again
into his muscular rings, his great flat head rising in the midst, and
slowly nodding, as it were, towards her, the eye still peering deeply into
her own;—the rattle still slightly ringing at intervals, and giving forth
that paralyzing sound, which, once heard, is remembered for ever. The
reptile all this while appeared to be conscious of, and to sport with,
while seeking to excite her terrors. Now, with its flat head, distended
mouth, and curving neck, would it dart forward its long form towards
her,—its fatal teeth, unfolding on either side of its upper jaws, seeming
to threaten her with instantaneous death, while its powerful eye shot
forth glances of that fatal power of fascination, malignantly bright,
which, by paralyzing, with a novel form of terror and of beauty, may
readily account for the spell it possesses of binding the feet of the timid,
and denying to fear even the privilege of flight. Could she have fled!
She felt the necessity; but the power of her limbs was gone! and there
still it lay, coiling and uncoiling, its arching neck glittering like a ring of

brazed copper, bright and lurid; and the dreadful beauty of its eye still fastened, eagerly contemplating the victim, while the pendulous rattle still rang the death note, as if to prepare the conscious mind for the fate which is momently approaching to the blow. Meanwhile the stillness became death-like with all surrounding objects. The bird had gone with its scream and rush. The breeze was silent. The vines ceased to wave. The leaves faintly quivered on their stems. The serpent once more lay still; but the eye was never once turned away from the victim. Its corded muscles are all in coil. They have but to unclasp suddenly, and the dreadful folds will be upon her, its full length, and the fatal teeth will strike, and the deadly venom which they secrete will mingle with the life blood in her veins.

The terrified damsel, her full consciousness restored, but not her strength, feels all the danger. She sees that the sport of the terrible reptile is at an end. She cannot now mistake the horrid expression of its eye. She strives to scream, but the voice dies away, a feeble gurgling in her throat. Her tongue is paralyzed; her lips are sealed—once more she strives for flight, but her limbs refuse their office. She has nothing left of life but its fearful consciousness. It is in her despair, that, a last effort, she succeeds to scream, a single wild cry, forced from her by the accumulated agony; she sinks down upon the grass before her enemy—her eyes, however, still open, and still looking upon those which he directs for ever upon them. She sees him approach—now advancing, now receding—now swelling in every part with something of anger, while his neck is arched beautifully like that of a wild horse under the curb; until, at length, tired as it were of play, like the cat with its victim, she sees the neck growing larger and becoming completely bronzed as about to strike—the huge jaws unclosing almost directly above her, the long tubulated fang, charged with venom, protruding from the cavernous mouth—and she sees no more! Insensibility came to her aid, and she lay almost lifeless under the very folds of the monster.

In that moment the copse parted—and an arrow, piercing the monster through and through the neck, bore his head forward to the ground, alongside of the maiden, while his spiral extremities, now unfolding in his own agony, were actually, in part, writhing upon her person. The arrow came from the fugitive Occonestoga, who had fortunately reached the spot, in season, on his way to the Block House. He rushed from the copse, as the snake fell, and, with a stick, fearlessly approached him where he lay tossing in agony upon the grass. Seeing him advance, the courageous reptile made an effort to regain his coil, shaking the fearful rattle violently at every evolution which he took for that purpose; but the arrow, completely passing through his neck, opposed an unyielding obstacle to the endeavour; and finding it hopeless, and seeing the new enemy about to assault him, with something of the spirit of the white man under like circumstances, he turned desperately round, and striking his charged fangs, so that they were riveted in the wound they made, into a susceptible part of his own body, he threw himself over with a single convulsion, and, a moment after, lay dead beside the utterly unconscious maiden.*

* The power of the rattlesnake to fascinate, is a frequent faith among the superstitious of the southern country-people. Of this capacity in reference to birds and insects, frogs, and the smaller reptiles, there is indeed little question. Its power over persons is not so well authenticated, although numberless instances of this sort are given by persons of very excellent veracity. The above is almost literally worded after a verbal narrative furnished the author by an old lady, who never dreamed, herself, of doubting the narration. It is more than probable, indeed, that the mind of a timid person, coming suddenly upon a reptile so highly venomous, would for a time be paralyzed by its consciousness of danger, sufficiently so to defeat exertion for a while, and deny escape. The authorities for this superstition are, however, quite sufficient for the romancer, and in a work like the present we need no other.

Chapter Twenty-one

"Come with me; thou shalt hear of my resolve."

WITHOUT giving more than a single glance to the maiden, Occonestoga approached the snake, and, drawing his knife, prepared to cut away the rattles, always a favourite Indian ornament, which terminated his elongated folds. He approached his victim with a deportment the most respectful, and, after the manner of his people, gravely, and in the utmost good faith, apologized in well set terms, in his own language, for the liberty he had already taken, and that which he was then about to take. He protested the necessity he had been under in destroying it; and, urging his desire to possess the excellent and only evidence of his own prowess in conquering so great a warrior, which the latter carried at his tail, he proceeded to cut away the rattles with as much tenderness as could have been shown by the most considerate operator, divesting a fellow-creature, still living, of his limbs. A proceeding like this, so amusing as it would seem to us, is readily accounted for, when we consider the prevailing sentiment among the Indians in reference to the rattlesnake. With them he is held the gentleman, the nobleman—the very prince of snakes. His attributes are devoutly esteemed among them, and many of their own habits derive their existence from models furnished by his peculiarities. He is brave, will never fly from an enemy, and for this they honour him. If approached, he holds his ground and is never unwilling for the combat. He does not begin the affray, and is content to defend himself against invasion. He will not strike without due warning of his intention, and when he strikes, the blow of his weapon is fatal. It is highly probable, indeed, that, even the war-whoop with which the

Indians preface their own onset, has been borrowed from the warning rattle of this fatal, but honourable enemy.*

Many minutes had not elapsed before the operation was completed, and the Indian became the possessor of the desired trophy. The snake had thirteen rattles, and a button, or incipient rattle; it was therefore fourteen years old—as it acquires the button during its first year, and each succeeding year yields it a new rattle. As Occonestoga drew the body of the serpent from that of Bess Matthews, her eyes unclosed, though but for an instant. The first object in her gaze was the swollen and distorted reptile, which the Indian was just then removing from her sight. Her terror was aroused anew, and with a single shriek she again closed her eyes in utter unconsciousness. At that moment, Harrison darted down the path. That single shriek had given wings to his movement, and rushing forward, and beholding her lifted in the arms of Occonestoga, who, at her cry, had come to her support, and had raised her partially from the ground—he sprang fiercely upon him, tore her from his hold, and sustaining her with one hand, wielded his hatchet fiercely in the other above his own head, while directing its edge upon that of the Indian. Occonestoga looked up indifferently, almost scornfully, and without exhibiting any wish to escape the blow. This appearance of indifference or recklessness arrested the arm of Harrison, and caused him to doubt and hesitate.

"Speak, young chief! speak, Occonestoga;—say what does this mean? What have you done to the maiden? Quickly speak, or I strike."

"Strike, Harrison!—the hatchet is good for Occonestoga. He has a death-song that is good. He can die like a man."

"What hast thou done with the maiden—tell me, Occonestoga, ere I hew thee down like a dog."

"Occonestoga is a dog. Sanutee, the father of Occonestoga, says he is a dog of the English. There is no fork in the tongue of Sanutee.

---

* This respect of the Indians for the rattlesnake, leading most usually to much forbearance when they encountered him, necessarily resulted in the greater longevity of this snake than of any other. In some cases, they have been found so overgrown from this forbearance, as to be capable of swallowing entire a young fawn. An instance of this description has been related by the early settlers of South Carolina, and, well authenticated, is to be found on record. The movements of the rattlesnake are usually very slow, and the circumstance of his taking prey so agile as the fawn, would be something in favour of an extensive fascinating faculty. That he takes birds with some such influence there is no sort of question.

Look! The war-rattle put his eye on the girl of the pale-face, and she cried out, for his eye was upon her to kill! Look, Harrison, it is the arrow of Occonestoga," and as he spoke he pointed to the shaft which still stuck in the neck of the serpent. Harrison, who before had not seen the snake, which the Indian had thrown aside under the neighbouring bush, now shivered as with a convulsion, while, almost afraid to speak, and his face paling like death as he did so, he cried to him in horror:—

"God of Heaven—tell me, Occonestoga—say—is she struck—is she struck?" and before he could hear the reply his tremors were so great that he was compelled to lay the still insensible form of the maiden, unequal then to her support, upon the grass beneath the tree.

The Indian smiled, with something of scornful satisfaction, as he replied—

"It was the swift arrow of Occonestoga—and the war-rattle had no bite for the girl of the pale-faces. The blood is good in her heart."

"Thank God—thank God! Young chief of the Yemassee, I thank thee—I thank thee, Occonestoga—thou shalt have a rich gift—a noble reward for this;" and, seizing the hand of the youth wildly, he pressed it with a tenacious gripe that well attested the sincerity of his feelings. But the gloom of the recreant savage was too deeply driven into his spirit by his recent treatment and fugitive privations, to experience much pleasure, either from the proffered friendship or the promised reward of the English. He had some feeling of nationality left, which a return to sobriety always made active.

"Occonestoga is a dog," said he; "death for Occonestoga!"

For a moment Harrison searched him narrowly with his eye; but as he saw in his look nothing but the one expression with which an Indian in the moment of excitement conceals all others, of sullen indifference to all things around him, he forebore further remark, and simply demanded assistance in the recovery of the maiden. Water was brought, and after a few moments her lover had the satisfaction of noting her returning consciousness. The colour came back to her cheeks, her eyes opened upon the light, her lips murmured in prayer,—a prayer for protection, as if she still felt the dangers present and threatening still, from which she had escaped so happily. But the glance of her lover reassured her.

"Oh, Gabriel, such a dream—such a horrible dream," and she shuddered and looked anxiously around her.

"Ay, dearest, such as I trust you will never again suffer. But fear not. You are now safe and entirely unhurt. Thanks to our brave friend Occonestoga here, whose arrow has been your safety."

"Thanks, thanks to thee, young chief—I know thee; I shall remember," and she looked gratefully to the Indian, whose head simply nodded a recognition of her acknowledgment.

"But where, Gabriel, is the monster? Oh! how its eye dazzled and ensnared me. I felt as if my feet were tied, and my knees had lost all their strength."

"There he lies, Bess, and a horrible monster he is, indeed. See there, his rattles, thirteen and a button—an old snake, whose blow must have been instant death!"

The maiden shuddered as she looked upon the reptile to whose venom she had so nearly fallen a victim. It was now swollen to a prodigious size from the natural effects of its own poison. In places about its body, which the fatal secretion had most easily affected, it had bulged out into putrid lumps, almost to bursting; while, from one end to the other of its attenuated length, the linked diamonds which form the ornament of its back, had, from the original dusky brown and sometimes bronze of their colour, now assumed a complexion of spotted green—livid and diseased. Its eyes, however, though glazed, had not yet lost all of that original and awful brightness, which, when looking forth in anger, nothing can surpass for terrific beauty of expression. The powers of this glance none may well express, and few imagine; and when we take into consideration the feeling of terror with which the timid mind is apt to contemplate an object known to be so fatal, it will not be difficult to account for its possession of the charm commonly ascribed to this reptile in the southern country, by which, it is the vulgar faith, he can compel the bird from the highest tree to leave his perch, shrieking with fear and full of the most dreadful consciousness, struggling with all the power of its wings, and at last, after every effort has proved fruitless, under the influence of that unswerving glance, to descend even into the jaws which lie waiting to receive it. Providence in this way has seemingly found it necessary to clothe even with a moral power the evanescent and merely animal nature of its creation; and, with a due wisdom, for, as the rattlesnake is singularly slow in its general movements, it might suffer frequently from want of food unless some such power had been assigned it. The study of all nature with a little more exactitude, would perhaps discover to us an enlarged instinct in every other form of life, which a narrow analysis might almost set down as the fullest evidence of an intellectual existence.

The interview between Harrison and Bess Matthews had been especially arranged with reference to a discussion of various matters, important to both, and affecting the relations which existed between them. But it was impossible, in the prostrate and nervous condition in which he found her, that much could be thought or said of other matters than those which had been of the last few moments' occurrence. Still they lingered, and still they strove to converse on their affairs; despite the presence of Occonestoga, who sat patiently at the foot of a tree without show of discontent or sign of hunger, though, for a term of at least eighteen hours, he had eaten nothing. In this lies one of the chief merits of an Indian warrior—

> "Severe the school that made him bear
> The ills of life without a tear—
> And stern the doctrine that denied
> The chieftain fame, the warrior pride;
> Who, urged by nature's wants expressed
> The need that hungered in his breast—
> Or, when beneath his foeman's knife,
> Who uttered recreant prayer for life—
> Or, in the chase, whose strength was spent,
> Or in the fight whose knee was bent,
> Or, when with tale of coming fight
> Who sought his allies' lodge by night,
> And ere his missives well were told,
> Complained of hunger, wet, and cold.
> A woman, if in fight his foe,
> Could give, yet not receive the blow—
> Or, if undext'rously and dull,
>   His hand and knife had failed to win
> The dripping, warm scalp from the scull
>   To trim his yellow mocasin."

Thus, a perfect embodiment of the character, so wrought and so described, Occonestoga, calm, sullen, and stern, sat beneath the tree, without look or word, significant of that fatigue and hunger under which he must have been seriously suffering. He surveyed, with something like scorn, those evidences between the lovers of that nice and delicate affection which belongs only to the highest forms of civilization. At length, bidding him wait his return, Harrison took the way with Bess, who was now sufficiently restored for the effort, to the cottage of her father. It was not long before he returned to the savage, whose hand he again shook cordially and affectionately, while repeating his grateful promise of reward. Then, turning to a subject at that time strongly present in his mind, he inquired into the recent demonstrations of his people.

"Occonestoga, what news is this of the Yemassee? He is angry, is he not?"

"Angry to kill, Harrison. Is not the scout on the path of Occonestoga—Occonestoga, the son of Sanutee?—look! the tomahawk of Sanutee shook in the eyes of Occonestoga.—The swift foot, the close bush, the thick swamp and the water—they were the friends of Occonestoga. Occonestoga is a dog.—The scouts of Yemassee look for him in the swamps."

"You must be hungry and weary, Occonestoga. Come with me to the Block House, where there are meat and drink."

"Harrison is friend to Occonestoga?"

"Surely I am," was the reply.

"The good friend will kill Occonestoga?" was the demand, uttered in tones of more solicitude than is common to the Indian.

"Kill you? no! why should I kill you?"

"It is good! knife Occonestoga, Englishman; put the sharp tooth here, in his heart, for the father of Occonestoga has a curse for his head! Sanutee has sworn him to Opitchi-Manneyto! will not the chief of the English put the sharp knife here?" The entreaty was earnestly made. The uttermost depths of despair seemed to have been sounded by the outcast.

"No, Occonestoga, no. I will do no such thing. Thou shalt live and do well, and be at friendship with thy father and thy people. Come with me to the Block House and get something to eat. We will talk over this affair of thy people. Come with me, young chief, all will be right ere many days. Come!"

The melancholy savage rose, passively resigned to any will, having none of his own. In silence he followed his conductor to the Block House, where, under the instructions of Harrison, Granger and his wife received him with the kindliest solicitude.

Chapter Twenty-two

*"And wherefore sings he that strange song of death,
That song of sorrow? Is the doom at hand?"*

THE wife of Granger soon provided refreshments for the young sav-age, of which he ate sparingly, and without much seeming con-sciousness of what he was doing. Harrison did not trouble him much with remark or inquiry, but busied himself in looking after the prepa-rations for the defence of the building. For this purpose, Hector and himself occupied an hour in the apartment adjoining that in which the household concerns of Granger were carried on. In this apartment Hector kept Dugdale, a famous bloodhound, supposed to have been brought from the Caribbees, which, when very young, Harrison had purchased from a Spanish trader. This dog was of a peculiar breed, and resembled in some respects the Irish wolf-hound, while having all the thirst and appetite for blood which distinguished the more ancient *Slute* or Sleuth-hound of the Scots. It is a mistake to suppose that the Spaniards brought these dogs to America. They found them here, actually in use by the Indians and for like purposes, and only perfected their training, while stimulating them in the pursuit of man. The dog Dugdale had been partially trained after their fashion to hunt the Indians, and even under his present owner, it was not deemed unbe-coming that he should be prepared for the purposes of war upon the savages, by the occasional exhibition of a stuffed figure, so made and painted as to resemble a naked Indian, around whose neck a lump of raw and bleeding beef was occasionally suspended. This was shown him while chained,—from any near approach he was withheld until his appetite had been so wrought upon that longer restraint would have been dangerous and impossible. The training of these dogs, as known to the early French and Spanish settlers, by both of whom they were in common use for the purpose of war with the natives, is exceeding curious; and so fierce under this sort of training did they become in process of time, that it was found necessary to restrain them in cages while thus stimulated, until the call to the field, and the prospect of immediate strife, should give an opportunity to the exercise of their unallayed rapacity. In the civil commotions of Hayti, the most formidable enemies known to the insurrectionists were the fierce dogs which had been so educated by the French. The dog of Harrison had not, however, been greatly exercised by his present owner after this fashion. He had been simply required to follow and attend upon his master, under the conduct of Hector, for both of whom his attachments had become singularly strong. But the early lessons of his Spanish masters had not been forgotten by Dugdale, who, in the war of the Carolinians with the Coosaws, following his master into battle, proved an unlooked-for auxiliar of the one, and an enemy whose very appearance struck terror into the other. So useful an ally was not to be neglected, and the stuffed figure which had formed a part of the property of the animal in the sale by his Spanish master, was brought into occasional exercise and use, under the charge of Hector, in confirming Dugdale's warlike propensities. In this exercise, with the figure of a naked Indian perched against one corner, and a part of a deer's entrails hanging around his neck, Hector, holding back the dog by a stout rope drawn around a beam, the better to embarrass him at pleasure, was stimulating at the same time his hunger and ferocity.

"Does Dugdale play to-day, Hector?" inquired his master.

"He hab fine sperits, maussa—berry fine sperits. I kin hardly keep 'em in. See da, now—" and, as the slave spoke, the dog broke away, dragging the rope suddenly through the hands of the holder, and, without remarking the meat, ran crouching to the feet of Harrison.

"Him nebber forgit you, maussa, ebber since you put your hand down he troat."

Harrison snapped his fingers, and motioning with his hand to the bleeding entrails of the deer around the neck of the figure, the hound sprang furiously upon it, and dragging it to the floor, planted himself across the body, while, with his formidable teeth, he tore away the bait from the neck where it was wound, lacerating the figure at every bite, in a manner which would have soon deprived the living man of all show of life. Having given some directions to the slave, Harrison returned to the apartment where he had left the Indian.

Occonestoga sat in a corner mournfully croning over, in an uncouth strain, something of a song, rude, sanguinary, in his own wild language. Something of the language was known to Harrison, but not enough to comprehend the burden of what he sang. But the look and the manner of the savage were so solemn and imposing, so strange yet so full of dignified thought, that the Englishman did not venture to interrupt him. He turned to Granger, who, with his wife, was partially employed in one corner of the apartment, folding up some of his wares and burnishing others.

"What does he sing, Granger?" he asked of the trader.

"His death song, sir. It is something very strange—but he has been at it now for some time; and the Indian does not employ that song unless with a near prospect of death. He has probably had some dream or warning, and they are very apt to believe in such things."

"Indeed!—his death-song—" murmured Harrison, while he listened attentively to the low chant which the Indian still kept up. At his request, forbearing his labour, Granger listened also, and translated at intervals the purport of many of the stanzas.

"What is the Seratee," in his uncouth lyric, sang the melancholy Indian—

> "What is the Seratee?—
> He is but a dog
> Sneaking in the long grass—
> I have stood before him,
> And he did not look—
> By his hair I took him,—
> By the single tuft—
> From his head I tore it,
> With it came the scalp,—
> On my thigh I wore it—
> With the chiefs I stood,
> And they gave me honour,
> Made of me a chief,
> To the sun they held me,
> And aloud the prophet
> Bade me be a chief—
> Chief of all the Yemassee—
> Feather chief and arrow chief—
> Chief of all the Yemassee,"

At the conclusion of this uncouth verse, he proceeded in a different tone and manner, and his present form of speech constituted a break or pause in the song.

"That Opitchi-Manneyto—wherefore is he wroth with the young chief who went on the war-path against the Seratee? He made slaves for him from the dogs of the long grass. Let Opitchi-Manneyto hear. Occonestoga is a brave chief, he hath struck his hatchet into the lodge of the Savannah, when there was a full sun in the forests."

"Now," said Granger, "he is going to tell us of another of his achievements." Occonestoga went on—

> "Hear, Opitchi-Manneyto,
> Hear Occonestoga speak—
> Who of the Savannah stood
> In the council, in the fight—
> With the gallant Suwannee?—
> Bravest he, of all the brave,
> Like an arrow path in fight—
> When he came, his tomahawk—
> (Hear, Opitchi-Manneyto,
> Not a forked tongue is mine—)
> Frighted the brave Yemassee—
> Till Occonestoga came—
> Till Occonestoga stood
> Face to face with Suwannee,
> By the old Satilla swamp.
> Then his eyes were in the mud—
> With these hands I tore away
> The war ringlet from his head—
> With it came the bleeding scalp—
> Suwannee is in the mud;
> Frighted back, his warriors run,
> Left him buried in the mud—
> Ho! the gray-wolf speaks aloud,
> Hear, Opitchi-Manneyto;
> He had plenty food that night,
> And for me he speaks aloud—
> Suwannee is in his jaw—
> Look, Opitchi-Manneyto—
> See him tear Suwannee's side,
> See him drink Suwannee's blood—

> With his paw upon his breast,
> Look, he pulls the heart away,
> And his nose is searching deep,
> Clammy, thick with bloody drink,
> In the hollow where it lay.
> Look Opitchi-Manneyto,
> Look, the grey-wolf speaks for me."

Then after this wild and barbarous chant, which, verse after verse, Granger rendered to Harrison, a pause of a few moments was suffered to succeed, in which, all the while in the profoundest silence, the young warrior continued to wave his head backwards and forwards at regular intervals.

"He has had a warning certainly, captain; I have seen them frequently go on so. Now, he begins again."

Not singing, but again addressing the evil deity, Occonestoga began with the usual adjuration.

"Arrows and feathers, burnt arrows and feathers—a bright flame for thee, Opitchi-Manneyto. Look not dark upon the young brave of Yemassee. Hear his song of the war path and the victory."

This said, he resumed the chant in a burden of less personal, and more national character, a more sounding and elevated strain, and which, in the translation of Granger, necessarily lost much of its native sublimity.

> "Mighty is the Yemassee,
> Strong in the trial,
> Fearless in the strife,
> Terrible in wrath—
> Look, Opitchi-Manneyto—
> He is like the rush of clouds,
> He is like the storm by night,
> When the tree-top bends and shivers,
> When the lodge goes down.
> The Westo and the Edisto,
> What are they to him?—
> Like the brown leaves to the cold,
> Look, they shrink before his touch,
> Shrink and shiver as he comes—
> Mighty is the Yemassee."

Harrison now ventured to interrupt the enthusiastic but still sullen warrior. He interrupted him with a compliment, confirming that which he had himself been uttering, to the prowess of his nation.

"That is a true song, Occonestoga—that in praise of your nation. They are indeed a brave people; but I fear under wild management now. But come—here is some drink, it will strengthen you."

"It is good," said he, drinking, "It is good—good for strength. The English is a friend to Occonestoga."

"We have always tried to be so, Occonestoga, as you should know by this time. But speak to me of Pocota-ligo. What have the people been doing there? What maddens them, and wherefore should they grow angry with their English brothers?"

"The Yemassee is like the wolf—he smells blood on the track of the hunter, when the young cub is carried away. He is blind, like the rattlesnake, with the poison of the long sleep, when he first comes out in the time of the green corn. He wants blood to drink—he would strike the enemy."

"I see. The Yemassees are impatient of peace. They would go upon the war-path, and strike the English as their enemies. Is this what you think, Occonestoga?"

"Harrison speaks! The English is a friend to Yemassee, but Yemassee will not hear the word of Occonestoga. Sanutee says the tongue of Occonestoga has a fork—he speaks in two voices."

"They are mad, young brave—but not so mad, I think, as to go on the war-path without an object. At this moment they could not hope to be successful, and would find it destructive."

"The thought of Occonestoga is here. They will go on the war-path against the English."

"Ha!—If you think so, Occonestoga, you must be our friend."

"Cha! Cha! Occonestoga is too much friend to the English."

"Not too much, not too much—not more than they will reward you for."

"Will the strong water of the English make Occonestoga to be the son of Sanutee? Will the meat carry Occonestoga to the young braves of the Yemassee? Will they sleep till he speaks for them to wake? Look, Harrison, the death-song is made for Occonestoga."

"Not so—there is no cause yet for you to sing the death-song of the young warrior."

"Occonestoga has said!—he has seen—it came to him when he ate meat from the hands of the trader."

"Ah! that is all owing to your fatigue and hunger, Occonestoga. You have long years of life before you, and still have some service to perform for your friends, the English. You must find out for us certainly whether your people mean to go on the war-path or not— where they will strike first, and when; and above all, whether any other tribes join with them. You must go for us back to Pocota-ligo. You must watch the steps of the chiefs, and bring word of what they intend."

An overpowering sense of his own shame as he listened to this requisition of Harrison, forced his head down upon his bosom, while the gloom grew darker upon his face. At length he exclaimed—

"It is no good talk: must Occonestoga be a dog for the English? The tomahawk of Sanutee is good for a dog."

"Wherefore this, young chief of the Yemassee?—What mean you by this speech?"

"Young chief of Yemassee!" exclaimed the savage, repeating the phrase of Harrison as if in derision— "said you not the young chief of Yemassee should hunt his people like a dog in the cover of the bush?"

"Not like a dog, Occonestoga, but like a good friend, as well to the English as to the Yemassee. Is not peace good for both? It is peace, not war, that the English desire; but if there be war, Occonestoga, they will take all the scalps of your nation."

"The English must look to his own scalp," cried the young man, fiercely,— "the hand of the Yemassee is ready;—" and as he spoke, for a moment his eye lightened up, and his form rose erect from the place where he had been sitting, while a strong feeling of nationality in his bosom aroused him into something like the warlike show of an eloquent chief inspiriting his tribe for the fight. But Granger, who had been watchful, came forward with a cup of spirits, which, without a word, he now handed him. The youth seized it hurriedly, drank it off at a single effort, and, in that act, the momentary enthusiasm which had lightened up, with a show of still surviving consciousness and soul, the otherwise desponding and degraded features, passed away; and sinking again into his seat, he replied to the other portion of the remark of Harrison:

"It is good, what the English speaks. Peace is good—peace for the

Yemassee—peace for the English—peace—peace for Occonestoga—Occonestoga speaks for peace."

"Then let Occonestoga do as I wish him. Let him go this very night to Pocota-ligo. Let his eye take the track of the chiefs, and look at their actions. Let him come back to-morrow, and say all that he has seen, and claim his reward from the English."

"There is death for Occonestoga if the Yemassee scout finds his track."

"But the young chief has an eye like the hawk—a foot like the sneaking panther, and a body limber as the snake. He can see his enemy afar—he can hide in the thick bush—he can lie still under the dead timber when the hunter steps over it."

"And rise to strike him in the heel like the yellow-belly moccasin. Yes! The young chief is a great warrior—the Seratee is a dog, the Savannah is a dog—Look, his legs have the scalp of Suwannee and Chareco. Occonestoga is a great warrior."

The vanity of the savage once enlisted, and his scruples were soon overcome. An additional cup of spirits which Granger again furnished him, concluded the argument, and he avowed himself ready for the proposed adventure. His preparations were soon completed, and when the night had fairly set in, the fugitive was on the scent, and again within the boundary lines of his nation, and cautiously threading his way, with all the skill and cunning of an Indian, among the paths of the people whom he had so grievously incensed. He knew the danger, but he was vain of his warrior and hunter skill. He did not fear death, for it is the habitual practice of the Indian's thought to regard it as a part of his existence; and his dying ceremonies form no inconsiderable part of the legacy of renown which is left to his children. But had he known the doom which had been pronounced against him, along with the other chiefs, and which had been already executed upon them by the infuriated people, he had never ventured for an instant upon so dangerous a commission.

Chapter Twenty-three

"What love is like a mother's? You may break
The heart that holds it—you may trample it
In shame and sorrow; but you may not tear
One single link away that keeps it there."

HALF conscious only of his design at starting, the young and profligate savage, on crossing to the opposite shore, which he did just at the Block House, grew more sensible, not only in reference to the object of his journey, but to the dangers which necessarily came along with it. Utterly ignorant, as yet, of that peculiar and unusual doom which had been pronounced against himself and the other chiefs, and already executed upon them, he had yet sufficient reason to apprehend that, if taken, his punishment, death probably, would be severe enough. Apprehending this probability, the fear which it inspired was not however sufficient to discourage him from an adventure which, though pledged for its performance in a moment of partial inebriation, was yet held by the simple Indian to be all-binding upon him. Firmly resolved, therefore, upon the fulfilment of his promise to Harrison, who, with Granger and others, had often before employed him, though on less dangerous missions, he went forward, preparing to watch the progress of events among the Yemassees, and to report duly the nature of their warlike proceedings.

The aim of Harrison was preparation, and the purpose was therefore of the highest importance upon which Occonestoga had been sent. The generally exposed situation of the whole frontier occupied by the whites, with the delay and difficulty of warlike preparation, rendered every precautionary measure essential on the part of the Carolinians. For this reason, a due and proper intelligence of the means, designs, and strength of their adversaries, became absolutely necessary; particularly as the capricious nature of savage affections makes it doubtful whether they can, for any length of time, continue in peace and friendship. How far Occonestoga may stand excused for the part which he had taken against his countrymen, whatever may have been the character of their cause, is a question not necessary for our consideration here. It is certain that the degradation consequent upon his intemperance, had greatly contributed towards blunting that feeling of nationality, which is no small part of the honest boast of every Indian warrior.

Night had fairly shrouded the forest when the young chief commenced his journey. But he knew the path, by night as by day, with a familiarity begun in childhood. His ear, quick, keen, and discriminating by his education, could distinguish between and identify the movement of every native of the woodland cover. He knew the slight and hurried rustle of the black snake, from the slow, dignified sweep of the rattle; and, drunk or sober, the bear in the thicket, or the buck bounding along the dry pine-land ridge, were never mistaken, one for the other, by our forest warrior. These, as they severally crossed or lay in his path—for the rattlesnake moves at his own pleasure—he drove aside or avoided; and when contradictory sounds met his ear, doubtful in character or significant of some dangerous proximity, then would the warrior sink down into the bush or under the cover of the fallen tree, or steal away into the sheltering shadow of the neighbouring copse, without so much as a breath or whisper. Such precautions as these became more and more necessary as he drew nigher to the homestead of his people. The traces of their presence thickened momently around him. Now the torch flared across his eye, and now the hum of voices came with the sudden gust; and, more than once, moving swiftly across his path, stole along a dusky figure like his own, bent upon some secret quest, and watchful like himself to avoid discovery. He too, perhaps, had been dimly seen in the same manner— not his features, for none in that depth of shadow in which he crept could well have made them out; but such partial glances, though he strove to avoid all observation, he did not so much heed, as he well knew that the thought of others, seeing him, without ascertaining who he was, would be apt to assign him a like pursuit with their own; possibly, the nocturnal amour; pursued by the Yemassees with a fastidious regard to secrecy, not because of any moral reserve, but that such a pursuit savours of a weakness unbecoming to manhood.

On a sudden he drew back from the way he was pursuing, and sank under the cover of a gigantic oak. A torch flamed across the path, and a dusky maiden carried it, followed by a young warrior. They passed directly beside the tree behind which Occonestoga had sought for shelter, and, at the first glance, he knew Hiwassee, the young maiden who was to have filled his own lodge, according to the expectations of the people. But he had lost sight of, and forgotten her in the practices which had weaned him from his brethren and bound him to the whites. What were the affections now to him? Yet he had regarded her with favour, and though he had never formally proposed to break with her the sacred wand of Checkamoysee,* which was to give her the title to his dwelling and make her his wife, yet such had been the expectation of his mother, her wish, and perhaps that of the damsel herself. He remembered this with a sad sinking of the heart. He remembered what he had been, what were his hopes and pride; what had been the expectations, in regard to him, of his parents and his people. It was with a bitter feeling of disappointment and self-reproach, that he heard the proposition of love as it was made to her by another.

"It is a brave chief, Hiwassee—a brave chief that would have you enter his lodge. The lodge of Echotee is ready for Hiwassee. Look! this is the stick of Checkamoysee; break it, take it in thy hands and break it, Hiwassee, and Echotee will quench the torch which thou bearest in the running water. Then shalt thou be the wife of a warrior, and the venison shall always be full in thy lodge. Break the stick of Checkamoysee, Hiwassee, and be the wife of Echotee."

And the dusky maiden needed little wooing. She broke the stick, and as she did so, seizing the blazing torch with a ready hand, Echotee hurried with it to a brook that trickled along at a little distance, and in the next instant it hissed in the water, and all was darkness. Without regarding what he was doing, or thinking of his own risk, Occonestoga, in the absence of her accepted lover, could not forbear a word, something of reproach, perhaps, in the ear of Hiwassee. She stood but a few paces off, under the shadow and on the opposite side of the same tree which gave him shelter; with the broken stick still in her hand in attestation of her wild forest nuptial. What he said was unheard save by her-

---

* Checkamoysee, the Yemassee Hymen.

self, but she screamed as she heard it; and, hearing her lover approach, and now duly conscious of his error, Occonestoga, in the next moment, had darted away from the place of their tryst, and was pursuing his route with all the vigour of a renewed and resolute spirit. The sense of what he had lost for ever, seemed to sting him into a sort of despairing energy which hurried him recklessly onward.

At length he approached the town of Pocota-ligo, but, at first, carefully avoiding its main entrance, which was upon the river—particularly as the throng of sounds reaching his ears from that quarter indicated a still active stir—he shot off circuitously into the thicker woods, so as to come into the immediate neighborhood of his father's dwelling. From a neighbouring thicket, after a little while, he looked down upon the cabin which had given a birth-place and shelter to his infancy; and the feeling of shame grew strong in his bosom as he thought upon the hopes defeated of his high-souled father, and of the affections thrown away of the gentle mother, with whom, however mortified and fruitless, they still continued to flourish for the outcast. Such thoughts, however, were not permitted to trouble him long; for, as he looked he beheld by the ruddy blaze of the pine torch which the boy carried before him, the person of his father emerge from the lodge, and take the well-known pathway leading to Pocota-ligo. If Occonestoga had no other virtue, that of love for his mother was, to a certain extent, sufficiently redeeming. His previous thoughts, his natural feeling, prepared him, whatever the risk, to take advantage of the opportunity thus offered him. In another instant, and the half penitent prodigal stood in the presence of Matiwan.

"Oh, boy—Occonestoga—thou art come—thou art come. Thou art not yet lost to Matiwan."

And she threw herself, with the exclamation, fondly, though but for a moment, upon his neck; the next, recovering herself, she spoke in hurried tones, full of grief and apprehension.

"Thou shouldst not come!—fly, boy—fly, Occonestoga—be a swift bird, that the night has overtaken far away from his bush. There is danger—there is death—not death—there is a curse for thee from Opitchi-Manneyto."

"Let not the grief stand in the eye of Matiwan. Occonestoga fears not death. He has a song for the Manneyto of the blessed valley; the great warriors shall clap their hands and cry 'Sangarrah-me, Sangarrah-me, Yemassee,' when they hear. Let not the grief stand in the eye of Matiwan."

"It is for thee, for thee, boy—for thee, Occonestoga. The sorrow of Matiwan is for thee. Thou hast been in this bosom, Occonestoga, and thine eyes opened first, when the green was on the young leaf and the yellow flower was hanging over the lodge in the strength of the sun."

"Know I not the song of Enoree-Mattee, when the eyes of Occonestoga looked up? Said he not—under the green leaf, under the yellow flower, the brave comes who shall have arrows with wings and a knife that has eyes? Occonestoga is here!"

"Matiwan was glad. Sanutee lifted thee to the sun, boy, and begged for thee his beams from the good Manneyto. The gladness is gone, Occonestoga—gone from Sanutee, gone from Matiwan,—gone with thee. There is no green on the leaf—my eyes look upon the yellow flowers no longer. Occonestoga, it is thou,—thou hast taken all this light from the eye of Matiwan. The gladness and the light are gone."

"Matiwan tells no lie—this dog is Occonestoga."

Thus he began, sinking back into the humiliating consciousness of his shame and degradation. But the gentle parent, tender even in the utterance of the truth, fearing she had gone too far, hastily and almost indignantly interrupted him in the melancholy self-condemnation he was uttering.

"No, no—Occonestoga is no dog. He is a brave—he is the son of Sanutee, the well-beloved of the Yemassee. Occonestoga has shut his eyes and gone upon the track of a foolish dream, but he will wake with the sun,—and Matiwan will see the green leaf and the yellow flower still hanging over the lodge of Sanutee;" and as she spoke she threw her arms about him affectionately, while the tears came to the relief of her heart and flowed freely down her cheeks. The youth gently but coldly disengaged her clasp, and proceeded to seat himself upon the broad skin lying upon the floor of the cabin; when, aroused by the movement, and with a return of her old apprehensions, she thrust him from it with an air of anxiety, if not horror, and shutting her eyes upon the wondering and somewhat indignant glance with which he now surveyed her, she exclaimed passionately—

"Go—fly—wherefore art thou here—here in the lodge of Sanutee—thou, the accursed—the—" and the words stuck in her throat, and, unarticulated, came forth chokingly.

"Is Matiwan mad—has the fever-pain gone into her temples?" he asked in astonishment.

"No, no, no—not mad, Occonestoga. But thou art cast out from the Yemassee. He does not know thee—the young warriors know thee not—the chiefs know thee not—Manneyto denies thee. They have said—thou art a Yemassee no longer. They have cast thee out."

"The Yemassee is great, but he cannot deny Occonestoga. Thou art mad, Matiwan. Look, woman, here is the broad arrow of Yemassee upon the shoulder of a chief."

"It is gone—it is gone from thee, Occonestoga. They have sworn by Opitchi-Manneyto, that Malatchie, the Clublifter, shall take it from thy shoulder."

The youth shrunk back, and his eyes started in horror, while his limbs trembled with a sentiment of fear not often felt by an Indian warrior. In another instant, however, he recovered from the stupor if not from the dread, which her intelligence occasioned.

"Ha, Matiwan, thou hast no fork in thy tongue. Thou speakest not to me with the voice of the Coonee-latee."

"Opitchi-Manneyto!—he hears the voice of Matiwan. The Yemassee has doomed thee."

"They dare not—they will not. I will go with them upon the war-path against the Santee and the Seratee. I will take up the hatchet against the English. I will lead the young warriors to battle. They shall know Occonestoga for a chief."

"Thou canst not, boy. They do not trust thee—they have doomed thee with the chiefs who sold the land to the English. Has not Malatchie cut with the knife, and burnt away with fire from their shoulders, the sacred and broad arrow of Yemassee, so that we know them no more?—Their fathers and their sons know them no more— the mothers that bore them know them no more—the other nations know them no more—they cannot enter the blessed valley of Manneyto, for Manneyto knows them not when he looks for the broad arrow of Yemassee, and finds it not upon their shoulders."

"Woman! thou liest!—thou art hissing lies in my ears, like the green snake, with a forked tongue. The Yemassee has not done this thing as thou say'st."

The voice of the woman sank into a low and husky murmur, and the always melancholy tones of the language of the red man, grew doubly so in her utterance, as she replied in a stern rebuke, though her attitude and manner were now entirely passionless:—

"When has Matiwan lied to Occonestoga? Occonestoga is a dog when he speaks of Matiwan as the forked tongue."

"He is a dog if thou hast *not* lied, Matiwan. Say that thou hast lied—that thou hast said a foolish thing to Occonestoga. Say, Matiwan, and the young arrow will be in thy hand even as the long shoots of the tree that weeps. Thou shalt make him what thou wilt."

With an expression the most humbled and imploring, and something more of warmth than is usually shown by the Indian warrior, the young chief took the hand of his mother, while uttering an appeal, virtually apologizing for the harsh language he had previously made use of. With the pause of an instant, and a passionate melancholy, almost amounting to the vehemence of despair, she replied:—

"Matiwan does not lie. The Yemassee has said the doom, which Enoree-Mattee, the prophet, brought from Opitchi-Manneyto. Has not Malatchie cut from the shoulders of the chiefs and burnt away with fire the broad arrow, so that never more may they be known by the Yemassee—never more by the Manneyto! The doom is for thee, Occonestoga. It is true. There is no fork in the tongue of Matiwan. Fly, boy—fly, Occonestoga. It is thy mother, it is Matiwan that prays thee to fly. Matiwan would not lose thee, Occonestoga, from the happy valley. Be the swift arrow on the path of flight—let them not see thee— let them not give thee to Malatchie."

Thus, passionately imploring him, the mother urged upon him the necessity of flight. But, for a few minutes, as if stunned by the intelligence which he could not now disbelieve, the young warrior stood in silence, with down-bending head, the very personification of despair. Then, quickly and fully recovering, with a kindling eye, and a manner well corresponding with his language, he started forward, erectly, in his fullest height, and with the action of a strong mood, for a moment assumed the attitude of that true dignity, from which, in his latter days and habits, he had but too much and too often departed.

"Ha! Is Occonestoga an arrow that is broken? Is he the old tree across the swamp, that the dog's foot runs over? Has he no strength— has the blood gone out of his heart? Has he no knife—where are the arrow and the tomahawk? They are here—I have them. The Yemassee shall not hold me down when I sleep. Occonestoga sleeps not. He will do battle against the Yemassee. His knife shall strike at the breast of Sanutee."

"Thou hast said a folly, boy—Occonestoga, wouldst thou strike at thy father?" said the mother, sternly.

"His hatchet shook over the head of Occonestoga in the lodge of council. He is the enemy of Occonestoga—a bad thorn in the path, ready for the foot that flies. I will slay him like a dog. He shall hear the scalp-song of Occonestoga—I will sing it in his ears, woman, like a bird that comes with the storm, while I send the long knife into his heart;" and fiercely, as he concluded this speech, he chanted a passage of the famous scalp-song of the Yemassee—

> "I go with the long knife,
> On the path of my enemy—
> In the cover of the brake,
> With the tooth of the war-rattle,
> I strike the death into his heel—
> Sangarrah-me, Sangarrah-me.
> I hear him groan, I see him gasp,
> I tear his throat, I drink his blood,
> He sings the song of his dying,
> To the glory of Occonestoga."

"Ha! thou hearest, Matiwan—this will I sing for Sanutee when my knee is upon his breast, when my knife is thick in his heart, when I tear the thin scalp from his forehead."

Thus, in a deep, fiercely impressive, but low tone, Occonestoga poured forth in his mother's ears the fulness of his paroxysm,—in his madness attributing, and with correctness, the doom which had been pronounced against him as coming from his father. In that fierce and bitter moment he forgot all the ties of kindred, and his look was that of the furious and fearful savage, already imbruing his hands in parental blood. The horror of Matiwan, beyond expression, could not, however, be kept from utterance:—

"Thou hast drunk madness, boy, from the cup of Opitchi-Manneyto. The devil of the white man's prophet has gone into thy heart. But thou art the child of Matiwan, and, though thou art in a foolish path, it is thy mother that would save thee. Go—fly, Occonestoga—keep on thy shoulder the broad arrow of Yemassee, so that thy mother may not lose thee from the blessed valley of Manneyto."

Before the young warrior, somewhat softened by this speech, could find words to reply it, his acute sense—acute enough at all times to savour of a supernatural faculty—detected an approaching sound; and, through an opening of the logs in the dwelling, the flare of a torch was seen approaching. Matiwan, much more apprehensive, with her anxieties now turned in a new direction, went quickly to the entrance, and returning instantly with great alarm, announced the approach of Sanutee.

"He comes to the hatchet of Occonestoga," cried the youth fiercely, his recent rage re-awakening.

"Wouldst thou slay Matiwan?" was the reply,—and the look, the tone, the words were sufficient. The fierce spirit was quelled and the youth suffered himself to follow quietly as she directed. She led him to a remote corner of the lodge, which, piled up with skins, furnished a fair chance and promise of security. With several of these, as he stretched himself at his length, she contrived to cover him in such a manner as effectually to conceal him from the casual observer. Having so done, she strove to resume her composure in time for the reception of the old chief, whose torch now blazed at the entrance.

Chapter Twenty-four

"They bind him, will they slay him? That old man,
His father, will he look upon and see
The danger of his child, nor lift his voice,
Nor lend his arm to save him?"

WITH a mind deeply taken up with the concerns of state, Sanutee threw himself upon the bearskin which formed a sort of carpet in the middle of the lodge, and failed utterly to remark the discomposure of Matiwan, which, otherwise, to the keen glance of the Indian, would not have remained very long concealed. She took her seat at his head, and croned low and musingly some familiar chant of forest song, unobtrusively, yet meant to soothe his ear. He heard—for this had long been a practice with her and a domestic indulgence with him—he heard, but did not seem to listen. His mind was away—busied in the events of the wild storm it had invoked, and the period of which was rapidly approaching. But there were other matters less important, that called for present attention; and, turning at length to his wife, and pointing at the same time to the pile of skins that lay confusedly huddled up over the crouching form of Occonestoga, he quietly remarked upon their loose and disordered appearance. The well-bred housewife of a city might have discovered something of rebuke to her domestic management in what he said on this subject; but the mind of Matiwan lost all sight of the reproach, in the apprehensions which such a reference had excited. He saw not her disorder, however, but proceeded to enumerate to himself their numbers, sorts, and qualities, with a simple air of business; until, suddenly labouring, as it appeared, under some deficiency of memory, he instructed her to go and ascertain the number of bearskins in the collection.

"The Spanish trader will buy from Sanutee with the next sun. Go, Matiwan."

To hear was to obey; and half dead with fear, yet rejoiced that he had not gone himself, she proceeded to tumble about the skins, with ready compliance, and an air of industry, the most praiseworthy in an Indian woman. Her labour was lengthened, so Sanutee seemed to think, somewhat beyond the time necessary to enumerate a lot of skins not exceeding fifteen or twenty in number, and with some little sternness at last he demanded of her the cause of the delay. Apprehensive that he would yet rise, and seek for himself a solution of the difficulty, she determined, as she had not yet ascertained, to guess at the fact, and immediately replied in a representation which did not at all accord with the calculation of the chief's own memory on the subject. The impatience of Occonestoga, in the meantime, was not less than that of Sanutee. He worried his mother not a little in his restlessness while she moved about him; and once, as she bent over him, removing this, and replacing that, he seized upon her hand, and would have spoken, but that so dangerous an experiment she would not permit. But she saw by his glance, and the settled firmness with which he grasped his hatchet, that his thought was that of defiance to his father, and a desire to throw aside the restraining cover of the skins, and assert his manhood. She drew away from him rapidly, with a finger uplifted as if in entreaty, while with one hand she threw over him a huge bearskin, which nearly suffocated him, and which he immediately, in part, threw aside. Sanutee, in the meantime, seem very imperfectly satisfied with the representation which she had made, and manifesting some doubt as to the correctness of her estimate, he was about to rise and look for himself into the matter. But, in some trepidation, the wary Matiwan prevented him.

"Wherefore should the chief toil at the task of a woman? Battle for the chief—wisdom in council for the chief; and the seat under the big tree, at the head of the lodge, when the great chiefs come to eat meat from his hands. Sit, well-beloved—wherefore should not Matiwan look for thee? The toil of the lodge is for Matiwan."

"Sanutee will look, Matiwan—the bearskin is heavy on thy hands," was the considerate reply.

"Go not, look not—" impatiently, rather too impatiently earnest, was the response of the woman; sufficiently so to awaken surprise, if not suspicion, in the mind of the old chief. She saw her error in the next instant, and proceeding to correct it, without, at the same time yielding the point, she said:

"Thou art weary, chief—all day long thou hast been upon the track of toil, and thy feet need rest. Rest thee. Matiwan is here—why shouldst thou not repose? Will she not look to the skins? She goes."

"Thou art good, Matiwan, but Sanutee will look with the eye that is true. He is not weary as thou say'st. Cha!" —he exclaimed, as she still endeavored to prevent him— "Cha!—Cha!" impatiently putting her aside with the exclamation, and turning to the very spot of Occonestoga's concealment. Hopeless of escape, Matiwan clasped her hands together, and the beatings of her heart grew more frequent and painful. Already his hands were upon the skins,—already had Occonestoga determined upon throwing aside his covering and grappling with his fate like a warrior, when a sudden yell of many voices, and the exciting blood-cry of Yemassee battle, "Sangarrah-me, Sangarrah-me,"— rang through the little apartment. Lights flared all around the lodge, and a confused, wild, approaching clamour, as of many voices, from without, drew the attention of all within, and diverted Sanutee from a further search at that time, which must have resulted in such a *dénouement* as would have tried severely, if not fatally, the several parties. But the respite afforded to Matiwan was very brief. The cry from without was of startling significance to the woman and her son.

"Sangarrah-me—he is here—the slave of Opitchi-Manneyto is here."

And a general howl, with a direct call for Sanutee, brought the old chief to the door of the lodge. It was surrounded by a crowd of the red men, in a state of intense excitement. Before the old chief could ask the purpose of their visit, and the cause of their clamour, he had heard it from a score of voices. They came to denounce the fugitive, they had tracked him to the lodge. The indiscretion of Occonestoga when speaking in the ear of the Indian maiden, Hiwassee, had brought about its legitimate consequences. In her surprise, and accounting for the shriek she gave, she had revealed the circumstance to her lover, and it was not long before he had again related it to another. The story flew, the crowd increased, and, gathering excitement from numbers, they rushed forward to the lodge of Matiwan, where, from his known love to his mother, they thought it probable he would be found, to claim the doomed slave of Opitchi-Manneyto. The old chief heard them with a stern and motionless calm of countenance; then, without an instant of reflection, throwing open the door of the lodge, he bade them enter upon the search for their victim.

The clamour and its occasion, in the meantime, had been made sufficiently and fearfully intelligible to those within. Matiwan sank down hopelessly in a corner of the apartment, while Occonestoga, with a rapid recovery of all his energies, throwing aside his covering of skins, and rising from his place of concealment, stood up once more, an upright and fearless Indian warrior. He freed the knife from its sheath, tightened the belt about his waist, grasped the tomahawk in his right hand, and placing himself conspicuously in the centre of the apartment, prepared manfully for the worst.

Such was his position, when, leading the way for the pursuers of the fugitive, Sanutee re-entered the cabin. A moment's glance sufficed to show him the truth of the statement made him, and at the same time accounted for the uneasiness of Matiwan, and her desire to prevent his examination of the skins. He darted a severe look upon her where she lay in the corner, and as the glance met her own, she crept silently towards him and would have clasped his knees; but the ire of Sanutee was too deeply awakened, and, regarding his profligate son, not merely in that character, but as the chief enemy and betrayer of his country to the English, he threw her aside, then approached and stretched forth his arm as if to secure him. But Occonestoga stood on the defensive; and with a skill and power, which, at one time, had procured for him a high reputation for warrior-like conduct, in a field where the competitors were numerous, he hurled the old chief back upon the crowd that followed him. Doubly incensed with the resistance thus offered, Sanutee re-advanced with a degree of anger which excluded the cautious consideration of the true warrior,—and as the approach was narrow, he re-advanced unsupported. The recollection of the terrible doom impending over his head—the knowledge of Sanutee's own share in its decree—the stern denunciations of his father in his own ears,—the fierce feeling of degraded pride consequent upon his recent and present mode of life, and the desperate mood induced by his complete isolation from all the sympathies of his people, evinced by their vindictive pursuit of him—all conspired to make him the reckless wretch who would rather seek than shrink from the contemplated parricide. His determination was evident in the glance of his eye; and while he threw back the tomahawk, so that the sharp pick on the opposite end rested upon his right shoulder, and its edge lay alongside his cheek, he muttered between his firmly set teeth, fragments of the fearful scalp-song which he had sung in his mother's ear before.

> "Sangarrah-me—Sangarrah-me,
> I hear him groan, I see him gasp,
> I tear his throat, I drink his blood—
> Sangarrah-me—Sangarrah-me."

But the fierce old chief, undiscouraged, roused by the insult he had received by the defiance of his own son, sprang again towards him. Even while he sang the bloody anthem of the Yemassee, the fugitive, with desperate strength and feeling grappled the father by his throat, crying aloud to him, as he shook the hatchet in his eyes—

"I hear thee groan—I see thee gasp—I tear thy throat—I drink thy blood; for I know thee as mine enemy. Thou art not Sanutee—thou art not the father of Occonestoga—but a black dog, sent on his path to tear. Die, thou dog—thou black dog—die—thus I slay thee—thus I slay thee, thou enemy of Occonestoga."

And, handling the old man with a strength beyond his power to contend with, he aimed the deadly stroke directly at the eyes of his father. But the song and the speech had aroused the yet conscious but suffering Matiwan, and starting up from the ground where she had been lying, almost between the feet of the combatants, with uplifted hands she interposed, just as the fell direction had been given to the weapon of her son. The piercing shriek of that fondly cherishing mother went to the very bones of the young warrior. Her interposition had the effect of a spell upon him, particularly as, at the moment—so timely for Sanutee had been her interposition—he who gave the blow could with difficulty arrest the impulse with which it had been given, and which must have made it a blow fatal to her. The narrow escape which he had made, sent through the youth an unnerving chill and shudder. The deadly instrument fell from his hand, and now rushing upon him, the crowd drew him to the ground, and taking from him every other weapon, pinioned his arms closely behind him. He turned away with something of horror in his countenance as he met the second gaze of his father, and his eyes rested with a painful solicitude upon the wo-begone visage of Matiwan, who had, after her late effort, again sunk down at the feet of Sanutee. He looked fondly, but sadly upon her, and, with a single sentence addressed to her, he offered no obstacle while his captors led him away.

"Matiwan—" said he,— "thou hast bound Occonestoga for his enemies. Thou hast given him up to Opitchi-Manneyto."

The woman heard no more, but, as they bore him off, she sank down in momentary insensibility upon the spot where she had been crouching through the greater part of the previous scene. Sanutee, meanwhile, with much of the character of ancient Roman patriotism, went forth with the rest, on the way to the council; one of the judges— indeed the chief arbiter upon the destinies of his son. There was no delay among the red men, in the work of justice. The midnight was not less sacred than the sunlight, when the victim was ready for the executioner.

Chapter Twenty-five

"The pain of death is nothing. To the chief,
The forest warrior, it is good to die—
To die as he has lived, battling and hoarse,
Shouting a song of triumph. But to live
Under such doom as this, were far beyond
Even his stoic, cold philosophy."

IT was a gloomy amphitheatre in the deep forests to which the assembled multitude bore the unfortunate Occonestoga. The whole scene was unique in that solemn grandeur, that sombre hue, that deep spiritual repose, in which the human imagination delights to invest the region which has been rendered remarkable for the deed of punishment or crime. A small swamp or morass hung upon one side of the wood, from the rank bosom of which, in numberless millions, the flickering fire-fly perpetually darted upwards, giving a brilliance and animation to the spot, which, at that moment, no assemblage of light or life could possibly enliven. The ancient oak, a bearded Druid, was there to contribute to the due solemnity of all associations—the green but gloomy cedar, the ghostly cypress, and here and there the overgrown pine,—all rose up in their primitive strength, and with an undergrowth around them of shrub and flower, that scarcely, at any time, in that sheltered and congenial habitation, had found it necessary to shrink from winter. In the centre of the area thus invested, rose a high and venerable mound, the tumulus of many preceding ages, from the washed sides of which might now and then be seen protruding the bleached bones of some ancient warrior or sage. A circle of trees, at a little distance, hedged it in,—made secure and sacred by the performance there of many of their religious rites and offices,—themselves, as they bore the broad arrow of the Yemassee, being free from all danger of overthrow or desecration by Indian hands.

Amid the confused cries of the multitude, they bore the captive to the foot of the tumulus, and bound him backward, half reclining upon a tree. An hundred warriors stood around, armed according to the manner of the nation, each with a tomahawk, and knife, and bow. They stood up as for battle, but spectators simply, and took no part in a proceeding which belonged entirely to the priesthood. In a wider and denser circle, gathered hundreds more—not the warriors, but the people—the old, the young, the women, and the children, all fiercely excited and anxious to see a ceremony, so awfully exciting to an Indian imagination; involving, as it did, not only the perpetual loss of human caste and national consideration, but the eternal doom, the degradation, the denial of, and the exile from, their simple forest heaven. Interspersed with this latter crowd, seemingly at regular intervals, and with an allotted labour assigned them, came a number of old women, not unmeet representatives, individually, for either of the weird sisters of the Scottish Thane,

> "So withered and so wild in their attire—"

and, regarding their cries and actions, of whom we may safely affirm, that they looked like any thing but inhabitants of earth! In their hands they bore, each of them, a flaming torch, of the rich and gummy pine; and these they waved over the heads of the multitude in a thousand various evolutions, accompanying each movement with a fearful cry, which, at regular periods, was chorussed by the assembled mass. A bugle, a native instrument of sound, five feet or more in length, hollowed out from the commonest timber—the cracks and breaks of which were carefully sealed up with the resinous gum oozing from their burning torches, and which, to this day, borrowed from the natives, our negroes employ on the southern waters with a peculiar compass and variety of note—was carried by one of the party, and gave forth at intervals, timed with much regularity, a long, protracted, single blast, adding greatly to the wild and picturesque character of the spectacle. At the articulation of these sounds, the circles continued to contract, though slowly; until, at length, but a brief space lay between the armed warriors, the crowd, and the unhappy victim.

The night grew dark of a sudden, and the sky was obscured by one of the brief tempests that usually usher in the summer, and mark the transition, in the south, of one season to another. A wild gust rushed along the wood. The leaves were whirled over the heads of the assemblage, and the trees bent downwards, until they cracked and groaned again beneath the wind. A feeling of natural superstition crossed the minds of the multitude, as the hurricane, though common enough in that region, passed hurriedly along; and a spontaneous and universal voice of chaunted prayer rose from the multitude, in their own wild and emphatic language, to the evil deity whose presence they beheld in its progress:

> "Thy wing, Opitchi-Manneyto,
> It o'erthrows the tall trees—
> Thy breath, Opitchi-Manneyto,
> Makes the waters tremble—
> Thou art in the hurricane,
> When the wigwam tumbles—
> Thou art in the arrow-fire,
> When the pine is shiver'd—
> But upon the Yemassee,
> Be thy coming gentle—
> Are they not thy well-beloved?
> Bring they not a slave to thee?
> Look! the slave is bound for thee,
> 'Tis the Yemassee that brings him.
> Pass, Opitchi-Manneyto—
> Pass, black spirit, pass from us—
> Be thy passage gentle."

And, as the uncouth strain rose at the conclusion into a diapason of unanimous and contending voices, of old and young, male and female, the brief summer tempest had gone by. A shout of self-gratulation, joined with warm acknowledgments, testified the popular sense and confidence in that especial Providence, which even the most barbarous nations claim as for ever working in their behalf.

At this moment, surrounded by the chiefs, and preceded by the great prophet or high-priest, Enoree-Mattee, came Sanutee, the well-beloved of the Yemassee, to preside over the destinies of his son. There was a due and becoming solemnity, but nothing of the peculiar feelings of the father, visible in his countenance. Blocks of wood were placed around as seats for the chiefs, but Sanutee and the prophet threw themselves, with more of imposing veneration in the proceeding, upon the edge of the tumulus, just where an overcharged spot, bulging out with the crowding bones of its inmates, had formed an elevation answering the purpose of couch or seat. They sat, directly looking upon the prisoner, who reclined, bound securely upon his back to a decapitated tree, at a little distance before them. A signal having been given, the women ceased their clamours, and approaching him, they waved their torches so closely above his head as to make all his features distinctly visible to the now watchful and silent multitude. He bore the examination with stern, unmoved features, which the sculptor in brass or marble might have been glad to transfer to his statue in the block. While the torches waved, one of the women now cried aloud, in a barbarous chant, above him:—

> "Is not this a Yemassee?
> Wherefore is he bound thus—
> Wherefore, with the broad arrow
> On his right arm growing,
> Wherefore is he bound thus—
> Is not this a Yemassee?"

A second woman now approached him, waving her torch in like manner, seeming closely to inspect his features, and actually passing her fingers over the emblem upon his shoulder, as if to ascertain more certainly the truth of the image. Having done this, she turned about to the crowd, and in the same barbarous sort of strain with the preceding, replied as follows:—

> "It is not the Yemassee,
> But a dog that runs away.
> From his right arm take the arrow,
> He is not the Yemassee."

As these words were uttered, the crowd of women and children around cried out for the execution of the judgment thus given, and once again flamed the torches wildly, and the shoutings were general among the multitude. When they had subsided, a huge Indian came forward, and sternly confronted the prisoner. This man was Malatchie, the executioner; and he looked the horrid trade which he professed. His garments were stained and smeared with blood and covered with scalps, which, connected together by slight strings, formed a loose robe over his shoulders. In one hand he carried a torch, in the other a knife. He came forward, under the instructions of Enoree-Mattee, the prophet, to claim the slave of Opitchi-Manneyto,—that is, in our language, the slave of hell. This he did in the following strain:—

> "'Tis Opitchi-Manneyto
> In Malatchie's ear that cries,
> This is not the Yemassee—
> And the woman's word is true—
> He's a dog that should be mine,
> I have hunted for him long.
> From his master he had run,
> With the stranger made his home,
> Now I have him, he is mine—
> Hear Opitchi-Manneyto."

And, as the besmeared and malignant executioner howled his fierce demand in the very ears of his victim, he hurled the knife which he carried, upwards with such dexterity into the air, that it rested, point downward, and sticking fast on its descent into the tree and just above the head of the doomed Occonestoga. With his hand, the next instant, he laid a resolute gripe upon the shoulder of the victim, as if to confirm and strengthen his claim by actual possession; while, at the same time, with a sort of malignant pleasure, he thrust his besmeared and distorted visage close into the face of his prisoner. Writhing against the ligaments which bound him fast, Occonestoga strove to turn his head aside from the disgusting and obtrusive presence; and the desperation of his effort, but that he had been too carefully secured, might have resulted in the release of some of his limbs; for the breast heaved and laboured, and every muscle of his arms and legs was wrought, by his severe action, into so many ropes, hard, full, and indicative of prodigious strength.

There was one person in that crowd who sympathized with the victim. This was Hiwassee, the maiden in whose ears he had uttered a word, which, in her thoughtless scream and subsequent declaration of the event, when she had identified him, had been the occasion of his captivity. Something of self-reproach for her share in his misfortune, and an old feeling of regard for Occonestoga, who had once been a favourite with the young of both sexes among his people, was at work in her bosom; and, turning to Echotee, her newly-accepted lover, as soon as the demand of Malatchie had been heard, she prayed him to resist the demand. In such cases, all that a warrior had to do was simply to join issue upon the claim, and the popular will then determines the question. Echotee could not resist an application so put to him, and by one who had just listened to a prayer of his own, so all-important to his own happiness; and being himself a noble youth, one who had been a rival of the captive in his better days, a feeling of generosity combined with the request of Hiwassee, and he boldly leaped forward. Seizing the knife of Malatchie, which stuck in the tree, he drew it forth and threw it upon the ground, thus removing the sign of property which the executioner had put up in behalf of the evil deity.

"Occonestoga is the brave of the Yemassee," exclaimed the young Echotee, while the eyes of the captive looked what his lips could not have said. "Occonestoga is a brave of Yemassee—he is no dog of Malatchie. Wherefore is the cord upon the limbs of a free warrior? Is not Occonestoga a free warrior of Yemassee? The eyes of Echotee have looked upon a warrior like Occonestoga, when he took many scalps. Did not Occonestoga lead the Yemassee against the Savannahs? The eyes of Echotee saw him slay the red-eyed Suwannee, the great chief of the Savannahs. Did not Occonestoga go on the war-path with our young braves against the Edistoes, the brown-foxes that came out of the swamp? The eyes of Echotee beheld him. Occonestoga is a brave, and a hunter of Yemassee—he is not the dog of Malatchie. He knows not fear. He hath an arrow with wings, and the panther he runs down in the chase. His tread is the tread of a sly serpent that comes, so that he hears him not, upon the track of the red deer, feeding down in the valley. Echotee knows the warrior—Echotee knows the hunter—he knows Occonestoga, but he knows no dog of Opitchi-Manneyto."

"He hath drunk of the poison drink of the pale-faces—his feet are gone from the good path of the Yemassee—he would sell his people to the English for a painted bird. He is the slave of Opitchi-Manneyto," cried Malatchie, in reply. Echotee was not satisfied to yield the point so soon, and he responded accordingly.

"It is true. The feet of the young warrior have gone away from the good paths of the Yemassee, but I see not the weakness of the chief, when my eye looks back upon the great deeds of the warrior. I see nothing but the shrinking body of Suwannee under the knee, under the knife of the Yemassee. I hear nothing but the war-whoop of the Yemassee, when we broke through the camp of the brown-foxes, and scalped them where they skulked in the swamp. I see this Yemassee strike the foe and take the scalp, and I know Occonestoga—Occonestoga, the son of the well-beloved—the great chief of the Yemassee."

"It is good—Occonestoga has thanks for Echotee—Echotee is a brave warrior!" murmured the captive to his champion, in tones of melancholy acknowledgment. The current of public feeling began to set somewhat in behalf of the victim, and an occasional whisper to that effect might be heard here and there among the multitude. Even Malatchie himself looked for a moment as if he thought it not improbable that he might be defrauded of his prey; and, while a free shout from many attested the compliment which all were willing to pay to Echotee for his magnanimous defence of one who had once been a rival—and not always successful—in the general estimation, the executioner turned to the prophet and to Sanutee, as if doubtful whether or not to proceed farther in his claim. But all doubt was soon quieted, as the stern father rose before the assembly. Every sound was stilled in expectation of his words on this so momentous an occasion to himself. They waited not long. The old man had tasked all the energies of the patriot, not less than of the stoic, and having once determined upon the necessity of the sacrifice, he had no hesitating fears or scruples palsying his determination. He seemed not to regard the imploring glance of his son, seen and felt by all besides in the assembly; but, with a voice entirely unaffected by the circumstances of his position, he spoke forth the doom of the victim in confirmation with that originally expressed.

"Echotee has spoken like a brave warrior with a tongue of truth, and a soul that has birth with the sun. But he speaks out of his own heart—and does not speak to the heart of the traitor. The Yemassee will all say for Echotee, but who can say for Occonestoga when Sanutee himself is silent? Does the Yemassee speak with a double tongue? Did not the Yemassee promise Occonestoga to Opitchi-Manneyto with the other chiefs? Where are they? They are gone into the swamp, where the sun shines not, and the eyes of Opitchi-Manneyto are upon them. He knows them for his slaves. The arrow is gone from their shoulders, and the Yemassee knows them no longer.

Shall the dog escape, who led the way to the English—who brought the poison drink to the chiefs, which made them dogs to the English and slaves to Opitchi-Manneyto? Shall he escape the doom the Yemassee hath put upon them? Sanutee speaks the voice of the Manneyto. Occonestoga is a dog, who would sell his father—who would make our women to carry water for the pale-faces. He is not the son of Sanutee—Sanutee knows him no more. Look,—Yemassees—the well-beloved has spoken!"

He paused, and turning away, sank down silently upon the little bank on which he had before rested; while Malatchie, without further opposition—for the renunciation of his own son by one so highly esteemed as Sanutee, was conclusive against the youth—advanced to execute the terrible judgment upon his victim.

"Oh! father, chief, Sanutee, the well-beloved!"—was the cry that now, for the first time, burst convulsively from the lips of the prisoner—"hear me, father—Occonestoga will go on the war-path with thee, and with the Yemassee—against the Edisto, against the Spaniard—hear, Sanutee—he will go with thee against the English." But the old man bent not—yielded not, and the crowd gathered nigher in the intensity of their interest.

"Wilt thou have no ear, Sanutee?—it is Occonestoga—it is the son of Matiwan that speaks to thee." Sanutee's head sank as the reference was made to Matiwan, but he showed no other sign of emotion. He moved not—he spoke not—and bitterly and hopelessly the youth exclaimed—

"Oh! thou art colder than the stone-house of the adder—and deafer than his ears. Father, Sanutee, wherefore wilt thou lose me, even as the tree its leaf, when the storm smites it in summer? Save me, my father."

And his head sank in despair, as he beheld the unchanging look of stern resolve with which the unbending sire regarded him. For a moment he was unmanned: until a loud shout of derision from the crowd, as they beheld the show of his weakness, came to the support of his pride. The Indian shrinks from humiliation, where he would not shrink from death; and, as the shout reached his ears, he shouted back his defiance, raised his head loftily in air, and with the most perfect composure, commenced singing his song of death, the song of many victories.

"Wherefore sings he his death-song?" was the cry from many voices,— "he is not to die!"

"Thou art the slave of Opitchi-Manneyto," cried Malatchie to the captive— "thou shalt sing no lie of thy victories in the ear of Yemassee. The slave of Opitchi-Manneyto has no triumph"—and the words of the song were effectually drowned, if not silenced, in the tremendous clamour which they raised about him. It was then that Malatchie claimed his victim—the doom had been already given, but the ceremony of expatriation and outlawry was yet to follow, and under the direction of the prophet, the various castes and classes of the nation prepared to take a final leave of one who could no longer be known among them. First of all came a band of young marriageable women, who, wheeling in a circle three times about him, sang together a wild apostrophe containing a bitter farewell, which nothing in our language could perfectly embody.

"Go,—thou hast no wife in Yemassee—thou hast given no lodge to the daughter of Yemassee—thou hast slain no meat for thy children. Thou hast no name—the women of Yemassee know thee no more. They know thee no more."

And the final sentence was reverberated from the entire assembly—

"They know thee no more—they know thee no more."

Then came a number of the ancient men—the patriarchs of the nation, who surrounded him in circular mazes three several times, singing as they did so a hymn of like import.

"Go—thou sittest not in the council of Yemassee—thou shalt not speak wisdom to the boy that comes. Thou hast no name in Yemassee—the fathers of Yemassee, they know thee no more."

And again the whole assembly cried out, as with one voice—

"They know thee no more, they know thee no more."

These were followed by the young warriors, his old associates, who now, in a solemn band, approached him to go through a like performance. His eyes were shut as they came—his blood was chilled in his heart, and the articulated farewell of their wild chant failed seemingly to reach his ear. Nothing but the last sentence he heard—

> "Thou that wast a brother,
> Thou art nothing now—
> The young warriors of Yemassee,
> They know thee no more."

And the crowd cried with them— "they know thee no more."

"Is no hatchet sharp for Occonestoga?"—moaned forth the suffering savage. But his trials were only then begun. Enoree-Mattee now approached him with the words, with which, as the representative of the good Manneyto, he renounced him,—with which he denied him access to the Indian heaven, and left him a slave and an outcast, a miserable wanderer amid the shadows and the swamps, and liable to all the dooms and terrors which come with the service of Opitchi-Manneyto.

"Thou wast the child of Manneyto"—

sung the high priest in a solemn chant, and with a deep-toned voice that thrilled strangely amid the silence of the scene.

> "Thou wast a child of Manneyto,
> He gave thee arrows and an eye,—
> Thou wast the strong son of Manneyto,
> He gave thee feathers and a wing—
> Thou wast a young brave of Manneyto,
> He gave thee scalps and a war-song—
> But he knows thee no more—he knows thee no more."

And the clustering multitude again gave back the last line in wild chorus. The prophet continued his chant:

> "That Opitchi-Manneyto!—
> He commands thee for his slave—
> And the Yemassee must hear him,
> Hear, and give thee for his slave—
> They will take from thee the arrow,
> The broad arrow of thy people—
> Thou shalt see no blessed valley,
> Where the plum-groves always bloom—
> Thou shalt hear no song of valour,
> From the ancient Yemassee—
> Father, mother, name, and people,
> Thou shalt lose with that broad arrow,
> Thou art lost to the Manneyto—
> He knows thee no more, he knows thee no more."

The despair of hell was in the face of the victim, and he howled forth, in a cry of agony, that, for a moment, silenced the wild chorus of the crowd around, the terrible consciousness in his mind of that privation which the doom entailed upon him. Every feature was convulsed with emotion; and the terrors of Opitchi-Manneyto's dominion seemed already in strong exercise upon the muscles of his heart, when Sanutee, the father, silently approached him, and with a pause of a few moments, stood gazing upon the son from whom he was to be separated eternally—whom not even the uniting, the restoring hand of death could possibly restore to him. And he—his once noble son—the pride of his heart, the gleam of his hope, the triumphant warrior, who was even to increase his own glory, and transmit the endearing title of well-beloved, which the Yemassee had given him, to a succeeding generation—he was to be lost for ever! These promises were all blasted, and the father was now present to yield him up eternally—to deny him—to forfeit him, in fearful penalty to the nation whose genius he had wronged, and whose rights he had violated. The old man stood for a moment, rather, we may suppose, for the recovery of his resolution, than with any desire for the contemplation of the pitiable form before him. The pride of the youth came back to him,— the pride of the strong mind in its desolation—as his eye caught the inflexible gaze of his unswerving father; and he exclaimed bitterly and loud:—

"Wherefore art thou come—thou hast been my foe, not my father—away—I would not behold thee!" and he closed his eyes after the speech, as if to relieve himself from a disgusting presence.

"Thou hast said well, Occonestoga—Sanutee is thy foe—he is not thy father. To say this in thy ears has he come. Look on him, Occonestoga—look up, and hear thy doom. The young and the old of the Yemassee—the warrior and the chief,—they have all denied thee— all given thee up to Opitchi-Manneyto! Occonestoga is no name for the Yemassee. The Yemassee gives it to his dog. The prophet of Manneyto has forgotten thee—thou art unknown to those who were thy people. And I, thy father—with this speech, I yield thee to Opitchi-Manneyto. Sanutee is no longer thy father—thy father knows thee no more"—and once more came to the ears of the victim that melancholy chorus of the multitude— "He knows thee no more—he knows thee no more." Sanutee turned quickly away as he had spoken; and, as if he suffered more than he was willing to show, the old man rapidly hastened to the little mound where he had been previously sitting, his eyes averted from the further spectacle. Occonestoga, goaded to madness by these several incidents, shrieked forth the bitterest execrations, until Enoree-Mattee, preceding Malatchie, again approached. Having given some directions in an under-tone to the latter, he retired, leaving the executioner alone with his victim. Malatchie, then, while all was silence in the crowd—a thick silence, in which even respiration seemed to be suspended—proceeded to his duty; and, lifting the feet of Occonestoga carefully from the ground, he placed a log under them—then addressing him, as he again bared his knife which he struck in the tree above his head, he sung—

> "I take from thee the earth of Yemassee—
> I take from thee the water of Yemassee—
> I take from thee the arrow of Yemassee—
> Thou art no longer a Yemassee—
> The Yemassee knows thee no more."

"The Yemassee knows thee no more," cried the multitude, and their universal shout was deafening upon the ear. Occonestoga said no word now—he could offer no resistance to the unnerving hands of Malatchie, who now bared the arm more completely of its covering. But his limbs were convulsed with the spasms of that dreadful terror of the future which was racking and raging in every pulse of his heart. He had full faith in the superstitions of his people. His terrors acknowledged the full horrors of their doom. A despairing agony, which no language could describe, had possession of his soul. Meanwhile, the silence of all indicated the general anxiety; and Malatchie prepared to seize the knife and perform the operation, when a confused murmur arose from the crowd around; the mass gave way and parted, and, rushing wildly into the area, came Matiwan, his mother—the long black hair streaming—the features, an astonishing likeness to his own, convulsed like his; and her action that of one reckless of all things in the way of the forward progress she was making to the person of her child. She cried aloud as she came—with a voice that rang like a sudden death-bell through the ring—

"Would you keep the mother from her boy, and he to be lost to her for ever? Shall she have no parting with the young brave she bore in her bosom? Away, keep me not back—I will look upon, I will love him. He shall have the blessing of Matiwan, though the Yemassee and the Manneyto curse."

The victim heard, and a momentary renovation of mental life, perhaps a renovation of hope, spoke out in the simple exclamation which fell from his lips—

"Oh, Matiwan—oh, mother!"

She rushed towards the spot where she heard his appeal, and thrusting the executioner aside, threw her arms desperately about his neck.

"Touch him not, Matiwan," was the general cry from the crowd.— "Touch him not, Matiwan—Manneyto knows him no more."

"But Matiwan knows him—the mother knows her child, though the Manneyto denies him. Oh, boy—oh, boy, boy, boy." And she sobbed like an infant on his neck.

"Thou art come, Matiwan—thou art come, but wherefore?—to curse like the father—to curse like the Manneyto?" mournfully said the captive.

"No, no, no! Not to curse—not to curse. When did mother curse the child she bore? Not to curse, but to bless thee.—To bless thee and forgive."

"Tear her away," cried the prophet; "let Opitchi-Manneyto have his slave."

"Tear her away, Malatchie," cried the crowd, now impatient for the execution. Malatchie approached.

"Not yet—not yet," appealed the woman. "Shall not the mother say farewell to the child she shall see no more?" and she waved Malatchie back, and in the next instant drew hastily from the drapery of her dress a small hatchet, which she had there carefully concealed.

"What wouldst thou do, Matiwan?" asked Occonestoga, as his eye caught the glare of the weapon.

"Save thee, my boy—save thee for thy mother, Occonestoga—save thee for the happy valley."

"Wouldst thou slay me, mother—wouldst strike the heart of thy son?" he asked, with a something of reluctance to receive death from the hands of a parent.

"I strike thee but to save thee, my son:—since they cannot take the totem from thee after the life is gone. Turn away from me thy head— let me not look upon thine eyes as I strike, lest my hands grow weak and tremble. Turn thine eyes away—I will not lose thee."

His eyes closed, and the fatal instrument, lifted above her head, was now visible in the sight of all. The executioner rushed forward to interpose, but he came too late. The tomahawk was driven deep into the skull, and but a single sentence from his lips preceded the final insensibility of the victim.

"It is good, Matiwan, it is good—thou hast saved me—the death is in my heart." And back he sank as he spoke, while a shriek of mingled joy and horror from the lips of the mother announced the success of her effort to defeat the doom, the most dreadful in the imagination of the Yemassee.

"He is not lost—he is not lost. They may not take the child from his mother. They may not keep him from the valley of Manneyto. He is free—he is free." And she fell back in a deep swoon into the arms of Sanutee, who by this time had approached. She had defrauded Opitchi-Manneyto of his victim, for they may not remove the badge of the nation from any but the living victim.

Chapter Twenty-six

"For love and war are twins, and both are made
Of a strange passion, which misleads the sense,
And makes the feeling madness. Thus they grow,
The thorn and flower together, wounding oft
When most seductive."

Some men only live for great occasions. They sleep in the calm—but awake to double life, and unlooked for activity, in the tempest. They are the zephyr in peace, the storm in war. They smile until you think it impossible they should ever do otherwise, and you are paralyzed when you behold the change which an hour brings about in them. Their whole life in public would seem a splendid deception; and as their minds and feelings are generally beyond those of the great mass which gathers about, and in the end depends upon them, so they continually dazzle the vision and distract the judgment of those who passingly observe them. Such men become the tyrants of all the rest, and, as there are two kinds of tyranny in the world, they either enslave to cherish or to destroy.

Of this class was Harrison,—erratic, daring, yet thoughtful,—and not to be measured by such a mind as that of the pastor Matthews. We have seen his agency—a leading agency—in much of the business of the preceding narrative. It was not an agency of the moment, but of continued exertion, the result of a due recognition of the duties required at his hands. Nor is this agency to be discontinued now. He is still busy, and, under his direction and with his assistance, the sound of the hammer, and the deep echo of the axe, in the hands of Granger, the smith, and Hector, were heard without intermission in the Block House, "closing rivets up," and putting all things in a state of preparation for those coming dangers to the colony, which his active mind had predicted. He was not to be deceived by the thousand shows which are apt to deceive others. He looked more deeply into principles and the play of moods in other men, than is the common habit; and while few of the borderers estimated with him the amount of danger and difficulty which he felt to be at hand, he gave himself not the slightest trouble in considering their vague speculations, to which a liberal courtesy might have yielded the name of opinions. His own thoughts were sufficient for him; and while this indifference may seem to have been the product of an excessive self-esteem, we shall find in the sequel that, in the present case, it arose from a strong conviction, the legitimate result of a calm survey of objects and actions, and a cool and deliberate judgment upon them.

We have beheld some of Harrison's anxieties in the strong manifestation which he gave to Occonestoga, when he despatched the unfortunate young savage as a spy, on an adventure which had found such an unhappy and unlooked-for termination. Entirely ignorant of the event, it was with no small impatience that his employer waited for his return during the entire night and the better portion of the ensuing day. The distance was not so great between the two places, but that the fleet-footed Indian might have readily overcome it in a night; giving him sufficient allowance of time also for all necessary discoveries; and, doubtless, such would have been the case but for his ill-advised whisper in the ear of Hiwassee, and the not less ill-advised visit to the cottage of Matiwan. The affection of the mother for the fugitive and outlawed son, certainly, deserved no less acknowledgment; but, while it merited the most grateful returns,—such as the young chief, whatever might have been his faults and vices, yet cheerfully and fondly gave her—the indiscreet visit was sadly in conflict with the best policy of the warrior. His failure—the extent yet unknown to Harrison—left the latter doubtful whether to ascribe it to his misfortune, or to treachery; and this doubt contributed greatly to his solicitude. In spite of the suggestions of Granger, who knew that bad faith was not among the vices of the young warrior, he could not help suspecting him of deserting from the English cause as the only means by which to secure himself a reinstatement in the confidence of his people; and this suspicion, while it led to new preparations for the final issue, on the part of Harrison, was fruitful, at the same time, of exaggerated anxiety in his mind. To much of the drudgery of hewing and hammering, therefore, he subjected himself with the rest; and, though cheerful in its performance, the most

casual observer could have readily seen how much station and education had made him superior to such employments. Having thus
laboured for some time, he proceeded to other parts of his assumed
duties, and, at length, mounting his steed,—a favourite and fine
chestnut—and followed by Dugdale, who had been carefully muzzled,
he took his way, in a fleet gallop, through the intricacies of the surrounding country.

The mystery was a singular one which hung over Harrison in all
that region. It was strange how people loved him—how popular he
had become, even while in all his individual relations and objects so
perfectly unknown. He had somehow won golden opinions from all
the borderers, wild, untameable, and like the savages, as in many
cases they were; and the utmost confidence was placed in his opinions, even when, as at this time was the case, they happened to differ
from the general tenor of their own. This confidence, indeed, had
been partially given him, in the first instance, from the circumstance
of his having taken their lead suddenly, at a moment of great danger
and panic; when all were stricken with terror but himself; and none
knew what to do, and no one undertook to guide. Then it was, that,
with an audacity that looked like madness (but which is the best policy in time of peril), he fearlessly led forth a small party, taking the
initiative, in an encounter with the Coosaws. This was a reduced but
brave and desperate tribe, which had risen, without any other warning than the war-whoop, upon the Beaufort settlement. His valour on
this occasion, obtained from the Indians themselves the *nom de
guerre* of *Coosah-moray-te,* or the Coosaw-killer. It was one that
seems to have been well deserved, for, in that affair, the tribe nearly
suffered annihilation, and but a single town, that of *Coosaw-hatchie,*
or the refuge of the Coosaws, was left them of all their possessions.
The poor remains of their people from that time became incorpo-
rated with the Yemassees. Harrison's reckless audacity, cheerful freedom, mingled at the same time so strangely with playfulness and cool
composure, while exciting the strongest interest, created the warmest
regard among the foresters; and, though in all respects of residence
and family utterly unknown except to one, or at the most, to two
among them—appearing as he did, only now and then, and as suddenly disappearing—yet all were glad when he came, and sorry when
he departed. Esteeming him thus, they gave him the command of the
"green jackets," the small corps which, in that neighbourhood, the

affair of the Coosaws had first brought into something like a regular organization. He accepted this trust readily, but frankly assured his men that he might not be present—such were his labours elsewhere— at all times to discharge the duties. Such, however, was his popularity among them, that a qualification like this failed to affect their choice. They took him on his own terms, called him Captain Harrison, or, more familiarly, captain, and never troubled themselves for a single instant to inquire whether that were his right name or not; though, if they had any doubts, they never suffered them to reach, certainly never to offend, the ears of their commander. The pastor, rather more scrupulous, as he reflected upon his daughter, and her affections, lacked something of this confidence. We have seen how his doubts grew as his inquiries had been baffled. The reader, if he has not been altogether inattentive to the general progress of the narrative, has probably, at this moment, a more perfect knowledge of our hero than either of these parties.

But to return. Harrison rode away into the neighbouring country, all the settlements of which he appeared perfectly to know. His first visit in that quarter had been the result of curiosity in part, and partly in consequence of some public responsibilities coming with an official station, as by this time the reader will have conjectured. A new and warmer interest came with these duties soon after he had made the acquaintance of the beautiful Bess Matthews; and having involved his own affections with that maiden, it was not long before he found himself able to command hers. The father of Miss Matthews objected, as we have seen, not simply because nothing was certainly known of the family and social position of the lover; but because the latter had by his free bearing and perfect *aplomb*, outraged the self-esteem and dignity of the clerical dignitary. But love seldom seriously listens to the objections of a papa; and though Bess Matthews was as dutiful a damsel as ever dreamed of happiness, still her affections were a little too strong for parental authority. She loved Gabriel Harrison with a faith which preferred to confide where the pastor required that she should question; and the exhortations of the old gentleman had only the effect of increasing a passion which grows vigorous from restraint, and acquires obstinacy from compulsion.

But the lover went not forth on this occasion in quest of his mistress. His labours were more imposing, if less grateful. He went forth among his troop and their families. He had a voice of warning for all the neighbouring cottagers—a warning of danger, and an exhortation to the borderers to be in perfect readiness for its encounter, at the well-known signal. But his warning was in a word—an emphatic sentence—which, once uttered, affected in no particular his usual manner. To one and another he had the cheerful encouragement of the brother soldier—the dry sarcasm for the rustic gallant—the innocuous jest to the half-won maiden; and, with the ancient grand-sire or grandam, the exciting inquiry into old times—merry old England, or hilarious Ireland—or whatever other foreign fatherland might claim to possess their affections.

This adjusted, and having prepared all minds for events which his own so readily foresaw—having counselled the more exposed and feeble to the shelter of the Block House at the first sign of danger,—the lover began to take the place of the commander, and in an hour we find him in the ancient grove—the well-known place of tryst, in the neighbourhood of the dwelling of old Matthews. And she was there—the girl of seventeen—confiding, yet blushing at her own confidence, with an affection as warm as it was unqualified and pure. She hung upon his arm—she sat beside him, and the waters of the little brooklet gushed into music as they trickled on by their feet. The air was full of a song of love—the birds sang it—the leaves sighed it—the earth echoed, in many a replication, its delicious burden, and they felt it. There is no life, if there be no love. Love is the life of nature—all is unnatural without it. The golden bowl has no wine, if love be not at its bottom—the instrument has no music if love come not with the strain. "Let me perish, let me perish," was the murmured chant of Harrison, "when I cease to love—when others cease to love me."

So thought the two—so felt they—and an hour of delicious dreaming threw into their mutual souls a linked hope, which promised not merely a future and a lasting union to their forms, but an undecaying life to their affections. They felt in reality that love must be the life of heaven!

"Thou unmann'st me, Bess—thou dost, my Armida—the air is enchanted about thee, and the active energy which keeps me ever in motion when away from thee, is gone, utterly gone, when thou art nigh. I could now lie down in these delicious groves, and dream away the hours—dream away life. Do nothing but dream! Wherefore is it so? Thou art my tyrant—I am weak before thee—full of fears, Bess—timid as a child in the dark."

"Full of hopes too, Gabriel, is it not? And what is the hope if there be no fear—no doubt? They sweeten each other. I thy tyrant, indeed—

when thou movest me as thou willest. When I have eyes only for thy coming, and tears only at thy departure."

"And hast thou these always, Bess, for such occasions? Do thy smiles always hail the one, and thy tears always follow the other?—I doubt, Bess, if always."

"And wherefore doubt—thou hast eyes for mine, and canst see for thyself."

"True, but knowest thou not that the lover looks most commonly for the beauty, and not often for the sentiment of his sweetheart's face? It is this which they mean when the poets tell of love's blindness. The light of thine eye dims and dazzles the gaze of mine, and I must take the tale from thy lips—"

"And safely thou mayest, Gabriel—"

"May I—I hardly looked to find thee so consenting, Bess—" exclaimed the lover, taking her response in a signification rather at variance with that which she contemplated, and, before she was aware, warmly pressing her rosy mouth beneath his own.

"Not so—not so—" confused and blushing she exclaimed, withdrawing quickly from his grasp. "I meant to say—"

"I know—I know,—thou wouldst have said, I might safely trust to the declaration of thy lips—and so I do, Bess—and want no other assurance. I am happy that thy words were indirect, but I am better assured as it is, of what thou wouldst have said."

"Thou wilt not love me, Gabriel, that thus I favour thee—thou seest how weak is the poor heart which so waits upon thine, and wilt cease to love what is so quickly won."

"It is so pretty, thy chiding, Bess, that to have thee go on, it were well to take another assurance from thy lips."

"Now, thou shalt not—it is not right, Gabriel; besides my father has said—"

"What he should not have said, and will be sorry for saying. He has said that he knows me not, and indeed he does not, and shall not, so long as in my thought it is unnecessary, and perhaps unwise that I should be known to him."

"But, why not to me—why shouldst thou keep thy secret from me, Gabriel? Thou couldst surely trust it to my keeping."

"Aye, safely, I know, were it proper for thee to know any thing which a daughter should of right withhold from a father. But as I may not give my secret to him, I keep it from thee; not fearing thy integrity, but as thou shouldst not hold a trust without sharing thy confidence with a parent. Trust me, ere long he shall know all; but now, I may not tell him or thee. I may not speak a name in this neighbourhood, where, if I greatly err not, its utterance would make me fine spoil for the cunning Indians, who are about some treachery."

"What, the Yemassees?"

"Even they, and of this I would have you speak to your father. I would not foolishly alarm you, but go to him. Persuade him to depart for the Block House, where I have been making preparations for your comfort. Let him only secure you all till this vessel takes herself off. By that time we shall see how things go."

"But what has this vessel to do with it, Gabriel?"

"A great deal, Bess, if my apprehensions are well grounded; but the reasons are tedious by which I come to think so, and would only fatigue your ear."

"Not so, Gabriel—I would like to hear them, for of this vessel, or rather of her captain, my father knows something. He knew him well in England."

"Aye!" eagerly responded Harrison— "I heard that, you know; but, in reality, what is he?—who is he?"

"His name is Chorley, as you have heard him say. My father knew him when both were young. They come from the same part of the country. He was a wild, ill-bred profligate, so my father said, in his youth; unmanageable, irregular—left his parents, and without their leave went into a ship and became a sailor. For many years nothing was seen of him—by my father at least—until the other day, when, by some means or other, he heard of us, and made himself known just before your appearance. I never saw him to know or remember him before, but he knew me when a child."

"And do you know what he is—and his vessel?"

"Nothing but this. He makes voyages from St. Augustine and Cuba, and trades almost entirely with the Spaniards in that quarter."

"But why should he have no connexion here with us of that nature, or why is he here at all if his business be not with our people? And it seems that he hath no traffic with us—no communion for us, though he doth apparently commune with the red men. This is one of the grounds of my apprehension—not to speak of the affair of Hector, which is enough of itself to prove him criminal of purpose."

"Ah—his crew is ignorant of the language, and then he says, so he told us, he seeks to trade for furs with the Indians."

"Still not enough. None of these reasons are sufficient to keep his vessel from the landing, his men from the shore, and himself mysteriously rambling in the woods without offering at any object, unless it be the smuggling of our slaves. I doubt not he comes to deal with the Indians, but he comes as an emissary from the Spaniards, and it is our skins and scalps he is after, if any thing."

"Speak not so, Gabriel, you frighten me."

"Nay, fear not. There is no danger if we keep our eyes open, and can get your obstinate old precisian of a father to open his."

"Hush, Gabriel, remember he is my father." And she looked the rebuke which her lips uttered.

"Aye, Bess, I do remember it, or I would not bother my head five seconds about him. I should gather you up in my arms as the Pagan of old gathered up his domestic gods when the earthquake came, and be off with you without long deliberating whether a father were necessary to your happiness or not."

"Speak not so lightly, Gabriel, the subject is too serious for jest."

"It is, Bess, quite too serious for jest, and I do not jest, or if I do I can't help it. I was born a jester, after a fashion. That is to say, I am somewhat given to mixing my laughter with my sorrows; and my wisdom, if I have any, is always mingled with my smiles, without, I trust, forfeiting any of its own virtue by the mixture. This, indeed, is one of your father's objections to me as your suitor. He thinks me irreverent when I am only cheerful. I do not tie up my visage when I look upon you, as if I sickened of the thing I looked on—and he well knows how I detest that hypocritical moral starch, with which our would-be saints contrive to let the world see that sunshine is sin, and a smile of inborn felicity a defiance thrown in the teeth of the very God that prompts it."

"But my father is no hypocrite, Gabriel."

"Then why hoist his colours? He is too good a man, Bess, to be the instrument of hypocrisy, and much I fear me that he sometimes is. He has too much of the regular roundhead—the genuine, never-end-the-sermon manner of an old Noll sanctifier. I would forego a kiss—the sweetest, Bess, that thy lips could give—to persuade the old man, your father, but for a single moment, into a hearty, manly, honest, unsophisticated, downright laugh. A man that can laugh out honestly and heartily is not wholly evil, I am sure."

"It is true, Gabriel, he laughs not, but then he does not frown."

"Not at thee, Bess, not at thee: who could? But he does at me, most ferociously, and his mouth puckers up when his eye rises to mine, in all the involutions of a pine bur. But forgive me: it is not of this I would speak now. I will forgive, though I may not forget his sourness, if you can persuade him into a little caution at the present moment. There is danger, I am sure, and to him and you particularly. Your situation here is an exposed one. This sailor-friend or acquaintance of yours, is no friend if he deal with the Spaniards of St. Augustine; is most certainly an enemy, and most probably a pirate. I suspect him to be the latter, and have my eyes on him accordingly. As to the trade with the Indians that he talks of, it is all false, else why should he lie here so many days without change of position or any open intercourse with them? And then, what better evidence against him than the kidnapping of Hector?"

"But he has changed his position—his vessel has gone higher up the river."

"Since when?"

"Within the last three hours. Her movement was pointed out by my father as we stood together on the bluff fronting the house."

"Indeed, this must be seen to, and requires despatch. Come with me, Bess. To your father at once, and say your strongest fears and look your sweetest loves. Be twice as timid as necessary, utter a thousand fears and misgivings, so that we may persuade him to the shelter of the Block House."

"Where I may be as much as possible in the company of Master Gabriel Harrison. Is it not so?" and she looked up archly into his face. For once the expression of his look was grave, and his eye gazed deeply down into her own. With a sobriety of manner not unmixed with solemnity, he spoke—

"Ah, Bess, if I lose thee, I am myself lost! But come with me, I will see thee to the wicket, safe, ere I leave thee, beyond the province of the rattlesnake."

"Speak not of that," she quickly replied, with an involuntary shudder, looking around her as she spoke, to the neighbouring wood, which was now more that ever present to her mind, with the memories of that scene of terror. Harrison conducted her to the end of the grove, within sight of her father's cottage, and his last words at leaving her were those of urgent entreaty, touching her removal to the Block House.

Chapter Twenty-seven

"Away! thou art the slave of a base thought,
And hast no will of truth. I scorn thee now,
With my whole soul, as once, with my whole soul,
I held thee worthy."

B UT Bess Matthews was not left to solitude, though left by her lover. A new party came upon the scene, in the person of Hugh Grayson, emerging from the neighbouring copse, from the cover of which he had witnessed the greater portion of the interview between Harrison and the maiden. This unhappy young man, always a creature of the fiercest impulses, in a moment of the wildest delirium of that passion for Bess which had so completely swallowed up his better judgment, not less than all sense of high propriety, had been guilty, though almost unconscious at the time of the woful error, of a degree of espionage, for which, the moment after, he felt many rebukings of shame and conscience. Hurried on, however, by the impetuous impulse of the passion so distracting him, the fine sense, which should have been an impassable barrier, rising up like a wall in the way of such an act, had foregone its better control for the moment, and he had lingered sufficiently long under cover to incur the stigma, as he now certainly felt the shame, of having played the part of a spy. But his error had its punishment even in its own progress. He had seen that which contributed still more to increase his mortification, and to embitter his soul against the more successful rival, whose felicities he had beheld—scarcely able to clench the teeth in silence which laboured all the while to gnash in agony. With a cheek in which shame and a purposeless fury alike showed themselves, and seemed struggling for mastery, he now came forward; and approaching the maiden, addressed her as he did so with some common phrase of formal courtesy, which had the desired effect of making her pause for his approach. He steeled his quivering muscles into something like rigidity, while a vain and vague effort at a smile, like lightning from the cloud, strove visibly upon his features.

"It is not solitude, then," said he, "that brings Miss Matthews into the forest. Its shelter—its secrecy alone, is perhaps its highest recommendation."

"What is it that you mean, Master Grayson, by your words?" replied the maiden, while something of a blush tinged slightly the otherwise pale and lily complexion of her face.

"Surely I have spoken nothing mysterious. My thought is plain enough, I should think, were my only evidence in the cheek of Miss Matthews herself."

"My cheek speaks nothing for me, Master Grayson, which my tongue should shame to utter; and if you have spoken simply in reference to Gabriel—Master Harrison I mean—you have been at much unnecessary trouble. Methinks too, there is something in your own face that tells of a misplaced watchfulness on your part, where your neighbour holds no watch to be necesssary."

"You are right, Miss Matthews—you are right. There is—there should be, at least—in my face, acknowledgment enough of the baseness which led me as a spy upon your path—upon *his* path!" replied the young man, while his cheek grew once more alternately from ashes to crimson. "It was base, it was unmanly—but it has had its punishment—its sufficient punishment, believe me—in the discovery which it has made. I have seen that, Miss Matthews, which I would not willingly have seen; and which the fear to see, alone, prompted to the accursed survey. Pardon me, then—pity me, pity if you can—though I can neither well pardon nor pity myself."

"I do pardon you, sir—freely pardon you—for an error which I should not have thought it in your nature intentionally to commit; but what to pity you for, saving for the self-reproach which must come with your consciousness, I do not so well see. Your language is singular, Master Grayson."

"Indeed! Would I could be so blind! You have not seen, then—you know not? Look at me, Miss Matthews—is there no madness in my eyes—on my tongue—in look, word, action? Have I not raved in your ears—never?"

"No, as I live, never!" responded the astonished maiden. "Speak not in this manner, Master Grayson—but leave me—permit me to retire."

"What! you would go to him once more!" he uttered with a sarcastic grin. "You would follow him!—Recal him! Hear me, Bess Matthews. Do you know him—this stranger—this adventurer—this haughty pretender, whose look is presumption? Would you trust to him you know not? What is he? Can you confide in one whom nobody speaks for— whom nobody knows? Would you throw yourself upon ruin—into the arms of a stranger—a—"

"Sir, Master Grayson—this is a liberty—"

"License, rather, lady! The license of madness; for I am mad, though you see it not—an abandoned madman; degraded, as you have seen, and almost reckless of all things and thoughts, as all may see in time. God! is it not true? True it is, and you—you, Bess Matthews— you are the cause."

"I?—" replied the maiden, in unmixed astonishment.

"Aye, you. Hear me. I love—I loved you, Miss Matthews—have long loved you. We have been together almost from infancy; and I had thought—forgive the vanity of that thought, Bess Matthews—I had thought that you might not altogether have been unkind to me. For years I had this thought—did you not know it?—for years I lived on in the sweet hope—the dear promise which it hourly brought me—for years I had no life, if I had not this expectation! In an evil hour came this stranger—this Harrison—it is not long since—and from that moment I trembled. It was an instinct that taught me to fear, who had never feared before. I saw, yet dreaded to believe in what I saw. I suspected, and shrunk back in terror from my own suspicions. But they haunted me like so many damned spectres. They were everywhere around me, goading me to madness. In my mood, under this spur, I sunk into the spy. I became degraded,—and saw all—all! I saw his lip resting upon yours—warmly, passionately—and yours,—yours grew to its pressure, Bess Matthews, and did not seek to be withdrawn."

"No more of this, Master Grayson—thou hast thought strange and foolish things, and though they surprise me, I forgive them—I forgive thee. Thou hadst no reason to think that I was more to thee than to a stranger, that I could be more—and I feel not any self-reproach, for I have done naught and said naught which could have ministered to thy error. Thy unwise, not to say thy unbecoming and unmanly curiosity, Master Grayson, makes me the less sorry that thou shouldst know a truth which thou findest so painful to know."

"Oh, be less proud—less stern, Bess Matthews. Thou hast taken from this haughty stranger some of his bold assumption of superiority, till thou even forgettest that erring affection may have its claim upon indulgence."

"But not upon justice. I am not proud—thou dost me wrong, Master Grayson, and canst neither understand me nor the noble gentleman of whom thy words are disrespectful."

"And what is he, that I should respect him? Am I not as free—a man,—an honest man—and what is he more,—even if he be so much? Is he more ready to do and to dare for thee?—Is he stronger?—Will he fight for thee? Ha! if he will!—"

"Thou shalt make me no game-prize, even in thy thought, Master Grayson—and thy words are less than grateful to my ears. Wilt thou not leave me?"

"Disrespectful to him, indeed—a proud and senseless swaggerer, presuming upon his betters. I—"

"Silence, sir! think what is proper to manhood, and try to appear that which thou art not," exclaimed the aroused maiden, in a tone which completely startled her companion, while she gathered herself up to her fullest height, and waved him off with her hand. "Go, sir—thou hast presumed greatly, and thy words are those of a ruffian, as thy late conduct has been that of the hireling and the spy. Thou think that I loved thee!—that I thought of a spirit so ignoble as thine;—and it is such as thou that wouldst slander and defame my Gabriel,—he, whose most wandering thought could never compass the tithe of that baseness which makes up thy whole soul."

And as she spoke words of such bitter import, her eye flashed and the beautiful lips curled in corresponding indignation, while her entire expression of countenance was that of a divine rebuke. The offender trembled with convulsive and contradictory emotions, and, for a few moments after her retort had been uttered, remained utterly speechless. He felt the justice of her severity, though every thought and feeling, in that instant, taught him how unequal he was to sustain it. He had, in truth, spoken without clear intent, and his language had been in no respect under the dominion of reason. But he regained his energies as he beheld her, with an eye still flashing fire and a face covered with inexpressible dignity, moving scornfully away. He recovered, though with a manner wild and purposeless—his hands and eyes lifted imploringly—and chokingly, thus addressed her:—

"Leave me not—not in anger, Bess Matthews, I implore you. I have done you wrong—done *him* wrong, perhaps; and I am bitterly sorry!—" it was with a desperate rapidity that he uttered the last passage— "I have spoken unjustly, and like a madman. But forgive me. Leave me not with an unforgiving thought, since, in truth, I regret my error as deeply as you can possibly reprove it."

Proud and lofty in her sense of propriety, the affections of Bess Matthews were, nevertheless, not less gentle than her soul was high. She at once turned to the speaker, and the prayer was granted by her glance, ere her lips had spoken.

"I do—I do forgive thee, Master Grayson, in consideration of the time when we were both children. But thou hast said bitter words in mine ear, which thou wilt not hold it strange if I do not over-soon forget. But doubt not that I do forgive thee; and pray thee for thy own sake—for thy good name, and thy duty to thyself and to the good understanding which thou hast, and the honourable feeling which thou shouldst have,—that thou err not again so sadly. Greatly do I sorrow that thou shouldst waste thy thoughts on me—thy affections. Recover them, I pray thee, and find some one more worthy and more willing to requite thy love."

He seized her hand convulsively, gave it a swift, hard pressure, then resigned it as suddenly, and exclaimed—

"I thank thee! I thank thee!" he rushed away, and was soon buried from sight in the adjacent thicket.

Chapter Twenty-eight

"Thus human reason, ever confident,
Holds its own side—half erring and half right—
Not tutored by a sweet humility,
That else might safely steer."

BRED up amid privation, and tutored as much by its necessities as by a careful superintendence, Bess Matthews was a girl of courage, not less than of feeling. She could endure and enjoy; and the two capacities were so happily balanced in her character, that, while neither of them invaded the authority of the other, they yet happily neutralized any tendency to excess on either side. Still, however, her susceptibilities were great; for at seventeen the affections are not apt to endure much provocation; and, deeply distressed with the previous scene, and with that gentleness which was her nature, she grieved sincerely at the condition of a youth, of whom she had heretofore thought so favourably—but not to such a degree as to warrant the hope which he had entertained, and certainly without having held out to him any show of encouragement— she re-entered her father's dwelling, and immediately proceeded to her chamber. Though too much excited by her thoughts to enter with her father upon the topic suggested by Harrison, and upon which he had dwelt with such emphasis, she was yet strong and calm enough for a close self-examination. Had she said or done anything which might have misled Hugh Grayson? This was the question which her fine sense of justice not less than of maidenly propriety, dictated for her answer; and with that close and calm analysis of her own thoughts and feelings, which must always be the result of a due acquisition of just principles in education, she referred to all those unerring standards of the mind which virtue and common sense establish, for the satisfaction of her conscience, against those suggestions of doubt with which her feelings had assailed it, on the subject of her relations with that person. Her feelings grew more and more composed as the scrutiny progressed, and she rose at last from the couch upon which she had thrown herself, with a heart lightened at least of the care which a momentary doubt of its own propriety had inspired.

There was another duty to perform, which also had its difficulties. She sought her father in the adjoining chamber, and if she blushed in the course of the recital, in justice to maidenly delicacy, she at least did not scruple to narrate fully in his ears all the particulars of her recent meeting with Harrison, with a sweet regard to maidenly truth. We do not pretend to say that she dwelt upon details, or gave the questions and replies—the musings and the madnesses of the conversation—for Bess had experience enough to know that in old ears, such matters are usually tedious enough, and in this respect, they differ sadly from young ones. She made no long story of the meeting, though she freely told the whole; and with all her warmth and earnestness, as Harrison had counselled, she proceeded to advise her father of the dangers from the Indians, precisely as her lover had counselled herself.

The old man heard, and was evidently less than satisfied with the frequency with which the parties met. He had not denied Bess this privilege—he was not stern enough for that; and, possibly, knowing his daughter's character not less than her heart, he was by no means unwilling to confide freely in her. But still he exhorted, in good set but general language, rather against Harrison than with direct reference to the intimacy between the two. He gave his opinion on that subject too, unfavourably to the habit, though without uttering any distinct command. As he went on and warmed with his own eloquence, his help-mate,—an excellent old lady, who loved her daughter too well to see her tears and be silent—joined freely in the discourse, and on the opposite side of the question: so that, on a small scale, we are favoured with the glimpse of a domestic flurry, a slight summer gust, which ruffles to compose, and irritates to smooth and pacify. Rough enough for a little while, it was happily of no great continuance; for the old people had lived too long together, and were quite too much dependent on their mutual sympathies, to suffer themselves to play long at cross purposes. In ceasing to squabble, however, Mrs. Matthews gave up no point; and was too much interested in the present subject readily to forego the argument upon it. She differed entirely from her husband with regard to Harrison, and readily sided with her daughter in favouring his pretensions. He had a happy and singular knack of endearing himself to most people; and the very levity which made him distasteful to the pastor, was, strange to say, one of the chief influences which commended him to his lady.

"Bess is wrong, my dear," at length said the pastor, in a tone and manner meant to be conclusive on the subject— "Bess is wrong— decidedly wrong. We know nothing of Master Harrison—neither of his family nor of his pursuits—and she should not encourage him."

"Bess is right, Mr. Matthews," responded the old lady, with a doggedness of manner meant equally to close the controversy, as she wound upon her fingers, from a little skreel in her lap, a small volume of the native silk.*— "Bess is right—Captain Harrison is a nice gentleman—always so lively, always so polite, and so pleasant. I declare, I don't see why you don't like him, and it must be only because you love to go against all other people."

"And so, my dear," gently enough responded the pastor, "you would have Bess married to a—nobody knows who or what."

"Why, dear me, John—what is it you don't know? I'm sure I know everything I want to know about the captain. His name's Harrison— and—"

"What more?" inquired the pastor with a smile, seeing that the old lady had finished her silk and speech at the same moment.

"Why nothing, John—but what we do know, you will admit, is highly creditable to him; and so, I do not see why you should be so quick to restrain the young people, when we can so easily require to know all that is necessary before we consent, or any decisive step is taken."

---

* The culture of silk was commenced in South Carolina as far back as the year 1702, and thirteen years before the date of this narrative. It was introduced by Sir Nathaniel Johnston, then holding the government of the province under the lords proprietors. This gentleman, apart from his own knowledge of the susceptibility, for its production, of that region, derived a stimulus to the prosecution of the enterprise from an exceeding great demand then prevailing in England for the article. The spontaneous and free growth of the mulberry in all parts of the southern country first led to the idea that silk might be made an important item in the improving list of its products. For a time he had every reason to calculate upon the entire success of the experiment, but after a while, the pursuit not becoming immediately productive, did not consort with the impatient nature of the southrons, and was given over—when perhaps wanting but little of complete success. The experiment, however, was prosecuted sufficiently long to show, though it did not become an object of national importance, how much might, with proper energy, be done towards making it such. Of late days, a new impulse has been given to the trial, and considerable quantities of silk are annually made in the middle country of South Carolina.

"But, my dear, the decisive step is taken when the affections of our daughter are involved."

The old lady could say nothing to this, but she had her word.

"He is such a nice, handsome gentleman, John."

"Handsome is as handsome does!" sneered the pastor, through a homely proverb.

"Well, but John, he's in no want of substance. He has money, good gold in plenty, for I've seen it myself—and I'm sure that's a sight for sore eyes, after we've been looking so long at the brown paper that the Assembly have been printing, and which they call money. Gold now is money, John, and Captain Harrison always has it."

"It would be well to know where it comes from," doggedly muttered the pastor.

"Oh, John, John—where's all your religion? How can you talk so? You are only vexed now—I'm certain that's it—because Master Harrison won't satisfy your curiosity."

"Elizabeth!"

"Well, don't be angry now, John. I didn't mean that exactly, but really you are so uncharitable. It's neither sensible nor Christian in you. Why will you be throwing up hills upon hills in the way of Bess's making a good match?"

"Is it a good match, Elizabeth?—that is the very point which makes me firm."

"Stubborn, you mean."

"Well, perhaps so, Elizabeth, but stubborn I will be until it is shown to be a good match, and then he may have her with all my heart. It is true, I love not his smart speeches, which are sometimes quite too free; and not reverend and scarcely respectful. But I shall not mind that, if I can find out certainly who he is, and that he comes of good family, and does nothing disreputable. Remember, Elizabeth, we come of good family ourselves—old England can't show a better; and we must be careful to do it no discredit by a connection for our child."

"That is all true and very sensible, Mr. Matthews, and I agree with you whenever you talk to the point. Now you will admit, I think, that I know when a gentleman is a gentleman, and when he is not—and I tell you that if Master Harrison is not a gentleman, then give me up, and don't mind my opinion again. I don't want spectacles to see that he comes of good family and is a gentleman."

"Yes, your opinion may be right; but still it is opinion only—not evidence; and, if it be wrong—what then? The evil will be past remedy."

"It can't be wrong. When I look upon him, I'm certain—so graceful and polite, and then his dignity and good-breeding."

"Good-breeding, indeed!" and this exclamation the pastor accompanied with a most irreverend chuckle, which had in it a touch of bitterness. "Go to your chamber, Bess, my dear," he said turning to his daughter, who, sitting in a corner rather behind her mother, with head turned downwards to the floor, had heard the preceding dialogue with no little interest and disquiet. She obeyed the mandate in silence, and when she had gone, the old man resumed his exclamation.

"Good-breeding, indeed! when he told me, to my face, that he would have Bess in spite of my teeth."

The old lady now chuckled in earnest, and the pastor's brow gloomed accordingly.

"Well, I declare, John, that only shows a fine-spirited fellow. Now, as I live, if I were a young man, in the same way, and were to be crossed after this fashion, I'd say the same thing. That I would. I tell you, John, I see no harm in it, and my memory's good, John, that you had some of the same spirit in our young days."

"Your memory's quite too good, Elizabeth, and the less you let it travel back the better for both of us," was the somewhat grave response. "But I have something to say of young Hugh—Hugh Grayson, I mean. Hugh really loves Bess—I'm certain quite as much as your Captain Harrison. Now, we know him?"

"Don't speak to me of Hugh Grayson, Mr. Matthews—for it's no use. Bess don't care a straw for him."

"A fine, sensible young man, very smart, and likely to do well."

"A sour, proud upstart—idle and sulky—who does nothing, though, as we all know, he's got nothing in the world."

"Has your Harrison any more?"

"And if he hasn't, John Matthews—let me tell you at least he's a very different person from Hugh Grayson, besides being born and bred a gentleman."

"I'd like to know, Elizabeth, how you come at that fact, that you speak it so confidently."

"Leave a woman alone for finding out a gentleman bred from one that is not; it don't want study and witnesses to tell the difference betwixt them. We can tell at a glance."

"Indeed! But I see it's of no use to talk with you now. You are bent on having things all your own way. As for the man, I believe you are almost as much in love with him as your daughter." And this was said with a smile meant for compromise; but the old lady went on gravely enough for earnest.

"And it's enough to make me, John, when you are running him down from morning to night, though you know we don't like it. But that's neither here nor there. His advice is good, and he certainly means it for our safety. Will you do as Bess said, and shall we go to the Block House, till the Indians become quiet again?"

"His advice, indeed! You help his plans wondrously. But I see through his object if you do not. He only desires us at the Block House, in order to be more with Bess than he possibly can be at present. He is always there, or in the neighbourhood."

"And you are sure, John, there's no danger from the Indians?"

"None, none in the world. They are as quiet as they well can be, under the repeated invasion of their grounds by the borderers, who are continually hunting in their woods. By the way, I must speak to young Grayson on the subject. He is quite too frequently over the bounds, and they like him not."

"Well, well—but this insurrection, John?"

"Was a momentary commotion, suppressed instantly by the old chief Sanutee, who is friendly to us, and whom they have just made their great chief, or king, in place of Huspah, whom they deposed. Were they unkindly disposed, they would have destroyed, and not have saved, the Commissioners."

"But Harrison knows a deal more of the Indians than any body else; and then they say that Sanutee himself drove Granger out of Pocota-ligo."

"Harrison says more than he can unsay, and pretends to more than he can ever know; and I heed not his opinion. As for the expulsion of Granger, I do not believe a word of it."

"I wish, John, you would not think so lightly of Harrison. You remember he saved us when the Coosaws broke out. His management did every thing then. Now, don't let your ill opinion of the man stand in the way of proper caution. Remember, John,—your wife—your child."

"I do, Elizabeth; but you are growing a child yourself."

"You don't mean to say I'm in my dotage?" said the old lady, quickly and sharply.

"No, no, not that," and he smiled for an instant— "only, that your timidity does not suit your experience. But I have thought seriously on the subject of this threatened outbreak, and, for myself, can see nothing to fear from the Yemassees. There is nothing to justify these suspicions of Master Harrison. On the contrary, they have not only always been friendly heretofore, but they appear friendly now. Several of them, as you know, have professed to me a serious conviction of the truth of those divine lessons which I have taught them; and when I know this, it would be a most shameful desertion of my duty were I to doubt those solemn avowals which they have made, through my poor instrumentality, to the Deity."

"Well, John, I hope you are right, and that Harrison is wrong; though, I confess, I'm dubious. To God I leave it to keep us from evil: in his hands there are peace and safety."

"Amen, amen!" fervently responded the pastor, as he spoke to his retiring dame, who, gathering up her working utensils, was about to pass into the adjoining chamber; but lingered, as the Parson followed her with a few more last words.

"Amen, Elizabeth—though, I must say, the tone of your expressed reliance upon God has still in it much that is doubting and unconfiding. Let us add to the prayer one for a better mood along with the better fortune."

Here the controversy ended; the old lady, as her husband alleged, still unsatisfied, and the preacher himself not altogether assured in his own mind that a lurking feeling of hostility to Harrison, rather than a just sense of his security, had not determined him to risk the danger from the Indians, in preference to a better hope of security in the shelter of the Block House.

Chapter Twenty-nine

"I must dare all myself. I cannot dare
Avoid the danger. There is in my soul,
That which may look on death, but not on shame."

As soon as his interview was over with Bess Matthews, Harrison hurried back to the Block House. He there received intelligence confirming that which she had given him, concerning the movements of Chorley and his craft. The strange vessel had indeed taken up anchors and changed her position. Availing herself of a favouring breeze, she had ascended the river, a few miles nigher to the settlements of the Yemassees, and now lay fronting the left wing of the pastor's cottage;—the right of it, as it stood upon the jutting tongue of land around which wound the river, she had before fronted from below. The new position could only have been chosen for the facility of intercourse with the Indians, which, from the lack of a good landing on this side of the river, had been wanting to her where she originally lay. In addition to this intelligence, Harrison learned that which still further quickened his anxieties. The wife of Granger, a woman of calm, stern, energetic disposition, who had been something more observant than her husband, informed him that there had been a considerable intercourse already between the vessel and the Indians since her remove—that their boats had been around her constantly during the morning, and that boxes and packages of sundry kinds had been carried from her to the shore; individual Indians, too, had been distinguished walking her decks; a privilege which, it was well known, had been denied to the whites, who had not been permitted the slightest intercourse with the stranger. All this confirmed the already active apprehensions of Harrison. He could no longer doubt of her intentions, or of the intentions of the Yemassees; yet, how to proceed—how to prepare—on whom to rely—in what quarter to look for the attack, and what was the extent of the proposed insurrection?—was it partial, or general? Did it include the Indian nations generally—twenty–eight of which, at that time, occupied the Carolinas—or was it confined to the Yemassees and Spaniards? and if the latter were concerned, were they to be looked for in force, and whether by land or by sea? These were the mutiplied questions, and to resolve them was the great difficulty in the way of Harrison. That there were now large grounds for suspicion, he could no longer doubt; but how to proceed in arousing the people, and whether it were necessary to arouse the colony at large, or only that portion of it more immediately in contact with the Indians—and how to inform them in time for the crisis which he now felt was at hand, and which might involve the fate of the infant colony—all depended upon the correctness of his acquired information;—and yet his fugitive spy came not back, sent no word, and might have betrayed his mission.

The doubts grew with their contemplation. The more he thought of the recent Yemassee discontents, the more he dreaded to think. He knew that this discontent was not confined to the Yemassee, but extended even to the waters of the Keowee and to the Apalachian mountains. The Indians had suffered on all sides from the obtrusive borderers, and had been treated, he felt conscious, with less than respect and justice by the provincial government itself. But a little time before, the voluntary hostages of the Cherokees had been entertained with indignity and harshness by the Assembly of Carolina; having been incarcerated in a dungeon, under cruel circumstances of privation, which the Cherokees at large did not appear to feel in a less degree than the suffering hostages themselves, and were pacified with extreme difficulty. The full array of these circumstances, to the mind of Harrison, satisfied him of the utter senselessness of any confidence in that friendly disposition of the natives, originally truly felt, but which had been so repeatedly abused as to be no longer entertained, or only entertained as a mask to shelter feelings directly opposite in character. The increasing consciousness of danger, and the failure of Occonestoga, on whose intelligence he had so greatly depended, momentarily added to his disquiet, by leaving him entirely at a loss, as to the time, direction, and character of that danger, which it had been his wish and province to provide against. Half soliloquizing as he thought, and half addressing Granger, who stood beside him in the upper and habitable room of the Block House, the anxieties of Harrison found their way to his lips.

"Bad enough, Granger—and yet what to do—how to move—for there's little use in moving without a purpose. We can do nothing without intelligence, and that we must have though we die for it. We must seek and find out their aim, their direction, their force, and what they depend upon. If they come alone we can manage them, unless they scatter simultaneously upon various points and take us by surprise, and this, if I mistake not, will be their course. But I fear this sailor-fellow brings them an ugly coadjutor in the power of the Spaniard. He comes from St. Augustine evidently; and may bring them men—a concealed force, and this accounts for his refusal to admit any of our people on board. The boxes too,—did you mark them well, Granger?"

"As well as I might, sir, from the Chief's Bluff."

"And what might they contain, think you?"

"Goods and wares, sir, I doubt not: blankets perhaps—"

"Or muskets and gunpowder. Your thoughts run upon nothing but stock in trade, and the chance of too much competition. Now, is it not quite as likely that those boxes held hatchets, and knives, and fire-arms? Were they not generally of one size and shape—long, narrow—eh? Did you note that?"

"They were, my lord, all of one size, as you described them. I saw that myself, and so I said to Richard, but he did not mind."

Thus spoke the wife of Granger, in reply to the question which had been addressed to her husband.

"Did you speak to me?" was the stern response of Harrison, in a tone of voice and severity not usually employed by the speaker, accompanying his speech by a keen penetrating glance, which, passing alternately from husband to wife, seemed meant to go through them both.

"I did speak to you, sir,—and you will forgive me for having addressed any other than Captain Harrison," she replied, composedly and calmly, though in a manner meant to conciliate and excuse the inadvertence of which she had been guilty in conferring upon him a title which in that region it seemed his policy to avoid. Then, as she beheld that his glance continued to rest in rebuke upon the shrinking features of her husband, she proceeded thus—

"You will forgive him too, sir, I pray you; but it is not so easy for a husband to keep any secret from his wife, and least of all, such as that which concerns a person who has provoked so much interest in us all."

"You are adroit, mistress, and your husband owes you much. A husband does find it difficult to keep any thing secret from his wife but his own virtues; and of these she seldom dreams. But pray, when was this wonderful revelation made to you?"

"You were known to me, sir, ever since the Foresters made you captain, just after the fight with the Coosaws at Tulifinnee Swamp."

"Indeed!" was the reply; "well, my good dame, you have had my secret long enough to keep it now. I am persuaded you can keep it better than your husband. How now, Granger! you would be a politician too, and I am to have the benefit of your counsels, and you would share mine. Is't not so—and yet, you would fly to your chamber, and share them with a tongue, which, in the better half of the sex, would wag it on every wind, from swamp to sea, until all points of the compass grew wiser upon it."

"Why, captain," replied the trader, half stupidly, half apologetically— "Moll is a close body enough."

"So is not Moll's worser half," was the reply. "But no more of this folly. There is much for both of us to do, and not a little for you in particular, if you will do it."

"Speak, sir, I will do much for you, captain."

"And for good pay. This it is. You must go to the Yemassees—to Pocota-ligo—see what they do, find out what they design, and look after Occonestoga—are you ready?"

"It were a great risk, captain, at this time."

"Why, true, and life itself is a risk. We breathe not an instant without hazard of its loss, and a plumstone, to an open mouth at dinner, is quite as perilous as the tenth bullet. Sleep is a risk, and one presses not his pillow o'nights, without a prayer against eternity before morning. Show me the land where we risk nothing, and I will risk all to get there."

"It's as much as my life's worth, captain."

"Psha! we can soon count up that. Thou art monstrous fond of thy carcass, now, and by this I know thou art growing wealthy. We shall add to thy gains, if thou wilt go on this service. The Assembly will pay thee well, as they have done before. Thou hast not lost by its service."

"Nothing, sir—but have gained greatly. In moderate adventure, I am willing to serve them now; but not in this. The Yemassees were friendly enough then, and so was Sanutee. It is different now, and all the favour I could look for from the old chief, would be a stroke of his hatchet, to save me from fire-torture."

"But why talk of detection? I do not desire that thou shouldst allow thyself to be taken. Think you, when I go into battle, the thought of being shot ever troubles me? No. If I thought that, I should not perhaps go. My only thought is how to shoot others; and you should think, in this venture, not of your own, but the danger of those around you. You are a good Indian hunter, and have practised all their arts. Take the swamp—hug the tree—line the thicket—see and hear, nor shout till you are out of the wood. There's no need to thrust your nose into the Indian kettles."

"It might be done, captain; but if caught, it would be so much the worse for me. I can't think of it, sir."

"Caught indeed! A button for the man who prefers fear rather than hope. Will not a hundred pounds teach thee reason? Look, man, it is here with thy wife—will that not move thee to it."

"Not five hundred, captain,—not five hundred," replied the trader, decisively. "I know too well the danger, and shan't forget the warning which old Sanutee gave me. I've seen enough of it to keep me back; and though I am willing to do a great deal, captain, for you as well as the Assembly, without any reward, as I have often done before,—for you have all done a great deal for me—yet it were death, and a horrible death, for me to undertake this. I must not—I do not say I will not—but in truth I cannot—I dare not."

Thus had the dialogue between Harrison and the trader gone on for some time, the former urging and the latter refusing. The wife of the latter all the while had looked on, and listened in silence, almost unnoticed by either, but her countenance during the discussion was full of eloquent speech. The colour in her cheeks now came and went, her eye sparkled, her lip quivered, and she moved to and fro, with emotion scarcely suppressed, until her husband came to his settled conclusion not to go, as above narrated, when she boldly advanced between him and Harrison, and with her eye settling somewhat scornfully upon him, where he stood, she thus addressed him:—

"Now out upon thee, Richard, for a mean spirit. Thou wouldst win money only when the game is easy and all thine own. Hast thou not had the pay of the Assembly, time upon time, and for little risk? and because the risk is now greater, wilt thou hold back like a man having no heart? I shame to think of what thou hast spoken. But the labour and the risk thou fearest shall be mine. I fear not the savages—I know their arts and can meet them, and so couldst thou, Granger, did thy own shadow not so frequently beset thee to scare. Give me the charge which thou hast, captain—and, Granger, touch not the pounds. Thou wilt keep them, my lord, for other service. I will go without the pay."

"Thou shalt not, Moll—thou shalt not," cried the trader, interposing.

"But I will, Richard, and thou knowest I will when my lips have said it. If there be danger, I have no children to feel my want, and it is but my own life, and even its loss might save many."

"Moll—Moll!" exclaimed the trader, half entreating, half commanding in his manner, but she heeded him not.

"And now, my lord, the duty. What is to be done?"

Harrison looked on as she spoke, in wonder and admiration, then replied, warmly seizing her hand as he did so:

"Now, by heaven, woman, but thou hast a soul—a noble, strong, manly soul, such as would shame thousands of the more presumptuous sex. But thy husband has said right in this. Thou shalt not go, and thy words have well taught me that the task should be mine own."

"What! my lord," exclaimed both the trader and his wife— "thou wilt not trust thy person in their hands?"

"No—certainly not. Not if I can help it—but whatever be the risk that seems so great to all, I should not seek to hazard the lives of others, where my own is as easily come at, and where my own is the greater stake. So, Granger, be at rest for thyself and wife. I put thyself first in safety, where I know thou wishest it. For thee—thou art a noble woman, and thy free proffer of service is indeed good service this hour to me, since it brings me to recollect my own duty. The hundred pounds are thine, Granger!"

"My lord!"

"No lording, man—no more of that, but hear me. In a few hours, and with the dusk, I shall be off. See that you keep good watch when I am gone, for the Block House will be the place of retreat for our people in the event of commotion, and will therefore most likely be a point of attack with the enemy. Several have been already warned, and will doubtless be here by night. Be certain you know whom you admit. Grimstead and Grayson, with several of the foresters, will come with their families, and with moderate caution you can make your defence. No more."

Thus counselling, and directing some additional preparations to the trader and his wife, he called for Hector, who, a moment after, made his appearance, as if hurried away from a grateful employ, with a mouth greased from ear to ear, and a huge mass of fat bacon still clutched tenaciously between his fingers.

"Hector!"

"Sa, maussa."

"Hast fed Dugdale to-day?"

"Jist done feed 'em, maussa."

"See that you give him nothing more—and get the horse in readiness. I go up the river-trace by the night."

"He done, maussa, as you tell me:" and the black retired to finish the meal, in the enjoyment of which he had been interrupted. At dusk, under the direction of his master—who now appeared gallantly mounted upon his noble steed—Hector led Dugdale behind him to the entrance of a little wood, where the river-trace began upon which his master was going. Alighting from his horse, Harrison played for a few moments with the strong and favourite dog, and thrusting his hand, among other things, down the now and then extended jaws of the animal, he seemed to practice a sport to which he was familiar. After this, he made the negro put Dugdale's nose upon the indented track, and then instructed him, in the event of his not returning by the moon-rise, to unmuzzle and place him upon the trace at the point he was leaving. This done, he set off at a rapid pace, Dugdale vainly struggling to follow close upon his footsteps.

Chapter Thirty

"School that fierce passion down, ere it unman,
Ere it o'erthrow thee. Thou art on a height
Most perilous, and beneath thee spreads the sea,
And the storm gathers."

L EAVING Bess Matthews, as we have seen, under the influence of a
sad and feverish spirit, Hugh Grayson, as if seeking to escape the
presence of a pursuing and painful thought, plunged deeper and
deeper into the forest, out of the pathway, though still in the direction
of his own home. His mind was now a complete chaos, in which vexation and disappointment, not to speak of self-reproach, were active
principles of misrule. He felt deeply the shame following upon the act
of espionage of which he had been guilty, and though conscious that it
was the consequence of a momentary paroxysm that might well offer
excuse, he was, nevertheless, too highly gifted with sensibility not to
reject those suggestions of his mind which at moments sought to
extenuate it. Perhaps, too, his feeling of abasement was not a little
exaggerated by the stern and mortifying rebuke which had fallen from
the lips of that being whose good opinion had been all the world to
him. With these feelings at work, his mood was in no sort enviable;
and when, at nightfall, he reached the dwelling of his mother, it was in
a condition of mind which drove him, a reckless savage, into a corner
of the apartment opposite that in which sat the old dame croning over
the pages of the sacred volume. She looked up at intervals, and curso-
rily surveyed, in brief glances, the features of her son; whose active
mind and feverish ambition, warring as they ever did against that condition of life imposed upon him by the necessities of his birth and
habitation, had ever been an object of great solicitude to his surviving
parent. He had been her pet in his childhood—her pride as he grew

older, and began to exhibit the energies and graces of a strongly-marked and highly original, though unschooled intellect. Not without ambition and an appreciation of public honours, the old woman could not but regard her son as promising to give elevation to the name of his then unknown family; a hope not entirely extravagant in a part of the world in which the necessities of life were such as to compel a sense of equality in all; and, indeed, if making an inequality anywhere, making it in favour rather of the bold and vigorous plebeian, than of the delicately-nurtured and usually unenterprising scion of aristocracy. Closing the book at length, the old lady turned to her son, and without remarking upon the peculiar unseemliness, not to say wildness, of his appearance, she thus addressed him:—

"Where hast thou been, Hughey, boy, since noon? Thy brother and thyself both from home—I have felt lonesome, and really began to look for the Indians that the young captain warned us of."

"Still the captain—nothing but the captain. Go where I may, he is in my sight, and his name within my ears. I am for ever haunted by his presence. His shadow is on the wall, and before me, whichever way I turn."

"And does it offend thee, Hughey, and wherefore? He is a goodly gentleman, and a gracious, and is so considerate. He smoothed my cushion when he saw it awry, and so well, I had thought him accustomed to it all his life. I see no harm in him."

"I doubt not, mother. He certainly knows well how to cheat old folks not less than young ones into confidence. That smoothing of thy cushion makes him in thy eyes for ever."

"And so it should, my son, for it shows consideration. What could he hope to get from an old woman like me, and wherefore should he think to find means to pleasure me, but that he is well-bred and a gentleman?"

"Aye, that is the word, mother—he is a gentleman—who knows, a lord in disguise—and is therefore superior to the poor peasant who is forced to dig his roots for life in the unproductive sands. Wherefore should his hands be unblistered, and mine asore? Wherefore should he come, and with a smile and silly speech win his way into people's hearts, when I, with a toiling affection of years, and a love that almost grows into a worship of its object, may not gather a single regard from any? Has nature given me life for this? Have I had a thought given me, bidding me ascend the eminence and look down upon the multitude, only for denial and torture? Wherefore is this cruelty, this injustice? Can you answer, mother—does the Bible tell you any thing on this subject?"

"Be not irreverent, my son, but take the sacred volume more frequently into you own hands if you desire an answer to your question. Why, Hughey, are you so perverse? making yourself and all unhappy about you, and still fevering with every thing you see."

"That is the question, mother, that I asked you but now. Why is it? Why am I not like my brother, who looks upon this Harrison as if he were a god, and will do his bidding, and fetch and carry for him like a spaniel? I am not so—yet thou hast taught us both—we have known no other teaching. Why does he love the laughter of the crowd, content to send up like sounds with the many, when I prefer the solitude, or if I go forth with the rest, go forth only to dissent and to deny, and to tutor my voice into a sound that shall be unlike any of theirs? Why is all this?"

"Nay, I know not, yet so it is, Hughey. Thou wert of this nature from thy cradle, and wouldst reject the toy which looked like that of thy brother, and quarrel with the sport which he had chosen."

"Yet thou wouldst have me like him—but I would rather perish with my own thoughts in the gloomiest dens of the forest, where the sun comes not; and better, far better that it were so—far better," he exclaimed, moodily.

"What say'st thou, Hughey—why this new sort of language? what has troubled thee?" inquired the old woman, affectionately.

"Mother, I am a slave—a dog—an accursed thing, and in the worst of bondage—I am nothing."

"How!—"

"I would be, and I am not. They keep me down—they refuse to hear—they do not heed me, and with a thought of command and a will of power in me, they yet pass me by, and I must give way to a bright wand and a gilded chain. Even here in these woods, with a poor neighbourhood, and surrounded by those who are unhonoured and unknown in society, they—the slaves that they are!—they seek for artificial forms, and bind themselves with constraints that can only have a sanction in the degradation of the many. They yield up the noble and true attributes of a generous nature, and make themselves subservient to a name and a mark—thus it is that fathers enslave their children; and but for this, our lords proprietors, whom God in His mercy take to himself, have dared to say, even in this wild land not yet their own, to the people who have battled its dangers—ye shall worship after our fashion, or your voices are unheard. Who is the tyrant in this?—not the ruler—not the ruler—but those base spirits who let him rule,—those weak and unworthy, who, taking care to show their weaknesses, have invited the oppression which otherwise could have no head. I would my thoughts were theirs—or, and perhaps it were better—I would their thoughts were mine."

"God's will be done, my son—but I would thou hadst this content of disposition—without which there is no happiness."

"Content, mother—how idle is that thought. Life itself is discontent—hope, which is one of our chief sources of enjoyment, is discontent, since it seeks that which it has not. Content is a sluggard, and should be a slave—a thing to eat and sleep, and perhaps to dream of eating and sleeping, but not a thing to live. Discontent is the life of enterprise, or achievement, of glory—ay, even of affection. I know the preachers say not this, and the cant of the books tells a different story; but I have thought of it, mother, and I know! Without discontent—a serious and unsleeping discontent—life would be a stagnant stream as untroubled as the back water of the swamps of Edistoh, and as full of the vilest reptiles."

"Thou art for ever thinking strange things, Hugh, and different from all other people, and somehow I can never sleep after I have been talking with thee."

"Because I have thought for myself, mother—in the woods, by the waters—and have not had my mind compressed into the old time-mould with which the pedant shapes the skulls of the imitative apes that courtesy considers human. My own mind is my teacher, and perhaps my tyrant. It is some satisfaction that I have no other—some satisfaction that I may still refuse to look out for idols such as Walter loves to seek and worship—demeaning a name and family which he thus can never honour."

"What reproach is this, Hughey? Wherefore art thou thus often speaking unkindly of thy brother? Thou dost wrong him."

"He wrongs me, mother, and the name of my father, when he thus for ever cringes to this captain of yours—this Harrison—whose name and image mingle in with his every thought, and whom he thrusts into my senses at every word which he utters."

"Let not thy dislike to Harrison make thee distrustful of thy brother. Beware, Hughey—beware, my son, that thou dost not teach thyself to hate where nature would have thee love!"

"Would I could—how much more happiness were mine! Could I hate where now I love—could I exchange affections, devotion, a passionate worship, for scorn, for hate, for indifference,—anything so it be change!" and the youth groaned at the conclusion of the sentence, while he thrust his face buried in his hands against the wall.

"Thou prayest for a bad spirit, Hughey; and a temper of sin—hear now what the good book says, just where I have been reading;" and she was about to read, but he hurriedly approached and interrupted her—

"Does it say why I should have senses, feelings, faculties of mind, moral, person, to be denied their aim, their exercise, their utterance, their life? Does it say why I should live, for persecution, for shame, for shackles? If it explain not this, mother,—read not—I will not hear— look! I shut my ears—I will not hear even thy voice—I am deaf, and would have thee dumb!"

"Hugh," responded the old woman, solemnly— "have I loved thee or not?"

"Wherefore the question, mother?" he returned, with a sudden change from passionate and tumultuous emotion, to a more gentle and humble expression.

"I would know from thy own lips, that thou thinkest me worthy only of thy unkind speech, and look, and gesture. If I have not loved thee well, and as my son, thy sharp words are good, and I deserve them; and I shall bear them without reproach or reply."

"Madness, mother, dear mother—hold me a madman, but not forgetful of thy love—thy too much love for one so undeserving. It is thy indulgence that makes me thus presuming. Hadst thou been less kind, I feel that I should have been less daring."

"Ah! Hugh, thou art wrestling with evil, and thou lovest too much its embrace!—but stay,—thou art not going forth again to-night?" she asked, seeing him about to leave the apartment.

"Yes, yes—I must—I must go."

"Where, I pray—"

"To the woods—to the woods. I must walk—out of sight—in the air—I must have fresh air, for I choke strangely."

"Sick, Hughey, my boy—stay, and let me get thee some medicine."

"No, no,—not sick, dear mother; keep me not back—fear not for me—I was never better—never better." And he supported her with an effort at moderation, back to her chair. She was forced to be satisfied with the assurance, which, however, could not quiet her.

"Thou wilt come back soon, Hughey, for I am all alone, and Walter is with the captain."

"The captain!—ay, ay, soon enough, soon enough," and as he spoke he was about to pass from the door of the apartment, when the ill-suppressed sigh which the mother uttered as she contemplated in him the workings of a passion too strong for her present power to suppress, arrested his steps. He turned quickly, looked back for an instant, then rushed towards her, and kneeling down by her side, pressed her hand to his lips, while he exclaimed—

"Bless me, mother—bless your son—pray for him, too—pray that he may not madden with the wild thoughts and wilder hopes that keep him watchful and sometimes make him wayward."

"I do, Hughey—I do, my son. May God in his mercy bless thee, as I do now!"

He pressed her hand once more to his lips, and passed from the apartment.

Chapter Thirty-one

"What have I done to thee, that thou shouldst lift
Thy hand against me? Wherefore wouldst thou strike
The heart that never wrong'd thee?"
                                    "'Tis a lie,
Thou art mine enemy, that evermore
Keep'st me awake o' nights. I cannot sleep,
While thou art in my thought."

FLYING from the house, as if by so doing he might lose the thoughts that had roused him there into a paroxysm of that fierce passion which too much indulgence had made habitual, he rambled, only half conscious of his direction, from cluster to cluster of the old trees, until the seductive breeze of the evening, coming up from the river, led him down into that quarter. The stream lay before him in the shadow of night, reflecting clearly the multitude of starry eyes looking down from the heavens upon it, and with but a slight ripple, under the influence of the evening breeze, crisping its otherwise settled bosom. How different from his—that wanderer! The disappointed love—the vexed ambition—the feverish thirst for the unknown, perhaps for the forbidden, increasing his agony at every stride which he took along those quiet waters. It was here in secret places, that his passion poured itself forth—with the crowd it was all kept down by the stronger pride, which shrank from the thought of making its feelings public property. With them he was simply cold and forbidding, or perhaps recklessly and inordinately gay. This was his policy. He well knew how great is the delight of the vulgar mind when it can search and tent the wound which it discovers you to possess. How it delights to see the victim writhe under its infliction, and, with how much pleasure its ears drink in the groans of suffering, particularly the suffering of the heart. He knew that men are never so well content, once apprised of the sore, as when they are probing it; unheeding the wincings, or enjoying them with the same sort of satisfaction with which the boy tortures the kitten—and he determined, in his case at least, to deprive them of that gratification. He had already learned how much we are the sport of the many, when we become the victims of the few.

The picture of the night around him was not for such a mood. There is a condition of mind necessary for the due appreciation of each object and enjoyment, and harmony is the life-principle, as well of man as of nature. That quiet stream, with its sweet and sleepless murmur—those watchful eyes, clustering in capricious and beautiful groups above, and peering down, attended by a thousand frail glories, into the mirrored waters beneath—those bending trees, whose matted arms and branches, fringing the river, made it a hallowed home for the dreaming solitary—they chimed not in with that spirit, which now, ruffled by crossing currents, felt not, saw not, desired not their influences. At another time, in another mood, he had worshipped them; now, their very repose and softness, by offering no interruption to the train of his own wild musings, rather contributed to their headstrong growth. The sudden tempest had done the work—the storm precedes a degree of quiet which in ordinary nature is unknown.

"Peace, peace—give me peace!" he cried, to the elements. The small echo from the opposite bank, cried back to him, in a tone of soothing, "peace" —but he waited not for its answer.

"Wherefore do I ask?" he murmured to himself, "and what is it that I ask? Peace, indeed! Repose, rather—release, escape—a free release from the accursed agony of this still pursuing thought. Is life peace, even with love attained, with conquest, with a high hope realized—with an ambition secure in all men's adoration! Peace, indeed! Thou liest, thou life! thou art an embodied lie,—wherefore dost thou talk to me of peace? Ye elements, that murmur on in falsehood,—stars and suns, streams, and ye gnarled monitors—ye are all false. Ye would soothe, and ye excite, lure, encourage, tempt, and deny. The peace of life is insensibility—the suicide of mind or affection. Is that a worse crime than the murder of the animal? Impossible. I may not rob the heart of its passion—the mind of its immortality; and the death of matter is absurd. Ha! there is but one to care—but one,—and she is old. A year—a month—and the loss is a loss no longer. There is too much light here for that. Why need these stars see—why should any see, or hear, or know? When I am silent they will shine—and the waters rove on, and she—she will be not less happy that I come not between her and——. A dark spot—gloomy and still, where the groan will have no echo, and no eye may trace the blood which streams from a heart that has only too much in it."

Thus soliloquizing, in the aberration of intellect, which was too apt to follow a state of high excitement in the individual before us, he plunged into a small, dark cavity of wood, lying not far from the river road, but well concealed, as it was partly under the contiguous swamp. Here, burying the handle of his bared knife in the thick ooze of the soil upon which he stood, the sharp point upwards, and so placed that it must have penetrated, he knelt down at a brief space from it, and, with a last thought upon the mother whom he could not then forbear to think upon, he strove to pray. But he could not—the words stuck in his throat, and he gave it up in despair. He turned to the fatal weapon, and throwing open his vest, so as to free the passage to his heart of all obstructions, with a swimming and indirect emotion of the brain, he prepared to cast himself, from the spot where he knelt, upon its unvarying edge, but at that moment came the quick tread of a horse's hoof to his ear; and with all that caprice which must belong to the mind which, usually good, has yet, even for an instant, purposed a crime not less foolish than foul, he rose at once to his feet.

The unlooked-for sounds had broken the spell of the scene and situation; and, seizing the bared weapon, he advanced to the edge of the swamp, where it looked down upon the road which ran alongside. The sounds rapidly increased in force; and at length, passing directly along before him, his eye distinguished the outline of a person whom he knew at once to be Harrison. The rider went by, but in a moment after, the sounds had ceased. His progress had been arrested; and with an emotion, strange, and still seemingly without purpose, and for which he did not seek to account, Grayson changed his position, and moved along the edge of the road to where the sounds of the horse had terminated. His fingers clutched the knife, bared for a different purpose, with a strange sort of ecstasy. A sanguinary picture of triumph and of terror rose up before his eyes; and the leaves and the trees, to his mind, seemed of the one hue, and dripping with gouts of blood. The demon was present in every thought. He had simply changed his plan of operations. A long train of circumstances and their concomitants crowded upon the mental vision of the youth—

circumstances of strife, concealment, future success—deep, long-looked for enjoyment—and still, with all, came the beautiful image of Bess Matthews.

> "Thus the one passion subject makes of all,
> And slaves of the strong sense—"

There was a delirious whirl—a rich, confused assemblage of the strange, the sweet, the wild, in his spirit, that, in his morbid condition, was a deep delight; and, without an effort to bring order to the adjustment of this confusion, as would have been the case with a well-regulated mind—without a purpose in his own view—he advanced cautiously and well concealed behind the trees, and approached the individual whom he had long since accustomed himself only to regard as an enemy. Concealment is a leading influence of crime with individuals not accustomed to refer all their feelings and thoughts to the control of just principles, and the remoteness and the silence, the secrecy of the scene, and the ease with which the crime could be covered up, were among the moving causes which prompted the man to murder, who had a little before meditated suicide.

Harrison had alighted from his horse, and was then busied in fastening his bridle to a swinging branch of the tree under which he stood. Having done this, and carefully thrown the stirrups across the saddle, he left him, and sauntering back a few paces to a spot of higher ground, he cast himself, with the composure of an old hunter, at full length upon the long grass, which tufted prettily the spot he had chosen. This done, he sounded merrily three several notes upon the horn which hung about his neck, and seemed then to await the coming of another.

The blast of the horn gave quickness to the approach of Hugh Grayson, who had been altogether unnoticed by Harrison; and he now stood in the shadow of a tree, closely observing the fine, manly outline, the graceful position, and the entire symmetry of his rival's extended person. He saw, and his passions grew more and more tumultuous with the survey. His impulses became stronger as his increasing thoughts grew more strange. There was a feeling of strife, and a dream of blood in his fancy—he longed for the one, and his eye saw the other—a rich, attractive, abundant stream, pouring, as it were, from the thousand arteries of some overshadowing tree. The reasoning powers all grew silent—the moral faculties were distorted with the survey; and the feelings were only so many winged arrows goading him on to evil. For a time, the guardian conscience—that high standard of moral education, without which we cease to be human, and are certainly unhappy—battled stoutly; and taking the shape of a thought, which told him continually of his mother, kept back, nervously restless, the hand which clutched the knife. But the fierce passions grew triumphant, with the utterance of a single name from the lips of Harrison,—that of Bess Matthews, mingled with a momentary catch of song, such as is poured forth, almost unconsciously, by the glad and ardent affection. Even as this little catch of song smote upon his senses, Hugh Grayson sprang from the shadow of the tree which had concealed him, and cast himself headlong upon the bosom of the prostrate man.

Harrison grappled his assailant, and struggled with powerful limbs, in his embrace, crying out, as he did so:

"Ha! why is this? Who art thou? Would'st thou murder me, ruffian?"

"Ay! murder is the word! Murder! I would have thy blood. I would drink it!"

Such was the answer of the madman, and the knife flashed in his grasp.

"Horrible! but thou wilt fight for it, murderer," was the reply of Harrison; while, struggling with prodigious effort, though at great disadvantage from the closely pressing form of Grayson, whose knee was upon his breast, he strove with one hand, at the same moment to free his own knife from its place in his bosom, while aiming to ward off with the other hand the stroke of his enemy. The whole affair had been so sudden, so perfectly unlooked-for by Harrison, who, not yet in the Indian country, had not expected danger, that he could not but conceive that the assailant had mistaken him for another. In the moment, therefore, he appealed to him.

"Thou hast erred, stranger. I am not he thou seekest."

"Thou liest," was the grim response of Grayson.

"Ha! who art thou?"

"Thy enemy—in life—in death—through the past, and for the long future, though it be endless,—still thine enemy. I hate—I will destroy thee. Thou hast lain in my path—thou hast darkened my hope—thou hast doomed me to eternal woe. Shalt thou have what thou hast denied me? Shalt thou live to win what I have lost? No—I have thee. There is no aid for thee. In another moment, and I am revenged. Die—die like a dog, since thou hast doomed me to live, and to feel like one. Die!"

The uplifted eyes of Harrison beheld the blade descending in the strong grasp of his enemy. One more effort, one last struggle; for the true mind never yields. While reason lasts, hope lives, for the natural ally of human reason is hope. But he struggled in vain. The hold taken by his assailant was unrelaxing—that of iron; and the thoughts of Harrison, though still he struggled, were strangely mingling with the prayer, and the sweet dream of a passion, now about to be defrauded of its joys for ever—but, just at the moment when he had given himself up as utterly lost, the grasp of his foe was withdrawn. The criminal had relented—the guardian conscience had resumed her sway in time for the safety of both the destroyer and his victim.

And what a revulsion of feeling and of sense! How terrible is passion—how terrible in its approach—how more terrible in its passage and departure! The fierce madman, a moment before ready to drink a goblet-draught from the heart of his enemy, now trembled before him, like a leaf half detached by the frost, and yielding at the first breathings of the approaching zephyr. Staggering back, as if himself struck with the sudden shaft of death, Grayson sank against the tree from which he had sprung in his first assault, and covered his hands in agony. His breast heaved like a wave of the ocean when the winds gather in their desperate frolic over its always sleepless bosom; and his whole frame was rocked to and fro, with the convulsions of his spirit. Harrison rose to his feet the moment he had been released, and with a curiosity not unmingled with caution, approached the unhappy man.

"What! Master Hugh Grayson!" he exclaimed naturally enough, as he found out who he was, "what has tempted thee to this madness—wherefore?"

"Ask me not—ask me not—in mercy, ask me not. Thou art safe, thou art safe. I have not thy blood upon my hands; thank God for that. It was her blessing that saved thee—that saved me; oh, mother, how I thank thee for that blessing. It took the madness from my spirit in the moment when I would have struck thee, Harrison, even with as fell a joy as the Indian strikes in battle. Go—thou art safe. Leave me, I pray thee. Leave me to my own dreadful thought—the thought which hates, and would just now have destroyed thee."

"But wherefore that thought, Master Grayson? Thou art but young to have such thoughts, and shouldst take counsel—and why such should be thy thoughts of me, I would know from thy own lips, which have already said so much that is strange and unwelcome."

"Strange, dost thou say," exclaimed the youth with a wild grin, "not strange—not strange. But go—go—leave me, lest the dreadful passion come back. Thou didst wrong me—thou hast done me the worst of wrongs, though, perchance, thou knowest it not. But it is over now—thou art safe. I ask thee not to forgive, but if thou wouldst serve me, Master Harrison—"

"Speak!" said the other, as the youth paused.

"If thou wouldst serve me,—think me thy foe, thy deadly foe; one waiting and in mood to slay, and so thinking, as one bound to preserve himself at all hazard, use thy knife upon my bosom now, as I would have used mine upon thee. Strike, if thou wouldst serve me." And he dashed his hand upon the bared breast violently as he spoke.

"Thou art mad, Master Grayson—to ask of me to do such folly. Hear me but a while"—

But the other heard him not,—he muttered to himself half incoherent words and sentences.

"First suicide—miserable wretch,—and then, God of Heaven! that I should have been so nigh to murder," and he sobbed like a child before the man he had striven to slay, until pity had completely taken the place of every other feeling in the bosom of Harrison. At this moment the waving of a torch-light appeared through the woods at a little distance. The criminal started as if in terror, and was about to fly from the spot, but Harrison interposed and prevented him.

"Stay, Master Grayson—go not. The light comes in the hands of thy brother, who is to put me across the river. Thou wilt return with him, and may thy mood grow gentler and thy thoughts wiser. Thou hast been rash and foolish, but I mistake not thy nature, which I hold meant for better things—I regard it not, therefore, to thy harm; and to keep thee from a thought which will trouble thee more than it can harm me now, I will crave of thee to lend all thy aid to assist thy mother from her present habitation, as she has agreed, upon the advice of thy brother and myself. Thou wast not so minded this morning, so thy brother assured me; but thou wilt take my word for it that the remove has grown essential to her safety. Walter will tell thee all. In the meanwhile, what has passed between us we hold to ourselves; and if, as thou hast said, thou hast had wrong at my hands, thou shalt have right at thy quest, when other duties will allow."

"Enough, enough!" cried the youth in a low tone impatiently, as he beheld his brother, carrying a torch, emerge from the cover.

"How now, Master Walter—thou hast been sluggard, and but for thy younger brother, whom I find a pleasant gentleman, I should have worn out good-humour in seeking for patience."

"What, Hugh here!" Walter exclaimed, regarding his brother with some astonishment, as he well knew the dislike in which he held Harrison.

"Ay," said the latter, "and he has grown more reasonable since morning, and is now,—if I so understand him—not unwilling to give aid in thy mother's remove. But come—let us away—we have no time for the fire. Of the horse, thy brother will take charge—keep him not here for me, but let him bear thy mother to the Block House. She will find him gentle. And now, Master Grayson—farewell! I hope to know thee better on my return, as I desire thou shalt know me. Come, Walter."

Concealed in the umbrage of the shrub trees which overhung the river, a canoe lay at the water's edge, into which Harrison leaped, followed by the elder Grayson. They were soon off—the skiff, like a fairy bark, gliding almost noiselessly across that Indian river. Watching their progress for a while, Hugh Grayson lingered until the skiff became a speck; then, with strangely mingled feelings of humiliation and satisfaction, leaping upon the steed which had been given him in charge, he took his way to the dwelling of his mother.

Chapter Thirty-two

"Be thy teeth firmly set; the time is come,
To rend and trample. We are ready all,
All, but the victim."

AT dark, Sanutee, Ishiagaska, Enoree-Mattee, the prophet and a few others of the Yemassee chiefs and leaders, all entertaining the same decided hostilities to the Carolinians, and all more or less already committed to the meditated enterprise against them, met at the lodge of Ishiagaska, in the town of Pocota-ligo, and discussed their further preparations at some length. The insurrection had ripened rapidly, and had nearly reached a head. All the neighbouring tribes, without an exception, had pledged themselves for the common object, and the greater number of those extending over Georgia and Florida, were also bound in the same dreadful contract. The enemies of the settlement, in this conspiracy, extended from Cape Fear to the mountains of Apalachia, and the disposable force of the Yemassees, under this league, amounted to at least six thousand warriors. These forces were gathering at various points according to arrangement, and large bodies from sundry tribes had already made their appearance at Pocota-ligo, from which it was settled that the first blow should be given. Nor were the Indians, thus assembling, bowmen merely. The Spanish authorities of St. Augustine, who were at the bottom of the conspiracy, had furnished them with a considerable supply of arms; and the conjectures of Harrison rightly saw in the boxes transferred by Chorley, the seaman, to the Yemassees, those weapons of massacre which the policy of the Carolinians had withheld usually from the hands of the redmen. These, however, were limited to the forest nobility—the several chiefs bound in the war;—to the commons, a knife or tomahawk was the assigned, and perhaps the more truly useful present. The musket, at that period, in the hands of the unpractised savage, was not half so dangerous as the bow. To this array of the forces gathered against the Carolinians, we must add those of the pirate Chorley—a desperado in every sense of the word, a profligate boy, a vicious and outlawed man—daring, criminal, and only engaging in the present adventure in the hope of the spoil and plunder which he hoped from it. In the feeble condition of the infant colony there was little risk in his present position. Without vessels of war of any sort, and only depending upon the mother country for such assistance, whenever a French or Spanish invasion took place, the province was lamentably defenceless. The visit of Chorley, in reference to this present weakness, had been admirably well-timed. He had waited until the departure of the Swallow, the English armed packet, which periodically traversed the ocean with advices from the sovereign to the subject. He then made his appearance in the waters of the colony, secure from that danger, and, indeed, if we may rely upon the historians of the period, almost secure from any other; for we are told that, in their wild abodes, the colonists were not always the scrupulous moralists which another region had made them. They did not scruple at this or at that sort of trade, so long as it was profitable; and Chorley, the pirate, would have had no difficulty, as he well knew by experience, so long as he avoided any overt performance, which should force upon the public sense a duty, which many of the people were but too well satisfied when they could avoid. It did not matter to many among those with whom he pursued his traffic, whether or not the article which they procured, at so cheap a rate, had been bought with blood and the strong hand. It was enough that the goods were to be had when wanted, of as fair quality, and fifty per cent. cheaper than those offered in the legitimate course of trade. To sum up all in little, our European ancestors were, in many respects, monstrous great rascals.

Chorley was present at this interview with the insurrectionary chiefs of Yemassee, and much good counsel he gave them. The meeting was preparatory, and here they prepared the grand *mouvement*, and settled the disposition of the subordinates. Here they arranged all those small matters of etiquette beforehand, by which to avoid little jealousies and disputes among their auxiliaries; for national pride, or rather the great glory of the clan, was as desperate a passion with the southern Indians, as with the yet more breechless Highlanders of Scotland. Nothing was neglected in this interview which, to the deliberate mind, seemed necessary to success; and they were prepared to break up their meeting, in order to attend the general assemblage of the people, to whom the formal and official announcement was to be given, when Ishiagaska recalled them to a matter which, to that fierce Indian, seemed much more important than any other. Chorley beheld, with interest, the animated glance—the savage grin,—of the red warrior, and though he knew not the signification of the words of the speaker, he yet needed no interpreter to convey to him the purport of his speech.

"The dog must smell the blood, or he tears not the throat. Ha! shall not the War-Manneyto have a feast?"

Sanutee looked disquieted, but said nothing, while the eye of Ishiagaska followed his glance and seemed to search him narrowly. He spoke again, approaching more nearly to the person of the "well-beloved:"

"The Yemassee hath gone on the track of the Swift Foot, and the English has run beside him. They have taken a name from the pale-face and called him brother. Brother is a strong word for Yemassee, and he must taste of his blood, or he will not hunt after the English. The War-Manneyto would feast upon the heart of a pale-face, to make strong the young braves of Yemassee."

"It is good—let the War-Manneyto have the feast upon the heart of the English!" exclaimed the prophet, and such seeming the general expression, Sanutee yielded, though reluctantly. They left the lodge, and in an hour a small party of young warriors, to whom, in his wild, prophetic manner, Enoree-Mattee had revealed the requisitions of the God he served, went forth to secure an English victim for the dreadful propitiatory sacrifice they proposed to offer,—with the hope, by this means, to render success certain,—to the Indian Moloch.

This done, the chiefs distributed themselves among the several bands of the people and their allies, stimulating by their arguments and eloquence, the fierce spirit which they now laboured to arouse in storm and tempest. We leave them to return to Harrison.

The adventure which he was now engaged in was sufficiently perilous. He knew the danger, and also felt that there were particular responsibilities in his case which increased it greatly. With this consciousness came a proportionate degree of caution. He was shrewd, to a proverb, among those who knew him—practised considerably in Indian stratagem—had been with them in frequent conflict, and could anticipate their arts—was resolute as well as daring, and, with much of their circumspection, had learned skilfully to imitate the thousand devices, whether of warfare or of the chase, which make the glory of the Indian brave. Having given as fair a warning as was in his power to those of his countrymen most immediately exposed to the danger, and done all that he could to assure their safety against the threatening danger, he was less reluctant to undertake the adventure. But had he been conscious of the near approach of the time fixed on by the enemy for the explosion—could he have dreamed that the conspiracy was so extensive and the outbreak so near at hand, his attitude would have been very different indeed. But this was the very knowledge, for the attainment of which, he had taken his present journey. The information sought was important in determining upon the degree of effort necessary for the defence, and for knowing in what quarter to apprehend the most pressing danger.

It was still early evening, when the canoe of Grayson, making into a little cove about a mile and a half below Pocota-ligo, enabled Harrison to land. With a last warning to remove as quickly as possible, and to urge as many more as he could to the shelter of the Block House, he left his companion to return to the settlement; then plunging into the woods, and carefully making a sweep out of his direct course, in order to come in upon the back of the Indian town, so as to avoid as much as practicable the frequented paths, he went fearlessly upon his way. For some time, proceeding with slow and heedful step, he went on without interruption, yet not without a close scrutiny into everything he saw. One thing struck him, however, and induced unpleasant reflection. He saw that many of the dwellings which he approached were without fires, and seemed deserted. The inhabitants were gone—he met with none; and he felt assured that a popular gathering was at hand or in progress. For two miles of his circuit he encountered no sign of human beings; and he had almost come to the conclusion that Pocota-ligo, which was only a mile or so farther, would be equally barren, when suddenly a torch flamed across his path, and with an Indian instinct he sank back into the shadow of a tree, and scanned curiously the scene before him. The torch grew into a blaze in a hollow of the wood, and around the fire, he beheld, in various positions, some fifteen or twenty warriors, making a small war encampment. Some lay at length, some "squat, like a toad," and all gathered around the friendly blaze which had just been kindled in time to prevent him from running headlong into the midst of them. From the cover of the tree, which perfectly concealed him, he could see by the light around which they clustered, not only the forms but the features of the warriors; and he soon made them out to be a band of his old acquaintance, the Coosaws—who, after the dreadful defeat which they sustained at his hands in the forks of Tullifinee, found refuge with the Yemassees, settled the village of Coosaw-hatchie, and being too small in number to call for the further hostility of the Carolinians, were suffered to remain in quiet. But they harboured a bitter malice against their conquerors, and the call to the field, with a promised gratification of their long slumbering revenges, was a pledge as grateful as it was exciting to their hearts. With a curious memory which recalled vividly his past adventure with the same people, he surveyed their diminutive persons, their small, quick, sparkling eyes, the dusky, but irritably red features, and the querulous upward turn of the nose—a most distinguishing feature with this clan, showing a feverish quarrelsomeness of disposition, and a want of becoming elevation in purpose. Harrison knew them well, and his intimacy had cost them dearly. It was probable, indeed, that the fifteen or twenty warriors then grouped before him were all that they could send into the field—all that had survived, women and children excepted, the severe chastisement which had annihilated them as a nation. But what they lacked in number they made up in valour—a fierce, sanguinary people, whose restless habits and love of strife were a proverb even among their savage neighbours, who were wont to describe a malignant man—one more so than usual,—as having a Coosaw tooth. But a single warrior of this party was in possession of a musket, a huge and cumbrous weapon, of which he seemed not a little proud. He was probably a chief. The rest were armed with bow and arrow, knife, and, here and there, a hatchet. The huge club stuck up conspicuously among them, besmeared with coarse paint, and surmounted with a human scalp, instructed Harrison sufficiently as to the purpose of the party. The war-club carried from hand to hand, and in this way transmitted from tribe to tribe, from nation to nation, by their swiftest runners, was a mode of organization not unlike that employed by the Scotch for a like object, and of which the muse of Scott has so eloquently sung. The spy was satisfied with the few glances which he gave to this little party; and as he could gather nothing distinctly from their language, which he heard imperfectly, and as imperfectly understood, he cautiously left his place of concealment, and once more darted forward on his journey. Digressing from his path as circumstances or prudence required, he pursued his course in a direct line towards Pocota-ligo, but had not well lost sight of the fire of the Coosaws, when another blaze appeared in the track just before him. Pursuing a like caution with that already given, he approached sufficiently nigh to distinguish a band of *Sewees*, something more numerous than the Coosaws, but still not strong, encamping in like manner around the painted post, the common ensign of approaching battle. He knew them by the number of shells which covered their garments, were twined in their hair, and formed a peculiar and favourite ornament to their persons, while at the same time declaring their usual *habitat*. They occupied one of the islands which still bear their name—the only relics of a nation which had its god and its glories, and believing in the Manneyto and the happy valley, can have no complaint that their old dwellings shall know them no more. The Sewees resembled the Coosaws in their general expression of face, but in person they were taller and more symmetrical, though slender. They did not exceed thirty in number.

The precautions of Harrison were necessarily increased, as he found himself in such a dangerous neighbourhood, but still he felt nothing of apprehension. He was one of those men, singularly constituted, in whom hope becomes a strong exciting principle, perpetually stimulating confidence and encouraging adventure into a forgetfulness of risk, and a general disregard to difficulty and opposition. On he went, until, at the very entrance to the village, he came upon an encampment of the Santees, a troop of about fifty warriors. These he knew by their greater size and muscle, being generally six feet or more in height, of broad shoulders, full, robust front, and forming—not less in their countenances, which were clear, open, and intelligent, than in their persons—a singular and marked contrast to the Sewees and Coosaws. They carried, along with the bow, another, and, in their hands, a more formidable weapon—a huge mace, four or five feet in length, of the heaviest wood, swelling into a large bulb, or knot, at the end. This was suspended by a thong of skin or sinews from the necks. A glance was enough to show their probable number, and desiring no more, Harrison sank away from further survey, and carefully avoiding the town, on the skirts of which he stood, he followed in the direction to which he was led by a loud uproar and confused clamour coming from the place. This was the place of general encampment, a little above the village, immediately upon the edge of the swamp from which the river wells, being the sacred ground of Yemassee, consecrated to their several Manneytos of war, peace, vengeance, and general power—which contained the great tumulus of Pocota-ligo, consecrated by a thousand awful sacrifices, for a thousand years preceding, and already known to us as the spot where Occonestoga, saved from perdition, met his death from the hands of his mother.

Chapter Thirty-three

"Battle-god Manneyto—
Here's a scalp, 'tis a scull,
This is blood, 'tis a heart,
Scalp, scull, blood, heart,
'Tis for thee, Manneyto—'tis for thee, Manneyto—
They shall make a feast for thee,
Battle-god Manneyto."
　　　　　YEMASSEE WAR-HYMN

THE preparatory rites of battle were about to take place around the tumulus. The warriors were about to propitiate the Yemassee God of War—the Battle-Manneyto—and the scene was now, if possible, more imposing than ever. It was with a due solemnity that they approached the awful rites with which they invoked this stern principle—doubly solemn, as they could not but feel that the existence of their nation was the stake at issue. They were prostrate—the thousand warriors of Yemassee—their wives, their children—their faces to the ground, but their eyes upward, bent upon the cone of the tumulus, where a faint flame, dimly flickering under the breath of the capricious winds, was struggling doubtfully into existence. Enoree-Mattee, the prophet, stood in anxious attendance—the only person in the neighbourhood of the fire—for the spot upon which he stood was holy. He moved around it, in attitudes now lofty, now grotesque—now impassioned, and now humbled—feeding the flame at intervals as he did so with fragments of wood, which had been consecrated by other rites, and sprinkling it, at the same time, with the dried leaves of the native and finely odorous vanella, which diffused a grateful perfume upon the gale. All this time he muttered a low, monotonous chant, which seemed an incantation—now and then, at pauses in his song, turning to the gathered multitude, over whose heads, as they lay in thick groups around the tumulus, he extended his arms as if in benediction. The flame all this while gathered but slowly, and this was a matter of discontent to both prophet and people; for the gathering of the fire was to indicate the satisfaction of the Manneyto with their proposed design. While its progress was doubtful, therefore, a silence entirely unbroken, and full of awe, prevailed throughout the crowd. But when it burst forth, growing and gathering—seizing with a ravenous rapidity upon the sticks and stubble with which it had been supplied— licking the long grass as it progressed, and running down the sides of the tumulus, until it completely encircled the savagely picturesque form of Enoree-Mattee as with a wreath of fire—when it sent its votive and odorous smoke in a thick, direct column, up to the heavens—a single, unanimous shout, that thrilled through and through the forest, even as the sudden uproar of one of its own terrible hurricanes, burst forth from that now exhilarated assembly, while each started at once to his feet, brandished his weapons with a fierce joy, and all united in that wild chorus of mixed fury and adoration, the battle-hymn of their nation:

> "Sangarrah-me, Yemassee,
> Sangarrah-me—Sangarrah-me—
> Battle-god Manneyto,
> Here's a scalp, here's a scull,
> This is blood, 'tis a heart,
> Scalp, scull, blood, heart,
> 'Tis for thee, battle-god,
> 'Tis to make the feast for thee,
> Battle-god of Yemassee!"

As they repeated the wild chant of battle, at the altars of their war-god, chorussed by the same recurring refrain, the sounds were caught up, as so many signals, by couriers, stationed along the route, who conveyed the sounds to others yet beyond. These were finally carried to the various encampments of their allies, who only waited to hear of the blazing of the sacred fire, to understand that they had the permission of the Yemassee deity to appear and join in the subsequent ceremonial—a ceremonial which affected and interested them, in the approaching conflict, equally with the Yemassees.

They came at length, the great body of that fierce but motley gathering. In so many clans, each marched apart, with the distinct emblem of its tribe. There came the subtle and the active Coosaw, with his small flaming black eye, in which gathered the most malignant fires. A stuffed rattlesnake in coil, with protruded fang, perched upon a staff, formed their emblem, and no bad characteristic, for they were equally fearless and equally fatal with that reptile. Then came the Combahee and the Edistoh, the Santee and the Seratee—the two latter kindred tribes bearing huge clubs, which they wielded with equal strength and agility, in addition to the knife and bow. Another and another cluster forming around, completed a grouping at once imposing and unique,—each body, as they severally came to behold the sacred fire, swelling upwards from the mound, precipitating themselves upon the earth where first it met their sight. The prophet still continued his incantations, until, at a given signal, when Sanutee, as chief of his people, ascended the tumulus, and bending his form reverently as he did so, approached him to know the result of his auguries. The appearance of the old chief was haggard in the extreme—his countenance bore all the traces of that anxiety which, at such a moment, the true patriot would be likely to feel—and a close eye might discern evidences of a deeper feeling working at his heart, equally vexing and of a more personal nature. Still his manner was firm and nobly commanding. He listened to the words of the prophet, which were in their own language. Then advancing in front, the chief delivered his response to the people. It was auspicious— Manneyto had promised them success against their enemies, and their offerings had all been accepted. He required but another sacrifice, and the victim assigned for this, the prophet assured them, was at hand. Again the shout went up to heaven, and the united warriors clashed their weapons and yelled aloud the triumph which they anticipated over their foes.

In a neighbouring copse, well concealed by the thicket, lay the person of Harrison. From this spot he surveyed the entire proceedings. With the aid of their numerous fires, he was able to calculate their numbers, and note the different nations engaged, whose emblems he generally knew. He listened impatiently for some evidences of their precise intention; but as they spoke only in their own, or a mixed language of the several tribes, he almost despaired of any discovery of this kind, which would serve him much, when a new party appeared upon the scene, in the person of Chorley, the captain of the sloop. He appeared dressed in a somewhat gaudy uniform—a pair of pistols stuck in his belt—a broad short sword at his side, and dagger—and, though evidently in complete military array, without having discarded the rich golden chain, which hung suspended ostentatiously around his thick, short, bull-shaped neck. The guise of Chorley was Spanish, and over his head, carried by one of his seamen in a group of twenty of them, which followed him, he bore the flag of Spain. This confirmed Harrison in all his apprehensions. He saw that once again the Spaniard was about to strike at the colony, in the assertion of an old claim put in by his monarch to all the country then in the possession of the English, northward as far as Virginia, and to the southwest the entire range, including the Mississippi and some portion even of the territory beyond it. Such was the vast ambition of nations in that day;—such the vague grasp which the imagination took, of geographical limits and expanse. In support of this claim, which, under the existing circumstances of European convention, the Spanish monarch could not proceed to urge by arms in any other manner—the two countries being then at peace at home—the governor of the one colony, that of Spain, was suffered and instigated to do that which his monarch immediately dared not attempt; and from St. Augustine innumerable inroads were daily projected into Georgia and the Carolinas: the Spaniards, with their Indian allies, penetrating, in some instances, almost to the gates of Charleston. The Carolinians were not idle, and similar inroads were made upon Florida; the two parent nations, looking composedly upon a warfare in the colonies, which gratified national animosity, without perilling national security, and indulged them at a favourite pastime, in a foreign battle field; where they could help, with contributions, their several champions, while sitting at home, cheek-by-jowl, on terms of seeming amity and good fellowship. This sort of warfare had been continued almost from the commencement of either settlement, and the result was a system of foray into the enemy's province from time to time—now of the Spaniards, and now of the Carolinians.

Harrison was soon taught to see by the evidence before him, that the Spaniard, on the present occasion, had more deeply matured his plans than he had ever anticipated; and that—taking advantage of the known discontents among the Indians, and of that unwise cessation of watchfulness, which too much indicated the confiding nature of the Carolinians, induced by a term of repose, protracted somewhat longer than usual—he had prepared a mine which, he fondly hoped, and with good reason, would result in the utter extermination of the intruders, whom they loved to destroy, as on one sanguinary occasion their own inscription phrased it, not so much because they were Englishmen, but "because they were heretics." His success in the present adventure, he felt assured, and correctly, would place the entire province in the possession, as in his thought it was already in the right, of his most Catholic Majesty.

Captain Chorley, the bucanier and Spanish emissary, for in those times and that region, the two characters were not always unlike, advanced boldly into the centre of the various assemblage. He was followed by twenty stout seamen, the greater part of his crew. These were armed chiefly with pikes and cutlasses. A few carried pistols, a few muskets; but generally speaking, the larger arms seemed to have been regarded as unnecessary, and perhaps inconvenient, in an affair requiring despatch and secrecy. As he approached, Sanutee descended from the mound and advanced towards him, with a degree of respect, which, while it was marked and gracious, subtracted nothing from the lofty carriage and the towering dignity which at the same time accompanied it. In a few words of broken English, he explained to Chorley sundry of their present and future proceedings—detailed what was required of him, in the rest of the ceremony; and having made him understand, which he did with some difficulty, he reascended the mound, resuming his place at the side of the prophet, who all the while, as if without noticing any thing going on around, had continued those fearful incantations to the war-god, which seemed to make of himself a victim. He was intoxicated with his own spells and incantations. His eye glared with the light of madness—his tongue hung forth between his clinched teeth, which seemed every moment, when parting and gnashing, as if about to sever it in two, while the slaver gathered about his mouth in thick foam, and all his features were convulsed. At a signal which he gave, while under this fury, a long procession of women, headed by Malatchie, the executioner, made their appearance from behind the hill, and advanced into the area. In their arms six of them bore a gigantic figure, rudely hewn out of a tree, with a head so carved as in some sort to resemble that of a man. With hatchet and fire a rude human face had been wrought out of the block, and by means of one paint or another, it had been stained into something like expression. The scalp of some slaughtered enemy was stuck upon the skull, and made to adhere, with pitch extracted from the pine. The body, from the neck, was left unhewn. This figure was stuck up in the midst of the assembly, in the sight of all, while the old women danced in wild contortions round it, uttering, as they did so, a thousand invectives in their own wild language. They charged it with all offences comprised in their system of ethics. It was a liar, and a thief—a traitor, and cheat—a murderer, and without a Manneyto—in short, in summary of their own—they called it "English—English— English." Having done this, they receded, leaving the area clear of all but the unconscious image which they had so denounced, and sinking back behind the armed circle, they remained for awhile in silence.

Previously taught in what he was to do, Chorley now advanced alone, and striking a hatchet full in the face of the figure, he cried aloud to the warriors around:

"Hark, at this English dog! I strike my hatchet into his skull. Who will do thus for the King of Spain?"

Malatchie acted as interpreter in the present instance, and the words had scarcely fallen from his lips, when Chinnabee, a chief of the Coosaws, his eyes darting fire, and his whole face full of malignant delight, rushed out from his clan, and seizing the hatchet, followed up the blow by another, which sunk it deeply into the unconscious block, crying aloud, as he did so, in his own language:

"The Coosaw,—ha! look, he strikes the skull of the English!" and the fierce war-whoop of "Coosaw—Sangarrah-me," followed up the speech.

"So strikes the Cherah!—Cherah-hah, Cherah-me!" cried the head warrior of that tribe, following the example of the Coosaw, and sinking his hatchet also into the skull of the image. Another and another, in like manner came forward, each chief, representing a tribe or nation, being required to do so, showing his assent to the war; until, in a moment of pause, believing that all were done, Chorley reapproached, and baring his cutlass as he did so, with a face full of the passion which one might be supposed to exhibit, when facing a deadly and a living foe, with a single stroke he lodged the weapon so deeply into the wood, that for a while its extrication was doubtful—at the same time exclaiming fiercely:

"And so strikes Richard Chorley, not for Spain, nor France, nor Indian—not for any body, but on his own log—for his own wrong, and so would he strike again if the necks of all England lay under his arm."

A strong armed Santee, who had impatiently waited his turn while Chorley spoke, now came forward with his club—a monstrous mace, gathered from the swamps, under the stroke of which the image went down prostrate. Its fall was the signal for a general shout and tumult among the crowd; scarcely quieted, as a new incident was brought in to enliven a performance, which, though of invariable exercise among the primitive Indians, preparatory to all great occasions like the present, was yet too monotonous not to need in the end some stirring variation.

Chapter Thirty-four

"And war is the great Moloch; for his feast,
Gather the human victims he requires,
With an unglutted appetite. He makes
Earth his grand table, spread with winding-sheets,
Man his attendant, who, with madness fit,
Serves his own brother up, nor heeds the prayer,
Groaned by a kindred nature, for reprieve."

BLOOD makes the taste for blood—we teach the hound to hunt the victim, for whose entrails he acquires an appetite. We acquire such tastes ourselves from like indulgences. There is a sort of intoxicating restlessness in crime that seldom suffers it to stop at a solitary excess. It craves repetition—and the relish so expands with indulgence, that exaggeration becomes essential to make it a stimulant. Until we have created this appetite, we sicken at its bare contemplation. But once created, it is impatient of employment, and it is wonderful to note its progress. Thus, the young Nero wept when first called upon to sign the warrant commanding the execution of a criminal. But the ice once broken, he never suffered it to close again. Murder was his companion—blood his banquet—his chief stimulant licentiousness—horrible licentiousness. He had found out a new luxury.

The philosophy which teaches this, is common to experience all the world over. It was not unknown to the Yemassees. Distrusting the strength of their hostility to the English, the chief instigators of the proposed insurrection, as we have seen, deemed it necessary to appeal to this appetite, along with a native superstition. Their battle-god called for a victim, and the prophet promulgated the decree. A chosen band of warriors was despatched to secure a white man; and in subjecting him to the fire-torture, the Yemassees were to feel the provocation of that thirsting impulse which craves a continual renewal of its stimulating indulgence. Perhaps one of the most natural and necessary agents of man, in his progress through life, is the desire to destroy. It is this which subjects the enemy—it is this that prompts him to adventure—which enables him to contend with danger, and to flout at death—which carries him into the interminable forest and impels the ingenuity into exercise which furnishes him with a weapon to contend with its savage possessors. It is not surprising, if, prompted by dangerous influences, in our ignorance, we pamper this natural agent into a disease, which preys at length upon ourselves.

The party despatched for this victim had been successful. The peculiar cry was, at length, heard from the thickets, indicating their success; and as it rang through the wide area, the crowd gave way and parted for the new comers, who were hailed with a degree of satisfaction, extravagant enough, unless we consider the importance generally attached by the red-men to the requisitions of the prophet, and the propitiation of their war-god. It was on the possession and sacrifice of a living victim, that they rested their hope of victory in the approaching conflict. Such was the prediction of the prophet—such the decree of their god of war—and for the due celebration of this terrible sacrifice, the preparatory ceremonies had been delayed.

They were delayed no longer. With shrill cries and the most savage contortions, not to say convulsions of body, the assembled multitude hailed the *entrée* of the detachment sent forth upon this expedition. They had been eminently successful; having taken their captive, without themselves losing a drop of blood. Upon this, the prediction had founded their success. Not so the prisoner. Though unarmed, he had fought desperately, and his enemies were compelled to wound in order to secure him. He was only overcome by numbers, and the sheer physical weight of their crowding bodies.

They dragged him into the ring, the war-dance all the time going on around him. From the copse, close at hand, in which he lay concealed, Harrison could distinguish, at intervals, the features of the captive. He knew him at a glance, as a poor labourer, named Macnamara, an Irishman, who had gone jobbing about, in various ways, throughout the settlement. He was a fine-looking, fresh, muscular man—not more than thirty. Surrounded by howling savages, threatened with a death the most terrible, the brave fellow sustained himself with the courage and firmness which belongs so generally to his countrymen. His long, black

hair, deeply saturated and matted with his blood, which oozed out from
sundry bludgeon-wounds upon the head, was wildly distributed in
masses over his face and forehead. His full, round cheeks, were marked
by knife-wounds, the result also of his fierce defence against his captors.
His hands were bound, but his tongue was unfettered; and as they
danced and howled about him, his eye gleamed forth in fury and derision, while his words were those of defiance and contempt.

"Ay! ye may screech and scream, ye red divils—ye'd be after seeing
how a jontleman would burn in the fire, would ye, for your idification
and delight. But it's not Teddy Macnamara, that your fires and your
arrows will iver scare, ye divils; so begin, boys, as soon as ye've a mind
to, and don't be too dilicate in your doings."

He spoke a language, so far as they understood it, perfectly congenial with their notion of what should become a warrior. His fearless
contempt of death, his haughty defiance of their skill in the arts of torture—his insolent abuse—were all so much in his favour. They were
proofs of the true brave, and they found, under the bias of their habits
and education, an added pleasure in the belief, that he would stand
well the torture, and afford them a protracted enjoyment of the spectacle. His execrations, poured forth freely as they forced him into the
area, were equivalent to one of their own death-songs, and they
regarded it as his.

He was not so easily compelled in the required direction. Unable
in any other way to oppose them, he gave them as much trouble as he
could, and in no way sought to promote his own progress. This was
good policy, perhaps; for this passive resistance—the most annoying
of all its forms,—was not unlikely to bring about an impatient blow,
which might save him from the torture. In another case, such might
have been the result of the course taken by Macnamara; but now, the
prophecy was too important an object; and the red men can be politic
enough in their passions when they will. Though they handled him
roughly enough, his captors yet forbore any excessive violence. Under
a shower of kicks, cuffs, and blows from every quarter, the poor fellow,
still cursing them to the last, hissing at and spitting upon them, was
forced to a tree; and in a few moments tightly lashed back against it. A
thick cord secured him around the body to its overgrown trunk, while
his hands, forced up in a direct line above his head, were fastened to
the tree with withes—the two palms turned outwards, nearly meeting,
and so well corded as to be perfectly immovable.

A cold chill ran through all the veins of Harrison, and he grasped his knife with a clutch as tenacious as that of his fast-clinched teeth, while he looked, from his place of concealment, upon these dreadful preparations for the Indian torture. The captive was seemingly less sensible of its terrors. All the while, with a tongue that seemed determined to supply, so far as it might, the forced inactivity of all other members, he shouted forth his scorn and execrations.

"The pale-face will sing his death-song," cried a young warrior in the ears of the victim, as he flourished his tomahawk around his head. The sturdy Irishman did not comprehend the language, but he did the action, and his answer seemed a full compliance with the requisitions. His speech was a shout or scream, and his words were those of desperate defiance.

"Ay, ye miserable red nagers,—ye don't frighten Teddy Macnamara now so aisily. He is none of yer spalpeens, honies, to be frightened by your bows and your pinted sticks, ye red nagers. It isn't your knives, nor your hatchets, that's going to make Teddy beg your pardon, and ax for yer marcies. I don't care for your knives, and your hatchets, at all at all, ye red divils. Not I—by my faith, and my own ould father, that was a Teddy before me."

They took him at his word, and their preparations were soon made for the torture. A hundred torches of the gummy pine were placed to kindle in a neighbouring fire—a hundred old women stood ready to employ them. These were to be applied as a sort of cautery, to the arrow and knife-wounds which the more youthful savages were expected, in their sports, to inflict. It was upon their captives, in this manner, that the youth of the nation was practised. It was in this school that the boys were prepared to become men—to inflict pain as well as to submit to it. To these two classes,—for this was one of the peculiar features of the Indian torture,—the fire-sacrifice, in its initial penalties, was commonly assigned; and both of them were ready at hand to engage in it. How beat the heart of Harrison with conflicting emotions, in the shelter of the adjacent bush, as he surveyed each step in the prosecution of these horrors!

They began. A dozen youth, none over sixteen, came forward and ranged themselves in front of the prisoner.

"And for what do ye face me down after that sort, ye dirty little red nagers?" cried the sanguine prisoner.

They answered him with a whoop—a single shriek, and the face of the brave fellow paled then, for a moment, with that sudden yell—that mere promise of war—the face which had not paled in the actual conflict through which he had already gone. But it was for a moment only, and he nerved himself for the proper endurance of the more dreadful trials which were to succeed and from which there was no escape. The whoop of the young savages was succeeded by a simultaneous discharge of all their arrows, aimed, as would appear from the result, only at those portions of his person which were not vital. This was the common exercise, and their adroitness was wonderful. They placed the shaft where they pleased. Thus, the arrow of one penetrated one palm, while that of another, almost at the same instant, was driven deep into the other. One cheek was grazed by a third, while a fourth scarified the opposite. A blunted shaft struck the victim full in the mouth, and arrested, in the middle, his usual execration— "Ye bloody red nagers!" and there never were fingers of a hand so evenly separated one from the other, as those of Macnamara, by the admirably-aimed arrows of those embryo warriors. But the endurance of the captive was proof against all their torture; and while every member of his person attested the felicity of their aim, he still continued to shout his abuse, not only to his immediate assailants, but to the old warriors, and the assembled multitude, gathering around, and looking composedly on—now approving this or that peculiar hit, and encouraging the young beginner with a cheer. He bore all his tortures with the most unflinching fortitude, and a courage that, extorting their freest admiration, was quite as much the subject of cheer with the warriors as were the arrow-shots which sometimes provoked its exhibition.

At length, throwing aside the one instrument, the young warriors came forward with the tomahawk. They were far more cautious in the use of this fatal weapon, for, as their present object was not less the prolonging of their own exercise than of the prisoner's tortures, it was their wish to avoid wounding him fatally or even severely. Their chief delight was in stinging the captive into an exhibition of imbecile and fruitless anger, or terrifying him into ludicrous apprehensions. They had no hope of the latter source of amusement from the firmness of the victim before them; and to rouse his impotent rage, was the chief study in their thought.

With words of mutual encouragement, and boasting, garrulously enough, each of his superior skill, they strove to rival one another in the nicety of their aim and execution. The chief object now, was barely to miss the part at which they aimed. One planted the tomahawk in the tree so directly over the head of his captive, as to divide the huge tuft of hair which stood up massively in that quarter: and great was their exultation and loud their laughter, when the head thus jeoparded, very naturally, under the momentary impulse, was writhed about from the stroke, just at the moment when another hatchet, aimed to lie on one side of his cheek, clove the ear which it would have barely escaped had the captive continued immovable. Bleeding and suffering from these blows and hurts, not a solitary groan however escaped the victim. The stout-hearted Irishman continued to defy and to denounce his tormentors in language which, if only partially comprehended by his enemies, was yet illustrated, with sufficient animation, by the fierce light gleaming from his eye with a blaze like that of madness, and in the unblenching firmness of his cheek.

"And what for do ye howl, ye red-skinned divils, as if ye never seed a jontleman in the troubles, in all yer born days before? Be aisy, now, and shoot away with your pinted sticks, ye nagers,—shoot away and bad luck to ye, ye spalpeens; sure it isn't Tedd Macnamara that's afeerd of what ye can do, ye red divils. If it's the fun ye'r after now, honeys,— the sport that's something like—why, put your knife over this thong, and help this dilicate little fist to one of the bit shilalahs yonder. Do now, pretty crathers, do—and see what fun will come out of it. Ye'll not be after loving it at all, at all, I'm thinking, ye monkeys, and ye alligators, and ye red nagers; and them's the best names for ye, ye ragamuffin divils that ye are."

There was little intermission in his abuse. It kept due pace with their tortures, which, all this time, continued. The tomahawks continued to whiz about him on every side; and each close approximation of the instrument only called from him a newer sort of curse. Harrison was more than once prompted to rush forth desperately, at all hazards, in the hope to rescue the fearless captive. His noble hardihood, his fierce courage, his brave defiance, commanded all the sympathies of the concealed spectator. But he had to withstand them. It would have been madness and useless self-sacrifice, to have shown himself at such a moment, and the game was suffered to proceed without interruption.

It happened, however, as it would seem in compliance with a part of one of the demands of the captive that one of the tomahawks, thrown so as to rest betwixt his two uplifted palms, fell short, and striking the hide, a few inches below, which fastened his wrists to the tree, entirely separated it, and gave freedom to his arms. Though still incapable of any effort for his release, as the thongs tightly girded his body, and were connected on the other side of the tree, the fearless sufferer, with his freed fingers, proceeded to pluck from his body, amid a shower of darts, the arrows which had penetrated him in every part. These, with a shout of defiance, he hurled back towards his assailants, they answering in similar style with another shout and a new discharge of arrows, which again penetrated his person in every direction, inflicting the greatest pain, though carefully avoiding any vital region. And now as if impatient of their forbearance, the boys were made to give way, and, each armed with her hissing and resinous torch, the old women approached, howling and dancing, with shrill voices and an action of body frightfully demoniac. One after another, they rushed up to the prisoner, and, with fiendish fervour, thrust the blazing torches to his shrinking body, wherever a knife, an arrow, or a tomahawk had left a wound. The torture of this infliction greatly exceeded all to which he had been previously subjected; and with a howl, the unavoidable acknowledgment forced from nature by the extremity of pain, scarcely less horrible than that which they unitedly sent up around him, the captive dashed out his hands, and grasping one of the most forward among his unsexed tormentors, he firmly held her with one hand, while with the other he possessed himself of the blazing torch which she bore. Hurling her backwards, in the next moment, among the crowd of his enemies, with a resolution from despair, he applied the torch to the thongs which bound him to the tree and while his garments shrivelled and flamed, and while the flesh was blistered and burned with the terrible application, resolute as desperate, he kept the flame riveted to the suffering part, until the wythes that fastened his body to the tree, began to crackle, to blaze in him, and finally to break and separate!

His limbs were free. There was life and hope in the consciousness. A tide of fresh and buoyant emotions, actually akin to joy, rushed through his bosom, and he shouted aloud, with a cry of delight and exultation, in the consciousness of freedom from bonds and a situation which had been a mockery to the manhood and courage in his soul. He bounded forward with the cry. His garments were on fire. The flames curled over him, but he did not seem to feel or fear them. While the red warriors wondered, not knowing what to expect, he still further confounded

them by that over head and heels evolution which is called the somer-
sault, which carried him, a mass of fire, into the centre of a crowded circle of men, boys, and women. This scattered them in wild confusion. A
few blows were struck at him aimlessly by warriors as they darted aside;
but they left him free, and with a clear track. The blazing mass was a
surprise and terror, and the captive rolled over with impunity, the
flames being soon extinguished in the long green grasses of the plain.
Sore, scorched, suffering, he rose to his feet, shook out his hands in defiance, and with a wild yell, not unworthy to have issued from the throats
of the savages themselves, the captive darted away in flight, and, for a
moment, without any obstacle to freedom.

But the hope was short-lived in the bosom of the fugitive. The old
warriors now took up the cudgels. They had suffered the boys to enjoy
their sports, which, but for this unexpected event, might have continued much longer; but they were not willing to lose the victim decreed
for sacrifice. As Macnamara darted away, they threw the youth out of
the path, and dashed after him in pursuit. Escape was impossible, even
had the Irishman possessed the best legs in the world. The plain was
filled with enemies, and though the forest lay immediately beside it,
and though the necessities as well as instincts of the fugitive prompted
him to seek its immediate shelter, yet how should he escape so many
pursuers, and these men born of the forest thickets? They were soon
upon his heels. The poor fellow was still singularly vigorous. He possessed rare powers of endurance, and his hurts were those of the flesh
only, many of them only skin deep. His very tortures proved so many
spurs and goads to flight. He was covered with blisters; and the arrow
smarts were stinging him in arms, and thighs, and legs, like so many
scarificators. But the effect was to work up his mind to a fearful
energy; despair endowing him with a strength which, under no other
condition, he could have displayed. Very desperate was his attempt at
flight. He shouted as he fled. He dashed away right and left; narrowly
grazing the great pine,—barely dodging the branches of the umbra-
geous and low-spreading oak, and bounding over bush and log with
the fleetness of the antelope. He used his newly-won freedom nimbly,
and with wonderful exercise of agility and muscle; but was doomed to
use it vainly. He could not escape; but he might involve another in his
fearful fate! His headlong flight conducted him to the very coppice in
which Harrison lay concealed!

The cavalier beheld his peril from this unexpected cause of danger; but there was no retreat or evasion. The event had occurred too suddenly. He prepared for the result with the utmost possible coolness. He drew his knife and kept close to the cover of the fallen tree alongside of which he had laid himself down. Had the flying Macnamara seen this tree so as to have avoided it, Harrison might still have maintained his concealment. But the fugitive, unhappily, looked out for no such obstruction. He thought only of flight, and his legs were exercised at the expense of his eyes. A long-extended branch, shooting out from the tree, interposed, and he saw it not. His feet were suddenly entangled, and he fell between the arm and the trunk of the tree. Before he could rise or recover, his pursuers were upon him. He had half gained his feet; and one of his hands, in promoting this object, rested upon the tree itself, on the opposite side of which Harrison lay quiet, while the head of Macnamara was just rising above it. At that moment a tall chief of the Seratees, with a huge club, dashed the now visible skull down upon the trunk. The blow was fatal—the victim uttered not even a groan, and the spattering brains were driven wide, and into the upturned face of Harrison.

There was no more concealment for the latter after that, and, starting to his feet, in another moment his knife was thrust deep into the bosom of the astonished Seratee, before he had resumed the swing of his ponderous weapon. The Indian sank back, with a single cry, upon those who followed him—half paralysed, with himself, at the new enemy whom they had conjured up. But their panic was momentary, and the next instant saw fifty of them crowding upon the Englishman. He placed himself against a tree, hopeless, but determined to struggle to the last. But he was surrounded in a moment—his arms pinioned from behind, and knives from all quarters glittering around him, and aiming at his breast. What might have been his fate under the excitement of the scene and circumstances may easily be conjectured, for the red men were greatly excited—they had tasted blood; and, already, the brother of the Seratee chief—a chief himself,—had rushed into the circle, and with uplifted mace, was about to assert his personal claim to revenge the death of his brother—a claim which all others were prepared to yield. But, fortunately for the captive, there were other motives of action among the red men beside revenge. The threatened death by the mace of the Seratee was arrested—the blow was averted—the weapon stricken aside and intercepted by the huge staff of no less a person than the prophet.

"He is mine—the ghost of Chaharattee, my brother, is waiting for that of his murderer. I must hang his teeth on my neck," was the fierce cry, in his own language, of the surviving Seratee, when his weapon was thus arrested. But the prophet had his answer in a sense not to be withstood by the superstitious savage.

"Does the prophet speak for himself or for Manneyto? Is Manneyto a woman that we may say, Wherefore thy word to the prophet? Has not Manneyto spoken, and will not the chief obey? Lo! this is our victim, and the words of Manneyto are truth. He hath said one victim—one English for the sacrifice,—and but one before we sing the battle-song—before we go on the war-path of our enemies. Is not his word truth? This blood says it is truth. We may not slay another, but on the red trail of the English. The knife must be drawn and the tomahawk lifted on the ground of the enemy, but the land of Manneyto is holy, unless for his sacrifice. Thou must not strike the captive. He is captive to the Yemassee."

"He is the captive to the brown lynx of Seratee—is he not under his club?" was the fierce reply.

"Will the Seratee stand up against Manneyto? Hear! That is his voice of thunder, and see, the eye which he sends forth in the lightning!"

The auspicious bursting of the cloud at that moment—the vivid flashes which lightened up the heavens and the forest with a blinding glory, seemed to confirm the solemn claim of the prophet. Sullenly the Seratee chief submitted to the power which he might not openly withstand. But baffled in his attempt on the life of the prisoner, he yet claimed him as his captive, and demanded possession of him. But to this the prophet had his answer also.

"He is the captive of the Manneyto of the Yemassee; on the ground sacred to Manneyto."

Chapter Thirty-five

"Cords for the warrior—he shall see the fray
His arm shall share not—a worse doom than death,
For him whose heart, at every stroke, must bleed—
Whose fortune is the stake, and yet denied
All throw to win it."

THERE was no resisting this decree of the Prophet. The Seratee chief was silenced. The people were submissive. They were given to understand that their new captive was to be reserved for the sacrifice at the close of the campaign, when, as they confidently expected, they were to celebrate their complete victory over the Carolinians. Meanwhile, he was taken back, and under proper custodians, to the place where the ceremonies were still to be continued. The war-dance was begun in the presence of the prisoner. He looked down upon the preparations for a conflict, no longer doubtful, between the savages and his people. He watched their movements, heard their arrangements, saw their direction, knew their design, yet had no power to strike in for the succour or the safety of those in whom only he lived. What were his emotions in that survey? Who shall describe them?

They began the war-dance, the young warriors, the boys, and women—that terrible but fantastic whirl—regulated by occasional strokes upon the uncouth drum and an attenuated blast from the more flexible native bugle. That dance of death—a dance, which, perfectly military in its character, calling for every possible position or movement common to Indian strategy, moves them all with an extravagant sort of grace; and if contemplated without reference to the savage purposes which it precedes, is singularly pompous and imposing; wild, it is true, but yet exceedingly unaffected and easy, as it is one of the most familiar practices of Indian education. In this way, by extreme physical exercise, they provoke a required degree of mental enthusiasm. With this object the aborigines have many kinds of dances, and others of even more interesting character. Among many of the tribes these exhibitions are literally so many chronicles. They are the only records, left by tradition, of leading events in their history which they were instituted to commemorate. An epoch in the national progress—a new discovery—a new achievement—was frequently distinguished by the invention of a dance or game, to which a name was given significant of the circumstance. Thus, any successful hunt, out of their usual routine, was embodied in a series of evolutions at the gathering for a feast, exhibiting frequently in sport, what had really taken place. In this way, handed from tribe to tribe, and from generation to generation, it constituted a portion, not merely of the history of the past, but of the education of the future. This education fitted them alike for the two great exercises of most barbarians,—the battle and the chase. The weapons of the former were also those of the latter pursuit, and the joy of success in either object was expressed in the same manner. The dance and song formed the beginning, as they certainly made the conclusion of all their adventures; and whether in defeat or victory, there was no omission of the practice. Thus we have the song of war—of scalp-taking—of victory—of death; not to speak of the thousand various forms by which their feelings were expressed in song, in the natural progress of the seasons. These songs, in most cases, called for corresponding dances; and the Indian warrior, otherwise seeming rather a machine than a mortal, adjusted, on an inspiring occasion, the strains of the prophet and the poet, to the wild and various action of the Pythia. The elements of all uncultivated people are the same. The early Greeks, in their stern endurance of torment, in their sports and exercises, were exceedingly like the North American savages. The Lacedæmonians went to battle with songs and dances; a similar practice obtained among the Jews; and one particularly, alike of the Danes and Saxons, was to usher in the combat with wild and discordant anthems.

The survey was curious to Harrison, but it was also terrible. Conscious as he was, not merely of his own, but of the danger of the colony, he could not help feeling the strange and striking romance of his own situation. Bound to a tree—helpless, hopeless—a stranger, a prisoner, and destined to the sacrifice—the thick night around him—a thousand enemies, dark, dusky, fierce savages, half intoxicated with that wild physical action which has its drunkenness, not less than wine. Their wild distortions—their hell-kindled eyes—their barbarous sports and weapons—the sudden and demoniac shrieks from the women—the occasional burst of song, pledging the singer to the most diabolical achievements, mingled up strangely in a discord which had its propriety, with the clatter of the drum, and the long melancholy note of the bugle. And then, that high tumulus—that place of skulls—the bleached bones of centuries past peering through its sides, and speaking for the abundant fulness of the capacious mansion-house of death within! The awful scene of torture, and the subsequent unscrupulous murder of the heroic Irishman—the presence of the gloomy prophet in attendance upon the sacred fire, which he nursed carefully upon the mound—the little knot of chiefs, consisting of Sanutee, Ishiagaska, and others, not to speak of the Spanish agent, Chorley—in close council in his sight, but removed from hearing—these, and the consciousness of his own situation, while they brought to the heart of the Cavalier an added feeling of hopelessness, could not fail to awaken in his mind a sentiment of wonder and admiration, the immediate result of his excited thoughts and fancy.

But the dance was over at a signal from the prophet. He saw that the proper feeling of excitation had been attained. The demon was aroused, and, once aroused, was sleepless. The old women waved their torches and rushed headlong through the woods—shouting and shrieking—while the warriors, darting about with the most savage yells, struck their knives and hatchets into the neighbouring trees, giving each the name of an Englishman whom he knew, and howling out the sanguinary promise of the scalp-song, at every stroke inflicted upon the unconscious trunk.

"*Sangarrah-me, Sangarrah-me, Yemassee,*" was the cry of each chief to his particular division; and as they arranged themselves under their several commands, Harrison was enabled to form some idea of the proposed destination of each party. To Ishiagaska and Chorley, he saw assigned a direction which he readily conjectured would lead them to the Block House, and the settlement in the immediate neighbourhood, as it was not reasonable to suppose that the latter would desire any duty carrying him far from his vessel. To another force the word Coosaw sufficiently indicated Beaufort as the point destined for its assault; and thus, party after party was despatched in one direction or another, until but a single spot of the whole colony remained unthreatened with an assailant,—and that was Charleston. The reservation was sufficiently accounted for, as Sanutee, and the largest division of the Yemassee forces, remained unappropriated. The old chief had reserved this, the most dangerous and important part of the adventure, to himself.

A shrill cry—an unusual sound—broke upon the silence, and the crowd was gone in that instant;—all the warriors, with Sanutee at their head. The copse concealed them from the sight of Harrison, who, in another moment, found himself more closely grappled than before. A couple of tomahawks waved before his eyes in the glare of torches borne in the hands of the warriors who secured him. No resistance could have availed him, and, cursing his ill fortune, and suffering the most excruciating of mental griefs as he thought of the progress of the fate which threatened his people, he made a merit of necessity, and offering no obstacle to the will of his captors, he was carried to Pocota-ligo—bound with thongs and destined for the sacrifice which was to follow hard upon their triumph. Such was the will of the prophet of Manneyto, and ignorance does not often question the decrees of superstition.

Borne along with the crowd, Harrison entered Pocota-ligo under a motley guard and guidance. He had been intrusted to the care of a few superannuated old warriors, who were deemed sufficient for the service of keeping him a prisoner; but they were numerously attended. The mob of the Yemassees—for they had their mobs as well as the more civilized—consisted of both sexes; and when we reflect upon the usual estimation placed upon women by all barbarous people, we shall not be surprised to know that, on the present occasion, the sex were by far the most noisy if not the most numerous. Their cries—savage and sometimes indecent gestures—their occasional brutality, and the freedom and frequency with which they inflicted blows upon the captive as he approached them on his way to prison, showed them to have reached a condition, in which they possessed all the passions of the one sex, without the possession of their powers;—to have lost the gentle nature of the woman without acquiring the magnanimity of the man, which is the result of his consciousness of strength. We must add, however, in justice to the sex, that the most active participants in the torture of the captives of the red-men are mostly old women and boys. The young girls rarely show themselves active in such employments. On the present occasion, these old hags, bearing torches which they waved wildly in air as they ran, hurried along by the side of Harrison, urging him on with smart blows, which were painful and annoying, rather than dangerous. Some of them sang for him in their own language, songs sometimes of taunt, but frequently of downright blackguardism. And here we may remark, that it is rather too much the habit to speak of the Indians, at home and in their native character, as sternly and indifferently cold—people after the fashion of the elder Cato, who used to say that he never suffered his wife to embrace him, except when it thundered—adding, by way of jest, that he was therefore never happy except when Jupiter was pleased to thunder. We should be careful not to speak of them as we casually see them,— when, conscious of our superiority, and unfamiliar with our language, they are necessarily taciturn; as it is the pride of an Indian to hide his deficiencies. With a proper policy, which might greatly benefit upon circulation, he conceals his ignorance in silence. In his own habitation, uninfluenced by drink or any form of degradation, and unrestrained by the presence of superiors, he is sometimes even a jester—delights in a joke, practical or otherwise, and is not scrupulous about its niceness or propriety. In his council he is fond of speaking; glories in long talks; and, as he grows old, if you incline a willing ear, even becomes garrulous. Of course, all these habits are restrained by circumstances. He does not chatter when he fights or hunts, and when he goes to make a treaty, and never presumes to say more than he has been taught by his people.

The customary habit of the Yemassees was not departed from on the present occasion. The mob had nothing of forbearance towards the prisoner, and they showed but little taciturnity. Hootings and howlings— shriekings and shoutings—confused cries—yells of laughter—hisses of scorn—here and there a fragment of song, either of battle or ridicule, gathering, as it were, by a common instinct, into a chorus of fifty voices—most effectually banished silence from her usual night dominion in the sacred town of Pocota-ligo. In every dwelling—for the hour was not yet late—the torch blazed brightly—the entrances were thronged with their inmates, and not a tree but gave shelter to its own peculiar assemblage. Curiosity to behold a prisoner, destined by the unquestionable will of the prophet to the great sacrifice which should give gratitude to the Manneyto for the victory which such a pledge was most confidently anticipated to secure,—led them forward in droves; so that, when Harrison arrived in the centre of the town, the path became almost entirely obstructed by the dense and still gathering masses pressing upon them. The way, indeed, would have been completely impassable but for the hurrying torches carried forward by the attending women; who, waving them about recklessly over the heads of the crowd, distributed the melted gum in every direction, and effectually compelled the more obtrusive to recede into less dangerous places.

Thus marshalled, his guards bore the captive onward to the safe-keeping of a sort of block-house—a cell of logs, some twelve feet square, rather more compactly built than was the wont of Indian dwellings usually, and without any aperture save the single one at which he was forced to enter. Not over secure, however, as a prison, it was yet made to answer the purpose, and what it lacked in strength and security was, perhaps, more than supplied in the presence of the guard put upon it. Thrusting their prisoner, through the narrow entrance, into a damp apartment, the earthen floor of which was strewn with pine trash, they secured the door with thongs on the outside, and with the patience of old warriors, they threw themselves directly before it. Seldom making captives, unless as slaves, and the punishments of their own people being usually of a summary character, will account for the want of skill among the Yemassees in the construction of their dungeon. The present answered all their purposes, simply, perhaps, because it had answered the purposes of their fathers. This is reason enough, in a thousand respects, with the more civilized. The prison-house to which Harrison was borne, had been in existence a century.

Chapter Thirty-six

"Why, this is magic, and it breaks his bonds,
It gives him freedom."

HARRISON was one of those true philosophers who know always how to keep themselves for better times. As he felt that resistance, at that moment, must certainly be without any good result, he quietly enough suffered himself to be borne to prison. He neither halted nor hesitated, nor pleaded, nor opposed, but went forward, offering no obstacle, with as much wholesome good-will and compliance as if the proceeding were perfectly agreeable to him. He endured, with no little show of patience, all the blows and buffetings so freely bestowed upon him by his feminine enemies; and if he did not altogether smile under the infliction, he at least took good care to avoid any ebullition of anger, which as it was there impotent, must necessarily have been a weakness, and would most certainly have been entirely thrown away. Among the Indians, this was by far the better policy. They can admire the courage, though they hate the possessor. Looking round amid the crowd, Harrison thought he could perceive many evidences of this sentiment. Sympathy and pity he also made out, in the looks of a few. One thing he did certainly observe—a generous degree of forbearance, as well of taunt as of buffet, on the part of all the better-looking among the spectators. Nor did he deceive himself. The insolent portion of the rabble formed a class especially for such purposes as the present; and to them, its duties were left exclusively. The forbearance of the residue looked to him like kindness, and with the elasticity of his nature, hope came with the idea.

Nor was he mistaken. Many eyes in that assembly looked upon him with regard and commiseration. The firm but light tread of his step—the upraised, unabashed, the almost laughing eye—the free play into liveliness of the muscles of his mouth—sometimes curled into contempt, and again closely compressed, as in defiance—together with his fine, manly form, and even carriage—were all calculated to call for respect, if for no warmer feeling of the spectators. They all knew the bravery of the *Coosah-moray-te,* or the Coosaw-killer—many of them had felt his kindness and liberality, and, but for the passionate nationality of the Indian character, the sympathy of a few might at that moment have worked actively in his favour, and with the view to his release.

There was one in particular, among the crowd, who regarded him with a melancholy satisfaction. It was Matiwan, the wife of Sanutee. As the whole nation had gathered to the sacred town, in which, during the absence of the warriors, they found shelter, she was now a resident of Pocota-ligo. One among, but not of the rabble, she surveyed the prisoner with an emotion which only the heart of the bereaved mother may define. "Ah!" she muttered to herself, in her own language,— "ah! even thus lofty, and handsome, and brave—thus with a big heart, and a bright eye,—walked and looked the son of Matiwan and the great chief, Sanutee, when the young chief was the beloved brave of the Yemassee. Is there a living mother of the *Coosah-moray-te,* beyond the great waters, who loves her son, as the poor Matiwan loved the boy Occonestoga?" The strange enquiry filled the thoughts of the woman. Sympathy has wings as well as tears, and her eyes took a long journey in imagination to that foreign land. She saw the mother of the captive with a grief at heart like her own; and her own sorrows grew deeper at the survey. Then came a strange wish to serve that pale mother—to save her from an anguish such as hers: then she looked upon the captive, and her memory grew active; she knew him—she had seen him before in the great town of the pale-faces—he appeared a chief among them, and so had been called by her father, the old Warrior Etiwee, who, always an excellent friend to the English, had taken her, with the boy Occonestoga—on a visit to Charleston. She had there seen Harrison, but under another name. He had been kind to her father— had made him many presents, and the beautiful little cross of red coral, which, without knowing anything of its symbolical associations, she had continued to wear in her bosom, had been the gift of him who was now the prisoner to her people. She knew him through his disguise— her father would have known—would have saved him, had he been living. She had heard his doom denounced to take place on the return of the war-party; she gazed upon the manly form, the noble features, the free, fearless carriage—she thought of Occonestoga—of the pale mother of the Englishman—of her own bereavement—and of a thousand other things belonging naturally to the same topics. The more she thought, the more her heart grew softened within her—the more aroused her brain—the more restless and unrestrainable her spirit.

She turned away from the crowd as the prisoner was hurried into the dungeon. She turned away in anguish of heart, and a strange commotion of thought. She sought the shelter of the neighbouring wood, and rambled unconsciously, as it were, among the old forests. But she had no peace—she was pursued by the thought which assailed her from the first. The image of Occonestoga haunted her footsteps, and she turned only to see his bloody form and gashed head for ever at her elbow. He looked appealingly to her, and she then thought of the English mother over the waters. He pointed in the direction of Pocota-ligo, and she then saw the prisoner, Harrison. She saw him in the dungeon, she saw him on the tumulus—the flames were gathering around him—a hundred torturing arrows were stuck in his person, and she beheld the descending hatchet, bringing him the *coup de grace*. These images were full of terror, and their contemplation still more phrenzied her intellect. She grew strong and fearless with the desperation which they brought, and rushing through the forest, she once more made her way into the heart of Pocota-ligo.

The scene was changed. The torches were either burnt out or decaying, and scattered over the ground. The noise was over—the crowd dispersed and gone. Silence and sleep had resumed their ancient empire. She trod, alone, along the great thoroughfare of the town. A single dog ran at her heels, baying at intervals; but him she hushed with a word of unconscious soothing,—ignorant when she uttered it. There were burning feelings in her bosom, at variance with reason—at variance with the limited duty which she owed to society—at variance with her own safety. But what of these? There is a holy instinct that helps us, sometimes, in the face of our common standards. Humanity is earlier in its origin, and holier in its claims than society. She felt the one, and forgot to obey the other.

She went forward, and the prison-house of the Englishman under the shelter of a venerable oak—the growth of several silent centuries—rose dimly before her. Securely fastened with stout thongs on the outside, the door was still farther guarded by a couple of warriors lying upon the grass before it. One of them seemed to sleep soundly, but the other was wakeful. He lay at full length, however, his head upraised, and resting upon one of his palms—his elbow lifting it from the ground. The other hand grasped the hatchet, which he employed occasionally in chopping the earth just before him. He was musing rather than meditative, and the action of his hand and hatchet, capricious and fitful, indicated a want of concentration in his thought. This was in her favour. Still, there was no possibility of present approach unperceived; and to succeed in a determination only half-formed in her bosom, and, in fact, undesigned in her head, the gentle but fearless woman had recourse to some of those highly ingenious arts, so well known to the savage, and which he borrows in most part from the nature around him. Receding, therefore, to a little distance, she carefully sheltered herself in a small clustering clump of bush and brush, at a convenient distance for her purpose, and proceeded more definitely to the adjustment of her design.

Meanwhile, the yet wakeful warrior looked round upon his comrade, who lay in a deep slumber between himself and the dungeon entrance. Fatigue and previous watchfulness had done their work with the veteran. The watcher himself began to feel these influences stealing upon him, though not in the same degree, perhaps, and with less rapidity. But, as he looked around, and witnessed the general silence, his ear detecting with difficulty the drowsy motion of the zephyr among the thick branches over head—as if that slept also—his own drowsiness crept more and more upon his senses. Nature is thronged with sympathies, and the undiseased sense finds its kindred at all hours and in every situation.

Suddenly, as he mused, a faint chirp, that of a single cricket, swelled upon his ear from the neighbouring grove. He answered it, for great were his imitative faculties. He answered it, and from an occasional note, it broke out into a regular succession of chirpings, sweetly timed, and breaking the general silence of the night with an effect utterly indescribable, except to watchers blessed with a quick imagination. To these, still musing and won by the interruption, he sent back a similar response; and his attention was suspended, as if for some return. But the chirping died away in a click scarcely perceptible. It was succeeded, after a brief interval, by the faint note of a mockbird—a sudden note, as if the minstrel, starting from sleep, had sent it forth unconsciously, or, in a dream, had thus given utterance to some sleepless emotion. It was soft and gentle as the breathings of a flower. Again came the chirping of the cricket—a broken strain—capricious in time, and now seeming near at hand, now remote and flying. Then rose the whizzing hum, as of a tribe of bees suddenly issuing from the hollow of some neighbouring tree; and then, the clear, distinct tap of the woodpecker—once, twice, and thrice. Silence, then,—and the burden of the cricket was resumed, at the moment when a lazy stir of the breeze in the branches above the half-drowsy warrior seemed to solicit the torpor from which it occasionally started. Gradually, the successive sounds, so natural to the situation, and so grateful and congenial to the ear of the hunter, hummed his senses into slumber. For a moment, his eyes were half re-opened, and he looked round vacantly upon the woods, and upon the dying flame of the scattered torches, and then upon his fast-sleeping comrade. The prospect gave additional stimulus to the dreamy nature of the influences growing about and gathering upon him. Finally, the trees danced away from before his vision—the clouds came down close to his face; and, gently accommodating his arm to the support of his dizzy and sinking head, he gradually and unconsciously sank beside his companion, and, in a few moments, enjoyed a slumber as oblivious.

Chapter Thirty-seven

"'Tis freedom that she brings him, but the pass
Is leaguered he must 'scape through. Foemen watch,
Ready to strike the hopeless fugitive."

WITH the repose to slumber of the warrior—the cricket and the bee, the mock-bird and the woodpecker, all at once grew silent. A few moments only had elapsed, when, cautious in approach, they made their simultaneous appearance from the bush in the person of Matiwan. It was her skill that had charmed the spirit of the watcher into sleep, by the employment of associations so admirably adapted to the spirit of the scene. With that ingenuity which is an instinct with the Indians, she had imitated, one after another, the various agents, whose notes, duly timed, had first won, then soothed, and then relaxed and quieted the senses of the prison-keeper. She had rightly judged in the employment of her several arts. The gradual beatitude of mind and lassitude of body, brought about with inevitable certainty, when once we have lulled the guardian senses of the animal, must always precede their complete unconsciousness; and the art of the Indian, in this way, is often employed, in cases of mental excitation and disease, with a like object. The knowledge of the power of sooth-ing, sweet sounds over the wandering mind, possessed, as the Hebrew strongly phrased it, of devils, was not confined to that people, nor to the melodious ministerings of their David. The Indian claims for it a still greater influence, when, with a single note, he bids the serpent uncoil from his purpose, and wind unharmingly away from the bosom of his victim.

She emerged from her place of concealment with a caution which marked something more of settled purpose than she had yet exhibited. She approached in the dim, flickering light, cast from the decaying torches which lay scattered without order along the ground. A few paces only divided her from the watchers, and she continued to approach, when one of them turned with a degree of restlessness which led her to apprehend that he had awakened. She sank back like a shadow, as fleet and silently, once more into the cover of the brush. But he still slept. She again approached—and the last flare of the torch burning most brightly before, quivered, sent up a little gust of flame, and then went out, leaving her only the star light for her further guidance. This light was imperfect, as the place of imprisonment lay under a thickly branching tree, and her progress was therefore more difficult. But, with added difficulty, to the strong mood, comes added determination. To this determination the mind of Matiwan brought increased caution; and treading with the lightness of some melancholy ghost, groping at midnight among old and deserted chambers of the heart, the Indian woman stepped onward to her purpose, over a spot as silent, if not so desolate. Carefully placing her feet so as to avoid the limbs of the sleeping guard—who lay side by side and directly across the door-way—a design only executed with great difficulty, she at length reached the door; and drawing from her side a knife, she separated the thick thongs of skin which had otherwise well secured it. In another moment she was in the centre of the apartment and in the presence of the captive.

He lay at length, though not asleep, upon the damp floor of the dungeon. Full of melancholy thought, and almost prostrate with despair, his mind and imagination continued to depict before his eyes the thousand forms of horror to which savage cruelty was probably, at that very moment, subjecting the form most dear to his affections, and the people at large, for whose lives he would freely have given up his own. He saw the flames of their desolation—he heard the cries of their despair. Their blood gushed along before his eyes, in streams that spoke to him appealingly, at least for vengeance. How many veins, the dearest in his worship, had been drained perchance to give volume to their currents. The thought was horrible, the picture too trying and too terrible for the contemplation of a spirit, which, fearless and firm, was yet gentle and affectionate. He covered his eyes with his extended palms, as if to shut from his physical what was perceptible only to his mental vision.

A gust aroused him. The person of Matiwan was before him, a dim outline, undistinguishable in feature by his darkened and disordered sight. Her voice, like a murmuring water lapsing away among the rushes, fell soothingly upon his senses. Herself half dreaming—for her proceeding had been a matter rather of impulse than premeditation—the single word, so gently yet so clearly articulated, with which she broke in upon the melancholy musings of the captive, and first announced her presence, proved sufficiently the characteristic direction of her own maternal spirit.

"Occonestoga?"

"Who speaks!" was the reply of Harrison, starting to his feet, and assuming an attitude of defiance and readiness, not less than doubt; for he had now no thought but that of fight, in connexion with the Yemassees. "Who speaks?"

"Ah!" and in the exclamation we see the restored consciousness which taught her that not Occonestoga, but the son of another mother, stood before her.

"Ah! the Coosah-moray-te shall go," she said, in broken English.

"Who—what is this?" responded the captive, as he felt rather than understood the kindness of the tones that met his ear; and he now more closely approached the speaker.

"Hush,"—she placed her hand upon his wrist, and looked to the door with an air of anxiety—then whisperingly, urged him to caution.

"Big warriors—tomahawks—they may lie in the grass for the English."

"And who art thou—woman? Is it freedom—life? Cut the cords, quick, quick—let me feel my liberty." And as she busied herself in cutting the sinews that tightly secured his wrists, he scarcely forbore his show of impatience.

"I am free—I am free. I thank thee, God—great, good Father, this is thy Providence! I thank—I praise thee! And thou—who art thou, my preserver—but wherefore ask? Thou art—"

"It is Matiwan!" she said humbly.

"The wife of Sanutee—how shall I thank—how reward thee, Matiwan!"

"Matiwan is the woman of the great chief, Sanutee—she makes free the English, that has a look and a tongue like the boy Occonestoga."

"And where is he, Matiwan—where is the young warrior? I came to see after him, and it is this which has brought me into my present difficulty."

"Take the knife, English—take the knife. Look! the blood is on the hand of Matiwan. It is the blood of the boy."

"Woman, thou hast not slain him—thou hast not slain the child of thy bosom!"

"Matiwan saved the boy," she said proudly.

"Then he lives."

"In the blessed valley with the Manneyto. He will build a great lodge for Matiwan."

"Give me the knife."

He took it hurriedly from her grasp, supposing her delirious, and failing utterly to comprehend the seeming contradiction in her language. She handed it to him with a shiver as she gave it up; then, telling him to follow, and at the same time pressing her hand upon his arm by way of caution, she led the way to the entrance, which she had carefully closed after her on first entering. With as much, if not more caution than before, slowly unclosing it, she showed him, in the dim light of the stars, the extended forms of the two keepers. They still slept, but not soundly; and in the momentary glance which she required the captive to take, with all Indian deliberateness, she seemed desirous of familiarizing his glance with the condition of the scene, and with all those difficulties in the aspect of surrounding objects with which he was probably destined to contend. With the strong excitement of renewed hope, coupled with his consciousness of freedom, Harrison would have leaped forward; but she restrained him, and just at that moment, a sudden, restless movement of one of the sleepers warned them to be heedful. Quick as thought, in that motion, Matiwan sank back into the shadow of the dungeon, closing the door with the same impulse. Pausing, for a few moments, until the renewed and deep breathings from without reassured her, she then again led the way; but, as she half opened the door, turning quietly, she said in a whisper to the impatient Harrison:

"The chief of the English—the pale mother loves him over the water?"

"She does, Matiwan—she loves him very much."

"And the chief—he keeps her here—" pointing to her heart.

"Always—deeply. I love her too, very much, my mother!"

"It is good. The chief will go on the waters—he will go to the mother that loves him. She will sing like a green bird for him, when the young corn comes out of the ground. So Matiwan sings for Occonestoga. Go, English—but look!—for the arrow of the Yemassee runs along the path."

He pressed her hand warmly, but his lips refused all other acknowledgment. A deep sigh attested her own share of feeling in those references which she had made to the son in connexion with the mother. Then, once more unclosing the entrance, she stepped fearlessly and successfully over the two sleeping sentinels.

He followed her, but with less good fortune. Whether it was that he saw indistinctly in that unaccustomed light, and brushed one of the men with his foot, or whether the latter had been restless before, and only in an imperfect slumber just then broken, may not now be said; but at that inauspicious moment he awakened. With waking comes instant consciousness to the Indian, who differs in this particular widely from the negro. He knew his prisoner at a glance, and grappled him, as he lay, by the leg. Harrison, with an instinct quite as ready, dashed his unobstructed heel into the face of the warrior, and though released, would have followed up his blow by a stroke from his uplifted and bared knife; but his arm was held back by Matiwan. Her instinct was gentler and wiser. In broken English, she bade him fly for his life. His own sense taught him in an instant the propriety of this course, and before the aroused Indian could recover from the blow of his heel, and while he strove to waken his comrade, the Englishman bounded down, with a desperate speed, along the great thoroughfare leading to the river. The warriors were soon at his heels, but the generous mood of Matiwan did not rest with what she had already done. She threw herself in their way, and thus gained him some little additional time. But they soon put her aside, and their quick tread in the pathway taken by the fugitive warned him to the exercise of all his efforts. At the same time he coolly calculated his course and its chances. As he thought thus he clutched the knife given him by Matiwan, with an emotion of confidence which the warrior must always feel, having his limbs, and grasping a weapon with which his hand has been familiar.

"At least," thought he, fiercely,— "they must battle for the life they take. They gain no easy prey."

Thus he did console himself in his flight with his pursuers hard behind him. In his confidence he gained new strength; and thus the well-exercised mind gives strength to the body which it informs. Harrison was swift of foot, also,—few of the whites were better practised or more admirably formed for the events and necessities of forest life. But the Indian has a constant exercise which makes him a prodigy in the use of his legs. In a journey of day after day, he can easily out-wind any horse. Harrison knew this,—but then he thought of his knife. They gained upon him, and, as he clutched the weapon firmly in his grasp, his teeth grew tightly fixed, and he began to feel the rapturous delirium which makes the desire for the strife. Still, the river was not far off, and though galled at the necessity of flight, he yet felt what was due to his people, at that very moment, most probably, under the stroke of their savage butchery. He had no time for individual conflict, in which nothing might be done for them. The fresh breeze now swelled up from the river, and re-encouraged him.

"Could I gain that," he muttered to himself,— "could I gain that, I were safe. Of God's surety, I may."

A look over his shoulder, and a new start. They were behind him, but not so close as he had thought. Coolly enough he bounded on, thinking aloud:—

"They cannot touch, but they may shoot. Well—if they do, they must stop, and a few seconds more will give me a cover in the waters. Let them shoot—let them shoot. The arrow is better than the stake." Thus muttering to himself, but in tones almost audible to his enemies, he kept his way with a heart something lighter from his momentary effort at philosophy. He did not perceive that his pursuers had with them no weapon but the tomahawk, or his consolations might have been more satisfactory.

In another moment he was upon the banks of the river; and there, propitiously enough, a few paces from the shore, lay a canoe tied to a pole that stood upright in the stream. He blessed his stars as he beheld it, and pausing not to doubt whether a paddle lay in its bottom or not, he plunged incontinently forward, wading almost to his middle before he reached it. He was soon snug enough in its bottom, and had succeeded in cutting the thong with his knife when the Indians appeared upon the bank. Dreading their arrows, for the broad glare of the now rising moon gave them sufficient light for their use had they been provided with them, he stretched himself at length along the bottom of the boat, and left it to the current, which set strongly downward. But a sudden plunge into the water of one and then the other of his pursuers, left him without the hope of getting off so easily. The danger came in a new shape, and he properly rose to meet it. Placing himself in a position which would enable him to turn readily upon any point which they might assail, he prepared for the encounter. One of the warriors was close upon him—swimming lustily, and carrying his tomahawk grasped by the handle in his teeth. The other came at a little distance, and promised soon to be up with him. The first pursuer at length struck the canoe, raised himself sufficiently on the water for that purpose, and his left hand grasped one of the sides, while the right prepared to take the hatchet from his jaws. But with the seizure of the boat by his foe came the stroke of Harrison. His knife drove half through the hand of the Indian, who released his grasp with a howl that made his companion hesitate. Just at that instant a third plunge into the water, as of some prodigious body, called for the attention of all parties anew. The pursuers now became the fugitives, as their quick senses perceived a new and dangerous enemy in the black mass surging towards them, with a power and rapidity which taught them the necessity of instant flight, and with no half effort. They well knew the fierce appetite and the tremendous jaws of the native alligator, the American crocodile,—one of the largest of which now came looming towards them. Self-preservation was the word. The captive was forgotten altogether in their own danger; and swimming with all their strength, and with all their skill, in a zigzag manner, so as to compel their unwieldy pursuer to make frequent and sudden turns in the chase, occasionally pausing to splash the water with as much noise as possible—a practice known to discourage his approach when not over-hungry—they contrived to baffle his pursuit, and half exhausted, the two warriors reached and clambered up the banks, just as their ferocious pursuer, close upon their heels, had opened his tremendous jaws, with an awful compass, ready to engulf them. They were safe though actually pursued even up the banks by the voracious and possibly half-starved monster. Their late captive, the fugitive, was now safe also. Paddling as well as he could with a broken flap-oar lying in the bottom of the boat, he shaped his course to strike at a point as far down the river as possible, without nearing the pirate craft of Chorley. In an hour, which seemed to him an age, he reached the opposite shore, a few miles from the Block House, not very much fatigued, and in perfect safety.

Chapter Thirty-eight

"'Tis an unruly mood, that will not hear,
In reason's spite, the honest word of truth—
Such mood will have its punishment, and time
Is never slow to bring it. It will come."

LET us somewhat retrace our steps, and go back to the time, when, made a prisoner in the camp of the Yemassees, Harrison was borne away to Pocota-ligo, a destined victim for the sacrifice to their god of victory. Having left him, as they thought, secure, the war-party, consisting, as already described, of detachments from a number of independent, though neighbouring nations, proceeded to scatter themselves over the country. In small bodies, they ran from dwelling to dwelling with the utmost rapidity—in this manner, by simultaneous attacks, everywhere preventing anything like union or organization among the borderers. One or two larger parties were designed for higher enterprises, and without permitting themselves to be drawn aside to these smaller matters, pursued their object with Indian inflexibility. These had for their object the surprise of the towns and villages; and so great had been their preparations, so well conducted their whole plan of warfare, that six thousand warriors had been thus got together, and, burning and slaying, they had made their way, in the progress of this insurrection, to the very gates of Charleston—the chief, indeed the only town, of any size or strength, in the colony. But this belongs not to the narrative immediately before us.

Two parties of some force took the direction given to our story, and making their way along the river Pocota-ligo, diverging for a few miles on the English side, had, in this manner, assailed every dwelling and settlement in their way to the Block House. One of these parties was commanded by Chorley, who, in addition to his seamen, was intrusted with the charge of twenty Indians. Equally savage with the party he commanded, the path of this ruffian was traced in blood. He offered no obstacle to the sanguinary indulgence, on the part of the Red men, of their habitual fury in war; but rather stimulated their ferocity by the indulgence of his own. Unaccustomed, however, to a march through the forests, the progress of the seamen was not so rapid as that of the other party despatched on the same route; and many of the dwellings, therefore, had been surprised and sacked some time before the sailor commander could make his appearance. The Indian leader who went before him was Ishiagaska, one of the most renowned warriors of the nation. He, indeed, was one of those who, making a journey to St. Augustine, had first been seduced by the persuasions of the Spanish governor of that station—a station denounced by the early Carolinians, from the perpetual forays upon their borders, by land and sea, issuing from that quarter—as another *Sallee*. He had sworn fidelity to the King of Spain while there, and from that point had been persuaded to visit the neighbouring tribes of the Creek, Apalachian, Euchee, and Cherokee Indians, with the war-belt, and a proposition of a common league against the English settlements—a proposition greedily accepted, when coming with innumerable presents of hatchets, knives, nails, and gaudy dresses, furnished by the Spaniards, who well knew how to tempt and work upon the appetites and imagination of the savages. Laden with similar presents, the chief had returned home, and with successful industry had succeeded, as we have seen, aided by Sanutee, in bringing many of his people to a similar way of thinking with himself. The frequent aggressions of the whites, the cheats practised by some of their traders, and other circumstances, had strongly co-operated to the desired end; and with his desire satisfied, Ishiagaska now headed one of the parties destined to carry the war to Port Royal Island, sweeping the track of the Pocotaligo settlements in his progress, and at length uniting with the main party of Sanutee before Charleston.

He was not slow in the performance of his mission; but fortunately for the English, warned by the counsels of Harrison, the greater number in this precinct had taken timely shelter in the Block House, and left but their empty dwellings to the fury of their invaders. Still, there were many not so fortunate; and, plying their way from house to house in their progress, with all the stealthy silence of the cat, the Indians drove their tomahawks into many of the defenceless cotters who came imprudently to the door in recognition of the conciliatory demand which they made for admission. Once in possession, their aim was indiscriminate slaughter, and one bed of death not unfrequently comprised the forms of an entire family—husband, wife, and children. Sometimes they fired the dwelling into which caution denied them entrance, and as the inmates fled from the flames, stood in watch and shot them down with their arrows. In this way, sparing none, whether young or old, male or female, the band led on by Ishiagaska appeared at length before the dwelling of the pastor, Matthews. Relying upon his reputation with the Indians, and indeed unapprehensive of any commotion, for he knew nothing of their arts of deception, we have seen him steadily sceptical, and almost rudely indifferent to the advice of Harrison. Regarding the cavalier in a light somewhat equivocal, it is more than probable that the source of the counsel was indeed the chief obstacle with him in the way of its adoption. Be that as it may, he stubbornly held out in his determination to abide where he was, though somewhat staggered in his confidence, when in their flight from their own more exposed situation to the shelter of the Block House, under Harrison's counsel, the old dame Grayson, with her elder son, stopped at his dwelling. He assisted the ancient lady to alight from her horse, and helped her into the house for refreshments, while her son busied himself with the animal.

"Why, what's the matter, dame? What brings you forth at this late season? To my mind, at your time of life, the bed would be the best place, certainly," was the address of the pastor as he handed her some refreshment.

"Oh, sure, parson, and it's a hard thing for such as me to be riding about the country on horseback at any time, much less at night—though to be sure Watty kept close to the bridle of the creature, which you see is a fine one, and goes like a cradle."

"Well, but what brings you out?—you have not told me that, yet. Something of great moment, doubtless."

"What, you haven't heard? Hasn't the captain told you? Well, that's strange! I thought you'd be one of the first to hear it all,—seeing that all say he thinks of nobody half so much as of your young lady there. Ah! my dear—well, you needn't blush now, nor look down, for he's a main fine gentleman, and you couldn't find a better in a long day's journey."

The pastor looked grave, while the old dame, whose tongue always received a new impulse when she met her neighbours, ran on in the most annoying manner. She stopped at last, and though very readily conjecturing now the occasion of her flight, the pastor did not conceive it improper to renew his question.

"Well, as I said, it's all owing to the captain's advice—Captain Harrison, you know—a sweet gentleman that, as ever lived. He it was—he came to me this morning, and he went to all the neighbours, and looked so serious—you know he don't often look serious—but he looked so serious as he told us all about the savages—the Yemassees, and the Coosaws—how they were thinking to rise and tomahawk us all in our beds; and then he offered to lend me his horse, seeing I had no creature, and it was so good of him—for he knew how feeble I was, and his animal is so gentle and easy."

"And so, with this wild story, he has made you travel over the country by night, when you should be in your bed. It is too bad—this young man takes quite too many liberties."

"Why, how now, parson—what's to do betwixt you and the captain?" asked the old lady in astonishment.

"Well—nothing of any moment," was the grave reply. "I only think that he is amusing himself at our expense, with a levity most improper, by alarming the country."

"My!—and you think the Indians don't mean to attack and tomahawk us in our beds?"

"That is my opinion, dame—I see no reason why they should. It is true, they have had some difficulties with the traders of late, but they have been civil to us. One or more have been here every day during the last week, and they seemed then as peaceably disposed as ever. They have listened with much patience to my poor exhortations, and, I flatter myself, with profit to their souls and understandings. I have no apprehension myself; though, had it been left to Bess and her mother, like you, we should have been all riding through the woods to the Block House, with the pleasure of riding back in the morning."

"Bless me! how you talk—well, I never thought to hear so badly of the captain. He did seem so good a gentleman, and was so sweetly spoken."

"Don't mistake me, dame,—I have said nothing unfavourable to the character of the gentleman—nothing bad of him. I know little about him, and this is one chief objection which I entertain to a greater intimacy. Another objection is that wild and indecorous levity, of which he never seems to divest himself, and which I think has given you to-night a fatiguing and unnecessary ramble."

"Well, if you think so, I don't care to go farther, for I don't expect to be at all comfortable in the Block House. So, if you can make me up a truck, here—"

"Surely, dame,—Bess, my dear—"

But the proposed arrangement was interrupted by Walter Grayson, who just then appeared, and who stoutly protested against his mother's stopping short of the original place of destination. The elder Grayson was a great advocate for Captain Harrison, who embodied all his ideal of what was worthy and magnificent, and in whom his faith was implicit—and he did not scruple to dilate with praiseworthy eloquence upon the scandal of such a proceeding as that proposed.

"You must not think of it, mother. How will it look? Besides, I'm sure the captain knows what's right, and wouldn't say what was not certain. It's only a mile and a bit—and when you can make sure, you must not stop short."

"But, Watty, boy—the parson says it's only the captain's fun, and we'll only have to take a longer ride in the morning if we go on further to-night."

The son looked scowlingly upon the pastor, as he responded:—

"Well, perhaps the parson knows better than any body else; but give me the opinion of those whose business it is to know. Now, I believe in the captain whenever fighting's going on, and I believe in the parson whenever preaching's going on—so, as it's fighting and not preaching now, I don't care who knows it, but I believe in the captain, and I won't believe in the parson. If it was preaching and not fighting, the parson should be my man."

"Now, Watty, don't be disrespectful. I'm sure the parson must be right, and so I think we had all better stay here when there's no use in going."

"Well now, mother, I'm sure the parson's wrong, and if you stay, it will only be to be tomahawked and scalped."

"Why alarm your mother with such language, young man? You are deceived—the Yemassees were never more peaceable than they are at present." Matthews thus broke in, but commanded little consideration from the son, and almost provoked a harsh retort:—

"I say, Parson Matthews—one man knows one thing, and another man another—but, curse me, if I believe in the man that pretends to know everything. Now fighting's the business, the very trade as I may say of Captain Harrison, of the Foresters, and I can tell you, if it will do you any good to hear, that he knows better how to handle these red-skins than any man in Granville county, let the other man come from whatever quarter he may. Now, preaching's your trade, though you can't do much at it, I think; yet, as it is your trade, nobody has a right to meddle—it's your business, not mine. But, I say, parson—I don't think it looks altogether respectful to try and undo, behind his back, the trade of another; and I think it little better than backbiting for any one to speak disreputably of the captain, just when he's gone into the very heart of the nation, to see what we are to expect, and all for our benefit."

Grayson was mightily indignant, and spoke his mind freely. The parson frowned and winced at the rather novel and nowise sparing commentary, but could say nothing precisely to the point beyond what he had said already. Preaching, and not fighting, was certainly his profession; and, to say the least of it, the previous labours of Harrison among the Indians, his success, and knowledge of their habits and character, justified the degree of confidence in his judgment, upon which Grayson so loudly insisted, and which old Matthews so sturdily withheld. A new speaker now came forward, however, in the person of Bess Matthews, who, without the slightest shrinking, advancing from the side of her mother, thus addressed the last speaker:—

"Where, Master Grayson, did you say Captain Harrison had gone?"

"Ah, Miss Bessy, I'm glad to see you. But you may well ask, for it's wonderful to me how any body can undervalue a noble gentleman just at the very time he's doing the best, and risking his own life for us all. Who knows but just at this moment the Yemassees are scalping him in Pocota-ligo, for it's there he is gone to see what we may expect."

"You do not speak certainly, Master Grayson—it is only your con-jecture?" was her inquiry, while the lip of the maiden trembled, and the colour fled hurriedly from her cheek.

"Ay, but I do, Miss Bessy, for I put him across the river myself, and it was then he lent me the horse for mother. Yes, there he is, and nobody knows in what difficulty—for my part, I'm vexed to the soul to hear people running down the man that's doing for them what they can't do for themselves, and all only for the good-will of the thing, and not for any pay."

"Nobody runs down your friend, Mr. Grayson."

"Just the same thing—but you may talk as you think proper; and if you don't choose to go, you may stay. I don't want to have any of mine scalped, and so, mother, let us be off."

The old woman half hesitated, and seemed rather inclined once more to change her decision and go with her son, but happening to detect a smile upon the lips of the pastor, she grew more obstinate than ever, and peremptorily declared her determination to stay where she was. Grayson seemed perfectly bewildered, and knew not what to say. What he did say seemed only to have the effect of making her more dogged in her opposition than ever, and he was beginning to despair of success, when an influential auxiliary appeared in the person of his younger brother. To him the elder instantly appealed, and a close observer might have detected another change in the countenance of the old dame at the approach of her younger son. The features grew more feminine, and there was an expression of conscious dependance in the lines of her cheek and the half parted lips, which necessarily grew out of the greater love which she bore to the one over the other child.

"And what do you say, Hughey, my son?" inquired the old dame, affectionately.

"What have I said, mother?" was the brief response.

"And we must go to the Block House, Hughey?"

"Did we not set out to go there?"

"But the parson thinks there is no danger, Hughey."

"That is, doubtless, what he thinks. There are others having quite as much experience, who think there is danger, and as you have come so far, it will not be much additional trouble to go farther and to a place of safety. Remember my father—he thought there was no danger, and he was scalped for it."

The young man spoke gravely and without hesitation, but with a manner the most respectful. His words were conclusive with his mother, whose jewel he unquestionably was, and his last reference was unnecessary. Drawing the strings of her hat, with a half suppressed sigh, she prepared to leave a circle somewhat larger and consequently somewhat more cheerful than that to which she had been accustomed. In the meantime, a little by-play had been going on between the elder brother and Bess Matthews, whose apprehensions, but poorly concealed, had been brought into acute activity on hearing of the precarious adventure which her lover had undertaken. This dialogue, however, was soon broken by the departure of Dame Grayson, attended by her elder son, the younger remaining behind, much against the desire of the anxious mother, though promising soon to follow. Their departure was succeeded by a few moments of profound and somewhat painful silence, for which each of the parties had a particular reason. The pastor, though obstinately resolved not to take the counsel given by Harrison, was yet not entirely satisfied with his determination; and the probability is, that a single circumstance occurring at that time, so as to furnish a corresponding authority from another, might have brought about a change in his decision. His wife was, comparatively speaking, a taciturn body, particularly when the widow Grayson was present. She was, just now, a little bewildered also, between the extremes of counsel,—Harrison's on the one hand and the Parson's on the other. She accordingly looked her bewilderment only, and said nothing, while Bess Matthews, filled only with apprehensions of her lover, in supposed danger form the Yemassees, was as little capable of thought or speech. She could contribute nothing to the discussion.

Young Grayson, too, had his peculiar cause of disquiet, and, with a warm passion, active yet denied, in his heart—and a fierce mood for ambition, kept within those limits which prescription and social artifice so frequently wind, as with the coil of the constrictor, around the lofty mind and the upsoaring spirit, keeping it down to earth, and chaining it in a bondage as degrading as it is unnatural—he felt in no humour to break through the restraints which fettered the goodly company about him. Still, the effort seemed properly demanded of him, and, referring to the common movement, he commenced the conversation by regretting, with a commonplace phraseology, the prospect held forth, so injurious to the settlement, by any approaching tumult among the Indians. The old pastor fortified his decision not to remove, by repeating his old confidence in their quiet:—

"The Indians," said he, "have been and are quiet enough. We have no reason to anticipate assault now. It is true, they have the feelings of men, and as they have been injured by some of our traders, and perhaps by some of our borderers, they may have cause of complaint, and a few of them may even be desirous of revenge. This is but natural. But, if this were the general feeling, we should have seen its proofs before now. They would seek it in individual enterprises, and would strike and slay those who wronged them. Generally speaking, they have nothing to complain of; for, since that excellent man, Charles Craven, has been governor, he has been their friend, even in spite of the Assembly, who, to say truth, have been nowise sparing of injustice wherever the savage has been concerned. Again, I say, I see not why we should apprehend danger from the Yemassees at this moment."

As if himself satisfied with the force of what he had said, the pastor threw himself back in his chair, and closed his eyes and crossed his hands in complacent style, his look wearing an appearance of most satisfactory conclusion—solemnly assured, and authoritatively content. Our parson had, we fear, quite as much pride in his head, as devotion in his heart. Grayson replied briefly:—

"Yet there are some evidences which should not be disregarded. Sanutee, notoriously friendly as he has been to us, no longer visits us—he keeps carefully away, and when seen, his manner is restrained, and his language anything but cordial. Ishiagaska, too, has been to St. Augustine, brought home large presents for himself and other of the chiefs, and has paid a visit to the Creeks, the Apalachian, and other tribes—besides bringing home with him Chigilli, the celebrated Creek war-chief, who has been among the Yemassees ever since. Now, to say the least of it, there is much that calls for attention in the simple intercourse of foes so inveterate hitherto as the Spaniards and Yemassees. Greater foes have not often been known, and this new friendship is therefore the more remarkable; conclusive, indeed, when we consider the coldness of the Yemassees towards us just as they have contracted this new acquaintance; the fury with which they revolutionized the nation, upon the late treaty for their lands, and the great difficulty which Sanutee had in restraining them from putting our commissioners to death."

"Ah, that was a bad business, but the fault was on our side. Our Assembly would inveigle with the young chiefs, and bribe them against the will of the old, though Governor Craven told them what they might expect, and warned them against the measure. I have seen his fine letter to the Assembly on that very point."

"We differ, Mr. Matthews, about the propriety of the measure, for it is utterly impossible that the whites and Indians should ever live together and agree. The nature of things is against it, and the very difference between the two, that of colour, perceptible to our most ready sentinel, the sight, must always constitute them an inferior caste in our minds. Apart from this, an obvious superiority in arts and education must soon force upon them the consciousness of their inferiority. When this relationship is considered, in connexion with the uncertainty of their resources and means of life, it will be seen that, after a while, they must not only be inferior, but they must become dependant. When this happens, and it will happen with the diminution of their hunting lands, circumscribed, daily, more and more, as they are by our approaches, they must become degraded, and sink into slavery and destitution. A few of them have become so now; they are degraded by brutal habits,—and the old chiefs have opened their eyes to the danger among their young men, from the seductive poisons introduced among them by our traders. They begin too, to become straitened in their hunting grounds. They lose by our contact in every way; and to my mind, the best thing we can do for them is to send them as far as possible from communion with our people."

"What! and deny them all the benefits of our blessed religion?"

"By no means, sir. The old apostles would have gone along with, or after them. Unless the vocation of the preacher be very much changed in times present from times past, they will not, therefore, be denied any of the benefits of religious education."

The answer somewhat changed the direction of our pastor's discourse, who, though a very well meaning, was yet a very sleek and highly providential person; and, while his wits furnished no ready answer to this suggestion, he was yet not prepared, himself, for an utter remove from all contact with civilization, and the good things known to the economy of a Christian kitchen. As he said nothing in reply, Grayson proceeded thus:—

"There is yet another circumstance upon which I have made no remark, yet which seems important at this moment of doubt, and possibly of danger. This guarda costa, lying in the river for so many days, without any intercourse with our people, and seemingly with no object, is at least singular. She is evidently Spanish; and the report is, that on her way, she was seen to put into every inlet along the coast— every bay and creek along the rivers—and here we find her, not coming to the shore, but moored in the stream, ready to cut cable and run at a moment. What can be her object?"

"You have been at some pains, Master Hugh Grayson, I see, to get evidence; but so far as this vessel or guarda costa is concerned, I think I may venture to say she is harmless. She is *not* a Spanish, but an English vessel. As to her putting into this creek or that, I can say nothing—she may have done so, and it is very probable, for she comes especially to get furs and skins from the Indians. I know her captain—at least I knew him when a boy—a wild youth from my own country—who took to the sea for the mere love of roving. He was wild, and perhaps a little vicious, when young, and may be so now; but I have his own word that his object is trade with the Indians for furs and skins, as I have told you."

"And why not with the whites for furs and skins? No, sir! He needs no furs, and of this I have evidence enough. I had a fine parcel, which I preferred rather to sell on the spot than send to Charleston, but he refused to buy from me on the most idle pretence. This, more than any thing else, makes me doubt; and, in his refusal, I feel assured there is more than we know of. Like yourself, I have been slow to give ear to these apprehensions, yet they have forced themselves upon me; and precaution is surely better, even though at some trouble, when safety is the object. My brother, from whom I have several facts of this kind within the last hour, is himself acquainted with much in the conduct of the Indians, calculated to create suspicion, and from Captain Harrison he gets the rest."

"Ay, Harrison again—no evidence is good without him. He is everywhere, and with him a good jest is authority enough at any time."

"I love him not, sir, any more than yourself," said Grayson, gloomily; "but there is reason in what he tells us now."

"Father!" said Bess, coming forward, and putting her hand tenderly on the old man's shoulder— "hear to Master Grayson—he speaks for the best. Let us go to the Block, only for the night, or at most two or three nights—for Gabriel said the danger would be soon over."

"Go to, girl, and be not foolish. Remember, too, to speak of gentlemen by their names in full, with a master before them, or such title as the law or usage gives them. Go!"

The manner in which Harrison had been referred to by the daughter, offended Grayson not less than it did her father, and, though now well satisfied of the position in which the parties stood, he could not prevent the muscles of his brow contracting sternly, and his eyes bending down sullenly upon her. The old lady now put in:—

"Really, John, you are too obstinate. Here are all against you, and there is so little trouble, and there may be so much risk. You may repent when it is too late."

"You will have something then to scold about, dame, and therefore should not complain. But all this is exceedingly childish, and you will do me the favour, Master Grayson, to discourse of other things, since, as I see not any necessity to fly from those who have been friends always, I shall, for this good night at least, remain just where I am. For you, wife, and you, Bess, if you will leave me, you are both at liberty to go."

"Leave you, father," exclaimed Bess, sinking on one knee by the old man's side— "Oh! do not speak unkindly. I will stay, and if there be danger, will freely share it with you, in whatever form it may chance to come."

"You are a good girl, Bess—a little timid, perhaps, but time will cure you of that," and patting her on the head, the old man rose, and took his way from the house into his cottage enclosure. Some household duties at the same moment demanding the consideration of the old lady in another room, she left the young people alone together.

Chapter Thirty-nine

"A cruel tale for an unwilling ear,
And maddening to the spirit. But go on—
Speak daggers to my soul, which, though it feels,
Thou can'st not warp to wrong by injuries."

THE departure of the pastor and his wife was productive of some little awkwardness in those who remained. For a few moments, a deathlike stillness succeeded. Well aware that her affections for Harrison were known to her present companion, a feeling not altogether unpleasant, of maiden bashfulness, led the eyes of Bess to the floor, and silenced her speech. A harsher mood, for a time, produced a like situation on the part of Grayson; but it lasted not long. With a sullen sort of resolution, gathering into some of that energetic passion, as he proceeded, which so much marked his character, he broke the silence at length with a word—a single word—uttered desperately, as it were, and with a half choking enunciation:—

"Miss Matthews—"

She looked up at the sound, and as she beheld the dark expression of his eye, the concentrated glance, the compressed lip—as if he dared not trust himself to utter that which he felt at the same time must be uttered—she half started, and the "Sir" with which she acknowledged his address was articulated timorously.

"Be not alarmed, Miss Matthews; be not alarmed. I see what I would not see. I see that I am an object rather of fear, rather of dislike—detestation it may be—than of any other of those sweeter feelings I would freely give my life to inspire in your heart."

"You wrong me, Master Grayson, indeed you do. I have no such feelings for you, as those you speak of. I do not dislike or detest you, and I should be very sorry to have you think so. Do not think so, I beg you."

"But you fear me—you fear me, Miss Matthews, and the feeling is much the same. Yet why should you fear me—what have I done, what said?"

"You startle me, Master Grayson—not that I fear you, for I have no cause to fear when I have no desire to harm. But, in truth, sir— when you look so wildly and speak so strangely, I feel unhappy and apprehensive; and yet—I do not fear you."

He looked upon her as she spoke with something of a smile—a derisive smile.

"Yet, if you knew all, Miss Matthews—if you had seen and heard all—ay, even of the occurrences of the last few hours, you would both fear and hate me."

"I do not fear to hear, Master Grayson, and therefore I beg that you will speak out. You cannot, surely, design to terrify me? Let me but think so, sir, though for a moment only, and you will as certainly fail."

"You are strong, but not strong enough to hear, without terror, the story I could tell you. I said you feared, and perhaps hated me— more—perhaps you despise me. I despise myself, sincerely, deeply, for some of my doings, of which you—my mad passion for you, rather— has been the cause."

"Speak no more of this, Master Grayson—freely did I forgive you that error—I would also forget it, sir,"

"That forgiveness was of no avail—my heart has grown more black, more malignant than ever; and no need for wonder! Let your thoughts go back and examine, along with mine, its history; for, though, in this search, I feel the accursed probe irritating anew at every touch the yet bleeding wound, I am not unwilling that my own hand should direct it. Hear me. We were children together, Bess Matthews.—In our infancy, in another land, we played happily together. When we came to this, unconscious almost of our remove, for at first we were not separated,—when the land was new, and our fathers felled the old trees and made a cabin in common for them both, for three happy years we played together under the same shelter. Day by day found us inseparate, and, at that time, mutual dependants. Each day gave us a new consciousness, and every new consciousness taught us a most unselfish division of our gains. I feel that such was your spirit, Bess Matthews—do me the justice to say, you believe such was my spirit also."

"It was—I believe it, Hugh—Master Grayson, I mean."

"Oh, be not so frigid—say Hugh—Hugh, as of old you used to say it," exclaimed the youth passionately, as she made the correction.

"Such was your spirit then, Hugh, I willingly say it. You were a most unselfish playmate. I have always done you justice in my thought. I am glad still to do so."

"Then our school-mate life—that came—three months to me in the year, with old Squire Downie, while you had all the year. I envied you that, Bess, though I joyed still in your advantages. What was my solace the rest of the year, when, without a feeling for my labour, I ran the furrows, and following my father's footsteps, dropped the grain into them? What was my solace then? Let me answer, as perhaps you know not. The thought of the night, when, unwearied by all exertion, I should fly over to your cottage, and chat with you the few hours between night-fall and bedtime. I loved you then.—That was love, though neither of us knew it. It was not the search after the playmate, but after the playmate's heart, that carried me there; for my brother, with whom you played not less than with myself,—he sank wearied to his bed, though older and stronger than myself. I was unfatigued, for I loved; and thus it is that the body, taking its temper from the affections, is strong or weak, bold or timid, as they warm into emotion, or freeze with indifference. But day after day, and night after night, I came; unrelaxing, unchanging, to watch your glance, to see the play of your lips—to be the adoring boy, afraid sometimes even to breathe, certainly to speak, through fear of breaking the spell, or possibly of offending the divinity to whom I owed so much, and sent up feelings in prayer so devoutly."

"Speak not thus extravagantly, Master Grayson, or I must leave you."

"Hugh—call me Hugh, will you not? It bears me back—back to the boyhood I would I had never risen from."

"Hugh, then, I will call you, and with a true pleasure. Ay, more, Hugh, I will be to you again the sister you found me then; but you must not run on so idly."

"Idly, indeed, Bess Matthews, when for a dearer and a sweeter name I must accept that of sister. But let me speak ere I madden. Time came with all his changes. The neighbourhood thickened, we were no longer few in number, and consequently no longer dependant upon one another. The worst change followed then, Bess Matthews—the change in you."

"How, Hugh—you saw no change in me. I have surely been the same always."

"No, no—many changes I saw in you. Every hour had its change, and most of them were improving changes. With every change you grew more beautiful; and the auburn of your hair in changing to a deep and glossy brown, and the soft pale of your girlish cheek in putting on a leaf of the most delicate rose, and the bright glance of your eye in assuming a soft and qualifying moisture in its expression,—were all so many exquisite changes of lovely to lovelier, and none of them unnoticed by me. My eyes were sentinels that slept not when watching yours. I saw every change, however unimportant—however unseen by others! Not a glance—not a feature—not a tone—not an expression did I leave unstudied; and every portraiture, indelibly fixed upon my memory, underwent comparison in my lingering reflection before slumbering at night. Need I tell you, that watching your person thus, your mind underwent a not less scrupulous examination. I weighed every sentence of your lips—every thought of your sense—every feeling of your heart. I could detect the unuttered emotion in your eyes; and the quiver of your lip, light as that of the rose when the earliest droppings of the night dew steal into its bosom, was perceptible to that keen glance of love which I kept for ever upon you. How gradual then was the change which I noted day by day. He came at length, and with a prescience which forms no small portion of the spirit of a true affection, I cursed him when I saw him. You saw him too, and then the change grew rapid—dreadfully rapid, to my eyes. He won you, as you had won me. There was an instinct in it. You no longer cared whether I came to you or not—"

"Nay, Hugh—there you are wrong again—I was always glad—always most happy to see you."

"You think so, Bess;—I am willing to believe you think so—but it is you who are wrong. I know that you cared not whether I came or not, for on the subject your thought never rested for a moment, or but for a moment. I soon discovered that you were also important in his sight, and I hated him the more for the discovery—I hated him the more for loving you. Till this day, however, I had not imagined the extent to which you had both gone—I had not feared, I had not felt all my desolation. I had only dreamed of and dreaded it. But when, in a paroxysm of madness, I looked upon you and saw—saw your mutual lips—"

"No more, Master Grayson,"—she interposed with dignity.

"I will not—forgive me; but you know how it maddened me, and how I erred, and how you rebuked me. How dreadful was that rebuke!—but it did not restrain the error—it impelled me to a new one—"

"What new one, Hugh?"

"Hear me! This man Harrison—that I should speak his name!—that I should speak it praisefully too!—he came to our cottage—showed our danger from the Yemassees to my mother, and would have persuaded her to fly this morning—but I interfered and prevented the removal. He saw my brother, however, and as Walter is almost his worshipper, he was more successful with him. Leaving you in a mood little short of madness this afternoon, I hurried home, but there I could not rest, and vexed with a thousand dreadful thoughts, I wandered from the house away into the woods. After a while came the tread of a horse rapidly driving up the river-trace, and near the spot where I wandered. The rider was Harrison. He alighted at a little distance from me, tied his horse to a shrub, and threw himself just before me upon the grass. A small tree stood between us, and my approach was unnoticed. I heard him murmuring, and with the same base spirit which prompted me to look down on your meeting to-day, I listened to his language. His words were words of tenderness and love—of triumphant love, and associated with your name—he spoke of you—God curse him! as his own."

The word "Gabriel" fell unconsciously from the lips of the maiden as she heard this part of the narrative. For a moment Grayson paused, and his brow grew black, while his teeth were compressed closely; but as she looked up, as if impatient for the rest of his narrative, he went on:—

"Then I maddened. Then I grew fiendish. I know not whence the impulse, but it must have been from hell. I sprang upon him, and with the energies of a tiger and with more than his ferocity, I pinioned him to the ground, my knee upon his breast—one hand upon his throat, and with my knife in the other—"

"Stay!—God—man—say that you slew him not! You struck not—oh! you kept back your hand—he lives!" Convulsed with terror, she clasped the arm of the speaker, while her face grew haggard with affright, and her eyes seemed starting from their sockets.

"I slew him not!" he replied solemnly.

"God bless you—God bless you!" was all that she could utter, as she sank back fainting upon the floor of the apartment.

Chapter Forty

"Thou hast not slain her with thy cruel word,—
She lives, she wakes—her eyes unclose again,
And I breathe freely."

PASSIONATE and thoughtless, Hugh Grayson had not calculated the consequences of his imprudent and exciting narrative upon a mind so sensitive. He was now aware of his error, and his alarm at her situation was extreme. He lifted her from the floor, and supported her to a seat, endeavouring, as well as he could, with due care and anxiety, to restore her to consciousness. While thus employed the pastor re-entered the apartment, and his surprise may be imagined.

"Ha! what is the matter with my child? what has happened? what alarmed her? Speak, Master Grayson! Tell me what has caused all this!—My child!—Bessy, my child! Look up! open your eyes. Tell me! say! see, it is thy old father that has thee now. Thou art safe, my child. Safe with thy father. There is no danger now. Look up, look up, my child, and speak to me!"

Without answering, Grayson resigned her to the hands of the pastor, and with folded arms and a face full of gloomy expression, stood gazing upon the scene in silence. The father supported her tenderly, and with a show of fervency not common to a habit which, from constant exercise, and the pruderies of a form of worship rather too much given to externals, had, in progress of time, usurped dominion over a temper originally rather passionate than phlegmatic. Exclaiming all the while to the unconscious girl—and now and then addressing Grayson in a series of broken sentences, the old man proved the possession of a degree of regard for his child which might have appeared doubtful before. Grayson, meanwhile, stood by,—an awed and silent spectator,—bitterly reproaching himself for his imprudence in making such a communication, and striving, in his own mind, to forge or force an apology at least to himself, for the heedlessness which had marked his conduct.

"What, Master Grayson, has been the cause of this? Speak out, sir—my daughter is my heart, and you have trifled with her. Beware, sir.—I am an old man, and a professor of a faith whose essence is peace; but I am still a man, sir—with the feelings and the passions of a man; and sooner than my child should suffer wrong, slight as a word, I will even throw aside that faith and become a man of blood. Speak, sir, what has made all this?"

The youth grew firmer under such an exhortation, for his was the nature to be won rather than commanded. He looked firmly into the face of the speaker, and his brow gathered to a frown. The old man saw it, and saw in the confidence his glance expressed that however he might have erred, he had at least intended no disrespect. As this conviction came to his mind, he immediately addressed his companion in a different character, while returning consciousness in his daughter's eyes warned him also to moderation.

"I have been harsh, Master Grayson—harsh, indeed, my son; but my daughter is dear to me as the fresh blood around my heart, and suffering with her is soreness and more than suffering to me. Forbear to say, at this time—I see that she has misunderstood you, or her sickness may have some other cause. Look—bring me some water, my son."

"My son!" muttered Grayson to himself as he proceeded to the sideboard where stood the pitcher. Pouring some of its contents into a glass, he approached the maiden, whose increasing sighs indicated increasing consciousness. The old man was about to take the glass from his hands when her unclosing eye rested upon him. With a shriek she started to her feet, and lifting her hand as if to prevent his approach, and averting her eye as if to shut his presence from her sight, she exclaimed—

"Away! thou cruel murderer—come not nigh me—look not on me—touch me not with thy hands of blood. Touch me not—away!"

"God of Heaven!" exclaimed Grayson, in like horror,— "what indeed have I done? Forgive me, Miss Matthews, forgive me—I am no murderer. He lives—I struck him not. Forgive me!"

"I have no forgiveness—none. Thou hast lifted thy hand against God's image—thou hast sought to slay a noble gentleman to whom thou art as nothing. Away—let me not look upon thee!"

"Be calm, Bess—my daughter. Thou dost mistake. This is no murderer—this is our young friend, thy old playmate, Hugh Grayson."

"Ay! he came with that old story, of how we played together, and spoke of his love and all—and then showed me a knife, and lifted his bloody hands to my face, and—Oh! it was too horrible." And she shivered at the association of terrible objects which her imagination continued to conjure up.

"Thou hast wrought upon her over much, Master Grayson, and though I think with no ill intent, yet it would seem with but small judgment."

"True, sir—and give me, I pray you, but a few moments with your daughter—a few moments alone, that I may seek to undo this cruel thought which she now appears to hold me in. But a few moments—believe me, I shall say nothing unkind or offensive."

"Leave me not, father—go not out—rather let him go where I may not see him, for he has been a base spy, and would have been a foul murderer, but that the good spirit held back his hand."

"Thou sayest rightly, Bess Matthews—I have been base and foul—but thou sayest ungently and against thy better nature, for I have scorned myself that I was so. Give me leave—let thy father go—turn thy head—close thine eyes. I ask thee not to look upon me, but hear me, and the quest which I claim rather from thy goodness than from any meritings of mine own."

There was a gloomy despondence in his looks, and a tone of wretched self-abandonment in his voice, that went to the heart of the maiden, as, while he spoke, she turned, and her eyes were bent upon him. Looking steadfastly upon his face for a few moments after he had ceased speaking, she appeared slowly to deliberate; then, as if satisfied, she turned to her father, and with a motion of her hand signified her consent. The old man retired, and Grayson would have led her to a seat; but rejecting his proffered aid with much firmness, she drew a chair, and motioning him also to one at a little distance, she prepared to hear him.

"I needed not this, Miss Matthews, to feel how deeply I had erred—how dreadfully I have been punished. When you know that I have had but one stake in life—that I have lived but for one object—and have lived in vain and am now denied,—you will not need to be told how completely unnecessary to my torture and trial is the suspicion of your heart, and the coldness of your look and manner. I came to-night and sought this interview, hopeless of anything beside, at least believing myself not altogether unworthy of your esteem. To prove this more certainly to your mind, I laid bare my own. I suppressed nothing—you saw my uncovered soul, and without concealment I resolutely pointed out to you all its blots—all its deformities. I spoke of my love for you, of its extent, not that I might claim any from you in return—for I saw that such hope was idle; and, indeed, knowing what I do, and how completely your heart is in the possession of another, were it offered to me at this moment, could I accept of it on any terms? Base as I have been for a moment—criminal, as at another moment I would have been, I value still too deeply my own affections to yield them to one who cannot make a like return, and with as few reservations. But I told you of my love that you should find something in its violence—say its madness—to extenuate, if not to excuse, the errors to which it has prompted me. I studiously declared those errors, the better to prove to you that I was no hypocrite, and the more certainly therefore to inspire your confidence in one who, if he did not avoid, was at least as little willing to defend them. I came to you for your pardon; and unable to win your love, I sought only for your esteem. I have spoken."

"Master Hugh Grayson—I have heard you, and am willing to believe in much that you have said; but I am not prepared to believe that in much that you have said you have not been practising upon yourself. You have said you loved me, and I believe it—sorry I am that you should love unprofitably anywhere—more sorry still that I should be the unwitting occasion of a misspent and profitless passion. But, look closely into yourself—into your own thoughts, and then ask how you loved me? Let me answer—not as a woman—not as a thinking and a feeling creature—but as a plaything, whom your inconsiderate passion might practise upon at will, and move to tears or smiles, as may best accord with a caprice that has never from childhood been conscious of any subjection. Even now, you come to me for my confidence—my esteem. Yet you studiously practise upon my affections and emotions—upon my woman weaknesses. You saw that I loved another—I shame not to say it, for I believe and feel it—and you watched me like a spy. You had there no regulating principle keeping down impulse, but with the caprice of a bad passion, consenting to a meanness, which is subject to punishment in our very slaves. Should I trust the man who, under any circumstances save those of another's good and safety, should deserve the epithet of eavesdropper?"

"Forbear—forbear—in mercy!"

"No, Master Grayson—let me not forbear. Were it principle and not pride that called upon me to forbear, I should obey it; but I have known you from childhood, Hugh, and I speak to you now with all the freedom—and, believe me—with all the affection of that period. I know your failing, and I speak to it. I would not wound your heart, I only aim at the amendment of your understanding. I would give it a true direction. I believe your heart to be in the right place—it only wants that your mind should never swerve from its place. Forgive me, therefore, if, speaking what I hold to be just, I should say that which should seem to be harsh also."

"Go on—go on, Miss Matthews—I can bear it all—anything from you."

"And but small return, Master Grayson, for I have borne much from you. Not content with the one error, which I freely forgave—so far as forgiveness may be yielded without amendment or repentance—you proceeded to another—to a crime; a dark, a dreadful crime. You sought the life of a fellow-creature, without provocation, and worse still, Master Grayson, without permitting your enemy the common footing of equality. In that one act there was malignity, murder, and—"

"No more—no more—speak it not—"

"Cowardice!"

"Thou art bent to crush me quite, Bess Matthews—thou wouldst have me in the dust—thy foot on my head, and the world seeing it. This is thy triumph."

"A sad one, Hugh Grayson—a sad one—for thou hast thy good—thy noble qualities, wert thou not a slave."

"Slave, too—malignant, murderer, coward, slave."

"Ay, to thy baser thoughts, and from these I would free thee. With thee—I believe—it is but to know the tyranny to overthrow it. Thy pride of independence would then be active, and in that particular most nobly exercised. But let me proceed."

"Is there more?"

"Yes,—and thou wilt better prove thy regard for my esteem, when thou wilt stand patiently to hear me out. Thou didst not kill, but all the feeling of death—the death of the mind—was undergone by thy destined victim. He felt himself under thee, he saw no hope, he looked up in the glance of thy descending knife, and knew not that the good mood would so soon return to save him from death, and thee from perdition. In his thought thou didst slay him, though thou struck no blow to his heart."

"True, true—I thought not of that."

"Yet thou camest to me, Hugh Grayson, and claimed merit for thy forbearance. Thou wert confident, because thou didst not all the crime thy first criminal spirit proposed to thee. Shall I suggest that the good angel which interposed was thy weakness—art thou sure that the dread of punishment, and not the feeling of good, stayed thee not?"

"No! as I live,—as I stand before thee, Bess Matthews, thou dost me wrong. God help me, no! I was bad enough, and base enough, without that—it was not the low fear of the hangman—not the rope—not the death. I am sure it was any thing but that."

"I believe you; but what was it brought you to me with all this story—the particulars at full,—the dreadful incidents one upon the other, until thou saw'st my agony under the uplifted knife aiming at the bosom of one as far above thee, Hugh Grayson, in all that makes the noble gentleman, as it is possible for principle to be above passion, and the love of God and good works superior to the fear of punishment.— Where was thy manliness in this recital? Thou hast no answer here."

"Thou speakest proudly for him, Bess Matthews—it is well he stands so high in thy sight."

"I forgive thee that sneer, too, Master Grayson, along with thy malignity, thy murder, and thy—manliness. Be thou forgiven of all— but let us say no more together. My regards are not with me to bestow—they belong to thy doings, and thou mayst command, not solicit, whenever thou dost deserve them. Let us speak no more together."

"Cruel—most heartless—am I so low in thy sight? See, I am at thy feet—trample me in the dust—I will not shrink—I will not reproach thee."

"Thou shouldst shame at this practice upon my feelings. Thou, Hugh Grayson—with thy mind, with thy pride—shouldst not aim to do by passionate entreaty what thou mayst not do by sense and right reason. Rise, sir—thou canst not move me now. Thou hast undone thyself in my sight—thou need'st not sink at my feet to have me look down upon thee."

Had a knife gone into the heart of the young man, a more agonizing expression could not have overshadowed his countenance. The firmness of the maiden had taught him her strength not less than his own weakness. He felt his error, and with the mind for which she had given him credit, he rose with a new determination to his feet.

"Thou art right, Miss Matthews—and in all that has passed, mine had been the error and the wrong. I will not ask for the regards which I should command; but thou shalt hear well of me henceforward, and wilt do me more grateful justice when we meet again."

"I take thy promise, Hugh, for I know thy independence of character, and such a promise will not be necessary now for thy good. Take my hand—I forgive thee. It is my weakness, perhaps, to do so—but I forgive thee."

He seized her hand, which she had, with a girlish frankness, extended to him, carried it suddenly to his lips, and immediately left the dwelling.

Chapter Forty-one

"The storm cloud gathers fast, the hour's at hand,
When it will burst in fury o'er the land;
Yet is the quiet beautiful—the rush
Of the sweet south is all disturbs the hush,
While, like pure spirits, the pale night-stars brood
O'er forests which the Indian bathes in blood."

A BRIEF and passing dialogue between Grayson and the pastor, at the entrance, partially explained to the latter the previous history. The disposition of Matthews in regard to the pretensions of Grayson to his daughter's hand—of which he had long been conscious—was rather favourable than otherwise. In this particular the suit of Grayson derived importance from the degree of ill-favour with which the old gentleman had been accustomed to consider that of Harrison. With strong prejudices, the pastor was quite satisfied to obey an impression, and to mistake, as with persons of strong prejudices is frequently the case, an impulse for an argument. Not that he could urge any thing against the suitor who was the favourite of his child—of that he felt satisfied—but, coming fairly under the description of the doggerel satirist, he did not dislike Harrison a jot less for having little reason to dislike him. And there is something in this.

It was, therefore, with no little regret, that he beheld the departure of Grayson under circumstances so unfavourable to his suit. From his own, and the lips of his daughter, alike, he had been taught to understand that she had objections; but the emotion of Grayson, and the openly-expressed indignation of Bess, at once satisfied him of the occurrence of that which effectually excluded the hope that time might effect some change for the better. He was content, therefore, simply to regret what his own good sense taught him he could not amend, and what his great regard for his child's peace persuaded him not to attempt.

Grayson, in the meantime, hurried away under strong excitement. He had felt deeply the denial, but far more deeply the rebukes of the maiden. She had searched narrowly into his inner mind—had probed close its weaknesses—had laid bare to his own eyes those silent motives of his conduct, which he had not himself dared to analyze or encounter. His pride was hurt by her reproaches, and he was ashamed of the discoveries which she had made. Though mortified to the soul, however, there was a redeeming principle at work within him. He had been the slave of his mood: but he determined, from that moment, upon the overthrow of the tyranny. To this she had counselled him; to this his own pride of character had also counselled him; and, though agonized with the defeated hopes clamouring in his bosom, he adopted a noble decision, and determined to be at least worthy of the love which he yet plainly felt he could never win. His course now was to adopt energetic measures in preparing for any contest that might happen with the Indians. Of this danger he was not altogether conscious. He did not imagine it so near at hand, and had only given in to precautionary measures with regard to his mother, in compliance with his brother's wish, and as no great inconvenience could result from their temporary removal. But the inflexible obstinacy of the pastor in refusing to take the shelter of the contiguous Block House, led him more closely to reflect upon the consequent exposure of Bess Matthews; and, from thus reflecting, the danger became magnified to his eyes. He threw himself upon the steed of Harrison, as soon as he reached the Block House; and without troubling himself to explain to any one his intentions, for he was too proud for that, he set off at once, and at full speed, to arouse such of the neighbouring foresters as had not yet made their appearance at the place of gathering, or had been too remotely situated for previous warning.

The old pastor, on parting with the disappointed youth, re-entered the dwelling, and without being perceived by his daughter. She stood in the middle of the apartment, her finger upon her lips, and absorbed in meditation as quiet as if she had never before been disturbed for an instant; like some one of those fine embodiments of heavenward devotion we meet with now and then in a Holy Family by one of the old masters. He approached her, and when his presence became evident, she knelt suddenly before him.

"Bless me, father—dear father—bless me, and let me retire."

"God bless you, Bess—and watch over and protect you—but what disturbs you? You are troubled."

"I know not, father—but I fear. I fear something terrible, yet know not what. My thoughts are all in confusion."

"You need sleep, my child, and quiet. These excitements and foolish reports have worried you; but a night's sleep will make all well again. Go now—go to your mother, and may the good angels keep you."

With the direction she arose, and threw her arms about his neck, and with a kiss, affectionately bidding him good night, she retired to her chamber, first passing a few brief moments with her mother in the adjoining room. Calling to the trusty negro who performed such offices in his household, the pastor gave orders for the securing of the house, and retired to his chamber also. July—the name of the negro— proceeded to fasten the windows.

This he did by means of a wooden bolt; and thrusting a thick bar of knotted pine into hooks on either side of the door, he coolly threw himself down to his own slumbers alongside of it. We need scarcely add, knowing the susceptibility of the black in this particular, that sleep was not slow in its approaches to the strongest tower in the citadel of his senses. The subtle deity soon mastered all his sentinels, and a snore, not the most scrupulous in the world, sent forth from the flattened but capacious nostrils, soon announced his entire conquest over the premises he had invaded.

But though she retired to her chamber, Bess Matthews in vain sought for sleep. Distressed by the previous circumstances, and warmly excited as she had been by the trying character of the scene through which she had recently passed, she had vainly endeavoured to find that degree of quiet, which she felt necessary to her mental not less than to her physical repose. After tossing fruitlessly on her couch for a fatiguing hour, she arose, and slightly unclosing the window, the only one in her chamber, she looked forth upon the night. It was clear, with many stars—a slight breeze bent the tree-tops, and their murmurs, as they swayed to and fro, were pleasant to her melancholy fancies. How could she sleep when she thought of the voluntary risk taken by Harrison? Where was he then—in what danger, surrounded by what deadly enemies?—perhaps under their very knives, and she not there to interpose—to implore for—to save him. How could she fail to love so much disinterested generosity—so much valour and adventure, taken, as with a pardonable vanity, she fondly thought, so much for her safety and for the benefit of hers. Thus musing, thus watching, she lingered at the window, looking forth, but half conscious as she gazed, upon the thick woods, stretching away in black masses, of those old Indian forests. Just then, the moon rose calmly and softly in the east—a fresher breeze rising along with, and gathering seemingly with her ascent. The river wound partly before her gaze, and there was a long bright shaft of light—a pure white gleam, which even its ripples could not overcome or dissipate, borrowed from the pale orb just then swelling above it. Suddenly a canoe shot across the water in the distance—then another, and another—quietly, and with as little show of life, as if they were only the gloomy shades of the past generation's warriors. Not a voice, not a whisper—not even the flap of an oar, disturbed the deep hush of the scene; and the little canoes that showed dimly in the river from afar, as soon as they had overshot the pale gleamy bar of the moon upon its bosom, were no longer perceptible. Musing upon these objects with a vague feeling of danger, and an oppressive sense at the same time of exhaustion, which forbade anything like a coherent estimate of the thoughts which set in upon her mind like so many warring currents, Bess left the window, and threw herself, listlessly yet sad, upon the couch, vainly soliciting that sleep which seemed so reluctant to come. How slow was its progress—how long before she felt the haze growing over her eyelids. A sort of stupor succeeded—she was conscious of the uncertainty of her perception, and though still, at intervals, the beams from the fast ascending moon caught her eyes, they flitted before her like spiritual forms that looked on and came but to depart. These at length went from her entirely as a sudden gust closed the shutter, and a difficult and not very sound slumber came at last to her relief.

A little before this, and with the first moment of the rise of the moon on the eastern summits, the watchful Hector, obedient to his orders, prepared to execute the charge which his master had given him at parting. Releasing Dugdale from the log to which he had been bound, he led the impatient and fierce animal down to the river's brink, and through the tangled route only known to the hunter. The single track, imperfectly visible in the partial light, impeded somewhat his progress, so that the moon was fairly visible by the time he reached the river. This circumstance was productive of some small inconvenience to the faithful slave, since it proved him something of a laggard in his duty, and at the same time, from the lateness of the hour, occasioned no little anxiety in his mind for his master's safety. With a few words, well understood seemingly by the well-trained animal, he cheered him on, and pushing him to the slight trench made by the horse's hoof, clearly defined upon the path, and which had before been shown him, he thrust his nose gently down upon it, while taking from his head the muzzle; without which he must have been a dangerous neighbour to the Indians, for whose pursuit he had been originally trained by the Spaniards, in a system, the policy of which was still in part continued, or rather, of late, revived, by his present owner.

"Now, go wid you, Dugdale; be off, da's a good dog, and look out for your maussa. Dis he track—hark—hark—hark, dog—dis de track ob he critter. Nose 'em, old boy—nose 'em well. Make yourself good nigger, for you hab blessed maussa. Soon you go now, better for bote. Hark 'em, boy, hark 'em, and hole 'em fast."

The animal seemed to comprehend—looked intelligently up into the face of his keeper, then stooping down, carefully drew a long breath as he scented the designated spot, coursed a few steps quickly around it, and then, as if perfectly assured, sent forth a long deep bay, and set off on the direct route with all the fleetness of a deer.

"Da good dog dat, dat same Dugdale. But he hab reason—Hector no gib 'em meat for not'ing. Spaniard no l'arn 'em better, and de Lord hab mercy 'pon dem Ingin, eff he once stick he teet in he troat. He better bin in de fire, for he neber leff off, long as he kin kick. Hark—da good dog, dat same Dugdale. Wonder way maussa pick up da name for 'em; speck he Spanish—in English, he bin Dogdale."

Thus soliloquizing, after his own fashion, the negro turned his eyes in the direction of the strange vessel, lying about a mile and a half above the bank upon which he stood, and now gracefully outlined by the soft light of the moon. She floated there, in the bosom of the stream, still and silent as a sheeted spectre, and to all appearance with quite as little life. Built after the finest models of her time, and with a distinct regard to the irregular pursuits in which she was engaged, her appearance carried to the mind an idea of lightness and swiftness which was not at variance with her character. The fairy-like tracery of her slender masts, her spars, and cordage, harmonized well with the quiet water upon which she rested like some native bird, and with the soft and luxuriant foliage covering the scenery around, just then coming out from shadow into the gathering moonbeams.

While the black looked, his eye was caught by a stir upon the bank directly opposite; and, at length, shooting out from the shelter of cane and brush which thickly fringed a small lagune in that direction, he distinctly saw eight or ten large double canoes making for the side of the river upon which he stood. They seemed filled with men, and their paddles were moved with a velocity only surpassed by the silence which accompanied their use. The mischief was now sufficiently apparent, even to a mind so obtuse as that of the negro; and, without risking any thing by personal delay, but now doubly aroused in anxiety for his master—whose predictions he saw were about to be verified—he took his way back to the Block House with a degree of hurry proportioned to what he felt was the urgency of the case. It did not take him long to reach the Block House, into which he soon found entrance, and gave the alarm. Proceeding to the quarter in which the wife of Granger kept her abode, he demanded from her a knife—all the weapon he wanted—while informing her, as he had already done those having charge of the fortress, of the approaching enemy.

"What do you want with the knife, Hector?"

"I want 'em, missis—da's all—I guine after maussa."

"What! the captain?—why, where is he, Hector?"

"Speck he in berry much trouble. I must go see a'ter 'em. Dugdale gone 'ready—Dugdale no better sarbant dan Hector. Gib me de knife, missis—dat same long one I hab for cut he meat."

"But, Hector, you can be of very little good if the Indians are out. You don't know where to look for the captain, and you'll tread on them as you go through the bush."

"I can't help it, missis—I must go. I hab hand and foot—I hab knife—I hab eye for see—I hab toot for bite—I 'trong, missis, and I must go look for maussa. God! missis, if any ting happen to maussa, wha Hector for do? where he guine—who be he new maussa? I must go, missis—gib me de knife."

"Well, Hector, if you will go, here's what you want. Here's the knife, and here's your master's gun. You must take that too," said the woman.

"No—I tank you for not'ing, missis. I no want gun; I 'fraid ob 'em; he kin shoot all sides. I no like 'em. Gi' me knife. I use to knife—I kin scalp dem Injin wid knife a'ter he own fashion. But I no use to gun."

"Well, but your master is used to it. You must carry it for him. He has no arms, and this may save his life. Hold it so, and there's no danger."

She showed the timid Hector how to carry the loaded weapon so as to avoid risk to himself, and, persuaded of its importance to his master, he ventured to take it in his hands.

"Well, da 'nough—I no want any more. I gone, missis, I gone—but 'member—ef maussa come back and Hector loss—'member, I say, I no runway—'member dat. I scalp—I drown—I dead—ebbery ting happen to me—but I no runway."

With these last words, the faithful black started upon his adventure of danger, resolute and strong, in the warm affection which he bore his master, to contend with every form of difficulty. He left the garrison at the Block House duly aroused to the conflict, which they were now satisfied was not far off.

Chapter Forty-two

"Oh! wherefore strike the beautiful, the young,
So innocent, unharming? Lift the knife,
If need be, 'gainst the warrior; but forbear
The trembling woman."

LET us now return to the chamber of Bess Matthews. She slept not soundly, but unconsciously, and heard not the distant but approaching cry— "Sangarrah-me—Sangarrah-me!" The war had begun; and in the spirit and with the words of Yemassee battle, the thirst for blood was universal among their warriors. From the war-dance, blessed by the prophet, stimulated by his exhortations, and warmed by the blood of their human sacrifice, they had started upon the war-path in every direction. The larger division, led on by Sanutee and the prophet, took their course directly for Charleston, while Ishiagaska, heading a smaller party, proceeded to the frontier settlements upon the Pocota-ligo, intending massacre along the whole line of the white borders, including the now flourishing town of Beaufort. From house to house, with the stealth of a cat, he led his band to indiscriminate slaughter, and, diverging with this object from one settlement to another, he contrived to reach every dwelling-place of the whites known to him in that neighbourhood. But in many places he had been foiled. The providential arrangements of Harrison, wherever, in the brief time allowed him, he had found it possible, had rendered their design in great part innocuous throughout that section, and, duly angered with his disappointment, it was not long before Ishiagaska came to the little cottage of the pastor. The lights had been all extinguished, and, save on the eastern side, the dwelling lay in the deepest shadow. The quiet of the whole scene formed an admirable contrast to the horrors gathering in perspective, and about to destroy its sacred and sweet repose for ever.

With the wonted caution of the Indian, Ishiagaska led on his band in silence. No sound was permitted to go before the assault. The war-whoop, with which they anticipate or accompany the stroke of battle, was not suffered, in the present instance, to prepare, with a salutary terror, the minds of their destined victims. Massacre, not battle, was the purpose, and the secret stratagem of the marauder usurped the fierce habit of the avowed warrior. Passing from cover to cover, the wily savage at length approached the cottage with his party. He sta-tioned them around it, concealed each under his tree. He alone advanced to the dwelling with the stealth of a panther. Avoiding the clear path of the moon, he availed himself, now of one and now of another shelter—the bush, the tree—whatever might afford a conceal-ing shadow in his approach; and where this was wanting, throwing himself flat upon the ground, he crawled on like a serpent—now lying snug and immoveable, now taking a new start and hurrying in his progress, and at last placing himself successfully alongside of the little white paling which fenced in the cottage, and ran at a little distance around it. He parted the thong which secured the wicket with his knife, ascended the little avenue, and then, giving ear to every quarter of the dwelling, and finding all still, proceeded on tiptoe to try the fas-tenings of every window. The door he felt was secure—so was each window in the body of the house, which he at length encompassed, noting every aperture in it. At length he came to the chamber where Bess Matthews slept,—a chamber forming one-half of the little shed, or addition to the main dwelling—the other half being occupied for the same purpose by her parents. He placed his hand gently upon the shutter, and with savage joy he felt it yield beneath his touch.

The moment Ishiagaska made this discovery, he silently retreated to a little distance from the dwelling, and with a signal which had been agreed upon—the single and melancholy note of the whip-poor-will—he gave notice to his band for their approach. Imitating his pre-vious caution, they came forward individually to the cottage, and gathering around him, under the shadow of a neighbouring tree, they duly arranged the method of surprise.

This done, under the guidance of Ishiagaska, they again approached the dwelling, and a party having been stationed at the door in silence, another party with their leader returned to the window which was accessible. Lifted quietly upon the shoulders of two of them, Ishiagaska was at once upon a level with it. He had already drawn it aside, and, by the light of the moon which streamed into the little apartment, he was enabled with a single glance to take in its contents. The half-slumbering girl felt conscious of a sudden gush of air—a rustling sound, and perhaps a darkening shadow; but the obtrusion was not sufficient to alarm into action faculties which had been so very much excited, and subsequently depressed, by the severe mental trials to which she had been subjected, and which did not cease to trouble her even while she slept. It was in her exhaustion only that sleep came to her relief. But even in her dreams there floated images of terror; and vague aspects that troubled or threatened, caused her to moan in her sleep, as at a danger still to be apprehended or deplored. She lay motionless, however, and the wily savage succeeded in gaining the floor of her chamber without disturbing the sleeper. Here he stood, silent for a while, surveying at his ease the composed and beautiful outline of his victim's person. And she was beautiful—the ancient worship might well have chosen such an offering in sacrifice to his choice demon. Never did her beauty show forth more exquisitely than now, when murder stood nigh, ready to blast it for ever—ready to wrest the sacred fire of life from the altar of that heart which had maintained itself so well worthy of the heaven from whence it came. Ishiagaska looked on, but with no feeling inconsistent with the previous aim which had brought him there. The dress had fallen low from her neck, and in the meek, spiritual light of the moon, the soft, wavelike heave of the scarce living principle within her bosom was like that of some blessed thing, susceptible of death, yet, at the same time, strong in the possession of the most exquisite developments of life. Her long tresses hung about her neck, relieving, but not concealing, its snowy whiteness. One arm fell over the side of the couch, nerveless, but soft and snowy as the frostwreath lifted by the capricious wind. The other lay pressed upon her bosom above her heart, as if restraining those trying apprehensions which had formed so large a portion of her prayers when she laid herself down to sleep. It was a picture for any eye but that of the savage—a picture softening any mood but that of the habitual murderer. It worked no change in the ferocious soul of Ishiagaska. He looked, but without emotion. Nor was he long disposed to hesitate. Assisting another of the Indians into the apartment, who passed at once through it into the hall adjoining, the door of which he was to unbar for the rest, Ishiagaska now approached the couch, and drawing his knife from the sheath, the broad blade was uplifted, shining bright in the moonbeams, and the inflexible point bore down upon that sweet, white round, in which all was loveliness, and where was all of life;—the fair bosom, the pure heart, where the sacred principles of purity and of vitality had at once their abiding place. With one hand he lifted aside the long white finger that lay upon it, and in the next instant the blow would have descended fatally, but that the maiden's sleep was less sound than it appeared. His footsteps had not disturbed her, but his touch did. The pressure of his grasp brought instant consciousness to her sense. This may have been assisted also by the glare of the moon across her eyes; the window, opened by the red man, remaining still wide. Turning uneasily beneath the glare, she felt the savage gripe upon her fingers. It was an instinct, swift as the lightning, that made her grasp the uplifted arm with a strength of despairing nature, not certainly her own. She started with a shriek, and the change of position accompanying her movement, and the unlooked-for direction and restraint given to his arm, when, in that nervous grasp, she seized it, partially diverted the down-descending weapon of death. It grazed slightly aside, inflicting a wound, of which, at that moment, she was perfectly unconscious. Again she cried out with a convulsive scream, as she saw him transfer the knife from the one to the other hand. For a few seconds her struggles were all-powerful, and kept back, for that period of time, the fate which had been so certain. But what could the frail spirit, the soft hand, the unexercised muscles avail or achieve against such an enemy and in such a contest? With another scream, as of one in a last agony, consciousness went from her in the conviction of the perfect fruitlessness of the contest. With a single apostrophe—

"God be merciful—oh! my father—oh! Gabriel, save me—Gabriel—Ah! God, God—he cannot—" her eye closed, and she lay supine under the knife of the savage.

But the first scream which she uttered had reached the ears of her father, who had been more sleepless than herself. The scream of his child had been sufficient to give renewed activity and life to the limbs of the aged pastor. Starting from his couch, and seizing upon a massive club which stood in the corner of his chamber, he rushed desperately into the apartment of Bess, and happily in time. Her own resistance had been sufficient to give pause for this new succour, and it ceased just when the old man, now made conscious of the danger, cried aloud in the spirit of his faith, while striking a blow which, effectually diverting Ishiagaska from the maiden, compelled him to defend himself.

"Strike with me, Father of Mercies," cried the old Puritan—
"strike with thy servant—thou who struck with David and with
Gideon, and who swept thy waters against Pharaoh—strike with the
arm of thy poor instrument. Make the savage to bite the dust, while I
strike—I slay in thy name, Oh! thou avenger—even in the name of the
Great Jehovah!"

And calling aloud in some such apostrophe upon the name of the
Deity at every effort which he made with his club, the old pastor gained
a temporary advantage over the savage, who, retreating from his first
furious assault to the opposite side of the couch, enabled him to place
himself alongside of his child. Without giving himself a moment even
to her restoration, with a paroxysm of fury that really seemed from
heaven, he advanced upon his enemy—the club swinging over his head
with an exhibition of strength that was remarkable in so old a man.
Ishiagaska, pressed thus, unwilling with his knife to venture within its
reach, had recourse to his tomahawk, which, hurriedly, he threw at the
head of his approaching assailant. But the aim was wide—the deadly
weapon flew into the opposite wall, and the blow of the club rang upon
the head of the Indian with sufficient effect, first to stagger, and then to
bring him down. This done, the old man rushed to the window, where
two other savages were labouring to elevate a third to the entrance;
and, with another sweep of his mace, he defeated their design, by
crushing down the elevated person whose head and hands were just
above the sill of the window. In their first confusion, he closed the
shutter, and securely bolted it, then turned, with all the aroused affections of a father, to the restoration of his child.

Meanwhile, the Indian who had undertaken to unclose the main
entrance for his companions, ignorant of the sleeping negro before it,
stumbled over him. July, who, like most negroes suddenly awakening,
was stupid and confused, rose, however, with a sort of instinct; rub-
bing his eyes with the fingers of one hand, he stretched out the other
to the bar, and, without being at all conscious of what he was doing,
lifted it from its socket. He was soon brought to a sense of his error, as
a troop of half-naked savages rushed through the opening, pushing
him aside with a degree of violence which soon taught him his danger.
He knew now that they were enemies; and, with the uplifted bar still in
his hand, he felled the foremost of those around him—who happened
to be the fellow who first stumbled over him—and rushed bravely
enough among the rest. But the weapon he made use of was an

unwieldy one, and not at all calculated for such a contest. He was soon taught to discover this, fatally, when it swung uselessly around, and was put aside by one of the more wily savages, who, adroitly closing in with the courageous negro, soon brought him to the ground. In falling, however, he contrived to grapple with his more powerful enemy, and the two went down in a close embrace together. But the hatchet was in the hand of the Indian, and a moment after his fall it crushed into the skull of the negro. Another and another blow followed, and soon ended the struggle. While the pulse was still quivering in his heart, and ere his eyes had yet closed in the swimming convulsions of death, the negro felt the sharp blade of the knife sweeping around his head. The conqueror was about to complete his triumph by taking off the scalp of his victim, "as ye peel the fig when the fruit is fresh," when a light, borne by the half-dressed wife of the pastor, appeared at the door. She gave new terrors, by her screams, to the scene of blood and strife going on in the hall. At the same moment, followed by his daughter, who vainly entreated him to remain in the chamber, the pastor rushed headlong forward, wielding the club, so successful already against one set of enemies, in contest with another.

"Go not, father—go not," she cried earnestly, now fully restored to the acutest consciousness, and clinging to him passionately all the while.

"Go not, John, I pray you—" implored the old lady, endeavouring to arrest him. But his impulse, under all circumstances, was the wisest policy. He could not hope for safety by hugging his chamber, and a bold struggle to the last—a fearless heart, ready hand, and teeth clenched with a fixed purpose—exhibit a proper reason when dealing with the avowed enemy. A furious inspiration seemed to fill his heart as he went forward, crying aloud—

"I fear not. The buckler of Jehovah is over his servant. I go under the banner—I fight in the service of God. Keep me not back, woman—has he not said—shall I misbelieve—he will protect his servant. He will strike with the shepherd, and the wolf shall be smitten from the fold. Avoid thee, savage—unloose thee from thy prey. The sword of the Lord and of Gideon!"

Thus saying, he rushed like one inspired upon the savage whose knife had already swept around the head of the negro. The scalping of July's head was a more difficult matter than the Indian had dreamed of, fighting in the dark. It was only when he laid hands upon it that he found the difficulty of taking secure hold. There was no war-tuft to seize upon, and the wool had been recently abridged by the judicious scissors. He had, accordingly, literally to peel away the scalp with the flesh itself. The pastor interposed just after he had begun the operation.

"Avoid thee, thou bloody Philistine—give up thy prey. The vengeance of the God of Jacob is upon thee. In his name I strike, I slay."

As he shouted he struck a headlong, a heavy blow, which, could it have taken effect, would most probably have been fatal. But the pastor knew nothing of the arts of war, and though on his knees over the negro, and almost under the feet of his new assailant, the Indian was too "cunning of fence," too well practised in strategy, to be overcome in this simple manner. With a single jerk which completed his labour, he tore the reeking scalp from the head of the negro, and dropping his own at the same instant on a level with the floor, the stroke of the pastor went clean over it; and the assailant himself, borne forward incontinently by the ill-advised effort, was hurried stunningly against the wall of the apartment, and in the thick of his enemies. In a moment they had him down—the club wrested from his hands, and exhaustion necessarily following such prodigious and unaccustomed efforts in so old a man, he now lay without strength or struggle under the knives of his captors.

As she beheld the condition of her father, all fear, all stupor, passed away instantly from the mind of Bess Matthews. She rushed forward—she threw herself between the red men and their victim, and entreated their knives to her heart rather than to his. Clasping the legs of the warrior immediately bestriding the body of the old man, with all a woman's and a daughter's eloquence she prayed for pity. But she spoke to unwilling ears, and to senses that, scorning any such appeals in their own cases, looked upon them with sovereign contempt when made by others. She saw this in the grim smile with which he heard her apostrophes. His white teeth, gleaming out between the dusky lips which enclosed them, looked to her fears like those of the hungry tiger, gnashing with delight at the banquet of blood at last spread before it. While yet she spoke, his hand tore away from her hair a long and glittering ornament which had confined it—another tore from her neck the clustering necklace which could not adorn it; and the vain fancies of the savage immediately appropriated them as decorations for his own person—her own head-ornament being stuck most fantastically in the long, single tuft of hair—the war-tuft, and all that is left at that period—of him who had seized it. She saw how much pleasure the bauble imparted, and a new suggestion of her thought gave her a momentary hope.

"Spare him—spare his life, and thou shalt have more—thou shalt have beads and rings. Look—look,"—and the jewelled ring from her finger, and another, a sacred pledge from Harrison, were given into his grasp. He seized them with avidity.

"Good—good—more!" cried the ferocious but frivolous savage, in the few words of broken English which he imperfectly uttered in reply to hers, and which he well understood; for such had been the degree of intimacy existing between the Yemassees and the settlers, that but few of the former were entirely ignorant of some portions of the language of the latter. So far, something had been gained in pleasing her enemy. She rushed to the chamber, and hurried forth with a little casket, containing a locket, and sundry other trifles commonly found in a lady's cabinet. Her mother, in the meanwhile, having arranged her dress, hurriedly came forth also, provided, in like manner, with all such jewels as seemed most calculated to win the mercy which they sought. They gave all into his hands, and, possibly, had he been alone, these concessions would have saved them,—their lives at least; for these—now the spoils of the individual savage to whom they were given—had they been found in the sack of the house, must have been common stock with all of them. But the rest of the band were not disposed for mercy when they beheld such an appropriation of their plunder, and while they were pleading with the savage for the life of the pastor, Ishiagaska, recovered from the blow which had stunned him, entering the apartment, immediately changed the prospects of all the party. He was inflamed to double ferocity by the stout defence which had been offered where he had been taught to anticipate so little; and, with a fierce cry, seizing Bess by her long hair, which, from the loss of her comb, now streamed over her shoulders, he waved the tomahawk in air, bidding his men follow his example and do execution upon the rest. Another savage, with the word, seized upon the old lady. These sights re-aroused the pastor. With a desperate effort he threw the knee of his enemy from his breast, and was about to rise, when the stroke of a stick from one of the captors descended stunningly, but not fatally, and sent him once more to the ground.

"Father—father!—God of mercy—look, mother! they have slain

him—they have slain my father!" and she wildly struggled with her captor, but without avail. There was but a moment now, and she saw the hatchet descending. That moment was for prayer, but the terror was too great; for as she beheld the whirling arm and the wave of glittering steel, she closed her eyes, and insensibility came to her relief, while she sank down under the feet of the savage—a simultaneous movement of the Indians placing both of her parents at the same moment in anticipation of the same awful destiny that threatened her.

Chapter Forty-three

"Captives, at midnight, whither lead you them,
Heedless of tears and pity, all unmoved
At their poor hearts' distress? Yet, spare their lives."

THE blow was stayed—the death, deemed inevitable, was averted—the captives lived. The descending arm was arrested; the weapon thrown aside, and a voice of authority, at the most interesting juncture in the lives of the prisoners, interposed for their safety. The new comer was Chorley, the captain of the pirate, heading his troop of marines, and a small additional force of Indians. He was quite as much rejoiced as the captives, that he came in time for their relief. It was not his policy, in the house of the pastor, to appear the man of blood, or to destroy, though mercilessly destructive wherever he appeared before. There were in the present instance many reasons to restrain him. The feeling of "auld lang syne" alone might have have had its effect upon his mood; and, though not sufficiently potent, perhaps, for purposes of pity in a bosom otherwise so pitiless, yet, strengthened by a passion for the person of Bess Matthews, it availed happily to save the little family of the pastor. Their safety, indeed, had been his object; and he had hurried towards their dwelling with the first signal of war, as he well knew the dangers to which they would be exposed, should he not arrive in season, from the indiscriminate fury of the savages. But the circuitous route which he had been compelled to take, together with the difficulties of the forest to sailors, to whom a march through the tangled woods was something unusual, left him considerably behind the party led on by Ishiagaska. Arriving in time to save, however, Chorley was not displeased that he had been delayed so long. There was a merit in his appearance at a moment so perilous, which promised him advantages he had not contemplated before. He could now urge a claim to the gratitude of the maiden, for her own and the safety of her parents, upon which he built strongly his desire to secure her person, if not her heart. This, at least, under all circumstances, he had certainly determined upon.

He came at the last moment, but he came in time. He was well fitted for such a moment, for he was bold and decisive. With muscles of iron he grasped the arm of the savage, and thrust him back from his more delicate victim, while, with a voice of thunder, sustained admirably by the close proximity of the muskets borne by the marines, he commanded the savages to yield their prisoners. A spear-thrust from one of his men enforced the command, which was otherwise disregarded in the case of the Indian bestriding Mr. Matthews, and the old pastor stood once more erect. But Ishiagaska, the first surprise being over, was not so disposed to yield his captives.

"Will the white brother take the scalps from Ishiagaska? Where was the white brother when Ishiagaska was here? He was on the blind path in the woods—I heard him cry like the lost child for the scouts of Ishiagaska. It was Ishiagaska who crept into the wigwam of the white prophet—look! The white prophet can strike—the mark of his club is on the head of a great chief—but not to slay. Ishiagaska has won the English—they are the slaves of the Yemassee—he can take their scalps—he can drink their blood—he can tear out their hearts!"

"I'll be d——d if he does, though, while I am here. Fear not, Matthews, old boy—and you, my beauty bird—have no fear. You are all safe—he takes my life before he puts hands on you, by Santiago, as the Spaniards swear. Hark ye, Ishiagaska—do you understand what I say?"

"The Yemassee has ears for his brother—let him speak," replied the chief, sullenly.

"That means that you understand me, I suppose—though it doesn't say so exactly. Well, then—listen. I'll take care of these prisoners, and account for them to the Governor of Saint Augustine."

"The white prophet and the women are for Ishiagaska. Let our brother take his own scalps. Ishiagaska strikes not for the Spaniard—he is a warrior of Yemassee."

"Well, then, I will account to your people for them, but they are my prisoners now."

"Is not Ishiagaska a chief of the Yemassee—shall the stranger speak for him to his people? Our white brother is like a cunning bird that is lazy. He looks out from the tree all day, and when the other bird catches the green fly, he steals it out of his teeth. Ishiagaska catches no fly for the teeth of the stranger."

"Well, as you please; but, by G——d, you may give them up civilly or not! They are mine now, and you may better yourself as you can."

The brow of the Indian, stormy enough before, put on new terrors, and without a word he rushed fiercely at the throat of the sailor, driving forward one hand for that purpose, while the other aimed a blow at his head with his hatchet. But the sailor was sufficiently familiar with Indian warfare, as well as with most other kinds; he was good at all weapons, as we may suppose, and was not unprepared. He seemed to have anticipated resistance to his authority, and was ready for the assault. His promptness in defence was quite equal to the suddenness of the attack of Ishiagaska. Adroitly evading the direct assault, he bore back the erring weapon with a stroke that sent it wide from the owner's hand, and grasping him by the throat, waved him to and fro as an infant in the grasp of a giant. The followers of the chief, not discouraged by this evidence of superiority, or by the greater number of seamen with their white ally, rushed forward to his rescue, and the probability is that the affair would have been one of mixed massacre but for the coolness of Chorley.

"Men—each his man! Short work, as I order. Drop muskets, and close handsomely."

The order was obeyed with promptitude, and the Indians were belted in, as by a hoop of iron, without room to lift a hatchet or brandish a knife, while each of the whites had singled out an enemy, at whose breast a pistol was presented. The sailor captain in the meanwhile appropriated Ishiagaska to himself, and closely encircled him with one powerful arm, while the muzzle of his pistol rested upon the Indian's head. But the affair was suffered to proceed no further, in this way, by him who had now the chief management. The Indians were awed, and though they still held out a sullen attitude of defiance, Chorley, whose desire was that control of the savages without which he could hope to do nothing, was satisfied of the adequacy of what he had done towards his object. Releasing his own captive, therefore, with a stentorian laugh, he addressed Ishiagaska:—

"That's the way, chief, to deal with the enemy. But we are no enemies of yours, and have had fun enough."

"It is fun for our white brother," was the stern and dry response.

"Ay, what else—devilish good fun, I say—though, to be sure, you did not seem to think so. But I suppose I am to have the prisoners."

"If our brother asks with his tongue, we say no—if he asks with his teeth, we say yes."

"Well, I care not, d——n my splinters, Ishy—whether you answer to tongue or teeth, so that you answer as I want you. I'm glad now that you speak what is reasonable."

"Will our brother take the white prophet and the women, and give nothing to the Yemassee? The English buy from the Yemassee, and the Yemassee gets when he gives."

"Ay, I see—you have learned to trade, and know how to drive a bargain. But you forget, chief, you have had all in the house."

"Good—and the prisoners—they are scalps for Ishiagaska. But our brother would have them for himself, and will give his small gun for them."

The offer to exchange the captives for the pistol in his hand, caused a momentary hesitation in the mind of the pirate. He saw the lurking malignity in the eye of the savage, and gazed fixedly upon him, then, suddenly seeming to determine, he exclaimed,—

"Well, it's a bargain. The captives are mine, and here's the pistol."

Scarcely had the weapon been placed in the hands of the wily savage, than he hastily thrust it at the head of the pirate, and crying aloud to his followers, who echoed it lustily, "Sangarrah-me—Yemassee," he drew the trigger. A loud laugh from Chorley was all the response that followed. He had seen enough of the Indian character to have anticipated the result of the exchange just made, and gave him a pistol therefore which had a little before been discharged. The innocuous effort upon his life, accordingly, had been looked for; and having made it, the Indian, whose pride of character had been deeply mortified by the indignity to which the sport of Chorley had just subjected him, folded his arms patiently as if in waiting for his death. This must have followed but for the ready and contemptuous laugh of the pirate; for his seamen, provoked to fury by the attempt, would otherwise undoubtedly have cut them all in pieces. The ready laugh, however—so unlooked-for—so seemingly out of place—kept them still; and, as much surprised as the Indians, they remained as stationary also. A slap upon the shoulder from the heavy hand of the seaman aroused Ishiagaska with a start.

"How now, my red brother—didst thou think I could be killed by such as thee? Go to—thou art a child—a little boy. The shot can't touch me—the sword can't cut—the knife can't stick—I have a charm from the prophet of the Spaniards. I bought it and a good wind, with a link of this blessed chain, and have had no reason to repent my bargain. Those are the priests, friend Matthews—now you don't pretend to such a trade. What good can your preaching do to sailors or soldiers, when we can get such bargains for so little?"

The pastor, employed hitherto in sustaining the form of his still but half-conscious daughter, had been a silent spectator of this strange scene. But he now, finding as long as it lasted that the nerves of Bess would continue unstrung, seized the opportunity afforded by this appeal, to implore that they might be relieved of their savage company.

"What, and you continue here?" replied the sailor. "No, no—that's impossible. They would murder you the moment I am gone."

"What then are we to do—where go—where find safety?"

"You must go with me—with my party alone will you be safe, and while on shore you must remain with us. After that, my vessel will give you shelter."

"Never—never—dear father, tell him no—better that we should die by the savage," was the whispered and hurried language of Bess to her father as she heard this suggestion. A portion of her speech, only, was audible to the seaman.

"What's that you say, my sweet bird of beauty—my bird of paradise? —Speak out, there is no danger."

"She only speaks to me, captain," said the pastor, unwilling that the only protector they had now should be offended by an indiscreet remark.

"Oh, father, that you had listened to Gabriel," murmured the maiden, as she beheld the preparations making for their departure with the soldiers.

"Reproach me not now, my child—my heart is sore enough for that error of my spirit. It was a wicked pride that kept me from hearing and doing justice to that friendly youth."

The kind word, in reference to her lover, almost banished all present fears from the mind of Bess Matthews; and with tears that now relieved her, and which before this she could not have shed, she buried her head in the bosom of the old man.

"We are friends again, Ishiagaska," extending his hand while he spoke, was the address of the seaman to the chief, as the latter took his departure from the dwelling on his way to the Block House. The proffered hand was scornfully rejected.

"Is Ishiagaska a dog that shall come when you whistle, and put his tail between his legs when you storm? The white chief has put mud on the head of Ishiagaska."

"Well, go and be d——d, who cares? By G——d, but for the bargain, and that the fellow may be useful, I could send a bullet through his red skin with appetite."

A few words now addressed to his captives, sufficed to instruct them as to the necessity of a present movement; and a few moments put them in as great a state of readiness for their departure as, under such circumstances, they could be expected to make. The sailor, in the meantime, gave due directions to his followers; and, picking up the pistol which the indignant Ishiagaska has thrown away, he contented himself, while reloading it, with another boisterous laugh at the expense of the savage. Giving the necessary orders to his men, he approached the group, and tendered his assistance, especially to Bess Matthews. But she shrank back with an appearance of horror, not surely justifiable, if reference is to be had only to his agency on the present occasion. But the instinctive delicacy of maidenly feeling had been more than once outraged in her bosom by the bold, licentious glance which Chorley had so frequently cast upon her charms; and now, heightened as they were by circumstances—by the dishevelled hair, and ill-adjusted garments—the daring look of his eye was enough to offend a spirit so delicately just, so sensitive, and so susceptible as hers.

"What, too much of a lady—too proud, miss, to take the arm of a sailor? Is it so, parson? Have you taught so much pride to your daughter?"

"It is not pride, Master Chorley, you should know—but Bess has not well got over her fright, and it's but natural that she should look to her father first for protection. It's not pride, not dislike, believe me," was the anxiously-spoken reply.

"But there's no sense in that now—for what sort of protection could you have afforded her if I hadn't come? You'd ha' been all scalped to death, or there's no fish in the sea!"

"You say true, indeed, Master Chorley. Our only hope was in God, who is above all,—to him we look—he will always find a protector for the innocent."

"And not much from him either, friend Matthews—for all your prayers would have done you little good under the knife of the redskins, if I had not come at the very moment."

"True—and you see, captain, that God did send us help at the last trying moment."

"Why, that's more than my mother ever said for me, parson—and more than I can ever say for myself. What, Dick Chorley the messenger of God!—Ha! ha! ha!—The old folks would say the devil rather, whose messenger I have been from stem to stern, man and boy, a matter now—but it's quite too far to go back."

"Do not, I pray, Master Chorley," said the old man, gravely— "and know, that Satan himself is God's messenger, and must do his bidding in spite of his own will."

"The deuse, you say. Old Nick, himself, God's messenger! Well, that's new to me, and what the Catechism and old Meg never once taught me to believe. But I won't doubt you, for, as it's your trade, you ought to know best, and we'll have no more talk on the subject. Come, old boy—my good Mrs. Matthews, and you, my sweet—all ready? Fall in, boys—be moving."

"Where go we now, Master Chorley?" inquired the pastor.

"With me, friend Matthews," was the simple and rather stern reply of the pirate, who arranged his troop around the little party, and gave orders to move. He would have taken his place alongside of the maiden, but she studiously passed to the opposite arm of her father, so as to throw the pastor's person between them. In this manner the party moved on, in the direction of the Block House, which the cupidity of Chorley hoped to find unguarded, and to which he hurried, with as much rapidity as possible, in order to be present at the sack. He felt that it must be full of the valuables of all those who had sought its shelter, and with this desire he did not scruple to compel the captives to keep pace with his party, as it was necessary, before proceeding to the assault, that he should place them in a condition of comparative safety. A small cottage lay on the banks of the river, a few miles from his vessel, and in sight of it. It was a rude frame of poles, covered with pine bark; such as the Indian hunters leave behind them all over the country. To this spot he hurried, and there, under the charge of three marines, well armed, he left the jaded family, dreading every change of condition as full as death, if not of other terrors even worse than death—and with scarcely a smaller apprehension of that condition itself. Having so done, he went onward to the work of destruction, where we shall again come up with him.

Chapter Forty-four

"Is all prepared—all ready—for they come,
I hear them in that strange cry through the wood."

THE inmates of the Block House, as we remember, had been warned by Hector of the probable approach of danger, and preparation was the word in consequence. But what was the preparation meant? Under no distinct command, every one had his own favourite idea of defence, and all was confusion in their councils. The absence of Harrison, to whose direction all parties would most willingly have turned their ears, was now of the most injurious tendency, as it left them unprovided with any head, and just at the moment when a high degree of excitement prevailed against the choice of any substitute. Great bustle and little execution took the place of good order, calm opinion, deliberate and decided action. The men were ready enough to fight, and this readiness was an evil of itself, circumstanced as they were. To fight would have been madness then—to protract the issue and gain time was the object; and few, among the defenders of the fortress, at that moment, were sufficiently collected to see this truth. In reason, there was really but a single spirit in the Block House, sufficiently deliberate for the occasion. That spirit was a woman's—the wife of Granger. She had been the child of poverty and privation—the severe school of that best tutor, necessity, had made her equable in mind and intrepid in spirit. She had looked suffering so long in the face, that she now regarded it without a tear. Her parents had never been known to her, and the most trying difficulties clung to her from infancy up to womanhood. So exercised, her mind grew strong in proportion to its trials, and she had learned, in the end, to regard them with a degree of fearlessness far beyond the capacities of any well-bred heir of prosperity and favouring fortune. The same trials attended her after marriage—since the pursuits of her husband carried her into dangers, to which even he could oppose far less ability than his wife. Her genius soared infinitely beyond his own, and to her teachings was he indebted for many of those successes which brought him wealth in after years. She counselled his enterprises, prompted or persuaded his proceedings, managed for him wisely and economically; in all respects, proved herself unselfish; and, if she did not at any time appear above the way of life they had adopted, she took care to maintain both of them from falling beneath it—a result too often following the exclusive pursuit of gain. Her experience throughout life, hitherto, served her admirably now, when all was confusion among the councils of the men. She descended to the court below, where they made a show of deliberation, and, in her own manner, with a just knowledge of human nature, proceeded to give her aid in their general progress. Knowing that any direct suggestion from a woman, and under circumstances of strife and trial, would necessarily offend the *amour propre* of the nobler animal, and provoke his derision, she pursued a sort of management which an experienced woman is usually found to employ as a kind of familiar—a wily little demon, that goes unseen at her bidding, and does her business, like another Ariel, the world all the while knowing nothing about it. Calling out from the crowd one of those whom she knew to be not only the most collected, but the one least annoyed by any unnecessary self-esteem, she was in a moment joined by Wat Grayson, and leading him aside, she proceeded to suggest various measures of preparation and defence, certainly the most prudent that had yet been made. This she did with so much unobtrusive modesty, that the worthy woodman took it for granted, all the while, that the ideas were properly his own. She concluded with insisting upon his taking the command.

"But Nichols will have it all to himself. That's one of our difficulties now."

"What of that? You may easily manage him, Master Grayson."

"How?" he asked.

"The greater number of the men here are of the 'Green Jackets?'"

"Yes—"

"And you are their lieutenant—next in command to Captain Harrison, and their first officer in his absence?"

"That's true."

"Command them as your troop exclusively, and don't mind the rest."

"But they will be offended."

"And if they are, Master Grayson, is this a time to heed their folly when the enemy's upon us? Let them. You do with your troop without heed to them, and they will fall into your ranks—they will work with you when the time comes."

"You are right," was the reply; and immediately going forward with a voice of authority, Grayson, calling only the "Green Jackets" around him, proceeded to organize them, and put himself in command, as first lieutenant of the only volunteer corps which the parish knew. The corps received the annunciation with a shout, and the majority readily recognized him. Nichols, alone, grumbled a little, but the minority was too small to offer any obstruction to Grayson's authority, so that he soon submitted with the rest. The command, all circumstances considered, was not improperly given. Grayson, though not overwise, was decisive in action; and, in matters of strife, wisdom itself must be subservient to resolution. Resolution in trial is wisdom. The new commander numbered his force, placed the feeble and the young in the least trying situations, assigned different bodies to different stations, and sent the women and children into the upper and most sheltered apartment. In a few moments, things were arranged for the approaching conflict with tolerable precision.

The force thus commanded by Grayson was small enough; the whole number of men in the Block House not exceeding twenty-five. The women and children within its shelter were probably twice that number. The population had been assembled in great part from the entire extent of country lying between the Block House and the Indian settlements. From the Block House downward to Port Royal Island, there had been no gathering to this point; the settlers in that section, necessarily, in the event of a like difficulty, seeking a retreat to the fort on the island, which had its garrison already, and was more secure, and in another respect much more safe, as it lay contiguous to the sea. The greater portion of the country immediately endangered from the Yemassees, had been duly warned, and none but the slow, the indifferent, and the obstinate, but had taken sufficient heed of the many warnings given them, and put themselves in safety. Numbers, however, coming under one or other of these classes, had fallen victims to their folly or temerity in the sudden onslaught which followed the first movement of the savages among them, who, scattering themselves over the country, had made their attack so nearly at the same time, as to defeat any thing like unity of action in the resistance which might have been offered them.

Grayson's first care in his new command was to get the women and children fairly out of the way. The close upper apartment of the Block House had been especially assigned them; and there they had assembled generally. But some few of the old ladies were not to be shut up; and his own good Puritan mother gave the busy commandant no little trouble. She went to and fro, interfering in this, preventing that, and altogether annoying the men to such a degree, that it became absolutely necessary to put on a show of sternness which, in a moment of less real danger and anxiety, would have been studiously forborne. With some difficulty and the assistance of Granger's wife, he at length got her out of the way, and to the great satisfaction of all parties, she worried herself to sleep in the midst of a Psalm, which she croned over to the dreariest tune in her whole collection. Sleep had also fortunately seized upon the children generally, and but few, in the room assigned to the women, were able to withstand the approaches of that subtle magician. The wife of the trader, almost alone, continued watchful; thoughtful in emergency, and with a ready degree of common sense, to contend with trial, and to prepare against it. The confused cluster of sleeping forms, in all positions, and of all sorts and sizes, that hour, in the apartment so occupied, was grotesque enough. One figure alone, sitting in the midst, and musing with a concentrated mind, gave dignity to the ludicrous grouping—the majestic figure of Mary Granger—her dark eye fixed upon the silent and sleeping collection, in doubt and pity—her black hair bound closely upon her head, and her broad forehead seeming to enlarge and grow with the busy thought at work within it. Her hand, too—strange association—rested upon a hatchet.

Having completed his arrangements with respect to the security of the women and children, and put them fairly out of his way, Grayson proceeded to call a sort of council of war for further deliberation; and having put sentinels along the picket, and at different points of the building, the more "sage, grave men" of the garrison proceeded to their further arrangements. These were four in number. One of them was Dick Grimstead, the blacksmith, who, in addition to a little farming (carried on when the humour took him) did the horse-shoeing and ironwork for his neighbours of ten miles round, and was in no small repute among them. He was something of a woodman too; and hunting, and perhaps drinking, occupied no small portion of the time which might, with more profit to himself, have been given to his farm and smithy. Nichols, the rival leader of Grayson, was also chosen, with the view rather to his pacification than with any hope of good counsel to be got out of him. Granger, the trader, made the third; and presiding somewhat as chairman, Grayson the fourth. We may add that the wife of the trader, who had descended to the lower apartment in the meantime, and had contrived to busy herself in one corner with some of the wares of her husband, was present throughout the debate. We may add, too, that, at frequent periods of the deliberation, Granger found it necessary to leave the consultations of the council for that of his wife.

"What are we to do?" was the general question.

"Let us send out a spy, and see what they are about," was the speech of one.

"Let us discharge a few pieces, to let them know that a free people are always ready for the enemy," was the sage advice of Nichols, who, though a doctor, was a demagogue also; the breed being known at a very early day in our history.

"No, d——n 'em," said the burly blacksmith, "don't waste, after that fashion, the powder for which a buck would say thank you. If we are to shoot, let's put it to the red-skins themselves. What do you say, Master Grayson?"

"I say, keep quiet, and make ready."

"Wouldn't a spy be of service?" suggested Granger, with great humility, recurring to his first proposition.

"Will you go?" was the blunt speech of the blacksmith. "I don't see any good a spy can do us."

"To see into their force."

"That won't strengthen ours. No! I hold, Wat Grayson, to my mind. We must give the dogs powder and shot when we see 'em. There's no other way—for here we are, and there they are. They're for fight, and will have our scalps, if we are not for fight too. We can't run, for there's no place to go to; and besides that, I'm not used to running, and won't try to run from a red-skin. He shall chaw my bullet first."

"To be sure," roared Nichols, growing remarkably valorous. "Battle, say I. Victory or death."

"Well, Nichols, don't waste your breath now—you may want it

before all's over—" growled the smith, with a most imperturbable composure of countenance,— "if it's only to beg quarter."

"I beg quarter—never!" cried the doctor, fiercely.

"It's agreed, then, that we are to fight—is that what we are to understand?" inquired Grayson, desirous to bring the debate to a close, and to hush the little acerbities going on between the doctor and the smith.

"Ay, to be sure—what else?" said Grimstead.

"What say you, Granger?"

"I say so too, sir—if they attack us—surely."

"And you, Nichols?"

"Ay, fight, I say. Battle to the last drop of blood—to the last moment of existence. Victory or death! that's my word."

"Blast me, Nichols—what a bellows," shouted the smith.

"Mind your own bellows, Grimstead—it will be the better for you. Don't trouble yourself to meddle with mine—you may burn your fingers," retorted the demagogue, angrily.

"Why, yes, if your breath holds hot long enough," was the sneering response of the smith, who seemed to enjoy the sport of teasing his windy comrade.

"Come, come, men, no words," soothingly said the commander. "Let us look to the enemy. You are all agreed that we are to fight; and, to say truth, we didn't want much thinking for that; but how, is the question—how are we to do the fighting? Can we send out a party for scouts—can we spare the men?"

"I think not," said the smith, soberly. "It will require all the men we have, and some of the women too, to keep watch at all the loopholes. Besides, we have not arms enough, have we?"

"Not muskets, but other arms in abundance. What say you, Nichols—can we send out scouts?"

"Impossible! we cannot spare them, and it will only expose them to be cut up by a superior enemy. No, sir, it will be the nobler spectacle to perish, like men, breast to breast. I, for one, am willing to die for the people. I will not survive my country."

"Brave man!" cried the smith— "but I'm not willing to die at all, and therefore I would keep snug and stand 'em here. I can't skulk in the bush, like Granger; I'm quite too fat for that. Though, I'm sure, if I were such a skeleton sort of fellow as Nichols there, I'd volunteer as a scout, and stand the Indian arrows all day."

"I won't volunteer," cried Nichols, hastily. "It will set a bad example, and my absence might be fatal."

"But what if all volunteer?" inquired the smith, scornfully.

"I stand or fall with the people," responded the demagogue, proudly. At that moment, a shrill scream of the whip-poor-will smote upon the senses of the council.

"It is the Indians—that is a favourite cry of the Yemassees," said the wife of Granger. The company started to their feet, and seized their weapons. As they were about to descend to the lower story, the woman seized upon the arm of Grayson, and craved his attendance in the adjoining apartment. He followed; and leading him to the only window in the room, without disturbing any around her, she pointed out a fallen pine-tree, evidently thrown down within the night, which barely rested upon the side of the log house, with all its branches, and but a few feet below the aperture through which they looked. The tree must have been cut previously, and so contrived as to fall gradually upon the dwelling. It was a small one, and by resting in its descent upon other intervening trees, its approach and contact with the dwelling had been unheard. This had probably taken place while the garrison had been squabbling below, with all the women and children listening and looking on. The apartment in which they stood, and against which the tree now depended, had been made, for greater security, without any loop-holes, the musketry being calculated for use in that adjoining and below. The danger arising from this new situation was perceptible at a glance.

"The window must be defended. Two stout men will answer. But they must have muskets," spoke the woman.

"They shall have them," said Grayson, in reply to the fearless and thoughtful person who spoke. "I will send Mason and your husband."

"Do—I will keep it till they come."

"You?" with some surprise, inquired Grayson.

"Yes, Master Grayson—is there anything strange in that? I have no fears. Go—send your men."

"But you will close the shutter."

"No—better, if they should come—better it should be open. If shut, we might be too apt to rest satisfied. Exposure compels watchfulness, and men make the best fortresses."

Full of his new command, and sufficiently impressed with its importance, Grayson descended to the arrangement of his forces; and, true to his promise, despatched Granger and Mason with muskets to the defence of the window, as had been agreed upon with the wife of the trader. They prepared to go up; but, to their consternation, Mason, who was a bulky man, had scarcely reached midway up the ladder leading to the apartment, when, snapping off in the middle, down it came; in its destruction, breaking off all communication between the upper and lower stories of the house until it could be repaired. To furnish a substitute was a difficult task, about which several of the men were set immediately. This accident deeply impressed the wife of the trader, even more than it did the defenders of the house below, with the dangers of their situation; and, in much anxiety, watchful and sad, she paced the room in which they were now virtually confined, in momentary expectation of the enemy.

Chapter Forty-five

"The deep woods saw their battle, and the night
Gave it a genial horror. Blood is there;
The path of battle is traced out in blood."

HUGH GRAYSON, with all his faults, and they were many, was in reality a noble fellow. Full of a high ambition—a craving for the unknown and the vast, which spread itself vaguely and perhaps unattainably before his imagination—his disappointments very naturally vexed him somewhat beyond prudence, and now and then beyond the restraint of right reason. He usually came to a knowledge of his error before it had led too far, and his repentance then was not less ready than his wrong. So in the present instance. The stern severity of those rebukes which had fallen from the lips of Bess Matthews, had the effect upon him which she had anticipated. They brought out the serious determination of his manhood, and, with due effort, he discarded those feeble and querulous fancies which had been productive of so much annoyance to her and others, and so much unhappiness to himself. He strove to forget the feelings of the jealous and disappointed lover, in the lately recollected duties of the man and citizen.

With the good steed of Harrison, which, in the present service, he did not scruple to employ, he set off on the lower route, in order to beat up recruits for the perilous strife which he now began to believe, the more he thought of it, was in reality at hand. The foresters were ready; for one condition of security in border life was the willingness to volunteer in defence of one another; and a five mile ride gave him as many followers. But his farther progress was stopped short by an unlooked-for circumstance. The tread of a body of horse reached the ears of his party, and they slunk into cover. Indistinctly, in the imperfect light, they discovered a mounted force of twenty or thirty men. Another survey made them out to be friends.

"Who goes there?" cried the leader, as Grayson emerged from the bush.

"Friends—well met. There is still time," was the reply.

"I hope so—I have pushed for it," said the commander, "as soon as Sir Edmund gave the orders."

"Ha! you were advised then of this, and come from"—

"Beaufort," cried the officer, "with a detachment of twenty–eight for the upper Block House. Is all well there?"

"Ay, when I left, but things are thought to look squally, and I have just been beating up volunteers for preparation."

"'Tis well—fall in, gentlemen, and good speed—but this cursed road is continually throwing me out. Will you undertake to guide us, so that no time may be lost?"

"Ay—follow—we are now seven miles from the Block, and I am as familiar with the road, dark and light, as with my own hands."

"Away then, men—away"—and, led by the younger Grayson, now fully aroused by the spirit of the scene, they hurried away at full speed through the narrow trace leading to the Block House. They had ridden something like two–thirds of the distance, when a distant shot, then a shout, reached their ears, and compelled a pause for counsel, in order to avoid rushing into ambuscade.

"A mile farther," cried Grayson— "a mile farther, and we must hide our horses in the woods, and take the bush on foot. Horse won't do here; we shall make too good a mark; and besides, riding ourselves, we should not be able to hear the approach of an enemy."

A few moments after and they descended, each fastening his horse to a tree in the shelter of a little bay; and hurriedly organizing under Grayson's direction, they proceeded, alive with expectation, in the direction of the fray.

It is high time that we now return to our fugitive, whose escape from his Indian prison has already been recorded. Paddling his canoe with difficulty, Harrison drew a long breath as it struck the opposite bank in safety. He had escaped one danger, but how many more, equally serious, had he not reason to anticipate in his farther progress. He knew too well the character of Indian warfare, and the mode of assault proposed by them at present, not to feel that all the woods around him were alive with his enemies; that they ran along in the shadow of the thicket, and lay in waiting, for the steps of the flyer, alongside of the fallen tree. He knew his danger, but he had a soul well calculated for its trials.

He leapt ashore, and, at the very first step which he took, a bright column of flame rose above the forests in the direction of the Graysons' cottage. It lay not directly in his path, but it reminded him of his duties, and he came to all the full decision marking his character, as he pushed forward in that quarter. He was not long in reaching it, and the prospect realized many of his fears. The Indians had left their traces, and the dwelling was wrapped in flame, illuminating with a deep glare the surrounding foliage. He looked for other signs of their progress, but in vain. There was no blood, no mark of struggle, and his conclusion was, therefore, that the family had been able to effect its escape from the dwelling before the arrival of the enemy. This conviction was instantaneous, and he gave no idle time in surveying a scene which was only full of a terrible warning. The thought of the whole frontier, and more than all, to his heart, the thought of Bess Matthews, and of the obstinate old father, drove him onward—the blazing ruins lighting his way some distance through the woods. The rush of the wind, as he went forward, brought to his ears, at each moment, and in various quarters, the whoops of the savages, reduced to faintness by distance or cross currents of the breeze, that came here and there, through dense clusters of foliage. Now on one side and now on the other, the sounds smote his ears, compelling him capriciously to veer from point to point in the hope of avoiding the danger. He had not gone far when a second and sudden volume of fire rushed up above the trees only a little distance from him on the left, and he could hear the crackling of the timber. Almost at the same instant, in an opposite direction, another burst of flame attested the mode of warfare adopted by the cunning savages, who, breaking into small parties of five or six in number, thus dispersed themselves over the country, making their attacks simultaneous. This was the mode of assault best adapted to their enterprise; and, but for the precautions taken in warning the more remote of the borderers to the protection of the Block House, their irruption, throughout its whole progress, would have been marked in blood. But few of the settlers could possibly have escaped their knives. Defrauded, however, of their prey, the Indians were thus compelled to wreak their fury upon the unoccupied dwellings.

Dreading to make new and more painful discoveries, but with a spirit nerved for any event, Harrison kept on his course with unrelaxing effort, till he came to the dwelling of an old German, an honest but poor settler, named Van Holten. The old man lay on his threshold insensible. His face was prone to the ground, and he was partially stripped of his clothing. Harrison turned him over, and discovered a deep wound upon his breast, made seemingly with a knife—a hatchet stroke appeared upon his forehead, and the scalp was gone—a red and dreadfully lacerated skull presented itself to his sight, and marked another of those features of war so terribly peculiar to the American border struggles. The man was quite dead; but the brand thrown into his cabin had failed, and the dwelling was unhurt by the fire. Harrison could bestow no time in mere regrets and sympathies, but hurried away, under increased anxieties, and roused to new exertions and efforts by a spectacle that made him tremble momently with the fear of new discoveries of the same sort. The cries of the savages grew more distinct as he proceeded, and his caution was necessarily redoubled. They now gathered between him and the white settlements, and the probability of coming upon his enemies was increased at every step in his progress. Apart from this, he knew but little of their precise position—now they were on one, and now on the other side of him—their whoops sounding, with the multiplied echoes of the wood, in every direction, and inspiring a hesitating dread, at every moment, that he should find himself suddenly among them. The anxiety thus stimulated was more decidedly painful than would have been the hand-to-hand encounter. It was so to the fearless heart of Harrison. Still, however, he kept his way, until, at length, emerging from the brush and foliage, a small lake lay before him, which he knew to be not more than three miles from the dwelling of Bess Matthews. He immediately prepared to take the path he had usually pursued, to the left, which carried him upon the banks of the river. At that moment his eye caught the motion of a small body of the savages in that very quarter. One third of the whole circuit of the lake lay between them and himself, and he now changed his course to the right, in the hope to avoid them. But they had been no less watchful than himself. They had seen, and prepared to intercept him. They divided for this purpose, and while, with shouts and fierce halloos, one party retraced their steps and came directly after him, another, in perfect silence, advanced on their course to the opposite quarter of the lake, in the hope to waylay him in front. Of this arrangement Harrison was

perfectly unaware, and upon this he did not calculate. Having the start
considerably of those who came behind, he did not feel so deeply the
risk of his situation; but, fearless and swift of foot, he cheerily went
forward, hoping to fall in with some of the whites, or at least to shelter
himself in a close cover of the woods before the red men could possibly come up with him. Through brake and bush, heath and water, he
went forward, now running, now walking, as the cries behind him of
his pursuers influenced his feelings. At length the circuit of the lake
was made, and he dashed again into the deeper forest, more secure, as
he was less obvious to the sight than when in the glare of the now high
ascending moon. The woods thickened into copse around him, and he
began to feel something more of hope. He could hear more distinctly
the cries of war, and he now fancied that many of the shouts that met
his ears were those of the English. In this thought he plunged forward,
and as one fierce halloo went up which he clearly felt to be from his
friends, he could not avoid the impulse which prompted him to shout
forth in response. At that moment, bounding over a fallen tree, he felt
his course arrested. His feet were caught by one who lay hid beside it,
and he came heavily to the ground. The Indian who had lain in
ambush was soon above him, and he had but time to ward with one
arm a blow aimed at his head, when another savage advanced upon
him. These two formed the detachment which had been sent forward
in front, for this very purpose, by the party in his rear. The prospect
was desperate, and feeling it so, the efforts of Harrison were herculean.
His only weapon was the knife of Matiwan, but he was a man of great
muscular power and exceedingly active. His faculties availed him now.
With a sudden evolution, he shook one of his assailants from his
breast, and opposed himself to the other while recovering his feet.
They drove against him with their united force, and one hatchet
grazed his cheek. The savage who threw it was borne forward by the
blow, and received the knife of Harrison in his side, but not sufficiently deep to disable him. They came to it again with renewed and
increased ferocity, one assailing him from behind, while the other
employed him in front. He would have gained a tree, but they watched
and kept him too busily exercised to allow of his design. A blow from a
club for a moment paralysed his arm, and he dropped his knife.
Stooping to recover it they pressed him to the ground, and so distributed themselves upon him, that further effort was unavailing. He
saw the uplifted hand, and felt that his senses swam with delirious

thought—his eyes were hazy, and he muttered a confused language. At that moment—did he dream or not?—it was the deep bay of his own favorite hound that reached his ears. The assailants heard it too—he felt assured of that, as, half starting from their hold upon him, they looked anxiously around. Another moment, and he had no farther doubt; the cry of thirst and anger—the mixed moan and roar of the well-known and evidently much-aroused animal, was closely at hand. One of the Indians sprang immediately to his feet—the other was about to strike, when, with a last effort, he grasped the uplifted arm and shouted "Dugdale!" aloud. Nor did he shout in vain. The favorite, with a howl of delight, bounded at the well-known voice, and in another instant Harrison felt the long hair and thick body pass directly over his face, then a single deep cry rang above him, and then he felt the struggle. He now strove again to take part in the fray, though one arm hung nervelessly beside him. He partially succeeded in freeing himself from the mass that had weighed him down; and looking up, saw the entire mouth and chin of the Indian in the jaws of the ferocious hound. The savage knew his deadliest enemy, and his struggle was, not to destroy the dog, but, under the sudden panic, to free himself from his hold. With this object his hatchet and knife had been dropped. His hands were vainly endeavouring to loosen the huge, steely jaws of his rough assailant from his own. The other Indian had fled with the first bay of the animal—probably the more willing to do so, as the momentary fainting of Harrison had led them to suppose him beyond further opposition. But he recovered; and, with recovering consciousness, resuming the firm grasp of his knife which had fallen beside him, seconded the efforts of Dugdale by driving it into the breast of their remaining enemy, who fell dead, with his chin still between the teeth of the hound. Staggering as much with the excitement of such a conflict, as with the blow he had received, Harrison with difficulty regained his feet. Dugdale held on to his prey, and before he would forego his hold, completely cut the throat which he had taken in his teeth. A single embrace of his master attested the deep gratitude which he felt for the good service of his favorite.

But there was no time for delay. The division which pursued him was at hand. He heard their shout from a neighbouring copse, and he bent his steps forward. The red men were soon apprised of his movement. Joined by the fugitive, and having heard his details, what was their surprise to find their own warrior a victim, bloody and perfectly dead upon the grass, where they had looked to have taken a scalp! Their rage knew no bounds, and they were now doubly earnest in pursuit. Feeble from the late struggle, Harrison did not possess his previous vigour—besides, he had run far through the woods, and though as hardy as any of the Indians, he was not so well calculated to endure a race of this nature. But, though they gained on him, he knew that he had a faithful ally at hand on whom he felt that he might safely depend. The hound, trained as was the custom, was formidable to the fears of the Indians. Like the elephant of old among the Asiatics, he inspired a degree of terror among the American aborigines, which, in great degree, deprived them of courage and conduct; and, had there been less inequality of force, the dog of Harrison alone would have been sufficient to have decided his present pursuers to choose a more guarded course, if not to a complete discontinuance of pursuit. But they heard the shouts of their own warriors all around them, and trusting that flying from one, the White Chief, the famous Coosah-moray-tee, must necessarily fall into the hands of some other party, they were stimulated still farther in the chase.

They had not miscalculated. The wild whoop of war—the "*Sangarrah-me, Yemassee*," rose directly in the path of Harrison, and, wearied with flight, the fugitive prepared himself for the worst. He leaned against a tree in exhaustion, while the dog took his place beside him, obedient to his master's command, though impatient to bound forward. Harrison kept him for a more concentrated struggle, and wreathing his hands in the thick collar about his neck, he held him back for individual assailants. In the meantime his pursuers approached, though with caution. His dog was concealed by the brush, on the skirts of which he had studiously placed him. They heard at intervals his long, deep bay, and it had an effect upon them not unlike that of their own war-whoop upon the whites. They paused, as if in council. Just then, their party in front set up another shout, and the confusion of a skirmish was evident to the senses as well of Harrison as of his pursuers. This to him was a favourable sign. It indicated the presence of friends. He heard at length one shot, then another, and another, and at the same time the huzzas of the Carolinians. These inspired him with new courage; and, with an impulse which is sometimes, and, in desperate cases, may be almost considered wisdom, he plunged forward through the brush which separated him from the unseen combatants, loudly cheering in the

English manner, and prompting the hound to set up a succession of cries, sufficiently imposing to inspire panic in the savages.

His movement was the signal to move also on the part of those who pursued him. But a few steps changed entirely the scene. He had rushed upon the rear of a band of the Yemassees, who, lying behind brush and logs, were skirmishing at advantage with a corps of foresters which we have seen led on by the younger Grayson. A single glance sufficed to put Harrison in possession of the true facts of the case, and, though hazarding every chance of life, he bounded directly among, and through, the ambushed Indians. Never was desperation more fortunate in its consequences. Not knowing the cause of such a movement, the Yemassees conceived themselves beset front and rear. They rose screaming from their hiding places, and yielded on each side of the fugitive. With an unhesitating hand he struck with his knife one of their chiefs who stood in his path. The hound leaping among them like a hungry panther, farther stimulated the panic, and for a moment they scattered about bewildered, and with a wholly purposeless action. The fierce and forward advance of that portion of their own allies who had been pursuing Harrison, still further contributed to impress them with the idea of an enemy in the rear; and, before they could recover, so as to arrest his progress and discover the true state of things, he had passed them, followed by the obedient dog. In another instant, almost fainting with fatigue, to the astonishment but satisfaction of all, he threw himself, with a laugh of mingled triumph and exhaustion, into the ranks of his sturdy band of foresters.

Without a pause he commanded their attention. Fully conscious of the confusion among the ambushers, he ordered an advance, and charged resolutely through the brush. The contest was now hand to hand, and the foresters took their tree when necessary, as well as their enemies. The presence of their captain gave them new courage, and the desperate manner in which he had charged through the party with which they fought, led them to despise their foes. This feeling imparted to the Carolinians a degree of recklessness, which, new to them in such warfare, was not less new to the Indians. Half frightened before, they needed but such an attack to determine them to retreat. They faltered, and at length fled—a few fought on awhile, single handed, perhaps not knowing how completely their force was scattered; but wounded and without encouragement, they too gave way, sullenly and slowly, and at length were brought up with their less resolute companions in the cover of a neighbouring and denser wood.

Harrison did not think it advisable to pursue them. Calling off his men, therefore, he led them on the route towards the Block House, which he relied upon as the chief rallying point of the settlers in that quarter. His anxieties, however, at that moment, had in them something selfish, and he proceeded hurriedly to the house of old Matthews. It was empty—its inmates were gone, and the marks of savage devastation were all around them. The building had been plundered, and a hasty attempt made to burn it by torches, but without success, the floors being only slightly scorched. He rushed through the apartments in despair, calling the family by name. What had been their fate—and where was she? The silence of everything around spoke to him to loudly, and, with the faintest possible hope that they had been sufficiently apprised of the approach of the Indians to have taken the shelter of the Block House, he proceeded to lead his men to that designated point.

Chapter Forty-six

"A sudden trial, and the danger comes,
Noiseless and nameless."

LET us go back once more to the Block House, and look into the condition of its defenders. We remember the breaking of the ladder, the only one in the possession of the garrison, which led to the upper story of the building. This accident left them in an ugly predicament, since some time must necessarily be taken up in its repair, and, in the meanwhile, the forces of the garrison were divided in the different apartments above and below. In the section devoted to the women and children, and somewhat endangered, as we have seen, from the exposed window and the fallen tree, they were its exclusive occupants. The opposite chamber held a few of the more sturdy and common sense defenders, while in the great hall below, a miscellaneous group of fifteen or twenty—the inferior spirits—were assembled. Two or three of these were busied in patching up the broken ladder, which was to renew the communication between the several parties, thus, of necessity, thrown asunder.

The watchers of the fortress, from their several loop-holes, looked forth, east and west, yet saw no enemy. All was soft in the picture, all was silent in the deep repose of the forest. The night was clear and lovely, and the vague and dim beauty with which, in the imperfect moonlight, the foliage of the woods spread away in distant shadows, or clung and clustered together as in groups, shrinking for concealment from her glances, touched the spirits even of those rude foresters. With them the poetry of the natural world is a matter of feeling—with the refined, it is an instrument of art. Hence it is, indeed, that the poetry of the early ages speaks in the simplest language, while that of civilization, becoming only the agent for artificial enjoyment, is ornate in its dress, and complex in its form and structure.

The night wore on, still calm and serene in all its aspects about the Block House. Far away in the distance, like glimpses of a spirit, little sweeps of the river, in its crooked windings, flashed upon the eye, streaking, with a sweet relief, the sombre foliage of the swampy forest through which it stole. A single note—the melancholy murmur of the chuck-will's-widow—the Carolina whippoorwill—broke fitfully upon the silence, to which it gave an added solemnity. That single note indicated to the keepers of the fortress a watchfulness corresponding with their own, of another living creature. Whether it were human or not— whether it were the deceptive lure and signal of the savage, or, in reality, the complaining cry of the solitary and sad night-bird which it so resembled, was, however, matter of nice question with those who listened to the strain.

"They are there—they are there;—hidden in that wood;" —cried Grayson— "I'll swear it. I've heard them quite too often not to know their cunning now. Hector was right, after all, boys."

"What, where?" —asked Nichols.

"There, in the bush to the left of the blasted oak—now, down to the bluff—and now, by the bay on the right. They are all round us."

"By what do you know, Wat?"

"The whippoorwill—that is their cry—their signal."

"It *is* the whippoorwill," said Nichols,— "there is but one of them; you never hear more than one at a time."

"Pshaw!" responded Grayson,— "you may hear half-a-dozen at a time, as I have done a thousand times. But that is from no throat of bird. It is the Indian. There is but a single note, you perceive; and it rises from three different quarters. Now it is to the Chief's Bluff—and now—it comes immediately from the old grove of scrubby oak. A few shot there would get an answer."

"Good! that is just my thought—let us give them a broadside, and disperse the scoundrels," cried Nichols.

"Not so fast, Nichols—you swallow your enemy without asking leave of his teeth. Have you inquired first whether we have powder and shot to throw away upon bushes that may be empty?" now exclaimed the blacksmith, joining in the question.

"A prudent thought, that, Grimstead," said Grayson,— "we have no ammunition to spare in that way. But I have a notion that may prove of profit. Where is the captain's straw man—here, Granger, bring out Dugdale's trainer."

The stuffed figure already described was brought forward, the window looking in the direction of the grove supposed to shelter the savages was thrown open, and the perfectly indifferent head of the automaton thrust incontinently through the opening. The *ruse* was completely successful. The foe could not well resist this temptation, and a flight of arrows, penetrating the figure in every portion of its breast and face, attested to the presence of the enemy and the truth of his aim. A wild and shuddering cry rang through the forest at the same instant—that cry, well known as the fearful war-whoop, the sound of which made the marrow curdle in the bones of the frontier settler, and prompted the mother with a nameless terror to hug closer to her bosom the form of her unconscious infant. It was at once answered from side to side, wherever their several parties had been stationed, and it struck terror even into the sheltered garrison which heard it—such terror as the traveller feels by night, when the shrill rattle of the lurking serpent, with that ubiquity of sound which is one of its fearful features, vibrates all around him, leaving him at a loss to say in what quarter his enemy lies in waiting, and teaching him to dread that the very next step which he takes may place him within the coil of death.

"Ay, there they are, sure enough—fifty of them at least, and we shall have them upon us, after this, monstrous quick, in some way or other," was the speech of Grayson, while a brief silence through all the party marked the deep influence upon them of the summons which they had heard.

"True—and we must be up and doing," said the smith; "we can now give them a shot, Wat Grayson, for they will dance out from the cover now, thinking they have killed one of us. The savages—they have thrown away some of *their* powder at least." As Grimstead spoke, he drew three arrows with no small difficulty from the bosom of the figure in which they were buried.

"Better there than in our ribs. But you are right. Stand back for a moment and let me have that loop—I shall waste no shot. Ha! I see—there is one—I see his arm and the edge of his hatchet—it rests upon his shoulder, I reckon, but that is concealed by the brush. He moves—he comes out, and slaps his hands against his thigh. The red devil, but he shall have it. Get ready, now, each at his loop, for if I hurt him they will rush out in fury."

The sharp click of the cock followed the words of Grayson, who was an able shot, and the next moment the full report came burdened with a dozen echoes from the crowding woods around. A cry of pain—then a shout of fury and the reiterated whoop followed; and as one of their leaders reeled and sank under the unerring bullet, the band in that station, as had been predicted by Grayson, rushed forth to where he stood, brandishing their weapons with ineffectual fury, and lifting their wounded comrade; as is their general custom, to bear him to a place of concealment, and preserve him from being scalped, by secret burial, in the event of his being dead. They paid for their temerity. Following the direction of their leader, whose decision necessarily commanded their obedience, the Carolinians took quite as much advantage of the exposure of their enemies, as the number of the loop-holes in that quarter of the building would admit. Five muskets told among the group, and a reiterated shout of fury indicated the good service which the discharge had done, and taught the savages a lesson of prudence, which, in the present instance, they had been too ready to disregard. They sank back into cover, taking care however to remove their hurt companions, so that, save by the peculiar cry which marks a loss among them, the garrison were unable to determine what had been the success of their discharges. Having driven them back into the brush, however, without loss to themselves, the latter were now sanguine, where, only a moment before, their confined and cheerless position had taught them a feeling of despondency not calculated to improve the comforts of their case.

The Indians had made their arrangements, on the other hand, with no little precaution. But they had been deceived and disappointed. Their scouts, who had previously inspected the fortress, had given a very different account of the defences and the watchfulness of their garrison, to what was actually the fact upon their appearance. The scouts, however, had spoken truth, and, but for the discovery made by Hector, the probability is that the Block House would have been surprised with little or no difficulty. Accustomed to obey Harrison as their only leader, the foresters present never dreamed of preparation for conflict unless under his guidance. The timely advice of the trader's wife, and the confident assumption of command on the part of Walter Grayson, completed their securities. But for this, a confusion of counsels, not less than of tongues, would have neutralized all action, and left them an easy prey, without head or direction, to the knives of their insidious enemy. Calculating upon surprise and cunning as the only means by which they could hope to balance the numerous advantages possessed by European warfare over their own, the Indians had relied rather more on the suddenness of their onset, and the craft peculiar to their education, than on the force of their valour. They felt themselves baffled, therefore, in their main hope, by the sleepless caution of the garrison, and now prepared themselves for other means.

They made their disposition of force with no little judgment. Small bodies, at equal distances, under cover, had been stationed all about the fortress. With the notes of the whippoorwill they had carried on their signals, and indicated the several stages of their preparation; while, in addition to this, another band—a sort of forlorn hope, consisting of the more desperate, who had various motives for signalizing their valour—creeping singly, from cover to cover, now reposing in the shadow of a log along the ground, now half buried in a clustering bush, made their way at length so closely under the walls of the log house as to be completely concealed from the garrison, which, unless by the window, had no mode of looking directly down upon them. As the windows were well watched by their comrades—having once attained their place of concealment—it followed that their position remained entirely concealed from those within. They lay in waiting for the favourable moment—silent as the grave, and sleepless—ready, when the garrison should determine upon a sally, to fall upon their rear; and in the meanwhile, quietly preparing dry fuel in quantity, gathering it from time to time, and piling it against the logs of the fortress, they prepared thus to fire the defences that shut them out from their prey.

There was yet another mode of finding entrance, which has been partially glimpsed at already. The scouts had done their office diligently in more than the required respects. Finding a slender pine twisted by a late storm, and scarcely sustained by a fragment of its shaft, they applied fire to the rich turpentine oozing from the wounded part of the tree, and carefully directing its fall, as it yielded to the fire, they lodged its extremest branches, as we have already seen, against the wall of the Block House and just beneath the window, the only one looking from that quarter of the fortress. Three of the bravest of their warriors were assigned for scaling this point and securing their entrance, and the attack was forborne by the rest of the band, while their present design, upon which they built greatly, was in progress.

Let us then turn to this quarter. We have already seen that the dangers of this position were duly estimated by Grayson, under the suggestion of Granger's wife. Unhappily for its defence, the fate of the ladder prevented that due attention to the subject, at once, which had been imperatively called for; and the subsequent excitement following the discovery of the immediate proximity of the Indians, had turned the consideration of the defenders to the opposite end of the building, from whence the partial attack of the enemy, as described, had come. It is true that the workmen were yet busy with the ladder; but the assault had suspended their operations, in the impatient curiosity which such an event would necessarily induce, even in the bosom of fear.

The wife of Granger, fully conscious of the danger, was alone sleepless in that apartment. The rest of the women, scarcely apprehensive of attack at all, and perfectly ignorant of the present condition of affairs, with all that heedlessness which marks the unreflecting character, had sunk to the repose (without an effort at watchfulness) which previous fatigues had, perhaps, made absolutely unavoidable. She, alone, sat thoughtful and silent—musing over present prospects—perhaps of the past—but still unforgetful of the difficulties and the dangers before her. With a calm temper she awaited the relief which, with the repair of the ladder, she looked for from below.

In the meantime hearing something of the alarm, together with the distant war-whoop, she had looked around her for some means of defence, in the event of any attempt being made upon the window before the aid promised could reach her. But a solitary weapon met her eye, in a long heavy hatchet, a clumsy instrument, rather more like the cleaver of a butcher than the light and slender tomahawk so familiar to the Indians. Having secured this, with the composure of that courage which had been in great part taught her by the necessities of fortune, she prepared to do without other assistance, and to forego the sentiment of dependance, which is perhaps one of the most marked characteristics of her sex. Calmly looking round upon the sleeping and defenceless crowd about her, she resumed her seat upon a low bench in a corner of the apartment, from which she had risen to secure the hatchet, and, extinguishing the only light in the room, fixed her eye upon the accessible window, while every thought of her mind prepared her for the danger which was at hand. She had not long been seated when she fancied that she heard a slight rustling of the branches of the fallen tree just beneath the window. She could not doubt her

senses, and her heart swelled and throbbed with the consciousness of
approaching danger. But still she was firm—her spirit grew more confirmed with the coming trial; and, coolly throwing the slippers from
her feet, grasping firmly her hatchet at the same time, she softly arose,
and keeping close in the shadow of the wall, she made her way to a
recess, a foot or so from the entrance, to which it was evident some
one was cautiously approaching along the attenuated body of the
yielding pine. In a few moments a shadow darkened the opening. She
edged more closely to the point, and prepared for the intruder. She
now beheld the head of the enemy—a fierce and foully painted savage—the war-tuft rising up into a ridge, something like a comb, and
his face smeared with colours in a style the most ferociously grotesque.
Still she could not strike, for, as he had not penetrated the window,
and as its entrance was quite too small to enable her to strike with any
hope of success at any distance through it, she felt that the effort
would be wholly without certainty; and failure might be of the worst
consequence. Though greatly excited, and struggling between doubt
and determination, she readily saw what would be the error of any
precipitation. But even as she mused thus apprehensively, the cunning
savage laid his hand upon the sill of the window, the better to raise
himself to its level. That sight tempted her in spite of her better sense,
to the very precipitation she had desired to avoid. In the moment that
she saw the hand of the red man upon the sill, the hatchet descended,
under an impulse scarcely her own. She struck too quickly. The blow
was given with all her force, and would certainly have separated the
hand from the arm had it taken effect. But the quick eye of the Indian
caught a glimpse of her movement at the very moment in which it was
made, and the hand was withdrawn before the hatchet descended. The
steel sank deep into the soft wood—so deeply that she could not disengage it. To try at this object would have exposed her at once to his
weapon, and leaving it where it stuck, she sunk back again into
shadow.

What now was she to do? To stay where she was would be of little
avail; but to cry out to those below, and seek to fly, was equally unproductive of good, besides warning the enemy of the defencelessness of
their condition, and thus inviting a renewal of the attack. The thought
came to her with the danger; and, without a word, she maintained her
position, in waiting for the progress of events. As the Indian had also
sunk from sight, and some moments had now elapsed without his

reappearance, she determined to make another effort for the recovery of the hatchet. She grasped it by the handle, and in the next moment the hand of the savage was upon her own. He felt that his grasp was on the fingers of a woman, and in a brief word and something of a chuckle, while he still maintained his hold upon it, he conveyed intelligence of the fact to those below. But it was a woman with a man's spirit with whom he contended, and her endeavour was successful to disengage herself. The same success did not attend her effort to recover the weapon. In the brief struggle with her enemy it had become disengaged from the wood, and while both strove to seize it, it slipped from their mutual hands, and sliding over the sill, in another instant was heard rattling through the intervening bushes. Descending upon the ground below, it became the spoil of those without, whose murmurs of gratulation she distinctly heard. But now came the tug of difficulty. The Indian, striving at the entrance, was necessarily encouraged by the discovery that his opponent was not a man; and assured, at the same time, by the forbearance, on the part of those within, to strike him effectually down from the tree, he now resolutely endeavoured to effect his entrance. His head was again fully in sight of the anxious woman—then his shoulders; and, at length, taking a firm grasp upon the sill, he strove to elevate himself by muscular strength, so as to secure him sufficient purchase for the entrance at which he aimed.

What could she do—weaponless, hopeless? The prospect was startling and terrible enough; but she was a strong-minded woman, and impulse served her when reflection would most probably have taught her to fly. She had but one resource; and as the Indian had gradually thrust one hand forward for the hold upon the sill, and raised the other up to the side of the window, she grasped the one nighest her own. She grasped it firmly, with all her might, and to advantage, as, having lifted himself on tiptoe for the purpose of ascent, he had necessarily lost much of the control which a secure hold for his feet must have given him. Her grasp sufficiently assisted him forward, to lessen still more greatly the security of his feet, while, at the same time, though bringing him still farther into the apartment, placing him in such a position—half in air—as to defeat much of the muscular exercise which his limbs would have possessed in any other situation. Her weapon now would have been all-important; and the brave woman mentally deplored the precipitancy with which she had acted in the first instance, and which had so unhappily deprived her of its use. But self-reproach was unavailing now, and she was satisfied if she could be able to retain her foe in his present position; by which, keeping him out, or in and out, as she did, she necessarily excluded all other foes from the aperture which he so completely filled up. The intruder, though desirous enough of entrance before, was rather reluctant to obtain it now, under existing circumstances. He strove desperately to effect a retreat, but had advanced too far, however, to be easily successful; and, in his confusion and disquiet, he spoke to those below, in his own language, explaining his difficulty, and directing their movement to his assistance. A sudden rush along the tree indicated to the conscious sense of the woman the new danger, in the approach of additional enemies, who must not only sustain, but push forward, the one with whom she contended. This warned her at once of the necessity of some sudden procedure, if she hoped to do any thing for her own and the safety of those around her—the women and the children; whom, amid all the contest, she had never once alarmed. Putting forth all her strength, therefore, though nothing in comparison with that of him whom she opposed, had he been in a condition to exert it, she strove to draw him still farther across the entrance, so as to exclude, if possible, the approach of those coming behind him. She hoped to gain time—sufficient time for those preparing the ladder to come to her relief; and with this hope, for the first time, she called aloud to Grayson and her husband.

The Indian, in the meanwhile, derived support for his person, as well from the grasp of the woman, as from his own hold upon the sill of the window. Her effort necessarily drawing him still farther forward, placed him so completely in the way of his allies that they could do him little service while things remained in this situation; and, to complete the difficulties of his predicament, while they had busied themselves in several efforts at his extrication, the branches of the little tree, resting against the dwelling, yielding suddenly to the unusual weight upon it—trembling and sinking away at last—cracked beneath the burden, and snapping off from its several holds, fell from under them, dragging against the building in the progress down; thus breaking their fall, but cutting off all their hope from this mode of entrance, and leaving their comrade awkwardly poised aloft, able neither to enter, nor to depart from the window. The tree finally settled heavily upon the ground; and with it went the three savages

who had so readily ascended to the assistance of their comrade—
bruised and very much hurt; while he, now without any support but
that which he derived from the sill, and what little his feet could
secure from the irregular crevices between the logs of which the
house had been built, was hung in air, unable to advance except at the
will of his woman opponent, and dreading a far worse fall from his
eminence than that which had already happened to his allies.
Desperate with his situation, he thrust his arm, as it was still held by
the woman, still farther into the window, and this enabled her with
both hands to secure and strengthen the grasp which she had originally taken upon it. This she did with a new courage and strength,
derived from the voices below, by which she understood a promise of
assistance. Excited and nerved, she drew the extended arm of the
Indian, in spite of all his struggles, directly over the sill, so as to turn
the elbow completely down upon it. With her whole weight thus
employed, bending down to the floor to strengthen herself to the
task, she pressed the arm across the window until her ears heard the
distinct, clear crack of the bone—until she heard the groan, and felt
the awful struggles of the suffering wretch, twisting himself round
with all his effort to obtain for the shattered arm, a natural and
relaxed position, and, with this object, leaving his hold upon every
thing; only sustained, indeed, by the grasp of his enemy. But the
movement of the woman had been quite too sudden, her nerves too
firm, and her strength too great, to suffer him to succeed. The jagged
splinters of the broken limb were thrust up, lacerating and tearing
through flesh and skin, while a howl of the acutest agony attested the
severity of that suffering which could extort such an acknowledgment
from the American savage. He fainted in his pain, and as the weight
increased upon the arm of the woman, the nature of her sex began to
resume its sway. With a shudder of every fibre, she released her hold
upon him. The effort of her soul was over—a strange sickness came
upon her; and she was conscious of a crashing fall of the heavy body
among the branches of the tree at the foot of the window, when she
staggered back fainting into the arms of her husband, who just at that
moment ascended to her relief.

Chapter Forty-seven

"He shouts, he strikes, he falls—his fields are o'er;
He dies in triumph, and he asks no more."

THESE slight defeats were sufficiently annoying in themselves to the invaders; they were more so, as they proved not only the inadequacy of their present mode of assault, but the watchfulness of the beleaguered garrison. Their hope had been to take the borderers by surprise. Failing to succeed in this, they were now thrown all aback. Their fury was consequently more than ever exaggerated by their losses, and, rushing forward in their desperation, through, and in defiance of, the fire from the Carolinians, the greater number placed themselves beneath the line of pickets, with so much celerity as to baffle, in most respects, the aim of the defenders. A few remained to bear away the wounded and slain to a place of safe shelter in the thick woods, while the rest lay, either in quiet under the walls of the Block House, secure there from the fire of the garrison, or amused themselves in unavailing cries of sarcasm to those within, while impotently expending blows upon the insensible logs between them. The elder Grayson, who directed solely the movements of the beleaguered, was not unwilling that the assailants should amuse themselves after this fashion, as the delay of the Indians was to them the gain of time, which was all they could expect at such a period, and, perhaps, in a predatory warfare like the present, all that they could desire.

But Ishiagaska with his force now came upon the scene, and somewhat changed the aspect of affairs. He took the entire command, reinvigorated the efforts of the red men, and considerably altered the mode and direction of attack. He was a subtle partisan, and the consequences of his appearance were soon perceptible in the development of events. The force immediately beneath the walls, and secure from the shot of the garrison, were reinforced, and in so cautious a manner, that the Carolinians were entirely ignorant of the increased strength of the enemy in that quarter. Creeping, as they did, from bush to bush—now lying prone and silent to the ground, in utter immobility—now rushing, as circumstances prompted, with all rapidity—they put themselves into cover, crossing the intervening space without the loss of a man. Having thus collected in force beneath the walls of the fortress, the greater number proceeded to gather up in piles, as they had begun to do before, immense quantities of the dry pine trash and the gummy turpentine wood which the neighbourhood readily afforded. Other parties watched the garrison, with bows ready, and arrows on the string. Meanwhile, the piles of combustible matter were heaped in thick masses around the more accessible points of the pickets; and the first intimation which the garrison had of their proceeding was a sudden gust of flame, blazing first about the gate of the area, on one side of the Block House, then rushing from point to point with amazing rapidity, sweeping and curling widely around the building itself. The gate, and the pickets all about it, made as they had been of the rich pine, for its great durability, were themselves as appropriate materials for the destructive element to feed upon, as the Indians could have desired; and, licked greedily by the fire, were soon ignited. Blazing impetuously, the flames soon aroused the indwellers to a more acute consciousness of the danger now at hand. A fierce shout of their assailants, as they beheld the rapid progress of the experiment, warned them to greater exertion if they hoped to escape the dreadful fate which threatened to engulf them. To remain where they were, was to be consumed in the flames; to rush forth, was to encounter the tomahawks of an enemy five times their number.

It was a moment of gloomy necessity, that which assembled the chief defenders of the fortress to a sort of war-council. They could only deliberate—to fight was out of the question. Their enemy was one to whom they could now oppose

> "————————Nor subtle wile,
> Nor arbitration strong."

The Indians showed no front for assault or aim, while the flames, rushing from point to point, and seizing upon numerous places at once, continued to advance with a degree of celerity which left it impossible, in the dry condition of its timber, that the Block House could possibly, for any length of time, escape. Upon the building itself the savages could not fix the fire at first. But two ends of it were directly accessible to them, and these were without any entrance, had been pierced with holes for musketry, and were well watched by the vigilant eyes within. The two sides were inclosed by the line of pickets, and had no need of other guardianship. The condition of affairs was deplorable. The women wept and prayed, the children screamed, and the men, assembling in the long apartment of the lower story, with heavy hearts and solemn faces, proceeded to ask counsel of one another in the last resort. Some lay around on the loose plank; here and there, along the floor, a bearskin formed the place of rest for a huge and sullen warrior, vexed with the possession of strength which he was not permitted to employ. A few watched at the musket holes, and others busied themselves in adjusting all things for the final necessity, so far as their thoughts or fancies could possibly divine its shape.

The principal men of the garrison were gathered in the centre of the hall, sitting with downcast heads and fronting one another, along two of the uncovered sleepers; their muskets resting idly between their legs, their attitudes and general expression of *abandon* signifying clearly the due increase of apprehension in their minds with the progress of the flames. Broad flashes of light from the surrounding conflagration illuminated, but could not enliven, the sombre character of that grouping. A general pause ensued after their assemblage, none seeming willing or able to offer counsel; and Grayson himself, the brave forester in command, was evidently at fault in the farther business before them. Nichols was the only man to break the silence, which he did in his usual manner.

"And why, my friends, are we here assembled?" was his sagacious inquiry, looking around as he spoke upon his inattentive co-adjutors. A forced smile on the faces of several, but not a word, attested their uniform estimate of the speaker. He proceeded:

"That is the question, my friends—why are we here assembled? I answer, for the good of the people. We are here to protect them if we can, and to perish for, and with them, if we must. I cannot forget my duties to my country, and to those in whose behalf I stand before the hatchet of the Indian, and the cannon of the Spaniard. These teach me, and I would teach it to you, my friends—to fight, to hold out to the last. We may not think of surrender, my friends, until other hope is gone. Whatever be the peril, till that moment be it mine to encounter it—whatever be the privation, till that moment I am the man to endure it. Be it for me, at least, though I stand alone in this particular, to do for the people whatever wisdom or valour may do until the moment comes which shall call on us for surrender. The question now, my friends, is simply this—has that moment come or not? I pause for a reply."

"Who talks of surrender?" growled the smith, as he cast a glance of ferocity at the speaker. "Who talks of surrender at all, to these cursed bloodhounds; the red-skins that hunt for nothing but our blood! We cannot surrender if we would—we must fight, die, do anything but surrender!"

"So say I—I am ready to fight and die for my country. I say it now, as I have said it a hundred times before, but—" The speech which Nichols had thus begun, the smith again interrupted with a greater bull-dog expression than ever.

"Ay, so you have, and so will say a hundred times more—with as little sense in it one time as another. We are all here to die, if there's any need for it; but that isn't the trouble. It's how we are to die—that's the question. Are we to stay here and be burnt to death like timber-rats—to sally out and be shot, or to volunteer, as I do now, axe in hand, to go out and cut down the pickets that immediately join the house? By that we may put a stop to the fire, and then we shall have a clear dig at the savages that lie behind them. I'm for that. If anybody's willing to go along with me, let him up hands—no talk—we have too much of that already."

"I'm ready—here!" cried Grayson, and his hands were thrust up at the instant.

"No, Wat," cried the smith— "not you—you must stay and manage here. Your head's the coolest, and though I'd sooner have your arm alongside of me in the rough time than any other two that I know of, 'twould not do to take you from the rest on this risk. Who else is ready?—let him come to the scratch, and no long talk about it. What do you say, Nichols? that's chance enough for you, if you really want to die for the people." And as Grimstead spoke, he thrust his head forward, while his eyes peered into the very bosom of the little doctor, and his axe descended to the joist over which he stood with a thundering emphasis that rang through the apartment.

"I can't use the axe," cried Nichols, hurriedly. "It's not my instrument. Sword or pistol for me. In their exercise I give way to no man, and in their use I ask for no leader. But I am neither woodman nor blacksmith."

"And this is your way of dying for the good of the people!" said the smith contemptuously.

"I am willing even now—I say it again, as I have before said, and as now I solemnly repeat it. But I must die for them after my own fashion, and under proper circumstances. With sword in hand crossing the perilous breach—with weapon befitting the use of a noble gentleman, I am ready; but I know not any rule in patriotism that would require of me to perish for my country with the broad axe of a woodchopper, the cleaver of a butcher, or the sledge of a blacksmith in my hands."

"Well, I'm no soldier," retorted the smith; "but I think a man, to be really willing to die for his country, shouldn't be too nice as to which way he does it. Now the sword and the pistol are of monstrous little use here. The muskets from these holes, above and below, will keep off the Indians, while a few of us cut down the stakes; so now, men, as time grows short. Grayson, you let the boys keep a sharp look out with the ticklers, and I'll for the timber, let him follow who will. There are boys enough, I take it, to go with Dick Grimstead, though they may none of them be very anxious to die for their country."

Thus saying, and having received the sanction of Grayson to this, the only project from which anything could be expected, the blacksmith pushed forward, throwing open the door leading to the area which the fire in great part now beleaguered—while Grayson made arrangements to command the group with his musketry, and to keep the entrance, thus opened for Grimstead and his party, with his choicest men. The blacksmith was one of those blunt, burly fellows, who take with the populace. It was not difficult for him to procure three men where twenty were ready. They had listened with much sympathy to the discussion narrated, and as the pomposity and assumption of Nichols had made him an object of vulgar ridicule, a desire to rebuke him, not less than a willingness to go with the smith, contributed readily to persuade them to the adventure. In a few moments the door was unbarred, and the party sallied forth through the entrance, which was kept ajar for their ingress, and well watched by half a dozen of the stoutest men in the garrison, Grayson at their head. Nichols went above to direct the musket-men, while his mind busied itself in conning over the form of capitulation, which he thought it not improbable that he should have to frame with the chiefs of the besieging army. In this labour he had but one cause of vexation, which arose from the necessity he would be under, in enumerating the prisoners, of putting himself after Grayson, the commander.

In the meanwhile, with sleeves rolled up, jacket off, and face that seemed not often to have been entirely free from the begriming blackness of his profession, Grimstead commenced his tremendous blows upon the contiguous pickets, followed with like zeal, if not equal power, by the three men who had volunteered along with him. Down went the first post beneath his arm, and as, with resolute spirit, he was about to assail another, a huge Santee warrior stood in the gap which he had made, and, with a powerful blow from the mace which he carried—had our blacksmith been less observant—would have soon finished his career. But Grimstead was a man of agility as well as strength and spirit, and, leaping aside from the blow, as his eye rose to the corresponding glance from that of his enemy, he gave due warning to his axe-men, who forbore their strokes under his command. The aperture was yet too small for any combat of the parties; and, ignorant of the force against him, surprised also at its appearance, he despatched one of his men to Grayson, and gave directions, which, had they been complied with, had certainly given the advantage to the garrison.

"Now, boys, you shall have fun—I have sent for some hand-to-hand men to do the fighting, while we do the chopping,—and Nichols, who loves dying so much, can't help coming along with them. He's the boy for sword and pistol—he's no woodcutter. Well, many a better chap than he's had to chop wood for an honest living. But we'll see now what he is good for. Let him come."

"Oh, he's all flash in the pan, Grimstead. His tongue is mustard-seed enough, but 'taint the shot. But what's that—?"

The speaker, who was one of Grimstead's comrades, might well ask, for first a crackling, then a whirling crash, announced the fall, at length, of the huge gate to the entrance of the court. A volume of flame and cinders, rising with the gust which it created, rushed up, obscuring for a moment, and blinding all things around it; but, as it subsided, the Indians lying in wait on the outside and whom no smoke could blind, leaped with uplifted tomahawks through the blazing ruins, and pushed forward to the half-opened entrance of the

Block House. The brave blacksmith, admirably supported, threw himself in the way, and was singled out by the huge warrior who had struck at him through the picket. The savage was brave and strong, but he had his match in the smith, whose courage was indomitable and lively, while his strength was surpassed by that of few. Wielding his axe with a degree of ease that, of itself, warned the enemy what he had to expect, it was but a moment before the Indian gave way before him. But the smith was not disposed to allow a mere acknowledgment of his superiority to pass for victory. He pressed him back upon his comrades, while his own three aids, strong and gallant themselves, following his example, drove the intruders upon the blaze which flamed furiously around them. Already had a severe wound, which almost severed the arm of the Santee warrior from its trunk, confirmed the advantage gained by the whites, while severe hatchet wounds had diminished not a little the courage of his Indian fellows, when, of a sudden, a new party came upon the scene of combat, changing entirely its face and character, and diminishing still more the chances of the Carolinians.

This was Chorley, the captain of the pirate. Having lodged his captives, as we have seen, in a little hovel on the river's brink, under a small guard of his own seamen, he had proceeded with all due speed upon the steps of Ishiagaska. He arrived opportunely for the band which had been placed along the walls of the Block House, in ambush, and whose daring had at length carried them into the outer defences of the fortress. A single shot from one of his men immediately warned the smith and his brave comrades of the new enemy before them, and while stimulating afresh the courage of their savage assailants, it materially diminished their own. They gave back—the three survivors— one of the party having fallen in the first discharge. The Indians rushed upon them, and thus throwing themselves between, for a time defeated the aim of Chorley's musketeers. Fighting like a lion, as he retreated to the door of the Block House, the brave smith continued to keep unharmed, making at the same time some little employment in the shape of ugly wounds to dress, in the persons of his rash assailants. Once more they gave back before him, and again the musketry of Chorley was enabled to tell upon him. A discharge from the Block House in the meantime retorted with good effect the attack of the sailors, and taught a lesson of caution to Chorley, of which he soon availed himself. Three of his men bit the dust in that single fire; and the Indians, suffering more severely, fled at the discharge. The brave smith reached the door with a single unwounded follower, himself unhurt. His comrades threw open the entrance for his reception, but an instant too late. A parting shot from the muskets of the seamen was made with a fatal effect. Grimstead sank down upon the threshold as the bullet passed through his body—the axe fell from his hand—he grasped at it convulsively, and lay extended in part upon the sill of the door, when Grayson drew him in safety within, and again securely closed it.

"You are not hurt, Dick, my old fellow," exclaimed Grayson, his voice trembling with the apprehensions which he felt.

"Hurt enough, Wat—bad enough. No more grist ground at that mill. But, hold in—don't be frightened—you can lick 'em yet. Ah," he groaned in a mortal agony.

They composed his limbs, and pouring some spirits down his throat, he recovered in a few moments, and convulsively inquired for his axe.

"I wouldn't lose it—it was dad's own axe, and must go to brother Tom when I die."

"Die indeed, Dick—don't speak of such a thing," said Grayson.

"I don't, Wat—I leave that to Nichols—but get the axe—ah! God—it's here—here—where's Tom?"

His brother, a youth of sixteen, came down to him from the upper apartment where he had been stationed, and kneeling over him, tried to support his head—but the blood gushed in a torrent from his mouth. He strove to speak, but choked in the effort. A single convulsion, which turned him upon his face, and the struggle was over. The battles of the smith were done.

Chapter Forty-eight

"The last blow for his country, and he dies,
Surviving not the ruin he must see."

THE force brought up by the younger Grayson, and now led by Harrison, came opportunely to the relief of the garrison. The flames had continued to rage, unrestrained, so rapidly around the building, that its walls were at length greedily seized upon by the furious element, and the dense smoke, gathering through all its apartments, was alone sufficient to compel the retreat of its defenders. Nothing now was left them in their desperation but to sally forth even upon the knives and hatchets of their merciless and expecting foe; and for this last adventure, so full of danger, so utterly wanting in a fair promise of any successful result, the sturdy forester prepared themselves, with all their courage. Fortunately for this movement, it was just about this period that the approach of Harrison, with his party, compelled the besiegers to change their position, in order the better to contend with him; and, however reluctant to suffer the escape of those so completely in their power, and for whose destruction they had already made so many sacrifices of time and life, they were compelled to do so in the reasonable fear of an assault upon two sides—from the garrison before them, impelled by desperation, and from the foe in their rear, described by their scouts as in rapid advance to the relief of the Block House. The command was shared jointly between Chorley and Ishiagaska. The former had fared much worse than his tawny allies; for, not so well skilled in the artifices of land and Indian warfare, seven out of the twenty warriors whom he commanded had fallen victims in the preceding conflicts. His discretion had become something more valuable, therefore, when reminded, by the scanty force remaining under his command, not only of his loss, but of his present weakness; a matter of no little concern, as he well knew that his Indian allies, in their capricious desperation, might not be willing to discriminate between the whites who had befriended, and those who had been their foes.

Thus counselled by necessity, the assailing chiefs drew off their forces from the Block House, and, sinking into cover, prepared to encounter their new enemies, after the fashion of their warfare. Ignorant, in the meantime, of the approach of Harrison or the force under him, Grayson wondered much at this movement of the besiegers, of which he soon had intelligence, and instantly prepared to avail himself of the privilege which it gave to the garrison of flight. He called his little force together, and having arranged, before leaving its shelter, the progress and general movement of his party, he carefully placed the women and children in the centre of his little troop, sallied boldly forth into the woods, conscious of all the dangers of the movement, but strengthened with all those thoughts of lofty cheer with which the good Providence, at all times, inspires the spirit of adventure, in the hour of its trying circumstance. There was something of pleasure in their very release from the confined circuit of the Block House, though now more immediately exposed to the tomahawk of the Indian; and with the pure air, and the absence of restraint, the greater number of the foresters grew even cheerful and glad—a change of mood in which even the women largely partook. Some few indeed of the more Puritanical among them, disposed to think themselves the especial charge of the Deity, and holding him not less willing than strong to save, under any circumstances, even went so far as to break out into a hymn of exultation and rejoicing, entirely forgetting the dangers still hanging around them, and absolutely contending warmly with Grayson when he undertook to restrain them. Not the least refractory of these was his own mother, who, in spite of all he could say, mouthed and muttered continually, and every now and then burst forth into starts of irrepressible psalmody, sufficient to set the entire tribe of Indians unerringly upon their track. The remonstrance of Grayson had little effect, except when he reminded her of his younger brother. The idolized Hugh, and his will, were her law in most things. Appealing to his authority and threatening complaint to him, he succeeded in making her silent—at least to a certain extent. Entire silence was scarcely possible with the old dame, who likened her escape from the flaming Block House, and, so far, from the hands of the savage, to every instance of Providential deliverance she had ever read of in the sacred volume; and still, under the stimulus of such a feeling, broke out every now and then, with sonorous emphasis, into song, from an old collection of the period, every atom of which she had familiarly at the end of her tongue. A moment had not well elapsed after the first suggestion of Grayson, when, as if unconsciously, she commenced again:—

> "'The Lord doth fight the foe for us,
> And smite the heathen down.'"

"Now, mother, in the name of common sense, can't you be quiet?"

"And wherefore should we not send up the hymn of rejoicing and thanksgiving for all his mercies, to the Father who has stood beside us in the hour of peril? Wherefore, I ask of you, Walter Grayson? Oh, my son, beware of self-conceit and pride of heart; and because you have here commanded earthly and human weapons, think not, in the vanity of your spirit, that the victory comes from such as these. The Saviour of men, my son—it is he that has fought this fight. It is his sword that has smitten the savage hip and thigh, and brought us free out of the land of bondage, even as he brought his people of old from the bondage of the Egyptians. He is mighty to save, and therefore should we rejoice with an exceeding strong voice."

And as if determined to sustain by her own example, the proceeding which she counselled, her lungs were tasked to the uttermost, in proclaiming—

> "'The Lord he comes with mighty power,
> The army of the saints is there—
> He speaks—'"

"For Heaven's sake, mother—hush your tongue—if it be in you to keep it quiet for a moment. Let it rest only for a little while, or we shall all be scalped. Wait till daylight, and you may then sing to your heart's content. It can't be long till daylight, and you can then begin, but not till then, or we shall have the savages on our track, and nothing can save us."

"Oh! thou of little faith—I tell thee, Walter, thou hast read but too little of thy Bible, and dependest too much upon the powers of earth—all of which are wicked and vain defences. Put thy trust in God; he is strong to save. Under his hand I fear not the savage—for, does he not tell us—" and she quavered again:—

> "'Unfold thine eye and see me here,
>   I do the battle for the just,
>   My people nothing have to fear—'"

"Mother, in the name of common sense." But she went on with double fervour, as if furious with the interruption:—

> "'If faithful in my word—'"

"Mother, mother, I say—" But she was bent seemingly to finish the line:—

> "'—they trust,'"

"Was there ever such an obstinate! I say, mother—"

"Well, my son?"

"Are you my mother?"

"Of a certainty, I am. What mean you by that question, Walter?"

"Do you want to see my scalp dangling upon the long pole of a savage?"

"God forbid, Walter, my son. Did I not bear thee—did I not suffer for thee?"

"Then, if you do not really desire to see me scalped, put some stop on your tongue, and move along as if death lay under every footstep. If the savages surround us now, we are gone, every mother's son of us—and all the saints, unless they are accustomed to Indian warfare, can do nothing in our behalf."

"Speak not irreverently, son Walter. The saints are blessed mediators for the sinner, and may move eternal mercy to save. Have they not fought for us already to-night—and are we not saved by their ministry from the bloody hands of the savage?"

"No—it's by our own hands, and our own good handiwork, mother. I owe the saints no thanks, and shall owe you still less, unless you stop that howling."

"Oh, Father, forgive him, he knows not what he says—he is yet in the bondage of sin—" and she hymned her prayer from her collection:—

"'Strike not the sinner in his youth,
   But bear him in thy mercy on,
'Till in the path of sacred truth,
   He sees—'"

"Mother, if you do not hush up, I will tell Hugh of your obstinacy. He shall know how little you mind his counsel."

"Well, well, Walter, my son, I am done. Thou are too hasty, I'm sure.—Oh, bless me—"

Her speech was cut short by a sudden and fierce whoop of the Indians, followed by the huzzas of the whites at a greater distance, and the rapid fire of musketry, scattered widely along the whole extended range of forest around them.

"Down, down, all of you, on your knees—one and all—" was the cry of Grayson to his party; and, accustomed to most of the leading difficulties and dangers of such a fight, the order was obeyed, as if instinctively, by all except Dame Grayson, who inflexibly maintained her position, and refused to move, alleging her objection to any prostration except for the purposes of prayer. Maddened by her obstinacy, Grayson, with very little scruple, placing his hand upon her shoulder, bore her down to the earth, exclaiming,—

"Then say your prayers, mother—do any thing but thwart what you cannot mend."

Thus humbled, the party crept along more closely into cover, until, at a spot where the trees were clustered along with underwood into something like a copse, Grayson ordered a halt, and proceeded to arrange his men and their weapons for active conflict. The war approached at intervals, and an occasional shot whistled over the heads of the party, conclusively proving the necessity of their position. The Indians seemed to lie betwixt them and the advancing Carolinians; and perceiving this to be the case, Grayson threw the non-combatants under shelter in such a manner as to interpose those who could fight in the way of the coming red men, in the event of their being driven back upon them. His party, in the meanwhile, well prepared, lay quietly under cover, and with their weapons ready to take advantage of any such event.

Harrison, as we may remember, had taken the command of the greater body of the force which had been brought up through the industrious and prodigious exertions of Hugh Grayson. This young man, stung and mortified as he had been by the rebuke of Bess

Matthews, with a degree of mental concentration, rather indicative of his character—though hopeless of those affections, which of all other human hopes he had most valued—had determined to do himself justice by doing his duty. Throwing aside, therefore, as well as he might, the passionate mood which was active in his soul, he had gone forth from the house of the pastor, resolute to make every exertion in procuring a force which might protect the family from an attack, which he had at length learned, as well as Harrison, greatly to apprehend. His pride suggested to him the gratification of saving the life of her who had scorned him, as an honourable revenge, not less than a fair blotting out of those errors of which, on her account, he had suffered himself to be guilty. His efforts, so far, had been crowned with success; but he had come too late for his prime object. The dwelling of the pastor had been sacked before his arrival, and, like Harrison, he was under the most horrible apprehensions for her safety. The latter person came upon him opportunely, in time to keep him from falling into the ambuscade through which he had himself so singularly passed in safety—and with more knowledge of Indian strife, Harrison took the command of a party which confided fully to his skill, and, of necessity, with a courage heightened proportionately when under his direction.

The cautious yet bold management of Harrison soon gave him the advantage. The foresters, guided by him, each took his tree after the manner of the Indians, and with the advantage of weapons more certain to kill, and equally, if not more certain, in aim. Apart from this, the Carolinian woodman knew enough of the savages to know that they were no opponents, generally speaking, to be feared in a trial of respective muscular strength. The life of the hunter fits him to endure rather than to contend. The white borderer was taught by his necessities to do both. He could wield the axe and overthrow the tree—a labour to which the Indian is averse. He could delve and dig, and such employment was a subject of scorn and contempt with the haughty aboriginal warrior. At the same time, he practised the same wanderings and the same felicity of aim, and in enduring the toils of the chase, he was fairly the equal of his tawny but less enterprising neighbour. The consciousness of these truths—a consciousness soon acquired from association—was not less familiar to the Indian than to the Carolinian; and the former, in consequence, despaired of success usually when required to oppose the white man hand to hand. His hope was in the midnight surprise—in the sudden onslaught—in the terror inspired by his fearful whoop—and in the awful scalp-song with which he approached, making the imagination of his foe an auxiliar to his own, as he told them how he should rend away the dripping locks from his skull, while his eyes swam in darkness, and the pulses were yet flickering at his heart.

From cover to cover—from tree to tree—the individual Carolinians rushed on against their retreating enemies. In this manner the fight became somewhat pell-mell, and the opponents grew strangely mingled together. Still, as each was busy with his particular enemy, no advantage could well be taken of the circumstance on either side; and the hatchets of the individual combatants clashed under neighbouring trees, and their knives were uplifted in the death-struggle over the same stump, without any hope of assistance from their friends in any form of their difficulty.

In this general state of things, there was one exception in the case of Harrison himself. He was approached resolutely in the course of the conflict by a Coosaw warrior—a man of inferior size, even with his tribe, the individuals of which were generally diminutive. The dark eye of the swarthy foe, as he advanced upon Harrison, was lighted up with a malignant audacity, to be understood only by a reference to the history of his people. That people were now almost exterminated. He was one of the few survivors—a chief—a bold, brave man—subtle, active, and distinguished for his skill as a warrior and hunter. He recognised in Harrison the renowned *Coosah-moray-te*—the leader of the force which had uprooted his nation, and had driven his warriors to the degrading necessity of merging their existence as a people with that of a neighbouring tribe. The old feeling of his country, and a former war, was at work in his bosom, and through all the mazes of the conflict he steadily kept his eye on the course of Harrison. He alone sought him—he alone singled him out for the fight. For a long time, the nature of the struggle had prevented their meeting; but he now approached the spot where Harrison stood, holding at bay a tall Chestatee warrior from the interior of Georgia. The Chestatee was armed with the common war-club, and had no other weapon. This weapon is chiefly useful when confusion has been introduced by the bowmen into the ranks of an enemy. It is about two feet in length, and bears at its end, and sometimes at both ends, a cross-piece of iron, usually without any distinct form, but sometimes resembling the blade of a spear, and not unfrequently that of a hatchet.

Harrison was armed with a sword, and had besides, in his possession, the knife—the same broad, cimeter-like weapon—which had been given him by Matiwan in his flight from Pocota-ligo. His rifle, which he had not had time to reload, leaned against a tree, at the foot of which stood Hector, with difficulty restraining, and keeping back, with all his might, the impatient dog Dugdale, which, by his master's orders, he had re-muzzled. This had been done in order to his safety. It was only in pursuit that his services would have been of avail; for though he might be of use in the moment of strife, the chances were that he would have been shot. Thus reposing, Hector was enabled to see the approach of the Coosaw, and by an occasional exhibition of his own person and that of the dog, to deter him from the attack which he had long meditated. But the strife between Harrison and the Chestatee was about to cease. That warrior, aiming a fierce blow at the person of his enemy, drove the spear-head of his club into the tree, and failing at the moment to disengage it, fell a victim to the quicksightedness of his opponent. Harrison's sword in that instant was sheathed in the bosom of the Chestatee, who, as he received the wound, sprang upwards from the ground, snapping the slender weapon short at the hilt, the blade still remaining buried in his body. Harrison drew his knife, and having for some time seen the purpose of the Coosaw, he fortunately turned to meet him at the very instant of his approach. Something surprised at the fearlessness with which his enemy advanced to the conflict, he spoke to him, as they both paused at a few paces from each other.

"Thou art a Coosaw,"—exclaimed Harrison,— "I know thee."

"Chinnabee is the last chief of the Coosaw. He wants blood for his people."

"Thou knowest me, then?" said Harrison.

"*Coosah-moray-te!*" was the simple response; and the dark eye glared, and the teeth of the savage gnashed like those of the hungered wolf, as the name stirred up all the recollections in his mind, of that war of extermination which the warrior before him had waged against his people.

"Ay—the *Coosah-moray-te* is before thee. Would Chinnabee follow his people?" exclaimed the Englishman.

"Chinnabee would have much blood for his people. He would drink blood from the skull of *Coosah-moray-te*—he would show the scalp of the Coosah-moray-te to the warriors of Coosaw, that wait for him in the Happy Valley."

"Thou shalt have no scalp of mine, friend Chinnabee. I'm sorry to disappoint you, but I must—I can't spare it. Come! I know you of old for a cunning snake—a snake lying in the dried bush. The foot of the Coosah-moray-te will trample on thy head."

Harrison spoke fearlessly, for who, contrasting the appearance of the two, would have thought the contest doubtful? The Indian was scarcely over five feet in height, slender, and not well set; while his opponent, fully six feet in height, a fine specimen of symmetrical manhood, seemed able to crush him with a finger. The Coosaw simply responded with something like a smile of scorn,—throwing himself at the same moment like a ball at the feet if his enemy—

"Good!—the snake is in the bush. Look! *Coosah-moray-te*—put the foot on his head."

The Englishman looked down upon him with something of surprise mingled in with his contempt, and made no show of assault; but he was too well acquainted with Indian trick and manœuvre to be thrown off his guard by this movement. Curious to see what would be the next effort of one who had studiously singled him out, he watched him carefully, and the Indian, something balked that the enemy had not taken him at his word and approached him while in his prostrate condition, slowly uncoiled himself from his fold, and had partially regained his feet, when Harrison, who had been looking for him fully to do so, was surprised in the next moment to find his wily enemy directly between his legs. The suddenness of such a movement, though it failed to throw him, as the Coosaw had calculated, yet disordered his position not a little; and before he could strike a blow, or do more than thrust one of his feet down upon him, his active adversary had passed from his reach, having made a desperate effort with his knife to hamstring his adversary, as he leaped aside and turned suddenly upon him. The rapidity of Harrison's movement alone saved him, though, even then, not entirely, since the knife grazed his leg, inflicting a sharp, though not dangerous wound. He barely turned in time to meet the preparations of the Coosaw for a second assault of similar character; and something more ready at this novel mode of attack, and vexed at its partial success, Harrison looked with some impatience for his enemy's approach, and felt a thrill of fierce delight as he saw him leave with a bound the spot upon which he stood. Sinking upon his knee as the savage rolled towards him, he presented his knife, edge upwards, to his advance. What was his surprise to find that in so stooping, he had only evaded a blow upon his bosom, which, from his position, and the direction which the Indian pursued, had he stood, the heels of his foe would certainly have inflicted.

He saw from this that he must now become the assailant; particularly as he perceived that his men were successfully pressing upon the enemy in every direction, and that the battle was progressing towards the river, and between it and the Block House. Active as most men, Harrison was also a man of ready decision; and with the thought came the execution. With a bound he grappled the Coosaw, who had not looked for an attack so sudden, and no doubt had been fatigued by previous efforts. Harrison drove him back against a tree with all the muscle of an extended arm, and thus forced the combat upon him on his own terms. But even then the subtlety of the savage did not fail him. He evaded the grasp, and contrived to double once or twice completely under the body of his opponent, until, exasperated by his pertinacity not less than at the agility with which the Indian eluded him, without stooping to where he wriggled like a snake around him, the Englishman leaped upon him with both feet, striking his heel securely down upon the narrow of his sinuous back, and in this way fastening him to the earth. In another instant and the knife would have finished the combat, when the conqueror received a severe blow with a club, upon his shoulder, from some unseen hand, which completely staggered him; and before he could recover, he was confronted by another warrior of the Coosaws, crying to him in his own language in the exultation of success deemed secure, and thus cheering his prostrate chief, Chinnabee—

"*Coosah-moray-te,*—I drink his blood, I tear his throat, I have his scalp—I hear his groan—Hi-chai!—'tis a dog for Opitchi-Manneyto!"

At the cry, the former opponent rose from the ground, not so much injured but that he could recommence the battle. They advanced at the same moment upon the Englishman, though from different quarters. They came upon him with all their subtlety and caution, for the two together could scarce have contended with the superior strength of Harrison. Taking his tree, he prepared for the worst; and with his left arm so severely paralysed by the blow that he could do little more than throw it up in defence, he yet held a good heart, and while he saw with what malignity the two Coosaws had singled him out, he had hope to meet them individually by the exercise of some of those adroit arts which he too could employ not less than the savage. But he was spared this trial. The very instant of their simultaneous approach, a gun-shot from the rear brought down the second assailant. The survivor, Chinnabee, as if exasperated beyond reason at the event, now precipitated himself forward, tomahawk in hand, upon his foe; was foiled by the ready agility which encountered him, put aside, and almost in the same instant hurled like a stone to the ground by the now fully aroused Englishman.

"Coosaw—thou art the last chief of thy people. The cunning serpent will die by the Coosah-moray-te, like the rest," said Harrison, addressing the conquered savage, who lay motionless, but still alive, at his feet.

"The Coosah-moray-te will strike. Chinnabee is the last chief of the Coosaw—his people have gone—they wait for him with the cry of a bird. Let the pale-face strike. Ah! ha!"

The knife was in his heart. Vainly the eyes rolled in a fruitless anger—the teeth fixed for ever, while gnashing in fury, in the death spasm. A short groan—a word, seemingly of song—and the race of the Coosaws was for ever ended.

Harrison rose and looked round for the person whose timely shot had saved him from the joint attack of the two warriors. He discovered him advancing in the person of Hector, who, having fastened Dugdale to a sapling, had reloaded the musketoon of his master, and by his intervention at the proper moment, had no doubt preserved his life. Unaccustomed, however, to the use of gunpowder, the black had overcharged the piece, and the recoil had given him a shock which, at the moment, he was certain could not have been a jot less severe than that which it inflicted upon the Coosaw he had slain. His jaws ached, he bitterly alleged, whenever, years after, he detailed the fight with the Yemassee on the banks of the Pocota-ligo.

"Hector—thou hast saved my life," said Harrison, as he came up to him.

"I berry glad, maussa," was the natural reply.

"Where's Dugdale?"

"In de tree—I hook 'em wid rope, when I load for shoot de Injin."

"Bring him, and set him loose."

The black did as he was told, and harking him on the track of the flying Indians, Harrison seized and reloaded his rifle, while Hector possessed himself of a knife and hatchet which he picked up upon the field. They then proceeded hastily to overtake the Carolinians, who, at a little distance, were pressing upon the retreating enemy. Harrison came in time to give his influence and energy where they were most needed. The flying force was met and strengthened by the party from the Block House, under Ishiagaska and the pirate, and the fight commenced anew—a sort of running fight, however, for the Indians grew weary of a contest in which they had none of those advantages of number or circumstance which usually encourage them to war; and so trifling was the force of whites now remaining with them under Chorley, that their presence rather induced despondency than hope. The pirate himself was much discouraged by the nature of the strife, for which he did not dream that the Carolinians would have been so well prepared; and the loss which he sustained, so disproportioned to his force, had not a little exaggerated his discontent. His disquiet was destined to find still further increase in the new assault; two more of his men, not so well sheltered as they should have been, or more venturous, having been shot down near a tree immediately adjoining that behind which he stood; and, though the Indians still continued to fight, he saw that they could not be encouraged to do so long; as, even if successful in killing, they had no opportunity of obtaining the scalps of the slain, the best evidence with them of their triumph. The Carolinians still pressed on, their numbers greatly increased by the presence of several slaves, who, volunteering even against the will of their masters, had armed themselves with knives or clubs, and, by their greater numbers, held forth a prospect of ultimately hemming in the smaller force of their enemy. This was an ally upon which the Spaniards had largely counted. They had no idea of that gentler form of treatment which, with the Carolinians, won the affections of their serviles; and, knowing no other principle in their own domestic government than that of fear, and assured of the instability of any confidence built upon such a relationship between the ruler and the serf, they had miscalculated greatly when they addressed their bribes and promises to the negroes, as well as to the Indians of Carolina. But few joined them—the greater number, volunteering for their owners, were taken actually into the employment of the colony, and subsequently rewarded in proportion to their services and merits.

The engagement became a flight. From point to point the Carolinians pursued their enemy—Chorley the seaman, and Ishiagaska, alone endeavouring, by the most ardent effort, to stimulate the courage of their followers, and maintain a show of fight. But in vain. The whites pressed closely upon the heels of the fugitives, who were at length suddenly brought up by a severe fire, directly upon their path, from the concealed party under Grayson. This completed their panic; and each darting in the direction given him by his fears, sought for individual safety. There was no longer the form of a battle array among them, and the negroes cleared the woods with their clubs, beating out the brains of those whom they overtook, almost without having any resistance offered them. The day dawned upon the forest, and every step of the route taken by the combatants was designated by blood.

Chapter Forty-nine

"Away, away,—I hold thee as my spoil,
To bless and cheer me—worthy of my toil—
Let them pursue—I have thee, thou art mine,
With life to keep, and but with life resign."

THE night of storm had been one of great brightness and natural beauty. Not less beautiful and bright was the day by which it was followed. The sun rose clearly and beautifully over the scattered bands of the forest. The Indians were fairly defeated, Ishiagaska slain, and Chorley, the pirate, uninfluenced by any of those feelings of nationality which governed the native red men, which would have prompted him to a desperate risk of his own person in a struggle so utterly unlooked-for, as soon as he saw the final and complete character of the defeat, silently withdrew, with his few remaining followers, from farther conflict. He had another care upon his hands besides that of his own safety. There was one reward—one spoil—with which he consoled himself for his disaster—and that was Bess Matthews. She was in his power!

Filled with fierce passion, as he thought of her, he took his way, unseen by the victorious Carolinians, towards the little cot on the river's edge, in which he had left his prisoners. Circumstances had materially altered from what they were at the time when they became so. He was no longer able to control, with an imposing and superior force, the progress, either of his Indian allies or of his Carolinian enemies. He had not foreseen, any more than the Yemassees, the state of preparation in which the settlers about the Pocota-ligo had met the invasion. He had looked to find invasion and conquest one—and had never dreamed of opposition, much less of a defence which would prove so completely successful. The energies of a single man, his address, farsightedness, and circumspection, had done all this. To the perseverance and prudence of Harrison—his devotedness to the cause he had undertaken—the borderers owed their safety. But of this the pirate chief knew nothing; and, anticipating no such provident management, he had fearlessly leagued himself with the savages, stimulated by passions as sanguinary as theirs, and without that redeeming sense of national character and feeling—that genuine love of country—which not only accounted for, but exculpated the people of whom he was the unworthy ally. But he had lost all that he came for—all objects but one. His best followers had fallen victims—his hope of spoil had in great part been defeated, and though he had shed blood, the quantity was as nothing to one with whom such had been a familiar indulgence. Yet, with a voluptuous appetite, he had won a prize which promised him enjoyment, if it could not compensate his losses. The beautiful Bess Matthews—the young, the budding, the sweet. She was in his power—a trembling dove in the grasp of the fowler. The thought was as so much fire to his fancy, and he sought the cottage in which he had secured her, with a fierce and feverish thirst—a brutal sense at work in his mind—stimulating him to an utter disregard of humanity, and prompting the complete violation of all ties of kindred, as he meditated to tear her away from the bosom of her parents.

About a mile from the hovel in which the family of the pastor was immured lay the guarda-costa. There was an air of bustle on board of her, in the unreefing of sails, and the waving and rustling of her ropes. The tide of battle had alternated from spot to spot along the banks of the river—now lost in the density of the forest, and now swelling, with all its clamours, along the bosom of the water. The firing had alarmed all parties, the seamen remaining on board, not less than the old pastor and his timid wife and trembling daughter, who, only conscious of the struggle, and not of its results, were filled with a thousand tearful anticipations.

To Bess Matthews, however, the strife brought with it a promise, since it proved that the Carolinians were prepared, in part at least, for their invaders—and many were the fluctuations of hope and fear in her soul, as the gathering clamour now approached and now receded in the distance. Love taught her that Harrison was the leader making such bold head against the enemy. Love promised her, as the battle dissipated, that he would come and rescue her from a position in which she did not well know whether to regard herself as a captive to the seaman, or as one owing him gratitude for her own and the preservation of her family. She remembered his lustful eye, and insolent speech and gesture, and she trembled as she thought of him. True, her father knew him in his boyhood, but his account of him was rather tolerant than favourable; and the subsequent life and conduct of the licentious rover—not to speak of the suspicions openly entertained of his true character by her lover—all taught her to fear the protection which he had given, and to dread, while she seemed to anticipate, the price of it.

She had no long time for doubt, and but little for deliberation. He came—bloody with conflict—covered with dust, blackened with gunpowder—the fierce flame of war in his eye, and in his hand the bared weapon, streaked with fresh stains, which he had only in part wiped away, with a handful of moss gathered from the trees. There was nothing encouraging in his aspect—nothing now of conciliation in his deportment. His manner was impatient and stern, as, without addressing either of his captives, he called aside and gave directions to his seamen. The pastor craved his attention, but he waved his hand impatiently, nor turned to him for an instant, until he had despatched two of his men to the edge of the stream, where, well concealed by the shrubbery upon its banks, lay the small boat of the vessel, which had been carefully placed there by his orders. They gave him a shrill whistle as they reached it, which he immediately returned—then approaching the pastor, he scrupled not an instant in the development of the foul design which he had all along meditated.

"Hark ye, Matthews—this is no place for us now—I can't protect ye any longer. I hav'n't the men—they are cut up—slashed—dead— eleven of the finest fellows—best men of my vessel—by this time, without a scalp among them. I have done my best to save you, but it's all over, and there's but one way—you must go with us on board."

"How, Chorley—go with you—and wherefore? I cannot—I will not."

"What, will not? Oh! ho! Do you suppose I am the man to listen to such an answer? No! no! I'll take care of you whether you will or no! Do you think I'll let you stay to lose your scalps, and this sweet darling here? No, by my soul, I were no man to suffer it. You shall go."

"What mean you, Chorley? Are the savages successful—have they defeated our men? And you—wherefore do you fly—how have you fought—with us—for our people?"

The old pastor, half bewildered, urged these questions incoherently, but yet with such directness of aim as almost to bewilder the person he addressed, who could not well answer them; even if he cared to do so. How, as the pastor argued with himself,—how, if the Yemassees have defeated the Carolinians—how was it that Chorley, who had evidently been their ally, could not exert his power and protect them? and, on the other hand, if the Carolinians had been the victors, wherefore should he and his family fly from their own people? Unable well to meet these propositions, the native fierce impetuosity of the pirate came to his relief, and throwing aside entirely the conciliatory manner of his first address, he proceeded in a style more congenial with his true character.

"Shall I stay all day disputing with you about this nonsense? I tell you, you shall go, whether you will or not. Look you, I have the power— look at these men—can you withstand them? In a word, they force you to the ship, and all your talking—ay, and all your struggling—will help you nothing. Come—away."

"Never—never! Oh! father, let us die first!" was the involuntary exclamation of the maiden, convulsively clinging to the old man's arm as the ruffian took a step towards her.

"Captain Chorley, I cannot think you mean this violence!" said the old man with dignity.

"May I be d——d," said he fiercely, "but I do! Violence, indeed! violence is my life,—my business! What, old man, shall I leave you here to be made mincemeat of by the Indians? No, no! I love you and your pretty daughter too well for that. Come, sweetheart, don't be shy—what! do you fear me then?"

"Touch me not—touch me not with your bloody hands. Away! I will not go—strike me dead first—strike me dead, but I will not go."

"But you shall! What! think you I am a child to be put off with great words and passionate speeches! What, ho! there, boys—do as I have told you."

In a moment, the pastor and his child were torn asunder.

"Father—help—help! I lose thee—mother—father—Gabriel!"

"Villain, release me—give me back my child. Undo your hold— you shall suffer for this. Ha! ha! ha! they come—they come! Hurry, hurry, my people. Here—here—we are here—they tear away my child. Where are you—oh, Harrison, but come now—come now, and she is yours—only save her from the hands of this fierce ruffian. God be praised! They come—they come!"

They did come—the broad glare of sunlight on the edge of the forest was darkened by approaching shadows. A shot—another and another was heard—and the fugitives, who were Indians flying from the pursuing Carolinians, rushed forward headlong; but as they saw the group of whites on the river's brink, thinking them new enemies, they darted aside, and taking another route, buried themselves in the forest, out of sight, just as their pursuers came forth upon the scene. A single glance of Bess Matthews, as the ruffian suddenly seized upon and bore her to the boat, distinguished the manly form of her lover darting out of the thicket and directly upon the path approaching them. That glance gave her new hope—new courage—new strength! She shrieked to him in a voice delirious with terror and hope, as the pirate, bearing her like an infant in his powerful grasp, strode into the boat, and bade the seamen who manned it, push off, and pull away with all their vigour.

"Come to me, Gabriel—save me, save me, or I perish. It is I—thy own Bess—ever thine—save me, save me."

She fell back fainting with exhaustion and excitement, and lay nerveless and almost senseless in the arms of her abductor. He sustained her with perfect ease with one arm, upon his bosom, while standing erect, for the boat scarce permitted him with his burden to do otherwise, he placed his foot upon the slender rudder and guided its progress, his men looking round occasionally and suggesting the course of the vessel. In this way he kept his eye upon shore, and beheld the progress of events in that quarter.

The cries of his betrothed had taught Harrison the condition of affairs. He saw her precarious situation at a glance, and, rushing down to the beach, followed by his men, the seamen fled along the banks higher up the river, and were soon out of sight, leaving the old pastor and his wife free. The scene before him was too imposing in the eye of Harrison to permit of his giving the fugitives a thought. But the pastor, now free from restraint, with a speechless agony, rushed forward and clasping his arm, pointed with his finger to the form of his daughter, hanging like a broken flower, supine and almost senseless, upon the shoulder of her Herculean captor. The action of Harrison was immediate, and in a moment, the rifle was lifted to his shoulder, his eye ranging upon the sight, and singling out the exposed breast of the pirate, which lay uncovered, but just alongside of the drooping head of the maiden. As the seaman saw the movement, he changed her position— she saw it too, and lifting her hand, placed it, with an emphasis not to be mistaken, upon her heart. The old pastor, terrified by what he saw, again seized Harrison by the arm, and cried to him convulsively, while the tears trickled down his cheeks—

"Stay thy hand—stay thy hand—shoot not; rather let me lose her, but let her live—thou wilt slay her, thou wilt slay my child—my own, my only child," and he tottered like an infant in his deep agony.

"Away, old man—give me room—away!" and with the words, with unscrupulous strength, Harrison hurled him from him upon the sands. Without a pause the fearful instrument was again uplifted—the aim was taken,—his finger rested on the trigger, but his heart sickened—his head swam—his eyes grew blind and dizzy ere he drew it; and with a shiver of convulsion, he let the weapon descend heavily to the ground.

The weakness was only momentary. A faint scream came to his ears over the water, and brought back with it all his strength. The maiden had watched closely all his motions, and the last had given her energy somewhat to direct them. That scream aroused him. He resumed his position and aim; and, fixing the sight upon that part of the bosom of his enemy least concealed, nerved himself to all the hazard, and resolutely drew the trigger. The effect was instantaneous. The next instant the maiden was seen released from the pirate's grasp and sinking down in the bottom of the boat, while he stood erect. The venerable pastor fainted, while, on her knees, his aged wife bent over him in silent prayer.

That moment was more than death to Harrison; but what was his emotion of delight when, at the next, he beheld the pirate, like some gigantic tree that has kept itself erect by its own exceeding weight, fall, like a tower, headlong, over the side of the boat, stiff and rigid, and without a struggle, sink deeply and silently down beneath the over-closing waters. But a new danger awaited the maiden; for in his fall, destroying the equipoise of the skiff, its entire contents were, at the next instant, precipitated into the stream; and while the two seamen, unhurt, struck off towards the vessel, the maiden lay in sight, sustained above the surface only by the buoyancy of her dress, and without exhibiting any other motion. A dozen sinewy arms from the shore at once struck the water, but which of all, nerved as he was by the highest stimulant of man's nature, could leave the fearless Harrison behind him? On he dashes—on—on—now he nears her,—another moment and she is saved; but while every eye was fixed as with a spell upon the prospect with an anxiety inexpressible, the sullen waters went over her, and a universal cry of horror arose from the shore. But she rose again in an instant, and with a show of consciousness, stretching out her hand, the name of "Gabriel," in a tone of imploring love, reached the ears of her lover. That tone, that word, was enough, and the next moment found her insensible in his arms. She was a child in his grasp, for the strength of his fearless and passionate spirit, not less than of his native vigour, was active to save her.

"Help—help," was his cry to the rest, and to the shore;—he sustained her till it came. It was not long ere she lay in the arms of her parents, whose mutual tears and congratulations came sweetly, along with their free consent, to make her preserver happy with the hand hitherto denied him.

Chapter Fifty

"Another stroke for triumph. It goes well,
The foe gives back—he yields. Another hour
Beholds us on his neck."

HARRISON, thus blessed with happiness, appropriated but little time, however, to its enjoyment. His mind was of that active sort, that even the sweets of love were to be enjoyed by him as a stimulant, rather than a clog to exertion. Conveying the little family to a recess in the woods, and out of sight of the craft of the pirate, he immediately proceeded—having first led the foresters aside—to explain his further desires to them in reference to their common duties.

"Joy, my brave fellows, and thanks to you, for this last night's good service. You have done well, and risked yourselves nobly. Grayson, give me your hand—you are a good soldier. Where's your brother?"

"Here!" was the single word of response spoken from the background by the lips of Hugh Grayson. The tone of the monosyllable was melancholy, but not sullen. Harrison advanced to him, and extended his hand.

"Master Grayson, to you we owe most of our safety to-day. But for you, the sun would have found few of us with a scalp on. Your activity in bringing up the men has saved us; for, though otherwise safe enough, the firing of the Block House must have been fatal to all within. For myself, I may freely acknowledge, my life, at this moment, is due to your timely appearance. Your command, too, was excellently managed for so young a soldier. Accept my thanks, sir, in behalf of the country not less than of myself. I shall speak to you again on this subject, and in regard to other services in which your aid will be required, after a while."

The youth looked upon Harrison with a degree of surprise, which prevented him from making any adequate answer. Whence came that air of conscious superiority in the speaker—that tone of command—of a power unquestionable, and held as if born with it in his possession? The manner of Harrison had all the ease and loftiness of a prince; and, scarcely less than the crowd around him, the proud-spirited youth felt a degree of respectful awe stealing over him, of which he began to grow ashamed. But, before he could recover, in time to exhibit any of that rash and imperious rusticity which the lowlier born of strong native mind is so apt to show in the presence of the conventional superior, the speaker had again addressed the crowd.

"And you, men, you have all done well for the country, and it owes you its gratitude."

"Ay, that it does, captain," said Nichols, advancing— "that it does. We have stood by her in the hour of her need. We have resisted the approach of the bloody invader, and with liberty or death for our motto, we have rushed to the conflict, sir, defying consequences."

"Ah, Nichols—you are welcome, both in what you have done and what you have said. I might have known that the country was safe in your hands, knowing as I do your general sentiments on the subject of the liberties of the people. Granville county, Nichols, must make you her representative after this, and I'm sure she will."

The speaker smiled sarcastically as he spoke, but Nichols had an easy faith, and was modestly content with a surface compliment, and never laboured to discover the occult adverse signification which it might conceal. He was wise after the usual fashion of the demagogue, and with great regard to proprieties of character, he replied in a speech.

"Ah, captain, 'twere an honour;—and could my fellow-countrymen be persuaded to look upon me with your eyes, proud would I be to stand up for their rights, and with the thunders of my voice, compel that justice from the Assembly which, in denying representation to all dissenters, they have most widely departed from. Ay, captain—fellow-citizens—permit me to address you now upon a few topics most important to your own liberties, and to the common benefit of humanity. My voice—"

"Must just at this moment be unheard," interrupted Harrison; "we have need of other thunders now. Hear me, gentlemen; for this I have called you together. I want from among you thirty volunteers—hardy, whole-souled fellows, who do not count heads in a scuffle. The enterprise is dangerous, and must be executed—very dangerous I say—and

I beg that none may offer but those who are perfectly ready at any moment—to use the words of Dr. Nichols—to die for the country. The doctor himself, however, must not go, as he is too important to us in his surgical capacity."

Nichols, well pleased with the exception thus made, was not however willing to appear so, and, glad of the opportunity, could not forbear making something of a popular hit.

"How, captain—this may not be. I am not one of those, sir, altogether content to be denied the privilege of dying for my country when occasion calls for it. Let me go on this service;—I insist. I am one of the people, and will forego none of their dangers."

"Oh, well, if you insist upon it, of course I can say nothing—we hold you pledged, therefore. There are now three of us—Master Hugh Grayson, I presume to place you, as one with myself and Dr. Nichols, volunteering upon this service. I understand you so."

The high compliment, and the delicate manner in which it was conveyed, totally disarmed young Grayson, who, softened considerably by the proceeding, bowed his head in assent, approaching by degrees to where Harrison stood. Nichols, on the other hand, had not contemplated so easily getting the permission which he called for, and, well knowing his man, Harrison barely gave it, as he foresaw it would not be long before he would assume new ground, which would bring about a ready evasion of his responsibility. The elder Grayson meanwhile volunteered also, followed by several others, and in a little time the required number was also complete. But the surgeon now demanded to know the nature of the service.

"What matters it, doctor—it is an honourable, because a dangerous service. You shall know in time."

"That does not suit me, captain. What,—shall I suffer myself to be led blindfold upon a duty, the propriety of which may be doubtful, not less than the policy? Sir—I object upon principle."

"Principle—indeed, doctor," said Harrison, smiling. "Why, what in the name of pounds and shillings has principle to do in this business?"

"Enough, sir—the rights of man—of the people of the country, are all involved. Do I not, sir, in thus volunteering upon a service of which I know nothing, put myself under the control of one who may make me a traitor to my country, a defier of the laws, and probably a murderer of my fellow-man? Sir, what security have I of the morality and the lawfulness of your proceeding?"

"Very true—you are right, and such being your opinions, I think you would err greatly to volunteer in this business," was the grave response of Harrison.

"Ah, I knew you would agree with me, captain—I knew it," cried the doctor, triumphantly.

"I want another man or two—we are something short."

As the leader spoke Hector came forward, his head hanging on one shoulder, as if he feared rebuff for his presumption, in the unlooked-for proffer of service which he now made.

"Maussa—you let Hector go, he glad too much. He no want stay here wid de doctor and de 'omans."

His reference to the demagogue, accompanied as it was with an ill-concealed chuckle of contempt, provoked the laughter of the crowd; and observing that the greater number looked favourably upon the proposal of the negro, Harrison consented.

"You will knock a Spaniard on the head, sir, if I bid you?"

"Yes, maussa, and scalp 'em too, jist like dem Injin."

"You shall go."

"Tankee—dat's a good maussa. Hello, da—" and perfectly over-joyed, he broke out with a stanza of negro minstrelsy, common, even now, to the slaves of Carolina—

> "He come rain—he come shine,
>   Hab a good maussa, who da care?
> De black is de white and de white is de black,
>   Hab a good maussa, who da care?
> But look out, nigger, when missis come—
> Hah! den de wedder will alter some—
> If she cross,—Oh!—who for say,
> You ebber again see sunshine day?"

How long Hector might have gone on with his uncouth, and, so far as the sex is interested, ungallant minstrelsy, may not well be said; but, seeing its direction, his master silenced it in a sufficiently potent manner.

"Be still, sirrah, or you shall feed on hickory."

"No hab 'tomach for 'em, maussa. I dumb."

"'Tis well. Now, men, see to your weapons—hatchets and knives for all—we shall need little else, but fearless hearts and strong hands. Our purpose is to seize upon that pirate vessel in the river."

The men started with one accord.

"Ay, no less. It's a perilous service, but not so perilous as it appears. I happen to know that there are now not two men on board of the vessel accustomed to the management of the guns—not fifteen on board in all. Granger has got us boats in plenty, and I have conceived a plan by which we shall attack her on all points. Something of our success will depend upon their consciousness of weakness. They are without a commander, and their men, accustomed to fighting, are in our woods dead or running, and in no ability to serve them. The show of numbers, and ten or a dozen boats with stout men approaching them, will do much with their fears. We shall thus board them with advantage; and though I hope not to escape with all of us unhurt, I am persuaded we shall be successful without much loss. Master Hugh Grayson will command three of the boats, Master Walter Grayson three others, and the rest will be with me. You have now heard. If, like the doctor here, any of you object to proceeding, on principle, against this pirate who has sought the destruction of our people, well and good—they are at liberty to withdraw, and we shall look for other men less scrupulous. Who is ready?"

The confident, almost careless manner of the speaker, was of more effect than his language. The cry was unanimous:

"Lead on—we are all ready."

"I thank you, my merry men, and old England for ever! Master Hugh Grayson, and you, friend Walter,—let us counsel here a moment."

He led them aside, and together they matured the plan of attack. Then leaving them to parcel off the men, Harrison stole away for a few moments into the silent grove where the pastor's family was sheltered. As we have no business there, we can only conjecture the motive of his visit. A press of the hand from the beloved one were much to one about to go upon an adventure of life and death. He returned in a few moments with increased alacrity, and led the way to the boats, eleven in number, which Granger in the meantime had selected from those employed by the Indians in crossing the preceding night. They were small, but sufficiently large for the men allotted to each. In their diminutiveness, too, lay much of their safety from the great guns of the vessel.

Leading the way, the boat of Harrison, followed by those in his charge, shot ahead of the rest, bearing down full upon the broadside of the pirate. This was the most dangerous point of approach. The two

Graysons led their separate forces, the one to reach the opposite side, the other at the stern lights, in order that the attack should be simultaneous at all vulnerable places. In this manner the several boats covered the various assailable points of the vessel, and necessarily, by dividing their force for the protection of each quarter, weakened the capacity of the seamen to contend with them.

The pirate lay at about a mile and a half below them upon the river—her form in perfect repose—and even weaker in her force than Harrison had conjectured. Bewildered with his situation, and unaccustomed to command, the inferior officer, left in temporary charge of her by Chorley, had done nothing, and indeed could do nothing, towards the defence of his vessel. The few men left with him had become refractory; and, with the reputed recklessness of men in their way of life, had proceeded, during the absence of Chorley, whom they feared rather than respected, to all manner of excess. Liquor, freely distributed by the commanding officer, with the hope to pacify, had only the effect of stimulating their violence; and the approach of the assailing party, magnified by their fears and excesses, found them without energy to resist, and scarcely ability to fly. The lieutenant did indeed endeavour to bring them to some order and show of defence. With his own hand he rigged up a gun, which he pointed among the approaching boats. The scattering and whizzing shot would have been fatal, had the aim been better; but apprehension and excitement had disturbed too greatly the mental equilibrium of officer and men alike; and, not anticipating such a result to their adventure, and having no thought themselves of being attacked, where they had come to be assailants, they fell into a panic from which they did not seek to recover. The failure of the shot to injure their enemies completed their apprehension; and as the little squadron of Harrison continued to approach, without fear and without obstruction, the refractory seamen let down their own boats in the direction of the opposite shore, and, so considerably in advance of the Carolinians as to defy pursuit, were seen by them pulling with all industry towards the Indian country. A single man, the lieutenant, appeared on board for a few moments after they had left the vessel; but whether he remained from choice, or that they refused to take him with them, was at that time a mystery to the assailing party. His design may be guessed at in the sequel.

Despatching the Graysons in pursuit of the flying pirates, whose number did not exceed ten men, Harrison brought his boat alongside the vessel, and resolutely leaped on board. But where was the lieutenant he had seen but a few minutes before? He called aloud, and traversed the deck in search of him, but in vain. He was about to descend to the cabin, when he felt himself suddenly seized upon by Hector, who, with looks of excited terror, dragged him forward to the side of the vessel, and with a directing finger and a single word, developed their full danger to his master.

"Maussa—de ship da burn—look at de smoke—jump, maussa, for dear life—jump in de water." It needed no second word—they sprang over the side of the vessel at the same instant that an immense body of dense sulphureous vapour ascended from below. The river received them, for their boat had been pushed off, with a proper precaution, to a little distance. Ere they were taken up, the catastrophe was over—the explosion had taken place, and the sky was blackened with the smoke and fragments of the vessel upon which, but a few moments before, they had stood in perfect safety. But where was the lieutenant?—where? He had been precipitate in his application of the match, and his desperation found but a single victim in himself!

Chapter Fifty-one

"It is the story's picture—we must group,
So that the eye may see what the quick mind
Hath chronicled before. The painter's art
Is twin unto the poet's—both were born,
That truth might have a tone of melody,
And fancy shape her motion into grace."

A MOTLEY assemblage gathered at the Chief's Bluff, upon the banks of the Pocota-ligo, at an early hour on the day so full of incident. A fine day after so foul a promise—the sun streamed brightly, and the skies without a cloud looked down peacefully over the settlement. But there was little sympathy among the minds of the borderers with such a prospect. They had suffered quite too much, and their sufferings were quite too fresh in their minds, properly to feel it. Worn out with fatigue, and not yet recovered from their trials and terrors—now struggling onward with great effort, and now borne in the arms of the more able-bodied among the men—came forward the women and children who had been sheltered in the Block House. That structure was now in ashes—so indeed, generally speaking, were all the dwellings between that point and Pocota-ligo. Below the former point, however—thanks to the manful courage and ready appearance of Hugh Grayson with the troop he had brought up—the horrors of the war had not extended. But, in all other quarters, the insurrection had been successful. Far and wide, scattering themselves in bands over every other part of the colony, the Yemassees and their numerous allies were carrying the terrors of their arms through the unprepared and unprotected settlement, down to the very gates of Charleston—the chief town and principal rallying point of the Carolinians; and there the inhabitants were literally walled in, unable to escape unless by sea, and then, only from the country. But this belongs elsewhere. The group now assembled upon the banks of the Pocota-ligo, absorbed as they were in their own grievances, had not thought of the condition of their neighbours. The straits and sufferings of the other settlements were utterly unimagined by them generally. But one person of all the group properly conjectured the extent of the insurrection—that was Harrison. He had been a part witness to the league—had counted the various tribes represented in that gloomy dance of death—the club and scalp-dance—the rites of demoniac conception and origin;—and he felt that the very escape of the people around him only arose from the concentration of the greater force of the savages upon the more populous settlements of the Carolinians. Full of satisfaction that so many had been saved, his mind was yet crowded with the thousand apprehensions that came with his knowledge of the greater danger to which the rest of the colony was exposed. He knew the strong body commanded by Sanutee to be gone in the direction of the Ashley river settlement. He knew that a force of Spaniards was expected to join them from St. Augustine; but whether by sea or land was yet to be determined. He felt the uncertainty of his position, and how doubtful was the condition of the province under such an array of enemies; but, with a mind still cheerful, he gave his orders for the immediate remove, by water, to the city; and, having completed his preparations as well as he might, and while the subordinates were busied in procuring boats, he gave himself for a brief time to the family of Bess Matthews.

Long and sweet was the murmuring conversation carried on between the lovers. Like a stream relieved from the pressure of the ice, her affections now poured themselves freely into his. The consent of her father had been given, even if his scruples had not been withdrawn; and that was enough. Her hand rested in the clasp of his, and the unrebuking eyes of the old Puritan gave it a sufficient sanction. Matthews may have sought, in what he then said, to satisfy himself of the necessity for his consent, if he had failed to satisfy his conscience.

"She is yours, Captain Harrison—she is yours! But for you, but for you, God knows, and I dread to think, what would have been her fate in the hands of that bad man. Bad from his cradle; for I knew him from that time, and knew that, mischief then, and crime when he grew older, were his familiar playmates, and his most companionable thoughts."

"You were slow in discovering it, sir," was the reply of Harrison—"certainly slow in acknowledging it to me."

"I had a hope, Master Harrison, that he had grown a wiser and a better man, and was therefore unwilling to mortify him with the recollection of the past, and to make it public to his ill-being. But let us speak of him no more. There are other topics far more grateful in the recollection of our escape from this dreadful night; and long and fervent should be our prayers to the benevolent Providence who has had us so affectionately in his care. But what now are we to do, Captain Harrison—what is our hope of safety, and where are we to go?"

"I have thought of all this, sir. There is but one course for us, and that is to place the young and feeble safely in Charleston. There is no safety short of that point."

"How—not at Port Royal Island?"

"No! not even there—we shall be compelled to hurry past it now as rapidly as possible in our way to the place of refuge—the only place that can now certainly be considered such."

"What—shall we go by water?"

"There is no other way. By this time, scarce a mile of wood between Pocota-ligo and Charleston itself but is filled by savages. I saw the force last night, and that with which we contended was nothing to the numbers pledged in this insurrection. They did not look for resistance here, and hence the smallness of their numbers in this quarter."

"And to your wise precautions, Master Harrison, we owe all this. How unjust I have been to you, sir!"

"Speak not of it, Master Matthews—you have more than atoned in the rich possession which I now hold. Ah, Bess!—I see you look for the promised secret. Well, it shall be told. But stay—I have a duty. Pardon me a while."

He rose as he spoke, and made a signal to Hector, who now came forward with the dog Dugdale, which had been wounded with an arrow in the side, not seriously, but painfully, as was evident from the writhings and occasional moanings of the animal, while Hector busied himself plastering the wound with the resinous gum of the pine-tree.

"Hector," said his master, as he approached— "give me Dugdale. Henceforward I shall take care of him myself."

"Sa! maussa," exclaimed the negro, with an expression almost of terrified amazement in his countenance.

"Yes, Hector,—you are now free. I give you your freedom, old fellow. Here is money, too, and in Charleston you shall have a house to live in for yourself."

"No, maussa; I can't go; I can't be free," replied the negro, shaking his head, and endeavouring to resume possession of the strong cord which secured the dog, and which Harrison had taken into his own hand.

"Why can't you, Hector? What do you mean? Am I not your master? Can't I make you free, and don't I tell you that I do make you free? From this moment you are your own master."

"Wha' for, maussa? Wha' Hector done, you guine turn um off dis time o' day?"

"Done! You have saved my life, old fellow—you have fought for me like a friend, and I am now your friend, and not any longer your master."

"Ki, maussa! enty you always been frien' to Hector! Enty you gib um physic when he sick, and come see and talk wid um, and do ebbery ting he want you for do! What more you guine do, now?"

"Yes, Hector, I have done for you all this—but I have done it because you were my slave, and because I was bound to do it."

"Ah, you no want to be boun' any longer. Da's it! I see. You want Hector for eat acorn wid de hog, and take de swamp wid de Injin, enty?"

"Not so, old fellow—but I cannot call you my slave when I would call you my friend. I shall get another slave to carry Dugdale, and you shall be free."

"I d——n to h——l, maussa, ef I guine to be free!" roared the adhesive black, in a tone of unrestrainable determination. "I can't loss you company, and who de debble Dugdale guine let feed him like Hector? 'Tis onpossible, maussa, and dere's no use for talk 'bout it. De ting aint right; and enty I know wha' kind of ting freedom is wid black man? Ha! you make Hector free, he turn wuss more nor poor buckrah—he tief out of de shop—he git drunk and lie in de ditch—den, if sick come, he roll, he toss in de wet grass of de stable. You come in de morning, Hector dead—and, who know—he no take physic, he no hab parson—who know, I say, maussa, but de debble fine em 'fore anybody else? No, maussa—you and Dugdale berry good company for Hector. I tank God he so good—I no want any better."

The negro's objections to the boon of liberty, with which he so little knew what to do, were not to be overcome; and his master, deeply affected with this evidence of his attachment, turned away in silence, offering no further obstruction to the desperate hold which Hector again took of the wounded Dugdale. Approaching the little group from which, but a few moments before, he had parted, he stood up in earnest conversation with the pastor, while the hand of Bess, in confiding happiness and innocence, was suffered to rest passively in his own. It was a moment of delirious rapture to both parties. But there was one who stood apart, yet surveying the scene, to whom it brought a pang little short of agony. This was the younger Grayson. Tears started to his eyes as he beheld the happy party, and he turned away from the group in a suffering anguish, that, for the moment, brought back those sterner feelings which he had hitherto so well suppressed. The eye of Harrison caught the movement, and readily divined its cause. Calling Granger to him, he demanded from him a small packet which he had intrusted to his care on leaving the Block House for Pocota-ligo the evening before. The question disturbed the trader not a little, who, at length, frankly confessed he had mislaid it.

"Say not so, man! think!—that packet is of value, and holds the last treaty of the colony with the Queen of St. Helena, and the Cassique of Combahee—not to speak of private despatches, set against which thy worthless life would have no value! Look, man, as thou lovest thy quiet!"

"It is here, sir—all in safety, as thou gavest it him," said the wife of the trader, coming forward. "In the hurry of the fight he gave it me for safe keeping, though too much worried to think afterwards of the trust."

"Thou art a strong-minded woman—and 'tis well for Granger that such as thou hast him in charge. Take my thanks for thy discharge of duties self-assumed, and not assigned thee. Thou shalt be remembered."

Possessing himself of the packet, he approached Hugh Grayson, who stood sullenly apart, and drawing from its folds a broad sheet of parchment, he thus addressed him:—

"Master Grayson, the colony owes thee thanks for thy good service, and would have more from thee. I know not one in whom, at such a time, its proprietary lords can better confide, in this contest, than in thee. Thou hast courage, enterprise, and conduct—art not too rash, nor yet too sluggish—but, to my poor mind, thou combinest happily all the materials which should make a good captain. Thou hast a little mistaken me in some things, and, perhaps, thou hast something erred in estimating thyself. But thou art young, and responsibility makes the man—nothing like responsibility! So thinking, and with a frank speech, I beg of thee to accept this commission. It confers on thee all military command in this county of Granville, to pursue the enemies of the colony with fire and sword—to control its people for the purposes of war in dangerous times like the present—and to do, so long as this insurrection shall continue, whatever may seem wise to thy mind, for the proprietors and for the people, as if they had spoken through thy own mouth. Is the trust agreeable to thee?"

"Who art thou?" was the surprised response of the youth, looking a degree of astonishment, corresponding with that upon the faces of all around, to whom the speaker had hitherto only been known as Gabriel Harrison.

"True—let me answer that question. The reply belongs to more than one. Bess, dearest, thou shalt now be satisfied; but in learning my secret, thou losest thy lover. Know, then, thou hast Gabriel Harrison no longer! My true name is Charles Craven!"

"The governor!"—faltered Grayson.

"Ha! what!" exclaimed the pastor.

"The Governor"—roared Nichols— "the Governor, himself—the Lord Palatine of Carolina!"

Bess Matthews only murmured— "Oh! Gabriel!" as she sank, with her heart full of silent happiness, into the arms of her lover. Meanwhile, the loud and joyful shout of all around attested the gratification with which the people recognised, in an old acquaintance, the most popular governor of the Carolinas, under the lords-proprietors, whom the Carolinians ever had.

"I take your commission, my lord," replied Grayson, with a degree of firm manliness, superseding his gloomy expression and clearing it away— "I take it, sir, and will proceed at once to the execution of its duties. Your present suggestions, sir, will be of value."

"You shall have them, Master Grayson, in few words," was the reply of the Palatine. "It will be your plan to move down with your present force along the river, taking with you, as you proceed, all the settlers, so as to secure their safety. Your point of rest and defence will be the fort at Port Royal, which now lacks most of its garrison from the draught made on it by my orders to Bellinger, and which gave you command of the brave men you brought up last night. I shall be at

Port Royal before you, and will do what I may there, in the meanwhile, towards its preparation, whether for friend or foe. With your present force, and what I shall send you on my arrival at Charleston, you will be adequate to its defence."

"Ahem, ahem!—My lord," cried Nichols, awkwardly approaching— "My lord, permit me, with all due humility, to suggest that the duties so assigned Master Grayson are heavy upon such young hands. Ahem! my lord—it is not now that I have to say that I have never yet shrunk from the service of the people. I would—"

"Ay, ay, Nichols—I know what you would say, and duly estimate your public spirit; but, as you are the only surgeon—indeed, the only medical man in the parish—to risk your life unnecessarily, in a command so full of peril as that assigned Master Grayson, would be very injudicious. We may spare a soldier—or even an officer—but the loss of a doctor is not so easily supplied—and"—here his voice sank into a whisper, as he finished the sentence in the ears of the patriot— "the probability is, that your commander, from the perilous service upon which he goes, will be the very first to claim your skill."

"Well, my lord, if I must, I must—but you can understand, though it does not become me to say, how readily I should meet death in behalf of the people."

"That I know—that I know, Nichols. Your patriotism is duly estimated. Enough, now—and farewell, gentlemen—God speed, and be your surety. Granger, let us have boats for the city."

"Young missis," whispered Hector, taking Bess Matthews aside— "let me beg you call Hector your sarbant—tell maussa you must hab me—dat you can't do widout me—and den, you see, missis, he wun't bodder me any more wid he foolish talk 'bout freedom. Den, you see, he can't turn me off, no how." She promised him as he desired, and he went off to the boats singing:—

> "Go hush you tongue, ole nigger,
> 	Wha' for you grumble so,
> You hab you own good maussa,
> 	And you hab good missis too:
> 'Che-weet, che-weet,' de little bird cry,
> 	When he put he nose under he wing,
> But he hab no song like Hector make,
> 	When de young misses yerry um sing."

"Well, good-by, Maussa Doctor, good-by! Dem Injins 'member you long time—dem dat you kill?"

"What do you mean, you black rascal!" cried Constantine Maximilian to the retreating negro, who saw the regretful expression with which the medical man surveyed the preparation for a departure from the scene of danger, in the securities of which he was not permitted to partake. Three cheers marked the first plunge of the boats from the banks, bearing off the gallant Palatine with his peerless forest-flower.

Chapter Fifty-two

"Truthe, this is an olde chronycle, ywritte
Ynne a strange lettere, whyche myne eyne have redde
Whenne birchen were a lessonne of the schoole,
Of nighe applyance. I doe note it welle,
'I faithe, evenne by that tokenne; albeit muche,
The type hath worne away to skeleton,
That once, lyke some fatte, punsy aldermanne,
Stoode uppe in twentie stonne."

OUR tale becomes history. The web of fiction is woven—the romance is nigh over. The old wizard may not trench upon the territories of truth. He stops short at her approach with a becoming reverence. It is for all things, even for the upsoaring fancy, to worship and keep to the truth. There is no security unless in its restraints. The fancy may play capriciously only with the unknown. Where history dare not go, it is then for poetry, borrowing a wild gleam from the blear eye of tradition, to couple with her own the wings of imagination, and overleap the boundaries of the defined and certain. We have done this in our written pages. We may do this no longer. The old chronicle is before us, and the sedate muse of history, from her graven tablets, dictates for the future. We write at her bidding now.

In safety, and with no long delay, Harrison,—or, as we should call him, the Palatine,—reached Charleston, the metropolis of Carolina. He found it in sad dilemma and dismay. As he had feared, the warlike savages were at its gates. The citizens were hemmed in—confined to the shelter of the seven forts which girdled its dwellings—half-starved, and kept in constant watchfulness against hourly surprise. The Indians had ravaged with fire and the tomahawk all the intervening country. Hundreds of the innocent and unthinking inhabitants had perished by deaths the most painful and protracted. The farmer had been shot down in the furrows where he sowed his corn. His child had been butchered upon the threshold, when, hearing the approaching footsteps, it had run to meet its father. The long hair of his young wife, grasped in the clutches of the murderer, became the decoration of a savage, which had once been the charm of an angel. Death and desolation smoked along the wide stretch of country bordering the coast, and designating the route of European settlement in the interior. In the neighbourhood of Pocota-ligo alone, ninety persons were slain. St. Bartholomew's parish was ravaged—the settlement of Stono, including the beautiful little church of that place, was entirely destroyed by fire, while but few of the inhabitants, even of the surrounding plantations, escaped the fury of the invaders. All the country about Dorchester, then new as a settlement, and forming the nucleus of that once beautiful and attractive, but thrice-doomed village, shared the same fate, until the invaders reached Goose Creek, when the sturdy militia of that parish, led on by Captain Chiquan, a gallant young Huguenot, gave them a repulse, and succeeding in throwing themselves between the savages and the city, reached Charleston, in time to assist in the preparations making for its defence.

The arrival of the Palatine gave a new life and fresh confidence to the people. His course was such as might have been expected from his decisive character. He at once proclaimed martial law—laid an embargo, preventing the departure of any of the male citizens, and the exportation of clothes, provisions, or anything which might be useful to the colonists in their existing condition. Waiting for no act of Assembly to authorize his proceedings, but trusting to their subsequent sense of right to acknowledge and ratify what he had done, he proceeded by draught, levy, and impressment, to raise an army of eleven hundred men, in addition to those employed in maintaining the capital. In this proceeding he still more signally showed his decision of character, by venturing upon an experiment sufficiently dangerous to alarm those not acquainted with the condition of the southern negro. Four hundred of the army so raised, consisted of slaves, drawn from the parishes according to assessment. Charleston gave thirty—Christ Church, sixteen—St. Thomas and St. Dennis, fifty–five—St. James, Goose Creek, fifty–five—St. Andrew's, eighty—St. John's, Berkley, sixty—St. Paul's, forty-five—St. James's, Santee, thirty–five—St. Bartholomew's, sixteen—St. Helena, eight—making

up the required total of four hundred. To these, add six hundred
Carolinians, and one hundred friendly Indians or allies; these latter
being Tuscaroras,* from North Carolina, almost the only Indian
nation in the south not in league against the colony. Other bodies of
men were also raised for stations, keeping possession of the Block
Houses at points most accessible to the foe, and where the defence was
most important. At the *Savano* Town, a corps of forty men were
stationed—a similar force at Rawlin's Bluff on the Edistoh; at Port
Royal; on the Combahee; at the Horseshoe, and other places, in like
manner; all forming so many certain garrisons to the end of the
war. All other steps taken by the Palatine were equally decisive; and
such were the severe and summary penalties annexed to the non-
performance of the duties required from the citizen, that there was no
evasion of their execution. Death was the doom, whether of desertion
from duty, or of a neglect to appear at the summons to the field. The
sinews of war in another respect were also provided by the Palatine.
He issued bills of credit for 30,000*l.* to raise supplies; the counterfeit-
ing of which, under the degree of the privy council, was punishable by
death without benefit of clergy. Having thus prepared for the contest,
he placed himself at the head of his rude levies, and with a word of
promise and sweet regret to his young bride, he marched out to meet
the enemy.

War with the American Indians was a matter of far greater
romance than modern European warfare possible can be. There was
nothing of regular array in such conflicts as those of the borderers
with the savages; and individual combats, such as give interest to story,
were common events in all such issues. The borderer singled out his
foe, and grappled with him in the full confidence of superior muscle.
With him, too, every ball was fated. He threw away no shot in line. His
eye conducted his finger; and he touched no trigger, unless he first
ranged the white drop at the muzzle of his piece upon some vital point
of his foe's person. War, really, was an art, and a highly ingenious one,
in the deep recesses and close swamps of the southern forests. There
was no bull-headed marching up to the mouth of the cannon. Their
pride was to get around it—to come in upon the rear—to insinuate—
to dodge—to play with fears or the false confidence of the foe, so as to

---

* Apart from his pay in this war, each Tuscarora received, on returning home, as a bounty, one
gun, one hatchet; and for every slave which he may have lost, an enemy's slave in return!

effect by surprise what could not be done by other means. These were the arts of the savages. It was fortunate for the Carolinians that their present leader knew them so well. Practised as he had been, the Palatine proceeded leisurely, but decisively, to contend with his enemies on their own ground, and after their own fashion. He omitted no caution which could insure against surprise, and, at the same time, he allowed himself no delay. Gradually advancing, with spies always out, he foiled all the efforts of his adversary. In vain did Sanutee put all his warrior skill in requisition. In vain did his most cunning braves gather along the sheltered path in ambuscade. In vain did they show themselves in small numbers, and invite pursuit by an exhibition of timidity. The ranks of the Carolinians remained unbroken. There was no exciting their leader to precipitation. His equanimity was invincible, and he kept his men steadily upon their way—still advancing—still backing their adversaries—and with courage and confidence in themselves, duly increasing with every successful step in their progress.

Sanutee did not desire battle, until the force promised by the Spaniards should arrive. He was in momentary expectation of its appearance. Still, he was reluctant to recede from his ground, so advantageously taken; particularly, too, as he knew that the Indians, only capable of sudden action, are not the warriors for a patient and protracted watch in the field, avoiding the conflict for which they have expressly come out. His anxieties grew with the situation forced upon him by the army and position of the Palatine; and gradually giving ground, he was compelled, very reluctantly, to fall back upon the river of Salke-hatchie, where the Yemassees had a small town, some twenty miles from Pocota-ligo. Here he formed his great camp, determined to recede no farther. His position was good. The river-swamp ran in an irregular sweep, so as partially to form in front of his array. His men he distributed through a thick copse running alongside of the river, which lay directly in his rear. In retreat, the swamps were secure fastnesses, and they were sufficiently contiguous.

The night had set in before he took his position. The Carolinians were advancing, and but a few miles divided the two armies. Sanutee felt secure from attack so long as he maintained his present position; and, sending out scouts, and preparing all things, like a true warrior, for every event, he threw himself, gloomy with conflicting thoughts, under the shadow of an old tree that rose up in front of his array.

While he mused, his ear caught the approach of a light footstep

behind him. He turned, and his eye rested upon Matiwan. She crept
humbly towards him, and lay at his feet. He did not repulse her; but
his tones, though gentle enough, were gloomily cold.

"Would Matiwan strike with a warrior, that she comes to the camp
of the Yemassee? Is there no lodge in Pocota-ligo for the woman of a
chief?"

"The lodge is not for Matiwan, if the chief be not there. Shall the
woman have no eyes? what can the eye of Matiwan behold if Sanutee
stand not up before it. The boy is not—"

"Cha! cha! It is the tongue of a foolish bird that sings out of his
season. Let the woman speak of the thing that is. Would the chief of
the Yemassee hear a song from the woman? It must be of the big club,
and the heavy blow. Blood must be in the song, and a thick cry."

"Matiwan has a song of blood and a thick cry, the song and cry of
Opitchi-Manneyto when he comes out of the black swamps of
Edistoh. She saw the black spirit with the last dark. He stood up before
her in the lodge, and he had a curse for the Woman, for Matiwan took
from him his slave. He had a curse for Matiwan—and a fire-word, oh,
well-beloved, for Sanutee."

"Cha, cha! Sanutee has no ear for the talk of a child."

"The Opitchi-Manneyto spoke of Yemassee," said the woman.

"Ha! what said the black spirit to the woman of Yemassee?" was
the question of the chief, with more earnestness.

"The scalps of the Yemassee were in his hand—the teeth of the
Yemassee were round his neck, and he carried an arrow that was broken."

"Thou liest—thou hast a forked tongue, and a double voice for
mine ear. The arrow of Yemassee is whole."

"The chief has a knife for the heart. Let the well-beloved strike the
bosom of Matiwan. Oh, chief—thou wilt see the red blood that is true.
Strike, and tell it to come. Is it not thine?" she bared her breast as she
spoke, and her eyes were fixed full upon his with a look of resignation
and of love, which spoke her truth. The old warrior put his hand tenderly upon the exposed bosom,—

"The blood is good under the hand of Sanutee. Speak, Matiwan."

"The scalps of Yemassee—and the long tuft of a chief were in the
hand of the Opitchi-Manneyto."

"What chief?" inquired Sanutee.

"The great chief, Sanutee—the well-beloved of the Yemassee," groaned the woman, as she denounced his own fate in the ears of the old warrior. She sank prostrate before him when she had spoken, her face prone to the ground. The chief was silent for an instant, after hearing the prediction conveyed by her vision, which the native superstition, and his own previous thoughts of gloom, did not permit him to question. Raising her after awhile, he simply exclaimed—

"It is good!"

"Shall Matiwan go back to the lodge in Pocota-ligo?" she asked, in a tone which plainly enough craved permission to remain.

"Matiwan will stay. The battle-god comes with the next sun, and the Happy Valley is open for the chief."

"Matiwan is glad. The Happy Valley is for the woman of the chief, and the boy—"

"Cha! it is good, Matiwan, that thou didst strike with the keen hatchet into the head of Occonestoga—Good! But the chief would not hear of him. Look—the bush is ready for thy sleep."

He pointed to the copse as he spoke, and his manner forbade further conversation. Leaving her, he took his way among the warriors, arranging the disposition of his camp and of future events.

Meanwhile, the Palatine approached the enemy slowly, but with certainty, and with the resolve to make him fight if possible. Confident, as he advanced, he nevertheless made his approaches sure. He took counsel of all matters calculated to affect or concern the controversies of war. He omitted no precaution—spared no pains—suffered nothing to divert him from the leading object in which his mind was interested. His scouts were ever in motion, and as he himself knew much of the country through which he marched, his information was at all times certain. He pitched his camp within a mile of the position chosen by the Yemassees, upon ground carefully selected so as to prevent surprise. His main force lay in the hollow of a wood, which spread in the rear of a small mucky bay, interposed directly between his own and the main position of the enemy. A thick copse hung upon either side, and here he scattered a chosen band of his best sharp-shooters. They had their instructions; and as he left as little as possible to chance, he took care that they fulfilled them. Such were his arrangements that night, as soon as his ground of encampment had been chosen.

At a given signal, the main body of the army retired to their tents. The blanket of each soldier, suspended from a crotch-stick, as was the custom of war in that region, formed his covering from the dews of night. The long grass constituted a bed sufficiently warm and soft in a clime, and at a season, so temperate. The fires were kindled, the roll of the drum in one direction, and the mellow tones of the bugle in another, announced the sufficient signal for repose. Weary with the long march of the day, the greater number were soon lulled into a slumber, as little restrained by thought as if all were free from danger and there were no enemy before them.

But the guardian watchers had been carefully selected by their provident leader, and they slept not. The Palatine himself was a sufficient eye over that slumbering host. He was unwearied and wakeful. He could not be otherwise. His thought kept busy note of the hours and of the responsibilities upon him. It is thus that the leading mind perpetually exhibits proofs of its immortality, maintaining the physical nature in its weakness, renewing its strength, feeding it with a fire that elevates its attributes, and almost secures it in immortality too. The Governor knew his enemy, and suspecting his wiles, he prepared his own counter-stratagems. His arrangements were well devised, and he looked with impatience for the progress of the hours which were to bring about the result he now contemplated as certain.

It was early morning, some three hours before the dawn, and the grey squirrel had already begun to scatter the decayed branches from the tree-tops in which he built his nest, when the Palatine roused his officers, and they in turn the men. They followed his bidding in quick movement, and without noise; they were marshalled in little groups, leaving their blanket tents standing precisely as when they lay beneath them. Under their several leaders they were marched forward, in single or Indian file, through the copse which ran along on either side of their place of encampment. They were halted, just as they marched, with their tents some few hundred yards behind them. Here they were dispersed through the forest, at given intervals, each warrior having his bush or tree assigned him. Thus stationed, they were taught to be watchful and to await the movements of the enemy.

The Palatine had judged rightly. He was satisfied that the Yemassees would be unwilling to have the battle forced upon them at Pocota-ligo, exposing their women and children to the horrors of an indiscriminate fight. To avoid this, it was necessary that they should anticipate his approach to that place. The Salke-hatchie was the last natural barrier which they could well oppose to his progress; and the swamps and thick fastnesses which marked the neighbourhood, indicated it well as the most fitting spot for Indian warfare. This was in the thought of the Palatine not less than of Sanutee; and in this lay one of the chief merits of the former as a captain. He thought for his enemy. He could not narrow his consideration of the game before him to his own play; and having determined what was good policy with his foe, he prepared his own to encounter it.

Sanutee had been greatly aided in the progress of this war by the counsels of the celebrated Creek chief, Chigilli, who led a small band of the lower Creeks and Euchees in the insurrection. With his advice, he determined upon attacking the Carolinian army before the dawn of the ensuing day. That night Sanutee arranged his proceedings, and, undaunted by the communication of his fate, revealed to him in the vision of Matiwan, and which, perhaps—with the subdued emotions of one who had survived his most absorbing affections—he was not unwilling to believe, he roused his warriors at a sufficiently early hour, and they set forward, retracing their steps, and well prepared to surprise their enemy. The voice of the whippoorwill regulated their progress through the doubtful and dark night, and without interruption they went on for a mile or more, until their scouts brought them word that the yellow blankets of the whites glimmered through the shadows of the trees before them. With increased caution, therefore, advancing, they came to a point commanding a full view of the place of repose of the Carolinian army. Here they halted, placing themselves carefully in cover, and waiting for the earliest show of dawn in which to commence the attack by a deadly and general fire upon the tents and their flying inmates. In taking such a position, they placed themselves directly between the two divisions of the Palatine's force, which, skirting the copse on either hand, formed a perfect ambush. The Yemassees did not suspect their enemy; who were so placed, that, whenever the red men should make their demonstration upon the tents, where the supposed sleepers lay, which they were wont to do just before the dawn—they would be prepared and ready to cover them with cross fires, and to come out upon their wings and rear, taking them at a vantage which must give a fatal blow to their enterprise.

It came at last, the day so long and patiently looked for by both parties. A faint gleam of light gushed through the trees, and a grey streak like a fine thread stole out upon the horizon. Then rose the cry, the fierce war-whoop of Yemassee and Creek. "*Sangarrah-me, Sangarrah-me!*" was the deafening shout of the savages with which they calculated to terrify the souls of those whom they thus awakened from bewildering sleep. Blood for the Yemassee, blood for the Cherokee, blood for the Creek—were the cries which, at a given moment, carried forward the thousand fierce and dusky warriors of the confederate nations upon the tents which they fondly imagined to contain their sleeping enemies. The shots penetrated the blankets in every direction—the arrows hurtled on all sides through the air, and, rapidly advancing with the first discharge, the Indians rushed to the tents, tomahawk in hand, to strike down the fugitives.

In that moment, the sudden hurrah of the Carolinians, in their rear and on their sides, aroused them to a knowledge of that stratagem which had anticipated their own. The shot told fatally on their exposed persons, and a fearful account of victims came with the very first discharge of the sharp-shooting foresters. Consternation, for a moment, followed the first consciousness which the Indians had of their predicament; but desperation took the place of surprise. Sanutee and Chigilli led them in every point, and wherever the face of the foe could be seen. Their valour was desperate but cool, and European warfare has never shown a more determined spirit of bravery than was then manifested by the wild warriors of Yemassee, striking the last blow for the glory and the existence of their once mighty nation. Driven back on one side and another, they yet returned fiercely and fearlessly to the conflict, with a new strength and an exaggerated degree of fury. Chigilli, raging like one of his own forest panthers, fell fighting, with his hand wreathed in the long hair of one of the borderers, whom he had grappled behind his tree, and for whose heart his knife was already flashing in the air. A random shot saved the borderer, by passing directly through the skull of the Indian. A howl of despairing vengeance went up from the tribe which he led, as they beheld him fall; and rushing upon the sheltered whites, as they sought to reclaim his body, they experienced the same fate to a man! For two hours after this the fight raged recklessly and fierce. The Indians were superior in number to the Carolinians, but the surprise of their first assault was productive of a panic from which they never perfectly recovered. This was more than an off-set to any disparity of force originally; and, as the position of the whites had been well taken, the Yemassees found it impossible in the end to force it. The sun, risen fairly above the forests, beheld them broken—without concert—hopeless of all further effort—flying in every direction; shot down as they ran into the open grounds, and crushed by the servile auxiliaries of the whites as they sought for shelter in the cover of the woods, assigned, for this very purpose, to the negroes.

A brief distance apart from the mêlée,—free from the flying crowd, as the point was more exposed to danger—one spot of the field of battle rose into a slight elevation. A little group rested upon it, consisting of four persons. Two of them were Yemassee subordinates. One of them was already dead. From the bosom of the other, in thick currents, freezing fast, the life was rapidly ebbing. He looked up as he expired, and his last broken words, in his own language, were those of homage and affection to the well-beloved of his people—the great chief, Sanutee.

It was the face of the "well-beloved" upon whom his glazed eyes were fixed with an expression of admiration, indicative of the feeling of his whole people, and truly signifying that of the dying Indian to the last. The old chief looked down on him encouragingly, as the warrior broke out into a start of song—the awful song of the dying. The spirit parted with effort, and Sanutee turned his eyes from the contemplation of the melancholy spectacle to the only living person beside him.

That person was Matiwan. She hung over the well-beloved warrior, with an affection as purely true, as warmly strong, as the grief of her soul was speechless and tearless. Her hand pressed closely upon his side, from which the vital torrent was pouring fast; and between the two, in a low moaning strain, in the Yemassee tongue, they bewailed the fortunes of their nation.

"The eye of Matiwan looked on, when the tomahawk was red— when the knife had a wing. She saw Chigilli, the brave of the Creeks— she saw him strike?" inquired the chief of the woman.

"Matiwan saw."

"Let the woman say of Sanutee, the well-beloved of Yemassee. Did Chigilli go before him? Was Sanutee a dog that runs? Was the hatchet of a chief slow? Did the well-beloved strike at the pale-face as if the red eye of Opitchi-Manneyto had looked on him for a slave?"

"The well-beloved is the great brave of Yemassee. The other chiefs came after. Matiwan saw him strike like a chief, when the battle was thick with a rush, and the hatchet was deep in the head of a pale warrior. Look, oh, well-beloved—is not this the bullet of the white man? The big knife is in the bosom of a chief, and the blood is like a rope on the fingers of Matiwan."

"It is from the heart of Sanutee!"

"Ah-cheray-me-ah-cheray-me!" groaned the woman, in savage lamentation, as she sank down beside the old warrior, one arm now enclasping his already rigid person.

"It is good, Matiwan. The well-beloved has no people. The Yemassee has bones in the thick woods, and there are no young braves to sing the song of his glory. The *Coosah-moray-te* is on the bosom of the Yemassee, with the foot of the great bear of Apalachia. He makes his bed in the old home of Pocota-ligo, like a fox that burrows in the hill-side. We may not drive him away. It is good for Sanutee to die with his people. Let the song of his dying be sung."

"Ah-cheray-me-ah-cheray-me!" was the only response of the woman, as, but partially equal to the effort, the chief began his song of many victories.

But the pursuers were at hand, in the negroes, now scouring the field of battle with their huge clubs and hatchets, knocking upon the head all of the Indians who yet exhibited any signs of life. As wild almost as the savages, they luxuriated in a pursuit to them so very novel—they hurried over the forests with a step as fleet, and a ferocity as dreadful—sparing none, whether they fought or pleaded, and frequently inflicting the most unnecessary blows, even upon the dying and the dead.

The eye of Matiwan, while watching the expiring blaze in that of the old warrior, discovered the approach of one of these sable enemies. She threw up her hand to arrest or impede the blow, declaring, as she did so, the name of the chief she defended. He himself feebly strove to grasp the hatchet, which had sunk from his hands, to defend himself, or at least to strike the assailant; but the expiring life had only gathered for a moment, stagnating about his heart. The arm was palsied; but the half-unclosing eye, which glowed wildly upon the black, and arrested his blow much more completely than the effort of Matiwan, attested the yet reluctant consciousness. Life went with the last effort, when, thinking only of the strife for his country, his lips parted feebly with the cry of battle— "Sangarrah-me, Yemassee—Sangarrah-me—Sangarrah-me!"

The eye was dim for ever. Looking no longer to the danger of the stroke from the club of the negro, Matiwan threw herself at length upon the body, now doubly sacred to that childless woman. At that moment the Lord Palatine came up, in time to arrest the blow of the servile which still threatened her.

"Matiwan," said the Palatine, stooping to raise her from the body— "Matiwan, it is the chief?"

"Ah-cheray-me, ah-cheray-me, Sanutee—Ah-cheray-me, ah-cheray-me, Yemassee!"

She was unconscious of all things, as they bore her tenderly away, save that the Yemassee was no longer the great nation. She only felt that the "well-beloved," as well of herself as of her people, looked forth, with Occonestoga, wondering that she came not, from the Blessed Valley of the Good Manneyto.

Afterword

It is not surprising that *The Yemassee* had an impact upon the American reading public in 1835; the young nation had a hunger for "undiluted Americanism"—for American history highlighted by violence committed in the name of high-minded patriotism. But what appeal does *The Yemassee* have for the more sophisticated reader of today with different artistic expectations, and—perhaps more important—different political agenda? If read with even a modicum of tolerance for nineteenth-century style and standards—cumbersome and cluttered though they appear to be—*The Yemassee* can have an astonishing hold on an audience now attuned more to the tragedy of Native Americans than were the readers of Simms's day. For, viewed through twentieth-century eyes, *The Yemassee* dramatically and unflinchingly bares the manipulation, exploitation, and eventual genocide of a proud indigenous nation that preferred extinction to the surrender of its lands and the subjection of its people. It is not that Simms is unsympathetic with South Carolina's first colonists or the challenges they faced, for he characterizes most of them as highly worthy individuals dedicated to their mission. The author celebrates their bravery, applauds their superior ingenuity and leadership, and vigorously defends their patriotism and honor, factors which contributed to the enthusiastic reception given the book upon its publication. While today's reader may appreciate Simms's tribute to their bravery, laud the stamina and fortitude of the men and women in facing the challenges of their existence, and acknowledge their contribution to the westward thrust of the young nation, it is in the depiction of the Indian and his plight where the book's greatest impact lies and where Simms's merit will be found. Today a generation acutely sensitive to racial injustice is struck by the breadth of Simms's vision in depicting, with graphic realism yet sympathetic insight, the plight of the American

Indian and the anguish in his realization of the inevitability of white dominance of his people and confiscation of his land.

In Simms's portrayal, when faced with the choice of death or dishonor, the Indian—whether a nation like the Yemassee or the Coosaw or an individual like Occonestoga or Chinnabee—invariably chose death. In his compassion for their unjust fate, however, Simms does not neglect the weaknesses of the Indian. He represents the Yemassee as capable of greed, treachery, cowardice, cruelty, hate, revenge, stubbornness, and jealousy as well as honor, trust, bravery, generosity, love, wisdom, compassion, and forgiveness. In short, Simms's Indians are believable individuals with flaws and virtues unrelated to race, tribe, or sex. There are good and bad Yemassees, Coosaws, men and women; little stereotyping exists in Simms's delineation. Perhaps the main thing—in addition to their belief in ritual and religion—that unites the Indians in *The Yemassee* is their universal victimization by whites, although the degree and method of exploitation may vary from tribe to tribe.

In keeping with his knowledge of Indian culture—to which he was exposed as a young man while visiting his father in Mississippi— Simms characterizes "the great chief of the Yemassees," the historical figure Sanutee, as rigid and unbending in his concept of honor and principle. Though generous and courteous almost to a fault in his initial meetings with the English, Sanutee proves tenaciously stubborn in his refusal to negotiate with the white colonists after he foresees the consequence of the continued barter of land for trinkets. One of the most memorable scenes in the novel occurs when Sanutee—"his eyes . . . now fully opened to his error" (69)—speaks at the house of council, before his traitorous fellow chiefs:

> Why comes the English to the lodge of our people? Why comes he with a red coat to the Chief—why brings he beads and paints for the eye of a little boy? Why brings he the strong water for the young man? Why makes he long speeches, full of smooth words—why does he call us brother? He wants our lands. But we have no lands to sell. The lands came from our fathers—they must go to our children. They do not belong to us to sell—they belong to our children to keep. [81]

Unsuccessful in his argument because jealousy and greed drive a majority of the chiefs to the decision to "sell the land to our English brothers," Sanutee retains composure and dignity with his single, acquiescent utterance, "It is well! It is well!" (83). But he is more determined than ever to thwart both the bribed chiefs and the bribing settlers. Meeting with his comrades in insurrection, high priest Enoree-Mattee and fellow chiefs Ishiagaska and Choluculla, Sanutee concocts "a moral earthquake" calculated to rouse the Yemassee nation to a religious frenzy and to strike terror in the hearts of the "sacrilegious" sellers of "the old burial-places of the Yemassee" (87). The war cry, "Sangarrah, Sangarrah-me, Yemassee—Sangarrah, Sangarrah-me—Yemassee," is raised by the frenetic tribesmen, followed by the shout, "They shall all die—have they not planted corn in the bosom of my mother?"

But Sanutee, of whom Simms says "no better politician lived in the nation" (90), astutely recognizes that death for the betraying chiefs is not in the interest of his people. Instead, Sanutee contrives to have the high priest Enoree-Mattee capture the attention of the masses by "writhing upon the ground . . . in the most horrible convulsions," as if seized by the will of the evil deity, Opitchi-Manneyto. Standing erect, "lifted, as it were, with inspiration," his eyes "spiritually bright," and his features "sublimed by a sacred fury," Enoree-Mattee chants "a wild rhythmic strain":

> "Let the Yemassee have ears,
> For Opitchi-Manneyto—
> 'Tis Opitchi-Manneyto,
> Not the prophet now that speaks,
> Hear Opitchi-Manneyto.
>
> "In my agony, he came,
> And he hurl'd me to the ground;
> Dragged me through the twisted bush,
> Put his hand upon my throat,
> Breathed his fire into my mouth—
> That Opitchi-Manneyto.
>
> "And he said to me in wrath,—
> Listen, what he said to me;
> Hear the prophet, Yemassees—

For he spoke to me in wrath;
He was angry with my sons,
For he saw them bent to slay,
Bent to strike the council-chiefs,
And he would not have them slain,
That Opitchi-Manneyto." [89–90]

At this surprising revelation, which seemed to deny the Yemassee people revenge upon the offending chiefs, Sanutee again displays his political acumen. Knowing well the value of a "show of concession," Sanutee steps forth to question Enoree-Mattee in a speech whose words are actually aimed for the ears of the multitude: "Wherefore, Enoree-Mattee, should Opitchi-Manneyto save the false chiefs who robbed their people? Shall we not have their blood—shall we not hang their scalps in the tree . . . ? Wherefore this strange word from Opitchi-Manneyto—wherefore would he save the traitors?" Enoree-Mattee's response is perhaps the most effective representation of Indian poetry to be found in our early literature; in it Simms seems to capture the mood, rhythm, and spirit of the Yemassee in stanzas embodying the righteous wrath of a proud, defiant people. The third and fourth epitomize the sacred nature of a revenge more terrifying than death:

"Death is for the gallant chief
Says Opitchi-Manneyto—
Life is for the traitor slave,
But a life that none may know—
With a shame that all may see.

"Thus Opitchi-Manneyto,
To his sons, the Yemassee—
Take the traitor chiefs, says he,
Make them slaves, to wait on me.
Bid Malatchie take the chiefs,
He, the executioner—
Take the chiefs and bind them down,
Cut the totem from each arm,
So that none may know the slaves,
Not their fathers, not their mothers—
Children, wives, that none may know—

Not the tribes that look upon,
Not the young men of their own,
Not the people, not the chiefs—
Nor the good Manneyto know.
. . . ." [91–92]

By thus sanctifying and refining "the art of punishment" (92), Sanutee is able to ensure a devastating victory over his rivals. His policy "to degrade [rather] than to destroy" allows the condemned chiefs no sympathy from the enraged citizenry and yet paralyzes them with a terror far greater than fear of death. The brutal melee that follows when the chiefs attempt to compel their own deaths is an example of the graphic depiction of violence which offended some readers of Simms's day. Only Manneywanto, the most "powerful and ferocious" of the fallen leaders, manfully battling "with a skill and struggle that knew no abatement," manages to coerce, or coax, an avenger to "[sever] his skull with a hatchet." The surviving chiefs are not so fortunate:

They found no mercy. They did not plead for mercy, nor for life. Death was implored, but in vain. The prophet—the people, were relentless. The knife sheared the broad arrow from breast and arm, and in a single hour they were expatriated men, flying desperately to the forests, homeless, nationless, outcasts from God and man, yet destined to live. [96]

Unsparing in his portrayal of cruelty as a part of life in frontier America, Simms provides other equally striking examples. Perhaps the most terrible scene of ritualistic cruelty by the Yemassees is the torture of the doughty Irishman Macnamara, white sacrifice to the God of War—the Battle-Manneyto. Teddy Macnamara's "fearless contempt of death, his haughty defiance of their skill in the arts of torture—his insolent abuse" serves only to ensure his crucifiers that "he would stand well the torture" and "afford them a protracted enjoyment of the spectacle" (259).[1] But in evincing the Indian's cruelty in ceremonial rituals sanctioned by deity, Simms points out that civilized man, too, follows the theory ("common to experience all the world over") that "Blood makes the taste for blood" (257). "There is a sort of intoxicating restlessness in crime that seldom suffers it to stop at a solitary excess," the author relates. "It craves repetition—and the relish so expands with indulgence, that exaggeration becomes essential to make it a stimulant" (257).

Yet—let it be noted—it is also the Yemassees' strict observance of ritual that halts the blood-thirstiness and spares the life of Gabriel Harrison. Captured immediately following Macnamara's agonizing death, he, too, appears doomed to a similar fate, but Enoree-Mattee, the prophet of the Yemassee, evokes the words of Manneyto, proclaiming, "He hath said one victim—one English for the sacrifice—and but one . . . before we go on the war-path of our enemies" (266); thus it is that obedience to the will of the war-god—who had called for "but one" sacrifice—prevents a second.

This strict honoring of principle also provides the basis for the extreme mental cruelty evidenced in the relationship between Sanutee and Occonestoga. Sanutee's disappointment in his son's failure to live up to expectations, and Occonestoga's resentment of his father's overbearing attitude—tensions between patriarch and male offspring frequently recorded in various cultures—contribute significantly to the rivalry; but much of the hostility between Yemassee chief and warrior son is rooted in the Indian code of honor. The first observable clash between highly respected chief and prodigal son occurs immediately after Sanutee's emotionally taut, well-articulated denunciation of the other Yemassee chiefs at the council meeting in Pocota-ligo. With Sanutee's oratory against the sale of land defeated by vote of the council of chiefs, a half-drunken Occonestoga staggers forth, in the presence of Sir Edmund Bellinger and other colonial leaders, to confront (and insult) his father with a eulogy on the English, whom he calls "the true friends and dear brothers of the Yemassees" (83). In anger at the insolence of his son, Sanutee springs forward, and, "with uplifted arm and descending blow, would have driven the hatchet deep into the skull of the only half-conscious youth" except for the intervention of Bellinger. To Bellinger's sharp question, "Wouldst thou slay thy own son, Sanutee?" the infuriated chief replies:

> He is thy slave—he is not the son of Sanutee. Thou hast made him a dog with thy poison drink, till he would sell thee his own mother to carry water for thy women. Hold me not, Englishman—I will strike the slave—I will strike thee, too, that art his master . . . [83–84]

Thus a line has been drawn between father and son, with each bearing partial responsibility for the hostility. When Occonestoga learns from Matiwan that Sanutee has condemned him to the doom of the traitorous chiefs—that is, to have the "sacred and broad arrow of the Yemassee" cut from arm and shoulder—the young warrior becomes "the very personification of despair." But recovering quickly, the defiant youth vows to "do battle against the Yemassee" and most of all, to "strike at the breast of Sanutee." When Matiwan sternly asks, ". . . wouldst thou strike at thy father?" Occonestoga reacts as violently as his father had: "He is the enemy of Occonestoga . . . I will slay him like a dog" (178–79). Thus the circle of hatred and animosity around Matiwan is complete; the wife-mother at the center hopelessly torn between love for her husband and love for her son.

Simms handles this family impasse with adroitness. Recognizing the sensitivities and motivations of each and without attributing guilt or issuing remonstrance, he manages to convey the ambivalences haunting all three. As leader of the Yemassee, Sanutee is obligated by Indian tradition to put the welfare of his nation above all else; he cannot, in performance of his covenant with his people, harbor special compassion, tolerate double standards, or seem affected by personal interests. Thus to spare a blood son guilty of the treason he has unequivocally condemned in others would be a violation of his sacred trust as chief. So well has Simms succeeded in delineating the dilemma Sanutee faces, the reader never ceases to sympathize with him. Despite stern demeanor and ruthless behavior, Sanutee is seen as an essentially noble human being, whose official sense of duty, love of nation, and worship of deity have obliterated any personal tenderness.

Yet in the final scene with Matiwan he displays both the passionate gentleness of conjugal love and the forgiving magnanimity of paternal love. Confronting her obdurate husband with a dreaded vision from Opitchi-Manneyto—a prophecy of the death of the Yemassee nation and of their chief—as proof of her truthfulness and submission Matiwan "bared her breast as she spoke, and her eyes were fixed full upon him with a look of resignation and of love." In response the "old warrior put his hand tenderly upon the exposed bosom," saying simply, "the blood is good under the hand of Sanutee." Greatly moved by his wife's demonstration of the bonding between them, Sanutee speaks to her a forbidden name in tones of forgiveness long withheld, thereby emphasizing his recognition of the significant place she held in his physical and spiritual life: ". . . it is good, Matiwan, that thou didst strike with the keen hatchet into the head of Occonestoga—Good!" (406–7). The family circle, broken on earth, will be restored—it is implied—in the Happy Valley of the Yemassee spirit.

In her conflicting roles as wife to ruling chief and mother to unruly chieftain, Matiwan reveals uncommon sensitivity, tact, and wisdom. To save a wayward son from the punishment decreed by his father, her husband, is not a small undertaking; at first glance it seems to have been a simple act of humanism, placing the welfare of her son before the principles of her husband. But Matiwan's decision to kill Occonestoga to free his spirit from disgrace only seems to be in defiance of Sanutee. In reality, it is a way of preserving Sanutee's integrity, of maintaining his honor and reputation as well-beloved chief of the Yemassees: while saving their only son from a fate worse than death, Matiwan through her daring rescues her husband from any responsibility—in his own eyes as much as in the eyes of his people—in the willful spurning of the wishes of Opitchi-Manneyto. Sanutee would never have violated his trust as leader of the Yemassee nation; he never admits to himself compassion for Occonestoga. But Matiwan, loving her husband as completely as she loves her son, recognizes in Sanutee what he could not acknowledge; and her action to "free" Occonestoga, to subvert the will of the gods, does not implicate her spouse. Matiwan comes close to being "a person upon whom nothing is lost" in the Jamesian sense in her social, moral, and ethical sensitivity to all nuances in a delicate but desperate situation. Her courageous and wise action not only benefits her son's spirit and eases her own conscience; in the long run, it is also a blessing and boon to her husband—eventually, even, in his own perception, as she is fortunate to discover before his death. Matiwan seems the prime example, in all Simms's writings, of the humanistic concept that no principle—moral, ethic, or religious—takes precedent over concern for a cherished human being. That she is a Native American makes Simms's achievement the more memorable.

But, in an ironic sense, it is Matiwan's unquestioning conviction of the validity of principle that determines her belief that her son is better off dead than disgraced; otherwise she could have "saved" him simply by cutting his bonds, not by cutting off his life. That she would place what she considered the welfare of her son above the principle of absolute allegiance to nation, religion, husband appears to illustrate, in Simms's words, that "Humanity is earlier in its origin, and holier in its claims than society. She felt the one, and forgot to obey the other" (275). It is specifically Matiwan's maternal instinct—as well as her general humanitarianism—that causes her to act in defiance of principle thoroughly embedded in her psyche.

Shortly after her rescue of Occonestoga, this maternal impulse leads Matiwan to violate Indian covenant once again. With the "image of Occonestoga" (275) haunting her and the question "Is there a living mother of the *Coosah-moray-te,* beyond the great waters, who loves her son, as the poor Matiwan loved the boy Occonestoga?" (274) uppermost in her thoughts, the "burning feelings in her bosom" cause Matiwan to identify with Harrison's mother and through her to see Harrison as a mother's son, and not as an enemy. Resolved, then, to spare the man who, during an earlier visit to Charleston by Matiwan and her father, "had been kind to her father" and had given her "the beautiful little cross" she still wore, Matiwan employs "highly ingenious arts" of woodcraft to outwit Harrison's sentinels. Slipping stealthily into his place of captivity, she whispers "Occonestoga?" (280) in the ear of the surprised captive Carolina governor-in-disguise just before she releases him from his destined ritualistic torture and death. Although compassion for two doomed young men—her actual son and the son of an English mother with whom she empathized— seemingly serves to separate herself from her people and her husband, Matiwan in the end pledges her allegiance. Her knowledge of the inevitable extinction of her nation motivates her to seek re-identification with Sanutee and his purposes, whatever the consequences. It might be argued that Matiwan's oneness with Occonestoga, with Sanutee, with the Yemassee had been tried and sorely tested, but never shattered.

Not so fully delineated as Sanutee and Matiwan, Occonestoga nevertheless emerges in *The Yemassee* as a comprehensible human being. His story is that of the heir to the kingdom who, after an auspicious beginning, disappoints both king and kingdom; of the youth who, lacking in self-confidence and willpower, rebels against a father image in a futile quest for self-knowledge and identity. Easily frustrated— primarily because of his addiction to the alcohol introduced by Europeans—Occonestoga is essentially an ineffectual moral weakling who craves respect and love from a proud, ambitious father displeased with the performance and not appeased by the honorable intentions of his son. Occonestoga's relationship with Matiwan exposes him as a sensitive person hungry for the love of women. After his embarrassing fall from his father's grace, this need is intensified by the alienation of Hiwassee, the young woman to whom he was once beholden. Her betrothal to another, coupled with Sanutee's harsh rejection, helps to destroy the self-image of the inexperienced youth. Unable to assuage his vulnerable feelings and assert a stoic self-control, he becomes suspicious and vindictive.

In one sense, Sanutee's disappointment in Occonestoga seems justified; mortified by the cruel and, in his eyes, unfair treatment he has received from his tribesmen and his father in particular, Occonestoga becomes an easy pawn in the hands of Harrison, who, perceiving the Indian's wounded ego, skillfully manipulates the embittered youth into an agreement to spy on his own people for the English. Foolhardy, vain, and resentful though he is, however, Occonestoga has redeeming qualities. His prowess and skill as a warrior are attested to not only by his early exploits in battle against the Savannahs, "against whom he distinguished himself" (146); but more particularly in the powerful, if melodramatic scene in which he saves the utterly transfixed Bess Matthews from death by piercing the head of a menacing rattlesnake with a single arrow—shot at the last possible moment with unerring accuracy. In addition, in Simms's own words, if Occonestoga "had no other virtue," he did possess one that "was, to a certain extent, sufficiently redeeming": love for his mother (175).

A characteristic ambivalence marks Occonestoga, however, even in his final moments with Matiwan: "Thou art come, Matiwan—thou art come, but wherefore?—to curse like the father . . . —to curse like the Manneyto? . . . . Wouldst thou slay me, mother—wouldst strike the heart of thy son?" (199). Somewhat unnerved by her son's questioning, the resolute Matiwan nevertheless completes her mission of merciful death, just as Occonestoga utters his last words: "thou hast saved me" (200). If it seems ironic—by one set of standards—that Occonestoga's murder by his mother occurs only after prayerful thought and planning, by her own standards based upon those of her people, Matiwan has not committed murder at all but a courageous, highly moral act of love. That this action should take the life of her only son (more victim than criminal) is surprising to no one steeped in Indian mythology as was Simms at the time of writing. It is indicative of how well the author has entered the mind and character of the Yemassee that to the reader of the novel the actions of Matiwan seem heroic and tragic—inspiring, not repelling.

The major appeal of *The Yemassee* to the modern reader is, as we
have seen, Simms's masterful treatment of the Native American. Yet
the popularity of the novel immediately upon publication, we have
also seen, owes more to its stirring epic portrayal of the heroics of the
colonists than to its dramatization of the tragedy of the Yemassee.
Setting aside, then, Simms's singular achievement in capturing the
essence of Yemassee culture, the salient reason for the novel's instant
success is its deftness in bringing to life a crucial episode in what
Simms called "our first American period in history"—specifically, in
this case, the early colonization of South Carolina by the English.[2]
What are the strengths and weaknesses of Simms's fictional embodiment of this epoch?

When he reread *The Yemassee* in 1853 to prepare it for a new edition, Simms himself purports to have been "absolutely angry" with
himself "at having spoiled and botched so much excellent material." It
is significant, however, that though "fully conscious" of the novel's
"defects and crudities," the author chose to make only "small" acci-
dental corrections in the original manuscript and to leave untouched
the "thoughts," "situations," and "style" which he identified as awkward or inappropriate and acknowledged needed improvement. Taken
at face value Simms's explanation for not substantially revising *The
Yemassee* is hardly adequate: "I see now a thousand passages, through
which had I the leisure, and could I muster courage for the effort, I
should draw the pen . . . . But . . . how coldly and reluctantly would
such a task be undertaken, by one who has survived his youth, and
who must economize all his enthusiasm for the new creations of his
fancy" (xxvii).

In the light of Simms's anger at critics who concentrate upon
small defects while missing the larger merit of a work, the novelist, it
seems almost certain, was writing tongue-in-cheek in lamenting that
he could "only bestow a touch of the pruning knife here and there" on
a book "long dismissed from his thoughts." Simms by 1853 well knew
that his strength as a novelist lay in boldness and vision, the power
and gusto of the creative surges that periodically dominated his imagination, allowing his pen to flash across the page spontaneously,
"writ[ing] usually as I talk" (*L*, VI, 27). An author thus knowledgeable
about his habits of composition and confident about his writing style
may well acknowledge weaknesses in a work long ago completed; he
may lament deficiencies pointed out by his critics; but he is unlikely to

spend much time and effort on revisions, particularly if he is already envisioning a new creation. Simms's creativity gushes forth explosively and extravagantly; yet the exuberance of the lavishly wasteful surge adds to the exhilarating effect. Any attempt by Simms to restrict, refine, or redirect this creative explosiveness usually seems to result in a loss of spontaneity and power without an appreciable gain in artistic mastery. Simms the writer understood himself well.

That detracting errors do exist in *The Yemassee* cannot be denied, however. They are abundant enough and apparent enough that the most blatant—needless repetition,[3] overuse of coincidence, heavy-handed authorial intrusion, awkward structure, sententious style, stilted dialogue of romanticized hero and heroine—may oppress the reader. One does not read a Simms or a Dickens or a Dreiser for artistic elegance; to retain an active readership, a novelist like Simms with stylistic and structural deficiencies must possess power, intensity, pictorial quality. Some tolerance of artistic imperfection is prerequisite to enjoyment of Simms's untamed, spirited prose. But the late twentieth-century bibliophile who can adapt intellectually to Simms's early nineteenth-century literary style and habits is rewarded by an extraordinary reading experience heightened by the fullness and the sharpness of Simms's vision of America.

The case has been made that Simms in *The Yemassee* is stirringly effective in characterizing Native Americans. Unfortunately, he is less impressive in the development of his white protagonists: the historical figure Charles Craven, governor of South Carolina who is in disguise throughout most of the action under the alias Gabriel Harrison, and Bess Matthews, the seventeen-year-old daughter of a conservative Presbyterian minister unreceptive to her desire to marry Harrison. Gabriel Harrison and Bess Matthews possess the Sir Walter Scott-prescribed ingredients for the gentleman-hero and the lady-heroine: he is a noble-minded man of thirty, dashing in appearance, forthright in manner, proud yet sensitive, resolute yet considerate, skilled in diplomacy, and courageous in battle; she is a charming, intelligent, high-spirited girl possessed of intuitive insight and a hint of rebelliousness in her gentle nature.

As if in recognition that his conventional lead characters lack verisimilitude, Simms focuses upon small characteristics that help lend them credibility. Harrison, for instance, enjoys debate and argumentation, sometimes at the expense of better judgment. Vain about his linguistic superiority, Harrison appears inappropriately condescending toward his stern-minded future father-in-law. Because at the time John Matthews had not yet consented to his daughter's marriage to Harrison, the religious discussion that takes place between the two men seems to call for more tact (perhaps more courtesy) than Harrison demonstrates when the minister objects to the younger man's "tone and language" disrespectful of religion. While admitting to "sometime levity, . . . playfulness, and . . . . thoughtlessness, perhaps," Harrison in his rebuttal directly challenges the goodwill of the venerable pastor at the very time he seeks his favorable opinion:

> I shall undertake to reform these, when you shall satisfy me that to laugh and sing, and seek and afford amusement, are inconsistent with my duties either to the Creator or the creature. On this head, . . . you are the criminal, not me. It is you, sir, and your sect, that are the true criminals. Denying, as you do, to the young, all those natural forms of enjoyment and amusement . . . , you cast a shadow over all things around you . . . . That I shall never be a Puritan . . . you may be assured, if it be only to avoid giving to my face the expression of a pine bur. [54–55]

Such an impolitic outburst from a public servant (in disguise) known for his diplomatic skill seems refreshingly human; on this rare occasion Harrison is so enamored of his rhetoric that he cannot forego a "cool and confident" squelch of his elder when his own interest dictates discretion.

Simms adds interest to his characterization of Bess Matthews by granting her a piquant sprightliness. In the initial stages of her courtship by Gabriel Harrison, she displays annoyance at the implication that, being female, she enjoys being coddled. When Harrison queries her, "And why not, my Beautiful?" the resourceful young woman chides him to "cease calling me nicknames, or I'll leave you. I won't suffer it. You make quite too free" (47). Later in their lively flirtation, when Harrison teasingly asserts that "the assurance [of love] is so sweet to your ears that you could not have it too often repeated," Bess playfully yet cleverly defends her sex: "Oh, abominable—thus it is, you destroy all the grace of your pretty speeches. But you mistake the sex, if you suppose we care for your vows on this subject knowing, as we do, that you are compelled to love us, we take the assurance for granted" (48). In this exchange Bess Matthews displays captivating archness as well as a distinct sense of self-worth. Later, this same prideful, independent spirit accounts for her aversion to the patronizing attitude of Richard Chorley: in Simms's words "Bess Matthews was a thinking, feeling woman, and he addressed her as a child" (110). Throughout, she demands that she be accorded respect as a mature human being, not looked upon as a mere object or as a child to be bribed and fondled; in a dramatic confrontation with Hugh Grayson, who professes to love her passionately and unconditionally, she artfully and accurately defines the nature of his love: ". . . look closely into yourself . . . and then ask how you loved me? Let me answer—not as a woman—not as a thinking and a feeling creature—but as a plaything, whom your inconsiderate passion might practise upon at will . . ." (305). Bess Matthews's insistence upon being considered a woman of intellect and imagination sets her apart from her otherwise conventional role as exemplary heroine.

Her father is in many ways a more intricate figure than Bess Matthews herself. In introducing John Matthews to the reader, Simms does full justice to the religious and political intolerance permeating colonial South Carolina—and consequently accounting for some of the prejudicial views held by the radical clergyman. Some of the best writing in the novel occurs in a perceptive passage capturing both the situation and its many nuances:

> there seemed a something of backwardness, a chilly repulsiveness in the manner of the old gentleman, quite repugnant to the habits of the country, and not less so to the feelings of Harrison. For a brief period, indeed, the cold deportment of the Pastor had the effect of . . . freezing the warm exuberant blood of the cavalier . . . . The old man was an ascetic—a stern Presbyterian—one of the ultra-nonconformists—and not a little annoyed at that period, and in the new country, by the course of government . . . . The leading proprietors were generally of the church of England, and, with all the bigotry of the zealot, forgetting . . . their strict pledges . . . not to interfere in the popular religion—they proceeded . . . to the establishment of a regular church, and . . . actually to exclude from all representation in the colonial assemblies, such portions of the country as were chiefly settled by other sects . . . . [Matthews] was a bigot himself, and, with the power, would doubtless have tyrannised after a similar fashion. The world within him was what he could take in with his eye, or control

> within the sound of his voice. He could not be brought to under-
> stand that climates and conditions should be various, and that
> the popular good . . . demanded that people should everywhere
> differ in manner and opinion. He wore clothes after a different
> fashion from those who ruled, and the difference was vital; but he
> perfectly agreed with those in power that there should be a pre-
> scribed standard by which the opinions of all persons should be
> regulated . . . . But though as great a bigot as any of his neigh-
> bours, Matthews yet felt how very uncomfortable it was to be in a
> minority; and the persecutions to which his sect had been
> exposed in Carolina . . . had made him not less hostile towards
> the government . . . . [49–50]

But though "as great a bigot as any of his neighbours" on matters
of religion, John Matthews, almost alone among the English, perceives
the grave injustice being done to the Native Americans. When
Harrison warns the old Puritan of the forthcoming uprising of the
Yemassee and gives evidence of their increasing hostility, Matthews
exclaims: "This but proves, Captain Harrison, that we may, if we
please, provoke them by our persecutions into insurrections. Why do
we thus seek to rob them of their lands?"

Though naive in his understanding of the dangers of living
unprotected on the frontier, Matthews is steadfast in his view that
the Europeans, not the Indians, are the guilty aggressors. In this
assessment—as history attests—the minister is essentially correct; but
his refusal to move his family to the relative safety of the Block House,
as urged by Harrison, borders on perversity. His closed mind contrasts
with the more open mind of Harrison: no powers of persuasion—no
amount of evidence—change Matthews's belief that the Indians
remain basically friendly; Harrison, too, acknowledges wrongdoing on
the part of the English, but—aware of the ferocity of the aroused
Yemassee—cautions against exposing loved ones to unnecessary risk.
It is ironic that during the Yemassee uprising Matthews is spared a terrible death from the hatchet of Ishiagaska only by the last-second
intervention of the churlish Chorley, whose unfulfilled lust for Bess
calls for the preservation of the minister and his family.

Another Matthews, Elizabeth, the pastor's good wife, is also inter-
estingly, if sketchily, drawn. Simms's quick brush outlines Elizabeth
Matthews with a few telling strokes: "The good old dame, a tidy, well-
preserved antique, received the visitor [Harrison] with regard and

kindness, and though evidently but half recovered from a sound nap, proceeded to chatter with him, and at him, with all the garrulous freedom of one who saw but little of the world . . ." (49). Even in a very minor role the talkative Mrs. Matthews captures one important scene in the novel: her amiable yet unyielding encounter with her husband over the qualifications of Gabriel Harrison as a suitor of their daughter:

> "Bess is wrong, my dear," at length said the pastor, in a tone and manner meant to be conclusive on the subject— "Bess is wrong—decidedly wrong. We know nothing of Master Harrison—neither of his family nor of his pursuits—and she should not encourage him."
>
> "Bess is right, Mr. Matthews," responded the old lady, with a doggedness of manner meant equally to close the controversy. . . . "Bess is right—Captain Harrison is a nice gentleman— always so lively, always so polite, and so pleasant. I declare, I don't see why you don't like him, and it must be only because you love to go against all other people." [217]

Without actually convincing Matthews in their family squabble (in which, however, she "gave up no point"), the knowing wife scores by asking her husband: "Oh, John, John—where's all your religion? . . . really you are so uncharitable. It's neither sensible nor Christian in you. Why will you be throwing up hills upon hills in the way of Bess's making a good match? . . . Now you will admit, I think, that I know when a gentleman is a gentleman, and when he is not—and I tell you that if Master Harrison is not a gentleman, then give me up, and don't mind my opinion again. I don't want spectacles to see that he comes of good family and is a gentleman" (218).

On the surface successful neither in certifying Harrison to Matthews's satisfaction nor in persuading the recalcitrant clergyman to heed Harrison's warning about the Yemassee, in actuality Elizabeth Matthews does plant in her husband a seed of doubt: ". . . the preacher himself not altogether assured in his own mind that a lurking feeling of hostility to Harrison, rather than a just sense of his security, had not determined him to risk the danger from the Indians . . ." (221). Nevertheless, even in this moment of partial self-awareness, the stubborn Matthews is not yet ready to admit error in judgment, or to heed advice.

Perhaps Simms's best-drawn characters among the English settlers are the frontiersmen themselves—or, at least in one extraordinary case, a frontierswoman. Mary or Moll Granger (the author calls her both) is another of Simms's exceptionally strong women who, living in the backwoods world of violence ostensibly dominated by men, quietly assert superiority in intelligence, will, and bravery. One example, of course, is the Indian Matiwan; but the female best compared to Granger is Harricane Nell Dean, the guerrilla fighter vividly portrayed in *Eutaw*. Moll Granger is quieter, less intense, less flamboyant than Nelly Dean; but Granger is probably superior to Dean in the conciliatory skills that assuage the male ego and permit the assertion of effective female leadership.

The reader first encounters the "tall, fine looking woman, of much masculine beauty"—the wife of Indian trader Richard Granger—when, in defiance of the will of chief commissioner Sir Edmund Bellinger, she performs an act indicative of her character. Recognizing the folly of Bellinger's decision not to return to Sanutee the wampum he demands, she takes matters into her own hands: "seizing upon the little skin of earth and the parchment at the same moment, without a word, she threw open the door, and cried out to Sanutee to receive them" (98). To Bellinger's outburst, "Woman, how durst thou do this!" Moll Granger politely but firmly replies: "My life is precious to me, Sir, though you may be regardless of yours. The treaty is nothing now to the Yemassees . . . To have kept it would have done no good, but must have been destructive to us all. Sanutee will keep his word, and our lives will be saved" (99). The superb discretionary sense of this uncommon woman is confirmed by an authorial comment: "It was evident that she was right, and Bellinger was wise enough to see it. He said nothing farther, glad, perhaps that the responsibility of the action had been thus taken from his shoulders."

If this instance reflects Moll Granger's wisdom, another displays her daring. When Harrison offers to reward Richard Granger to spy upon the Yemassee, to "find out what they design," the trader refuses on the ground that "it were death, and a horrible death, for me to undertake this. I must not—I do not say I will not—but in truth I cannot—I dare not." Her husband has no sooner spoken than Moll Granger scornfully volunteers to undertake the assignment he has rejected—

   . . . the labour and the risk thou fearest shall be mine. I fear not

the savages—I know their arts and can meet them, and so couldst
thou, Granger, did thy own shadow not so frequently beset thee
to scare. Give me the charge which thou hast, captain—and,
Granger, touch not the pounds. Thou wilt keep them, my lord,
for other service. I will go without pay. [226–27]

The mollified Granger frantically protests, but his wife ignores
him, focusing solely upon Harrison: "And now, my lord, the duty.
What is to be done?" That Harrison—much impressed by Moll
Granger's "noble, strong, manly soul, such as would shame thousands
of the more presumptuous sex"—decides to undertake the risky
assignment himself detracts neither from her willingness to tackle the
dangerous, nor from her effectiveness in instilling a sense of responsibility in her male companions.

Moll Granger's awareness of sensitivities of gender is once again
evident in her adroit handling of Wat Grayson when she sees need for
assuming direction of the strategy for defending the Block House. In
describing the perilous situation at the Block House, Simms recounts
the experiences and circumstances that molded the character of a
woman acclimated to hardship and danger:

> She had been a child of poverty and privation—the severe school
> of that best tutor, necessity, had made her equable in mind and
> intrepid in spirit. She had looked suffering so long in the face,
> that she now regarded it without a tear. Her parents had never
> been known to her, and the most trying difficulties clung to her
> from infancy up to womanhood. So exercised, her mind grew
> strong in proportion to its trials, and she had learned, in the end,
> to regard them with a degree of fearlessness far beyond the capac-
> ities of any well-bred heir of prosperity. . . . The same trials
> attended her after marriage—since the pursuits of her husband
> carried her into dangers, to which even he could oppose far less
> ability than his wife. Her genius soared infinitely beyond his own
> . . . . She counselled his enterprises, prompted or persuaded his
> proceedings, managed for him wisely and economically. . . . Her
> experience throughout life, hitherto, served her admirably now,
> when all was confusion among the councils of the men. [332–33]

In establishing the resolute Wat Grayson as the perceived commander of the Block House (in a move designed to palliate masculine

amour-propre), Moll Granger so positions herself that she can initiate action when the occasion demands. It is only she, for instance, who foresees the consequences of the fallen pine tree against the side of the Block House, and attempts to limit the danger of a Yemassee attack through this avenue. "The window must be defended. Two stout men will answer," she says to Grayson. "But they must have muskets." Grayson is not surprised at these instructions, having come to rely upon Moll Granger, but even he is not prepared for her assertion that she would defend the spot alone until assistance arrives. "You?" he asks. "Yes, Master Grayson—is there anything strange in that? I have no fears," replies the calm and resourceful frontierswoman. "Go— send your men."

It is in this precarious position that the will, the physical strength, and the courage of Mary Granger come to harrowing test. As she had feared, a wily Yemassee attacker seeks to use the fallen tree for ingress into the Block House. Pitting her skill against his, she manages to manuever the athletic Indian into an awkward situation in which she holds fast to his arm: he is "poised aloft, able neither to enter, nor to depart from the window":

> Desperate with his situation, he thrust his arm, as it was still held by the woman, still farther into the window, and this enabled her with both hands to secure and strengthen the grasp which she had originally taken upon it. . . . Excited and nerved, she drew the extended arm of the Indian, in spite of all his struggles, directly over the sill, so as to turn the elbow completely down upon it. With her whole weight thus employed, bending down to the floor to strengthen herself to the task, she pressed the arm across the window until her ears heard the distinct, clear crack of the bone—until she heard the groan, and felt the awful struggles of the suffering wretch, twisting himself round with all his effort to obtain for the shattered arm, a natural and relaxed position. . . . The jagged splinters of the broken limb were thrust up, lacerating and tearing through flesh and skin, while a howl of the acutest agony attested to the severity of that suffering which could extort such an acknowledgment from the American savage. He fainted in his pain. . . . [358]

This graphic description of frontier violence is a classic example of the kind of realism that shocked some of Simms's contemporary readers.

But Moll Granger is not the only frontiersperson whose fortitude and audacity Simms extolls in grimly realistic detail, yet heroic
dimensions. The hardy blacksmith Dick Grimstead stands in sharp
contrast to the bombastic medical man, Constantine Maximilian
Nichols, whose patriotic blathering succeeds neither in covering his
cowardice nor in diverting from him the derision of his companions. Though vociferous, Grimstead is blunt and direct, skeptical of
the pusillanimous doctor's proclamations of courage and without
pretense about his own. Yet in the most desperate of situations he
volunteers to lead a group out from the Block House "axe in hand"
in an effort to "cut down the pickets" near the gate. Such a measure,
Grimstead surmises, is better than "to stay here and be burnt to
death like timber-rats" (362). Grimstead and all but one of his
squad of four are killed in their almost suicidal undertaking, but
not before the burly smith, "wielding his axe with a degree of ease,"
has struck enough terror in the astounded attackers to force them to
fall back temporarily, thereby gaining precious time for the besieged
settlers.

Wat Grayson himself—as opposed to his idealistic younger
brother, Hugh, who is hypersensitive to the pangs of unrequited love
and jealousy—is another of Simms's stolid backwoodsmen—purveyors
of homespun wisdom. After listening at length to John Matthews's
bullheaded arguments against heeding the precautions recommended
by Harrison, the elder Grayson slowly and respectfully—yet with a
tinge of scorn—enunciates his opinion:

> Well, perhaps the parson knows better than any body
> else; but give me the opinion of those whose business it is to
> know. Now, I believe in the captain whenever fighting's going on,
> and I believe in the parson whenever preaching's going on—so, as
> it's fighting and not preaching now, I don't care who knows it, but
> I believe in the captain, and I won't believe in the parson. [289]

When Grayson's mother injects, "Now, Watty, don't be disrespectful. I'm sure the parson must be right, and so I think we had
better stay here when there's no use in going," he retorts: "Well now,
mother, I'm sure the parson's wrong, and if you stay, it will only be
to be tomahawked and scalped." Wat Grayson's patience finally
breaks completely, however, at Matthews's obtuse rebuttal, "Why

alarm your mother with such language, young man? You are deceived—the Yemassees were never more peaceful than they are at present." The pithy words of the frontiersman have a sting of their own:

> I say, Parson Matthews—one man knows one thing, and another man another—but, curse me, if I believe in the man that pretends to know everything . . . . Now, preaching's your trade . . . [and] nobody has a right to meddle—it's your business, not mine. But, I say, parson—I don't think it looks altogether respectful to try and undo, behind his back, the trade of another; and I think it little better than backbiting for any one to speak disreputably of the captain . . . [289–90]

The pragmatism of her elder son later becomes the source of Simms's satire on the loudly sanctimonious proclamations of Dame Grayson, who—praising the "blessed . . . saints for the rebuff of the attacking Yemassees"—asks her son, ". . . are we not saved by their ministry from the bloody hands of the savage?" Once again down-to-earth practicality provides Wat Grayson his answer: "No—it's by our own hands, and our own good handiwork, mother. I owe the saints no thanks, and shall owe you still less, unless you stop that howling" (370).

It is with characters such as these, and the conversations Simms attributes to them, that the reader today as well as in Simms's own day is drawn into the life of the American frontier, with its richness of experience, its brutality and wit, its strengths and weaknesses. It is a depiction in which realistic detail sparing no sensibilities blends with indications of Simms's own views and assessments.

In *Views and Reviews* Simms writes that the "chief value of history consists in its proper employment for the purposes of art!" (34). This audacious statement demonstrates unequivocally Simms's values and priorities—he is a creative writer first and foremost, a historian only secondarily. But there can be no doubt that Simms had done his historical homework before commencing to write *The Yemassee*. As he freely acknowledges, he read and drew extensively from the early histories of South Carolina by Hewatt, Drayton, Ramsay, Moultrie, and Archdale. Not only does he faithfully follow the actual outlines of the Yemassee War itself; he bases his characterizations of principal historical figures on his own perceptions of history—Craven and Bellinger among the English; Sanutee, Ishiagaska, and Huspar among the Indians. In addition Simms seemingly models other characters and incidents upon real or legendary people and events: for instance, Richard Chorley, the English pirate in league with the Spanish and the Yemassee against the English in *The Yemassee,* is probably based upon an actual pirate named Richard Worley, who with Steed Bonnett had taken possession of the mouth of the Cape Fear River in 1717.[4] The excruciating death of Teddy Macnamara is strikingly similar to that of Thomas Nairne, a Scotsman agent for Indian affairs at Pocotaligo, whose slow torture as a white sacrifice was witnessed by a friend in hiding, much as Harrison under cover watched the racking of Macnamara; and both Richard and Moll Granger may have been suggested by a trader named John Fraser and his new wife, both of whom (according to Hewatt among other historians) were befriended by Yemassee chief Sanute (or Sanutee) and warned to seek safety before the outbreak of war.

All these examples illustrate Simms's thesis that the artist is "the true historian":

> It is he who gives shape to the unknown fact, who yields relation to the scattered fragments,—who unites the parts in coherent dependency, and endows, with life and action, the otherwise motionless automata of history. It is by such artists, indeed, that nations live. [36]

Though frequently Simms's theories of art are couched in romantic terms (a vocabulary for realism was not in vogue), when Simms writes "with his sleeves rolled up" what comes out is realistic in language, tone, and mode—witness nearly all scenes in *The Yemassee* dealing with frontier action, away from the drawing room with its polite conversation and pretense of noble sentiment. Though mistaken in some of his assessments of Simms, Parrington was correct—first among academic critics—in recognizing and hailing Simms's innate realism as his forte.

What Simms thrust upon the American literary market in 1834 and 1835 were two historical novels (he called them romances) imbued with realism—*Guy Rivers* and *The Yemassee.* His fascination with romanticism is apparent in his definition of "the soul of art" as the creative faculty that "binds periods and places [of history] together"; but what Simms accomplishes—in his Revolutionary novels as well as in *The Yemassee* and his other border writings—is a realistic, vivid, and comprehensive portrayal of America's development as a nation.

NOTES

1. Although Louis D. Rubin, Jr., in *The Edge of the Swamp: A Study in the Literature and Society of the Old South* (Baton Rouge: Louisiana State University Press, 1988), 115–16, states of Macnamara (unlike Simms, Rubin has it McNamara), "It seems clear that he constitutes . . . a tribute to Simms's own Irish-born father out in Mississippi," no real evidence is offered to support the contention.

2. See "The Four Periods of American History," part iii of "The Epochs and Events of American History, as Suited to the Purposes of Art in Fiction," *Views and Reviews in American Literature, History and Fiction*, First Series, ed. C. Hugh Holman (Cambridge: Harvard University Press, 1962), 75–86. (*Views and Reviews* was originally published by Wiley and Putnam in New York in 1845.)

In this visionary essay Simms outlines the four stages in the development of America as a nation that he was to focus upon in a lifetime of fiction writing. It is noteworthy that Simms depicted in fiction not only the early attempts at colonization by the English (in *The Cassique of Kiawah* [1859] as well as in *The Yemassee*); he also delineated the pioneer efforts at colonization by the Spanish (in *Vasconselos* [1853]), and by the French (in *The Lily and the Totem* [1850]). His fictional portrait of precolonial and colonial America is by far the most complete and most authentic in our literature.

3. Chapter 48 alone affords numerous examples of Simms's repetitiveness: in its opening sentence, we are told that the Carolinian force "is now led by Harrison" (367); shortly thereafter we are reminded that "with more knowledge of Indian strife, Harrison took the command . . ." (372). Another striking example is Hector's "difficulty restraining, and keeping back, with all his might, the impatient dog Dugdale" (374). In yet another example, the word *adversary* is used twice within three

lines but with different references: ". . . his active adversary had passed from his reach, having made a desperate effort with his knife to hamstring his adversary, as he leaped aside and turned suddenly upon him" (375). Despite these careless oversights by Simms, Chapter 48 performs its function of highlighting the liberation of the Block House. Redundancy and repetitiveness were not uncommon in the fiction of mid-nineteenth-century England and America.

4. In keeping with his early interest in the psychology of crime, as demonstrated in "The Confessions of a Murderer" (1827), *Martin Faber: The Story of a Criminal* (1833) and *Guy Rivers* (1834), Simms focuses upon Chorley's abuse, neglect, and ridicule as a child in England as a contributing factor in his development as a criminal. A key to understanding Chorley's motivating resentment is his statement of Matthews: "Blast me! old man, but you don't think I'm the same ragged urchin that the parish fed and flogged—that broke his master's head, and was the laughing-stock and the scapegoat of every gentleman rascal in the shire? . . . They put me in the stocks, then expected me to be a good citizen" (112–13).

Simms's emphasis upon the influence of environment in the formation of the criminal character is consistent throughout his fiction; particularly notable examples among his later works include *Richard Hurdis, Helen Halsey, Confession,* and *Voltmeier.*

Historical Background

The Yamassees[1] were coastal Indians of Muskoghean stock. In the late 1600s and early 1700s, they occupied the coastal areas of South Carolina on the west side of the Savannah River, near its mouth. The Yamassee settlement consisted of five upper and five lower towns, with Pocotaligo serving as the principal upper town. They had previously lived off the coast of Georgia, under the control of Spain, but by 1685 they revolted, settling on the southern border of South Carolina and becoming the colony's most reliable allies. They raided Spanish missions in Florida with the English, and a number of them fought the Tuscarora Indians in North Carolina under Col. John Barnwell four years prior to the Yamassee War.

Though history has credited the Spanish with instigating the Yamassee uprising, it has equally asserted that the Yamassees acted in response to the abuses they suffered at the hands of the Indian traders. That these traders were occasionally less than fair with the Yamassees is evident in the Indian Trade Commission journals of the time, which contain instructions that a gift from the Indians should be reciprocated with one not exceeding half the value of the Indian gift. The most serious offenses, however, included abusing Indian women and selling rum. Those who could not pay immediately were permitted to

---

[1] The preferred spelling of this tribe is "Yamassee," though Simms's spelling is also legitimate.

accumulate sizeable debts, not suspecting that their wives and children would be seized and sold into slavery as payment for those debts.

In 1714 Yamassee chiefs began to visit the Spanish in St. Augustine, Florida, and meet with their Indian allies. According to Alexander Hewatt's *History of South Carolina,* the Yamassee chief Sanute warned trader John Fraser and his wife that the outbreak of the war was near, advising them to leave immediately.

The Creeks planned and incited the war, but it was the Yamassees who made the first strike. At daybreak on Good Friday, April 15, 1715, they attacked Pocotaligo, capturing and killing South Carolina government representatives who had gathered there to address and resolve the Indians' complaints. Several of those captured were tortured. The execution of Indian agent Thomas Nairne lasted several days: he was burned at the stake with small fires. At least a dozen traders were massacred, and more than one hundred settlers were captured.

Gov. Charles Craven himself led approximately 250 men toward Pocotaligo, having sent Capt. Alexander Mackay and Col. John Barnwell by water to mount the attack from the south. Though Craven's men were ambushed by the Yamassees at the head of the Salkehatchie or Combahee River, his forces rallied to defeat the Indians and drive them into the swamps, while Mackay took Pocotaligo.

The South Carolina settlement was preserved by Craven's leadership. The governor declared martial law, forbade settlers to leave, and sent his experienced Indian fighters to take on the Yamassees and their allies. But the war had not yet come to an end. Many other tribes had joined the Yamassees, and in June, their allies attacked the Santee border. By mid-June, however, the Yamassees left South Carolina and fled to Florida after their defeat at the battle of Dawfuskey Island. The coastal Siouan tribes withdrew from the war following their defeat at the battle of the Ponds. The conflict became, essentially, a war with the Creeks. Militia from North Carolina and Virginia took part in subsequent battles. The war would last through 1716.

In January 1716 a delegation of Creeks and Yamassees traveled to the lower Cherokee town of Tugaloo, with the ostensible aim of securing peace, but instead they urged their hosts to join the struggle. The Cherokees murdered them in the council house, thus effecting a peace with the whites. In the face of a Cherokee-Carolina alliance, the other warring Indian nations soon negotiated peace treaties with South Carolina. The Creeks, in 1717, were among the last to make peace.

The Yamassees who remained settled near St. Augustine, occasionally making raids on South Carolina. In 1719 and 1728 English expeditions from South Carolina destroyed the Yamassee towns near St. Augustine. The Chickasaw nation also raided the Yamassees at this time. According to some historical accounts, the Yamassees were threatened with extinction at this point, and by 1761 many of them were wiped out by the Creeks. A small number of the Yamassee women who remained bore children to Creeks and Seminoles. Some Yamassee survivors are also thought to have been absorbed by the Catawbas.

REFERENCES

Crane, Verner W. *The Southern Frontier, 1670–1732* (Durham: Duke University Press, 1928).

Heard, J. Norman. *Handbook of the American Frontier: Four Centuries of Indian-White Relationships.* Volume I: The Southeastern Woodlands (Metuchen, New Jersey: Scarecrow Press, 1987).

Hewatt, Alexander. "An Historical Account of the Rise and Progress of the Colonies of South Carolina and Georgia" (London: A. Donaldson, 1779). [Reprinted in Bartholomew Rivers Carroll, ed., comp., *Historical Collections of South Carolina* (New York: Harper & Brothers, 1836).]

Milling, Chapman J. *Red Carolinians* (Chapel Hill: University of North Carolina Press, 1940).

Reid, John Phillip. *A Better Kind of Hatchet* (University Park: Pennsylvania State University Press, 1976).

John R. Swanton, *The Indians of the Southeastern United States* (Washington, D.C.: Government Printing Office, 1946). [Smithsonian Institution Bureau of American Ethnology: Bulletin 137]

Explanatory Notes

The footnotes that appear in the text itself are Simms's own.

CHAPTER ONE

p. 2, line 6 Sayle: William Sayle, the first governor of Carolina (1669–1771).

p. 4, line 2 Edisto: a river in southern South Carolina, flowing southeast into the Atlantic Ocean.

p. 4, line 27 Charleston: Founded in 1680 and located approximately forty-five to fifty miles above Beaufort, Charleston became the center of both the deerskin trade and the Indian slave trade, largely because of its harbor and its access to the Indian tribes.

p. 6, line 13 Pocota-ligo: the main town of the upper towns of the Yemassee, located approximately twenty-five miles north of Beaufort.

CHAPTER TWO

p. 7, line 7 Coosaw-hatchie: an island which was part of the Yemassee lands.

p. 10, line 18 Sanutee: This name is probably derived from the Yemassee chief Sanute in Alexander Hewatt's *History of South Carolina.*

p. 11, line 11 Manneyto: the Yemassee's beneficent deity.

p. 11, line 37 Ishiagaska: Hewatt's *History* describes Ishiagaska as one of the chief warriors of the Yemassee.

CHAPTER FIVE

p. 28, line 29 Pepperbox: a temperamental or highly emotional person.

p. 29, line 26 Xerxes: king of Persia from 486 to 465 B.C.

p. 29, line 34 Jamaica: rum.

p. 30, line 24 Coosaw-killer: It seems unlikely that Charles Craven actually participated in the Coosaw War, which took place in 1675.

p. 30, line 40 stiver: something of little value; an insignificant or worthless part.

p. 31, line 15 clear your joints: leave, depart.

p. 31, line 22 pay out rope: to unwind a coil of rope.

p. 34, line 15 According to Hewatt's *History of South Carolina,* Ishiagaska was one of the Yemassee warriors who frequently visited the Spaniards in St. Augustine and persuaded the Creek Indians to take part in Spain's plans to destroy the English settlers.

CHAPTER SIX

p. 39, line 15 (including poetry counted as lines) Ashepoo: the region between the Combahee and Edisto rivers on the Ashepoo River, a small river running parallel to the Combahee and flowing into the Atlantic.

p. 40, line 29 St. Mary's: a river on the border of Florida and Georgia, flowing from the Okefenokee swamp to the Atlantic.

p. 40, line 29 Hatteras: an island in North Carolina, between Pamlico Sound and the Atlantic.

p. 41, line 32 pettiauger: a dugout canoe.

CHAPTER SEVEN

p. 51, line 20 Queen Anne: Queen of Great Britain from 1702 to 1714.

p. 51, line 23 Elector of Hanover: England was ruled by the house of Hanover beginning in 1714, with the accession of George I.

CHAPTER NINE

p. 68, line 40 Logan: a Mingo chief in the Ohio region. He was friendly with the whites until 1774, when Daniel Greathouse and other white men lured his family and his people across the Ohio River with liquor. After the Indians became drunk, they were slaughtered.

CHAPTER TEN

p. 76, line 23 Mackintosh: An Indian chief who fought with the whites against his Red Stick kinsmen in the Creek War of 1813–1814.

Though warned by his people that he would be executed if he signed a second treaty, which seceded his lands for lands in Oklahoma, he accepted the protection of the American government. On May 1, 1825, Indians set fire to his home and shot him to death when he fled.

CHAPTER TWELVE

p. 99, line 30 This warning to Granger and his wife closely parallels Sanute's warning to trader John Fraser and his wife in Hewatt's *History of South Carolina*. The Journals of the Commissioners of the Indian Trade, which comprise part of the colonial records of South Carolina, state that such a warning was given to the wife of trader William Bray, though the Yemassee Indian who informed her of the danger is not specifically named.

CHAPTER THIRTEEN

p. 104, line 11 bilbo: a finely tempered sword.

p. 108, line 9 Plutus: In Homer, Plutus is the son of Demeter and Iasion; his name means "Wealth," usually in reference to good harvests, the riches of the soil.

CHAPTER FIFTEEN

p. 115, line 1 tacky: shabby, seedy.

p. 115, line 3 Esculapius: (Asclepius) the god of healing, son of Apollo and Coronis.

p. 116, line 27 Tulifinee: one of the lower towns of the Yemassee settlement.

p 117, line 7 Decius: Roman emperor from 249 to 251.

p. 118, line 33 *secundem artem*: (Latin) according to the accepted practice of a profession or trade.

CHAPTER SIXTEEN

p. 122, line 15 filibustier: a variant form of "filibuster," a pillager, pirate, or irregular military adventurer; here, an organizer or member of a hostile expedition to a country with which his own is at peace.

p. 122, line 33 Jupiter Ammon: Zeus

p. 123, line 31 Port Royal Island: a settlement on the southern coast of South Carolina near Beaufort and St. Helena, approximately fifty miles below Charleston.

p. 126, line 37 snow-ball: a humorous term for Negro, used in the South.

p. 127, line 18 *Quod erat demonstrandum*: (Latin) which was to be proved.

CHAPTER SEVENTEEN

p. 129, lines 30–32 Harrison's implication suggests that the character of Chorley is based on Richard Worley, who collaborated with Bonnett, according to Hewatt's *History of South Carolina*.

p. 131, line 25 tacky: a small pony or inferior horse.

CHAPTER EIGHTEEN

p. 143, line 28 stays: large, strong ropes attached to something as a brace or guide.

CHAPTER NINETEEN

p. 146, line 27 Occonestoga: It seems likely that Simms obtained the basic elements of this character from the Cherokee chief Oconostota, also known as the Great Warrior of Chote and the Man-Killer of Tellico. Oconostota served as principal warrior chief from 1755 until his death in 1782. He was generally despised by his own people (including his own father) for his dealings with the French and English. The Journals of the Commissioners of the Indian Trade reveal a fear that his own brother would kill him. He is nowhere described as a drunkard, though he did insist that the English honor their promises to pay his people in rum.

CHAPTER TWENTY-ONE

p. 160, line 17 gripe: Simms's variation of "grip."

CHAPTER TWENTY-SIX

p. 203, line 25 *nom de guerre*: (French) pseudonym (literally, "war name").

p. 205, line 32 Armida: a beautiful sorceress in medieval legend.

p. 208, line 11 precisian: a person who stresses or practices scrupulous adherence to a strict standard, especially of religious observance or morality.

p. 208, lines 34–35 "Roundhead" and "old Noll" refer to followers of Oliver Cromwell, the lord protector of England from 1653 to 1658.

CHAPTER TWENTY-NINE

p. 225, line 17 Moll: "Moll" is a nickname for Mary.

p. 227, lines 8–10 Simms's use of Mary Granger is, to an extent, historically accurate. Colonial records report that in John Barnwell's 1719 expedition against the Yemassees who had fled to Florida, he was to receive help from the wife of one of his scouts at Pocotaligo; however, the Spaniards became suspicious of the woman's conduct, and Barnwell lost the element of surprise.

CHAPTER THIRTY-TWO

p. 243, line 11 Cape Fear: A cape in southeastern North Carolina, approximately 150 miles above Charleston, on the Cape Fear River, which flows southeast into the Atlantic.

p. 245, line 28 Moloch: a Semitic god to whom children were sacrificed.

CHAPTER THIRTY-THREE

p. 254, line 9 bucainer: Simms's variation of "buccaneer."

p. 255, line 26 Cherah: a hostile Sioux tribe of the region.

CHAPTER THIRTY-FOUR

p. 258, line 34 Macnamara: The character of Teddy Macnamara is probably based on the historical personage of Thomas Nairne, an Indian agent who was burned to death with small fires after the manner here described. Several of Nairne's colleagues hid from the Indians in nearby bushes, remaining concealed there for several days to avoid capture, and witnessing Nairne's prolonged torture and eventual death.

CHAPTER THIRTY-EIGHT

p. 286, line 15 Sallee: the seaport of northwest Morocco, at one time known for its pirates.

p. 293, line 18 Chigilli: (also spelled Chigelly or Chekilli) The Creek Emperor Brims planned the Yemassee War; Chigilli was his brother. Chigilli's attack on the South Carolina settlements during the war reached nearly as far as Charleston. He later succeeded his brother as Emperor.

CHAPTER FORTY-FOUR

p. 333, lines 17–18 *amour propre*: (French) pride, self-esteem.

p. 337, line 2 beg quarter: to ask for mercy.

CHAPTER FORTY-SEVEN

p. 362, line 34 scratch: the devil.

p. 364, lines 30–31 flash in the pan: This term derives from the firing of the priming in the pan of a flintlock musket without discharging the piece. Though his tongue is acrid enough, Nichols is, finally, all talk.

CHAPTER FIFTY-ONE

p. 395, lines 16–17 Ashley River settlement: a settlement on the Ashley, a river in southern South Carolina flowing southeast into the Charleston harbor.

CHAPTER FIFTY-TWO

p. 403, line 17 Chiquan: George Chicken.

p. 404, line 7 Savano Town: Founded in 1685, Savano Town was located on the left bank of the Savannah River, approximately one hundred miles north of Beaufort and nearly opposite the present site of Augusta, Georgia, to encourage trade with the Cherokees and the Creeks.

p. 405, lines 24–25 Simms's account is largely accurate here. Craven did defeat the Yemassee at Salkehatchie, a Yemassee town near the Combahee (or Salkehatchie) River. Several important chiefs were killed in the battle that took place at the mouth of the river, but the South Carolina militia lost only one man. The Yemassee War continued for at least another seven or eight months.

Textual Notes

The Yemassee: A Romance of Carolina was first published in 1835 in two volumes by Harper & Brothers in New York; copy-text for the Arkansas Edition is the "New and Revised Edition" published in one volume by Redfield in 1853, also in New York. In preparing the Redfield edition, Simms made relatively few substantive changes, probably the most important occurring in the dedicatory letter to Samuel Henry Dickson.

I. A Partial List of Substantive Changes

Listed below are the most important substantive changes Simms made in the 1835 edition in revising it for the 1853 Redfield edition (copy-text). Passages from the original edition revised by Simms are reproduced as they appear in the 1835 edition, followed by page and line reference to the revised passage as printed in the Arkansas Edition.

In the 1853 edition, chapter numbers appear as Roman numerals; throughout the Arkansas Edition, chapter numbers are spelled out.

ARKANSAS EDITION
p. xxvii, line 1–p. xxvii, line 27
This passage does not appear in the original edition; Simms added it in his 1853 revision.

ORIGINAL EDITION
Volume I, Advertisement, p. v, line 22–p. vi, line 44
. . . a distinguished writer of this country gravely remarks, in a leading periodical—"Magic is now beyond the credulity of eight

years,"—and yet, the author set out to make a story of the supernatural, and never contemplated, for a moment, the deception of any good citizen!

For the comparable passage as revised by Simms, see the Arkansas Edition, p. xxix, lines 10–15.

ORIGINAL EDITION
Volume I, Advertisement, p. vi, lines 12–19
The domestic novel of those writers, confined to the felicitous narration of common and daily occurring events, is altogether a different sort of composition; and if such a reader happens to pin his faith, in a strange simplicity and singleness of spirit, to such writers alone, the works of Maturin, of Scott, of Bulwer, and the rest, are only so much incoherent nonsense.

For the comparable passage as revised by Simms, see the Arkansas Edition, p. xxix, lines 24–32.

ORIGINAL EDITION
Volume I, Advertisement, p. vi, lines 20–25
The modern romance is a poem in every sense of the word. It is only with those who insist upon poetry as rhyme, and rhyme as poetry, that the identity fails to be perceptible. Its standards are precisely those of the epic.

For the comparable passage as revised by Simms, see the Arkansas Edition, p. xxix, line 33–p. xxx, line 7.

ARKANSAS EDITION
Dedicatory letter, p. xxx, line 37–p. xxxi, line 4
This passage does not appear in the original edition; Simms added it in his 1853 revision.

ORIGINAL EDITION
Volume I, Chapter I, p. 9, line13–p. 10, line 5
There is a small section of country now comprised within the limits of Beaufort District, in the State of South Carolina, which, to this day, goes by the name of Indian Land. The authorities are numerous which show this district, running along, as it does, and on its southern

side bounded by, the Atlantic Ocean, to have been the very first in North America, distinguished by an European settlement. The design is attributed to the celebrated Coligni, Admiral of France, who, in the reign of Charles IX., conceived the project with the ulterior view of securing a sanctuary for the Huguenots, when they should be compelled, as he foresaw they soon would, by the anti-religious persecutions of the time, to fly from their native into foreign regions.

For the comparable passage as revised by Simms, see the Arkansas Edition, p. 1, line 13–p. 2, line 1.

ORIGINAL EDITION

Volume I, Chapter I, p. 9, lines 10–25, and p. 10, lines 34–41 (footnote)

Dr. Melligan, one of the historians of South Carolina, says farther, that a French settlement, under the same auspices, was actually made at Charleston, and that the country received the name of La Caroline, in honour of Charles IX. This is not so plausible, however, for as the settlement was made by Huguenots, and under the auspices of Coligni, it savours of extravagant courtesy to suppose that they would pay so high a compliment to one of the most bitter enemies of that religious toleration, in pursuit of which they deserted their country. Charleston took its name from Charles II, the reigning English monarch at the time. Its earliest designation was Oyster Point town, from the marine formation of its soil. Dr. Hewatt—another of the early historians of Carolina, who possessed many advantages in his work not common to other writers, having been a careful gatherer of local and miscellaneous history—places the first settlement of Jasper de Coligni, under the conduct of Jean Ribaud, at the mouth of a river called Albemarle, which, strangely enough, the narration finds in Florida. Here Ribaud is said to have built a fort, and by him the country was called Carolina. May river, another alleged place of original location for this colony, has been sometimes identified with the St. John's and other waters of Florida or Virginia; but opinion in Carolina settles down in favour of a stream still bearing that name, and in Beaufort District, not far from the subsequent permanent settlement. Old ruins, evidently French in their origin, still exist in the neighbourhood.

Simms deleted this passage from his 1853 edition.

ARKANSAS EDITION (FOOTNOTE)
Chapter One, p. 1, lines 11–17
This passage does not appear in the original edition; Simms added it in his 1853 revision.

ORIGINAL EDITION
Chapter I, p. 12, lines 7–15
They were politic and brave—their sway was unquestioned, and even with the Europeans, then grown equal to their defense along the coast, they were ranked as allies rather than auxiliaries. As such they had taken up arms with the Carolinians against the Spaniards, who, from St. Augustine, perpetually harassed the settlements.
For the comparable passage as revised by Simms, see the Arkansas Edition, p. 3, lines 19–30.

ORIGINAL EDITION
Volume I, Chapter II, p. 16, lines 16–21
Within its limits—that is to say, with the circuit of a narrow ditch, which had carefully prescribed the bounds around it—the murderer found safety; and the hatchet of his pursuer, and the club of justice, alike, were to him equally innocuous while he remained within its protection.
For the comparable passage as revised by Simms, see the Arkansas Edition, p. 7, line 15–p. 8, line 5.

ORIGINAL EDITION
Volume I, Chapter II, p. 16, lines 30–43 (footnote)
These cities of refuge are, even now, said to exist among the Cherokees. Certain rites, common to most of the Indian tribes, are so clearly identical with many of those known to the Asiatics, that an opinion has been entertained, with much plausibility and force, which holds the North Americans to have come from the lost tribes of Israel. Dr. Barton, in his Materia Medica, referring to some traditions of the Carolina Indians respecting their medical knowledge of certain plants, holds it to be sufficient ground for the conjecture. The theorists on this subject have even pointed out the route of emigration from the east, by way of Kamtschatka, descending south along the shores of the

Pacific to Cape Horn. The great difficulty, however, is in accounting for the rapid falling back of any people into such extreme barbarism, from a comparative condition of civilization.

For the comparable passage as revised by Simms, see the Arkansas Edition, p. 7, lines 18–23.

ORIGINAL EDITION
Volume I, Chapter II, p. 17, lines 20–29
. . . and though the various parts of the dress were secured together by small strings of the deer sinew, passed rudely through opposite holes, every two having their distinct tie, yet the imitation had been close enough to answer all purposes of necessity, and in no way to destroy the claim of the whites to the originating of the improvement.

For the comparable passage as revised by Simms, see the Arkansas Edition, p. 8, lines 30–33.

ORIGINAL EDITION
Volume I, Chapter II, p. 19, lines 16–19
Sometimes the name of the Long Knife was conferred by the Indians, in a complimentary sense, upon the English, in due acknowledgement of the importance of their gift.

Simms deleted this passage from the 1853 edition.

ARKANSAS EDITION
Chapter Two, p. 10, lines 7–12
This passage does not appear in the original edition; Simms added it in his 1853 revision.

ARKANSAS EDITION
Chapter Three, p. 16, lines 9–20
This passage does not appear in the original edition; Simms added it in his 1853 revision.

ARKANSAS EDITION
Chapter Three, p. 18, lines 26–31
This passage does not appear in the original edition; Simms added it in his 1853 revision.

ORIGINAL EDITION
Volume I, Chapter IV, p. 32, lines 15–22
. . . then releasing his hold upon him, which all the while he had maintained with the most iron inflexibility of nerve, he left the expiring dog, to which the stroke had been fatal, to perish on the grass.
For the comparable passage as revised by Simms, see the Arkansas Edition, p. 22, line 36–p. 23, line 3.

ARKANSAS EDITION
Chapter Four, p. 25, line 37–p. 26, line 14
This passage does not appear in the original edition; Simms added it in his 1853 revision.

ORIGINAL EDITION
Volume I, Chapter IV, p. 36, lines 2–11
Sanutee threw up his arm, but the aim in this quarter had been a feint; for, turning the direction of the weapon, he passed the sharp steel directly upon the side of the warrior, and almost immediately under his own knee. The chief discovered the deception, and feeling that all hope was over, began muttering, with a seeming instinct, in his own language, the words of triumphant song, which every Indian prepares beforehand for the hour of his final passage. But he still lived.
For the comparable passage as revised by Simms, see the Arkansas Edition, p. 26, lines 15–21.

ARKANSAS EDITION
Chapter Five, p. 29, lines 23–35
This passage does not appear in the original edition; Simms added it in his 1853 revision.

ARKANSAS EDITION
Chapter Five, p. 32, lines 3–11
This passage does not appear in the original edition; Simms added it in his 1853 revision.

ORIGINAL EDITION
Volume I, Chapter VII, p. 60, lines 4–5

"Have you forgotten your manners, Betsy?"

For the comparable passage as revised by Simms, see the Arkansas Edition, p. 48, lines 38–39.

ORIGINAL EDITION

Volume I, Chapter VII, p. 67, lines 6–14

"As for my irreverence, and so forth—If it be so, it were a grievous fault, and I am grievously sorry for it. But I am free to say that I am not conscious of it. If you make a saint out of a murderer, as the Yemassee makes a God out of the devil, whom he worships as frequently and with more fervour than he does any other, I am not therefore irreverent when I doubt and deny."

For the comparable passage as revised by Simms, see the Arkansas Edition, p. 54, line 39–p. 55, line 9.

ARKANSAS EDITION

Chapter Seven, p. 55, lines 30–36

This passage does not appear in the original edition; Simms added it in his 1853 revision.

ORIGINAL EDITION

Volume I, Chapter VIII, p. 72, lines 5–15

. . . and under the general name of wampum, among all the Indians formed a common language, in which their treaties, whether of peace, war, or alliance, were commonly effected. Each tribe, indicated by some hieroglyphic of this sort, supposed to be particularly emblematic of its general pursuit or character, pledges itself and its people after this fashion, and affixes to the compact agreed upon between them a seal, which is significant of their intentions, and as faithfully binding as the more legitimate characters known among the civilized.

For the comparable passage as revised by Simms, see the Arkansas Edition, p. 59, lines 27–37.

ARKANSAS EDITION

Chapter Nine, p. 69, lines 6–14

This passage does not appear in the original edition; Simms added it in his 1853 revision.

ORIGINAL EDITION
Volume I, Chapter X, p. 95, lines 14–15
"Fear,—Sanutee has no fear of the English—he fears not the Manneyto."
For the comparable passage as revised by Simms, see the Arkansas Edition, p. 80, lines 32–33.

ARKANSAS EDITION
Chapter Twelve, p. 96, lines 1–11
This passage does not appear in the original edition; Simms added it in his 1853 revision.

ARKANSAS EDITION
Chapter Twelve, p. 99, lines 19–21
This passage does not appear in the original edition; Simms added it in his 1853 revision.

ARKANSAS EDITION
Chapter Sixteen, p. 125, lines 35–37
This passage does not appear in the original edition; Simms added it in his 1853 revision.

ORIGINAL EDITION
Volume I, Chapter XVIII, p. 162, lines 10–20
"Be off now, young one, before I send you a supply of lead not so much to your liking. If you don't take this chance and put about, you'll never catch stays again. I'll send a shot through your timber-trunk and scuttle her at once."

The fierce spirit of Grayson ill brooked such treatment, but he had no remedy save in words. He did not scruple to denounce the seaman as a low churl and an illnatured ruffian. Coolly then, and with the utmost deliberation, paddling himself round, with a disappointed heart, he made once more for the cottage landing.

For the comparable passage as revised by Simms, see the Arkansas Edition, p. 143, line 25–p. 144, line 5.

ORIGINAL EDITION
Volume I, Chapter XIX, p. 165, lines 9–15
But the soul was debased, and if it were possible at all, in the thought of an Indian, for a moment to meditate the commission of suicide, there was that in the countenance and expression of Occonestoga, as he rose from the morass, on the diversion from his track of the pursuers, almost to warrant the belief that his detestation of life had driven him to such a determination.

For the comparable passage as revised by Simms, see the Arkansas Edition, p. 147, lines 13–28.

ORIGINAL EDITION
Volume I, Chapter XX, p. 171, line 40–p. 172, line 6
Things grew indistinct to her wandering eye—the thought was turned inward—and the musing spirit denying the governing sense to the external agents and conductors, they failed duly to appreciate the forms that rose, and floated, and glided before them.

For the comparable passage as revised by Simms, see the Arkansas Edition, p. 153, lines 12–17.

ORIGINAL EDITION
Volume I, Chapter XX, p. 172, lines 14–27
She saw or thought she saw, at moments, through the bright green of the leaves, a star-like glance, a small bright ray, subtile, sharp, beautiful—an eye of the leaf itself, darting the most searching looks into her own. Now the leaves shook and the vines waved elastically and in beautiful forms before her, but the star-like eye was there, bright and gorgeous, and still glancing up to her own. How beautiful—how strange, did it appear to the maiden. She watched it still with a dreaming sense, but with a spirit strangely attracted by its beauty—with a feeling in which awe and admiration were equally commingled.

For the comparable passage as revised by Simms, see the Arkansas Edition, p. 153, line 26–p. 154, line 7.

ORIGINAL EDITION
Volume I, Chapter XX, p. 176, lines 9–15
. . . he turned recklessly round, and striking his charged fangs, so that they were riveted in the wound they made, into a susceptible part of his own body, he threw himself over upon his back with a single con-

vulsion, and, a moment after, lay dead upon the person of the maiden.

For the comparable passage as revised by Simms, see the Arkansas Edition, p. 157, lines 1–11.

ARKANSAS EDITION
Chapter Twenty-one, p. 163, lines 24–27
This passage does not appear in the original edition; Simms added it in his 1853 revision.

ORIGINAL EDITION
Volume I, Chapter XXI, p. 184, lines 34–37
A curious work, found in the Charleston Library, devoted to the history of that time and province, is illustrated with several plates which show the training common with the animal.
Simms deleted this passage from the 1853 edition.

ARKANSAS EDITION
Chapter Twenty-three, p. 175, lines 5–6
This passage does not appear in the original edition; Simms added it in his 1853 revision.

ARKANSAS EDITION
Chapter Twenty-seven, p. 214, lines 19–22
This passage does not appear in the original edition; Simms added it in his 1853 revision.

ORIGINAL EDITION
Volume II, Chapter II, p. 18, lines 22–25
"I thank thee—I thank thee,"—was all he said, as he carried the frankly extended hand of the maiden to his lips, and then rushed hurriedly into the adjacent thicket.
For the comparable passage as revised by Simms, see the Arkansas Edition, p. 214, lines 25–26.

ORIGINAL EDITION
Volume II, Chapter VI, p. 46, lines 18–29
. . . —that of Bess, linked with the tenderest epithets of affection. With

a fierce fury as he heard it, Grayson sprung forth from the tree, and his form went heavily down upon the breast of the prostrate man.

[one paragraph omitted]*

"Thy blood—thy blood!" was the only answer, as the knife was uplifted.

For the comparable passage as revised by Simms, see the Arkansas Edition, p. 239, lines 6–18.

ORIGINAL EDITION

Volume II, Chapter VIII, p. 61, line 39–p. 62, line 5

The Carolinians were not idle, and similar inroads were made upon Florida; the two parents looking quietly on the strife of the colonies, as it gratified the national animosity of either nation, who, seemingly quiet enough at home, yet mutually contributed to the means of annoyance and defence, as their colonies severally needed them.

For the comparable passage as revised by Simms, see the Arkansas Edition, p. 253, lines 23–30.

ORIGINAL EDITION

Volume II, Chapter IX, p. 67, lines 13–20

He was a fine-looking, fresh, muscular man—not more than thirty, and sustaining well, amid that fierce assemblage, surrounded with foes, and threatened with a torture to which European ingenuity could not often attain, unless in the Inquisitorial dungeons, the fearless character which is a distinguishing feature with his countrymen.

For the comparable passage as revised by Simms, see the Arkansas Edition, p. 258, lines 36–39.

ORIGINAL EDITION

Volume II, Chapter IX, p. 72, line 40–p. 73, line 35

. . . he maintained it on the spot until the withes crackled, blazed, and separated.

[one paragraph omitted]

But the old warriors now took up the matter. They had suffered the game to go on as was their usage, for the tutoring of the youthful

---

* For passages of three or more paragraphs in the original edition, only the first and last paragraphs are reproduced for identification purposes.

savage in those arts which are to be the employment of his life. But their own appetite now gave them speed, and they soon gathered upon the heels of the fugitive. Fortunately, he was still vigorous, and his hurts were those only of the flesh. His tortures only stimulated him into a daring disregard of any fate which might follow, and, looking once over his shoulder, and with a halloo not unlike their own whoop, Macnamara bounded forward directly upon the coppice which concealed Harrison. The latter saw his danger from this approach, but it was too late to retreat. He drew his knife and kept close to the cover of the fallen tree alongside of which he had laid himself down. Had the flying Macnamara seen this tree so as to have avoided it, Harrison might still have maintained his concealment.

For the comparable passage as revised by Simms, see the Arkansas Edition, p. 263, line 29–p. 265, line 18.

ORIGINAL EDITION
Volume II, Chapter IX, p. 75, lines 20–32
Thus confirmed in his words by the solemn auguries to which he referred, and which, just at that moment came, as if in fulfilment and support of his decision, the Seratee obeyed, while all around grew silent and serious. But he insisted that, though compelled to forbear his blood, he was at least his captive. This, too, the prophet denied. The prisoner was made such upon the sacred ground of the Yemassees, and was therefore, doubly their captive. He was reserved for sacrifice to the Manneyto at the conclusion of their present enterprise, when his doom would add to the solemnity of their thanksgiving for the anticipated victory.

For the comparable passage as revised by Simms, see the Arkansas Edition, p. 266, lines 22–30.

ARKANSAS EDITION
Chapter Thirty-five, p. 267, lines 1–7
This passage does not appear in the original edition; Simms added it in his 1853 revision.

ORIGINAL EDITION
Volume II, Chapter X, p. 80, lines 14–25
. . . might find, with no little appropriateness, a choice similitude in the blackguardism of the Eleusinian mysteries—the occasional exercises of a

far more pretending people than that under our eye. They ran, many of them, with torches waving wildly above their heads, on each side of the prisoner, some urging him with blows and stripes, less dangerous, it is true, than annoying. Many of them, in their own language, poured forth all manner of strains, chiefly of taunt and battle, but frequently of downright indecency.

For the comparable passage as revised by Simms, see the Arkansas Edition, p. 270, line 31–p. 271, line 4.

ORIGINAL EDITION
Volume II, Chapter XIII, p. 107, lines 13–22
"A few of them have become so now, and one chief cause of complaint among the Yemassees, is the employment by our people of several of their warriors to carry messages and hunt our runaway slaves—both of them employments, which their own sense readily informs them, are necessarily degrading to their character, and calculated to make them a nation of mercenaries. To my mind, the best thing we can do for them is to send them as far as possible from contact with our people."

For the comparable passage as revised by Simms, see the Arkansas Edition, p. 294, lines 8–14.

ARKANSAS EDITION
Chapter Thirty-eight, p. 294, lines 38–39
This passage does not appear in the original edition; Simms added it in his 1853 revision.

ORIGINAL EDITION
Volume II, Chapter XVII, p. 134, lines 17–23
The half-slumbering girl felt conscious of a sudden press of air—a rustling sound, and perhaps a darkening shadow; but the obtrusion was not sufficient to alarm into action, faculties which had been so very much unbraced and overborne by previous exertion, under the exciting thoughts which had so stimulated, and afterward so frustrated them.

For the comparable passage as revised by Simms, see the Arkansas Edition, p. 318, lines 2–7.

ARKANSAS EDITION
Chapter Forty-two, p. 318, lines 7–11
This passage does not appear in the original edition; Simms added it in his 1853 revision.

ORIGINAL EDITION
Volume II, Chapter XVII, p. 135, lines 24–31
With one hand he lifted aside the long white finger that lay upon it, and in the next instant the blow was given; but the pressure of his grasp, and at the same moment the dazzling light of the moon, direct from the blade under her very lids, brought instant consciousness to the maiden. It was an instinct that made her grasp the uplifted arm with a strength of despairing nature, not certainly her own.
For the comparable passage as revised by Simms, see the Arkansas Edition, p. 319, lines 3–13.

ORIGINAL EDITION
Volume II, Chapter XXI, p. 175, lines 39–40
The wife of Grayson, fully conscious of the danger, was alone sleepless in that apartment.
For the comparable passage as revised by Simms, see the Arkansas Edition, p. 354, lines 12–13.

ORIGINAL EDITION
Volume II, Chapter XXI, p. 180, lines 10–20
. . . and finally settling heavily upon the ground. Down went the three savages who had so readily ascended to the assistance of their comrade—bruised and very much hurt;—while he, now without any support but that which he derived from the sill, and what little his feet could secure from the irregular crevices between the logs of which the house had been built, was hung in air, unable to advance except at the will of his woman opponent, and dreading a far worse fall from his eminence than that which had already happened to his allies.
For the comparable passage as revised by Simms, see the Arkansas Edition, p. 357, line 36–p. 358, line 7.

ORIGINAL EDITION
Volume II, Chapter XXIII, p. 193, lines 25–28
And as if determined to sustain amply the propriety she insisted on, her lungs were never more tasked than when she sung.
For the comparable passage as revised by Simms, see the Arkansas Edition, p. 369, lines 22–27.

ORIGINAL EDITION
Volume II, Chapter XXIV, p. 207, line 40–p. 208, line 1
. . . only partially covered with the sand through which it had been drawn.
For the comparable passage as revised by Simms, see the Arkansas Edition, p. 382, lines 12–13.

ORIGINAL EDITION
Volume II, p. 238, lines 33–40
In taking such a position, they placed themselves directly between the two divisions of the palatine's force, which, skirting the copse on either hand, stood in no less readiness than themselves, with their movement, to effect its own; and when the savages advanced upon the unconscious camp, to come out upon their wings and read, taking them at a vantage which must give a fatal defeat to their enterprise.
For the comparable passage as revised by Simms, see the Arkansas Edition, p. 409, lines 25–33.

II. Emendations

Listed below to the left of the brackets are accidentals as they appear in the 1853 Redfield edition; to the right of the brackets are emendations by the editor for the Arkansas Edition. The citation in the left-hand margin is to the page and line in the Arkansas Edition on which the emendation occurs.

xxix.35	thoroughly, and] thoroughly,
10.05	that] that were
33.14	Harrison] "Harrison
34.16	name] name.
38.15	sailor-follow] sailor-fellow

42.08	to-night] to-night that
46.27	secresy] secrecy (see "secrecy," 53.31 and 254.16)
53.21	Harrision] Harrison
76.11	regulation] regulation.
86.15	Sanute] Sanutee
95.14	Ths] This
101.Headnote	on.] on."
102.25	no other] any other
107.02	safe y] safely
107.08	gentleman.] gentleman,
134.38	some] some of
145.Headnote	form"] form."
166.10	Granger?'] Granger?"
190.21	Yemassee?] Yemassee?"
205.03	utterred] uttered
243.Headnote	trample] trample.
245.01	to] to attend
321.16	hall,] hall.
336.10	himself] herself
350.19	Nicholas] Nichols
350.24	Nicholas] Nichols
351.28	Hugh] Wat
354.12	Grayson] Granger
355.08	moments and] moments
363.26	thowing] throwing
366.21	Hugh] Wat
409.10	arranged] Sanutee arranged

Select Bibliography

LETTERS

The Letters of William Gilmore Simms. Ed. Mary C. Simms Oliphant, Alfred Taylor Odell, and T. C. Duncan Eaves. 5 vols. Columbia: University of South Carolina Press, 1952–1956. (Cited in Introduction and Afterword as *L*, followed by volume and page number.)

The Letters of William Gilmore Simms. Ed. Mary C. Simms Oliphant and T. C. Duncan Eaves. Supplement, Vol. VI. Columbia: University of South Carolina Press, 1982.

MODERN COLLECTIONS

Selected Poems of William Gilmore Simms. Ed. James Everett Kibler, Jr. Athens: University of Georgia Press, 1990.

Stories and Tales. Ed. John Caldwell Guilds (Vol. V of *The Writings of William Gilmore Simms: Centennial Edition*). Columbia: University of South Carolina Press, 1974.

BIOGRAPHY

Guilds, John Caldwell. *Simms: A Literary Life.* Fayetteville: University of Arkansas Press, 1992.

Trent, William P. *William Gilmore Simms* (American Men of Letters Series). Boston: Houghton Mifflin, 1892.

GENERAL CRITICISM AND STUDIES

Davidson, Donald. "Introduction." In *The Letters of William Gilmore Simms*, Vol. I. Columbia: University of South Carolina Press, 1952. [see xxxi–clii; early, highly appreciative estimate of Simms's fiction]

Faust, Drew Gilpin. *A Sacred Circle: The Dilemma of the Intellectual in the Old South, 1840–1860*. Baltimore: Johns Hopkins University Press, 1977. [deals extensively and perceptively with Simms as Southern intellectual]

Gray, Richard. *Writing the South: Ideas of an American Region*. Cambridge: Cambridge University Press, 1986. [see "To Speak of Arcadia: William Gilmore Simms and Some Plantation Novelists," 45–62]

Guilds, John Caldwell, ed. *"Long Years of Neglect": The Work and Reputation of William Gilmore Simms*. Fayetteville: University of Arkansas Press, 1988. [evaluative essays by Guilds, James B. Meriwether, Anne M. Blythe, Linda E. McDaniel, Nicholas G. Meriwether, James E. Kibler, Jr., David Moltke-Hansen, Mary Ann Wimsatt, Rayburn S. Moore, Miriam J. Shillingsburg, John McCardell, and Louis D. Rubin, Jr.]

Guilds, John Caldwell, and Caroline Collins, eds. *William Gilmore Simms and the American Frontier: Papers of the Inaugural Simms Society Symposium*. Lewiston, N.Y.: Edwin Mellen Press, 1993. [twenty articles by literary and historical scholars treating the general theme of the American frontier and the significance of Simms's portrayal of it]

Hubbell, Jay B. *The South in American Literature, 1607–1900*. [Durham]: Duke University Press, 1954. [chapter on Simms, 572–602; still one of the best short essays on the author]

Keiser, Albert. *The Indian in American Literature*. New York: Oxford University Press, 1933. [see the discussion of *The Yemassee* in the chapter entitled "Simms' Romantic Naturalism," 154–74]

Kolodny, Annette. *The Lay of the Land: Metaphors as Experience and History in American Life and Letters.* Chapel Hill: University of North Carolina Press, 1975. [see 115–32; feminist study of Simms's depiction of landscape]

————. "Letting Go Our Grand Obsessions: Notes toward a New Literary History of the American Frontiers." *American Literature* 64 (March 1992): 1–18. [a seminal call for re-defining the American frontier and its place in our literary history; though Simms is not mentioned, his frontier writings reveal his recognition of the multi-cultural and multi-lingual elements at work]

Kreyling, Michael. *Figures of the Hero in Southern Narrative.* Baton Rouge: Louisiana State University Press, 1987. [see "William Gilmore Simms: Writer and Hero," 30–51]

McHaney, Thomas L. "William Gilmore Simms." In *The Chief Glory of Every People: Essays on Classic American Writers.* Ed. Matthew J. Bruccoli. Carbondale: Southern Illinois University Press, 1973, pp. 173–90. [notable for its recognition of the significance of Border novels such as *Guy Rivers*]

Parrington, Vernon L. *The Romantic Revolution in America, 1800–1860.* New York: Harcourt, Brace, 1927. Vol. II of *Main Currents in American Thought.* 3 vols. 1927–1930. [chapter on Simms, 125–36; an important early assessment of his achievements]

Ridgely, J. V. *William Gilmore Simms.* (Twayne's United States Authors Series). New York: Twayne, 1962.

Rubin, Louis D., Jr. *The Edge of the Swamp: A Study in the Literature and Society of the Old South.* Baton Rouge: Louisiana State University Press, 1989. [see "The Dream of the Plantation: Simms, Hammond, Charleston," 54–102; and "The Romance of the Frontier: Simms, Cooper, and the Wilderness," 103–26]

Wakelyn, Jon L. *The Politics of a Literary Man: William Gilmore Simms.* Westport, Conn.: Greenwood, 1973.

Wimsatt, Mary Ann. *The Major Fiction of William Gilmore Simms: Cultural Traditions and Literary Form.* Baton Rouge: Louisiana State University Press, 1989. [valuable study focusing on the Revolutionary Romances and Simms's use of humor throughout his fiction]

REFERENCE WORK

Butterworth, Keen, and James E. Kibler, Jr. *William Gilmore Simms: A Reference Guide.* Boston: G. K. Hall, 1980. [contemporary reviews of *The Yemassee* are listed and very briefly summarized, 28–32, 34, 37, 40, 55–56, 58–59, 66, 69–70, 84, 90–92, 94, 100]